THE IMMORTA...

This is respectfully dedicated to the "American Cowboy." His was the saga sparked by the turmoil that followed the Civil War, and the passing of more than a century has by no means diminished the flame.

———◈———

True, the old days and the old ways are but treasured memories, and the old trails have grown dim with the ravages of time, but the spirit of the cowboy lives on.

———◈———

In my travels—to Texas, Oklahoma, Kansas, Nebraska, Colorado, Wyoming, New Mexico, and Arizona—I always find something that reminds me of the Old West. While I am walking these plains and mountains for the first time, there is this feeling that a part of me is eternal, that I have known these old trails before. I believe it is the undying spirit of the frontier calling me, through the mind's eye, to step back into time. What is the appeal of the Old West of the American frontier?

———◈———

It has been epitomized by some as the dark and bloody period in American history. Its heroes—Crockett, Bowie, Hickok, Earp—have been reviled and criticized. Yet the Old West lives on, larger than life.

———◈———

It has become a symbol of freedom, when there was always another mountain to climb and another river to cross; when a dispute between two men was settled not with expensive lawyers, but with fists, knives, or guns. Barbaric? Maybe. But some things never change. When the cowboy rode into the pages of American history, he left behind a legacy that lives within the hearts of us all.

—*Ralph Compton*

RALPH COMPTON DOUBLE

ROUGH JUSTICE #1

TWO WESTERNS BY
RALPH COMPTON
AND
RALPH COTTON

BERKLEY

NEW YORK

BERKLEY

An imprint of Penguin Random House LLC

penguinrandomhouse.com

ISBN: 9780593441176

First Edition: November 2022

Printed in the United States of America
1st Printing

Book design by George Towne

CONTENTS

DEATH RIDES A CHESTNUT MARE

THE SHADOW OF A NOOSE

DEATH RIDES A CHESTNUT MARE

PROLOGUE

ST. JOSEPH, MISSOURI. APRIL 1, 1870.

Margaret," said Daniel Strange to his wife, "Texas cattle can be had for three dollars a head in Texas. Drive them north to the railroad, and they'll bring thirty dollars and more. I can't pass up a chance at that kind of money."

"But you're the best gunsmith in Missouri," Margaret said, "and you've taught all the children the trade. Your father was a gunsmith and his father before him. Why must you give it all up and travel hundreds of miles for a herd of Texas cows? Why, you're one of the most respected men in town."

"And the most taken for granted," said Daniel Strange. "I'm owed thousands of dollars, and nobody pays. I've already arranged to sell the shop for five thousand dollars, which is more than it's worth. I can leave fifteen hundred dollars for you to manage on until I can bring the cattle north."

"But there's just *you*, Daniel. You'll need men to help you drive the cattle."

"Texas is suffering through Reconstruction," Daniel said. "From what I've heard, I can get riders aplenty, paying them at the end of the drive."

"I have a bad feeling about this, Daniel," said Margaret. "Like if you go, I'll never see you again."

But Daniel Strange's mind was made up. On April 10, he rode out on a chestnut mare his daughter, Danielle, had named

Sundown, bound for Texas. His wife, Margaret, wept; his twin sons, Jed and Tim, cussed the fate that kept them from going; and Danielle said not a word. While Jed and Tim had their father's blue eyes, they were not as tall. Danielle, on the other hand, had her father's height. With hat and boots, she was almost six feet. Her hair was dark as a raven's wing, and she had her mother's green eyes.

"Damn it, Ma," said thirteen-year-old Jed, "Tim and me should be goin' with him."

"Don't you swear at me, young man," Margaret snapped. "You and your brother will remain here and go to school, just as your father ordered. You don't see Danielle wanting to ride off on a cattle drive."

"She's just a girl," Tim scoffed. "What does she know about cattle, or anything else?"

Danielle turned and walked away, saying nothing. She had shared her mother's misgivings regarding Daniel Strange's journey to Texas, but she knew her father too well to try to cross him. She sat down on the front steps, watching the evening sun sink below the mountains far to the west. Despite her mother's objections, she had taken to wearing her gun belt with the Colt her father had taught her to use. She thought fondly of the days Daniel Strange had spent teaching her to draw and cock the weapon in a single motion. There had been countless days of constant practice, with advice on cleaning and oiling the weapon as well. There was practice shooting with her brothers, and Daniel Strange had been delighted when Danielle had outshot both of them. Not only had he been a master gunsmith; he had been a master of the weapon itself. Thus the offspring of Daniel Strange were proud of their ability to pull a Colt and fire in a split second. Instead of going back into the house, where Jed and Tim still complained, Danielle leaned on the corral fence, her eyes looking away into the distance, where she had last seen her father.

Daniel Strange regretted taking the chestnut mare, for it was the best horse they had, and he had given it to his daughter,

Danielle. From St. Joe, he would ride almost due south, crossing Indian Territory into north Texas. The thirty-five hundred dollars in his wallet would more than pay for the anticipated herd. There would be money enough for a chuck wagon and grub for the journey to Kansas. Dan Strange well knew the dangers of crossing Indian Territory, but trail herds were doing it on a regular basis. There was no other route that wouldn't be hundreds of miles longer. He simply had to be careful. Taking care to rest the chestnut mare, he made swift progress. After Daniel entered Indian Territory at the extreme northeastern corner, a four-day ride had taken him well into the heart of the Territory. He had seen nobody since leaving southern Missouri. His cook fires were small, and he doused them before dark. He had just lighted a fire to make his breakfast coffee when the chestnut mare nickered. There was an answering nicker, and Dan Strange drew his Colt. He well knew the Territory was a haven for renegades and killers, and prepared to bluff his way out if he could. His heart sank when a dozen riders reined up a few yards away. They had the look of men on the dodge. Some of them wore two guns, and every man had a rifle in his saddle boot. Dan looked longingly at his own saddle and the Winchester in the boot, but he dared not risk going for it. Finally, the lead rider spoke.

"What are you doin' here in the Territory all by your lonesome, mister?"

"I'm not the law if that's what's botherin' you," Dan said.

"Haw, haw," one of the men cackled. "Would you admit it if you was?"

"I have nothing to hide," said Dan. "I didn't cotton to the war, and I laid out up in St. Joe, Missouri. But I got lonesome for Texas, and that's where I'm headed."

To further his bluff, Dan holstered the Colt he still held in his hand.

"I'm Bart Scovill," the lead rider said, "and I've always had a hankerin' for a chestnut mare just like that one of yours."

"Good luck finding one," said Dan.

While Scovill had been talking, two of the mounted men had

sidestepped their horses so that they had a clear shot, and it was these men Daniel Strange was watching. When they went for their guns, Dan drew with lightning swiftness and shot them both out of their saddles. But the other mounted men were firing now, and a slug ripped into Daniel Strange's shoulder, slamming him to the ground. Four of them were on him before he was able to move.

"Jasper," said Scovill, "tie a good thirteen-knot noose. Rufe, bring me that chestnut mare that this pilgrim's willing to die for."

"Take the horse," Dan Strange said desperately. "Let me go."

"A mite late for that," said Scovill. "You gunned down Reece Quay and Corbin Rucker, and the Good Book says an eye for an eye. They was my friends."

Rufe had saddled the chestnut mare, leading it to where Dan lay on the ground.

"Byler," Scovill said, "search him. He might have enough on him to buy all of us a drink or two."

Dan fought his way loose and was on his knees when Byler slugged him with the heavy muzzle of a Colt. The outlaws shouted in glee when Byler took the sheaf of bills from Dan's old wallet.

"Here," said Scovill. "Gimme that for safekeeping. Get him in his saddle. We'll string him up, take his horse, and ride."

Byler hoisted Dan Strange into his saddle, leading the chestnut mare to a giant oak. The noose was placed around Dan's neck, and the loose end of the rope flung over a limb. Bart Scovill slapped the flank of the chestnut, and the mare broke into a gallop, leaving the unconscious Daniel Strange dangling at the end of a rope. The outlaws were watching in morbid fascination, and nobody remembered the mare until the animal had a good head start.

"Damn it," Scovill shouted, "some of you catch that mare."

But the chestnut mare didn't like these men, and riderless, the animal lit out in a fast gallop toward home. The pursuing outlaws were quickly left behind. Finally, they gave up the search and returned to join their comrades. Dan Strange's dead body turned slowly, one way and then the other, in the light breeze from the west. Byler still held the empty wallet, and he flung it to the ground beneath the dangling corpse. The remaining ten outlaws didn't even bury Quay and Rucker, but mounted their horses and rode south.

INDIAN TERRITORY. APRIL 15, 1870.

Deputy U.S. Marshal Buck Jordan smelled the stench before he came upon the grisly mass of flesh hanging from an oak limb. His horse snorted, backstepping, and Jordan led the skittish animal well away from the scene of death. He tied his bandanna over his nose and mouth and started back toward the hanging tree. That was when he saw what remained of the pair of outlaws Daniel Strange had shot.

"My God," said the lawman aloud, "the buzzards and coyotes have already got too much of you gents. They might as well have the rest."

Jordan cut the rope, easing Daniel Strange's body to the ground, and that was when he saw the empty wallet. He opened it and found a card that read *Daniel Strange, Gunsmith, St. Joseph, Missouri.*

"Well, old son," Jordan said to the lifeless man, "the bastards took everything but your shirt, britches, and boots. All I can do is bury you and try to get word to your next of kin."

Jordan carried a small folding spade behind his saddle for just such a need as this, and he buried Daniel Strange beneath the oak where he had died. Jordan then studied the sign left by the riders.

"Twelve horses left here, but two saddles were empty," Jordan said aloud. "That was good shootin', Daniel Strange. A damn shame there had to be so many of them, but it's the way of yellow coyotes to travel in packs."

FORT SMITH, ARKANSAS. APRIL 17, 1870.

Buck Jordan turned in his report to his superior and, having no better address, sent the empty wallet to the *Family of Daniel*

Strange, Gunsmith, St. Joe, Missouri. With it he enclosed a letter explaining the circumstances and signed his name.

ST. JOSEPH, MISSOURI. APRIL 20, 1870.

It was already dark outside when the chestnut mare reached her home corral. Gaunt and trail weary, she nickered.

"That's Sundown!" Danielle cried

"Oh, dear God," said Margaret Strange, "something's happened to Daniel."

"Maybe not," Danielle said. "I'll get a lantern."

Trailed by Margaret, Jed, Tim, and Danielle hurried to the corral. The mare nickered again, for she was among friends.

"She's stepped on the reins and broken them," said Danielle. "She's come a long way riderless."

"Pa's hurt somewhere," Tim said. "We got to go find him."

"No," said Margaret, biting her lip to hold back the tears. "Your father's dead."

"I'll ride into town tomorrow," Danielle said, "and see if there's anything the sheriff can do."

It was a long, miserable night during which none of them slept. Danielle was ready to ride at dawn.

"Why is she ridin' in to talk to the sheriff?" Tim cried. "It ought to be Jed or me. This is man's work, and she's just a . . . a girl."

"Stop botherin' Ma," shouted Danielle. "Can't you see she's sick?"

Margaret Strange was ill with grief and worry. Upon reaching town, Danielle went first to Dr. Soble's office and told him the circumstances.

"I'll prescribe a sedative and look in on her," the physician promised.

Danielle then went to the sheriff's office, and he confirmed her fears.

"This parcel came yesterday," Sheriff Connally said. "It has no address except St. Joe, and the postmaster give it to me to deliver. He reckoned it might be important."

Danielle ripped away the brown paper, revealing her father's old wallet. She collapsed in a ladder-back chair, weeping. Sheriff Connally gathered up the brown paper wrapping, which still contained the letter from Deputy U.S. Marshal Buck Jordan. Swiftly he read it, waiting for Danielle to compose herself. When she had, the old sheriff handed her the brief letter. As Danielle read the letter from Buck Jordan, her tears were replaced with fury.

"The low-down, murdering bastards!" she shouted. "There must be *something* we can do to make them pay."

"Now, girl," Sheriff Connally soothed, "it happened in Indian Territory. It's plumb full of thieves and killers, and there's no way of finding the varmints, even if we knowed who they are."

"There *must* be some way to find them, to make them pay," cried Danielle.

"Danielle," the old sheriff said, "your daddy's gone. There's nothing you can do that'll change that. Now, don't go off and do somethin' foolish."

Danielle knew if the sheriff had any idea of the thirst for vengeance that possessed her, he would somehow foil the plan that was taking shape in her mind.

"I won't do anything foolish, Sheriff," said Danielle. "Thank you for your concern."

She mounted the chestnut mare and rode away. Connally watched her go. Despite her suddenly mild demeanor, he suspected trouble. He sighed. The girl was ready to raise hell and kick a chunk under it, and there was nothing he could do.

When Danielle returned home, Dr. Soble's buckboard stood in the yard. Jed and Tim met Danielle at the corral.

"You can't go in," said Tim. "Doc Soble ran us out. Did you learn anything in town?"

Wordlessly, not trusting herself to speak, Danielle handed them their father's beat-up old wallet. Tim took the ragged billfold, and both boys stared helplessly at it. Jed finally spoke.

"How . . . where . . . did you get it?"

"From the sheriff," Danielle said. "It came through the mail. Here's the letter that came with it."

She passed the letter to Jed, and Tim read it over his brother's shoulder. Finished, they spoke not a word, for their teeth were clenched in anger and tears crept down their cheeks. Suddenly, the front door opened, and Dr. Soble emerged. Danielle, Tim, and Jed waited at the doctor's buckboard.

"How is she?" Danielle asked anxiously.

"In shock," said Dr. Soble. "She has a weak heart, and another such shock could kill her. She's in bed. See that she stays there. I left some medication, and I'll be back the day after tomorrow."

Danielle, Jed, and Tim watched the doctor drive away. Not until his buckboard was lost to distance did anyone speak.

"We got to find the sons of bitches that done Pa in," Tim said.

"Damn right," said Jed. "I'm ready."

"Neither of you will be fourteen until June fifth," said Danielle, "and you're not going anywhere. You heard what Doc said about another shock killing Ma."

"But them bastards got to pay for what they done," Jed said.

"They will," said Danielle, "but we're not going to discuss it anymore until Ma's able to hear of it without it killing her. If either of you breaks the news to her, I can promise you there'll be hell to pay. Not from Doc, but from me."

They went on into the house, looking in on their sleeping mother. She seemed so thin and frail, Danielle wondered if she would *ever* be strong enough to learn the terrible truth of what had happened to Daniel Strange.

ST. JOSEPH, MISSOURI. APRIL 30, 1870.

It was ten days before Dr. Soble allowed Danielle to show Margaret Strange Dan's wallet and the letter that came with it. She wept long and hard, ceasing only when Jed and Tim entered the room.

"Ma," said Jed, "old man Summerfield's hired Tim and me to do his gunsmithing."

"Yeah," Tim said. "Business is awful. I think he's regrettin' ever buying the place from Pa. Jed and me ain't as good as Pa was, but we're better gunsmiths than old Summerfield or anybody else in town."

"The two of you are staying in school," Margaret Strange said. "It's what your father would want. Let Summerfield find someone else to do his gunsmithing."

"Ma," said Tim, "it takes money to live. Jed and me will each earn ten dollars a week with a raise when business gets better."

It suited Danielle's plans for her brothers to take the gunsmithing work, for it would ease the shock when Danielle revealed her plans to her mother.

"Let them hire on as gunsmiths, Ma," Danielle said. "They're already near as good as Pa was, and they can read, write, and do sums. They're the men of the house now, and we'll need the money more than they need the schooling."

It was the inescapable truth, and Margaret Strange reluctantly gave in.

Danielle waited a month more before revealing her plans to avenge her father's death. Margaret, Danielle, Jed, and Tim had just finished supper and were gathered around the table while Margaret read a chapter aloud from the family Bible.

"I have something to say," Danielle told them. "I was seventeen years old the thirtieth day of April, and I'm a woman. I'm as good with a gun as Pa was. I aim to find and punish his killers if it takes me the rest of my life."

"No," said Margaret. "This is no task for a woman. I forbid it."

"Woman, my eye," Tim said. "You're just a shirttail girl with big feet."

"I won't be going as a woman," said Danielle. "I'll cut my hair and dress like a man."

Jed laughed. "Some man. When you walk, your chest jiggles like two cougars fightin' in a sack."

Margaret slapped him. Hard. Despite her tough talk, Danielle found herself blushing furiously. Tim grinned broadly, obviously wishing to comment, but didn't speak lest he, too, incurred his mother's wrath. Danielle said no more about her vendetta until her brothers had ridden to St. Joseph to attend to their gunsmithing duties. Her mother would be difficult enough to win over without the embarrassing comments of her brothers.

"Ma," said Danielle, "I haven't changed my mind about finding Pa's murderers."

"I said no, and I haven't changed *my* mind," Margaret Strange said. "Whatever gave you the idea you can function in a man's world? Why, every time you walk—"

"Oh, damn it, Ma, don't start that again," said Danielle. "I'll make myself a binder for my chest and wear a shirt a size too big. Nobody will ever know."*

"If you get shot and somebody has to undress you, they'll know," Margaret insisted.

"I don't aim to get shot," said Danielle. "You know how fast Pa was with a gun, and you know that I'm faster than he was."

Margaret Strange sighed. "I know you can take care of yourself under ordinary circumstances, and so could your father, but not against an outlaw gang. If I give my permission and anything happens to you, it would be the finish of me."

"I tell you, nothing's going to happen to me," Danielle said. "I know it was a gang that killed Pa, but I aim to find out who they are and go after them one at a time. I'm more grown-up than you think, and I'm not about to do something foolish that could get me killed."

"But you have no money," said Margaret, "and with your father gone, we're going to need the little that we have."

"I have a hundred dollars," Danielle said. "Remember, Pa gave me fifty dollars for my birthday last year, and the year before. Besides,

---

* A binder was a band of cloth women used to flatten their breasts.

I'm good enough with a horse and rope to find work on a ranch if I have to."

Slowly but surely, Danielle overcame all her mother's objections. Margaret reluctantly cut the girl's hair to a length that might have suited a man. Using strong fabric, Danielle doubled the material and then sewed it securely. Under one of her father's too-big shirts, there wouldn't be any "jiggling" going on.

Danielle wisely said nothing to Jed and Tim of her plans and cautioned her mother not to. It would be difficult enough for Margaret when her sons realized Danielle was gone to perform a task that they fancied their responsibility.

ST. JOSEPH, MISSOURI. JUNE 30, 1870.

Much against her wishes, Margaret helped Danielle prepare for her journey.

"You'd better take these shears with you to trim your hair," Margaret said.

Danielle wore one of her father's shirts and placed two more in her saddlebag, with her extra Levi's. She buckled the gun belt around her lean waist, tying down the holster just above her right knee. A black wide-brimmed Stetson completed her attire.

"Land sakes," said Margaret, "you *do* look like a man. Just be careful when and where you take your clothes off."

"Oh, Ma," Danielle said, embarrassed.

When all else had been done, Danielle went to the barn and saddled the chestnut mare. The good-byes had been said, and Margaret stood on the porch, watching Danielle ride away. Before crossing a ridge, Danielle turned and waved. There were tears in her eyes, a lump in her throat, and a nagging premonition that she might never see her mother again. Danielle carefully avoided St. Joseph, for there was hardly a person in town who wouldn't recognize the chestnut mare. She rode almost due south, bound for Fort Smith. Once there, she would talk to Deputy U.S. Marshal Buck Jordan.

FORT SMITH, ARKANSAS. JULY 5, 1870.

D anielle was directed to the courthouse in which the marshal's office was located. A lawman sat behind a desk, barely
noticing as she entered.

"What can I do for you, son?"

"Where can I find Deputy Marshal Buck Jordan?" Danielle
inquired. Her voice was naturally low, like that of Daniel Strange
himself, and she made it even lower to sound as much like a man
as possible.

"The hotel, likely," said the lawman. "It's across the street, where
he generally stays when he's in town."

"Jordan's in room four," the desk clerk told Danielle after she
inquired about the deputy marshal.

Danielle knocked on the door several times before a voice answered from within.

"Who are you, and what do you want?"

"I'm Dan Strange," Danielle answered, making her voice hus-
kier again. "You buried my father, and I want to talk to you if I may."

"I remember," said Jordan. "Come on in."

Danielle entered, and was dismayed to find Jordan sitting on
the edge of the bed, wearing only his undershirt. She fought back
a blush, forcing her eyes to meet his. She quickly explained her
reason for being there.

"The only thing I didn't put in the letter," Jordan said, "was that
your pa killed a pair of the bunch before they got him. Ten others
rode away, leading two horses with empty saddles."

"Which way did they go?" Danielle asked.

"South," said Jordan. "Deeper into Indian Territory."

"You didn't pursue them?"

"They had a one-, maybe two-day start," Jordan said, "and there
was ten of 'em. There was also rain that night, washing out their
tracks."

"So they murdered my pa, and they're gettin' away with it," said
Danielle.

"Look, kid," Jordan said, "Indian Territory's one hell of a big place. Outlaws come and go. You could spend years there without finding that particular bunch of killers, even if you could identify them. Besides, they may have ridden on to Texas, Kansas, or New Mexico."

"I appreciate what you did," said Danielle. "Now, would you do me one more favor and draw me a map so I can find my pa's grave?"

"Yeah," said Jordan. "Reach me my shirt off of that chair."

Danielle handed him the shirt, and from the pocket, he took a notebook and the stub of a pencil. Quickly, he drew the map and tore the page from the notebook.

"Look for a big oak tree," Jordan said. "It's been hit by lightning, and one side of it's dead. Like I showed it on the map, it's almost due west from here."

"Thanks," said Danielle. Without a backward look, she walked out.

He had done little enough, but Danielle realized the lawman had been honest with her. There was no way of knowing where the outlaws had gone. Her only clue was her father's silver-mounted Colt, with an inlaid letter "D" in both grips.

"One of you took his Colt," she muttered under her breath. "When I find you, you son of a bitch, you'll tell me the names of the others before I kill you."

As she calmed down, aware of the vow she had just made, it occurred to her that she had never fired a gun in anger, nor had she ever killed. It wasn't going to be enough, just looking like a man. She would have to think like a man, like a killer. Finding a mercantile, she laid her Colt on the counter.

"I want two tins of shells for it," she told the storekeeper in her man's voice.

"That's a handsome piece," said the storekeeper.

He brought the shells, and after buying enough supplies to last a week, Danielle rode out of Fort Smith, riding west along the Arkansas River. Darkness caught up with her before she found the landmark oak Jordan had mentioned. Rather than risk a fire, she ate a handful of jerked beef and drank from the river. Finding some decent graze, she picketed the chestnut mare, knowing that Sundown would warn her by nickering if anyone came near. She then lay down on one of her blankets, drawing the other one over her. She had removed only her hat and gun belt and held the fully loaded Colt in her hand. Sometime near dawn, the chestnut mare snorted a warning. Danielle rolled to the left just as two slugs ripped into the blanket on which she had been lying. She took in the situation in a heartbeat. There were two men, both with weapons drawn. They fired again, the slugs kicking dirt in her face. Belly down, Danielle fired twice and the deadly duo was flung backward into the brush by the force of the lead. Danielle was on her feet in an instant, fearing there might be more men, but all was quiet except for the restless Sundown, who smelled blood. With trembling hands, Danielle thumbed out the empty casings, replacing them with more shells. Bushwhacking was a cowardly act, and she had no doubt the pair were outlaws of some stripe, but why had they tried to kill her? She had acted swiftly, doing what she had to do, but as she looked at the two dead men, she became deathly ill, heaving. She forced herself to breathe deeply, and finally, after washing her face in the river, she mounted Sundown and again rode west.

It was late in the afternoon when Danielle reached the lightning-struck oak where Dan Strange had died. The mound—already grassed over—was where Jordan had told her it would be. She removed her hat, wiping tears from her eyes on the sleeve of her shirt.

"I'll get them for you, Pa," she said aloud. "If God's merciful and lets me live, I swear I'll gun them down to the last man."

CHAPTER 1

Danielle spent her second night in Indian Territory unmolested. As she lay looking at the glittering stars, it occurred to her she might actually have to join a band of outlaws to find the men she sought. Somewhere, one of the killers carried her father's Colt, and it was a unique piece that a man who lived by the gun would remember. *Could* she pass herself off as an outlaw among killers and thieves? It seemed the only way. She remembered Buck Jordan sitting on the edge of his bed, wearing only his undershirt. She realized she had led a sheltered life, and that men on the frontier were likely more crude than she even imagined. The kind of men she must associate with would soon become suspicious of her furious blushing. She drifted off to sleep. Tomorrow she would begin looking for a band of outlaws. The distressing thought crossed her mind that she might die the same senseless death as her father had, but that was the chance she had to take.

INDIAN TERRITORY. JULY 8, 1870.

Three days into Indian Territory, Danielle encountered a group of men who could only be outlaws. It was late in the day when she smelled woodsmoke. Dismounting, leading the mare, she called out a challenge.

"Hello, the camp!"

A rustling in the brush was proof enough that one or more of the outlaws were preparing to cover her.

"Come in closer where we can see you," a voice shouted. "Strangers ain't welcome."

"I'm Dan Strange," Danielle shouted back, "and my grub's running low. I was hoping for an invite to supper."

"Come on in," the voice invited, "but don't get too busy with your hands. We got you covered."

There were four men in camp, and two more who came out of the brush.

"Hell," said one of the men, "it's a shirttail kid that ain't old enough to shave."

"What are you doin' in the Territory, kid?" a second outlaw asked. "You won't find nobody here to change your diapers."

"I shot two *hombres* near Fort Smith," said Danielle, "and they had friends. It seemed like a good idea to move on."

It was time for a test, and one of the outlaws reached for his Colt. He froze before he cleared leather, for Danielle already had him covered.

"You're awful damn sudden with that iron, kid," said the man who had been about to draw. "Put it away. I was just testin' you. Part of our business is bein' suspicious. Who was the two *hombres* you gunned down?"

"I have no idea," Danielle said. "They came after me with guns drawn, so I shot them."

"*You* shot *them* while they had the drop on you?"

"I did," said Danielle. "Wouldn't you?"

"If I was fast enough," the outlaw said.

The rest of the men laughed and relaxed. It was the kind of action they could relate to, and the outlaw who had just been outdrawn introduced the bunch.

"I'm Caney Font. To your left is Cude Nations, Slack Hitchfelt, and Peavey Oden. The two varmints that just come out of the brush is Hargis Cox and Cletus Kirby."

"I've already told you my name," said Danielle.

"That's an unusual iron you're carryin'," Kirby said. "Mind if I have a look at it?"

"Nobody takes my Colt," said Danielle.

"The kid's smarter than he looks," Cude Nations said.

"Hell," said Kirby, "I never seen but one pistol like that, and I wanted a closer look. It looks like the same gun Bart Scovill had."

"Well, it's not." Danielle said. "A gunsmith in St. Joe made only four of these."

"I reckoned Scovill likely stole the one he had," said Kirby. "He ain't the kind to lay out money on a fancy iron. He claimed he had it made special just for him, and it *did* have a letter 'D' inlaid in the butt plates."

Danielle's ears pricked up at the mention of the gun.

"That don't make sense," Hargis Cox said. "Bart Scovill's got no 'D' in his name."

"You ain't knowed him as long as I have," said Caney Font. "His middle name is David, and there's times he calls himself Bart Davis."

"Where are you bound, kid?" Cude Nations asked.

"Away from Fort Smith," said Danielle.

The outlaws laughed. Her answer had told them nothing, and it was the kind of humor they could appreciate.

"We don't eat too high on the hog, kid," Caney Font said, "but you're welcome to stay to what there is."

The food was bacon, beans, and sourdough biscuits, washed down with coffee. Danielle was ravenous, having had no breakfast.

"Kid," Caney Font said after they had eaten, "we might could use that fast gun of yours. That is, if you ain't playin' games."

"Pick a target," said Danielle.

"What about this tin the beans was in?" Slack Hitchfelt said.

Without warning, Hitchfelt threw the tin into the air. In a split second, Danielle fired twice, drilling the can with both shots before it touched the ground.

"My God, that's some shootin'," said Caney Font. "How'd you learn to shoot like that, kid?"

"Practice," Danielle said, punching out the empty casings and reloading.

"How'd you like to ride with us to Wichita on a bank job?" asked Caney Font.

"I don't think so," Danielle said. "I have other business."

Cletus Kirby laughed. "What business is more important than money?"

"Killing the bastards that murdered my father," said Danielle.

"Then I reckon you ain't interested in joinin' us," Slack Hitchfelt said.

"No," said Danielle.

"Then I reckon it's unfortunate for you, kid," said Caney Font. "One word to the law in Wichita, and it'll all be over for us."

"I'm not going to Wichita," Danielle said.

"You're a sure enough killer, but you ain't no outlaw," said Peavey Oden.

Danielle saw it coming. She had refused to throw in with them, and having revealed their plans, they had to kill her. If they all drew simultaneously, she was doomed. But they had no prearranged signal. Peavy Oden drew first, with Hargis Cox and Cletus Kirby a second behind. Danielle fired three times in a drumroll of sound, while the men who had drawn against her hadn't even gotten off a shot. The remaining three outlaws were careful not to move their hands.

"The rest of you—Font, Nations, and Hitchfelt—are welcome to saddle up and ride," said Danielle. "Make the mistake of following me, and now that I know your intentions, I'll gun you down without warning."

"We ain't about to follow you, kid," said Caney Font. "At least, I ain't."

"Me neither," Nations and Hitchfelt said in a single voice.

"Then saddle up and ride," said Danielle.

Careful to keep their hands free of their weapons, the trio saddled their horses and rode into the night. Danielle's hands trembled as she reloaded her Colt. While she had a lead toward one of her father's killers, she had already gunned down five men. When and where would it end? She saddled the chestnut mare and was about to mount when it occurred to her that she should search the dead outlaws. As distasteful as the task was, she found a total of a hundred and twenty dollars in the pockets of the dead men. Common sense soon overcame her guilt and she took the money.

Already tired of killing and outlaws, she rode south, toward the Red River and Texas. There was a chance the men she hunted had traveled as far from the scene of their crime as they could, and Texas was by far larger than Indian Territory. Danielle forded the Red at the familiar cattle crossing, near Doan's Store. Taking some of the money she had, she bought supplies she had been doing without, such as a small coffeepot, coffee, a skillet, canned beans, and some cornmeal. On second thought, sparing her bacon, she bought half a ham, which was all the chestnut mare could comfortably carry.

The storekeeper eyed her curiously, for he had seen all kinds come and go. They were getting younger all the time, he decided with a sigh.

Danielle continued riding south. Eventually, she came to the village of Paris, Texas. There were a general store, a livery, a hotel, and a sheriff's office. Adjoining the hotel was a café. Already tired of her own cooking, Danielle went to the café and ordered a meal. Once finished, she had a question for the owner.

"I'm looking for a gent name of Bart Scovill. His middle name is Dave, and sometimes he goes by that."

"Can't help you there," said the café's cook. "You might try Sheriff Monroe. He knows everybody within two hundred miles."

Danielle took a room at the hotel and went looking for Sheriff Monroe, finding him in his office, cleaning his Winchester.

"Barton Scovill is sheriff over to Mineral Wells, in Palo Pinto County. His kid run off up north somewhere to stay out of the war. I ain't seen him in near ten years. He'd be near thirty by now."

"I'd hate to ride all the way over there and find out he's the wrong *hombre*," Danielle said. "Do you know if his middle name is Dave or David?"

"I got no idea," said Sheriff Monroe. "To tell the truth, my own son was killed in the war, and I got no respect for them that run off to avoid it."

"I can't say I blame you, Sheriff," Danielle said. "Thanks for your help."

Danielle took the chestnut mare to the livery, rubbed her down, and ordered a double portion of grain for her. She then took her saddlebags and Winchester to the small room she had rented. Clouds were building up in the west, and there would be rain before dark. She felt the need of a good night's rest in a warm bed, with a stall and grain for the chestnut mare. The first thing she did was lock the door, draw the window shade, and strip off all her clothes. She was well-endowed enough that the binder was extremely uncomfortable, and she took it off gratefully. She then sat on the bed naked and cross-legged, cleaning and oiling her Colt. Again, she fully loaded it with six shells. Outside, the wind was screaming around the eaves, and there was the first pattering of rain on the windowpane. Danielle delayed supper until the rain subsided, enjoying the comfort of the rickety bed. By the time she reached the café, the rain had started again. Dusk was falling as she left the café, and that and the rain were all that saved her. Two slugs slammed into the café's wall, just inches from her head. Instantly, Danielle had her Colt out, but with the rain and darkness, there was no target. Reaching her room, she removed only her hat, boots, and gun belt. The Colt she placed under her pillow. But the night was peaceful, and Danielle lay awake, wondering who had fired the shots at her the day before. Carefully, she made her way to the café for breakfast, and then to her room for her saddlebags and Winchester. She saddled the chestnut mare and rode east toward Dallas.

DALLAS, TEXAS. JULY 11, 1870.

Dallas was the largest town Danielle had ever visited, and she was somewhat in awe of it. She dismounted before a livery, and the first person she saw was Slack Hitchfelt.

"Hold it, kid," he said, his hands raised. "I don't want no trouble."

"You missed last night," said Danielle. "Sure you don't want to try again?"

"I ain't drawin' on you, kid, now or ever," Hitchfelt said.

"Where's your scruffy partners, Font and Nations?"

"I dunno," said Hitchfelt. "We busted up. Said they was ridin' north. To Dodge City likely."

"I'm sorry to hear that," Danielle said. "You deserved one another."

Danielle kept her eye on Hitchfelt until he rode away. She then left the chestnut mare at the livery, taking her saddlebags and her Winchester. The rain had continued most of the day, with every indication it would last the night. Danielle got herself a cheap room in an out-of-the-way hotel, returning to it after supper. She propped a ladder-back chair under the doorknob and slept with her Colt in her hand.

MINERAL WELLS, TEXAS. JULY 13, 1870.

It wasn't difficult to find the sheriff's office. Danielle had bought a second Colt, and she placed the gun her father had given her in her saddlebag, replacing it with the ordinary Colt in her holster. If Bart—or Dave—Scovill was around, the fancy weapon would immediately arouse his suspicion. She would use her mother's maiden name if there was a chance her true family name might reveal her mission to the killers.

"Sheriff," she said, "I'm Daniel Faulkner, and I'm looking for work of just any kind. Do you know of anybody that's hiring?"

"Not a soul, kid," said the sheriff. "The war chewed everybody up and spit 'em out. Nobody has anything but a few cows, and they're all but worthless unless you can get 'em to the railroad, and it takes money to do that."

While Danielle was in the sheriff's office, a young man reined up outside and came in. Two things about him immediately caught Danielle's attention. A lawman's star was pinned on his vest, and in his holster was the silver-mounted Colt with a "D" on the grip. This man was one of her father's killers!

"Excuse my poor manners," said the sheriff. "I'm Barton Scovill, and this is my son, Dave, who's also my deputy. Dave, this is Daniel Faulkner."

The younger Scovill nodded. Not trusting herself to speak, Danielle stepped out the door, closing it behind her. She paused by the chestnut mare, seeking to calm herself and ease her shaking hands. The irony of it struck her, and it might have been amusing under different circumstances, but as things stood, the first of the men she must kill to avenge her father was a deputy sheriff. There was no mistaking the pistol that had belonged to her father, and no doubt she'd get the rope if she were captured for killing Scovill. She had to devise a plan, and so she went looking for a livery for the chestnut mare, and an obscure hotel for herself. Finding both, she took her saddlebags and Winchester to her room, where she stretched out on the bed to think.

"Damn it," she said aloud, "I must get close enough to do the job, and still manage to escape without being seen."

Just then she recalled seeing a notice posted on the hotel's front window. Saturday night there was to be a Palo Pinto County dance. She got up and went downstairs.

"What about that Palo Pinto dance?" she asked the desk clerk. "Would it be worth my time, staying over for it?"

"If you like pretty girls," said the desk clerk. "They'll be here from all over."

"Then I reckon I'll stay," Danielle said.

DALLAS, TEXAS. JULY 16, 1870.

D anielle hated to part with the money, but she needed some fashionable female clothes, and she couldn't afford to be seen buying them in Mineral Wells. In Dallas, her first item was a bonnet to conceal her short-cropped hair. It wasn't uncommon for a cowboy to buy clothing for his intended, and nobody gave this "cowboy" a second look. Danielle bought a divided riding skirt in pale green to match her eyes, and a white blouse with fancy white ruffles. Finally, she bought a pair of fancy half boots. She bought no underclothing, and the blouse was the actual size she wore. The "jiggle" that so amused her brothers suited her purpose, and other women would brand her a brazen hussy, but she must intrigue her intended victim enough to draw him away from the dance. Taking her purchases, she rode back to Mineral Wells. She entered the rear door to the hotel, making her way up the back stairs. In her room, she tried on the clothes, tying the bonnet so as to best conceal her short hair. Finally, she stood admiring herself in a cracked mirror on the dresser.

"Danielle Strange," she said aloud, "you look like a whore, but to a man that's a killer low-down enough to have hanged my pa, a whore would be just his style."

Now there was nothing to do except wait four days for the planned dance. Meanwhile, Danielle learned it was to be a street dance at the farthest end of town, near a second livery across from a general store. A visit to the livery revealed overhead beams that were suited to Danielle's purpose.

MINERAL WELLS, TEXAS. JULY 20, 1870.

D anielle waited until the dance was in full swing before slipping out the hotel's back door and down the stairs. Soon she was mingling with the crowd. A bandstand had been built in front of the livery, and besides the caller, there were four musicians. One played a guitar, the second a banjo, the third a fiddle, and the fourth a mouth harp. A sixth man was beating time with the straws on the fiddle.*

The moment the men spotted Danielle, there was almost a fistfight over who was to have the first dance. It was a while before Scovill got his chance.

"Tarnation," said Scovill, "where have you been all my life?"

"Around," Danielle said coolly. "Where have *you* been?"

"I was in the war," said Scovill, lying.

"The war ended five years ago," Danielle said. "Did you get home crawling on your belly?"

"By God, if you was a man, I wouldn't take that."

Danielle laughed tauntingly. "If I was a man, folks would be wondering if you stand or squat."

"You brazen bitch," he said, shoving her away from him.

But there were a dozen men waiting to take his place, and despite Danielle's macabre reason for being there, she was beginning to enjoy the dance. As she had expected, Scovill couldn't stay away.

"Do you drink whiskey?" he asked.

Danielle laughed. "What do you think?"

Danielle had never tasted whiskey in her life, but it might be her only chance to get Scovill away from the crowd.

"I got a bottle stashed in a rear stall in the livery barn," Scovill said. "Give me a few minutes and come on back. Be careful you ain't seen. Whiskey ain't allowed."

After Scovill had been gone for what she judged ten minutes, Danielle ducked into the shadow of the barn roof's overhang. The two swinging front doors of the livery were closed. Only a full moon lighted the wide-open doors in the rear.

"Here," said Scovill. "Have a drink."

---

* In traditional hoedowns, sometimes the only instrument would be a fiddle. The "straws" were often porcupine quills. A man "beating the straws" stood beside the fiddler, tapping the "straws" against the body of the instrument. It created a drumlike effect, providing the fiddler some rhythm.

"Not yet," Danielle said.

She loosened the waist of her divided skirt, allowing it to drop to the ground. She wore nothing beneath it, and Scovill caught his breath.

Scovill laughed. "The drink can wait. There's an empty stall over there with some hay."

In the stall, he quickly shucked his gun belt and was bent over, tugging at his boots. Danielle took the opportunity to grab her father's Colt from Scovill's holster and struck him across the back of the head with it. He folded like an empty sack. Quickly, Danielle dressed herself and, taking a rope hanging outside the stall door, fashioned a noose. She had never tied one before, but the result would serve the purpose. Once she had the business end of it around Scovill's neck, she threw the loose end over an overhead beam. It took all her strength to hoist Scovill off the ground. She then tied the loose end of the rope to one of the poles separating the stalls and, with a leather thong, tied Scovill's hands behind his back. He began to groan as he came to his senses. His eyes began to bulge, and he kicked as the cruel rope bit into his throat.

"Now you know how my father felt when you hanged him in Indian Territory," Danielle said.

Taking her father's gun belt, holster, and the silver-mounted Colt, she slipped out the livery's back door. Keeping to darkened areas, she hurried back to her hotel. Going up the back stairs to her room, she saw nobody. Everybody was still at the dance. Once in her room, she locked the door and stripped off her female finery. She placed it all in her saddlebags and donned her cowboy clothing. Carefully, she placed her father's gun belt and Colt with her female clothes and her own initialed silver-mounted Colt. Again, the Colt she placed in her holster was the plain one. Being caught with either of the silver-mounted Colts would brand her as Scovill's killer.

Danielle lay awake, unable to sleep, in her mind's eye watching Dave Scovill strangle to death. Near midnight, the dance broke up. Suddenly, there were three distant shots. It was a signal for trouble, and it was from the livery where Scovill had been hanged. Obviously, he had been found when the livery closed. Come the dawn, Danielle went to the mercantile and bought a knee-length duster. Returning to her hotel room, she buckled the Colt her father had made for her on her right hip. She then buckled her father's belt around her waist so that the weapon was butt forward for a cross-hand draw. Trying on the knee-length duster, she found it adequately concealed the two fancy weapons.

Wearing the duster, Danielle sought out a café for breakfast. She passed the sheriff's office and was astounded to find the place packed and men milling around outside.

"What's happened?" she innocently asked a bystander.

"Last night during the dance, some bastard hanged Sheriff Scovill's kid in the livery barn right while the dance was goin' on."

"Any idea who did it?"

"The sheriff figures it might have been some men back from the war. Dave Scovill run off up north until the war was over and didn't come back until a few days ago. There's a lot of folks that lost kin in the war, and they didn't like Scovill. Trouble is, they all got alibis. Wasn't robbery. He still had money in his pockets, but whoever done him in took his fancy silver-mounted pistol."

It was time for Danielle to saddle up and ride on. Looking back, she realized she had made one bad mistake. In her hurry to hang Scovill, she had neglected to force from him the names of his nine companions. From now on, her task would be doubly hard. Finished with breakfast, she saddled the chestnut mare and rode northwest toward Dodge. Scovill had returned to Texas because it was his home. With Reconstruction going on in Texas, might not the rest of the outlaws have ridden to Dodge, Abilene, or Wichita?

DODGE CITY, KANSAS. JULY 24, 1870.

Danielle reached Dodge late in the afternoon and, taking a room at the Dodge House, went to Delmonico's for supper.

Afterward, she found the sheriff's office. Sheriff Harrington was a friendly man, well-liked by the town.

"Sheriff," said Danielle, "I'm Daniel Faulkner. I'm looking for men returned from the war. Some of them knew my father, and I owe them."

"If they don't have names," Harrington said, "you won't have much luck."

"No, I don't have any names," said Danielle, "but I owe them."

"Why not run some ads in the weekly newspaper?" Harrington suggested. It was a brilliant idea.

Danielle found the newspaper office, asked for pencil and paper, and carefully composed an ad that read:

> To whom it may concern: am interested in finding men who rode with Bart Scovill in Indian Territory recently. Payment involved. Ask for Faulkner, at Dodge House.

There was a three-day wait until the paper came out on Saturday, with a few more days to see if anybody went after the bait. The stay in Dodge had eaten a hole in Danielle's wallet. In another two weeks, she would be forced to find work just to eat. Thursday came and went with no response to her advertising. Not until Friday was there a nibble.

"Who's there?" Danielle asked in response to a knock on her door.

"I'm answerin' your ad," said a voice. "Do I come in or not?"

Danielle unlocked and opened the door.

The man had the look of a down-and-out cowboy, with a Colt tied down on his right hip. He stood in the doorway, looking around as though expecting a trap.

"There's nobody here but me," Danielle said. "Shut the door."

He closed the door and stood leaning against it, saying nothing.

"I'm Daniel Faulkner," said Danielle. "Who are you?"

"I'm Levi Jasper, and it's me that's entitled to ask the questions. Why are you looking for Scovill's friends?"

"Scovill and me had a job planned. He claimed he could get a gang together that he used to ride with. Then the damn fool got himself killed by some bounty hunter looking for draft dodgers. Now there's still a twenty-five-thousand-dollar military payroll that will soon be on its way to Fort Worth, and I can't handle it alone. Can you find the rest of the outfit?"

"I dunno," said Jasper, "and don't know that they'll be interested. They're scattered all over the West. They could be in St. Louis, New Orleans, Kansas City, Denver, and God knows where else."

"Are *you* interested?"

"Maybe, after I learn more about it. You ramroddin' the deal?"

"Not necessarily," Danielle said. "I just want a piece of it."

"Good," said Jasper. "I ain't sure the boys would ride with a shirttail *segundo*, even if we can find 'em. You aim to advertise in more newspapers?"

"If I had some specific names, I would," Danielle said. "Scovill never told me the names of the men he had in mind. I took a long chance, advertising for you. Tell me the names of the *hombres* I'm looking for so I can ask for them by name."

"I dunno. . . ."

"Oh, hell," said Danielle, "just forget it. I'm just seventeen years old, and if you're so afraid of me, I don't want you on this job. I'll find somebody else."

"Damn it, nobody accuses Levi Jasper of bein' afraid. I can give you the names of the Scovill gang, and we'll pull this damn job of yours. One thing, though. I'm the *segundo*. When you find these varmints, tell 'em about Scovill, and that you're part of the gang. Let 'em believe I planned the thing."

"I will," said Danielle. "Now write down those names and where you expect me to find them. We don't have that much time."

CHAPTER 2

Danielle saddled the chestnut mare and rode east to Kansas City. She regretted losing out on Levi Jasper, but she had alerted the sheriff to her presence. Undoubtedly, Jasper had asked for her at the hotel, leaving her wide open to suspicion had anything happened to him. At least she had the names of the rest of the gang that had murdered her father. Levi Jasper would have to wait for another time and place. With her money running low, Danielle made her camp by a stream and picketed the chestnut mare nearby. She had no idea what she would use for money. Worse, if she was lucky enough to find work, the trail she followed would grow colder by the day.

Suddenly, the chestnut mare snorted. Danielle rolled to her left, her Colt in her hand, as the intruder's weapon roared twice. He had anticipated her move, and both slugs struck the ground just inches from her. There was no moon, but the starlight and muzzle flash were enough. Danielle fired twice. There was a groan and the sound of Jasper's body striking the ground. What had she said or done that had warned Levi Jasper? After having thought about it, the outlaw had apparently become suspicious, and whatever he had perceived as a mistake on his part, he had tried to undo. But Danielle still had the names—real or fictitious—of the remaining eight outlaws. She wouldn't need to spend anything more on advertising.

"Since you won't be needin' it, Jasper, I'll just see how much money you have in your pockets."

There was a considerable roll of bills, and Danielle took it without remorse. Saddling the chestnut mare, she continued east toward Kansas City. She must lose her trail among many others before Levi Jasper's body was discovered. Two hours later, she reached a little river town whose name she didn't know. But it had a hotel of sorts, a livery, a café, and some other buildings, including a general store. One sleepy old hostler was dozing in a chair before the livery. He sat up and looked around when he heard the chestnut mare coming.

"Stay where you are, old-timer," said Danielle. "I'll unsaddle her, put her in a stall, and fork down some hay."

"I'm obliged," the hostler said.

With the mare safely in the livery, Danielle took a room at the one-story hotel. By the light of a lamp, feeling a little guilty, Danielle separated the roll of bills on the bed and was astounded to find there was more than six hundred dollars! Undoubtedly it was stolen, but from whom, when, and where? Her conscience bothered her some, but there was no way to return the money, and besides, Danielle needed it desperately.

"The Lord works in mysterious ways," her mother was fond of saying, and Danielle said a silent prayer of thanks. Slowly, she began changing her mind about riding to Kansas City. She would be very close to St. Joe and home, and getting under way again would be hell without Jed and Tim finding her and following. With that in mind, she changed directions, riding to the southeast. Since she had no idea where to go next, why not New Orleans?

SPRINGFIELD, MISSOURI. JULY 28, 1870.

Reaching Springfield, she left the chestnut mare at a livery and rented herself a modest hotel room. She had lived in Missouri all her life, but had never been south. A huge lump rose in her throat when she recalled what her father had once said.

"Someday, Danielle, when we've got money, we'll all board one of the big steamers and ride all the way to New Orleans."

But Daniel Strange's good intentions died with him, and there would be no steamboat ride to New Orleans. Instead, Danielle was riding obscure trails, seeking his cold-blooded killers. Eight of them remained at large, and she had no idea how long her quest would take. Jed and Tim might be grown and her mother dead by the time vengeance was hers, which was a chilling thought.

After supper, there seemed little to do except go to bed or make the rounds of the various saloons. Danielle chose the saloons, and since she didn't drink, she invested a few dollars in games of chance. A one-dollar bet on a roulette wheel won her ten dollars, more than she had lost all night. There were poker games in progress, and never having played before, Danielle left them alone. She could watch, however, listening to the conversation of the players. One of them mentioned a name that immediately caught her attention.

"Too bad about that killing in Indian Territory a while back. But they got just one of the men. Pete Rizner rode like hell and escaped. The law ain't done nothin', and Pete's mad as hell. He's swearin' one of the bunch of renegades was Rufe Gaddis, from right here in Missouri."

"Pardner," said Danielle, "my pa was killed by outlaws in Indian Territory not too long ago, and I'm wondering if the outfit you're talking abut might not be the same lot. I'd like to talk to Pete Rizner. Where can I find him?"

"Likely at the Busted Flush Saloon," one of the men said. "His brother owns it. Good luck, kid."

The Busted Flush wasn't doing a thriving business, and all the occupants watched as Danielle entered. She went immediately to the barkeep.

"Where can I find Pete Rizner?" she asked.

"Who wants to know and why?" asked the barkeep.

"I'm Daniel Strange, and I'm after the bastards that killed my pa in Indian Territory a few months ago. I'd like to know if they're still there, or if they've scattered."

A man slid his chair back and stood up, and when Danielle looked at him, he spoke.

"I'm Rizner, kid. Take a seat, and I'll tell you all I know."

Danielle drew back a chair and sat down at the table.

"Drink?" Rizner asked.

"No, thanks," said Danielle.

"It was gettin' on toward dark," Rizner said. "We seen these riders coming, and they all had their Winchesters out. There was eight of 'em, and I yelled for my pard to mount up and ride. I jumped on my horse and lit out, but my partner grabbed his Winchester and tried to stand 'em off. They rode him down, and he didn't get a one of 'em. I'd swear on a Bible the lead rider was Rufe Gaddis. You know him?"

"No," Danielle said. "I'm after the bunch that robbed and murdered my Pa. It looks as though it could be the same outfit. Where were you attacked?"

"Maybe a hundred miles north of Dallas, not too far north of the Red," said Rizner. "Ride careful, kid, and good luck."

Danielle didn't bother with any more saloons. From the information she had received, it seemed almost a certainty that the outlaws she was seeking had never left Indian Territory, or had soon returned. Danielle prepared to ride out at first light. Unless there had been rain in the Territory recently, there still might be tracks.

INDIAN TERRITORY. AUGUST 1, 1870.*

Weary after more than three hundred miles, Danielle was looking for a stream by which she might spend the night

---

* Near present-day town of Lawton, Oklahoma.

when she came upon a grisly scene that made her blood run cold. There was a scattering of human bones, and a skull that still had its hair. There were the ripped, shredded remains of a man's clothing. The leg bones from the knees down were still shrouded in run-over knee-length boots. There were tracks in abundance, and they all led south. Sundown, the chestnut mare, snorted, not liking this place of death. It was too late to follow the trail with darkness, but a few minutes away and far to the west, golden fingers of lightning galloped across the horizon. Danielle mounted and rode south, following the trail as long as she could see. There would be rain before dawn, and the trail would be washed out. Danielle made her camp on the north bank of Red River, wondering why the outlaws had suddenly returned to Texas after the killing.

She covered herself with her slicker for some protection against the expected rain, which started about midnight. There was no dry wood for a fire, which was just as well, for the smoke would have announced her presence. Breakfast was a handful of jerked beef, and through a drizzling rain, she crossed the Red River into Texas. She had ridden three or four miles when a voice suddenly spoke from a nearby thicket.

"You're covered. Rein up and identify yourself."

Danielle reined up, carefully keeping her hands on her saddle horn.

A young man stepped out with a Winchester, and he looked no older than Danielle.

"What are you doing here?" he asked.

"I'm Daniel Strange," said Danielle, "and I'm no outlaw or killer. Last April my pa was robbed and killed in Indian Territory, and I'm after the bastards who did it. I found what I thought was their trail late yesterday, but the rain last night washed it out. They all rode south, and having no trail to follow, I was just taking my chances."

"I'm Tuck Carlyle," the young man said, leaning the Winchester against a shrub. "This is our spread, for what it's worth. I live here with my sister, Carrie, and Audrey, my ma. Pa went off to war and never come back. The damn outlaws from Indian Territory have been rustlin' us blind. They hit us again night before last and already had the jump on me before I found out what they'd done."

"If it's the same bunch I'm after," said Danielle, "there's eight of them. That's a hell of an outfit for just you to be trailing them."

Tuck laughed. "Then there's at least one more gent that's as big a fool as I am, and that's *you*. You're trailing them, too."

"There wasn't anyone else," Danielle said. "My two brothers are barely fourteen."

"You don't look much older than that yourself," said Tuck.

"I'm just barely seventeen," Danielle said, "but I can ride, rope, and shoot."

"I believe you," said Tuck. "Have you caught up to any of the killers yet?"

"Two of them," Danielle said, "and I know the names of the others. Or at least the names they're using."

Tuck Carlyle whistled long and low. Westerners did not ask or answer foolish questions, and this young rider being alive was proof enough that two outlaws were dead.

"Trailing the varmints after last night's rain is a waste of time," Tuck said. "Why don't you ride on back to the house with me? You can meet Ma and my sister, Carrie, and have some breakfast."

"You talked me into it," said Danielle. "All I've had is a little jerked beef."

"Let's ride, then," Tuck said. "God, could I use a cup of hot coffee, but we haven't had any since before the war."

"The war's been over for five years," said Danielle.

"No money," Tuck said gloomily. "Texans don't have a damn thing to sell except cows, and us little ranchers can't get 'em to market. We'd have to drive to Abilene, right across Indian Territory. Them damn outlaws would love having them delivered instead of having to come and get 'em."

"Are other small ranchers having the same problem getting their cows to market?"

"All I know of," said Tuck. "Nobody has money for an outfit, and they can't afford the riders they'd need for a gather."

"If maybe half a dozen small ranchers went in together," Danielle said, "you might have enough riders to gather everybody's cows, one ranch at a time. With the gather done, you could take a rider or two from every ranch and drive the herd to Abilene."

"By God, that might work," said Tuck. "I can think of four others that's as desperate as we are."

"How big is your spread?" Danielle asked.

"A full section," said Tuck. "It's six hundred forty acres."

"Hell's bells," Danielle said, "if that's a small ranch, how large is a *big* one?"

Tuck laughed. "When I call us a small outfit, I mean we don't have that much stock."

"You could sell some of the land if you had to," said Danielle.

"We may have it taken from us," Tuck said, "but we'll never sell. This section of land has been in our family for four generations. It has an everlasting spring, with the best water for fifty miles around. The only potential buyer is Upton Wilks. He owns sections to the east and west of ours, and he's sittin' back like a damned old buzzard, just waitin' for us to default on our taxes."

"If it's not improper for me to ask," Danielle said, "how *are* you paying your taxes?"

"My aunt in St. Louis—Ma's sister—married well," said Tuck. "She's kept our taxes paid, God bless her, so we wouldn't lose the place. Now this damned Upton Wilks is tired of waiting. He's trying to force my sister, Carrie, to marry him, and that would just about amount to *giving* him our spread."

"How does Carrie feel about him?"

"She hates his guts," Tuck said. "He's old enough to be her daddy, drinks like a fish, and goes to a whorehouse in Dallas every Saturday night. That's his good points."

Danielle laughed in spite of herself.

"I'd give the place up before I'd have her marry that sorry old bastard," said Tuck.

"I don't blame you," Danielle said. "A girl shouldn't have to make a sacrifice like that. There must be some other way. Since we're both after the same gang, maybe I'll stick around for a few days if I won't be in the way."

"You won't be," said Tuck. "We don't have a bunkhouse, but we have a big log ranch house. There's plenty of room."

"I'll contribute something toward my keep," Danielle said. "I don't have a lot of money, but I do have a five-pound sack of coffee beans."

"Merciful God," said Tuck, "if you was a girl, I'd marry you for that."

Danielle laughed, feeling more at ease with him all the time. She was truly amazed that she had adapted so well to the ways of men. They were generally crude, and without even a shred of modesty among their own kind. She no longer blushed at anything said or done in her presence. She had already acquired enough swear words to hold her own with the best of them. Prior to leaving home, she hadn't been around men except for her father and brothers. She recalled the time when she had been fifteen and her brothers, Jed and Tim, were twelve. She had followed them to the creek that July, watched them strip and splash around. But to her horror, the boys discovered her. When they told her mother, Margaret Strange caught the tail of Danielle's skirt, lifted it waist high, and spanked her bare bottom. Jed and Tim had never let her forget it. She now felt old and wise in the ways of men, her childhood gone forever.

The Carlyle ranch house, when they reached it, was truly grand, the product of a bygone era. A huge wraparound porch covered the front and each side of the house. Danielle had a sudden attack of homesickness. Tuck's mother stood on the porch, watching them ride up, reminding the girl of her own mother.

"I brought some company, Ma," said Tuck. "This is Daniel Strange. He's hunting that same bunch of outlaws that's stealing our cattle."

"Welcome, Daniel," Mrs. Carlyle said. "Get down and come in."

A young girl—obviously Tuck's sister, Carrie—stepped out on the porch. She looked at Danielle with obvious interest, making Danielle nervous.

"Daniel," said Tuck, "this is my sister, Carrie. We're trying to marry her off to somebody so Upton Wilks will leave her alone."

The implication was obvious, and Carrie hung her head, blushing furiously.

"Tuck," said Mrs. Carlyle, "don't tease your sister about that. You and Daniel come on into the house, and I'll scare up some breakfast. We have bacon, ham, and eggs, but we've been out of coffee for years."

"Flour, too," Carrie added.

"I have some supplies, including flour and coffee," said Danielle. "It's risky building a fire to cook when you're tracking outlaws in the Territory."

"We surely will appreciate the coffee and flour," said Mrs. Carlyle, "and you're welcome to stay with us as long as you like, sharing what we have."

"Lord," Danielle said, "I haven't had an egg since I left St. Joe, Missouri."

"Your home is there?" Mrs. Carlyle asked.

"Yes," said Danielle. "My mother and two brothers are there."

"You're so young, your mother must be worried sick," Mrs. Carlyle said. "What have those outlaws done to bring you this far from home?"

"They robbed and murdered my pa in Indian Territory," said Danielle. "Jed and Tim, my twin brothers, are only fourteen."

"You don't look much older than that yourself," Mrs. Carlyle said.

"I'm a little past seventeen," said Danielle, "and there was nobody else to track down Pa's killers."

"He's already killed two of them and learned the names of the others," Tuck said.

Danielle spread out the provisions from her saddlebags on the big kitchen table. Every eye was on the five-pound bag of coffee beans, and Danielle was glad she had bought them.

"Ma," said Carrie, "I'll make us some coffee. The rest can wait."

"It sure can," Tuck said. "Do we even have a coffeepot anymore?"

"Yes," said Mrs. Carlyle, "but I have no idea where it is."

"You can search for it later," Tuck said. "For now, boil it in an open pot, and we'll add some cold water to settle the grounds."

"I'll go ahead and start breakfast," said Mrs. Carlyle. "Carrie and I have already eaten, but I'd dearly love to have a biscuit."

"Ma," Tuck said, "I've told Daniel our problems here, and he's come up with a way we can get our cows to market at Abilene. Tell her what you told me, Daniel."

"Dear God, yes," said Mrs. Carlyle.

Quickly, Danielle repeated what she had suggested to Tuck as they had ridden in.

"But we have no money for an outfit," Carrie said.

"I have some money," said Danielle. "It would buy enough grub to get you there with your herds."

"But you'll need what you have as you search for those killers," Mrs. Carlyle said. "It wouldn't be fair to you."

"I believe it would be more than fair," Danielle said. "I think that bunch of outlaws in Indian Territory will come after the herd. So you see, I have a selfish reason for wanting you to make that drive to Abilene. I'll be going with you."

"God bless you for making the offer," Mrs. Carlyle said. "Tuck, what do you think?"

"I think we'd better talk to Elmer Dumont, Cyrus Baldwin, Enos Chadman, and Wallace Flagg," said Tuck. "It'll take all of us, I think, and since Daniel has offered to stake us with the necessary grub, the first hundred head of cattle we gather should be his."

"No," Danielle said. "You'll need your money. Besides, your herd will be bait enough to attract that bunch of outlaws I'm trailing."

"No matter," said Mrs. Carlyle. "You've brought us hope, and there will be five of us small ranchers. Any one of us can spare you twenty head. Tuck, when you talk to the others, be sure you tell them Daniel has a stake in this drive."

"But I feel guilty, taking some of your stock," Danielle protested.

"Without your help, we couldn't raise enough money for the

drive, and neither could the others," said Tuck. "I'll want you to go with me and talk to the others. This sounds like the makings of a miracle, and I'm not sure they'll take me serious."

"Then I'll go with you," Danielle said. "We must have a couple of pack mules, and each rider will need spare horses. We must see how many can be had."

"Damn the luck," said Carrie. "We won't have enough horses, and I don't know of anybody with mules."

"We'll find them," Danielle replied. "First, let's see if we can line up those other ranchers for the drive."

"I'd like to go," said Carrie, "but there won't be enough horses."

"Somebody must have a wagon," Danielle said. "We could fix it up with seats for some of you, and still have room for our grub."

"That's a better idea than pack mules," said Tuck. "I doubt the others will be willing to leave their families behind."

"Besides the three of you," Danielle said, "how many other people will be involved?"

"Elmer Dumont has a wife and a son about my age," said Tuck. "Cyrus Baldwin has a wife and two sons old enough to work cattle. Enos Chadman has a wife, a daughter, and a son. Wallace Flagg has a wife and two sons."

"Including me, there'll be nineteen of us," Danielle said. "For those who don't have a horse, the wagon will have to do."

"Every girl my age can tend cattle," said Carrie. "The wives can go in the wagon."

"We'll suggest that," Tuck added. "With us so close to Indian Territory, a man would object to leaving his wife and daughters behind. We'll need plenty of ammunition, too."

"I thought Texans weren't allowed to have guns during Reconstruction," said Danielle.

"Only those who served in the war against the Union," Tuck said. "I have a Colt and a Henry rifle. I'm sure the others will be armed, but they may lack ammunition."

"I have three hundred dollars to buy what we'll need," said Danielle.

"That should be more than enough," Tuck said, "but we may have to go to Dallas for the ammunition."

"Then take a wagon and go to Dallas after everything," said Mrs. Carlyle. "None of us are that well-known in Dallas, while going to a smaller town would be like telling everybody what we intend to do."

"Everybody will know anyway, Ma," Tuck explained. "You can't keep a roundup secret, but we can try. We'll buy supplies in Dallas, and the way I see it, we have four weeks to get the herd together. It's already the first week in August. If we can't get away from here by September first, there'll be snow before we can reach Abilene."

"Then let's pay a visit to those other four ranchers today," Danielle said. "If each of the five of you can get cattle to market this fall, you'll have the money for a much bigger drive next spring."

"Bless you, son," Mrs. Carlyle beamed. "It will be our salvation."

"There's a rider coming," Carrie announced. "Oh, God, it's Upton Wilks. Please, Tuck, don't you or Daniel leave while he's here."

"We'll wait awhile, then," said Tuck. "He *would* show up now."

From his very attitude, Danielle decided she didn't like Upton Wilks. He wore a fancy silk shirt and new boots. As though he owned all of Texas, he reined up, dismounted, and pounded on the door. He had the ruddy face of a drinking man, and most of his hair was gone. Tuck opened the door.

"What do you want, Wilks?" Tuck demanded. "You know you're not welcome here."

"Maybe I'll wait for Miss Carrie to tell me that," retorted Wilks. "I'm here to call on her."

Carrie rose to the occasion, responding in a manner that shocked them all, especially Danielle.

"I choose not to see you, Mr. Wilks. This young man, Daniel Strange, is now working for us, and I prefer his company to yours. Now please go."

Wilks's eyes narrowed and fixed on Danielle. "What Upton Wilks wants, Upton Wilks gets," he said.

"Not necessarily," said Danielle, her cold green eyes boring into his. "Carrie's told you to leave. Now go while you still can."

"I don't take orders from no snot-nosed kid," Wilks said. "You want me to go, why don't you make me?"

With blinding speed, Danielle drew her right-hand Colt. Wilks's left earlobe vanished with a spurt of blood.

"Damn you," Wilks bawled. "You shot me!"

He clawed for his Colt and Danielle held her fire until he cleared leather. Then she shot the gun from his hand. Ruined, it clattered to the floor. Wilks's ear had bled heavily down his face so that it looked as though his throat had been cut.

With a deathly white face, he backed toward the door, his voice shaking with anger. "You'd better go back to where you come from, you young fool. I'll have you hunted down like a yellow coyote."

"Mr. Wilks pays others to do what he's not man enough to do himself," Carrie said. "Just be sure you watch your back, Daniel."

Speech failed Wilks. He mounted his horse and, spurring the animal cruelly, galloped away.

"Carrie," scolded Mrs. Carlyle, "you shouldn't have antagonized him. Having him think Daniel's here to see you wasn't the truth. You might have gotten him killed."

Tuck laughed. "I don't think so, Ma. I saw John Wesley Hardin draw once, and he was slow as molasses compared to Daniel."

"I'm sorry, Daniel," said Carrie, "but what I said was the truth. Everybody that's ever been on the outs with Upton Wilks has ended up dead. He hires a lot of men, some of them no better than outlaws."

"Carrie," Danielle said, "if you have to stomp a snake, don't put it off till the varmint bites you. I wouldn't be surprised to find Wilks behind the rustling."

"He has enough riders," said Tuck.

"No matter," Danielle said. "We'll go ahead with our plans. If Wilks is on the prod, I'll take care of him when the time comes.

Tuck, you and me had better have some of that hot coffee and go calling on those other ranchers."

The first of the four ranchers they called on was Elmer Dumont. All of them—including Dumont's son, Barney, and his wife, Anthea—gathered around the dining table. Danielle and Tuck, speaking by turns, revealed the proposed plan to the Dumont family.

"Count us in," Elmer Dumont said. "If somethin' ain't done, we can't last the winter."

"We got maybe seven hundred head left, Pa," said Barney.

"I think we'd better limit the drive to five hundred head per outfit," Daniel said. "We'll be shy on remuda horses. Twenty-five hundred head will be more than enough to see all of you through the winter and provide enough money for another drive in the spring."

"With Daniel puttin' up money for grub and ammunition, I aim to see that he gets the first hundred head when we reach Abilene," Tuck said. "Does anybody disagree with that?"

"My God, no," said Dumont. "I'd give fifty head myself."

"We'll be back," Tuck said. "We're callin' on Cyrus Baldwin, Enos Chadman, and Wallace Flagg. Then we'll all meet together and lay some plans."

CHAPTER 3

C yrus Baldwin, his wife, Teresa, and his sons, Abram and Clement, listened while Tuck Carlyle and Danielle outlined the plan to save the small ranchers by driving a trail herd to Abilene.

"It's a great plan," Baldwin said. "We should be ashamed of ourselves for not thinking of it on our own, instead of sitting here starving."

"Before you give me too much credit," said Danielle, "remember that my purpose is to lure that bunch of outlaws into the open. I figure a herd of cattle will do it."

"Let them come," Baldwin said. "At least we'll have a chance to fight for our herds. As it is now, they're stealing us blind. The only way we can stop that is to take our own cows to market, and to kill as many of these thieving bastards as we can."

"We can count on you, then," said Tuck.

"You sure can," said the four Baldwins together.

"We'll need extra horses, a team of good mules, and a wagon," Danielle said. "Can you help us?"

"If we're all going on the drive," Baldwin said, "we can take all four of our horses. I believe both Enos Chadman and Wallace Flagg have wagons and mules."

"We're calling on them next," said Tuck. "Unless you hear something different from us, then be at our place at noon tomorrow. We must start the gather soon, and finish the drive, if we're going to do it before snow flies."

Enos Chadman, his wife, Maureen, their son, Eric, and their daughter, Katrina, received the news of the proposed gather and drive with enthusiasm.

"We have a wagon and a team of mules," said Chadman. "You're welcome to make use of them."

"Wallace Flagg also has a wagon and mules," Maureen said. "Perhaps we can take both the wagons."

"We may have to," said Chadman. "With all you ladies going, you may be riding the wagons so that the riders can have an extra horse or two."

"We'll talk to Wallace about maybe using his mules and wagon," Tuck said. "Unless we tell you otherwise, be at our place at noon tomorrow. We have to make plans and decide what supplies we'll need."

"While the rest of you start the gather, Tuck and me can go to Dallas for supplies and ammunition," said Danielle.

Wallace Flagg, his sons, Floyd and Edward, and wife, Tilda, were as responsive as the other small ranchers had been.

"We'll be glad to take our mules and wagon," Flagg said, "but be sure when you go for supplies that you get a couple of sacks of grain."

"We'll get the grain," said Tuck. "I figure each animal should have a ration of grain three times a week."

THE CARLYLE RANCH. NORTH TEXAS. AUGUST 5, 1870.

Wallace Flagg, along with his sons and wife, arrived first. Tilda Flagg drove the wagon. Next came Enos Chadman, his wife, his son, and daughter. His wife drove the wagon. Cyrus Baldwin and his family were next to arrive. Last to arrive was Elmer Dumont, with his wife and son. There was an impressive display of livestock, about eight mules and eighteen horses in total.

Some of the horses were being led, because most of the women rode on the wagons.

"Thanks to Daniel," Mrs. Carlyle announced, "we have coffee."

There were whoops of joy from all those gathered, for they had been forced to do without many things before, during, and after the war. Sipping their coffee, they gathered on the porch. There were chairs for the ladies while the men hunkered down, rocking back on their bootheels.

"Ma has paper and pencil," said Tuck, "and she'll make the list. Each of you sing out the provisions you think we'll need. Don't bother with ammunition. We'll get to that and the weapons after we've decided on everything else."

As the list grew, Danielle worried that the three hundred dollars she had promised to provide wouldn't be nearly enough. Finally, they were ready to discuss weapons and ammunition.

"Thanks to the Comanches, every damn one of us has a rifle," said Wallace Flagg, "and if I ain't mistaken, they're all sixteen-shot Henrys."

"Anybody got any other kind?" Tuck asked.

Nobody spoke, and they quickly moved on to revolvers.

"Now," said Tuck, "all of you with pistols raise your hands."

All the men and their sons raised their hands.

"That's twelve including me," Danielle said. "What make?"

"Colt," they all answered at once.

"All of them may not work," said Wallace Flagg. "We ain't been able to afford parts."

"Anybody with a weapon that doesn't work," Danielle said, "give Mrs. Carlyle your name. My pa was a gunsmith, and I learned the trade. We'll hold off on our trip to Dallas until we know which gun parts we need. Between Indians and outlaws, we need every weapon in perfect condition."

Before day's end, Danielle and Tuck had their list of needed provisions and a second list of necessary gun parts.

"Take my wagon," Wallace Flagg offered. "The bed's a little longer than usual."

"I'll take my wagon and teams home," said Enos Chadman, "but we'll plan on using them for the drive. If nothing else, we can put the canvas up, keepin' our bedrolls dry."

"I feel good about this drive," Mrs. Carlyle said when the last of their visitors had gone.

"So do I," said Tuck. "These other ranchers are all older than Daniel or me, yet they have agreed to throw in with us. I think we should head for Dallas in the morning."

"How far?" Danielle asked.

"About eighty miles," said Tuck. "Figure three days there with an empty wagon, maybe five days returning with a load."

"We could be gone a week or more then," Danielle said. "As it is, we'll be until the middle of August starting the drive."

"No help for that," Tuck said. "We'll need time for the gather. Maybe we can make up some of what we've lost after we're on the trail."

When supper was over at the Carlyle place, Mrs. Carlyle spoke.

"Tuck, you and Daniel should get to bed early, getting as much rest as you can."

"I aim to do just that," said Tuck. "You coming, Daniel?"

"Not yet," Danielle said. "This is my favorite time of the day, and I think I'll sit on the porch for a while."

Danielle went out, thankful the Carlyles had a large house. What would she have done had Mrs. Carlyle suggested Danielle share a room with Tuck? She sat down on the porch steps as the last rosy glow of the Western sun gave way to purple twilight. To her total surprise, Carrie Carlyle came out and sat down beside Danielle. Uncomfortably close.

"May I sit with you?" Carrie asked.

"It's all right with me," said Danielle.

"What will you do when you've tracked down the men who murdered your pa?" Carrie asked.

"I haven't thought much about it," said Danielle. "It may take me a lifetime."

"Then you'd never have a home, wife, or family," Carrie said.

"I reckon not," replied Danielle. "Is that what you want, a place of your own?"

Danielle could have kicked herself for asking such a perfectly ridiculous question.

"I want a place of my own and a man," Carrie said, moving even closer. "That's why I was thinking . . . hoping . . . you might come back here. I've never been with a man before, and I'd like you to . . . to . . ." Her voice trailed off.

"Carrie," said Danielle uncomfortably, "you're still young. I'll have to settle somewhere after this search is done. I can't say I won't come back here, but I can't make any promise either."

"I hope you do," Carrie said. "There's nobody around here my age except Dumont's son, Barney, Baldwin's sons, Abram and Clement, Chadman's son, Eric, and the sons of old Wallace Flagg, Floyd and Edward."

Danielle laughed. "Hell, Carrie, there's six of them. Can't you be comfortable with at least one?"

"Damn it, you don't understand," said Carrie. "They've all been looking at me, but all they want is to get me in the hayloft with my clothes off. You're not like that, are you?"

"No," Danielle said, more uncomfortable than ever. "I've sworn to find Pa's killers, and that comes ahead of any plans of my own. Until you find a man who appeals to you, stay out of the hayloft."

"I've found one, and he doesn't want me," said Carrie miserably.

It was well past time to put an end to the conversation, and Danielle did so.

"With Tuck and me getting an early start, I'd better get some sleep."

Tuck and Danielle were ready to start at first light. Along the way, they rattled past the Wallace place, waving their hats. Traveling due south, they stopped only to rest the mules. They saw nobody else. Reaching a creek just before sundown, they unharnessed the mules, allowing the tired animals to roll.

"I aim to dunk myself in that creek for a few minutes," Tuck said. "How about you?"

"No," said Danielle, her heart beating fast. "I'm hungry, and I'll get supper started."

She tried her best not to notice Tuck Carlyle as he shucked his boots and clothing, but found it an impossible task. She watched him splash around in the creek, and unfamiliar feelings crept over her, sending chills up her spine. Tuck caught her watching him, and he struck a ridiculous, exaggerated pose. Danielle forced herself to laugh, hoping she was far enough away that he couldn't see her blush. Never having had experience with a man, she was becoming far too interested in Tucker Carlyle. She tried to rid him from her mind, but there was always that vision of him standing there naked in the creek, laughing at her. She lay awake long after Tuck began snoring, and when she finally slept, he crept into her troubled dreams.

DALLAS, TEXAS. AUGUST 10, 1870.

There was no trouble along the trail to Dallas. The only difficulty was Danielle's newly discovered infatuation with Tuck Carlyle. There were times when she dreamed of donning her female clothing, telling him the truth, and allowing him to have his way with her. But she quickly put all such thoughts from her mind. She must avenge her father before she did anything else. But there was a troublesome possibility that kept raising its ugly head. Suppose—now or later—when Tuck learned she was a woman, he didn't want her? There was no accounting for male pride. She swore like a man, looked, sounded, and acted like a man, and could draw and shoot like hell wouldn't have it. She found herself worrying more and more what the consequences might be of her having assumed the role of a man. Just as they were approaching Dallas, Tuck caught her off guard with a question.

"Dan, you want to find a cheap hotel room? Ma gave me the few dollars she had."

"Save it," Danielle said. "The weather's warm, and our camp won't cost anything. With so much to buy, you may have to add your few dollars to mine."

"Yeah," said Tuck, "I keep forgetting just how much we need. Since we have all of the afternoon ahead of us, let's find a mercantile and get them started on our provisions and ammunition list. Meanwhile, we can track down a gunsmith for the parts we need."

With the roll of bills she had taken from Levi Jasper, Danielle had well over six hundred dollars, but she had set a limit of three hundred for the trail drive. However it came out, she would still need money to keep herself fed and supplied with ammunition. But there was much to be gained. Unanimously, she had been promised a hundred head of cattle, and if they brought as much as thirty dollars a head, that would be three thousand dollars! They left the wagon at the mercantile with instructions to load the supplies and ammunition as their list specified.

"Dallas is a right smart of a town," Tuck said. "If we ride, it'll have to be bareback, on a couple of the mules."

"Then let's ride the mules," said Danielle.

Tuck laughed. "We won't have to worry about robbers. They'll figure if we had anything worth stealing, we wouldn't be riding mules without saddles."

Eventually they found a gunsmith and, for fifteen dollars, got the springs and various other parts needed to restore all their Colts to working condition. Tuck insisted on paying the gunsmith from the little money his mother had given him.

"You should have let me pay for that," Danielle said.

"We'll be lucky if you have enough to pay for all the provisions we're getting at the mercantile," said Tuck. "It's still too soon to return to the mercantile. Let's go into some of the big saloons and see what they're like."

"I don't drink," Danielle said.

"Neither do I," said Tuck, "but I may never get to Dallas again, and I'd like to have a look at some of it."

They entered a prosperous-looking place called the Four Aces, and it being early in the afternoon, there were few patrons. Five men sat at a table, playing poker. Two women sat on barstools and eyed the new arrivals with interest.

"Let's watch the poker game a few minutes," Tuck said. "Maybe I can sit in for a hand or two. I still have five dollars."

"Table stakes, dollar limit," said the house dealer as Tuck and Danielle approached.

"I'll stand back out of the way and watch," said Danielle.

She didn't approve of Tuck taking part in the game, and she was sure Mrs. Carlyle had not given Tuck her last few dollars for such a purpose. But she said nothing. Tuck hooked the rung of a chair with his boot, pulled it out, and sat down. He lost three pots before he started winning. He seemed to have forgotten Danielle as she stood with her back to the wall, watching the game. To her dismay, one of the painted women approached her.

"Hello, cowboy," drawled the woman. "I'm Viola. While your friend's at the table, I can show you a good time upstairs. Just twenty-five dollars."

"No," Danielle replied. "I'm not interested."

"So you don't have twenty-five dollars," said the whore. "How about fifteen?"

"Ma'am," Danielle said coldly, "I wouldn't have it if it was free. Now leave me the hell alone."

Viola slapped Danielle across the face, and Danielle had to grit her teeth to avoid a similar response. A man didn't strike a woman—not even an insolent saloon whore. It was time to leave the saloon, and Danielle did so, waiting outside on the boardwalk for Tuck. He soon joined her.

"I won fifty dollars," he said. "What got the saloon woman on the prod?"

"She wanted to take me upstairs for twenty-five dollars," said

Danielle, "and when I refused, she came down to fifteen dollars. I told her I wouldn't go upstairs with her if she was free."

Tuck laughed. "Sooner or later, you'll have to get your ashes hauled."

"My *what*?"

"Oh, hell," said Tuck, "you *know*. Get with a woman."

"There's no time or money for that," Danielle said, "even if I was so inclined. I reckon you've already been there, have you?"

"No," said Tuck sheepishly, "but I did look through a window once, watching Carrie taking a bath in a washtub."

Danielle laughed. "I don't think that counts. A man shouldn't do that to his sister."

"Damn it," said Tuck, "there's not a female within riding distance of our place, except Katrina Chadman."

"She's pretty," Danielle said, trying mightily to hide her jealousy.

"She's also just sixteen," said Tuck. "From what I hear, I think her ma dresses her in cast-iron underpants."

Danielle laughed, slapping her thighs with her hat, as a man would do.

"Give her another year or two," Tuck continued, "and some varmint will have his loop on her. Barney Dumont, Eric Chadman, Abram and Clement Baldwin, and the Flagg boys, Floyd and Edward, are all makin' eyes at her. What chance would I have?"

"None, if you don't get off your hunkers and make a bid," said Danielle. "You could always take her swimming. You don't look too bad in your bare hide."

"I might have known if anybody ever said that to me, it'd be some *hombre*," Tuck said.

"You have fifty dollars," said Danielle. "While you're here, you could always buy yourself a heavy hammer and a good chisel."

"What for?" Tuck demanded.

Danielle chuckled. "For the cast-iron underpants."

Tuck laughed in spite of himself. They reined up before the

mercantile, where the other two mules were tied to a hitch rail. The canvas on their wagon had been raised, and one look told them the loading—or most of it—had been done. Barrels of flour sat on the floor of the wagon bed, while lighter goods were piled as high as the wagon bows would permit.

"My God," said Tuck, "I hope we can pay for all this."

"We might as well find out," Danielle said. "Come on."

"Three hundred and thirty-five dollars," said the storekeeper. "I had to cut back to half the sugar and coffee beans you wanted, so's I'd have some for my regular customers."

Wordlessly, Tuck handed Danielle thirty-five dollars with a wink while she counted out the three hundred. It was ironic that the fifty dollars he had won in the saloon had paid for the needed gun parts, with enough left to pay the mercantile.

They harnessed the mules, and only when they mounted the wagon box did Tuck say anything.

"Well, I'm broke. There goes the hammer and chisel."

Danielle laughed. "Maybe you won't need it until we reach Abilene. By then, you'll have the money. Or maybe you can get in solid enough with Enos Chadman, he'll let you have the key."

Tuck Carlyle actually blushed, and Danielle laughed. She had learned much in the ways of men, and when it came to cowboy humor, she was giving as good as she got.

"There'll be rain sometime tonight," said Tuck, changing the subject.

"At least we have a wagon canvas to protect the load," Danielle said. "I reckon we'll get wet, but we'll be wet many more times before we get to Abilene."

NORTH OF DALLAS. AUGUST 14, 1870.

W e're making good time," said Tuck. "All the way from our ranch to Dallas and back to here in four days. We've come a good twenty-five miles today. If the rain don't bring mud hub deep, we'll be home in another two days."

But the rain started just before dark and didn't diminish until the next morning.

"Damn," Tuck groaned, "we ain't going anywhere with this load. Not until there's been a couple of days of sun."

They picketed the mules and sat down on the wagon tongue, allowing the morning sun to dry their sodden hats, boots, and clothing.

By way of conversation, Danielle spoke.

"If we find and gun these varmints down, there may be others who'll continue rustling your cattle. What of them?"

"If we make this drive successfully," Tuck said, "we'll have money to hire riders and protect our stock. With cows selling for three dollars a head in Texas, we might actually buy some. Three thousand dollars would buy a thousand head. That many cows driven to the railroad in Kansas, my God, that's thirty thousand dollars."

"Don't let me gun down your dreams," said Danielle, "but we'll be reaching the railroad late in the season. Cattle buyers may not be paying as much as we're expecting."

"Maybe not," Tuck said, "but there's a chance they'll pay *more* than we're expecting. There likely won't be another herd until spring."

Conversation lagged. Having already commented on the rain, the mud, the delay, the rustlers, and the possible price of cattle in Kansas, there seemed little else to say.

"That night, while I was on the porch, Carrie sat with me awhile," said Danielle. "She tried to make me promise I'd come back to your place after I've avenged my pa."

Tuck laughed. "You could do worse. Carrie's two years younger than me. By the time you get back to our place, Carrie will be a prize for some varmint. She'll be chomping at the bit to do something."

"She's chomping at the bit *now*," Danielle said. "She's likely to do something foolish."

"I reckon," said Tuck. "Has any woman ever done anything else when it comes to a man? She'll likely be wantin' to share your blankets before we reach Abilene."

"Tuck Carlyle, that's no way to speak of your sister," Danielle said heatedly.

"Whoa," said Tuck. "Don't go jumping on me. It was you that suggested she's after you like an old hen after a grasshopper. If she aims to bed down with some *hombre*, then I hope it's you, instead of one of the Dumont, Baldwin, Chadman, or Flagg boys."

"Sorry," Danielle said, "but I'm not beddin' with anybody until I've found and disposed of my pa's killers. Why don't you talk to Carrie, and give her some advice?"

"She'd tell me where to stick my advice," said Tuck. "She always has before. If you promised to come back here, it might keep her out of trouble."

"I can't use a lie to protect her," Danielle said. "Before my search ends, I could be dead. Besides, after I'm gone, she'll forget. The Dumont, Baldwin, Chadman, and Flagg boys may begin to look a little more promising."

Tuck laughed. "All any of them wants is to take her somewhere and get her clothes off. Ain't you old enough to figure that out?"

"I reckon," said Danielle, holding on to her temper. "While you're in Abilene, buy her some of those cast-iron underpants with the money and throw away the key."

That silenced him, and for a long time, neither of them spoke.

"There's more clouds over yonder to the west. Unless it rains itself out before it gets to us, there could be more rain late tonight," Tuck finally said.

"Oh, damn it," Danielle said, "we'll *never* get to Abilene. We may never get back to your ranch."

But the rain ceased before it reached them, and the following morning Tuck came up with an idea.

"Why don't we hitch up the teams and see how far we can get

today? I don't think I can stand another day sittin' on that wagon tongue, discussing cast-iron underpants for my sister, Carrie."

Danielle laughed. "Maybe I'll tell her that's what you aim to buy for her in Abilene."

"I don't care a damn," said Tuck. "I've done told her everything a girl should know and maybe more. I told her if she wants a snot-nose kid before she's seventeen to just do anything that strikes her fancy. I got cussed out for my efforts."

D espite the still muddy ground, Tuck and Danielle harnessed the teams and began their journey to the north. Tuck drove, steering the teams away from low places and keeping to high ground.

"You're good with a team and wagon," Danielle said.

"I'm good at most everything I've tried," said Tuck. "Of course," he said, winking, "I got a few things I ain't tried."

"One of them being Katrina, I suppose," Danielle said.

"Hell, I can dream, can't I?" said Tuck. "I saw her watching you while we were there at the Chadmans'. Chadman's impressed with you. By the time we get to Abilene, you may have already been inside those underpants."

"Maybe," Danielle said, for once not blushing, "but I'll tell everybody else what I've told you and Carrie. My pa's killers come first."

Despite the mud, Tuck's expert handling of the teams managed to keep the wagon on high ground. He continued on until after sundown before unharnessing the tired mules.

"I figure we're not more than thirty-five miles from the ranch," said Tuck. "If all goes well, we'll be there late tomorrow. Not bad, three days to Dallas and four back, returning with a loaded wagon."

W here *are* they, Ma?" Carrie complained. "They've been gone a week today."

Mrs. Carlyle laughed. "Who are you missing? Tuck or Daniel?"

"I miss them both," said Carrie. "The rest of the ranchers have gathered their five hundred head, and they're waiting on us."

"They've also promised to help Tuck and Daniel with our herd," Mrs. Carlyle said. "It shouldn't be more than a day, with so many riders."

"There was a full night of rain to the south of here, night before last," said Carrie. "The mud may be deep. They may still be three days away."

"We'll just have to wait and see," Mrs. Carlyle replied. "I'm sure they'll be here as soon as they can."

THE CARLYLE RANCH. NORTH TEXAS. AUGUST 18, 1870.

It was late in the evening, sundown not more than an hour away. Despite the scolding of Mrs. Carlyle, Carrie stayed rooted to her spot, continuing to look to the south as far as she could see. Finally, on the horizon, a moving speck became visible. It eventually turned into two teams of mules and a wagon.

"They're coming, Ma! They're coming!" Carrie shouted, running for the house.

Mrs. Carlyle and Carrie were waiting on the porch when Tuck reined up the tired and sweating teams. He was alone on the wagon box.

"Where's Daniel?" Carrie inquired in a quavering voice.

"Oh, he met a girl in Dallas and decided to spend a few days with her."

"No," Carrie cried, bursting into tears.

"Tuck," Mrs. Carlyle scolded, "don't tease your sister. Daniel's horse is still out there in our barn."

The joke was over, and Danielle managed to squeeze out of the wagon, where she had concealed herself.

"Damn you, Tuck Carlyle, I hate you," Carrie shouted.

"It was partly my idea," said Danielle.

"Then I hate you, too," Carrie snarled.

"We got to find her a man somewhere, Ma," said Tuck, apparently deadly serious, "else there's no tellin' what will be takin' her to the hayloft."

It was more than Carrie could stand. Speechless, her face flaming red, she ran into the house.

CHAPTER 4

THE CARLYLE RANCH. NORTH TEXAS. AUGUST 19, 1870.

The first thing we'd better do," Tuck said, "is get the word to Dumont, Baldwin, Chadman, and Flagg that we're back. If they'll help us gather our herd, we'll be on the trail to Abilene tomorrow."

"They promised," said Mrs. Carlyle.

"Maybe we'd better remind them we're ready to begin," Danielle said.

"Then let's go," said Tuck. "We're losing more time."

Only Carrie said nothing, but stared vacantly out the window.

Tuck and Danielle weren't even off the Carlyle spread when they met Barney Dumont.

"I was just comin' to see if you'd made it back," Barney said. "Pa said if you was back that I'm to take the word to Baldwin, Chadman, and Flagg. We can start your gather today, getting on the trail that much quicker."

"We're ready," said Tuck, "and we have the needed parts for the Colts, besides the wagonload of provisions and ammunition."

"Then I'll tell the others to get on over to your place just as quick as they can," said Barney.

"*Bueno,*" Tuck said. "It's the moment of truth. We'll have to find out if we have cows enough to make the drive."

At Upton Wilks's ranch, Wilks was receiving a report from Kazman, his *segundo*.

"They're gettin' ready for a drive," said Kazman. "Four of the outfits has rounded up at least five hundred head. There's nobody left 'cept the Carlyles."

"Why not the Carlyles?"

"Tuck and the young gent stayin' with 'em took off south a week ago, in old man Flagg's wagon. Today they come back. From the tracks, I'd say the wagon's loaded to the bows. They likely been to Dallas, buyin' food and ammunition."

"Where the hell would they get the money?" Wilks demanded.

"Somebody staked 'em," said Kazman. "Maybe that new gent that's stayin' with 'em."

"Looks like we'll have to take care of him," Wilks said. "Give 'em a couple of days on the trail, but before the herd becomes trail-wise and settles down, stampede the lot of them from here to yonder."

"It'll be hell finding them longhorns in Indian Territory," said Kazman. "I was hopin' we could grab the herd and take 'em on to Abilene ourselves."

"Maybe we can," Wilks said, "but we'll need more riders. Not countin' you and me, we got eight riders. There's nineteen in that outfit, and every one of them, even including the women, can shoot. We'll wait until they're practically out of Indian Territory before we take the herd. Let them do most of the hard work."

"I like it," said Kazman. "Ambush?"

"Yes," Wilks replied. "Shoot them all dead. Then when they default on their taxes, I'll take over all their ranches dirt cheap. Take a pair of riders with you and ride into Indian Territory. We'll need four or five more riders. No petty thieves. We want killers."

Within the hour, riders began showing up at the Carlyle ranch. The Dumonts were the first to arrive, followed by the Baldwins. The Chadmans were next, followed closely by the Flaggs.

"I'll need daylight to repair your Colts," Danielle said. "The rest of you begin gathering the cattle. When I'm done with the Colts, I'll join you."

"It's important we have those Colts ready," Tuck said. "Go ahead and fix them."

Danielle spread out a blanket on the grass beneath a tree. She then began work on the half dozen Colts, breaking them down one at a time. Finished with one, she started on the second one before Carrie joined her.

"I thought you hated me," said Danielle mildly.

"I don't, really," Carrie said. "I'm just disappointed in you."

"I'm sorry to have disappointed you," said Danielle, "but you knew when I first rode in that I was after my pa's killers. I won't find them settin' on my hunkers here."

"I suppose not," Carrie said with a sigh. With Danielle being busy, the conversation lagged, and Carrie wandered back to the house.

An hour past noon, the riders drove in the cattle they had gathered.

"More than two hundred head," said Tuck proudly. "We got to gather the rest, run all the five herds together, and post guards. The rustlers could clean us all out in one night."

After a hurried dinner, the riders went to finish the gather before dark, if they could. Danielle, having finished repairing the Colts, went with them.

"Most of the varmints are holed up in thickets where there's shade," said Tuck. "We'll have to run them out of there."

"I've never worked cattle," Danielle said. "I don't know how much help I'll be here or on the trail to Abilene."

"The secret to trail driving," said Tuck, "is keepin' the varmints bunched. Keep 'em on the heels of one another so that every critter has a pair of horns right at her behind. It generally takes a few days—maybe a week—for them to get trail-wise and settle down."

Danielle rode into the brush with the other riders and was amazed at all the longhorns they flushed out. Some of the riders circled the growing gather, seeing to it that none of the cattle made a break for the thickets. With many riders, the gather proceeded quickly.

"I think we got enough," said Tuck, an hour before sundown. "Let's run a tally."

"I count five hundred and thirty head," Elmer Dumont said.

"I count five hundred and twenty-seven," said Cyrus Baldwin.

"Five hundred and thirty-two," Enos Chadman said.

"I count five hundred and twenty-five," said Wallace.

"Our herds has got a few more than five hundred," Elmer Dumont concluded. "We generally accept the lowest tally. Does that suit you, Tuck?"

"Yeah," said Tuck. "I'm glad to see this many. I was afraid, with all the rustling, we'd have trouble finding five hundred."

"You got lots of scrub thickets, especially near the spring runoff," said Wallace Flagg. "I believe we could drag out another five hundred if we had to."

"Let the others wait until spring," Tuck said. "It's important to get our gather on the trail to Abilene as soon as we can."

The gather was driven to the Carlyle ranch and herded in with more than two thousand of their kind.

"We got twelve men," said Enos Chadman. "We got to keep watch. I think with the herd bunched right here near the barn, we can get by with six men and two watches."

"It's always the men," Carrie Carlyle said. "I can shoot as well as any man here."

"No doubt you can, ma'am," said Chadman, "and I expect you'll get a chance to prove it before we reach Abilene. Get yourself one last good night's sleep in a bed."

THE TRAIL NORTH. AUGUST 20, 1870.

The first day on the trail, the cattle were predictably wild, seeking to break away and return to their old grazing meadows and shaded thickets. At her own request, Danielle rode drag. The chestnut mare quickly learned what was expected of her. When a cow quit the bunch, the mare was after her. Danielle had little more to do than just stay in the saddle.

"I reckon we've come ten miles," Enos Chadman said when they had bedded down the herd for the night.

"Lucky to do as well as that with a new herd," said Cyrus Baldwin.

"Starting tonight," Carrie said, "we'll need more than six on each watch. I'm offering to stand either watch."

"So am I," Katrina Chadman said.

"We may not need you," said Tuck. "We have enough men for a first and a second watch. The rest of you can just sleep with your guns handy."

"No," Katrina said. "We've already decided the women will do the cooking, and I can ride better than I can cook."

Her response brought a roar of laughter, and the question was finally resolved when it was decided that Carrie would join the first watch, and Katrina the second.

"You ladies ride careful," said Enos Chadman. "If one of you gets spooked and shoots a cow, you'll end up washing dishes the rest of the way to Abilene."

On the first watch were Danielle, Tuck, Katrina, Elmer Dumont and his son, Barney, Chadman's son, Eric, and Wallace Flagg's sons, Floyd and Edward. Carrie had hoped to be part of the first watch, and she watched Katrina Chadman with some envy. Katrina was a year older than Carrie, and Carrie wanted to prove herself in front of Danielle.

Supper was over, and it was time for the first watch to mount up. The cattle were restless, being on the trail for the first time, and the riders were kept busy by bunch quitters. Danielle's task was made simpler by the chestnut mare. The horse seemed to sense when a cow was about to break away, and was there to head her. There was a moon, and it was Danielle's first opportunity to see Katrina Chadman close up. The girl had long blond hair that she wore in a single braid, and she rode her horse like she was part of it. For a few minutes Tuck rode alongside her, the two of them laughing. Danielle suffered a new emotion. As she watched them, flames of jealousy rose up, threatening to engulf her.

"Damn you, Katrina," said Danielle under her breath. "You haven't seen him jaybird naked in the creek."

The cattle finally settled down, and by the time the second watch came on at midnight, there were no more bunch quitters. Breakfast was an orderly affair, with Anthea Dumont, Teresa Baldwin, Maureen Chadman, Tilda Flagg, and Audrey Carlyle doing the cooking.

"This is the best I been fed in ten years," said Elmer Dumont. "A man could start to liking these trail drives."

"A man generally don't have his womenfolks along to fix the grub," said Tuck. "We all know it's hard times in Texas, and we didn't dare leave them there."

"There's a stronger reason than that," Maureen Chadman said. "Katrina and me haven't had a stitch of new clothes since before the war, and we're practically naked. Surely we'll get enough for the herd so we don't go home in rags."

"We'll just have to hope we get a good price," said Enos Chadman uncomfortably.

"Katrina's cast-iron underpants are startin' to rust," Tuck said softly, standing behind Danielle.

"If anybody would know, it would be you," said Danielle coldly. "You spent the night following her around, instead of watching the herd."

"So what the hell is it to you?" Tuck demanded. "Sooner or later, she's got to give in to some *hombre*. Why not me? You reckon I can't do her justice?"

"I don't doubt that you can," said Danielle. "And neither does she. I just want to get this damn herd to Abilene so I can get on with my life."

"You mean, to get on with your killing," Tuck said.

"Well, just what the hell would *you* have done if your pa had been strung up without cause?"

"I deserved that," said Tuck. "I'd do the same thing you're doing."

Their second day on the trail was little better than the first. "We should reach Red River tomorrow," Elmer Dumont said. "From there on, every night will be a danger. They can even set up an ambush and pick us off in broad daylight."

"There's always the old Indian trick," said Wallace Flagg. "Stampede the herd, and when we separate to gather them, get us one at a time."

The third day on the trail, the cattle had begun to settle down. The drive reached the Red River, making camp on the Texas side.

"This could be our last peaceful night," Cyrus Baldwin warned. "From here on, it could be Indians, outlaws, or both."

The night was still, and Danielle lay in her blankets, unable to sleep. She kept hearing Katrina laugh, and had no doubt Tuck Carlyle was keeping her amused. On Danielle's mind was the sobering realization that unless that murdering pack of outlaws died somewhere in Indian Territory, she would have to ride away and leave Tuck to the wiles of Katrina. At midnight, when it was time to change watches, Danielle spoke to Tuck.

"Well, did you get the key?"

"Not tonight," Tuck said cheerfully. "Maybe tomorrow night."

"Damn it," said Danielle, "like most men, you have only one thing on your mind."

"Then I reckon you don't," Tuck said. "Are you one of them fool *hombres* that prefers *other hombres* to women?"

"Tuck Carlyle, if we weren't on watch, I'd pistol-whip you for saying that."

"Just watch your damn tongue," said Tuck. "You're startin' to sound like a jealous female, and anytime you're of a mind to pistol-whip *me*, just keep in mind that I have a pistol, too."

It silenced Danielle. Already, Tuck was suspicious of her. It was difficult playing the part of a man when she most yearned to be a woman, but her resolve to find her father's killers was just as strong as ever. She would have to keep her silence, whatever Tuck and

Katrina did. Danielle didn't realize it, but Tuck and Katrina were actually talking about her.

"I'd like to know Dan Strange a little better," Katrina said. "He keeps watching me, and he seems so nice."

"I reckon I'm not," said Tuck grimly.

"Sometimes you are," Katrina said, "and other times you're not. You think I haven't heard all the talk about my cast-iron underpants?"

"I didn't start that," said Tuck.

"I wouldn't expect you to admit it," Katrina said angrily, "but you repeated it."

"Hell, it's a reputation you created for yourself," said Tuck. "Your look-at-me-but-don't-touch attitude scares the hell out of men."

"Everybody except you," Katrina said.

"And I'm gettin' exactly nowhere," said Tuck angrily. "Build yourself a reputation as a man-hater, and you won't need them cast-iron underpants."

Katrina laughed. "I'll give the key to the right man. Just don't get your hopes up too high, Tuck Carlyle."

INDIAN TERRITORY. AUGUST 23, 1870.

The Red River crossing had been used many times before, and there was a shallows that allowed even the wagons to cross without difficulty. There was a trail of sorts left by previous drives, and they followed it closely. Tuck was the point rider, and with the herd still behaving, he rode far ahead, seeking out a possible ambush. But all during their first day in Indian Territory, they saw nobody.

"From here on," said Elmer Dumont, "all of you on watch mustn't let anybody through your guard. Our lives and the herd are depending on you. No talking and no smoking, and when it's your turn to sleep, keep your horses saddled and picketed."

A t the Wilks ranch, Kazman had just returned from Indian Territory. With him were four men, and he introduced them.

"These gents is Mitch Vesper, Elihu Dooling, Burt Keleing, and Chunk Peeler. I done told them what we got to do."

"Nothin' ain't been said about the pay," Dooling said. "This ain't one of them thirty-and-found jobs, is it?"

"Forty and found," said Wilks.

"Fifty and found," Dooling said. "If I got to shoot somebody, it'd better be worth my while."

There was quick agreement from Vesper, Keleing, and Peeler.

"Fifty and found, then," said Wilks, "but damn it, I want results."

"We can leave now and be in Indian Territory by midnight," Kazman said.

"I want you to get ahead of the herd and stampede them south," said Wilks. "There'll be no moon tonight, so don't go after the riders. Scatter the herd, and the riders will have to split up, looking for them. That's when we pick them off one or two at a time."

"Thirteen of us," Chunk Peeler said. "That's an unlucky number."

"Only if you don't do what you been hired to do," said Wilks. "Now get the rest of the bunch out of the bunkhouse, Kazman, and ride."

Within minutes, thirteen heavily armed men rode north toward Indian Territory.

D anielle noticed there was not much conversation between Tuck and Katrina, and she wasn't sure if it was by command or by choice. She was awake an hour before the second watch took to the saddle, and lay there listening. There was nothing to disturb the silence of the night except the occasional bawling of a cow.

An hour after the second watch had gone on duty, the raiders struck, riding in from the north. Bending low over the necks of their horses, they fired their pistols until it sounded like a small war in progress. The second watch fired at the elusive targets, their own shooting spooking the cattle all the more. The herd was on its feet in an instant, running south, seeking to escape these demons who swooped after them from the north. Tuck Carlyle and Wallace Flagg got ahead of the running longhorns, but they wouldn't be headed off, and the two cowboys had to ride for their lives to escape being trampled. The stampede thundered on while those responsible for it fell back and vanished into the darkness. Slowly, the night watch made its way back to camp.

"Damn it," said Enos Chadman, "we didn't get a one of 'em."

"Well, at least they didn't get any of us either," Elmer Dumont said. "That tells me that when we split up to gather the scattered herd, they'll try to gun us down."

"That bein' the case," said Tuck, "maybe we'd better let the cows go for a couple of days and trail the varmints that stampeded 'em."

"That's good thinking, up to a point," Wallace Flagg said, "but there's two problems. There must have been a dozen or more of the varmints, and you can be sure they'll split up, making it necessary for us to divide our forces. That will make it easy enough for them to gun us down from ambush."

"He's dead right," Cyrus Baldwin said.

"Damn it, we have to do *something*," said Tuck. "If we go after the cattle or the rustlers, we're goin' to be split up. If it takes the whole outfit to pick up one cow at a time, we'll still be here *next* August."

"I think they stampeded the herd south, so it'll be easier rounding them up once they have disposed of us," Enos Chadman said. "When the herd begins to scatter, the riders will split up and get ahead of us somewhere in Indian Territory."

"Maybe," said Wallace Flagg, "but I don't think so. Why scatter the herd all to hell and gone unless they aim to scatter us for bushwhacking purposes during the gather?"

"Mr. Flagg's talking sense," Tuck Carlyle said. "I think if we separate while gathering the herd, that we'll be picked off one at a time."

"You think we should go after the rustlers, then," said Wallace Flagg. "So do I. After we've gathered the herd, what's to stop them from stampeding it all over again? I think where we find one of these varmints, we'll find them all."

The argument raged back and forth until a decision was reached. Those from the first and second watches would trail the outlaws. The women—except for Katrina—would stay with the wagons. The tracks of shod horses were plain enough in the wake of the stampede, and as Flagg had predicted, once the herd had scattered, so had the riders.

"There's thirteen of us," Flagg said. "Let's split up into two groups, with each group tracking one rider. Unless they all come together in a bunch, we'll nail at least two of them."

Again Danielle was denied an opportunity to ride with Tuck, for he was on the first watch with Katrina. The sun was an hour high when they reached the point where the herd had begun to scatter. None of the tracks of shod horses continued south, but turned east or west.

"Damn it," said Elmer Dumont, "they're expecting us. They'll be holed up somewhere in Indian Territory."

"Give me one rider," Tuck said, "and if it's an ambush, we'll spring it."

"I'll go," said Danielle.

"You got it," Tuck said. "Ride a mile east of here, and then ride north. Look for the tracks of a rider who may have doubled back. I'll ride west and then north, doin' the same as you. As long as they're split up, they're at the same disadvantage we are."

Danielle rode east for almost a mile before turning north. Her Henry was cocked and ready, and she carried it under her arm. For several miles, there was no sign. Suddenly, she saw the tracks of a shod horse coming from the southeast. The tracks were fresh. It had to be one of the renegades bound for a rendezvous somewhere to the north.

To the west, Tuck Carlyle had made a similar discovery. His rifle ready, he cautiously followed the trail of the single horse. His first and only warning came almost too late. His horse suddenly nickered, and somewhere ahead, another answered. There was a blaze of gunfire barely missing him, and Tuck rolled out of the saddle. There was no sound of hoofbeats, which meant his man was holed up within rifle range.

"Come on," shouted Wallace Flagg back in the camp. "Tuck's flushed somebody."

To the west, Danielle had no warning. The first slug snatched the hat from her head, and the second whipped through the baggy front of her shirt, leaving her thankful she had an uncomfortable binder around her chest. She rolled out of the saddle as though she had been hit, taking her Henry with her. She lay still, counting on her adversary to show himself. When she heard footsteps, she resisted the temptation to turn her head. Whoever was coming to see if she was alive or dead must soon come within her view. He did finally.

"Just a damn kid," he said aloud.

"With a gun," said Danielle. She drew her Colt from flat on her back and fired twice.

She waited a few minutes, Colt in her hand, until she decided the bushwhacker had been alone. She then knelt beside him and began going through his pockets. She found only a bill of sale for a horse and an envelope addressed to Mitch Vesper. There was nothing in the envelope. On the back of it had been scribbled meaningless numbers. She then mounted the chestnut mare and rode back to meet her comrades. They had joined Tuck and were all looking at the bushwhacker he had shot.

"Did you find a name on him?" Danielle asked.

"Elihu Dooling," said Tuck. "Is he one of the bunch you're after?"

"No," Danielle said, "and neither is the one I shot. Either I'm barking up the wrong tree, or this bunch has added some new faces."

"They had more than eight men last night," said Tuck. "That means they've added to their gang."

"Daniel and Tuck," Elmer Dumont said, "that was a good piece of work. The rest of the varmints will have to come together sooner or later. I say we run 'em down, one at a time if we have to."

"It could become a Mexican standoff," said Cyrus Baldwin. "If they're after the herd, they can't round 'em up while they're dodgin' lead. Neither can we."

"It all comes down to who can hold out the longest," Wallace Flagg said. "This bunch will be just as aware as we are that we're not much more than a month away from snow. Every day we spend tracking them is one day less before snow flies."

"Well, damn it," said Enos Chadman, "what choice do we have? We know this bunch of owlhoots stampeded the herd with one thought in mind. They're countin' on us to split up in ones and twos, gathering the herd. That's when they'll come gunning for us."

"Then we have no choice except to track them down first," Danielle said.

"That's how it looks to me," said Chadman, his grateful eyes on Danielle.

"I'll agree with that," Wallace Flagg said. "Hell, I'd rather make the drive through the snow than to dodge bushwhacker bullets from here to Abilene."

It was a sentiment they all shared, and they again began seeking tracks of shod horses that belonged to the outlaws. Elmer Dumont and his son, Barney, were the next to flush out one of the rustlers. Barney took a slug through his left thigh, while Elmer was unscathed. It was he who had killed the bushwhacker. Quickly, the rest of the outfit gathered. Elmer went through the dead man's pockets, finding only a pocketknife and a few dollars.

"No name, then," said Danielle, disappointed.

"None," Elmer said. "Barney, you'd better ride back to the wagons and have your ma take care of that leg wound."

"There's a medicine kit and a gallon jug of whiskey in the wagon," said Tuck. "Barney, can you make it alone?"

"I can make it," the white-faced Barney said. "Go after the others."

Danielle sneaked a look at Katrina, and the girl's face was ashen.

Tuck helped Barney mount his horse, and when he had ridden away, the others mounted, leaving the dead outlaw where he lay.

"The buzzards and coyotes will eat well," Wallace Flagg said. "If we can gun down two or three more, it might make believers of the others."

Losing Barney Dumont, they had twelve riders.

"We're at a disadvantage," said Tuck, "because they can be holed up under cover. For that reason, I think we should ride in pairs."

"I'll vote for that," Danielle replied. "With two of us after the same bushwhacker, he'll be forced to divide his attention."

"Katrina rides with me," stated Enos Chadman.

Nobody disagreed or complained, for Katrina was still pale and obviously afraid. She gripped her saddle horn with both hands, keeping her head down, refusing to look at any of them. Danielle felt sorry for her, but she thought Tuck looked a little disgusted.

Floyd and Edward Flagg rode into the next ambush, coming out of the fight unscathed. They were searching the dead outlaw when the rest of their outfit arrived.

"Does he have a name?" Danielle asked anxiously.

"Yeah," said Floyd. "It's in his wallet. Chunk Peeler."

"Damn," Danielle said, "four of them, and not one of the eight I'm looking for."

"All of these might be the killers you're looking for," said Tuck. "The names you have may not even be their real names."

"I know," Danielle said softly. "I know. But I won't give up the search until I'm certain each of the men who killed my father is dead."

CHAPTER 5

INDIAN TERRITORY. AUGUST 24, 1870.

The riders found no more of the outlaws, and sundown wasn't more than an hour distant. Wallace Flagg spoke.

"We'd better get back to the wagons if we want supper. We can't afford a fire after dark. We haven't seen any of that bunch, but that don't mean they won't be throwing lead our way."

"It's cloudy in the west," Danielle said, "and there's the smell of rain. It'll wash out all the tracks by morning."

"Probably," said Flagg, "but it'll be dark soon. We can't trail them at night."

Disappointed as Danielle was, there was no denying the truth of Flagg's words. When they returned to the wagons, supper was almost ready.

"I think we'd all better stand watch all night," Enos Chadman said. "It'd be just like the varmints to wait for the rain, and using it for cover, storm the camp."

"I agree with that," said Elmer Dumont. "I'd feel safer wide-awake, with my old Henry rifle cocked and ready."

"We have a dozen men," Cyrus Baldwin said. "That's a pretty strong defense."

"Don't forget the women," said Teresa, his wife. "There's not a woman among us who can't shoot. I can't speak for anyone else, but I'm staying awake with my rifle."

All the women—even Katrina—added their voices to the clamor.

"Then it's settled," Wallace said. "Every one of us will be waiting, weapons ready for a possible attack."

Danielle said nothing, hoping the outlaws *would* attack. It might be her last chance, for ahead of her might lie long, hopeless trails.

Two hours into the night, the rain started. It came down in torrents, but still there was no sign of the outlaws.

Kazman and his remaining eight men were quarreling among themselves as to what their next move would be.

"Using the rain for cover, we can fire into their camp," Kazman argued.

"Yeah," said Rufe Gaddis. "Givin' 'em a muzzle flash to shoot at. We already lost four men, without saltin' down one of them. I don't aim to become the fifth."

"Me neither," Julius Byler said. "I'm gettin' out of here now while I got this rain to cover my tracks. Trail-herdin' cattle is hard work, at best. They can have it."

Quickly, the rest of the outlaws agreed to the proposal.

"Upton Wilks ain't gonna like this," Kazman warned. "For fifty and found, he expects a lot of a man."

"Don't make a damn to me *what* Wilks thinks," said Chancy Burke, "'cause I won't be goin' back there. Fifty dollars a month, my aching hindquarters. I need ten times that just to live like I want to."

There were shouts of approval from the other seven outlaws, and they began saddling their horses. They rode west, across Indian Territory, toward the little panhandle town of Mobeetie, Texas. Kazman stood there cursing them, dreading to face Upton Wilks. Finally, he mounted his horse and, riding wide of the cow camp, used the storm as cover to return to the Wilks place. Kazman reached Wilks's bunkhouse well after midnight. The house was dark, and in the morning he would have to face the wrath of Upton Wilks. He unsaddled his horse in the barn and went to the bunkhouse to get what sleep he could.

So the bastards walked out on me," Wilks stormed, "and you let them go?"

"What the hell was I supposed to do?" Kazman demanded. "There was eight of them and one of me, and they'd just seen them shirttail ranchers gun down four of our outfit. I come back to tell you, which was all I could do. While I'm at it, I might as well tell you I ain't ridin' back to Indian Territory to round up more killers. This is a hell-for-leather outfit you sent us after. There's nineteen of 'em, and even the women can shoot. And I got a little more to say to you. What you want calls for gun wages, and you're just too damn cheap to pay."

"Are you finished?" Wilks inquired in a dangerously low voice.

"I am and in more ways than one," said Kazman. "I've had more than enough of you and your dirty work. I'm drifting."

Kazman started for the door, but some sixth sense warned him. When Kazman turned, Wilks already had his pistol in his hand. Kazman drew and fired twice, and not until he was sure Wilks was dead did he make a move. He then proceeded to rip apart the Wilks house, eventually finding three hundred dollars.

"Thanks, you cheap old bastard," said Kazman. "This will see me through to somethin' better."

Kazman rode out, elated when the storm started again. When Wilks was discovered, the rain would have washed away the tracks of Kazman's horse. The law might be suspicious of him, but suspicion wasn't proof. Besides, it was a big land, this frontier, and the law would never find him in Arizona or California.

I think they've given up on us," said Wallace Flagg. "It's rained all night without a shot bein' fired, and they couldn't ask for better cover than this rain."

"There's a muzzle flash, even in the rain," Elmer Dumont said. "They'd have been some mighty good targets for return fire."

"It looks like the rain's set in for the rest of the day," said Cyrus Baldwin, "and I'm not the kind to set here and wait on outlaws who may or may not still be around. I say we begin gathering the herd and get on with the drive."

"By God, I'm with Cyrus," Wallace Flagg said.

The women kept their silence, while the rest of the men agreed to continue the drive as soon as the herd could be rounded up. There was enough dry wood in the possum belly of one of the wagons, so they had breakfast with hot coffee.

"It's unlikely any of the herd would have run far enough to cross the Red River," Elmer Dumont said, "so we should find them between here and there. Barney, you stay here, and stay off that wounded leg."

"Aw, hell," said Barney, "I ain't hurt that bad." But he obeyed his father.

The others saddled up, mounted, and rode south.

"Cows have a habit of drifting with a storm," Wallace Flagg said. "I think we should be riding toward the east."

Accepting Flagg's suggestion, they rode southeast and were soon rewarded by finding their first small bunch of cattle.

"We can pick these up on our way back," said Enos Chadman. "We should find the rest of 'em a mite farther down, maybe grazing alongside the Red."

Chadman's optimism was justified, for the grass was good along the north bank of the Red, and the cattle hadn't crossed the river. But the small herd had the wind and rain at their backs, and they resisted all efforts to turn them around.

"Damn it," Wallace Flagg said, "as long as the wind's blowing that rain out of the west, this bunch of critters ain't of a mind to go with us."

"But somehow we *got* to turn 'em around," said Tuck Carlyle. "If we don't, they'll just drift with the storm, taking them farther and farther away."

"There's maybe three hundred in that bunch," Enos Chadman

said. "Let's get ahead of them and start firing our rifles. We got to make them more afraid of us than they are of the storm."

When the dozen men began firing their rifles, the cattle bawled in confusion. Finally, they turned and, facing the storm, galloped west.

"She's clearin' up back yonder to the west," said Cyrus Baldwin. "Give it another hour or so, and the rain will be done."

Baldwin's prediction proved accurate, and before noon the wind had died to a whisper and the rain had ceased entirely.

"No way we'll round up the rest of 'em today," Tuck said.

"We couldn't move out tomorrow, even if we had 'em all rounded up," said Wallace Flagg. "After all this rain, our supply wagon would soon be hub deep in mud. While we gather the herd, the sun may dry the ground enough for us to start the day after tomorrow."

The riders continued their gather until almost sundown.

"Let's run a tally," Tuck Carlyle suggested. "I'd like to know how many more we got to find."

"Go to it," said Flagg. "Elmer, you and Cyrus run tallies, too, and we'll take whatever is the low count."

Tuck had the low count of seven hundred head. "Not bad, considerin' the storm," Enos Chadman said. "That's almost a third of 'em. I expect we'll get the rest tomorrow."

It was too late to ride after another bunch of cows, and supper would soon be ready. The riders unsaddled their horses, rubbed them down, and turned them loose to graze. The sun had been shining since noon, and much of the standing water had begun to dry up. As the riders settled down to supper, Katrina made it a point to sit next to Tuck Carlyle. For all the good it did her, she might as well not have existed.

"Tuck," Katrina said softly, "I'm sorry for the . . . things I said."

"Don't be," said Tuck. "I say what I think, and you have the same right."

The conversation immediately stopped, for Katrina feared she would drive him even farther away if she said anything more. Because of Barney Dumont's wound, he soon had a fever, and Danielle was moved to the first watch. As they circled the gathered herd, it was only a matter of time before Danielle found Katrina riding beside her.

"Tuck's angry with me," said Katrina. "Has he said anything . . . about me?"

"Not to me," Danielle said. "I think he's the kind to settle his own problems. Maybe you should talk to him."

"He won't talk to me," said Katrina miserably. "I was scared silly when the shooting started, and everybody was watching me. I'm a disgrace."

"It's a good time to be scared, when the lead starts flying," Danielle said. "Besides, you're just a girl, and it's not your place to be gunning down rustlers."

"That's the trouble," said Katrina. "Everybody sees me as a fool-ish girl who can't do much of anything, and I've proven them right. In case you haven't heard what the other men are saying, I wear cast-iron underpants."

Danielle laughed. "Do you?"

"Hell no," Katrina said. "There's nothing under my Levi's but my own hide. They call me names because I won't go into the hayloft with any two-legged critter that asks me."

"It's a woman's right to refuse," said Danielle.

"You sure don't talk like the rest of the men around here," Ka-trina said. "I thought Tuck was different, but I'm changing my mind. I like you better than I do him. You're good with a gun, but there's a gentle side to you. Something only a woman would notice."

Danielle's heart beat fast, for she was treading on dangerous ground. All she needed was for poor, confused Katrina to develop a romantic interest in her, if only to make Tuck jealous.

Weighing her words carefully, Danielle spoke. "Why don't you just leave Tuck Carlyle alone for a while? He's still young, and so are you. Besides Tuck's sister, Carrie, you're the only unattached female on this drive. Leave Tuck be, and it'll worry the hell out of him."

Katrina laughed. "Thanks. I'll do that, and if you don't mind, perhaps I'll build a fire under him by talking to you."

"That might work," said Danielle, "but don't push him too far."
Katrina rode away grinning.

Danielle felt sick to her stomach. She saw herself as a hypocrite,
telling Katrina how to win Tucker Carlyle while she—Danielle—was
interested in Tuck herself. But Katrina had an edge. She would be
there long after Danielle had ridden away in search of her father's
killers. Danielle bit her lower lip and said some words under her
breath that would have shocked her mother beyond recovery. Danielle
didn't know Tuck was nearby until he spoke to her from the darkness.

"Well, *amigo*, did you get the key to the cast-iron underpants?"

"Tuck," Danielle said, "it's cruel of you to keep repeating that.
She needs a friend."

"And now she has one," said Tuck. "You."

"Only if you play the part of a damn fool and drive her away,"
Danielle said. "But I'll be riding on once we reach Abilene. I can't
afford to have Katrina interested in me for a number of reasons."

"We still may run into that bunch of outlaws," said Tuck, changing the subject.

"I'm doubting it more and more," Danielle said. "There's too
many of us, and we're all armed. The bunch I'm lookin' for is the
kind who would kill and rob one man, like they did my pa. If the
odds aren't favoring them, they'll back off."

INDIAN TERRITORY. AUGUST 26, 1870.

The next morning the outfit set out downriver, seeking the rest
of their herd. Their women would stand watch over the seven
hundred cattle they had gathered the day before. When the sun
had been up an hour, both riders and horses were sweating. The
cattle, when they began finding them, were scattered. Single cows
grazed alone.

"We got our work cut out for us," Enos Chadman said. "It'll be
one damn cow at a time. We'll be lucky if we find the rest of 'em
in two or three days."

The riders split up, each going after one or two cows. Danielle watched Katrina as she went after the wandering cattle. Danielle felt some envy. While Katrina had been frightened during the gunfire, she was adept at gathering the strays. With doubled lariat, she swatted the behinds of troublesome steers and cows, bending them to her will. She would make some proud rancher a worthy wife, Danielle thought gloomily.

"Time for another tally before we herd these in with what we got yesterday," Wallace Flagg said.

Enos Chadman had the low count of six hundred and twenty-five.

"Just barely half of them," said Cyrus Baldwin. "Two more days, if the rest are all over hell, like those we found today."

"We're just almighty lucky they stopped shy of crossin' the Red," Enos Chadman said. "Otherwise and we might have been trailing them all the way to their home range, starting this drive from the very beginning."

"We might have been deeper into Indian Territory at the time of the stampede," said Tuck. "I've never been there, but I've heard it's hell, tracking stampeded cattle. The deeper you are into the Territory, the more danger."

"I've ridden across it," Danielle said, "and parts of it are wilderness. A cow—or a man—could hide there forever without being found."

Their day's gather was driven back to camp and bedded down with those gathered the day before. Barney Dumont was still feverish and would have to drink some of the whiskey during the night. Danielle remained on the first watch and wasn't in the least surprised when she again found Katrina riding alongside her.

"I've been watching how well you handle cattle," Danielle said. "My pa was a gunsmith, and I'm having to learn this business by watching the rest of you."

"Thank you," said Katrina. "You're better at it than you think. I remember what you said about leaving Tuck alone, and I caught him watching me all day."

Danielle laughed uneasily. "He thought he had you hooked, and now he's not quite so sure. Most men don't like it when things don't work out the way they've planned."

"You say some curious things, to be a man," Katrina said. "Most men will fight until hell freezes, even when they know they're wrong. I have the feeling you're not like that at all."

"I try not to be," said Danielle. "Ma tried to change my pa's mind about selling his gunsmithing business and going to Texas for a herd of cattle. The more she tried, the more stubborn he became. All his pride and stubbornness got him was a lonely grave here in Indian Territory."

"I'm surprised you weren't riding with him," Katrina said. "If it had been my pa, my brother, Eric, would have been hell-bent on going along."

Danielle thought fast. "He didn't want my mother left here alone. Then, after we knew Pa was dead, Ma changed her mind about me going, because she knew I'd be going anyway."

Katrina laughed. "You just described yourself the same way you have described most other men. Prideful and stubborn."

"Damn," said Danielle, "you've discovered my secret. I'm just like all the others."

"No," Katrina said. "There's something strangely different about you."

Danielle sighed. Was this curious girl seeing through her disguise, looking beyond her lowered voice, her man's clothing, and fast gun? She made a silent resolution to avoid Katrina as much as she could, hoping—yet dreading—that Tuck Carlyle's interest in her might be renewed.

INDIAN TERRITORY. AUGUST 28, 1870.

Gathering the remainder of the herd required two more days. "We started with 2,625 head," said Wallace Flagg, "and we now have 2,605. I think we'd better end this gather, take our small loss, and head for Abilene. I'd hate to be here looking for those twenty cows when the first snow flies."

Flagg's suggestion was met with unanimous approval, and the next morning, the drive again headed north. The hot August sun had sucked up standing puddles of water, there was no mud, and the wagons followed the herd without difficulty. The first and second watches were continued, and there was no further sign of the expected outlaws. Danielle was glad for the sake of the small ranchers, but disappointed with her own position. She had been virtually certain the outlaws would try to take the herd. Now, having seen four of their number quickly shot down, the others had apparently given up. Tuck had barely spoken to her since she had begun talking to Katrina, and Danielle was surprised to find him riding beside her in drag position.

"What are you doing with the drag?" Danielle asked. "You think these cows will find their way to Abilene without you leading them?"

Tuck laughed. "They'll have about as much chance with me leading 'em. I've never been to Abilene. I just hope we can avoid any more outlaws and stampedes."

"I just wish I knew whether or not the bunch of outlaws that stampeded the herd is the same outfit that murdered my pa. The more I think about it, the more certain I am that the killers aren't using their real names. The names I have may mean exactly nothing."

"Yet, when we reach Abilene, you still aim to go looking for them," Tuck stated.

"Yes," said Danielle. "I made a promise, and I'll live or die by it."

Tuck's sister, Carrie, had said virtually nothing to Danielle since the drive had begun, and it came as a surprise when she found Carrie riding along beside her during the first watch.

"You've been avoiding me," Carrie said. "What does Katrina Chadman have that I don't have? Besides the cast-iron underpants, of course."

"She has feelings for that thickheaded brother of yours," said

Danielle. "She needs somebody to tell her there's nothing wrong with her. She needs a friend, and I haven't seen any of the rest of you being overly friendly."

"I've never been her friend, because she seemed snooty and stuck-up," Carrie said. "I can't see that she has anything I *don't* have, but she acts like she does."

"It's a defense against the way she's been treated," said Danielle. "How would *you* feel if men started spreading the word that *you* have cast-iron underpants?"

"I think I'd be flattered," Carrie said. "Nobody notices me except Barney Dumont, and he's about as romantic as a corral post."

Danielle laughed. "Do you want me to spread the word that you have cast-iron underpants, too?"

Carrie sighed. "I suppose not. Perhaps someday a man will see me for what I am. Whatever that may be. Do you still plan to leave us when we reach Abilene?"

"I must," said Danielle, "unless somewhere between here and there, I run into those outlaws who murdered my pa."

"I'll hate to see you go," Carrie said. "You're too nice to be shot in the back by some devil of an outlaw."

"I've learned to watch my back," said Danielle, "but I appreciate the kind words."

ABILENE, KANSAS. SEPTEMBER 15, 1870.

The outfit reached Abilene without further stampede, Indian attacks, or outlaw trouble. There were two cattle buyers who hadn't left town, and Wallace Flagg called on both of them.

"I got us a deal," Flagg said. "We're definitely the last herd of the season, and all our beef is prime. We're getting thirty-five dollars a head."

Flagg collected the money, and the first thing he did was count out thirty-five hundred dollars of it to Danielle. He then divided what was left by five, and the five ranchers each had a little more than eighteen thousand dollars.

"Dear God," said Wallace Flagg's wife, weeping, "I never expected to see so much in my whole life."

"We have Dan Strange to thank for suggesting this drive," Tuck Carlyle said. "All of us, on our own, were sittin' there starving, waiting for the rustlers to drive off the cattle we had left. Now we'll have enough to make a bigger drive next year."

Amid shouting and cheering, Danielle felt a little guilty. She had taken thirty-five hundred dollars of their money, after investing only three hundred dollars. But she was grateful and told them so.

"I don't feel like I've earned this money," Danielle said, "but God bless every one of you for it. Now I won't have to always sleep on the ground, living on jerked beef."

The time had come for Danielle to say good-bye, and she found it far more difficult than she had expected. Carrie and Katrina further dampened her enthusiasm by weeping, while all she got from Tuck was a handshake. Mounting the chestnut mare, she rode west, having no destination in mind. Far beyond the Kansas plains lay Colorado. She had heard Denver was a thriving town, and being so far west, it might be the very place that would appeal to outlaws ready to hole up for the winter. She would go there, but her progress was interrupted by a blizzard that had blown in from the high plains. She fought snow and howling wind for the last few miles, before reaching the little town of Hays.

HAYS, KANSAS. SEPTEMBER 20, 1870.

With the Union Pacific Railroad coming through Hays, there were many cafés, hotels, and boardinghouses. After leaving her horse at a nearby livery, Danielle took a room on the first floor of one of the hotels. There was already a foot of snow on the ground, and a man from the restaurant was shoveling a path to the hotel. Danielle decided to go ahead and eat before the storm became more intense. In the café sat a man she had seen in the hotel lobby. He wore at least a three-day beard and a pair of tied-down Colts, and he eyed Danielle as he had in the hotel lobby. He left the café before Danielle finished her meal. When she left, darkness had fallen, and the swirling snow blinded her. There was a sudden muzzle flash in the whiteout, and quickly returning the fire, Danielle dropped to her knees, unhurt. She heard the unmistakable sound of a body thudding to the ground. She waited to see if anyone had been drawn by the shooting, although she was unable to see the front of the café or the hotel. Minutes passed and nobody appeared. She approached the inert form and saw that it was the man from the café, his intense eyes now rolled back. Searching the dead man quickly, Danielle found only a worn wallet. She placed it in the pocket of her Levi's and hurried on to the hotel. She found a fire had already been started in the stove in her room, and that it was comfortably warm. Locking the door, she lighted a lamp and sat down on the bed to find out whom she had killed. The dead man's wallet contained no identification. There was a hundred dollars, however, and she took it. From the man's behavior, she was virtually certain he was on the dodge, but why had he come after her? She was leaving yet another dead man along her back trail, without the slightest idea why he had tried to kill her. She added more chunks of wood to the already glowing stove and prepared for bed. She thought of the many nights she had slept in her clothes and, despite the risk, stripped them all off. She had worn the binder around her chest so tight, her ribs were sore, and she sighed in blessed relief when she was without the bothersome binder. When she lay down for the night, the howling wind whipped snow against the window, and she was doubly thankful for a soft bed and a warm room.

When Danielle awakened next morning, the fire in the stove had apparently gone out, for the room was cold. She lay there dreading to get up. Finally, wrapping a blanket about herself, she got up and looked out the window. There was an unbroken expanse of snow, and it was still falling. Some buildings had drifts all the way up to the windowsills. The room was colder than Danielle had imagined, and hurrying back to the bed, she lay there shivering. Unanswered questions still galloped through her mind. Who *was* the gunman she had been forced to shoot, and why had he tried to kill her? An obvious answer was that he was probably an outlaw who feared being followed by a lawman. But Danielle had said or done nothing to lead the stranger to suspect she represented the law. It would be to her advantage to leave town before the melting snow revealed the dead man, but she dared not attempt it with snow up to a horse's belly. She considered the possible ways the law might connect her to the killing, and decided there was only one. While she had been in the café, the man had scarcely taken his eyes off her. There had been others in the café, including several cooks. Had any of them noticed the dead man's interest in the stranger with a tied-down Colt?

Resuming her identity as a man, Danielle donned the sheepskin-lined coat and gloves she had bought in Abilene. She then left the hotel for the café. She was dismayed when she discovered the only other person in the café wore a lawman's star. One of the cooks spoke to the sheriff, and he stood up, coming toward Danielle's table.

"I'm Sheriff Edelman," said the lawman. "Yesterday, there was a killer in town name of Gib Hunter, wanted in Texas, Missouri, and Kansas. When he left the café, he never went back to his hotel room. His horse is still at the livery. Do you know anything about him?"

"Only what you've just told me," Danielle said. "I'm Dan Strange, from St. Joe, and I got caught in this blizzard on my way west. Why would you expect me to know anything about this Gib Hunter?"

"I've been told Hunter had his eyes on you last night after you came in for supper," said the lawman. "Since I have no other clues, I thought there might be a connection."

"I saw him watching me," Danielle said, "and I can't imagine why unless he mistook me for somebody else. He left the café ahead of me, and I went straight to the hotel."

"Snowin' like it was, a man with killing on his mind could stage one hell of an ambush, couldn't he?"

CHAPTER 6

Sheriff Edelman's question took Danielle by surprise, and she recovered as quickly as she could.

"I'm not a bounty hunter, Sheriff, if that's what you're thinking."

"Glad to hear it," Edelman said, "and the possibility *had* crossed my mind. All over the frontier, there are men who are man hunters. They make their living hunting down wanted men with prices on their heads. Texas is willing to pay a thousand dollars for Gib Hunter, dead or alive."

"From what you've told me," said Danielle, "Hunter had been here several days. If you recognized him, why didn't you arrest him then?"

"I wanted to be sure," Sheriff Edelman said, "so I sent telegrams to authorities in Texas, Kansas, and Missouri. It took a while to get answers."

"Maybe one of the bounty hunters got him," said Danielle.

"I doubt it," Sheriff Edelman said. "He was in the café last night, and even then, snow was up to a sow's ear. Something happened to him after he left the café and before he reached the hotel. His bed hasn't been slept in."

"So I'm a suspect," said Danielle.

"Frankly, yes," Sheriff Edelman said. "It has all the earmarks of a bounty killing. You and Gib Hunter were the only strangers in town. Maybe you *ain't* a bounty hunter, but this owlhoot had no way of knowin' that. It could have well been his reason for watching you in the café, and reason enough for him to use the storm as cover, bushwhacking you when you left."

"Well, he's gone," said Danielle. "Can't you be satisfied with that?"

"It ain't that easy for a lawman," Sheriff Edelman said. "Wanted men are unpredictable. You never know when they're goin' to get suspicious, like Hunter was last night, and it's damn near impossible to prove one of 'em's dead if you can't produce a body. Come on, kid, tell me what happened after you left the café last night."

Danielle sighed. She had fired in self-defense, and Hunter's Colt would prove it. There seemed little doubt that Sheriff Edelman would not stop short of hearing the truth of it. It was time for a decision, and Danielle made it.

"All right, Sheriff," said Danielle. "When I left the café, it was snowing so hard that I couldn't see my hand in front of my face. Somebody fired at me, and even through the swirling snow, I could see the muzzle flash, so I returned fire. You'll find him there just a few feet from the western wall of the hotel. I'd never seen the man until last night, and I'm claiming self-defense."

"I won't dispute that," Sheriff Edelman said. "I just need to find him so we can close the book. There'll be an inquest in the morning, and you'll have to testify. But with deep snow and maybe more comin', you can't go anywhere. Besides, soon as I can verify that Hunter's dead, the state of Texas will owe you a thousand dollars."

"I told you I'm no bounty hunter," said Danielle, "and I don't want any reward. All I did was defend myself. Claim the reward in my name, and then see that it goes to a needy cause, such as an orphanage or church."

"I'll do that," Sheriff Edelman said. "I'll see you at half past eight tomorrow morning, and we'll go to the courthouse for the inquest. Now I'd better get some men with shovels to dig out Gib Hunter."

Somehow, Danielle felt better for having told the lawman the truth. He was right about the snow, and there was no way she could leave until it began to melt. By then, Hunter's body would have been found. The snow finally ceased in the late afternoon and there was a dramatic drop in the temperature. A big thermometer outside the hotel's front door said it was ten below zero. Danielle kept to herself, never allowing the fire in her stove to burn too low.

True to his word, Sheriff Edelman was at the hotel the next morning. Danielle was in the hotel lobby, waiting.

"We'd better get started," Sheriff Edelman said. "Snow's still mighty deep."

"I reckon you found him, then," said Danielle.

"Yeah," Sheriff Edelman said, "and there's proof enough of what you told me. His Colt had been fired and was still in his hand. I'll testify to that."

With Danielle's story and Sheriff Edelman's testimony, the inquest lasted not more than a quarter hour. Hunter's death was ruled self-defense. With some relief, she started back toward the hotel. There was little to do until the snow began to melt, and not until the following day did the clouds begin to break up enough for the sun to emerge. Danielle was thoroughly sick of the hotel and the café next door, silently vowing to ride out if some of the snow had melted.

MOBEETIE, TEXAS. SEPTEMBER 25, 1870.

The eight outlaws who had deserted Upton Wilks had reached Mobeetie just in time to hole up in the hotel before the snowstorm had begun.

"If we ain't goin' back to Indian Territory," Rufe Gaddis said, "I think we should split up. Eight of us in a bunch attract too much attention. I've already heard talk here in the hotel. Somebody's wonderin' who we are and why we're here."

"I think you're right," said Julius Byler. "We'd better split."

Chancy Burke, Saul Delmano, Newt Grago, Snakehead Kalpana, Blade Hogue, and Brice Levan quickly agreed.

"I crave warm weather," said Snakehead Kalpana. "I'm bound for south Texas."

"Yeah," Newt Grago said. "You aim to run them Mex horses across the border into Texas. Better men than you have been strung up for that."

When the snow had finally melted enough to permit travel, the eight outlaws split up, each going his separate way.

HAYS, KANSAS. SEPTEMBER 25, 1870.

Danielle judged the snow had melted enough for her to continue her journey to Denver. Before riding out, she paused at the sheriff's office to tell Edelman she was leaving.

"Good luck, kid," Sheriff Edelman said. "Don't turn your back on strangers."

The hotel clerk had told Danielle it was just a little under three hundred miles to Denver, so Danielle took her time. There were still snowdrifts so deep, it was necessary to dismount and lead the chestnut mare. An hour before sundown, Danielle found a secluded canyon where there was water. The canyon rim was high enough to keep out the cold night wind. After a hurried supper, she put out her fire. The chestnut mare had been picketed near the stream where there was still some graze. Confident that the horse would warn her of any danger, Danielle rolled in her blankets at the foot of the canyon rim where the snow had melted and the ground was dry. She slept undisturbed, awakening as the first gray light of dawn crept into the eastern sky. After a quick breakfast, she again rode west. Much of the snow had melted, being replaced with mud as the sun thawed the ground and sucked up the moisture. About two hours before sundown she came upon two sets of horse tracks leading from the southeast. While catching up to them could possibly be dangerous, they might be two of the very outlaws she sought. Her first warning came when the chestnut mare nickered and a distant horse answered. Danielle reined up.

"Hello, the camp!" Danielle shouted. "I come in peace."

"Come on," said a cautious voice. "Just keep your hands where I can see 'em."

Both men stood with their revolvers cocked and ready.

"My name is Dan Strange, and I'm from St. Joe, Missouri, on my way to Denver."

The men were young, in their early twenties, Danielle judged, and they looked like out-of-work line-riding cowboys. Danielle had made no threatening moves, and the pair slid their weapons back into their holsters.

"I'm Herb Sellers," said the rider who had called out the challenge. "My *amigo* here is Jesse Burris. Our grub's running low and we're out of coffee, but you're welcome to take part in what there is."

"I just left a trail drive in Abilene," Danielle said, "and I stocked up on supplies. Why don't you let me supply the grub for supper? I have coffee, too."

"That's the best offer I've had lately," said Sellers. "We holed up in Dodge, waiting out the storm, and town living just about busted us."

"Yeah," Burris said. "We done been starved out of Texas. Where in tarnation did you find a trail herd bound for Abilene? Ain't no money in Texas. It's been picked clean, and the buzzards is still there."

"Five small ranchers risked everything they had, driving twenty-six hundred head to Abilene," said Danielle. "Come spring, they'll have money enough to take a larger herd."

"Straight across Indian Territory," said Sellers. "Any trouble with rustlers?"

"Some," Danielle admitted. "After we killed four of them, the others decided to ride on to other parts."

The two men laughed, appreciating the droll humor.

"We aim to do some bounty hunting," said Sellers. "Catching

outlaws pays rewards, and I don't know of nobody needin' it worse than we do. We heard that Gib Hunter had been seen in Dodge and might be headed for Denver. That's a thousand-dollar bounty."

"No more," Danielle said. "Hunter tried to bushwhack somebody during the storm and was gunned down in Hays. I was waiting out the storm myself."

"Damn the luck," said Sellers. "We're having trouble getting the names of outlaws with prices on their heads. Lawmen don't like bounty hunters."

"That's one reason we're bound for Denver," Burris said. "I got an uncle there, and he's working for the Pinkertons. We're hoping he can supply us a list of outlaws and the bounties on their heads."

While Danielle wasn't concerned with the bounty, the possibility of a list of the names of outlaws on the dodge appealed to her. These two down-at-the-heels cowboys seemed to be exactly as they had described themselves. Danielle decided to take a chance and, after supper, told the pair of her search for the outlaws who had murdered her father.

"I'm not after these men for the bounty," Danielle said. "I don't know if there's bounty on them, but of the ten of them still loose, I can tell you the names they were using in Indian Territory."

"Then maybe we can work out a trade," Burris said. "If my uncle in Denver can get us a list of wanted men with bounties on their heads, you can compare the names you have to the names on the list."

"I'd be obliged," said Danielle. "I'm hunting them down because I don't want any of them to go free. If there's money on their heads, then you're welcome to it. I just want them dead."

On a page from a small notebook, Danielle wrote down the names of the outlaws that she remembered.

"Nobody on here I've ever heard of," Jesse Burris said, "but that don't mean anything. Outlaws change their names like the rest of us change our socks. It'll be something to compare to our list if we're lucky enough to get one."

Danielle had no cause to doubt the sincerity of the two young bounty hunters, but she slept with her Colt in her hand. Danielle supplied the food and coffee for breakfast, and the trio set out for Denver. Except for deep canyons where the sun didn't often shine, the snow had melted, leaving a quagmire of mud.

DENVER, COLORADO. SEPTEMBER 27, 1870.

There was nothing fancy about the Denver House, but its rooms weren't expensive, and Danielle rented two of them.

"You shouldn't've done that," said Herb Sellers. "We can't repay you until we collect some bounties."

"Let me look at your list of known outlaws," Danielle said, "and that will be payment enough."

"I aim to call on the Pinkertons and talk to my uncle in the morning," Burris said.

The more Danielle thought about it, the less likely it seemed the Pinkerton listing of known outlaws would be of any value. From what she had heard, the Pinkerton Agency was most often called upon to seek out bank and train robbers. The outlaws who had hanged Daniel Strange in Indian Territory began to seem more and more like a ragtag lot of renegades left over from those infamous days following the war. But Danielle had not a single lead, and a Pinkerton list would be better than nothing. Danielle bought supper for the three of them at a small café.

"Jesse and me aim to hit some of the saloons tonight," Herb said. "Want to come with us?"

"I reckon not," said Danielle. "I'm tired of sleeping on the ground, and I want to enjoy a warm bed."

If the two were out of grub and low on money, the last place they should be going was to a saloon, Danielle thought. But it was the way of the frontier not to offer advice or opinions unless asked.

After the recent snow, there had been a warming trend and it seemed a shame to retire to her room so early. After Herb Sellers and Jesse Burris had left, Danielle changed her mind. Without taking her chestnut from the livery stable, she would walk to the places of business nearest the hotel. One of them—the Pretty Girl Saloon* —was across the street from her hotel. The Pretty Girl was a two-story affair, and the bottom floor was well lighted. There was a bar all along one side of the room, while the rest of it was occupied by a roulette wheel, several billiard tables, and more than a dozen tables topped with green felt for poker and blackjack. A winding staircase led to the second floor. Waitresses dressed in flowing fancy gowns carried drinks to tables where the different games were in progress. Danielle stopped one of the waitresses.

"What's upstairs?"

"High-stakes poker and faro," the waitress said. "It'll cost you a hundred dollars to go up there, but you get a hundred dollars' worth of credit at the poker or faro tables."

While Danielle didn't care for poker, she had played faro—or "twenty-one"—with her father and brothers many times, and she understood the game. She still had more than thirty-three hundred dollars, and feeling bold, she took five double eagles from her Levi's pocket and exchanged them for chips.

"First door on the left, at the head of the stairs," the waitress said.

Danielle climbed the stairs, opened the door, and got the shock of her life. All over the huge gambling hall there were young women who wore nothing except a short jacket that covered the arms and shoulders, and red slippers on their feet. Danielle had no interest in naked women and was about to leave, when she recalled she had paid a hundred dollars to come to the second floor. Obviously, the girls were there to take a man's mind off how much he had lost or was likely to lose. Danielle took her handful of five-dollar chips to one of the faro tables.

"Minimum bet five dollars," said the dealer.

---

* The first Pretty Girl Saloon was in New Orleans. They caught on rapidly in the West.

Danielle lost five times in a row, and then she started winning. One of the naked girls was at her side, urging her to visit the bar, but Danielle wouldn't be distracted. Not until she had won more than three hundred dollars did she leave the table. There were some vain attempts to lure her to the poker tables, where the saloon might recover some of its money, but Danielle wasn't tempted. With a last look at the naked women, she stepped out into the hall, closing the door behind her. Reaching the street, she walked for an hour before returning to the hotel. She secretly hoped Sellers and Burris were as broke as they had implied, so that Burris wouldn't be hungover and sick when it was time to visit the Pinkerton office.

D anielle was awake at first light. She was sitting on the bed, tugging on her boots, when there was a knock on her door.

"Who's there?" she inquired.

"Sellers and Burris," said a voice.

Danielle got up, unlocked the door, and let them in.

"We got in a poker game and, between us, won more'n five hundred dollars," Jesse Burris said.

"That's risky when you can't afford to lose," said Danielle.

"Hell, we know that," Sellers said, "but we had so little, it didn't make much difference between that and stone broke. Let's get breakfast. We're buying."

After eating, they returned to the hotel, where they paid for another night.

"You want to go with us to the Pinkerton office?" Jesse Burris asked.

"I reckon not," said Danielle. "You'll likely be more successful if they don't think you have a gang of bounty hunters. I'll be here when you return."

Danielle waited for almost four hours before the young bounty hunters returned.

"We got a list of thirty men with prices on their heads," Jesse Burris said. "Look at it and see if any of the names sound familiar."

Eagerly, Danielle took the list, reading it twice.

"Well," said Herb, "have you found any of 'em?"

"Just two," Danielle said. "Rufe Gaddis and Julius Byler."

"Since you already knew their names, and the same names are on the Pinkerton list, it sounds like they're using their real names," said Jesse Burris.

"It does seem that way," Danielle said. "I just wonder if some of the others on this list are the men I want, using different names."

"One thing I learned from the Pinkertons might be helpful to you," Jesse Burris said. "In southern New Mexico, southern Arizona, and other territories where there's a lot of silver and gold mining going on, there's plenty of outlaws."

"I'm surprised the Pinkertons would tell you that," said Danielle. "Seems to me they'd be anxious to cover that territory themselves."

"They've tried," Burris said. "Three Pinkerton men were sent there almost six months ago, and they haven't been heard from. They're presumed dead."

"Damn," said Danielle, "I can't believe the Pinkertons would take that without fighting back. I thought they were tougher than that."

"They're plenty tough and dedicated," Burris said, "but they bleed just like anybody else when they're bushwhacked or shot in the back."

Danielle sighed. "I don't know where to start."

"Neither do we," said Herb Sellers. "Now that we got a stake, we're gonna stay here one more night and try our luck at the poker tables."

"Don't risk all you have," Danielle cautioned. "These outlaws may be scattered from here to yonder, and it may take some time to collect a bounty."

"That's good advice," said Jesse Burris. "I think we'll do well to take it."

"I think so, too," Herb Sellers said. "You've been a lot of help to us, Dan. In a way, I reckon we're all in the same business. If you ever get your tail caught in a crack, be sure we'll side you till hell freezes."

"I'm obliged," said Danielle. "If I'm there, and you need me and my gun, you got it."

Danielle had supper with Sellers and Burris. Afterward, the pair set out for the saloons and poker tables. Danielle, still two hundred dollars ahead after the previous night at the Pretty Girl Saloon, decided to return there. It seemed immoral to her, naked women wandering among the tables, fetching drinks. More and more, however, Danielle was becoming accustomed to this man's world. The naked girls drew men like flies drawn to a honey jug. She wondered how a man kept his mind on the game, with a naked female to distract him. Suppose they discovered she wasn't a man? Would she be asked to leave?

Reaching the saloon, Danielle paid her hundred dollars, received her credit in chips, and made her way up the stairs. She opened the door into the gambling hall, and immediately a pair of the naked women was there to greet her.

"I remember you from last night, cowboy," said one of the women. "You won big."

"I reckon," Danielle said. "You just have to keep your mind on the game."

Danielle headed for a faro table, while the two naked women looked at each other questioningly. It had been their specific duty to watch for the return of this stranger who seemed to have no interest in naked women and kept his mind on the game. The naked pair hurried to the faro table and watched Danielle win the first three hands. She lost one and then won the next two. Occasionally she lost a hand, but won more often than she lost. So engrossed was she in the game, she failed to see the man with a tied-down revolver quietly leave the hall. Danielle decided it was time to back off after she had won four hundred dollars.

"You're on a roll, cowboy," one of the girls said. "Don't be in a hurry."

"Thanks," Danielle said, "but it's past my bedtime."

She had taken seven hundred dollars of the saloon's money in two days, and she fully understood the hard looks she had received from the dealers as she prepared to leave. She had ignored the naked women, defied the odds, and won. Now she had only to cross the street to her hotel. She felt like her luck had run out at the Pretty Girl Saloon. Her feeling was confirmed when, from the darkness between the hotel and the building adjoining it, there came a blaze of gunfire. The first slug ripped through Danielle's left arm between wrist and elbow, but it didn't affect her aim. Lightning quick, she drew her Colt and fired twice. Once to the left and then once to the right of the muzzle flash. Three men—one of them the desk clerk—rushed out of the hotel.

"What's going on out here?" the desk clerk demanded.

"Somebody tried to bushwhack me," replied Danielle, "and I shot back. I reckon you'd better send for the sheriff."

Sheriff Hollis arrived soon after with a lantern. Scarcely looking at Danielle, Hollis headed for the dark area between the hotel and the adjoining building. There he hunkered down, and in the pale light from the lantern, it became obvious he was examining the body of a man. Slowly the sheriff returned to the street where Danielle stood, blood dripping off the fingers of her left hand.

"Come on," said Sheriff Hollis. "We'll have Doc take care of your wound. Then you'll go to my office and tell me what this is all about."

"It's about me being bushwhacked," Danielle said. "I fired back."

"Two hits in the dark," said Sheriff Hollis. "I don't often see shooting like that."

Danielle said nothing. When they reached the doctor's house, he quickly cleaned and bandaged Danielle's wounded arm. Danielle then followed Sheriff Hollis back to his office.

"Now," Sheriff Hollis said, "you have some talking to do. Start with your name."

"Daniel Strange. I had just left the Pretty Girl Saloon and was on my way back to my hotel. I didn't fire until somebody fired at me."

"I believe you," said Sheriff Hollis. "This is not the first time this has happened here, but it's the first time anybody's nailed a bushwhacker. His name is Belk Sanders. Have you heard of him?"

"Not until just now," Danielle said. "I'd just won four hundred dollars playing blackjack at the Pretty Girl Saloon. Sanders must have been there, leaving ahead of me. But the cost of going upstairs is a hundred dollars' worth of gambling chips. I doubt anyone would be able to afford that very often, and it makes me wonder if the saloon didn't hire him to bushwhack the winners and take back the money."

"I've thought of that myself," Sheriff Hollis said, "but there's no proof. Tonight's the fourth time a winner from the Pretty Girl has been bushwhacked. The first three weren't as sudden with a pistol as you."

"How long has this Belk Sanders been around here?" Danielle asked. "What does he do besides hang around in saloons?"

"Nothing as far as I know," said Sheriff Hollis, "but he always seemed to be flush. I think maybe you solved one of my problems tonight."

"Will you need me for an inquest?" Danielle asked. "I'm claiming self-defense."

"You'll have no trouble with the court," said Sheriff Hollis, "and I don't think you'll have to be here. Three men in the hotel, including the desk clerk, saw the muzzle flash from Sanders's gun before you fired. I've never seen a more obvious case of self-defense."

"I'll be at the hotel tonight, and until sometime tomorrow, if you need me," Danielle said. "I want to be sure this wound is going to heal before I ride on."

"Good thinking," said Sheriff Hollis. "Get yourself a quart of whiskey. It'll take care of a fever and kill any infection."

Danielle returned to the Pretty Girl Saloon, but only for some whiskey, which she was able to buy at the downstairs bar. From there, she returned to her hotel. By then, her wounded arm had begun to hurt, and she took a dose of the laudanum the doctor had given her. The quart of whiskey she placed on the table beside the bed. She awakened the next morning with a temperature, and forced herself to drink some of the liquor. It was a terrible experience, for Danielle had never tasted whiskey before. She choked the stuff down, wondering if it wouldn't do more harm to her insides than the bullet had done to her arm. She counted her blessings, for Sanders had fired twice. Had his second shot hit her, it might have been necessary for the doctor to undress her in order to treat the wound. That would have given the lawman and the town something to talk about, and would have explained why the Pretty Girl Saloon's naked women hadn't taken her mind off her game of twenty-one. Danielle was soon sick from the whiskey, and long before she was ready to get up, there was a knock on her door.

"It's Herb and Jesse," a voice said. "We're invitin' you to breakfast."

"I can't eat," said Danielle. "I had some whiskey last night, and I'm sick. I reckon I'll be here another night. If you're still here at suppertime, I'll join you."

The day dragged on, and it was late afternoon before Danielle felt like getting up. But when there was a knock on her door, she was ready.

"Burris and Sellers," said a voice through the door. "It's suppertime."

Danielle let them in, and although her shirtsleeve concealed her bandaged arm, the two of them looked at her with renewed interest.

"We heard what happened last night," Jesse Burris said. "The desk clerk's talking about it to anybody who'll listen."

"My God, that was some shootin'," said Herb Sellers enthusiastically. "You nailed the varmint twice, with only a muzzle flash to shoot at. When you start teachin' lessons for using a six-gun, I aim to sign up."

Danielle laughed. "My pa was the best gunsmith in all of Missouri. He taught me to draw and shoot."

"Maybe there's a reward on this gent you shot last night," Jesse Burris said.

"If there is, I don't want it," said Danielle. "I shot him because he shot at me. Now tell me about your night at the poker tables."

"Nothin' to brag about," Herb Sellers said. "Between us, we lost a hundred dollars, and when we managed to win it back, we quit. Is that Pretty Girl Saloon all it's cracked up to be?"

"I don't know about the poker," said Danielle, "but the faro game is honest. You have to play with a naked woman beside you."

CHAPTER 7

DENVER, COLORADO. SEPTEMBER 30, 1870.

Danielle spent one more night in Denver, feeling the need to visit some more saloons. It was unlikely the men she was hunting would be well-heeled enough to visit the Pretty Girl Saloon, and she silently rebuked herself for having spent two nights there. However, her stake was now thirty-six hundred dollars. Wisely spent, it would last her many months. One of the first saloons she found was the Broken Spoke, and as she entered, one of the bouncers spoke.

"Poker tables are in the back, behind the curtain, kid."

Since Danielle had sworn off any further bouts with whiskey, there was no excuse for hanging around the bar, so pushing aside the curtain, she went on to the poker area.

"Table stakes, dollar limit," said one of the dealers.

"Too rich for my blood," Danielle said. "I'd like to watch for a while. Maybe I'll learn something."

"I don't want you lookin' over my shoulder," said one of the players. "It makes me nervous."

One of the other men laughed. "Levan's nervous because he ain't won a pot tonight, and the way he's playin' his cards, he ain't likely to."

Levan! Could it be Brice Levan, from the death list? Danielle stayed there a few more minutes without learning anything more about Levan. Finally, she left the saloon, hiding in the darkness near where the horses were tied. Sooner or later, Levan would have to leave, and if he was playing poker badly, it shouldn't be long. When he finally exited the saloon, he staggered a little. He had tied his horse's reins securely to the hitching rail, and cursing, he fumbled with the knot. Danielle stepped out of the shadows with a Colt steady in her hand.

"I'm looking for a man named Levan," Danielle said. "What's your first name?"

"None of your damn business," said Levan.

"I'm making it my business," Danielle said. "Identify yourself and tell me where you've been during the past year. If you don't, I'll shoot you just on general principles."

Danielle cocked the Colt for effect, and Levan spoke.

"My name's Henry Levan, and I'm called Hank. Up to the first of September, I was in Alamosa, at Clay Allison's horse ranch. I was there most of a year, and was let go when Allison sold most of his stock. Does that satisfy you?"*

"Not entirely," said Danielle, "but I suppose it'll have to do. Where do you come from, Levan?"

"Down south of Santa Fe, along the Rio," Levan said. "Too damn many sheep down there to suit me."

"Then mount up and ride," said Danielle. "You're not the man I'm looking for."

Levan fumbled with his horse's reins. Danielle held her Colt on him until he had freed the reins and mounted his horse. When he rode away, she followed at a safe distance. The shabby boarding-house where Levan eventually reined up had an unattended stable, and he led his horse inside. When he came out, starting for the

---

* Clay Allison was a dangerous man with a gun. Discharged from the Confederacy for insanity, he moved to New Mexico. There, he killed a sheriff who came to arrest him for another killing. He then left New Mexico and started a horse ranch in southern Colorado.

boardinghouse, he carried only his rifle. When he was gone, Danielle slipped into the stable, seeking Levan's horse. When she found it, the saddle was on a nearby rail, with saddlebags intact. She fumbled around in the dark, avoiding a change of clothes and a box of shells. Finally, her hands touched paper that felt like an envelope. Removing that, she felt around, seeking something more, but there was nothing. Quickly slipping out of the stable, Danielle rode back to the Denver House. Leaving the chestnut mare in the nearby livery, she hurried up to her room and lighted a lamp. What she had retrieved from Levan's saddlebag was actually a letter. It had been postmarked in Santa Fe and was addressed to Henry Levan, Alamosa, Colorado.

"Oh, damn," said Danielle in disgust. "Damn the luck."

Then, as though by divine inspiration, a thought came to her mind. There had to be other Levans somewhere near Santa Fe for Henry Levan to be receiving mail from there. Without feeling guilty, she withdrew the single sheet of paper and read the letter. It was dated May 1, 1870, and, from its tone, had been written by Levan's mother. She urged Henry Levan to come home. One sentence quickly caught Danielle's eye: *Your brother has been gone for two months, riding to Texas with a bunch of outlaws.*

Danielle read the letter several more times without learning anything new. Everything pointed to Henry Levan's brother as one of the men Danielle was after, but where was he? Had he returned home, or was he still with the band of outlaws?

"Damn it, I'll ride to Santa Fe and find out," Danielle said aloud.

Inquiring, she learned that Alamosa was a little more than two hundred miles due south of Denver. Since she was bound for Santa Fe, even farther south, she decided to stop at the Allison ranch in Alamosa. Allison should be able to confirm or deny that Levan had been there for almost a year. Danielle made the rounds of half a dozen other saloons without learning anything helpful. At dawn, after riding to the mercantile to replenish her supplies, she rode south.

ALAMOSA, COLORADO. OCTOBER 3, 1870.

Alamosa wasn't a large town, and it was near dark when Danielle rode in. She took a room in the only hotel and led the chestnut mare across the street to the livery. She had no desire to go looking for the Allison ranch in the dark. There were several cafés, and she chose the one nearest the hotel. There were few patrons, and they left well ahead of Danielle. After paying for her meal, she questioned the cook about the Allison place.

"Allison's place is maybe ten miles east of here," the cook said, "but if you're looking for work, you won't find it there. He's done let most of his riders go. Old Crazy Clay may be gettin' ready to move on. He's about wore out his welcome around here."

"What's he done?" Danielle asked.

"It'd be easier to tell you what he *ain't* done," said the cook. "Two Saturdays in a row he's hoorawed the town. He rode in wearin' nothing but his hat and boots, screeching and shootin' like a crazy man. Swore he'd shoot anybody lookin' out the windows at him, but most of the ladies in town looked anyway. He didn't shoot nobody, but he's just so damn unpredictable as to what he'll do next. Ain't been long since he killed a man with a Bowie knife."

"Why?" Danielle asked.

"Him and his neighbor had an argument over a land boundary. To settle it, they dug a grave and the both of 'em got down in it with knives. The winner had to bury the loser, and old Clay's still walkin'."

"Maybe you can tell me what I need to know," said Danielle. "There used to be a gent name of Henry Levan working there. I need to know if he's still there, or if he's left, where he went."

"He's gone, far as I know," the cook said. "September first, Allison let four riders go, and they stopped here for grub. Levan was one of 'em."

"How long was Levan here?" Danielle asked.

"Not quite a year, as I recall. You ain't the law, are you?"

Danielle laughed. "No. I'm pretty well acquainted with Levan, and I reckoned I'd talk to him if he was still around."

"I expect he's gone looking for a place to hole up for the winter," said the cook.

THE CLAY ALLISON RANCH. OCTOBER 4, 1870.

Allison stood on the porch, watching Danielle ride in. With his fancy garb, sandy hair, and smoothly shaven face, he was a handsome man. Danielle thought with amusement of him riding naked through town, women peeking at him. Danielle reined up.

"Step down," Allison said.

Danielle dismounted, but stopped short of the porch, noting that he carried two tied-down revolvers. Allison said nothing, so she spoke.

"My name is Daniel Strange, and I'm looking for a gent named Levan. I was told that he worked here for a while."

"Are you the law? I'm Clay Allison, and lawmen aren't welcome on my property."

"No," Danielle said, "I'm not the law."

"Levan worked for me not quite a year," said Allison. "I let him and three others go on September first. I got no idea where they went, but I know Levan has kin somewhere south of Santa Fe. Now I'd suggest you mount up and ride on."

In the West, it was considered rude not to invite a stranger in, if only for a drink of cold water, but being asked to leave for no reason was unthinkable. Danielle decided she didn't like Clay Allison. Without a word, she mounted Sundown and rode south.

SANTA FE, NEW MEXICO. OCTOBER 5, 1870.

The ride from Alamosa to Santa Fe was a little more than a hundred miles. Taking the time to rest the horse, Danielle rode in just as the first stars began appearing in the purple heavens. Santa Fe was an old, old town, established by the Spanish, and their influence was still everywhere. To Danielle it looked as big as Denver. Eventually, she found a little hotel with a café directly across the street. She left the chestnut mare at a livery on the street that ran behind the hotel and, walking back to the lobby, took a room for the night. The wind from the west was cold, and there was a dirty smudge of clouds far to the west as the setting sun slipped over the horizon. It looked like another storm might be on the way. If that was the case, it should be obvious by morning. Danielle had no desire to be caught in the wilds somewhere to the south if there was snow. She would wait out the storm in Santa Fe, where there was shelter and warm food.

By dawn, a flurry of snow was blowing out of the west, and by the time Danielle had breakfast, the flakes were much larger. The wind was cold, slipping its icy fingers beneath her sheepskin-lined coat. Danielle returned to her room at the hotel and, from the wood stacked in the hall, built up the fire in the stove. She brought in more wood for the night and, after locking the door, slid the back of a chair under the knob. She then treated herself to the luxury of stripping off all her clothing and removing the hated binder, finally freeing her breasts of its constricting grasp. With the storm raging outside and the wind howling around the eaves, there was little to do except sleep, and Danielle did just that. Undisturbed, she slumbered the day through, arising in the late afternoon. One look out the window told her that not only had the storm continued to blow; it had become more intense. Starting with the binder, she dressed. She buckled on her Colt, pulled her hat down low, and then added her heavy coat and gloves. She had to get to the café for supper, and it was a fight, for the snow was already to her knees. There was nobody inside the café except the cook.

"You might as well close and go home," Danielle said.

"I can't," said the cook. "This *is* home. I live in the back of the place."

Two more men came in while Danielle was eating, and one of

them wore a lawman's star. The two ordered their meal and took seats at one of the tables, gratefully sipping hot coffee.

"Charlie," said the cook to the lawman, "how's it goin' with them cattlemen and sheepmen down along the Rio?"

"Not worth a damn," Charlie said. "Me and Vince rode down there for nothin', havin' to fight our way back through a blizzard. Old man Levan's killin' mad, and he's ready to go after the cattlemen with guns when he can't prove anything. Somebody rimrocked near a thousand head of his sheep."*

"Maybe he's right," said Vince, the lawman's companion. "Who else but the cattlemen would've done that?"

"Hell, I don't know," the lawman said. "All I know is this whole damn country is under my jurisdiction, and I can't spend all my time with old man Levan's sheep. I've done all I can do to avoid a range war between sheepmen and cattlemen. I reckon the winner will be whoever can afford the most hired guns."

Danielle listened with interest, a plan taking shape in her mind. Suppose she asked for and got a gunman's role with the sheepmen or cattlemen? Sooner or later, if he was alive, Brice Levan would be coming home. Even if he did not, some of the other killers hired by one side or the other might be men on her death list. Danielle returned to her hotel room, preparing for another dreary day of waiting out the storm.

To the south, on the eastern bank of the Rio Grande, Sam Levan's hired guns kept a roaring fire going in the bunkhouse stove. There were Gus Haddock, Dud Menges, Warnell Prinz, Sal Wooler, and Jasper Witheres.

"Old man Sam's mad enough to walk into hell and slap the devil's face," Dud Menges said. "By the time the sheriff and his

---

* "Rim-rocking" consisted of driving a herd of sheep off a cliff.

deputy got here, the snow had covered the tracks of that bunch that rim-rocked the sheep. Wasn't nothing could be done."

"He'll end up blamin' us," said Gus Haddock, "and there's no way in hell so few of us can keep watch over three sheep camps at the same time. Markwardt's cow nurses just hit one of the un-guarded camps, and by the time we can get there, they're gone. They'll split up, and like the sheriff says, there ain't a damn bit of evidence."

"He's got two Mex sheepherders at each of the three camps," Dud Menges said. "If he wasn't so damn cheap, he could arm them with Winchesters."

"But we get fightin' wages," said Warnell Prinz. "The sheep-herders don't."

"We need more men," Sal Wooler said.

"There's folks in hell wantin' cold spring water," Jasper With-eres said. "Their chance of gettin' it is about the equal of old Sam hirin' more guns. I think, once this storm has passed, he'll send us to the Adolph Markwardt spread to raise hell with or without any evidence. Who else but a bunch of cow nurses would want to run a flock of woolies off a bluff?"

At Adolph Markwardt's bunkhouse, there was considerable jubilation. Markwardt himself had come to congratulate his men. With him, he had brought two bottles of whiskey.

"You won't be able to ride for a couple of days," Markwardt said. "Get all the rest you can, for you've earned it. The sheriff was by here in the midst of the storm, and was on his way back to Santa Fe. Naturally I told him all of you was in the bunkhouse, waiting out the storm. I told him he could see for himself, but he didn't bother. It's a comfort knowin' we're law-abidin' folks, ain't it?"

"It is, for a fact," said Nat Horan. "Wasn't our fault them sheep didn't have the sense to stop running when they got to that drop-off."

"The damn four-legged locusts don't belong in cattle country," Lon McLean said.

"Yeah," said his brother, Oscar, "but what we're fightin' for is open range. Accordin' to the law, sheep have as much right there as cattle, but we *need* that range. We got just too many cows for the six hundred forty acres we have. We need two more sections."

"The sheepmen have set up camp there," Isaac Taylor said, "and they ain't likely to be movin' until there's some shootin' in their direction."

"After we've gunned down a few of them," said Joel Wells, "that's when the sheriff will come lookin' for us."

"Not if it's self-defense," Markwardt said. "We raise enough hell with them sheep, and Sam Levan will send his riders after us. For anybody trespassin' on my property, tryin' to gun us down, we got the right to shoot in self-defense."

Nat Horan laughed. "From ambush?"

"Whatever suits your fancy," said Markwardt. "I think after we rim-rock another two or three flocks of sheep, Sam Levan and his bunch will come looking for us."

During the second day of the storm, the snow ceased. With nothing to do but eat and sleep, Danielle was fed up with the inactivity. But the snow was deep, and travel would be all but impossible. Danielle went to the livery and requested a measure of grain every day for the chestnut mare. She would need it, because of the intense cold. The temperature was already well below zero. The day after the snow ceased, the sun came out, but had little effect, for the snow was at least two feet and frozen solid. Danielle waited another two days before deciding to resume her journey. She had not asked directions to either camp, for she had heard the sheriff say that the feud was taking place in his county. There was little doubt the bleating of sheep would lead her to Sam Levan's spread. If he refused to hire her, she must then seek out the cattlemen. During the cold months, even wanted men looked for a place to hole up, and the chance to draw gun wages might be tempting to the men on her death list. Within less than an hour, she could see the fair-sized herd of sheep. Two shepherds and two sheepdogs were with the flock, which looked to number a thousand or more. Danielle reined up, and one of the shepherds raised his eyebrows in question.

"Where might I find Mr. Levan, the owner of these sheep?" Danielle asked.

"At the *rancho, señor*," said the Mexican, pointing.

Well before Danielle reached the Levan house, a pack of dogs came yelping to greet her.

"Here, you dogs," a bull voice bellowed. "Get the hell back to the house."

The pack turned and trotted back the way they had come, allowing Danielle to ride to within a few feet of the porch. Sam Levan looked her over thoroughly before he spoke, and there was no friendliness in his voice.

"Who are you, and what do you want?"

"I'm Daniel Strange, and I'm looking for work."

"You should know there's a range war goin' on here," Levan said. "I pay gun wages of a hundred a month, plus ammunition."

"I can live with that," said Danielle.

"You don't look like no gunman to me," Levan said. "Hell, you ain't even old enough to shave."

"That has nothing to do with drawing and firing a gun," said Danielle.

Sam Levan didn't see her hand move, yet he found himself looking into the muzzle of a Colt. Danielle slipped the weapon back into its holster.

"Not bad," Levan said, "but a fast draw don't mean you can hit what you shoot at."

"True enough," said Danielle. "Choose me a target."

Wordlessly, Levan took a silver dollar from his pocket and flung it into the air. As it started its descent, Danielle drew and fired once. When Sam Levan recovered the coin, there was a dent in the center of it. He eyed Danielle with grudging respect, and then he spoke.

"You'll do, kid. The missus will feed you breakfast and supper in the kitchen. There's five other men, and plenty of room in the bunkhouse."

"Thanks," Danielle said. "Am I allowed to keep my horse in your barn?"

"Yes," said Levan. "There's a couple of sacks of grain in the tack room."

Danielle led the chestnut mare to the barn, found an empty stall, and took the time to rub the animal down. She was in no hurry to meet the five strangers in the bunkhouse. The five were seated around the stove in various stages of undress. One of the men took a look at her youthful face and laughed. Gus Haddock suddenly found himself face-to-face with a cocked, rock-steady Colt.

"What is it about me that you find so funny?" Danielle demanded.

"Not a thing, kid," said Haddock, now serious. "Not a damn thing."

"I'm Daniel Strange," Danielle said, holstering the Colt. "Are any of you *segundo*?"

"No," said Dud Menges. "Sam Levan gives all the orders."

Starting with himself, Menges introduced the small outfit to Danielle.

"Why are all of you hanging around in the bunkhouse?" Danielle asked. "Enough of the snow's melted for you to be riding."

"We ride when Levan says," said Warnell Prinz, "and he ain't said."

Danielle said no more. In the snow on the ground, and in the mud that would follow, it would be impossible for riders not to leave abundant horse tracks. At suppertime the outfit trooped into the kitchen, lining up to use the washbasin and towel. A thin woman was carrying dishes of food from the big stove to a long X-frame table. Along each side of the table was a backless bench.

"Eppie," said Levan, "this is Daniel Strange, a new rider I just hired."

Eppie barely nodded, saying nothing. She looked exactly like the harried woman who might have written the pathetic letter Danielle had taken from Henry Levan's saddlebag. It was an uncomfortable meal for Danielle, for the dark eyes of Eppie Levan seemed to have been stricken with a thousand years of heartbreak and despair. Danielle was much younger than the other riders and suspected Eppie Levan was seeing in her the faces of her own sons, who seemed lost to her. Suppose Brice Levan gave up his outlaw ways and, in coming home, found himself face-to-face with Danielle? Could she kill him for his part in murdering her father? After supper, the outfit returned to the bunkhouse. There were enough bunks for a dozen men, and Danielle chose an empty one farthest from the stove. It would be reason enough to sleep fully dressed.

LEVAN'S SHEEP RANCH. OCTOBER 10, 1870.

When the snow had melted and most of the mud had dried up, Sam Levan came looking for his riders.

"I want all of you to spend the next few days riding from one sheep camp to another," said Levan. "I know what Markwardt's trying to do. He reckons if he costs me enough, I'll come after him and his bunch. Then he'll call in the law."

"You reckon they aim to rim-rock more sheep, then?" Warnell Prinz said.

"I do," said Levan. "They know I can't go on taking losses like the last one, and that I can't call in the law without proof. Our only chance, short of attacking the Markwardt outfit, is to catch them stampeding our sheep. Then I figure we're justified in shooting the varmints without answering to the law."

It was sound thinking, and Danielle admired the old sheepman for seeking a way out of what seemed an impossible situation without breaking the law. Danielle followed the rest of the outfit along the Rio to the first sheep camp, and seeing no danger there, they rode on to the second and third camps. Still, there was no sign of trouble.

"Instead of three separate camps," said Danielle, "why not combine all the shepherds and all the sheep into one bunch? They'd be easier to protect, wouldn't they?"

"Kid, you don't know much about sheep, do you?" Gus Haddock said. "Get all them woolies into one pile, and they'd eat the grass down to the roots and beyond. Scatterin' them into three camps, they still got to be moved every other day. That's why we need the range the damn cattlemen don't aim for us to have."

"I can understand why they feel that way," said Danielle. "Does it bother you, forcing sheep onto range where they're not wanted, where you might be shot?"

"Kid, there ain't nothin' sacred about cows," Haddock said, "and I don't like or dislike sheep. I'm here because it pays a hundred a month an' found. I been shot at for a hell of a lot less."

Haddock's companions laughed, and it gave Danielle something to think about. Suppose the rest of the men she had sworn to kill had sold their guns somewhere on the frontier? Already, she could understand a drifting rider's need to hire on somewhere for the winter, but it made her task far more difficult. She had no way of knowing whether or not Brice Levan would *ever* come home. Riding with outlaws, perhaps he was already dead. There had to be a limit as to how long she could remain with Levan before giving up and moving on.

When they reached the third sheep camp and finding all was well, there was nothing to do except return to the first camp.

"What about tonight?" Danielle asked. "After we've been in the saddle all day, are we expected to ride all night?"

"So far," said Warnell Prinz, "the cattlemen have only stampeded the sheep during the daytime. We don't know why."

"I do," Sal Wooler said. "Them Mex herders has got dogs. Without 'em, it's hell tryin' to keep all them sheep headed the same way. I wouldn't want to try it at night."

Three days and nights passed without the Markwardt outfit bothering any of the three sheep camps. The strain was beginning to tell on old Sam Levan, and he spoke to all his riders at suppertime.

"I'm a patient man, but if Markwardt's bunch ain't made some move by sundown tomorrow, then we're goin' to."

"I reckon you aim to rim-rock some cows, then," said Dud Menges.

"Only if we have to," Levan said. "We'll start with a stampede tomorrow night. I want his herd scattered from here to the Mexican border. If *that* don't get his attention, then we'll try somethin' else."

"Then he'll be sendin' the law after us," said Gus Haddock.

"He can't send the law after us for stampedin' his cows any more than we could send the law after him for rim-rocking our sheep," Levan said. "At least his damn cows will be alive wherever they end up. That's more than can be said for my sheep."

"Unless it rains, they'll have tracks to follow," said Sal Wooler.

"Let them follow," Levan said. "I want to put *them* in the position of having to break the law by coming after us."

"You mean with guns," said Jasper Witheres.

"That's exactly what I mean," Levan said. "When an *hombre* shoots at you, whatever his reason, then you got the right to shoot back. It's just the way things is."

Supper was a somber meal. Eppie Levan looked more harried than ever, and each of the men seemed lost in his own thoughts. Danielle had hired out her gun, and now there was a very real chance she would be using it for a purpose she had never intended.

THE ADOLPH MARKWARDT RANCH. OCTOBER 14, 1870.

S tartin' tonight," Markwardt told his riders, "we're going to be watching our herds after dark."

"Hell," said Oscar McLean, "there ain't but six of us. Who's gonna be watching them in the daytime?"

"Nobody," Markwardt said. "You don't need daylight to scatter cows from here to yonder, and I reckon Sam Levan knows that. If him and his outfit show up on my range with mischief on their minds, then we can gun the varmints down."

"It'll be the start of a range war," said Nat Horan.

"Then so be it," Markwardt said. "This is the frontier, and a man can't claim nothin' he ain't strong enough to hold on to."

CHAPTER 8

Most of Adolph Markwardt's cattle were strung out along the Rio Grande, where there was still a little graze. Markwardt's outfit was watching from the west side of the river, and since there was no moon, they were not immediately aware of the Levan sheep outfit's arrival. Suddenly, the night blossomed with gunfire, and the spooked cattle lit out downriver, picking up others as they went.

"Let's go get 'em!" Nat Horan shouted.

He and his four companions galloped across the river, drawing their guns when they judged they were within range. But the marauders made poor targets, leaning over the necks of their horses. Finally, when the galloping herd was thoroughly spooked, they split up. Knowing the futility of pursuing them individually in the dark, Markwardt's outfit reined up to rest their heaving horses.

"Damn," spat Isaac Taylor, "old Adolph will have our heads on a plate."

"Not mine," Oscar McLean said.

"Nor mine," echoed his brother, Lon. "It's pitch-dark out here. A man can't fight what he can't see."

"Well," Joel Wells asked, "do we ride in and admit they got the jump on us?"

"Not me," said Nat Horan. "I been cussed by Markwardt before, and I ain't about to take it again. I say we wait for first light, round up them cows, and drive 'em up yonder where they was."

"Without telling Markwardt?" Joel Wells asked.

"Not unless one of you wants to volunteer," replied Nat Horan. "After all, they just run the hell out of the herd. None of 'em's likely to die from that."

"That's an invite for them to come back tonight and stampede 'em again," Joel Wells said. "Hell, we'll be up all night listening to the cattle run, and all the next day rounding them up."

"No, we won't," said Nat Horan. "Tonight we'll be over there among the cows, ridin' around the herd. At first sign of any riders, we cut down on them."

"With graze so damn skimpy, that bunch will be strung out for miles downriver," Oscar said. "How do you aim to keep 'em together long enough for just five of us to keep watch on them all?"

"We get down here a couple of hours before dark and bunch the varmints," Nat Horan said. "The only time we can legally shoot them damn sheepmen is when they're over here on Markwardt's holdings."

"They ain't exactly a wet-behind-the-ears bunch," said Joel Wells. "Old Adolph ain't done enough thinkin' on this. Soon as we gun down one of them sheepmen, it'll be hell from then on."

"Not if we gun 'em down on Adolph's spread, stampedin' his cattle," Nat Horan said. "The law can't touch us."

"It ain't the law that bothers me," said Joel Wells. "It's a range war. A man has to live like a hermit, afraid to ride to town on Saturday night, 'cause he never knows when he'll be shot in the back. There ain't no damn rules. It's shoot or be shot, every day, seven days a week."

"You can always take your bedroll and drift," Lon McLean said, "but you'll have to winter somewhere. It ain't often a man can draw a hundred and found."

"You're right about that," said Joel Wells, "and I ain't got enough money to even keep me alive until spring. I reckon I'll stay and take the risk with the rest of you."

The five of them set out at first light, driving the scattered cattle back upriver. It was two hours past sunrise when they finally gathered the last of them, and before they could merge the new arrivals with those already gathered, Adolph Markwardt rode out from behind some brush. He reined up and, for an uncomfortably long time, said nothing. Finally, he spoke.

"So they stampeded the herd right under your noses."

"It was black as the inside of a stovepipe last night," Nat Horan said. "A man can't shoot what he can't see, and they never fired back. They just scattered the herd."

"So all of you decided to keep it from me by rounding them up on the quiet," Adolph said.

"We done the best we could," said Oscar McLean.

"Yeah," his brother, Lon said. "It's easy to cuss somebody else because he fails to do something *you* couldn't've done yourself."

Adolph Markwardt's hand trembled over the butt of his revolver, but he knew better. He had hired these men for their deadly speed and accuracy with a gun. He relaxed, and when he spoke, there was no anger in his voice.

"Maybe you're right, McLean. Tonight and every night, until this thing is finished, I'll be ridin' watch with you. Now herd them cows together and git on to the house. The cook is holdin' breakfast for you. After that, git what sleep you can. We got a night's work ahead of us."

With that, he wheeled his horse and rode away. Not until he was well beyond hearing did any of his riders speak.

"Hell's bells on a tomcat," said Joel Wells. "I looked for him to spout fire and brimstone."

Oscar McLean laughed. "Maybe the old dragon's fire went out."

"I wouldn't get too cocky too soon," Nat Horan said. "He'll keep us circlin' them cows so long, we won't even have time to dismount and go to the bushes."

LEVAN'S SHEEP CAMP. OCTOBER 17, 1870.

I don't understand it," said Sam Levan at breakfast. "After we scattered his herd halfway to Mexico, old Adolph should've raised hell. I reckon we'll give him another dose tonight. There's *got* to be a limit to how much of that he'll take before comin' after us."

His riders said nothing. In a gunfight with Markwardt's outfit, any or all of them could die. It was the price a man might have to pay for having sold his gun. Danielle had begun wearing her father's Colt in addition to her own. Her own weapon was tied down on her right hip while her father's was tied down on her left hip, butt forward for a cross-hand draw. None of this had escaped the others.

"Kid," said Gus Haddock, "you're mighty young to be totin' a matched pair of irons like that. Where'd you get 'em?"

"My pa made four of them," Danielle said. "He was a gunsmith."

"They're fine-lookin' weapons," said Sal Wooler, "but they could get you killed. The last damn thing a man on the dodge needs is a brace of pistols with his initial carved into the grips."

"I'm not on the dodge," Danielle said.

"You likely will be before this thing between Sam Levan and Adolph Markwardt's over and done," said Jasper Witheres.

Danielle had mixed emotions, not doubting what Wooler had said about the danger of going on the dodge with a pair of fancy pistols. But there was a reason for her toting what appeared to be a matched pair of Colts. With a silver initial inlaid in the grips, they weren't the kind that a man was likely to forget, once having seen them. Wouldn't the men who had murdered her father remember the fancy Colt with inlaid silver? It was a calculated risk, but the killers might recognize the weapon as having belonged to Daniel Strange and, suspecting her vow of vengeance, come after *her*. If she couldn't find them, then let them begin looking for her.

"I'd bet my saddle old Markwardt give his riders hell for us stampedin' his herd," Dud Menges said. "I'm bettin' they're just waitin' for our patience to wear thin, figurin' we'll be back, just like Sam Levan aims for us to do tonight."

Levan's outfit spent the day riding from one of Levan's sheep camps to another, seeing nobody except the sheepherders.

Two hours after midnight, Sam Levan and his riders saddled

their horses and crossed the Rio Grande. At the time of their last raid, cattle had been strung out for several miles along the river. Tonight they saw no cattle. Levan reined up, his outfit gathered around him.

"They've bunched the varmints upriver," said Levan. "It may be a mite harder for us to get them running. We'll circle around, comin' in from the north. Keep your heads down and your pistols blazing."

They rode a mile east of the river before riding north. Somewhere ahead, a cow bawled. The riders slowed their horses. They were getting close, and in the small hours of the morning, any sound—even the creak of saddle leather—could be heard from a great distance. Again there was no moon, and the meager starlight would be of little or no help to the Markwardt outfit. Sam Levan was the lead rider, and when he saw the dim shadows that made up the dozing cattle herd, he cut loose with a fearful shriek and began firing his revolver. The cattle scrambled to their feet and noticed the six riders closing in on them. They began to mill in confusion, and the muzzle flashes from the guns of Levan's riders offered excellent targets for the defenders. It was a standoff, for Markwardt and his riders had headed the herd before they could run. Two of Levan's riders were sagging in their saddles as though hard hit. Shouting a warning, Levan wheeled his horse and galloped upriver, the way he had come. His riders immediately followed. Danielle had not been hit, keeping her head low on the neck of the chestnut mare. They reached the Levan ranch house, and in the light from the window, Danielle could see that it was Gus Haddock and Dud Menges who had been hit. They slid from their saddles and would have fallen, had they not been supported by their comrades.

"Get them into the house," Levan ordered. "Then a couple of you take their horses to the barn and rub them down."

Once the wounded men were inside, Danielle, Warnell Prinz, Sal Wooler, and Jasper Witheres left to tend to the horses.

"My God," said Eppie Levan as she beheld the bloody shirts of the wounded men. "We must get a doctor for them."

"No," Sam Levan said. "When there's shooting involved, the doc will go straight to the law. Old Markwardt couldn't ask for any better evidence than that. We'll have to take care of them ourselves."

With his knife, Levan cut away the shirts of the wounded men, and to his relief, the injuries didn't look fatal. Both men had shoulder wounds, and the lead had evidently gone on through without striking bone. Eppie brought the medicine chest, and with disinfectant, Levan cleansed the wounds. He then bound them tight, using strips of an old sheet.

"We'll keep them here in the house for a day or two," Levan said. "They're likely to have some fever, and will need whiskey to kill any infection."

Eppie Levan seldom questioned anything the temperamental Levan did, but with her eyes on the wounded men, she spoke.

"It's started, Sam. One day you'll be brought in, tied across your saddle."

"Maybe," said Sam, "but I didn't start it. Markwardt's bunch rim-rocked a thousand head of our sheep. We only stampeded his cows. Tonight we couldn't do even that. The varmints was ready for us."

"And they'll be ready the next time," Eppie said. "Can't we make do with the section of land we own, and let them *have* the free range?"

"Hell no," said Levan defiantly. "Just because Markwardt raises cows, that don't give him divine right to all the free grass. Soon as Haddock and Menges is well enough to ride, we'll be goin' after them again."

Having unsaddled, rubbed down, and put away the horses, the rest of Levan's riders returned to the house to see how their wounded comrades had fared.

"They'll make it," Levan said. "Some of you help me get them into a spare bedroom."

Levan and Warnell Prinz carried Gus Haddock to the bed, while Sal Wooler and Jasper Witheres carried Dud Menges. Once the injured were in bed, Levan forced each man to take half a bottle of laudanum. They would sleep through much of the after-shock and pain. Prinz, Wooler, and Witheres returned to the parlor, where Danielle waited. With two of the outfit wounded, they awaited orders from Sam Levan. They weren't long in coming.

"I want the rest of you to keep as close a watch on the sheep camps as you can," said Levan. "It's high time Markwardt and his outfit was comin' after us."

"We're considerably outgunned," Sal Wooler said.

"Damn it, I *know* that," Levan said. "I don't want a man of you killed over a few sheep, but do your best to keep them cow nurses from rim-rocking another flock."

After breakfast, Danielle, Prinz, Wooler, and Witheres rode out to begin their watch over the three sheep camps.

THE MARKWARDT RANCH. OCTOBER 18, 1870.

L et's go get some sleep," Adolph Markwardt said an hour after they had headed the intended stampede. "They won't be back tonight."

"We may have hit some of them," said Nat Horan. "We were within range, and all their muzzle flashes made pretty good targets."

"You boys done well," Markwardt said. "We may have just put an end to these late-night stampedes."

"I doubt it," said Oscar McLean. "Levan needs that free grass more than we do."

"All right by me," Markwardt said, "long as he's willing to risk his damn neck for it."

"Are we goin' after them now?" Isaac Taylor asked.

"Not yet," said Markwardt. "Give 'em a few days to lick their wounds, and they'll figure some other way of comin' after us."

S am Levan rode into Santa Fe, to the mercantile.
    "I need some dynamite," Levan said.

"Ain't got much," the storekeeper said. "Miners buy it up as quick as it comes in. I reckon I got a dozen sticks."

"That'll be enough," said Levan.

When Levan reached his ranch, he went to the bunkhouse, where he had the necessary privacy to cap and fuse the dynamite. Finished, he left it there. Had he taken it to the house, there would have been yet another tirade from Eppie. Just at sundown Danielle, Warnell Prinz, Sal Wooler, and Jasper Witheres rode in.

"Nothin' happened at any of the sheep camps today," said Jasper Witheres.

"I didn't expect it to," Sam Levan said. "We ain't pushed it far enough, but I think we will tonight. I'll meet you in the bunkhouse after supper."

"How's Gus and Dud?" Danielle asked.

"Better," said Levan. "Eppie's been dosin' 'em with whiskey, and they're sweatin' like mules."

Supper was a silent affair, the four remaining riders wondering what old Sam Levan had in mind for them, with two of their companions out of the fight. Levan finished first, and by the time his riders left the supper table, Levan was waiting in the bunkhouse. His remaining four riders looked skeptical. Levan reached under one of the bunks, dragging out a gunnysack. From it, he took a stick of capped and fused dynamite.

"A dozen sticks," said Levan, "each with a seven-second fuse. All we got to do is fling three or four of these into the air above the Markwardt herd, and they'll run like hell wouldn't have it. This time, they won't have muzzle flashes to shoot at."

"My God," Warnell Prinz said, "the concussion from that could kill some cows. Maybe even a man."

"Damn it," said Levan, "ridin' in, shouting, and shooting ain't got us nothing but two of the outfit shot. We can get close enough to fling this dynamite before they got any idea that we're there."

"No doubt we can," Jasper Witheres said, "but ain't you forgettin' we got two men out of the fight with wounds? This dynamite throwin' could be the very thing that'll blow old Adolph's mind. Why don't we wait until Haddock and Menges is healed? Then if them cow chasers comes after us, we won't be shorthanded."

"That makes sense to me," said Sal Wooler.

"And to me," Warnell Prinz agreed.

Danielle said nothing, and Sam Levan turned on her.

"Well, kid, ain't you standin' with the others?"

"I agree with their thinking," said Danielle, "but I'll ride with you. I don't cross a man who's paying me wages."

"Well, God bless my soul," Levan said. "The kid's got more sand than any of you."

"Aw, hell," said Warnell Prinz. "I still think we're bitin' off more than we can chew, but I'll ride with you."

Sam Levan looked at Sal Wooler and Jasper Witheres, and they nodded.

"I don't reckon they'll be expecting us again tonight," Levan said, "and we'll have that in our favor. We ride at midnight."

Danielle and her three companions retired to their bunks to get as much sleep as they could. For a long time Danielle lay thinking, pondering the wisdom of using dynamite. It seemed a cowardly thing to do, but nothing else had drawn the Markwardt outfit into an expected fight. When Danielle had ridden out of St. Joe, her mission seemed simple. All she had to do was track down the killers who had murdered her father, and extract revenge. Now she was about to take part in a raid that might cost innocent men their lives. Tonight she would ride with Sam Levan, but the more she thought about it, the more convinced she became that she should just ride on. If some of the Markwardt outfit died, it would be reason enough for the county sheriff to come looking for Sam Levan. The very last thing Danielle wanted was to become a fugitive from the law. So sobering were her thoughts, she was wide-awake when Sam Levan came to the bunkhouse at midnight.

"Each of us will take one stick of dynamite," Levan said. "We'll light the fuses, throw the dynamite, and get away from there before they know what's happening. Here's a block of Lucifers.* Each of you be sure and take some."

Danielle took her stick of dynamite and broke off six of the Lucifers.

"Now let's saddle up and ride," said Levan. "Let's be done with this."

Danielle thought Levan seemed nervous, as though his iron-fisted resolve was not quite as strong as it had been. There was a very real possibility that so much exploding dynamite could kill Markwardt or some of his men. The county sheriff was well aware of the increasing bitterness between sheepmen and cattlemen. If one or more of the cattlemen died tonight, the lawman would most certainly come looking for Sam Levan, along with any of his outfit who had ridden with him. The five of them rode out, nobody speaking, Levan taking the lead.

Adolph Markwardt and his five riders had most of the cows bedded down along the riverbank, and they rode from one end of the herd to the other, and back again.

"I still think we nailed a couple of 'em the last time they was here," Nat Horan said, "and I don't look for 'em to come back short-handed."

"Never underestimate a damn sheepman," said Markwardt. "The varmints could give mules lessons in bein' stubborn."

The rest of the men laughed. In his own mind, each doubted there was a sheepman anywhere in the world who was more stubborn than Adolph Markwardt.

"It's hell, spendin' the night ridin' from one herd to the other," said Oscar McLean. "I think we ought to wait at one end."

"Oh, hell, don't give me that," Markwardt growled. "That's how

---

* "Lucifers" were the first matches, invented by an Englishman in 1827. In blocks, they could be separated, one or more, as needed.

they stampeded the herd the first time, with all of you gathered in a bunch at the wrong place. We don't know from what direction they're likely to ride in."

"They come in from the north last time," Joel Wells said. "I look for 'em to come in from the south if they try it again."

"I don't," said Isaac Taylor. "That would stampede the herd back toward the ranch."

"Isaac's probably right," Markwardt said. "I expect we'd better spend a little more time to the north of the herd."

Markwardt and his outfit had begun circling the herd toward the north when the first explosion came. Flung high into the air, the short-fused dynamite exploded directly over the herd. Five times explosions rocked the night and the cattle went crazy. To the south they ran, Markwardt and his riders frantically trying to head them off. But there was no stopping the stampede, and it thundered on.

"Damn them," said Markwardt. "The scurvy yellow coyotes."

"My God," Nat Horan said, "if we'd been any closer to the north end of the herd, we'd all be dead men."

"Yeah," said Oscar McLean, "and that bunch didn't know we wasn't right there where they was throwin' the dynamite. How much longer before we ride over there and deliver a dose of lead?"

"Not much longer," Markwardt said. "The rest of you ride in and get what sleep you can. I expect them blasts killed some cows, and I aim to be here at first light to find out just how many. Then I'll ride in for a talk with the sheriff. I'm bettin' Sam Levan bought that explosive in Santa Fe. If we can tie him to that, it may be the proof we'll need."

As Sam Levan and his companions rode away, nobody spoke. There had been no shots fired in response to the blasts, so none of them knew whether or not Markwardt's riders had been close enough to be hurt. While not lacking in courage, Danielle didn't want to find herself on the wrong side of the law for having been part of Sam Levan's outfit. Her quest—a vow of vengeance—was dangerous enough, without having to go on the dodge. As they drew near the Levan house, they could see lamplight streaming from several of the windows.

"Damn," said Levan, "I hope nothing's gone wrong here."

"A little soon for that, I think," Warnell Prinz said. "You want the rest of us to ride on to the house with you?"

"No," said Levan. "Go on to the bunkhouse and get what sleep you can."

When Levan entered the house, he heard voices in the kitchen, one of them Eppie's.

"What's goin' on in there?" Levan demanded.

"Oh, Sam," Eppie cried joyously, "Brice is here. He's come back to us."

When Sam Levan entered the kitchen, a lanky rider got up from the table. He was thin and hungry-looking, his clothing tattered and dirty and his boots run over. Nothing was in order but the tied-down Colt on his right hip.

"Son, I'm glad to see you," said Levan, taking the young man's hand. "We got a fight in the making with old man Markwardt's cow outfit. I need all the help I can get."

"No," Eppie cried. "You're goin' to get yourself killed, Sam, and I won't let you take Brice with you."

"Ma," said Brice, "I can take care of myself. It's hard times in Texas, with no work for a line rider, so I'm back, asking for a bunk and grub for a while. I'll help Pa do whatever has to be done."

Eppie Levan said no more, for her wayward son was too much like his stubborn sire. Sam Levan grinned at Brice, and the two shook hands again.

Gus Haddock and Dub Menges had healed to the extent that they were able to come to the breakfast table, and were there when Levan and the rest of the outfit joined them. As they were about to begin eating, Brice Levan entered the kitchen.

"Any of you that ain't met him," said Sam, "this is my oldest son, Brice. He's . . . uh . . . been away."

With the exception of Danielle, all the riders nodded. Apparently they knew the new arrival. Looking directly at Danielle, Brice Levan spoke.

"Who's the kid?"

"I'm almighty damn tired of being called 'the kid,'" Danielle said, getting to her feet. "My name is Daniel Strange."

"Uh . . . sorry," said Brice Levan. "No offense intended."

There was no doubt in Danielle's mind that Brice had seen her pair of Colts with silver initials inlaid in the grips, for his face went a shade whiter. She waited for Levan to sit down before seating herself on the other side of the table. He ate very little and seemed uncomfortable, for several times, he found Danielle staring directly at him. He was first to leave the table, returning to his room. Sam Levan knew something was wrong, but wasn't sure exactly what. He eyed Danielle with suspicion, and she ignored his curious stares.

Adolph Markwardt counted fifteen dead cows. He then mounted his horse and rode north toward Santa Fe. Arriving there, he rode directly to the office of Charlie Murdock, the county sheriff. Murdock listened patiently as Markwardt spoke, telling the lawman of his suspicions.

"Fifteen cows, huh?" said Murdock. "That still ain't quite as bad as a thousand sheep. I don't have a doubt in my mind that it was your outfit that rim-rocked them sheep, but I don't have any proof. Likewise, I don't have anything but your suspicions as to who it was that stampeded your cows. I can't arrest a man on *my* suspicions. What the hell am I supposed to do with yours?"

"If it ain't expecting too much," Markwardt growled, "you could ask around town and see who's been buying dynamite."

"There's no law against having dynamite," Sheriff Murdock said. "Every miner in the territory's got a few sticks of the stuff. You and Levan had better settle your differences before somebody's hurt or killed. I reckon you're a big man in the territory, but you let me find you've broken the law, I'll throw you in the hoosegow as quick as I would a line-ridin' cowboy on Saturday night."

At Sam Levan's place, he and his outfit prepared to ride out to the various sheep camps. Gus Haddock and Dud Menges were still unable to ride, and remained at the house.

"What are we waitin' for?" Warnell Prinz demanded. "After what we done last night, them sheep are likely to catch hell."

"We're waitin' for Brice," said Sam. "Brice, where the hell are you?" he shouted.

Levan and his three companions were mounted while Danielle still stood beside the chestnut mare. Brice Levan left the house, but instead of going to the corral for a horse, he started toward the mounted riders, his hard eyes on Danielle. A dozen yards away, he halted. Then he spoke.

"I don't like you, kid, and I won't ride with any outfit as long as you're in it."

"Oh," said Danielle calmly, "I reckon I remind you of somebody a bunch of cutthroat outlaws robbed and murdered in Indian Territory. He was my pa, and this left-hand Colt was his."

His face a mask of fury, Brice Levan drew. Danielle waited until the muzzle of his revolver had cleared leather, but he didn't get off a shot. With a cross-hand draw, Danielle drew her father's gleaming Colt. She fired twice, both slugs striking Levan in the chest. He stumbled, his knees gave away, and he fell.

CHAPTER 9

There was a shocked silence. Warnell Prinz, Sal Wooler, and Jasper Witheres made no move toward their guns. Dying, Brice Levan was trying to speak, and Sam knelt over him.

"It was . . . like he said, Pa," Brice said. "My bunch . . . robbed and hung . . . a man in Indian Territory. . . ."

They were his final words. Sam Levan got to his feet and faced Danielle.

"Mount up and ride out," said Levan.

"I'll wait until the sheriff comes," Danielle said. "I want it understood that he was the first to draw."

"The sheriff won't be comin'," Levan said. "Four of us saw it, and it was a clear case of self-defense. That, and Brice confessed. I hate what you've done, but I can't fault you for doin' it. Now mount up and ride."

Danielle got on the chestnut mare and, nodding to her former companions, rode away. Eppie Levan had just left the house, and in the distance, Danielle could hear her anguished screams. Before she had left St. Joe, it had all seemed so simple—find the outlaws who had hanged her father and make them pay. Now she had to face the disturbing possibility that these seven other men might have families, just as Brice Levan had. It was a somber thought. She had hired on with Levan to pursue his best interests. Now she felt as if she had betrayed his trust, even though Brice Levan had admitted his guilt. She silently vowed never to sell her gun again for any reason. She rode south along the Rio Grande, having heard one of the men say they were two days' ride from El Paso.

EL PASO, TEXAS. OCTOBER 22, 1870.

Weary, Danielle stabled the chestnut mare, skipped supper, and, finding a hotel, slept the night through. As she started through the hotel lobby, the clerk spoke to her.

"Be careful. John Wesley Hardin's been seen in town."*

"Thanks," Danielle said. "I'll try to stay out of his way."

Danielle had heard of the gunman, for his reputation had been such that newspapers in St. Louis and Kansas City had carried stories about him. He carried two guns, and Danielle recalled a story that made her blood run cold. Inside a gunsmith's shop, testing a new pair of Colts, Hardin had chosen for a target an innocent man on the boardwalk outside. That was just one of many cruel acts attributed to the legendary gunman. After breakfast, Danielle went back to her hotel room, for few if any of the saloons would be open until noon. At eleven o'clock, she left the hotel and sought out the sheriff's office.

"I'm Daniel Strange."

"I'm Buford Powell," said the lawman. "What can I do for you?"

Danielle decided to tell the truth. She gave the lawman the names of the seven men on her death list, and told him of her vow to hunt them down.

"None of those names sounds familiar," Sheriff Powell said, "but with outlaws, you can't be sure they aren't using other names. I know that between here and Laredo, Mex horses are being run across the border and sold in Texas, while Texas horses are being rustled and sold in Mexico. We have no names, and they wait for

---

* Called the most dangerous gunman of his time, Hardin killed thirty-one men.

the dark of the moon. Not even the Texas Rangers have been able to stop them."

"It might be possible to join them and gather evidence," said Danielle.

"One of the rangers tried that," Sheriff Powell said. "He was never seen or heard from again. Was I you, I wouldn't go gettin' no similar ideas."

"Thanks for the information, Sheriff," said Danielle.

She quickly left the sheriff's office before the lawman got around to questioning her about her intentions. By then, the saloons were open. The Texas was one of the largest, and she went there first. She walked in, and then as though looking for someone she couldn't find, she left. There were no poker or faro games in progress, for it was still early, and being a nondrinker, Danielle couldn't justify her presence. She had to wait until evening. After supper, she found the saloons had come alive. In the Texas, two poker tables and a faro table were busy. The men seemed talkative enough, and hoping to learn something useful, Danielle sat in at the faro table.

"Two-dollar limit," said the dealer. "Table stakes."

Danielle quickly lost twenty dollars. Then she began winning, recovering her losses plus thirty dollars more. The rest of the men were looking at her with a mix of respect and anger, for all of them had lost money to her. At least one of the men was broke, and he appealed to the dealer.

"I got a pair of hosses—matched blacks—that I picked up in Mexico. They're worth a hundred dollars apiece. Will you take them for security?"

Danielle's eyes shot to the man at the mention of the horses' origins.

"We don't usually do this, Black Jack," said the dealer. "I'll grant you a hundred in credit for both of them."

"Done," Black Jack said. He sighed with relief as he suddenly began winning. When his winnings exceeded his losses, he dropped out and went to the bar.

Danielle was ahead by fifty dollars, and when Black Jack left the saloon, she also withdrew from the game. Following Black Jack wasn't difficult. He had left his horse and the pair of blacks at a livery, and to Danielle's practiced eye, they indeed were worth a hundred dollars each, if not more. With the pair on lead ropes, Black Jack rode southeast, toward the border. Danielle followed at a safe distance, and not until she had crossed the border did she see Black Jack again. From behind a clump of brush, Black Jack suddenly stepped out, a Winchester leveled at her.

"Why are you followin' me, kid? Make it good, or I'll cut you in half."

"I like the looks of the pair of blacks you picked up in Mexico," Danielle said, "and I'd like to pick up a few for myself."

Without warning, with blinding speed, Danielle drew her right-hand Colt and fired. The lead slammed into the muzzle of the Winchester, tearing it out of Black Jack's hands. Her Colt holstered, Danielle eyed him calmly.

"Damn you," Black Jack bawled, "if you've ruint my Winchester . . ."

Danielle laughed. "You'll have to get yourself another one."

Ignoring Danielle, Black Jack retrieved the weapon, examining it critically. Satisfied it wasn't seriously damaged, he again faced Danielle.

"Tarnation," said Black Jack, "I never seen such shootin'. Maybe there *is* as place for you, but it can't be just on my say-so. You'll have to prove yourself to my *amigos*."

"Lead on," Danielle said.

The outlaw camp was only a few miles south of the border. As they approached, there was a nicker from a distant horse, and Black Jack's horse responded. They rode on until they were challenged.

"Identify yourself," a voice shouted.

"Black Jack," the outlaw replied, "and I got company."

"Dismount and leave your horses there," the voice commanded.

Black Jack and Danielle dismounted. Ahead, in a small clearing beside a stream, stood four men. A coffeepot simmered over a small fire.

"Now," one of the men said, "who are you, and why are you here?"

"During a faro game, I heard Black Jack talking about picking up that pair of blacks in Mexico," said Danielle, "and I figured I'd like a hand in the game."

One of the outlaws laughed. "A kid that ain't even shaved, packin' two guns. Boy, one of them *Mejicanos* will have you for breakfast."

"I don't think so," said Black Jack. "I had the drop, had a Winchester coverin' him, and without me seein' him move, he shot the Winchester out of my hands."

Danielle said nothing, waiting for the outlaws to digest this new revelation. Quickly, they reached a decision, and they nodded at Black Jack.

"Who are you, kid, and where you from?" Black Jack asked.

"I don't answer to 'kid,'" said Danielle. "I'm Daniel Strange, and I'm from Missouri."

"I'm Black Jack Landis," said the outlaw. "The others is Joel Votaw, Revis Bronson, Hez Deshea, and Wes Pryor. Joel's our *segundo*."

"Black Jack," Votaw said, "I've warned you about leading horses through El Paso. With so many *Mejicanos* there, sooner or later, one of them's bound to recognize a horse, and then there'll be hell to pay. From now on, when you got the urge to ride to town, ride from here."

"Hell, there ain't nobody wise to me," said Black Jack.

"Oh?" Votaw said. "Then how come this two-gun man followed you back to camp? If he heard you shootin' off your mouth, then others heard. Next time, the *hombre* trailing you could be a ranger."

"After the war with Mexico, I've heard Americans can't legally cross the border into Mexico, and that Mexicans can't cross the border into the United States," said Danielle.

"That's the law," Revis Bronson said, "but it applies only if you get caught. There was at least one ranger that stepped over the line, and he ain't been seen since."

"You don't get shot at very often, then," said Danielle.

Black Jack Landis laughed. "Almost never. We take the horses at night. By first light, when the *Mejicanos* find our tracks, we are already across the river, in Texas. *Mejicanos* raise some very fine horses, but they're not fools. They don't consider 'em worth a dose of lead poisoning."

"I've heard talk that some sell Mexican horses in Texas and Texas horses in Mexico," Danielle said. "Anything to that?"

"Some do," said Joel Votaw, "but we don't. Believe me, there ain't no love between the state of Texas and Mexico, and most Texans don't give a damn what happens on the other side of the border. As it is, if things get touchy in Mexico, we can cross the river into Texas, and the Mexes can't touch us. That could change almighty quick, if we was to run Texas horses across the border into Mexico."

"Damn right it could," Hez Deshea said.

"You're avoiding the law in Texas," said Danielle, "but what about Mexico?"

"Too much border," Wes Pryor said. "There's no way they can watch it all. *Mejicanos* cross the river into Texas, drivin' Texas horses into Mexico. They can't complain to the United States that Texans are violatin' their boundaries, because they're violatin' the Texas boundary. That's why nobody—not even the rangers—can stop it."

"Why are you camped in Mexico instead of Texas?" Danielle asked.

"You ain't earned the right to know that," said Joel Votaw. "Not until you've told us the truth. What's a younker that ain't old enough to shave and totin' two irons doin' in old Mexico?"

Danielle sighed. None of these men were the killers she sought. She quickly decided to tell them the truth. Or most of it. She told them of her father's murder and of her vow to track down the killers.

"I need money to continue my search," Danielle said. "There's seven more killers, and I'll never find them if I have to stop regular for a thirty-and-found riding job."

"That makes sense," said Joel Votaw, "but how do we know if

you throw in with us, you won't shoot some *hombre* that'll attract the attention of the law? We can't allow that."

"If there's ever a possibility of the law stepping in, I'll vamoose," Danielle said.

Black Jack laughed. "I think we'd all vamoose if that happened."

"The men I'm after are outlaws and killers," said Danielle. "They're not going to call on the law for help."

"We been splittin' the money equal," Wes Pryor said. "If you join up with us, there'll be less money, split six ways."

"Show me what you're doing," said Danielle, "and I'll pull my weight. Your share may be even more."

"You've made a good case for yourself," Joel Votaw said. "I think we'll take you in for a while, as long as you don't get gun happy and draw attention to us."

"I've never shot anybody except in self-defense," said Danielle.

"Bueno," Votaw said. "So far, we've took the horses we wanted without us doing any shooting. How good are you with horses?"

"I grew up with them," said Danielle. "I trained the chestnut mare I'm riding."

"We don't take a whole herd of horses," Votaw said, "because it's hard to control a herd at night. Each of us will take two lead ropes and lead two horses away. Come first light, when they can follow our tracks, we'll be across the border, in Texas."

"Only twelve horses for a night's work," said Danielle.

"The right horses will bring a hundred dollars apiece," Votaw said. "Two hundred for you for one night's work. At thirty and found, that's near seven months of line riding. If you can find the work."

"I've already learned the truth of that," said Danielle. "Where are you finding all these hundred-dollar horses?"

"A rich Spaniard, Alonzo Elfego, owns about half of Mexico," Votaw said, "and all his horses are blooded stock."

"Why doesn't he have riders watching them at night?" Danielle asked.

"There's too many of them, and they're scattered," said Votaw. "Besides, he has no idea when we're coming to visit him. We'll go tonight, and then give him a rest. There are other *ranchos* with plenty of good horses."

"Black Jack," said Hez Deshea, "why did you bring that pair of blacks with you? They should've brought top dollar in Texas."

"Cheap old bastard that was interested in 'em tried to knock my askin' price down to seventy-five dollars," Black Jack said. "That, and he got a little too interested in them Mex brands. I mounted up, rode out, and left him standin' there."

"You done right," said Votaw. "Brands are none of his damn business as long as he's gettin' a bill of sale."

"Where do you get bills of sale?" Danielle asked.

"A jackleg printer in El Paso makes 'em up for us," said Votaw.

Danielle nodded, digesting the information. Horse stealing was a hanging offense, but it seemed that these thieves had it down to a fine art. The only question in her mind was whether or not her alliance with the horse thieves would enable her to find any of the remaining men on her death list. Again Votaw spoke.

"Black Jack, you'd better take that pair of blacks back across the border, where we'll meet after tonight's raid. The rest of you get what sleep you can."

Black Jack mounted his horse, and with the pair of blacks following on lead ropes, he rode north. Danielle picketed the chestnut mare and, resting her head on her saddle, tipped her hat down over her eyes. After the blizzards on the high plains, the mild climate of old Mexico and the warm sun were welcome. She drifted off to sleep, rousing only when she heard a horse coming. Black Jack was returning. Shortly afterward, one of the bunch got a supper fire going. It was small, under a tree so the leaves would dissipate the smoke, and as soon as the coffee was hot, Revis Bronson put out the fire.

"When will we be going?" Danielle asked.

"Midnight," said Joel Votaw. "We ain't more than fifteen miles away."

Black Jack laughed. "Hell, we may be camped on Elfego's holdings right now."

The horse thieves all laughed, finding such a possibility amusing. Danielle had nothing more to say, and except for an occasional comment from one of the others, there was only silence. Danielle watched the stars, unable to sleep, thinking of the changes in her life. She might easily step over the line, becoming an outlaw, but how else was she to ever find the outlaws who had murdered her father without associating with outlaws herself? Finally, Votaw gave an order.

"It's near midnight. Time to saddle up and ride."

Votaw gave each of them a pair of lead ropes. They then saddled their horses, mounted, and rode south. There was no moon, and riding behind the others, Danielle could barely see them. They took their time, eventually reining up in the shadow of a stand of trees.

"We go from here on foot," Votaw said. "Once you've taken your horses, bring them here until we're all ready to ride."

Danielle had to concede that the thieves were smart. By starlight, it would be difficult to see men afoot, even if the herd was being watched. Dark as it was, they could still see the dim shapes of grazing horses. The horses raised their heads and snorted as they were approached. Danielle began to speak softly in a soothing tone that had proven effective in her handling of the chestnut mare. Suddenly, the night came alive with gunfire. Winchesters blazed from three different directions. There were entirely too many defenders. Danielle did not return the fire, for muzzle flashes would have been the finish of her. Besides, she had no intention of killing men for defending what was theirs. She reached the stand of trees where the horses had been picketed without being hit. Black Jack Landis hadn't been quite so lucky. He lay on the ground, groaning.

"Hard hit?" Danielle asked.

"My thigh," said Black Jack. "I can't mount my horse."

"Here, I'll help you," Danielle said.

By the time Black Jack was mounted, the rest of the horse

thieves were galloping away to the north. None of them had horses except the ones they rode. Black Jack knew where they were headed, and Danielle followed him. There was a shallows in the river, and there they crossed the border into Texas. They reined up before a shack that had seen better days. The roof sagged in the middle, and what had once been a front porch had fallen in.

"All right," said Joel Votaw, "who's been hit and how bad?"

"In the thigh," Black Jack said, "and it hurts like hell."

None of the others had been wounded.

"Bronson," said Votaw, "get a fire going in the fireplace. Then put some water on to boil so we can take care of Black Jack's wound."

"This is the first time we ever been shot at by old Alonzo Elfego's outfit," Black Jack said. "What the hell went wrong?"

"We got too damn overconfident," said Votaw. "It's been only a week since we took ten of Elfego's horses. Now we got to stay away until he's convinced we've backed off. I'd say he had a dozen men staked out with Winchesters. One of us could've been shot right through the head just as easy as Black Jack took one through his thigh."

"But Elfego's is the biggest horse ranch in Mexico," said Hez Deshea. "If we can't take horses from there, where else can we go?"

"I didn't say we can't go there again," Votaw said. "We'll just have to wait a month or so until Elfego takes away them Mexes with Winchesters."

"Damn it," said Wes Pryor, "I'm near broke. I can't wait a month or two."

"Neither can I," Revis Bronson said as he stepped out of the dilapidated cabin. "When we started doin' this, we was selling horses every week."

"I need money, too," said Joel Votaw, "but I don't need it bad enough to be shot dead. Any of you that can't wait a few days until Elfego's cooled down, feel free to ride out on your own."

"I ain't wantin' to bust up the outfit," Bronson said. "I reckon I can wait a few days."

"Then I'll stay on, too," said Pryor.

"I reckon I'll ride on," Danielle said, "but I won't be competing with any of you. I'll be riding to south Texas, looking for the bunch that killed my pa."

"Good luck," said Votaw. "Watch your back."

Votaw went into the shack. The water was boiling, and after cleansing Black Jack's leg wound, he bound it tight. Danielle stretched out, her head on her saddle, awaiting first light. Votaw came out, took a bottle of whiskey from his saddlebag, and returned to the cabin. Like Danielle, Bronson, Deshea, and Pryor tried to rest. Danielle lay awake, unsure as to the effect of her decision to ride on. As the eastern horizon began to gray with the first light of dawn, Danielle saddled the chestnut mare.

"Good luck," called Danielle to the others as she rode away.

Until she was out of sight, chills ran up and down her spine. It would have been easy for one of them to shoot her in the back, taking the chestnut mare and the money in her saddlebag. But there were no shots. Danielle rode back to El Paso. Stabling the chestnut mare, she took a hotel room and slept until late afternoon. After supper, she again visited some of the saloons. Every saloon seemed to have a poster in the window, and Danielle stopped to read one. It was simple and to the point.

Señor Alonzo Elfego of Mexico will pay one thousand pesos for any hombre, dead or alive, who steals his horses.

Danielle felt a moment of guilt, for it had been only an act of providence that had kept her from stepping over the line and becoming a horse thief. She stopped at another saloon, the Rio, where a faro game was in progress. Danielle dragged out a chair and sat down.

"Five-dollar limit, kid," said the dealer. "No credit."

"I don't recall asking for any credit," Danielle said, dropping five double eagles on the green felt that lined the tabletop.

Several of the men at the table grinned, expecting this arrogant newcomer to soon get what he deserved. But their grins faded as

Danielle won five of the next six pots. Every time she lost a pot, she more than recovered her losses by winning the next three or four.

"I'm gettin' out of this," one of the gamblers snarled, kicking back his chair. "I think the damn house is slick-dealing cards to the kid. I ain't never seen anybody win so often."

"Hank," said the house dealer, getting to his feet, "I never slick-deal to anybody. Some folks is just better at the game than others, and if you can't afford to lose, then just stay the hell away from the tables. Now get out of here."

"If there's a problem," Danielle said, "I'll drop out."

"The problem's leavin', kid," said the dealer. "Win or lose, you're welcome to stay as long as you can cover your bets."

Danielle recovered her original hundred dollars, and won two hundred more. Leaving the saloon, she walked along the boardwalk. Suddenly a shadow moved from between two deserted buildings, and a voice spoke.

"Turn around, kid, and keep your hands where I can see 'em. I'm taking back all my money."

Danielle turned around slowly. The disgruntled gambler held a revolver on her. Quickly, she dropped to the ground as the pistol roared, almost in her ear. Before he could fire again, Danielle threw herself at his legs, and off-balance, he fell. His head slammed into the strong wood of the boardwalk, and he lay still. The shot had been heard, and the sheriff, Buford Powell, was the first to arrive. Almost immediately, some of the men from the Rio Saloon were there, arriving in time to hear Danielle's explanation. The sheriff had a lantern, and set it down on the boardwalk.

"Let me see your guns, kid."

Danielle handed him the weapons. They were fully loaded and had not been fired. The sheriff then took the gun from Hank's limp hand and found one load missing. There were many ways a man could fall from favor on the frontier, but there were three that stood head and shoulders above the rest: hitting a woman, mistreating a horse, or being a sore loser.

"The kid's lucky to be alive, Sheriff," said one of the men from the saloon. "I think Hank should be told when he wakes up that he's to stay away from the poker and faro tables in this town. This time, it was the kid. Next time, it could be any one of us."

"A couple of you tote him over to the jail," Sheriff Powell said. "I'll have some strong talk with him in the morning."

The sheriff took the gambler's revolver and followed the two men who lugged the still unconscious gambler. Some of the men from the saloon seemed inclined to further discuss the incident, but Danielle walked away. It seemed a good time to return to her room at the hotel.

"Well," said the desk clerk, "I see you didn't meet up with John Wesley Hardin. It's generally peaceful enough, except when he's in town."

For a long time Danielle lay awake, considering what her next move should be. When she had joined the horse thieves, she had felt there was a chance that one or more of the men she had sworn to kill might be in old Mexico. But after the raid on Elfego's horses had gone sour, she was forced to change her opinion. Not only was it illegal for persons from the United States to cross into Mexico; any American south of the border might be considered a horse thief and shot on sight. She was convinced the men she sought were still scattered across the Southwest.

Returning from breakfast the next morning, Danielle stopped to question the young man at the lobby desk.

"How far is it to San Antonio?"

"Well over five hundred miles, and nothing much in between," said the desk clerk. "If you're ridin', you'd best take plenty of grub. But there's a stage once a week."

"Thanks," Danielle said.

Stage fares were expensive, so Danielle dismissed that possibility. It was a hot, dusty, and uncomfortable way to travel. She would ride, allowing the chestnut mare to take her time. Checking her saddlebags, Danielle found she was low on some items and rode by a mercantile to replenish them. To her dismay, as she was leaving the store, she met Hank, the sore loser from the saloon the night before. He had a bandage around his head, and his holster was empty. Apparently Sheriff Powell had kept his revolver.

"You young coyote," the gambler snarled, "nobody treats Hank Marshall like you done. One day, we'll meet up where you can't hide behind the law. Then you'll pay."

"Then you'd better shoot me in the back," said Danielle, "because you don't have the guts to face me. Try it, and I'll kill you."

Without a word, Marshall went on into the mercantile. Danielle mounted the chestnut mare and rode eastward. She was soon out of El Paso, and the plains before her looked bleak. There was no sign of human habitation for as far as she could see. As barren as the land appeared, there was water, but little or no wood for a fire. Danielle had a cold supper without coffee. There was no graze for the chestnut mare, and Danielle fed the animal a ration of grain she had brought along for that purpose. Picketing the mare nearby, she rolled in her blankets, her head on her saddle.

When Danielle arose the next morning, the weather was still mild, but far to the west, there was a dirty smudge of gray on the horizon. She saddled and mounted the chestnut mare and rode on toward San Antonio.

CHAPTER 10

THE TRAIL TO SAN ANTONIO. OCTOBER 24, 1870.

By early afternoon, Danielle judged that she was fifty miles out of El Paso and that sometime during the coming night, she would be in for a soaking. The dark clouds from the west had begun moving in, and the wind was getting stronger. Danielle began looking for a place that might offer a little shelter, but there was nothing. It was then that she heard what sounded like a distant gunshot. She reined up, listening. The single shot was followed by a dozen more in quick succession. Somebody was under siege, and the odds didn't appear anywhere close to equal.

"Horse," said Danielle, "we ought to mind our own business, but somebody's in trouble down yonder toward the border."

Danielle kicked the chestnut into a slow gallop, reining her down to a walk as they drew nearer the shooting. Reaching a rise, she could see a shack below, and from brush that surrounded the shack, there were puffs of white smoke. There appeared to be three defenders, while the attackers numbered twice that many, perhaps more. Adjoining the shack was a corral, and in it were six horses, nickering in fear. The three men nearest the shack were in poor positions, for the attackers were on the opposite side of a ridge, where there was broken land and huge stones to cover them. From powder smoke, Danielle counted eight riflemen firing toward the cabin. As one of the attackers shifted position, she saw the high crown of a Mexican sombrero. Danielle dismounted and, drawing her Henry rifle from the boot, set out to even up the odds. Her position was far better than that of the three defenders below, for the ridge on which she stood was higher than that on which the attackers were concealed. Her first shot ripped the Mexican's sombrero from his head, while her second shot slammed into the top of the stone behind which he was hiding, filling his eyes with dust. Danielle's intervention seemed to have given the three defenders renewed hope, for their firing grew more intense. Danielle held her fire, settling down on the rise, for if the attackers on the opposite ridge moved, she could see them. Suddenly, one of them did, seeking to get nearer the shack. Danielle fired, and the attacker fell, throwing up his hands. Another tried to improve his position, and Danielle's shot struck him in the shoulder, turning him around. He leaped for the stone behind which he had been concealed. Danielle quickly accounted for a third man, while the three men below continued firing. One of them scored a direct hit, and the four that remained ceased firing. Their attempts to move in closer had proven disastrous. It was time to back off.

"You on the ridge," shouted a voice from near the cabin, "can you see 'em? Have they retreated?"

"I think so," Danielle said. "Who were they, and who are you?"

"They're Mexicans that chased us across the border," said the voice. "I'm Roy Carnes, and my *amigos* are Jake Kazman and Maury Lyles."

"You've been rustling horses in Mexico, then, and driving them across the border," Danielle said. "Maybe I should have stayed out of it and let them take you."

"I swear we ain't rustled nobody's horses," Carnes shouted back. "Three of the horses in the corral are our personal mounts. The other three are wild as Texas jacks, without any brands. We trapped 'em wild, and before we could get 'em across the border, the damn Mexicans caught up to us. Come on down. There'll be a storm pretty quick."

The invitation was difficult to refuse, for the black clouds out of the west appeared to be dropping lower and lower. Already they had obscured the sun, and it was as though twilight had descended on the land. Leading the chestnut mare, Danielle descended the slope to the cabin below. The three men were waiting for her.

"Not a very good place for a cabin," Danielle said. "It's hard to defend."

"We know," said Carnes, "but there's water handy. We never expected them Mexes to foller us across the border. They never have before."

"Maybe you'd better think long and hard before crossing the border for more horses," Danielle said.

"I expect we will," Carnes said. "Who are you?"

"I'm Daniel Strange, bound for San Antonio."

"You're welcome to wait out the storm here with us," said Carnes. "We ain't got a bunk for you, but we can offer you a dry place to spread your blankets. Turn your horse into the corral with ours."

"Thanks," Danielle said. "It's looking pretty black over there. I'll accept your invite."

Removing her saddle and saddlebags, Danielle led the chestnut mare into the corral. It was a good time to see if Carnes had been lying about the newly acquired horses. But the trio appeared wild, and there wasn't a sign of a brand on any of them. Danielle followed the three men into the shack, finding it larger than she had expected. Danielle dropped her saddle and saddlebags in a corner. Carnes started a fire in the fireplace.

"Kazman," said Danielle, "your name's mighty familiar. I spent some time with friends north of Dallas, and I seem to recall having heard your name."

"No," Kazman said, a little too hurriedly. "I'm from south Texas, near San Antone."

"We ain't got much to offer in the way of grub," said Carnes. "When we break these wild horses, we got to ride into El Paso and stock up on supplies."

"I bought pretty heavy before leaving there," Danielle said.

"While I'm here, and you're providing me shelter, I'll supply the grub. You got a coffeepot?"

"Yeah," said Maury Lyles, "but we been out of coffee beans for a week."

"I have some," Danielle said. "Maybe I can spare you enough to get you to El Paso."

"We'd be obliged," said Roy Carnes.

Outside, the wind had risen to a shriek, driving sheets of rain against the side of the cabin. Danielle felt the floor tremble beneath her feet. They all sat on the benches on each side of the table, Danielle covertly watching Jake Kazman. Without appearing to, he shifted his eyes toward Danielle's saddle and saddlebags, and then looked away. Danielle observed him from the corner of her eye, and realized if he *had* been in north Texas, he might well know of the trail drive in which Danielle had taken part. He might also suspect that she had earned considerable money when the cattle had been sold in Abilene. Outside, the storm roared on. Using Danielle's supplies, Carnes prepared supper. After eating, the conversation dribbled away to nothing. While Carnes and Lyles were at ease, Kazman was restless, and more than once Danielle caught him watching her.

"We might as well turn in for the night," Lyles said, "unless the rest of you want to light the lantern and play some low-stakes poker."

"Thanks," said Danielle, "but I don't play poker."

"I don't play for low stakes," Carnes said, "and these other two jaybirds are likely as broke as I am. Besides, we've had a hard day, and I can use the sleep."

The three retired to their bunks, while Danielle took her place in the corner, her head on her saddle. The fire was allowed to burn itself out, and soon the cabin was in complete darkness. In the early hours of the morning, Danielle awakened, unsure as to what had disturbed her. The storm had ceased, for there was no roar of the wind or the sound of rain on the roof. Danielle lay on her back and, without moving the rest of her body, very slowly moved her right hand until it reached the butt of her Colt. Slowly she drew the weapon, and again she heard the sound that had awakened her. A floorboard creaked.

"You're covered," Danielle said. "A step closer, and I'll shoot."

"Hell," said Jake Kazman, "I was just goin' outside."

"Then turn around," Danielle said. "The door's behind you."

"Kazman," said Carnes, who was awake now, "I don't hold with botherin' an *hombre* that's stood by me or been a help to me in any way."

"Neither do I," Lyles added. "Nothin' but a flea-bitten yellow coyote eats another man's grub and then tries to rob him."

"You can't prove I had any such thing in mind," Kazman shouted, "and I won't take a charge from nobody. Nobody, by God!"

"You've been watching me ever since I got here," Danielle said, "and I'm accusing you of coming after me in the dark. When you say you don't know me or don't know of me, you lie. If you're still here come daylight, be wearing your pistol. You'll need it."

"I ain't goin' nowhere without one of them wild horses," said Kazman. "One of them belongs to me."

"Then catch one of them, saddle your horse, and get the hell out of here," Roy Carnes said.

"That goes for me as well," said Maury Lyles. "I never liked you much, Kazman, and now I know why."

Carnes stirred up the coals and added some wood to the fire. Without a word, Kazman took his saddle and left the shack.

"You reckon we ought to watch the varmint?" Lyles asked. "He's likely to take all the horses. Maybe our mounts, too."

"I'll watch him," said Carnes, taking his Winchester and stepping out the door.

"I swear we didn't know what he was when he joined up with us," said Lyles.

"I don't fault you and Carnes," Danielle said. "Despite what Kazman said, I still think he's from north Texas. Several weeks ago, I joined some Texas ranchers in gathering and getting a trail herd to Abilene. We gunned down four outlaws in Indian Territory, and I'm sure Kazman was one of those who escaped."

Nothing more was said until Carnes returned to the cabin.

"He's got his work cut out for him with that wild horse," said Carnes.

"That's his problem," Lyles said. "I'm glad to be rid of him."

"He seems like a man that carries a grudge," said Danielle. "He's liable to sneak back and bushwhack one or both of you."

"You'd better watch your back trail," Carnes said. "He knows where you're headed, and I wouldn't put it past him, trailing you."

"I'll keep that in mind," said Danielle. "There's still time to get some sleep before first light. But I think we should shove the table up against the door."

It was still dark outside when the nickering of a horse awakened Danielle. She pulled on her boots, aware that Carnes and Lyles were moving about. Nobody spoke. Danielle heard her companions cocking their Winchesters, and she followed them outside. There was a frightened nicker from the chestnut mare, for a shadowy rider was attempting to mount the animal. Danielle whistled once, and the mare broke into a frenzy of bucking, flinging the would-be thief to the ground.

"Get up, you thieving bastard," Carnes shouted.

But there was a muzzle flash, and Carnes stumbled back against the cabin wall. In only a split second, Danielle drew and fired twice, to the right and the left of the muzzle flash. For a moment none of them moved, lest the intruder still lived. Finally, Maury Lyles spoke.

"How hard was you hit, Roy?"

"Shoulder," said Carnes.

"I'll get the lantern," Lyles said, "but I think we all know who the coyote is."

Lyles lighted the lantern, and they found themselves looking into the dead face of Jake Kazman. He had been shot twice.

"Tarnation, that's some shootin' in the dark," said Lyles to Danielle. "That skunk really had it in for you."

"Do you know if Kazman was his real name?" Danielle asked.

"That's the name he gave us," said Lyles. "I'd better patch up your shoulder, Roy."

After dragging Kazman away from the corral, they returned to the cabin. Lyles stirred up the fire and put on a pot of water to boil.

"I have a quart of whiskey in my saddlebag," Danielle said, "and I'll leave it with you. There may be infection."

"We're obliged," said Carnes. "We won't be ridin' to town until we break those three wild horses."

After dressing Carnes's wound, Lyles built up the fire and started breakfast, since first light wasn't far away. In the brightening sky, the stars had begun to retreat into the distant heavens. By the time they finished breakfast, the eastern horizon was illuminated with the first light of dawn.

"I have plenty of coffee beans," Danielle said. "I'll leave some with you to last until you can get to town. Do you want me to bury Kazman before I go?"

"No," said Lyles, "I'll take care of it. You've done us some mighty big favors, and we are obliged."

Carnes added, "If you hadn't come along and spooked Kazman, he might have shot us both in the back and took *all* the horses. You sure you can't stay and join in our horse hunting?"

"No," said Danielle. "My pa was robbed and murdered in Indian Territory by outlaws, and I aim to track them down. There's seven of them still alive, unless Kazman was one of them, using another name."

"Before you leave, I'll search Kazman," Lyles said. "You never know what you'll find in a dead man's pockets."

Lyles took a little more than an hour, digging a shallow grave and burying Kazman. He returned to the cabin and dropped six gold double eagles on the table.

"That's all he had on him," said Lyles. "I reckon it's yours, Daniel, since you gave him what he deserved."

"I don't want it," Danielle said. "Use it to stock up on grub and coffee beans."

Shortly afterward, Danielle rode away. She genuinely hated leaving the two genial cowboys, but she wanted nothing more to do with taking horses—wild or gentled—from old Mexico. She had thought at first that some of the killers she sought might have crossed the border into Mexico, and were hiding there. But now, with Mexicans so hostile toward all Americans, it seemed unlikely. Texas itself was large enough to hide the whole bunch, and she rode on toward San Antonio.

SAN ANTONIO, TEXAS. OCTOBER 30, 1870.

Danielle took a room on the second floor of the Cattleman's Hotel. It was the exception among frontier hotels, for there was a dining room on the first floor. Every room had a deep pile carpet on the floor, with matching drapes at the window. Danielle sat down on the bed, which was firm enough that it didn't sag under her weight. It would be a welcome comfort, after four nights on the ground. There were a washbasin and a porcelain pitcher of water, and she took advantage of them, washing away the trail dust. One look in the mirror told her that her hair was getting entirely too long. She had to visit a barbershop, and soon. Since there was still daylight left, she decided to go for a haircut and be done with it. It was nearing the supper hour, and there were no other patrons in the shop.

"Cut it short," Danielle said. "I'm having trouble getting my hat to fit."

"Shave?" the barber asked.

"No," Danielle said. "Just cut my hair."

"There's a bathhouse in back, with plenty of soap and hot water," the barber said.

"Maybe later," said Danielle. "It's near suppertime, and I'm hungry."

The door opened, and a lanky man entered. A Colt was tied low on each hip.

"Haircut," said the stranger.

"You're next," the barber replied.

"King Fisher don't like to wait," said the new arrival. "I'll get in that other chair, and you take care of me. Then you can get back to the shavetail you're working on now."

"I was here first," Danielle said, "and he's goin' to finish with me. If you don't like it, wait until I'm out of this chair and settle with me."

Under her barber's cloth, there was the ominous sound of a Colt being cocked. There was no fear in Danielle's cold green eyes as they bored into King Fisher's.

"I'll come back another time," said King Fisher. Turning, he walked out the door.

"My God," the barber said, "do you know who that was?"

"I believe he said his name is King Fisher," Danielle said. "It means nothing to me."

"It should," said the barber. "He don't carry them two guns just for show, and at this particular time, Ben Thompson's in town. Him and King Fisher are friends. Sober, they're decent, but let 'em get drunk, and the devil couldn't ask for no better disciples."*

Danielle left the barbershop and returned to the hotel, where she took a table in the dining room. She had not even been served when King Fisher entered. With him was a smaller man, dressed all in black, with a frock coat and black silk top hat. The two took a table next to Danielle's, and she couldn't help hearing their talk.

"The kid at the next table pulled a gun and run me out of the barbershop," said King Fisher loud enough for Danielle to hear.

Fisher's companion found that uproariously funny, pounding

---

* King Fisher and Ben Thompson (born in Knottingley, England, November 2, 1842) were dangerous men. Both were confirmed killers noted for their swiftness with a gun. They were notorious gamblers, and they each walked on both sides of the law, wearing the star until some drunken brawl or random killing got them dismissed. Both men were ambushed in a theater in San Antonio, in 1884. The killers were never caught.

the table with his fist, but when he spoke, his voice was like cold steel.

"Nobody drives Ben Thompson away if he wants to go on living."

Danielle tried her best to ignore the pair, taking her time with her meal. As she got up to leave, Thompson spoke.

"I never seen a man with a butt-forward pistol who had any speed with a cross-hand draw."

In an instant, he found himself facing the barrel end of the butt-forward Colt from Danielle's left hip.

"There are exceptions," Danielle said coldly. She border-shifted the Colt back to her left hand, deftly slipping the weapon back into its holster, again butt forward.

It was King Fisher's turn to laugh. "Who *are* you, kid?"

"My name is not 'kid.' I'm Daniel Strange."

"I'm King Fisher, and the little *hombre* in the stovepipe hat is Ben Thompson. Let word of this get around, and Thompson may have to go back to England."

"I've never seen a fancy pair of irons like that," Thompson said. "May I see one?"

"Look all you like," said Danielle, "but they stay where they are."

Thompson's ruddy face turned ugly, but King Fisher took the edge off his anger.

"Come on, Thompson, let's go play some poker. This two-gun man's too tough for a pair of old dogs like us."

Danielle waited, allowing the pair to leave ahead of her. Referring to her youth, King Fisher had been just as insulting as Ben Thompson, and she didn't like either of them. The evening was still young, and there was little to occupy one's time except gambling tables in the various saloons. Danielle still had almost four thousand dollars, thanks to her success at the faro tables, and a town like San Antonio had many saloons. With a self-imposed limit of a hundred dollars, she set out to make the rounds. She had learned that the fancier the saloon, the higher the stakes. The first place she entered was called the Oro Palace and the faro dealer was asking for—and getting—ten-dollar bets. When a player left the table,

Danielle sat down, dropping five double eagles on the felt-topped table before her. The other players paid her no attention until she won three pots in a row. She still had sixty dollars of her original hundred, plus her winnings. She lost two pots, and then won four in a row. The dealer had been watching her suspiciously but it was he, after all, who was dealing the cards. After winning back her initial hundred dollars and taking another two hundred from the house, Danielle dropped out. The house dealer seemed relieved.

Danielle found most saloons unpleasant, with brash, insensitive women determined to lead her upstairs. But the saloons were where men gathered, and as she sat at the faro table, she listened to talk around her, hoping for some word of the men who had killed her father. Quickly tiring, she returned to her hotel. In the lobby was a stack of newspapers.

"Take one," the clerk invited. "They're fresh in from Dallas."

Danielle took one, finding it to be larger than the average frontier newspaper. With news items from all over, one in particular caught her eye. It was datelined Wichita, and concerned the robbery of a Kansas Pacific train. She read the article twice, grinding her teeth.

. . . two men—Rufe Gaddis and Julius Byler—were believed to be involved, but they had none of the gold, and refused to talk. They were released for lack of evidence.

Both the men were on Danielle's death list, but after their brush with the law, they would be long gone from Wichita. The Kansas town was almost at the edge of Indian Territory, and the pair might have gone there to hide. On the other hand, they might have gone west, or perhaps back east, toward St. Louis. Danielle lay down to sleep, wondering if she was wasting her time in south Texas.

The next morning, after breakfast, Danielle found the Texas Ranger office. A ranger sat at a battered desk, reading a newspaper. He looked up as she entered.

"I'm Daniel Strange."

"I'm Sage Jennings," said the ranger.

"I'm looking for some men—outlaws—who robbed and murdered my pa in Indian Territory," Danielle said. "There are seven of them still alive, and although I've managed to learn their names, I don't know that they aren't using other names by now. Do you have any wanted dodgers that I'd be allowed to see?"

"You're welcome to look through what I have," Jennings said, "but I doubt they'll be of much help. These are only outlaws wanted by the state of Texas."

"I'd like to look at them anyway," said Danielle.

Jennings brought out the dodgers, many of them yellowed with age. Some of them had a rough sketch of the wanted man, but the majority had only a name, the nature of the crime, and the reward, if any. Almost immediately, Danielle found a pair of yellowed pages with the names of Rufe Gaddis and Julius Byler. There was a thousand dollars on the heads of each of them.

"This is two of them on my list," said Danielle.

"Those dodgers are mighty old," Jennings said. "Chances are, they're using some other names by now."

"No," said Danielle. "Yesterday, I saw both their names in a story in a Dallas newspaper. Gaddis and Byler were suspected of robbing a Kansas Pacific train, but were let go for lack of evidence. The law in Wichita had them."

"By now they're somewhere in Indian Territory," Jennings said.

Danielle thumbed through the rest of the wanted dodgers without finding the names of any more of the men she sought.

"Just those two," said Danielle. "I'm obliged."

"A ranger keeps records of his own," Jennings said. "I'll check out Bible Two."*

From his shirt pocket, he took a small notebook and began thumbing through it.

---

* Every Texas Ranger carried a personal Bible. In addition, he kept a record of outlaws wanted by the rangers, and this notebook was referred to as "Bible Two."

"Here's something that might be of interest to you," said Jennings, "and it brings back some unpleasant memories for me. Gaddis and Byler didn't take part in the war. They're both Texans, and they stayed here and raised hell. When they finally stepped over the line to become thieves and killers, we haven't seen them since. Another *hombre* known to the rangers as Chancy Burke generally rode with them."

"Burke's on my list with Gaddis and Byler," said Danielle. "If they're all Texans, then I may not be wasting my time in Texas, after all. What part of Texas did they call home?"

"In and around Waco," Jennings said, "and you may be right. They still have families—law-abiding folks—living there, and I wouldn't be surprised if all of them don't slip back home for an occasional visit."

"I'm obliged to you for the information," said Danielle. "Maybe I'll ride to Waco and see what I can find."

"Then take some advice from somebody that's been there," Jennings said, "and don't tell anybody why you're in town. Everybody in the county is loyal to them three young varmints, and hostile as hell toward the rangers and other lawmen."

"I reckon they didn't do their hell-raising close to home," said Danielle.

"They didn't," Jennings said. "Their kin will admit they're wild, but they won't lift a hand to help the law track them down."

"Thanks," said Danielle. "I'll keep my silence."

"If you're successful in finding any or all three of them, I'd appreciate your sending me word," Jennings said.

"I will," said Danielle.

On the way to her hotel, Danielle met King Fisher and Ben Thompson walking unsteadily along the boardwalk. The pair looked as though they might have been up all night.

"Well, by God," King Fisher said, slapping his thigh with his hat, "it's the kid with the two big guns."

"He'll bleed like anybody else with a slug in him," said Thompson, fixing his bloodshot eyes on Danielle.

Danielle walked around them, chills racing up and down her spine. Would the drunken Thompson shoot her in the back? Nothing happened, and she began to relax.

Danielle saw no advantage to remaining in San Antonio. Remaining there, she might be confronted with either Ben Thompson or King Fisher, a confrontation that would profit her nothing. So taking her bedroll and saddlebags, she went to the livery where she had left the chestnut mare. Saddling the animal, she mounted and rode north, toward Waco.

CHAPTER 11

WACO, TEXAS. NOVEMBER 3, 1870.

Reaching Waco, Danielle stabled the chestnut mare and took a hotel room not too far away. Danielle found a café and had supper. While Waco wasn't nearly as large as San Antonio, it had its share of saloons. Recalling the warning from Sage Jennings, the Texas Ranger in San Antonio, she would make the rounds of the saloons first. Only then, if she learned nothing, would she speak to the county sheriff.

The first saloon she entered was the Bull's Horn, and except for a poker game, there was nothing going on. She watched for a few minutes, but nobody spoke, except for an occasional grunt of satisfaction as one of the men won a hand and raked in the money. The rest of the saloons in town proved to be much like the first. There were faro games going on in several of them, but Danielle avoided them, lest she draw attention to herself. People in Waco seemed especially closemouthed, and she expected some hostility when she had to ask questions. Since it seemed there was no other way, the next morning after breakfast, she set out to find the sheriff's office. It was small, with a pair of barred cells behind it.

"Sheriff, I'm Daniel Strange, and I need to ask a favor."

The lawman had gray hair, and the years had taken their toll on his body. A Colt was tied down on his right hip. He looked Danielle over carefully before he spoke.

"I'm Sheriff Rucker. The last two-gun man through here got strung up. Now what do you want of me?"

"I'm looking for some word of Rufe Gaddis, Julius Byler, and Chancy Burke. They're from this area, I'm told."

"Far from here," Rucker said. "I ain't seen any of 'em for three years. Mind telling me why you're interested in them?"

There it was. There was no holding back the truth, which Rucker likely suspected already. Danielle sighed, then spoke.

"They were part of a group of men who robbed and hanged my pa in Indian Territory last spring."

"I reckon you got proof," said Sheriff Rucker.

"To my satisfaction," Danielle said. "I've tracked down three of them, and the second one gave me the names of the others. Where do you stand?"

"Right here in this county," said Sheriff Rucker. "I got no jurisdiction anywhere else, and unless some *hombres* ride in here to raise hell, I leave 'em alone."

"Even if they're wanted by the *rangers* for crimes in other places?"

"Even then," Rucker said. "Hell, the *rangers* ain't been sanctified. It wouldn't be the first time they've gone after the wrong men."

"How well are the Gaddis, Byler, and Burke families known around here?" Danielle asked.

"They're known and respected all over the county," said Rucker, "and they look after their own. They're clannish, and when you cut one, they all bleed."

"And they all vote," Danielle said.

"Yeah," said Sheriff Rucker, his face going red. "I won this office ten years ago, and an *hombre* like you could lose it for me in one day."

"Oh, I won't drag you into it," Danielle said in disgust.

She turned and left the office. When the liveryman brought her the chestnut mare, she had a question for him.

"I'm looking for work. Who are the most prominent ranchers in these parts?"

"Silas Burke, Damon Byler, and Luke Gaddis," said the livery-man, "but they won't be hiring. They can't afford no riders."

"Give me some directions anyway," Danielle said, "and I'll see for myself. I'm needin' to hire on somewhere for the winter."

It wasn't an unusual request from an unemployed drifting rider, and the liveryman gave Danielle directions. The Burke spread was the closest, and she rode there first. When Danielle rode in, a man with graying hair and a body gone to fat stood on the front porch, a Winchester under his arm. Danielle reined up a few yards away.

"Who are you and what do you want?" the man growled.

"I'm Daniel Strange, and I'm looking for some line riding to see me through winter."

"I'm Silas Burke, and I ain't hiring. If I was, I wouldn't hire no two-gun stranger. We got too many cowboys here in the county that's needin' work. Had you asked, you could've learned that in town."

Two young men—Benjamin and Monroe—looking like younger versions of Silas, came out and stood beside their father.

"He looks like one of them damn rangers, Pa," said Benjamin. "Two guns."

"A mite unusual for a line rider," Silas said. "Boy, are you the law?"

"No," said Danielle, "and I'm not a bounty hunter. Why are you afraid of the law?"

"I ain't afraid of the law," Silas growled, "and if I was, it wouldn't be no business of yours. Now turn that horse around and ride."

There was no help for it. Danielle wheeled the chestnut mare, riding back the way she had come. After she was well out of sight, a horseman rode out of a thicket where he had been waiting, and rode on to the Burke place. Sheriff Rucker had some news for old Silas Burke.

Danielle rode on to the Byler spread, where she received the same cold reception.

"I ain't hiring," said Damon Byler, "and if I was, it wouldn't be no two-gun shavetail passin' through. Ride on."

Reaching the Gaddis ranch, Danielle prepared herself for yet another rebuff, and it wasn't long in coming. Luke Gaddis was waiting for her to ride in, and before she had a chance to speak, Gaddis shifted the shotgun under his arm.

"I ain't hiring," said Gaddis bluntly.

"You don't even know me," Danielle said.

"No," said Gaddis, "but I know *of* you and your kind. Sheriff Rucker's told me about you. Now turn your horse around and ride."

Danielle rode away, furious. Sheriff Rucker had violated a confidence, knowing well the effect it would have on the Burke, Byler, and Gaddis families. There was nothing more to do except ride back to town, and Danielle did so, unsure as to what her next move would be. If the three men she sought *did* return to Texas, they would immediately learn that they were being hunted. But Danielle still had some unpleasant surprises ahead. She reined up and dismounted at the livery.

"I got no room for another horse," the liveryman said.

Danielle made up her mind to remain in Waco one more night. Returning to the hotel, she requested a room.

"Sorry," the desk clerk said. "We're full."

Danielle received the same treatment at other hotels and boardinghouses. She stopped at the café where she had eaten breakfast, and before she could sit down, one of the cooks spoke.

"You're not welcome here. Move on."

Danielle left, mounted the chestnut mare, and rode to the mercantile to replenish her supplies, including a bag of grain for the chestnut mare. She would sleep on the ground and prepare her own meals. But the store owner, looking embarrassed, turned her away.

"I got to live in this town," he said, "and I can't afford havin' them that don't like you comin' down on me. Sorry."

"The whole damn bunch of you deserves one another," spat Danielle in disgust.

She considered riding back to San Antonio and reporting the

sheriff's behavior to Sage Jennings, the Texas Ranger, but changed her mind. Jennings had almost surely been to this town and, beyond a doubt, had met with the same hostility. Recalling that Fort Worth was only ninety miles north, Danielle decided to go there. If the gold taken from the train by Gaddis and Byler had been a government payroll, surely the post commander at Fort Worth would know. He might even be sympathetic to her cause.

FORT WORTH, TEXAS. NOVEMBER 5, 1870.

Arriving in Fort Worth, Danielle asked to speak to the post commander. Following a Sergeant Waymont, she was taken through the orderly room. Sergeant Waymont knocked on a door, and from inside the office, a voice spoke.

"Yes, who is it?"

"Sergeant Waymont, sir, and I have someone with me who wants to talk to you."

"Come in, Sergeant," the officer said.

Waymont entered, saluted, and had it returned. He stepped out the door, closing it behind him. Danielle was on her own. She spoke.

"I'm Daniel Strange, from St. Joe, Missouri."

"I'm Captain Ferguson. Sit down and tell me what you want of me."

"Maybe you can help me track down three killers I'm looking for," said Danielle.

"The military does not assist bounty hunters," Ferguson said.

"I'm not a bounty hunter," said Danielle. "The men I'm searching for were part of a gang that robbed and murdered my pa in Indian Territory."

"You are justified in your search for them, then," Ferguson said, "but I don't understand what you want of me. I presume you have no evidence."

"Only the confession of one of the men," said Danielle.

"Oh," Ferguson said. "Where is he?"

Danielle sighed. "He's dead."

"Then we're right back where we started," said Ferguson.

"Not quite," Danielle said. "When I was in San Antonio, in a Dallas newspaper, I found a story about a train robbery near Wichita. Gaddis and Byler, two of the men I'm after, were involved in that holdup. They stole a military payroll, didn't they?"

After a long moment of silence and just when Danielle had decided Ferguson wasn't going to reply, he did.

"I don't think I'm violating any rules telling you this. Yes, it was a military payroll, bound for Fort Dodge. A military escort was to have intercepted it at the end of track."*

"Those outlaws were successful in one train robbery," said Danielle, "and it's a safe bet they'll plan another one. How can I find out when there'll be another shipment?"

"You can't," Ferguson said. "That's confidential information."

"Not confidential enough to keep the outlaws from knowing it," said Danielle.

"No," Ferguson said with a sigh. "Privately, I believe we're being sold out by somebody with the Kansas Pacific in Kansas City. But the railroad refuses to consider such a possibility, because there's no proof."

"Except that the thieves always seem to know which train is carrying a payroll," said Danielle. "Can you get me the names of the men employed by the railroad?"

"Probably," Ferguson said, "but for what purpose?"

"I want to see if any of the men I'm searching for are on that list," Danielle said. "If a name on that list matches a name on my list, he could well be the traitor that's selling out to the train robbers."

"I'll secure a list of the Kansas Pacific employees on one condition," said Ferguson.

---

* The Kansas Pacific rails didn't reach Dodge until 1872.

"I'm listening," Danielle said.

"Should we actually find on this list the name of one of the men you're searching for," said Ferguson, "I want him arrested by the proper authorities, not gunned down."

"If the proper authorities can take him, welcome," Danielle said. "If they can't, then he belongs to me. In case you don't know, three of the varmints on my list are from Waco, and two of them stole your last payroll. Your 'proper authority'—the county sheriff—is more concerned with keeping his star than he is in tracking down hometown boys who are thieves and murderers."

"See here, young man," said Captain Ferguson coldly, "it is not the responsibility of military personnel to track down civilian thieves. Asking for an employee list from Kansas Pacific would be exceeding my authority, and under the circumstances, I don't believe it is justified."

"Thank you for seeing me, Captain," Danielle said, getting to her feet.

"I'm not finished with you," said Ferguson.

"Maybe not," Danielle said, "but I'm finished with you. You're about as much help as that no-account sheriff in Waco."

Danielle left the office, mounted the chestnut mare, and rode north, bound for Indian Territory.

Meanwhile, Rufe Gaddis and Julius Byler had established a camp in Indian Territory, a few miles south of Wichita. Passing a bottle back and forth, they contemplated their next move.

"Damn it," Byler said, "if it wasn't for owin' Chancy Burke a third of what we got, we could take that twenty-five thousand and ride on."

Gaddis laughed. "We could ride on anyway, taking it all. What would Burke do? For sure he couldn't complain to the law that we took his share of the money he helped us steal from the railroad."

"No," Byler agreed, "but he wouldn't feed us any more information about when there's a gold shipment coming. This is a sweet setup, and us gettin' greedy could ruin it."

"One thing bothers me," said Gaddis. "There ain't been a word out of the railroad after we took that twenty-five thousand. We can always stop the train by blocking the track or ripping out a rail, but what happens if there's a dozen armed guards in that mail coach?"

"I reckon that's all the more reason for Burke to get his share," Byler said. "It'll be up to him to warn us if the train's swarming with Pinkertons or soldiers."

"Tomorrow, then," Gaddis said, "we'd better ride to Kansas City and have some words with him. If a shipment's under heavy guard, he's got to warn us."

Leaving Fort Worth, Danielle reached the Red River before sundown. Rather than enter Indian Territory so near dark, she made camp on the south bank of the Red. Tomorrow, she would continue her journey to Wichita. The story she had read in the Dallas paper was somehow incomplete. It had provided the names of the thieves—Rufe Gaddis and Julius Byler—but how had that been possible? For certain, the two had not introduced themselves. She hoped the sheriff in Wichita could and would fill in the missing information.

The following morning, after a hurried breakfast, Danielle saddled the chestnut mare and crossed the Red. It was a good two-day ride just getting across Indian Territory. She wanted to get as much of the Territory behind her as she could on the first day. She kept the chestnut mare at a mile-eating gait, stopping once every hour to rest the animal. Near sundown, she found a spring and, not wishing to risk a fire, ate jerked beef and drank cold water. There was no graze, and she fed the horse the last of the grain.

"Sorry, old girl," said Danielle. "That will have to hold you until we reach Wichita."

WICHITA, KANSAS. NOVEMBER 8, 1870.

The first stars were already twinkling when Danielle rode into Wichita. Her initial concern was for the horse, and she left the mare at a livery, paying for extra rations of grain and a rub-down. The newer buildings in Wichita were strung out along the railroad track, with several cafés and a hotel among them. Danielle took a room, then went to the nearest café. She was hungry, having eaten little but jerked beef since her first night in Waco. After eating, she decided against returning to the hotel immediately, going to a nearby saloon instead. In an obvious play for railroad business, it had been named the Railroad Saloon, and a sign in the plate-glass window proclaimed it the largest and fanciest in Wichita. It wasn't much past the supper hour, but the place was already crowded with an abundance of poker and faro games in progress. So as not to attract unwanted attention, Danielle sat in on one of the faro games. Sticking to her limit, she dropped her five double eagles on the felt-topped table.

"Five-dollar limit," said the dealer.

Danielle won and lost, won and lost, and finally dropped out, breaking even. She was about to leave the saloon when a pair of familiar faces caught her eye. At one of the poker tables sat Herb Sellers and Jesse Burris, the two would-be bounty hunters she had last seen in Denver. Danielle slipped up behind Burris and poked him between his shoulder blades with her finger.

"You're under arrest, you varmint."

"Not now damn it," said Burris. "I'm ahead."

Herb Sellers looked up and smiled, recognition in his eyes, but he remained where he was. For the next few hands, Danielle stood back and watched. Evidently, Herb and Jesse were doing well at the table, and it was almost an hour before they withdrew from the game.

"Well," Danielle said after they had left the saloon, "how's the bounty hunting going?"

"Not worth a damn," said Burris. "We're surviving because we've been lucky at the poker tables, but how long does a run of luck last?"

"What about your manhunt, Daniel?" Sellers asked.

"I caught up to one of the outfit in New Mexico," said Danielle, "but that's all. I came here because there was a short story in a Dallas newspaper about two *hombres* robbing a Kansas Pacific train of a government payroll. The newspaper printed the names of two of the men I'm searching for, so I came here to see what I could learn. Mostly, I want to know how the newspaper discovered their names."

"I can tell you that," said Burris. "Herb and me got here yesterday because there's a twenty-five-hundred-dollar bounty on the heads of each of the train robbers. They stopped the train four or five miles east of here, and after the robbery, the engineer backed the train into town. The sheriff got a quick posse together and picked up the trail of the robbers, who were bound for Indian Territory. But they found tracks of three horses, and eventually caught up to a woman whose horse had gone lame. She had been with the robbers, but hadn't taken part in the train robbery. She told the sheriff as much as she could—including the names of the train robbers—and the sheriff let her go."

"The newspaper account didn't tell it all," Danielle said. "There was no mention of the woman. She had to talk about Gaddis and Byler, but she might also have known something about the rest of that bunch that hanged my pa."

"She left last night on the eastbound train," said Herb. "The sheriff wouldn't even tell us her name."

"Sounds like the kind of treatment I got in Waco," Danielle said. "Rufe Gaddis, Julius Byler, and Chancy Burke are all from there, and they're all part of the gang that hanged my pa. I made the mistake of telling the sheriff why I was looking for them, and he made it a point to tell the whole damn county why I was there. The Gaddis, Byler, and Burke families tell everybody when to jump and how high. I couldn't stable my horse, rent a room, or buy myself a meal."

"Then what did you do?" Jesse Burris asked.

"I rode to Fort Worth and met with Captain Ferguson, the post commander. He finally admitted it was a military payroll that Gaddis and Byler took, but he wasn't interested in the plan I had. I think Gaddis and Byler are being fed information by someone working for the railroad. I wanted Captain Ferguson to use his influence to get a list of the names of men who are involved with the Kansas Pacific, but I couldn't meet his conditions. He wants to do everything by the book, allowing the authorities to make proper arrests. I don't care a damn about Gaddis and Byler being arrested for train robbery. I want the bastards dead."

"Burris and me was in that saloon right through supper," said Herb, "and I'm starved. Let's get somethin' to eat and talk about this some more."

"I've had supper," Danielle said, "but I can always use some more coffee."

They stopped at one of the cafés near the railroad. While Sellers and Burris waited for their food, the three of them sipped hot coffee.

"A damn shame the military wouldn't work with you," Burris said. "If Gaddis and Byler have somebody connected with the railroad feeding them information, they'll know when a train's carrying a payroll. But suppose we managed to get the names of every man with the Kansas Pacific, and none of them are the men you're hunting? We still wouldn't have a clue as to who the Judas is, and you'd be no closer to finding the bunch you're looking for."

"True," Danielle said, "but at least I'd know that they're likely not in Kansas. Since I learned nothing in Waco, I'm really not sure where to go from here. I'm thinking of going directly to the Kansas Pacific and asking them if any of the men on my list are involved with the railroad."

"Maybe we'll go with you," said Burris.

"No," Danielle said. "Some folks frown on bounty hunting, and that might interfere with my learning anything. If I learn something you can use, I'll pass it on."

"Then why don't we ride to Kansas City in the morning?" Herb suggested. "I doubt we'll learn anything more here."

KANSAS CITY, KANSAS. NOVEMBER 10, 1870.

The trio reached Kansas City in the late afternoon. There was the shriek of a whistle and the clanging of a bell as a train pulled out for the end of track.

"Let's find a hotel and get the horses stabled," Danielle said. "Then I'll see what I can learn from the railroad."

The town was large and growing, evidence enough of the prosperity that followed the coming of the rails. Danielle and her companions took rooms in one of the hotels not far from the railroad yard. It was close enough for Danielle to walk, and she did. Railroad offices were housed in a larger building that was also the terminal, and Danielle went in. A little man with spectacles looked up from the telegraph instrument on the table before him.

"I'm looking for someone who might be working for the railroad," Danielle said. "Who do I need to talk to about him?"

"Alan Steele," said the telegrapher. "He's personnel manager, but he's gone for the day. Nobody here but me."

Danielle sighed. "I'll try again tomorrow."

Slowly, she walked back to the hotel, her spirits at a low ebb. It was becoming more and more difficult to live up to her vow to find the men who had hanged her father. Herb and Jesse were eagerly awaiting her return.

"All I learned," said Danielle, "is that I'll have to talk to the personnel director, and he's gone for the day."

"Some bounty hunters we are," Burris said. "We spend all our time waitin' for something or somebody, and now we're ridin' your shirttail, hoping you'll lead us to *hombres* we can't seem to find on our own."

"Hell, I'm about ready to ride into Indian Territory and join a bunch of outlaws," said Sellers. "There must be plenty of them with prices on their heads."

"I don't recommend that," Danielle said. "I've tried that, and if they take you in, you'll have to take part in whatever they're doing. You could end up on the wrong side of the law with prices on *your* heads."

"I haven't put that much thought into it," said Sellers, "but I reckon you're right. I'm just not sure I'm cut out for bounty hunting. It all seemed so easy. You take a varmint in and collect the bounty. Trouble is, I never shot at a man in my life, and I wonder if I actually could. I doubt that any man with a price on his head will surrender, and that means he'll have to be brought in dead."

"I think so," Danielle agreed, "but you never know what you can do until it's shoot or be shot. The first *hombre* I shot was trying to kill me, and that left me no choice. If we can track down Gaddis and Byler, I'll let the two of you turn them in—or what's left of them—for the bounty."

"That's white of you," Sellers said, "but I don't take money that I ain't earned."

"Me neither," said Burris.

"Damn it," said Danielle, "you're looking at this all wrong. I'm not bounty hunting, and I'll not be claiming any bounty. I want some varmints dead, and I won't take money just for keeping a vow I made on my pa's grave. If you're with me, and there's a bounty, you can take it or leave it. I don't want it. I'd feel like I was selling my pa's life for the money."

"I reckon that makes sense," Sellers said. "You're a generous man, Daniel Strange."

"Let's get some supper," said Burris, "and then check out the games in the saloons. It won't seem so much like we're wasting time if we can win some money."

"I'll risk a hundred, but no more," Danielle said.

The Wagon Wheel was the biggest and fanciest saloon in town, and that's where the trio went. Sellers and Burris took their seats at a table where a poker game was going on, while Danielle approached one of the faro tables.

"Five-dollar limit," said the dealer. "Show me your money."

Danielle dropped five double eagles on the green felt that covered the table. Some of the men around her cast sidelong glances at the twin Colts tied down on each hip. Losing the first three hands, Danielle then began to win. Sellers and Burris remained in the poker game as Danielle continued winning at faro. When her hundred-dollar stake increased to three hundred, she withdrew from the game. The relief on the dealer's face was obvious. She headed for the poker table where Sellers and Burris seemed engrossed in the game. They seemed to be doing well, especially Burris. There was a huge pile of chips before him, and as Danielle watched, he won another pot.

"I'm out," said one of the players in disgust.

But as he slid back his chair, Danielle could see that he held a revolver under the table, and he wasted no time in using it. He stood up.

"Bucko," he said to Burris, "you're just a little too damn lucky to suit me."

Burris was caught totally by surprise, and as he went for his gun, his opponent fired.

But a second shot blended with his own, and he fell across the poker table. All eyes turned to Danielle, who still held a smoking Colt steady in her hand. Sellers was already kneeling over Burris.

"Is he alive?" Danielle asked.

"Yeah," said Sellers, "and he wasn't cheating. Some of you take a look at his cards."

They examined the cards Burris was holding, shaking their heads.

"That damn Winters had to be the worst poker player in town," said the house dealer. "When he's a big loser—which is most of the time—he's got to have a dog to kick."

"He won't be drawing any more bad poker hands," one of the men said. "He's stone-cold dead."

One man had gone for a doctor, while another had gone for the sheriff. Dr. Avery and Sheriff Barnes arrived together.

"He'll live," the doctor said after examining Burris.

"Who's responsible for this?" the sheriff asked, his eyes on the dead gambler.

CHAPTER 12

I shot him after he gunned down a friend of mine, Sheriff," Danielle said.

"The *hombre* Elmo Winters shot wasn't cheating, Sheriff," said a house dealer. "Elmo had a mad on because he was losing, like he usually does."

"I'll want you to come with me to the office," Sheriff Barnes told Danielle.

"Not until I've seen my friend back to the hotel," said Danielle.

"Me and the doctor can handle that," Herb Sellers said. "You got a stretcher, Doc?"

"Yes," said Dr. Avery. "I'll go get it."

"Some of you tote Elmo Winters over yonder to the carpenter shop," Sheriff Barnes said. "I'll ride out in the morning and see what Jubal and Ebeau wants to do with him."

Danielle followed Sheriff Barnes to his office, the lawman saying nothing until they were inside. Then he spoke.

"You can start by telling me who you are and what you're doing in town."

"I'm Daniel Strange, Sheriff. I mostly make my living gambling. You have some fine saloons here."

"We also have some snake-mean hell-raisers here," said Sheriff Barnes. "Elmo Winters, the *hombre* you shot, has family. There's his pa, Jubal, and his older brother, Ebeau. I'll tell you this for your own good, kid. Don't stay in town long enough for Jubal and Eb-eau to find out you shot Elmo."

"I had cause to shoot him," Danielle said. "Are you denying that?"

"No," said Sheriff Barnes, "he's had that coming for a long time. But his old daddy and his brother won't settle for anything less than an eye for an eye. I'll ride out in the morning and tell them, so you got a little time."

"I have business here, Sheriff," Danielle said, "and I'm not leav-ing until I've seen to it. I want peace, but not the kind that comes with the grave. You can tell Elmo's kin that if they come gunning for me, they'd better be wearing their burying clothes. Now, is there anything more you need from me?"

"I reckon not," Sheriff Barnes said. "There'll be an inquest to-morrow, but I think I'll be able to justify the shooting to the satis-faction of the court. There's witnesses aplenty."

"I'll be here at least through tomorrow if you want anything more of me."

Leaving the sheriff's office, Danielle returned to the hotel, knock-ing on the door to the room occupied by Herb Sellers and Jesse Burris. Herb opened the door and Danielle closed it behind her.

"How is he?" Danielle asked.

"Better than you'd expect, him being shot at such close range," said Herb. "I want to thank you for buying in. I'm sorry to say it took me as much by surprise as it did Jesse, and if Winters had got off a second shot, it would've been the end of Jesse Burris. What did the sheriff want?"

"Mostly to warn me to get out of town," Danielle said. "Elmo's pa, Jubal, and his brother, Ebeau, are the kind who'll likely come looking for me."

Jesse Burris slept, the doctor having given him some laudanum, and for a long moment, Herb looked at his sleeping friend. Finally, he spoke.

"Jesse will be sorry he dragged you into his fight, Daniel, and I'm sorry, too. Both of us are big enough to stomp our own snakes."

"We've all been taking our chances," Danielle said. "Some men are poor losers. Elmo Winters was one of them. If his pa and brother come looking for trouble, they'll find it. How long does the doctor think Jesse will be laid up?"

"Maybe a week," Herb said. "I cashed in his chips, and he'd won more than four hundred dollars. I won about half that, so we'll be able to afford the hotel until he's healed. Do you still aim to visit the Kansas Pacific tomorrow?"

"Yes," said Danielle. "I aim to learn something helpful if I can. If I can't, then I want to know it. Then I can move on."

"I'll stay close by," Herb said. "If Winters's kin come looking for you, I promise you'll not have to face them alone."

"I'm obliged," said Danielle, "but it was me that shot Elmo Winters, and I bought in of my own choosing. I'm not afraid of his pa or his brother. The only way they'll get me is to shoot me in the back."

Danielle returned to her own room. She bolted the door from inside and placed the back of a chair under the knob of the door. For a long time she lay awake, unable to sleep, yet too exhausted not to.

D anielle was awakened by a knock on her door.
"Who is it?" she asked.

"Herb," a voice replied. "I'm about to have breakfast and thought you might join me."

"I will," Danielle said. "Give me time to get up and get dressed."

Danielle dressed hurriedly and found Herb waiting in the hall.

"How's Jesse this morning?"

"Sleeping," said Herb. "No fever yet. The doctor's coming by sometime today."

Danielle and Herb had breakfast in a café, neither talking much, for it seemed there was little to be said. Danielle was thinking ahead to her meeting with Alan Steele, at the Kansas Pacific offices, and was at a loss as to what she must do or where she must go if the railroad man refused to cooperate with her. Herb interrupted her thoughts.

"How long do you aim to stay here?"

"At least today and tonight," Danielle said. "It's near nine o'clock, and when I leave here, I'm going straight to the Kansas Pacific offices. Go on back to the hotel, and I'll tell you what I learn, if anything."

The railroad terminal was a bustle of activity when Danielle arrived. In the outer office, a different telegrapher sat at the instrument, which was clattering out a message. Danielle waited until the machine was silent before speaking to the telegrapher.

"I'm Daniel Strange, and I need to talk to Alan Steele. Tell him it has to do with the recent train robbery."

The telegrapher wasted no time in getting the message to Steele, and Danielle was led down a hall to Steele's office. She entered, closing the door behind her. Steele nodded to a chair, and she sat down. Steele was a heavy man with bushy eyebrows and a ruddy face. His eyes met hers, and Danielle spoke.

"Mr. Steele, I'd like to help you find the men who recently took a military payroll from one of your trains."

"You're a bounty hunter, then," said Steele.

"No," Danielle said. "Last spring, a gang of outlaws robbed and murdered my pa. I have the names of those who are still alive. Gaddis and Byler, who robbed you, were part of the bunch I'm looking for. Another is Chancy Burke. All three men are from Waco, and they've been riding together. I have reason to believe they were working together on this robbery, and that they may be planning others."

"But you have no proof," said Steele.

"No," Danielle said, "and that's why I'm here. I want you to help me get that proof."

"And how do you propose I do that?"

"I think Gaddis and Byler are being fed information about these payroll shipments by someone on the inside," said Danielle. "Someone who works for the railroad."

"Now, see here," Steele said, becoming indignant. "This is all speculation. The payrolls are all brought here from Fort Leavenworth. If there's a leak, it could well be coming from that end."

"True," said Danielle, "but not likely. Will you allow me to see a list of the names of the men who work for the railroad?"

"No," Steele said. "I won't be a party to you killing someone purely on speculation and suspicion."

"Then take the names of the outlaws I'm looking for, and compare them to those of the men working for the railroad," Danielle said. "If none of these seven names appear on your roster, then I'll say no more."

"I suppose I can do that," said Steele.

Danielle handed him a sheet of paper on which she had written the names.

Steele studied the list, comparing it to his own. Finally, he looked up, and when he spoke, Danielle thought he seemed nervous, for his eyes didn't exactly meet hers.

"Nobody on your list works for the railroad," he said.

Danielle sighed. "I'm sorry to have taken your time, Mr. Steele."

Danielle closed the door behind her as she left the office. Steele waited until she was gone before he summoned a secretary. She looked at him questioningly, and he spoke.

"A few weeks ago we hired a freight handler, name of Chancy Burke. I want to see him here in my office, just as soon as possible."

Steele waited, clenching and unclenching his fists. The Kansas Pacific already had too much bad press as a result of the payroll robberies. The last thing the railroad needed was for word to get out that one of its own employees was in cahoots with the men who had robbed the train. When Chancy Burke entered the room, there was an arrogance in his manner that Steele didn't like. A Colt was tied down on his right hip, and despite his having been in town for several months, he still dressed like a down-at-the-heels cowboy.

"Burke," said Steele, "I have it on good authority that you have been consorting with thieves and outlaws. I have learned that two of your closest companions—Rufe Gaddis and Julius Byler—may have gotten information from you on that payroll that was stolen. Do you have anything to say?"

"Not a damn thing," Burke said, "except you got no proof. I deny doin' anything."

"Then take a look at this," said Steele, handing to him the names of the seven outlaws Danielle had given him.

Quickly, Burke read the list of names, and when he again faced Steele, he had lost much of his arrogance.

"So you threw my name in with six other *hombres* I never heard of," Burke said. "That don't prove anything."

"I think it does," Steele said. "I got this list from a young man who intends to kill all the men on that list, including you, and I don't want you involved with the railroad in any way when it happens. As of this moment, you're fired, and if you're still in town after today, I'll see that the sheriff knows what you've done. Now get out."

"I'll go," said Burke, "but before I do, I owe you something. You know too much, Mr. Railroad Man."

Burke drew his Colt and fired twice, the slugs striking Steele in the chest. Burke then left the office on the run, exiting the building and making his way across the tracks to the railroad yard. His horse had been tied there, and he mounted in one leap, kicking the animal into a gallop. In the Kansas Pacific offices, there was total confusion. Women screamed and men cursed. One of the telegraphers ran to find the sheriff and a doctor, but Sheriff Barnes had already ridden out to the Winters place. Dr. Avery took one look at the bloody body of Alan Steele and shook his head.

"He died instantly," said Dr. Avery. "This is a case for the sheriff."

Sheriff Barnes didn't relish reporting Elmo's death, and his confrontation with Elmo's kin was even stormier than he had expected.

"Fine damn sheriff you are," Jubal Winters bawled. "A man

can't go to town for a friendly game of cards without bein' shot dead."

"It wasn't what I'd call a friendly game," said Sheriff Barnes. "Elmo had a mad on for no other reason than he was a big loser. He shot a man without cause."

"The other *hombre* was cheatin'," Ebeau Winters said.

"Not according to what the witnesses and the house dealer said," the sheriff replied. "I had Elmo taken to the carpenter shop so a coffin could be built. Do you aim to come and get him, or will the county have to bury him?"

"We'll come and get him," Jubal snarled. "We don't want a damn thing from you but the name of the bastard that killed Elmo."

"So you can ride to town and raise hell," said the sheriff. "No, I don't think so."

"Then we'll find out on our own," Jubal said. "The next damn coffin you build will be his."

"Elmo's dead from a case of bad judgment," said the sheriff, "and I'm asking you to let it go. If the two of you show up in town with killing on your minds, I swear I'll throw both of you in the *calabozo*, leaving you there till the Second Coming."

With that, Sheriff Barnes rode away, fully aware of the whispered cursing of Jubal and Ebeau Winters. He had no doubt the pair would defy him, or that when they came for Elmo's body, they would come seeking vengeance. When Sheriff Barnes rode in, he had most of the town watching for him. One of the railroad's telegraphers got to him first.

"Sheriff, Alan Steele's been shot and killed in his office."

Wearily, Sheriff Barnes nodded. He then rode toward the railroad terminal and began asking questions. He quickly learned that the young gunman who had shot Elmo Winters had been in Steele's office, and when he had left, Steele had sent for Chancy Burke, one of several newly hired freight handlers.

"So this *hombre* Burke did the killing," Sheriff Barnes said.

"Yeah," said one of the telegraphers. "After the shooting, I saw him running down the hall toward the back of the building, into the railroad yards. His horse is gone."

Sheriff Barnes found the death list Danielle had given Steele on the floor behind Steele's desk. Burke's name was on that list, and Barnes believed it had been a factor in the killing of Steele. Daniel Strange had visited Steele in his office, and immediately following Daniel's leaving, Steele had sent for Chancy Burke. It was time for a serious talk with the young rider who had killed Elmo Winters, and Sheriff Barnes headed for the hotel where the wounded Jesse Burris had been taken.

D anielle found Herb waiting for her, and she broke the bad news.

"Well, damn, I reckon that does it," said Herb.

"I don't think so," Danielle said. "When Steele read those names from my list, I was watching his face. Something in his eyes told me he was lying when he said none of the men on my list worked for the railroad."

"But without his help, there's nothing you can do," said Herb.

Suddenly, there was a knock on Danielle's door.

"Who's there?" Danielle asked.

"Sheriff Barnes."

Danielle opened the door, and Sheriff Barnes closed it behind him as he entered.

"You know my *amigo* Herb Sellers, Sheriff," said Danielle.

"Yes," Sheriff Barnes said, "and he might want to leave the room. I have some serious questions to ask you."

"Let Herb stay, Sheriff," said Danielle. "I'll answer your questions."

"I know you were in Alan Steele's office at Kansas Pacific earlier this morning. Why?"

"I wanted a favor from him, which he denied," Danielle said. "You knew I believed there might be an outlaw on the railroad payroll, feeding information to train robbers. I wanted Steele to let me go over a list of men who work for the railroad, but he refused. He requested that I give him a list of the suspects, which I did. He assured me that none of them worked for the railroad."

"Is this the list?" Sheriff Barnes asked, holding out the sheet of paper.

"It is," said Danielle. "Where did you get it?"

"I found it on the floor behind Steele's desk," Sheriff Barnes said. "After you left, he had a freight handler Chancy Burke report to his office. Burke shot and killed him, and then ran for it."

Danielle looked at Herb, and he seemed pleased. Danielle's suspicions had just been confirmed. But Sheriff Barnes wasn't finished. His eyes on Danielle, he came up with the question she had been expecting.

"The men on this list—why are you hunting them?"

"They robbed and murdered my pa in Indian Territory last spring," Danielle said. "On my pa's grave, I swore I'd track them down and that they'd all die."

"What give you the idea that one of them worked for the railroad?" the sheriff asked.

"When I learned Rufe Gaddis and Julius Byler robbed a Kansas Pacific train," Danielle said. "Gaddis, Byler, and Burke are all from Waco, Texas, and usually ride together. I had an idea Burke had a hand in the robbery, and the only logical answer seemed that he must be working for the railroad."

"Good thinking," Sheriff Barnes said. "It's a damn shame Steele didn't use what he had learned to a better advantage. After that robbery, the railroad's a mite skittish, afraid of more bad publicity."

"There'll be plenty of it now," said Danielle. "There'll be no hiding the fact that the railroad hired a thief and a murderer. It won't help the confidence of the military if they aim to ship future payrolls."

"I expect future payrolls to Dodge will go by wagon with a military escort," Barnes said. "It won't be as quick as by train, but the military can protect it better. How much of what you've told me do you intend to tell the newspapers?"

"None of it if it can be avoided," said Danielle.

"I'm afraid it can't," Sheriff Barnes said. "Indirectly, you were responsible for Steele's death, but it wasn't your fault that he used your information as he did. Still, it's expected of the law to come up with a motive for the killing, and I can't do that without you. The newspaper people are already at Kansas Pacific, and they're going to be told that you were in Steele's office just before he sent for Chancy Burke. What will you tell them?"

"The truth, I reckon," Danielle said. "You have the list that I gave Steele, and Chancy Burke's name is on it. We can piece together the rest."

"Except for one thing," said Sheriff Barnes. "Why did Burke shoot Steele? Being fired is one thing, but I can't understand the need to kill a man. Steele wasn't even armed. I'm at a loss to explain why Burke didn't accept his dismissal and just quietly ride away. It seems that's probably what Steele expected. Now there'll be a murder charge against him."

There came a knock on Danielle's door.

"Who is it?" Danielle asked.

"Newspaper reporter," said the voice.

"You might as well get it over with," Sheriff Barnes said.

Danielle went to the door and let the man in. He was tall and thin, and had a nervous twitch. His head darted back and forth like that of an inquisitive rooster. But there was nothing slow about him.

"I'm Jud Dubose," he said, "and I'm here regarding the shooting of Alan Steele earlier today. You were in Steele's office just ahead of Chancy Burke, and we believe something you said or did caused Steele to summon Burke to the office. Would you tell me just how you fit into all this?"

"Yes," said Danielle, and she repeated everything she had told Sheriff Barnes.

"So Steele tried to cover it up, handling Burke on his own,"

Dubose said, "and Burke shot and killed him. May I see that death list you gave Steele to compare with names of employees on the railroad's payroll?"

"No," said Danielle. "Why should I allow you to publish it in the newspaper when it would only make things more difficult for me? These outlaws would change their names."

"That's suppressing evidence," Dubose said.

"Wrong," said Sheriff Barnes. "You can mention the list, and that Chancy Burke is one of the names on it, and it was he who did the shooting. But the rest of the names aren't any of your business. You know the motive, and you know the killer."

Clearly, Dubose didn't like it, but even without the rest of the names on the list, he had his story. Bowing to them all, he got up and left the hotel room.

"I'm obliged, Sheriff," Danielle said.

"You got enough trouble already," Sheriff Barnes said. "I rode out this morning to the Winters place. Jubal and Ebeau are killing mad and are vowing revenge. Was I you, I'd stay close to the hotel for a while."

C hancy Burke rode to the outskirts of town, where he had a room in a cheap boardinghouse. To his surprise, he found his door unlocked. Drawing and cocking his Colt, he then kicked the door open. Rufe Gaddis and Julius Byler sat on the bed.

"What are you doin' here so early in the day?" Gaddis inquired.

"They got wise to me," said Burke, "and I had to shoot the varmint that fired me."

"Had to or wanted to?" Byler asked.

"He knew too damn much," said Burke. "Somebody's huntin' all of our old gang. The death list he showed me included *hombres* we rode with in Indian Territory. Three names was missing. Bart Scovill, Levi Jasper, and Brice Levan wasn't on it, but I was, along with both of you."

"If somebody had the names of seven of us, he had them all," Gaddis said. "I reckon Scovill, Jasper, and Levan are dead."

"I think so, too," said Byler, "and thanks to you shootin' that railroad man, we'll likely have every damn bounty hunter and Pinkerton in the country after us."

"Then I'll just go my way, and you gents can go yours," Burke said, "but I won't be leavin' until I get my share of that twenty-five thousand you took from the train."

"You'll get it," said Gaddis, "and whether or not you go your own way is up to you. We know somebody's after us, maybe a bounty hunter, and we might be safer not ridin' alone."

"I'll likely have a price on my head before the day's done," Burke said. "Let's get out of here and head for Indian Territory for a while."

"We'll have to," said Byler. "That's where the gold's hid."

"I think we ought to wait until dark," Gaddis said. "There's a storm building, and it'll be raining by tonight. Somebody might discover our trail and decide to track us."

"I'm going down to the parlor for an evening paper," said Burke. "I'd like to see just how much they know about me, and if there's a price on my head."

The story was on page one, and they all gathered around to read it.

"Damn," Burke said, "there's a five-thousand-dollar bounty on me."

Gaddis laughed. "If they raise it to ten thousand, I'll take you in myself."

"Whoa," said Byler, "this ain't so damn funny. That death list the sheriff found on the floor of Steele's office come from a young gunman who's looking for us. Somehow, he's found out we're ridin' together."

"Yeah," Burke said, "and how does he know we're ridin' together?"

"He's likely been through Waco," said Gaddis. "It wouldn't take a man long to find out all of us are from there."

"This young gun thrower's smart," Burke said. "Without any evidence, he figured out that I was keeping you gents informed about the gold shipments. I owe Steele something. If he had gone directly to the sheriff and had allowed the sheriff to move in, I'd likely be in jail by now."

"The law's got our names on that death list now," said Gaddis, "and I think we should get the hell out of Kansas. That newspaper's linked all our names together, and the three of us have prices on our heads totaling ten thousand dollars."

"Then let's ride," Burke said. "Remember, that varmint that gave Alan Steele the list with all our names is still in town."

The three mounted and rode away toward Indian Territory.

Danielle whiled away her time in her hotel room, regretting having promised the sheriff she would remain in town another day. Looking out the window, she could see a gathering of clouds far to the west. She had considered circling the town, seeking the tracks of Burke's horse, but with rain on the way, it would be of little use. Tomorrow she'd have to begin her search all over again. But there was the problem with Elmo Winters's kin. Noon came and went without a sign of them. Then there was a knock on her door.

"Who is it?" Danielle asked.

"Sheriff Barnes."

Danielle opened the door, allowing the lawman to enter.

"Well," said Sheriff Barnes, "they're here. They brought a wagon, and they're over at the carpenter shop, loadin' Elmo to take him home."

"How should I handle this, Sheriff?" Danielle asked.

"Any way you have to," said Barnes, "but don't go gunning for them. Let them make the first move, and if you're forced to shoot, then shoot. Everybody around here knows how they are, and if they come after you with guns, there's not a court in Kansas that'll blame you for defending yourself."

"Then I might as well circulate around town," Danielle said. "Otherwise, they'll likely come here to the hotel, and somebody here might be hurt."

"I wouldn't spend too much time on the street," said Sheriff Barnes. "Trouble with the Winters family has never gone this far before, so I can't predict what they might do. They might climb up on a roof and bushwhack you."

"I don't believe in putting off something that must be done," Danielle said. "I'll go on and face them, and be done with it."

"Then I'll go with you," said Sheriff Barnes, "to be sure it's a fair fight."

Herb Sellers had heard the sheriff at Danielle's door, and had waited in the hall.

"I'm going along, too," Herb said.

Sheriff Barnes nodded, and the trio left the hotel. The walk to the carpenter shop was short, and Jubal and Ebeau Winters were there standing beside a wagon, arguing with someone from the carpenter shop. As Sheriff Barnes and his companions drew near, Jubal spoke.

"Sheriff, this varmint's expecting me to pay ten dollars for Elmo's coffin, and I ain't gonna do it. I didn't ask him to build it."

"I did," said Sheriff Barnes, "and I'll pay the ten dollars. Now you and Ebeau get out of town. I want no more trouble."

"We ain't goin' nowhere until we take care of the bastard that killed Elmo," Jubal said.

"That would be me," said Danielle.

Sheriff Barnes and Herb moved out of the line of fire. Ebeau walked toward Danielle.

"Jubal," Sheriff Barnes said, "this is going to be fair, just between the two of them. If you pull iron, I'll shoot you myself."

Danielle waited, thumbs hooked in her gun belt. Her green eyes bored into Ebeau's, and he halted a dozen yards away.

"Draw, damn you," Ebeau shouted.

Danielle continued to wait while Ebeau cursed. Then Danielle turned and began walking away, and that's when Ebeau Winters went for his gun.

"Daniel!" Herb shouted.

Danielle hit the ground and rolled, coming up with her right-hand Colt blazing. Ebeau had fired twice, but there was no third shot. Ebeau had died on his feet.

CHAPTER 13

As Ebeau Winters slumped to the ground, Jubal bawled like a fresh-cut bull and went for his gun. But Sheriff Barnes had been expecting that.

"Don't do it, Jubal," Barnes warned.

Jubal fought the urge to draw, finally dropping his shaking hands to his sides. His old face a mask of grief, he stared at the body of his second son.

"I'll help you get him in the wagon, Jubal," said Sheriff Barnes. "Then I'll ride out and help you bury them."

"I don't need no help from the likes of you," Jubal said.

But he couldn't handle Ebeau's body by himself, and he didn't object when Barnes lent a hand in getting Ebeau into the wagon beside Elmo's coffin. Wordlessly, Jubal climbed to the wagon seat, took the reins, and clucked to the team. Sheriff Barnes mounted his horse and followed the wagon.

"God, he took it hard," said Herb Sellers. "I thought you'd likely have to shoot him."

"I didn't want to shoot either of them," Danielle said.

"You didn't have any choice," said Herb. "He'd have shot you if he could. I reckon it's the curse of a man carryin' a gun. You got to shoot a man just so's he don't shoot you."

"Let's get on back to the hotel," Danielle said. "I want to say *adios* to Jesse before I ride out."

"There's a storm comin'," said Herb. "Why don't you wait until tomorrow?"

"I don't want to have to shoot Jubal Winters," Danielle said.

But it was already afternoon, and dark clouds hid the sun. The wind coming out of the southwest had begun to rise. Herb and Danielle had barely reached the hotel when the first drops of rain kicked up puffs of dust in the street.

"It's gonna blow long and hard," said Herb. "You'd better reconsider and lay over."

"I reckon you're right," Danielle said. "I'll likely spend enough time soaked to the hide, so I'd better enjoy a roof over my head while I can."

Suppertime was two hours away. When Danielle and Herb returned to the room that he shared with Jesse Burris, they found him awake, sitting on the edge of the bed, dressed except for his boots and hat.

"Where in tarnation do you think you're goin'?" Herb demanded.

"Out of this bed, and out of this hotel," said Jesse.

"I don't think so," Herb said. "The doc says you need a week to heal, and you ain't had any fever yet."

"No matter," said Jesse. "I was the cause of that shootin' in the saloon, and I reckon if that *hombre* that was shot has kin, they'll be ridin' in to settle up with somebody."

"You didn't shoot anybody," Danielle said. "I did."

"Elmo's pa and brother rode in looking for trouble earlier," said Herb, "and Daniel had to shoot Ebeau. Sheriff Barnes followed Jubal Winters home to help bury Elmo and Ebeau."

"All this over a damn poker game," Jesse said. "I wish I'd stayed out of it."

"You don't feel any worse than I do," said Danielle, "but some men have no business at a poker table, and Elmo Winters was one of them. I'm sorry for his pa's sake."

"There should be a newspaper out today," Herb said. "I'll go to the lobby for one. I'd like to see what's been written about that shooting at the Kansas Pacific offices."

"What shooting?" Jesse asked.

"Tell him about it, Daniel, while I go for the paper," said Herb.

Quickly, Danielle explained what had happened. By then, Herb had returned with the day's edition of the newspaper. He read the front-page account aloud while Danielle and Jesse listened.

"At least they didn't print the rest of the names on your death list," Jesse said.

"No," said Danielle, "but they figured out the connection between Chancy Burke and Gaddis and Byler. Now the three of them know their names are on my list."

"Alan Steele died for nothing," Herb said. "If he had told Daniel the straight of it, he'd have saved the railroad any bad publicity. Now the very thing he tried to hide is printed in the newspaper for everybody to read."

"Some good may come of that," said Danielle. "While they printed only the names of Gaddis, Byler, and Burke, that may warn the rest of them they're being hunted. If I can't find them, maybe they'll find me."

"You'll need somebody to watch your back," Jesse said, "and I'm beholden to you. If you can wait until the doc lets me get out of this bed, Herb and me can ride with you."

"I'm obliged," said Danielle, "but I aim to ride out in the morning, as soon as the storm blows itself out."

"There won't be any trail," Jesse said. "Where do you aim to start?"

"I reckon I'll ride back through Wichita, and from there into Indian Territory," said Danielle. "I figure that's the only place Chancy Burke will feel safe with a bounty on his head and a murder on his back trail."

"It's a hell of a place for one man to ride alone," Herb said.

"I have no choice," said Danielle, "and I have no right to ask you and Jesse to risk your lives for a cause that will gain you nothing but a bullet in the back."

S heriff Barnes showed up at the hotel, water dripping off his slicker. He knocked on Danielle's door.

"Who is it?"

"The sheriff," Barnes said.

Danielle unlocked and opened the door, allowing the sheriff to enter.

"Remove your slicker and sit down," Danielle invited.

"I won't be here that long," said Barnes. "I just want to know how long you aim to stay in town."

"Until the storm blows itself out," Danielle said. "Why?"

"I got me a gut feeling Jubal Winters ain't finished with you," said Sheriff Barnes. "All the time I was with Jubal, helpin' him bury his boys, he didn't say a word. Something's on his mind, and I think it involves you."

"The last thing I want is to have to shoot Jubal Winters, Sheriff," said Danielle. "I aim to ride out in the morning, storm or not."

"You've been a decent *hombre*, and I hate to rush you, but I think it's for the best."

"So do I, Sheriff," Danielle said.

J esse Burris was able to join Herb and Danielle at breakfast. There was little talk, for these young men had grown fond of Danielle, and she of them.

"Before you go," said Jesse, "write out the names of those seven men you're hunting. If we learn anything about them, we'll telegraph the Texas Ranger outpost in San Antonio."

"*Bueno,*" Danielle said. "Send it to Captain Sage Jennings. He knows me and what I have to do. I aim to cross Indian Territory and spend some tine in south Texas. Chancy Burke, Rufe Gaddis, and Julius Byler have kin there, and sooner or later, they'll be going back."

The sky was overcast with the threat of more rain as Danielle saddled the chestnut mare. Having already bid farewell to Herb and Jesse, she mounted and rode toward Wichita by simply following the Kansas Pacific tracks.

But vengeful eyes had watched Danielle ride out of the livery. When she finally rode out of sight, Jubal Winters mounted his horse and followed. In his saddle boot was a fully loaded Winchester.

WICHITA, KANSAS. NOVEMBER 15, 1870.

Danielle estimated the distance to Wichita at close to a hundred and fifty miles. Taking her time and sparing the chestnut mare, she rode what she felt was halfway, and there made camp for the night. She picketed the horse so that the mare might warn her of any approaching danger. After a day of cold, miserable drizzle, the rain had finally ceased, and stars in the purple sky overhead were a welcome sight. Having no dry wood for a fire, Danielle ate jerked beef for breakfast, washing it down with water from a spring. She quickly fed the mare a measure of grain, and when the horse had eaten, she saddled up and rode on toward Wichita. She arrived in the late afternoon of the second day and decided to spend the night there, for she was not more than twenty miles from Indian Territory. She hadn't bothered talking to the sheriff of Wichita before riding on to Kansas City. She thought the sheriff might supply some additional details about the train robbery and the thieves, so she went looking for him.

"I didn't know a thing about the robbery," said Sheriff Bart Devlin. "By the time the engineer backed the train from end of track to here, the thieves were long gone. A posse and me followed 'em as far as Indian Territory, and it was comin' on dark."

"What about the woman you captured?" Danielle asked.

"Her horse went lame, and they left her behind," said Sheriff Devlin. "She was furious at them for leaving her, and she told me their names. She didn't seem to know anything else, so I let her go. What's your interest in this? Are you with the railroad?"

"No," Danielle said. "This is personal."

She then told the lawman of tracking the men who had murdered her father.

"I read about you in the Kansas City paper," said Devlin, "but they didn't say exactly why you were hunting the outlaws. They did say you was responsible for rooting out one of the varmints that worked for the railroad, passing along information on gold shipments."

"His name is Chancy Burke," Danielle said, "and like Gaddis and Byler, he's from near Waco."

"That would be a good place to go looking for them," said Sheriff Devlin.

"I've already been there," Danielle said. "If they're riding together, it seemed like a good idea to see if Chancy Burke might be working for the railroad. If the railroad hadn't called Burke's hand, he might have been captured or killed."

"The sheriff in Waco was of no help to you?"

"None," said Danielle. "He went out of his way to warn the kin of Gaddis, Byler, and Burke that I was there, and I was practically run out of town."

"Damn such a lawman," Sheriff Devlin muttered. "It's enough to give us all a bad name."

"The woman you captured told you nothing except the names of the thieves? Where did she team up with Gaddis and Byler?"

"In St. Louis," said Sheriff Devlin, "and she was goin' back there."

"She didn't tell you where Gaddis and Byler were holed up before the robbery?"

"She didn't seem to know," Sheriff Devlin said. "She wasn't familiar with the country, and from her description, it sounded like

Indian Territory. She said they rode less than an hour before reaching the Kansas Pacific tracks."

"I'm obliged, Sheriff," said Danielle.

"Good luck," Sheriff Devlin said. "I hope you find them. The railroad's on my back because I can't catch the thieves, but I'm just a county sheriff. I can't watch their damn railroad all the way from Kansas City to end of track."

"They may get as far from here as they can," said Danielle. "After killing that Kansas Pacific man, Burke's got a price on his head, just like Gaddis and Byler."

Danielle stabled Sundown and took a room in one of the hastily built hotels that faced the Kansas Pacific tracks. She entered a café and had supper, and it was already dark when she left. The Railroad Saloon was ablaze with light. Lighted lanterns had been hung along the eaves of the building and across the top of its false front. There was a distant jangling of a piano that was sorely in need of tuning. From within the saloon, shouts mingled with the clinks of glasses and bottles. Danielle went in, finding the place packed, a large number of the men appearing to have come in from end of track. Three poker games were in progress, but only one faro game. Danielle waited until one of the men kicked back his chair and left the table.

"I'm buying in," Danielle said.

"Welcome, kid, long as you got money," said the dealer. "Five-dollar bets."

Danielle dropped her five double eagles on the table and, in ten straight hands, lost half her stake.

"We know one thing for damn sure," said one of the players, "the kid ain't cheatin'."

Danielle kept her silence and, within an hour, had won back her stake and more than two hundred dollars additional. She then withdrew from the game.

"I've never seen such a run of luck," one of the gamblers said, his eyes on the house dealer. "It's almost like you was slick-dealing to the kid."

It was an open invitation to a fistfight or a shooting, so Danielle hurriedly left the saloon and returned to her hotel room. She might well meet one of the disgruntled gamblers on the street and be forced into another senseless killing. Already, the Kansas City paper had referred to her as a "fast-gun artist," and "a killer riding a vengeance trail."

Danielle arose early, had her breakfast, and rode out. She was only a few miles north of Indian Territory, but chose to ride west, toward the end of track. She would learn nothing from the railroad men, for they would surely be hostile toward her for indirectly being the cause of Alan Steele's death. However, before reaching end of track, she would ride south toward Indian Territory. There would be no tracks, no trail, and little chance of her finding any of the men she sought. But they were all Westerners, and she fully expected them to be holed up in Indian Territory or in Texas. At this moment, the trio responsible for the train robbery might be at home in Waco.

As Danielle entered Indian Territory, chills crept up her spine, for it was a massive tangle of vines, thickets, brush, and tall trees. It was gloomy even when the sun was shining, for only a little sunlight filtered through the dense foliage. She reined up to rest the chestnut mare and stood beside the horse, looking back the way she had come. She saw nothing and, mounting, rode on. But something was bothering her, a strange foreboding that dug its claws into her and wouldn't let go. Again she reined up, dismounted, and walked a ways along her back trail without seeing anyone. She was about to mount and ride on when the stillness was shattered by the roar of a rifle just ahead of her. The lead tore its way through her left thigh, and a second slug ripped into her right side, making a ragged exit wound. She fell on her back, remaining still, for she believed the bushwhacker would come close enough to be sure she was dead. She was losing blood, but dared not move. Finally she heard cautious footsteps approaching and, through half-closed eyes, could see the haggard, grinning face of Jubal Winters.

"You damn gunslick," he snarled. "Kill my boys, will you?"

Jacking a shell into the chamber of the Winchester, he was about to shoot Danielle a third time when Danielle drew her right-hand Colt and fired twice. The slugs struck Jubal in the chest, and he died with a look of total surprise on his face. Danielle struggled to her feet and, using a rawhide thong from her saddle, wrapped and tied it tightly above the bleeding wound in her left thigh. But there was little she could do about the wound in her right side. The chestnut mare, spooked by the smell of blood, backstepped.

"Damn it, Sundown," Danielle gasped, "hold still."

Three times she tried to mount the horse, and three times her left leg failed her. Using her right leg for support, she mounted from the off side. She felt cold all over, and there was a growing weakness in her body. She turned the chestnut mare back the way she had come, hoping to reach Wichita before bleeding to death. She blacked out, holding to the saddle horn with both hands. Danielle had raised Sundown from a colt, and the horse knew something was terribly wrong. The animal stopped, perking up her ears. In the distance, a dog barked. The mare listened a moment and then, as though making up her mind, turned and trotted back into Indian Territory, toward the sound of the barking dog. The dog barked furiously as Sundown neared a run-down cabin.

"That awful man is coming back, Ma," said nine-year-old Anita Willard.

"Perhaps not," said her mother, Ann. "It doesn't sound like his horse."

The cabin's windows had no glass, and she had to open a shutter to see outside. Even with the threat of the dog, the chestnut mare waited patiently at the front stoop, seeking help for her young rider. Even as Ann Willard watched, Danielle fell from the saddle and lay still.

"Come on," said Ann. "He's hurt, and we must get him inside."

Once they had Danielle inside and stretched out on a bunk, Anita unsaddled the mare and led her to a corral where there were two other horses. Returning to the house, she found Ann Willard had stripped the injured rider and simply stood there staring.

"He . . . he's a woman," Anita said aghast.

"Yes," said Ann, "and we must do what we can for her and get her out of here before Eph Snell returns. Stir up the fire and put some water on to boil."

When the water was hot, Ann cleansed the wounds as best she could, disinfecting them with whiskey from a jug Eph Snell kept under his bunk. There was no other medicine, and Danielle moaned in her sleep. She didn't awaken until near dawn of the next day, her face flushed and her eyes bright with fever.

"Water," she begged.

Anita brought a tin cup of water, and Danielle drank it gratefully. Again she spoke.

"Where . . . am I, and who . . . are you?"

"I'm Ann Willard, and this is my daughter, Anita."

"I . . . I'm Danielle Strange. Do you . . . live here alone?" Danielle asked.

"Only when Eph Snell's gone," said Ann.

"Eph Snell's a damn horse thief, and when he's here, he's always drunk. I hate him," Anita said.

"Anita," said Ann, "that's no way for a young lady to talk."

"Then I ain't a young lady," Anita said. "I want to grow up and carry a gun so's I can shoot the varmints I don't like."

Despite being racked with fever and pain, Danielle laughed.

"Anita," said Ann, "go get the jug of whiskey."

"I'll get it," Anita said, "but old Eph's gonna raise hell when he finds we've been into his jug."

"God help us," said Ann with a sigh. "She's picking up Snell's bad habits."

"Why are the two of you living with such a man?" Danielle asked.

"My husband never returned from the war, and Anita and me

were starving back in New Orleans. I met Snell, and he promised me a better life. Am I permitted to know why you dress as a man?"

But Anita returned with the jug of whiskey just then, and Danielle was forced to drink a cupful. Then, as Ann and Anita listened, she told them her story and of becoming Daniel Strange.

"Dear God," Ann said, "how old are you, Danielle?"

"Just past seventeen," said Danielle.

"See, Ma?" Anita cried. "She's only eight years older than me."

"I'm trusting the two of you to keep my secret," said Danielle. "As soon as I'm able to ride, I'll move on. I don't want to cause any trouble."

"There'll be trouble whether you're here or not," Anita said. "Last time, he beat Ma up something terrible."

"Don't you have somewhere else you can go?" Danielle asked.

"I have a sister in St. Louis who would take us in, but I don't know how we'd ever get there," said Ann.

"I'll help you as soon as I'm able," Danielle said. "Do you have horses?"

"Two, but only because Eph hasn't sold them," said Ann. "He's gone after more."

"He steals them in Texas," Anita said helpfully.

"That's a long ride from here," said Danielle. "When do you expect him to return?"

"Perhaps in another week," Ann said. "He's usually away for two weeks, and he's been gone only six days."

"Then maybe I can get the two of you on the way to St. Louis before he returns," said Danielle.

"But we have no money," Ann said.

"I do," said Danielle, "and all we have to do is reach Wichita. From there, you can take the train to Kansas City, and another on to St. Louis."

"You are so kind," said Ann. "I fear we can never repay you."

"You already have," Danielle said. "It's me that'll never be able to repay *you*, because you saved my life."

"You need food," said Ann. "I'll make you some chicken soup."

She started toward the kitchen, but not before Danielle saw the tears on her cheeks. It was an opportune time for nine-year-old Anita to speak to this strange girl who dressed like a man and carried tied-down Colts. She sat down on the foot of the bed and spoke.

"Ma didn't tell you all of it. The last time Eph Snell came in drunk, he said I was old enough to be a woman, and he tore off all my clothes. Ma tried to stop him, and he beat her so bad, she couldn't get up off the floor."

"A poor excuse for a man," said Danielle. "Did he . . . bother you?"

"He was going to," Anita said, "but I ran outside and hid in the brush, naked. When he saddled his horse and rode away, I went back to take care of Ma."

"He won't lay a hand on either of you as long as I'm alive," said Danielle.

"Oh, I'm so glad you found us," Anita said. "The next time, I might not be able to get away from him."

Ann returned with a bowl of soup and a wedge of corn bread. Sore as Danielle was, she sat up long enough to eat, and immediately felt better.

"Now," said Ann, "we're going to leave you alone so you can sleep off that fever."

Danielle slept all day and part of the night. She awakened, sweating. Ann sat on the foot of the bed, and she spoke.

"The fever's broken. Now all you have to do is heal."

"I'm obliged," Danielle said. "You've done all this for me without knowing whether I've told you the truth about myself or not."

"I saw the truth in your eyes," said Ann, "but I'd have helped you even if you were an outlaw. The Good Book says we should not judge as we be not judged. It wasn't up to me to decide if you were deserving or not. All I saw was the need."

"You're a good woman, Ann Willard," Danielle said.

"I'm a sinful woman," said Ann, her hands covering her face. "For five years I've been with Eph Snell because Anita and me were starving. I thought anything was better than that, but I don't anymore. Snell's a thief and a killer, and I fear what he may do if he comes back and finds you here."

"Put my guns where I can reach them," Danielle said, "and I'll promise you he'll get the surprise of his life."

"It's none of my business," said Ann, "but can you tell me who shot you, and why?"

"It's something I'm not proud of," Danielle said, "but I'll tell you the story."

For the next few minutes she told of having to shoot Elmo and Ebeau Winters, and finally of the necessity of killing old Jubal after he had bushwhacked her.

"You didn't shoot anybody that didn't deserve it," said Anita from behind the door.

"You're supposed to be in bed asleep," Ann said.

"I'm too excited to sleep," said Anita. "When can we leave?"

"Not until Danielle heals enough to ride," Ann said.

"Three more days," said Danielle. "Just so I'm healed enough that the wounds won't start bleeding again."

The three days came and went without a sign of Eph Snell. Danielle was up and limping about, again with her binder in place, dressed like a man.

"It's time we were going," Danielle said. "Do you have saddles for your horses?"

"No," said Ann, "but I'd crawl from here to Wichita on my hands and knees. We can ride bareback."

Ann gathered her own and Anita's few belongings, stuffing them in a gunnysack. The trio then rode north toward Wichita.

"I'll stay with you in Wichita until there's an eastbound train," Danielle said. "Once we reach town, you can sell the horses you're riding. That'll give you some extra money. I'll buy your train tickets from Wichita to St. Louis."

"You're too generous," said Ann. "I'd gladly sell the horses, but I don't have any bills of sale. I'm sure Eph stole them somewhere."

"I'll write you some bills of sale," Danielle said. "By the time

Snell figures it all out, you'll be on your way to St. Louis and well out of his reach."

The trio reached Wichita. Inquiring, Danielle learned the next eastbound from the end of track wouldn't reach Wichita until the following morning. Danielle bought two tickets to St. Louis, and Ann Willard wept for her generosity.

"Now I'll get us a hotel room for the night," said Danielle, "and we'll see about selling those two horses."

The bills of sale were not questioned, and Danielle collected seventy-five dollars for each of the horses.

"Here," Danielle said, handing the money to Ann. "The horses brought a hundred and fifty dollars, and I've added some to that."

Ann Willard was completely overwhelmed, and Anita's eyes sparkled like stars.

Leading three horses, Eph Snell reached the deserted cabin in Indian Territory. He swore when he found the corral empty, and it took him only a few minutes to find tracks of three horses heading north. Leaving the three newly arrived horses in the corral, he mounted his horse and rode north, toward Wichita. He also carried a pair of tied-down Colts, and he had killing on his mind.

CHAPTER 14

WICHITA, KANSAS. NOVEMBER 22, 1870.

The eastbound was due at ten o'clock. Danielle had accompanied Ann and Anita to the railroad depot to await the train. Far down the track, they could hear the whistle blowing for the stop at Wichita.

"I can't believe we're actually leaving," Ann said. "I feel like I'm dreaming."

"We ain't gone yet," said Anita. "I won't feel safe until we're on the train and it's on its way."

With the clanging of its bell, the eastbound rolled in, and the locomotive began taking on water. The conductor stepped down from the one passenger coach, lowering the metal steps so that the passengers might enter. Up the track, beyond the train's caboose, there came a horseman at a fast gallop.

"Ma," Anita cried, "it's him!"

"Dear God," said Ann, "it's Eph Snell."

"Get aboard the train," Danielle said. "I'll delay him until you're gone."

"I can't let you do it," said Ann. "He'll kill you."

"I'll risk it," Danielle said. "Now get aboard the train."

Ann and Anita had just entered the passenger coach when Snell reined up. Dismounting, he started toward Danielle. She spoke quietly.

"That's far enough, Snell."

Snell laughed. "So you know me."

"I know *of* you," Danielle said. "You're a damn yellow-bellied, woman-beating coyote that walks on his hind legs like a man."

It was the ultimate insult, and Snell drew. He was fast—incredibly fast—but Danielle had her Colt roaring by the time Snell pulled the trigger. His slug spouted dust on the ground in front of him. From the locomotive, the fireman and the engineer had watched the entire affair. Suddenly, Ann and Anita were out of the coach, running toward Danielle. At the sound of shooting, the station agent came running from the depot. He eyed Danielle as she reloaded her Colt, directing his question at her.

"What's the meaning of this?"

"Get the sheriff," Danielle said, "and I'll explain it all to him. I reckon you'd best keep this train here until the sheriff's talked to the fireman and the engineer. They saw it all."

"I want to talk to the sheriff, too," said Ann to Danielle. "I won't leave until I know the law's not holding you responsible."

Others had heard the sound of distant gunfire, and men came on the run. One of them was Sheriff Bart Devlin. He eyed Danielle and spoke.

"Who's the dead man?"

"Eph Snell, a horse thief and likely a killer," Danielle said. "This is Ann and Anita Willard. I helped them to escape Snell, but he caught up to us and drew on me."

"He pulled iron first, Sheriff," the engineer said. "We saw him, didn't we, Slim?"

"Yeah," the fireman said, "and he was a fool. This young gent here could shoot the ears off John Wesley Hardin."

"Now, ma'am," Sheriff Devlin said to Ann, "suppose you tell me where you figure into all this."

Ann spoke swiftly, her eyes meeting those of Sheriff Devlin. When she paused to catch her breath, Anita spoke.

"He tore all my clothes off, and I had to hide from him in the woods."

Shouts of anger erupted from the men who had gathered around.

"Sheriff," said the station agent, "this train needs to be on its way. What more do you need of the fireman and the engineer?"

"Probably nothing," Sheriff Devlin said, "but just in case, write down their names and addresses for me. Then they can go."

"I'm not going until I know you're not in trouble for shooting him," Ann told Danielle.

"Neither am I," said Anita defiantly.

"I know this young gent," Sheriff Devlin said, "and from what I've heard, I believe I can safely promise you there'll be no charges filed. In fact, if this dead varmint's been hiding out in Indian Territory, I may have a wanted dodger on him."

The fireman and the engineer had mounted to the locomotive's cabin. A clanging of its bell and two blasts from the whistle announced the train's departure.

"Ann, it's time for you and Anita to get aboard," Danielle said. "Go in peace."

The two mounted the steps into the passenger coach, and as the train pulled out, they waved to Danielle for as long as they could see her. Two men had volunteered to remove Snell's body, taking it to the carpenter shop, where a coffin would be built. Sheriff Devlin spoke to Danielle.

"Come on to the office with me, and let's see if there's a dodger on Snell. Might even be a reward."

"I'm not concerned with a reward, Sheriff," Danielle said. "I shot him only to save my friends."

"A fine piece of work and a noble reason," said Sheriff Devlin, "but if there's a reward, it belongs to you."

Danielle waited while Sheriff Devlin fanned through a stack of wanted dodgers.

"Ah," Devlin said, "here he is. He's wanted in Missouri and Texas for murder. There's a five-hundred-dollar reward, but it'll take me a few days to collect it."

"When you do," said Danielle, "send it to Ann Willard, in St. Louis. Send it to this address."

"I will," Devlin said, "and it's a fine thing you're doing. Ride careful, kid."

Danielle genuinely liked the old sheriff and didn't object to him calling her "kid." She had not completely healed from her wounds, and the drawing and firing of the Colt had somehow inflamed the wound in her right side. She felt a dull, throbbing ache, and after leaving the sheriff's office, she took a room at a hotel, for she dared not go to a doctor. First, she stabled Sundown. She then went to a saloon and, as much as she hated the stuff, bought a quart of whiskey. At the mercantile she bought a bottle of laudanum and returned to the hotel. She was hungry, but in no mood to eat. She didn't yet have a fever, and dosing herself with the laudanum, she went to bed and slept far into the night. When she awakened, her throat was dry and inflamed, and her face felt like it was afire. She drank a third of the bottle of whiskey and returned to the bed. When she again awakened, the sun beamed in through the room's single window, for she had slept well into the day. Her fever had broken, and her body was soaked with sweat. The ache of the wound in her side was gone, allowing her to sit up without pain. On the dresser was a porcelain pitcher half full of water, and she drank it all, right from the pitcher. Her belly grumbled, reminding her she had eaten nothing since her meager breakfast with Ann and Anita the day before. Taking her time, she went to a café. After a satisfying meal of ham, eggs, biscuits, and hot coffee, she felt much better. She was tempted to ride on, but after having the wound in her side flare up again, she was reluctant to go until she had completely healed. She paid for another night at the hotel and spent most of the day stretched out on the bed, resting. In the late afternoon, there was a knock on her door.

"Who is it, and what do you want?"

"I'm Casper DeVero, and I want to talk to you," said a voice outside the door.

"About what?" Danielle asked, suspecting she already knew.

"About the heroic thing you did yesterday," said DeVero.

"I don't want to talk about it," Danielle said.

"Damn it," said DeVero, "the sheriff said you'd left town, and I had a hell of a time finding you. I'm a stringer for one of the Kansas City newspapers, and this is just the kind of human-interest story they'll like. You'll be famous."

"I don't *want* to be famous," Danielle shouted. "Now leave me alone."

"Your choice," said DeVero. "Talk to me, and you'll get a sympathetic ear. But I can piece the story together if I have to, and you may not like some of the turns it takes. I will see that the story's published, with or without your help."

"Then do it without my help," Danielle shouted, "and leave me alone."

Later, feeling better, Danielle went out for supper, encountering Sheriff Devlin in the café.

"I didn't know you were still in town," said Devlin. "We got a gent here name of DeVero, and he sells stories to the Kansas City newspapers. He's been looking for you."

"Unfortunately, he found me," Danielle said, "but I refused to talk to him. I'm still here only because I decided to rest a couple of days before riding on."

"I don't usually give advice unless it's asked for," said Devlin, "but it might have been better if you had talked to DeVero. There's certain gossipy folks in town that are likely to give you a reputation you won't like."

"Then they lie," Danielle said. "I did what was right."

"I believe you," said Sheriff Devlin, "but don't be surprised if DeVero hints at some funny business between you and this woman, Ann Willard."

"My God," Danielle said, "Ann's old enough to be my mother. If that yellow-bellied, two-legged coyote prints anything close to that, I'll kill him."

"Then I'd have to arrest you," said Devlin. "It's kind of a Mexican standoff. While he can't prove there was anything goin' on, you can't prove there wasn't. Writers have a way of hinting at things without actually accusing anybody, and this Ann Willard is an almighty handsome woman."

Sheriff Devlin departed, leaving Danielle alone with her thoughts. No longer hungry, she forced herself to eat, knowing her body had to gain strength. As she thought of DeVero and the lies he might tell, she decided to remain in Wichita long enough to read what he had to say. While she couldn't stop him from making her look bad in the press, she had no intention for it to appear she was running away.

WICHITA, KANSAS. NOVEMBER 27, 1870.

When the story appeared in the Kansas City newspaper, it was even worse than Sheriff Devlin had suggested it might be. Danielle was furious, and one particular paragraph made her killing mad. It said:

> It appears the young gunman, Daniel Strange, may have
> gunned down Eph Snell over a woman they both wanted.
> Had Strange been consorting with a woman of question-
> able morals when Eph Snell caught them?

There was much more, but Danielle refused to read it. A companion piece exploited the killing of Elmo and Ebeau Winters in Kansas City, suggesting that their father, Jubal, was also dead, since he had apparently disappeared. The only redeeming feature was a few lines quoting Sheriff Barnes, in which he stated flatly that Danielle had fired in self-defense. Grinding her teeth in frustration, Danielle went to supper. Tomorrow she would ride out, but the day wasn't over, and she expected the worst. It wasn't long in coming. There were half a dozen men in the café, and they grinned openly at her. Ordering her supper, she sat down to wait. In the distance there was a locomotive whistle, as the train neared

Wichita on its way to the end of track. She had just begun to eat when the door opened and she was confronted by Herb Sellers and Jesse Burris.

"We put our horses in a boxcar and come here on the train," Jesse said. "We didn't know if you'd still be here or not." Uninvited, the two pulled out chairs and sat down.

"You read about me in the paper, I reckon," said Danielle bitterly. "Believe it if you like. I don't give a damn anymore."

"We'll believe it like *you* tell it," Herb said, "and we'll stomp hell out of anybody that makes anything more of it."

"I'm obliged," said Danielle, "but I don't want either of you in trouble with the law because of me. The sheriff's already told me I can't shoot the no-account bastard that wrote the story, and that's the only thing that would give me any real satisfaction."

"We'll hit 'em where it hurts," Jesse Burris said. "When we've had supper, we'll make the rounds of all the saloons and win a pile of their money."

"You and Herb go ahead," said Danielle. "I'm going back to the hotel and rest. I aim to ride out early tomorrow."

After supper, Danielle parted company with the two genial bounty hunters. Her wound seemed to have healed, but there was still some weakness in her right arm. The wound in her left thigh had healed to the extent that she no longer limped. Locking her door and placing a ladder-back chair under the doorknob, she stripped off her clothes and got into bed. It was a blessed relief, being rid of the hated binder, and she suspected the pressure of it had slowed the healing of the wound in her right side. But there was no help for that. She thought fondly of Ann and Anita Willard, and the secret that they kept.

WICHITA, KANSAS. NOVEMBER 29, 1870.

Danielle was awakened by a knock on her door.

"Who is it, and what do you want?" she asked.

"Jesse and me," said Herb Sellers. "We was big winners last night, and we'll buy your breakfast."

"I'll eat with you," Danielle said, "but I'm barely awake. Wait for me in the lobby."

Danielle got up, feeling stronger. With the binder back in place, she was soon ready. She tipped her hat low over her eyes, buckled on her gun belts, and removed the back of the chair from beneath the doorknob. It was later than Danielle had believed, for the sun was already several hours high, its rays beaming through the lobby's open door.

"Herb and me slept late," Jesse said. "We won a pile last night, and we had to give the varmints a chance to win their money back."

Herb laughed. "They didn't win none of it back. Fact is, they lost some more, and we didn't run out. We stayed until the saloon closed."

The trio had breakfast at one of the cafés alongside the Kansas Pacific tracks. There was little talk until they finished eating, and it was Herb who spoke.

"Would you take kindly to Jesse and me ridin' with you? We got nothing to hold us here, and I think we'd better avoid that saloon tonight."

"I reckon you're welcome to ride with me," said Danielle, "but I want one thing understood. Bounty or not, when I find these yellow coyotes I'm looking for, they'll belong to me. Then you're welcome to any bounty. All I want is their scurvy hides."

"When you find 'em, Herb and me will stand aside and let you get your satisfaction," Jesse said.

The bank was across the railroad tracks from the hotel, and as Danielle, Herb, and Jesse neared the hotel entrance, Herb stopped.

"What is it?" Jesse asked.

"Them three *hombres* that's headin' for the bank's front door just left their horses behind the building, and the hitch rail's out front," said Herb.

"No law against that," Jesse said.

"No," said Herb, "but somethin' about this don't look right. Let's wait a minute."

Across the tracks, the three men entered the bank. Facing the tellers, they drew their guns.

"Don't nobody try nothin' foolish," yelled one of the thieves, "and nobody gets hurt. We want them cash drawers opened, and we want only the big bills."

But one of the tellers had a Colt in his cash drawer. When he drew it, one of the outlaws shot him. The teller's slug went wild, shattering the bank's front window with a tinkling crash. Fearfully, the other two tellers had emptied their cash drawers of large bills, and the outlaws scooped them up.

"The varmints are robbin' the bank!" Herb shouted as the echo of the shots faded.

Of a single mind, Herb, Jesse, and Danielle drew their Colts. Seconds later, the three robbers swung the bank's front door open, but before they could make a break for their horses, Herb challenged them.

"Halt, you varmints. You're covered."

But the three went for their guns. Danielle's Colt was roaring, and when Herb and Jesse began firing a second later, it sounded like rolling thunder. The three bank robbers went down as men poured from nearby saloons and businesses. A man stepped through the bank's front door with a shotgun under his arm, just as Sheriff Bart Devlin arrived. Devlin paid no attention to anybody except the three men who had been gunned down after leaving the bank. He found the trio dead, with the bills they had taken scattered about. The sheriff then turned his attention to the trio in front of the hotel. They were calmly reloading their Colts. The banker who had stepped out the door with the shotgun was the first to speak.

"Jenkins, one of my tellers, is hard hit, Sheriff. But for those three young men before the hotel, these thieves would have escaped."

The sheriff said nothing; then after crossing the street, he spoke to Danielle.

"I know you, but who are your friends?"

"Herb Sellers and Jesse Burris," Danielle said. "We just had breakfast, and it was Herb who thought there was something unusual about those three men leaving their horses behind the bank. When we heard the shots, we knew they were robbing the bank."

"A fine piece of work you gents have done," said Sheriff Devlin. "You just gunned down the Fenner gang. Three brothers gone bad, wanted for robbery and murder. I want to talk to all of you in my office after these dead men are removed."

Some of the same men who had laughed at the cruel story in the Kansas City paper no longer laughed at Danielle. They moved aside respectfully, allowing Danielle, Herb, and Jesse to proceed along the boardwalk to Sheriff Devlin's office.

"There's a reward for them three *hombres*," Sheriff Devlin said when he returned to his office, "but I don't know how much. I'll have to look it up, and it'll take a few days to collect the money."

"I aim to ride out this morning," said Danielle. "See that Herb and Jesse get the reward. If Herb hadn't been suspicious, all of us would have been in the hotel when the robbery took place."

Sheriff Devlin sat down at his desk and began going through wanted dodgers. He found the one he was seeking and spread it out on the desk. The trio had been wanted for murder and robbery in Kansas, Missouri, and Texas. The combined rewards were more than six thousand dollars.

"Daniel, it ain't fair, Jesse and me takin' all that," said Herb. "Part of it's yours."

"No," Danielle said. "There's only one thing I want. If this Casper DeVero comes asking questions, don't tell him anything about me. I don't like him or his habits."

"There'll likely be no avoiding him," said Sheriff Devlin, "but I'll see that nothing is said to him that will be damaging to you. Anything he says about you in print is goin' to leave him looking like a fool after that last piece he wrote. These varmints the three of you gunned down took twenty thousand dollars from that same bank last year. Morrison, the bank president, is grateful to you. He saw the whole thing as it happened. I'll see that Morrison gives DeVero a firsthand account."

Danielle, Herb, and Jesse left the sheriff's office and started back toward the hotel.

"I reckon the two of you made a pretty good start at bounty hunting," said Danielle.

"It's still not fair, us taking all the bounty," Jesse said.

"It is as far as I'm concerned," said Danielle. "I'm not of a mind to stay here longer than it takes to saddle my horse. That bounty will be enough eating money until you can track down some more outlaws with a price on their heads."

"I have a problem I never expected," Herb said. "I feel . . . well . . . guilty, gunning down a man for money."

"You shouldn't," said Danielle. "None of us *knew* there was a reward when we bought into that fight. We did the right thing, and if we hadn't taken those thieves by surprise, it might be one or all of us lying dead."

"That's right," Jesse said. "This same bunch robbed the same bank last year, but they won't ever do it again. Maybe it'll send a message to the rest of the thieves and killers holed up in Indian Territory."

The trio reached the hotel. Herb and Jesse waited in the hall while Danielle went into her room for her few belongings and saddlebags. It was time for parting, and Danielle was anxious to be gone. She genuinely liked these two cowboys, and while she didn't condemn them for bounty hunting, their motivation was entirely different from her own. How often had she read of men like Bill Hickok, John Wesley Hardin, and Ben Thompson who had become legends as a result of their speed and accuracy with a gun? It was just such a name she didn't want, and yet the more often she had to use her guns, the more likely she was to find herself with the very same unwanted reputation. Reaching the livery, she paid her bill and saddled Sundown. She rode out quietly, glad to be escaping any further contact with the newspaperman Casper DeVero. St. Joe wasn't that far from Kansas City, and for the first time, she wondered what her mother and brothers would think of the ridiculous story DeVero had written.

INDIAN TERRITORY. DECEMBER 1, 1870.

Danielle chose not to light a fire. Finding a source of water, she ate jerked beef for her supper. She then fed the chestnut mare a measure of grain. She had no illusions about finding any of the men she sought in Indian Territory, for it was a gloomy, dreary place. A man could remain there only so long, for thieves who had money would be eager to get to a town with saloons and whorehouses. Danielle spread her blankets near where Sundown was picketed, depending on the horse to warn her of any impending danger. But the night passed peacefully, and Danielle then rode south. Despite the difficulties she had experienced in Waco, she still believed some of the outlaws she was hunting were in Texas, and it was there she intended to go. She now regretted having left south Texas so quickly, for there was a good chance some of the fugitives from her list might be there. With only the river between Texas and old Mexico—despite her riding into an ambush while with Joel Votaw's outfit—she still believed that horse rustling flourished along the border. Done properly, there was little risk from authorities on either side of the river. Suddenly a distant horse nickered, and the chestnut mare answered. It was all the warning Danielle had. A rifle roared, and she rolled out of the saddle, going belly down. One of the slugs had grazed Sundown, and the animal galloped away.

"All right, *hombre*," a voice challenged, "git up, keepin' your hands high."

There was no help for it, and Danielle got to her feet, careful to keep her hands away from the butts of her Colts. That these men were outlaws, she had no doubt.

"Now, come on," said the voice, "and don't do nothin' foolish."

There was a small clearing through which a stream flowed, and four men stood there with their hands near the butts of their revolvers. One of them spoke.

"Come on, Leroy. We got him covered."

A fifth man stepped out of the brush, carrying a Winchester. He wasted no time. His hard eyes met Danielle's, and Leroy spoke.

"Who are you, kid, and what are you doin' here?"

"I'm not the law if that's what's botherin' you," Danielle said. "Thanks to you and your damned shooting, my horse ran away. Now get your no-account carcass out there and find her."

The rest of the outlaws laughed uproariously, and Leroy's face went bright red.

"Leroy," one of his companions said, "I never realized your daddy was so young."

That brought on a new round of laughter, and some violent cursing from Leroy. When they all became silent, Danielle was standing there with her thumbs hooked in her gun belts just above the butts of her Colts.

"I hope you're done shootin', Leroy," said Danielle, "because I aim to shoot back."

But Leroy was furious. Dropping the Winchester, he went for his Colt. Danielle waited until he cleared leather and then, with blinding speed, shot the gun out of his hand.

"Anybody else?" Danielle asked, covering them.

Leroy stood there, looking unbelievingly at his mangled Colt on the ground, while the other four men regarded Danielle with grudging respect.

"No need to get your tail feathers ruffled, kid," said one of the strangers warily. "Put away the iron. Sometimes, Leroy's a mite hard to convince. I'm Cass Herring, and these three gents beside me is Stubbs Potter, Jarvis Brooking, and Watt Slacker. Leroy Lomax you've already met."

Danielle punched out the empty shell casing and reloaded her Colt. Now there was no empty chamber, for the weapon was fully loaded, an observation that meant something to the five men who watched. Holstering the weapon, Danielle spoke.

"I'm Daniel Strange. Who you gents are and what you're doing here is of no interest to me. I'm on my way to Texas, and thanks to Leroy here, I have no horse. Whatever you're riding, Leroy, saddle it and find my horse."

"Damned if I will," Leroy snarled.

"You're damned if you don't," said Danielle, her green eyes regarding him coldly. "It's cost you a Colt so far. If you're still not convinced, I can shoot off a finger or a thumb."

Cass Herring laughed. "Leroy, I think you'd better round up the kid's horse."

Leroy stomped off into the brush, cursing as he went. Danielle relaxed. None of the other four men made any hostile moves. Instead, they regarded her curiously. It was Watt Slacker who finally spoke.

"Kid, where in tarnation did you learn to shoot like that?"

"My pa was a gunsmith in St. Joe, and he taught me," Danielle said. "He was robbed and hanged in Indian Territory last April. Seven of the coyotes that killed him are alive somewhere, and I'm after them."

"I reckon you got some way of knowin' who they are, then," Stubbs Potter said.

"I have their names," said Danielle. "At least the names they were using."

"Name them," Cass Herring said. "We might be of some help to you. We been down to Laredo, where we got into a disagreement over the ownership of some horses."

Danielle named the men on her death list.

"One of them *hombres* I've heard of," said Herring. "This Snakehead Kalpana has been down to Brownsville, driving Mex horses across the border into Texas."

"Yeah," Stubbs Potter said. "The damn Spaniard loused up everything by gunning down a Texas lawman. They'll overlook a gent picking up a few Mex horses, but when he kills a man behind the star, he's in trouble."

"I'm obliged," said Danielle.

At that point, Leroy returned, leading Sundown. Without a word, he passed the reins to Danielle.

"We're bound for north Texas, kid," Cass Herring said, "and you're welcome to ride with us. It ain't safe for a man alone here in Indian Territory."

"I'm obliged, and I'll join you," said Danielle. "Does that suit you, Leroy?"

"Hell no," Leroy snarled. "You humiliated me, and I owe you for that."

"When you're ready," said Danielle. "I'll give you a head start."

CHAPTER 15

Danielle allowed the five men to lead out, for she didn't trust Leroy behind her out of her sight. She didn't like the way he had cut down on her with a Winchester, not knowing if she was friend or foe. The other four men seemed of a more even temperament.

"I figure we're maybe two hundred and fifty miles north of Fort Worth," Cass Herring said when they had made camp for the night.

"You're bound for Fort Worth, then," said Danielle.

"Yeah," Herring replied. "For the time being anyway. It gets god-awful cold here in the Territory when them snowstorms blow down from the high plains."

"Hell, it snows in Texas, too," said Leroy sullenly.

"Not near as much as it does to the north," Herring replied. "If it gets bad enough, we can always ride farther south."

"I don't like south Texas," said Leroy. "Too damn many rangers there."

"You can always strike off on your own and go any place you damn please," Herring said, "but if you get gun happy in Texas and get us in trouble with the rangers, then I'll personally gutshoot you."

While none of them had admitted it, Danielle believed they had been in Laredo—on the Mexican border—rustling Mexican horses and selling them in Texas. They had then rode into Indian

Territory to avoid any retribution for the lawman who had been shot. Danielle wondered if Leroy had done the killing, but there was no way of finding out unless she asked. For her own well-being, she couldn't afford to show too much interest in these men, who were undoubtedly on the dodge.

"We used the last of our coffee this morning," Cass Herring said. "How are you fixed for grub, kid?"

"I have enough coffee to see us through to Fort Worth," said Danielle. "I've got some jerked beef, bacon, and hardtack I'll share."*

"That's generous of you," Jarvis Brooking said. "We're near 'bout out of everything."

They rode on, stopping only to rest their horses, making night camp near a spring or a stream. At the end of the second day, Danielle estimated they were within fifty miles of Fort Worth. She had no reason for returning to the fort, since Captain Ferguson—the post commander—had refused her any help. Still, the sutler's store would be the nearest source of supplies, and sharing with her five companions had all but emptied her saddlebags. With much of the frontier still unsettled, civilians were allowed to buy supplies and goods from a military outpost's store.

FORT WORTH, TEXAS. DECEMBER 4, 1870.

In back of the sutler's store was a saloon, and Danielle's five companions went there first. Danielle had no intention of remaining at the fort overnight and, in the sutler's store, began replenishing her supplies. The very last person she wished to see was Captain Ferguson, but she soon heard footsteps behind her, and there he was. His manner was different, and when he spoke, there was some friendliness in his voice.

"You've been busy, young man. I received the Kansas City

---

* Hardtack was an early version of today's soda crackers.

newspaper that told of the killing of a Kansas Pacific railroad man. He refused to cooperate with you, didn't he?"

"Yes," Danielle said. "He didn't want any bad publicity for the railroad, but he got it anyway. One of the men on my list is Chancy Burke, and I was told by Alan Steele that Burke didn't work for the railroad. Steele confronted Burke himself, and after he shot and killed Steele, Burke escaped."

"I suppose I owe you an apology," said Ferguson. "If you had gone to Kansas City knowing Burke was with the railroad and feeding information to his outlaw friends, Steele might be alive today. I'm sorry I didn't make some effort to get that list of railroad men for you."

"We all make mistakes, Captain," Danielle said. "Your apology is accepted. Now I want to ask you something. Did you know Rufe Gaddis, Julius Byler, and Chancy Burke are all from Waco and that they have families there?"

"No," said Ferguson. "It's news to me. Perhaps that's where they are now."

"I wouldn't be surprised," Danielle said, "but a lot of good it'll do me. I visited the Gaddis, Byler, and Burke families and was ordered out of town. I couldn't stable my horse, buy a meal, or rent a room."

"Waco has an elected sheriff," said Ferguson. "You got no help there?"

"None, and no promise of any," Danielle said. "The sheriff's concerned only with the next election, and it was him that told the town I was looking for Gaddis, Byler, and Burke. He also made it a point to warn the families of the three outlaws, and their kin were waiting for me with guns."

"I can't promise you any help," said Captain Ferguson. "I suspect there are outlaws all over Texas, but there's nothing the military can do. We're already undermanned, and with Quanah Parker and his Comanche followers raising hell, local lawmen and the rangers will have to deal with the outlaws."

"I understand," Danielle said, "but even the rangers have failed in Waco."

Shaking his head in frustration, Captain Ferguson walked away. When Danielle had her purchases bought and wrapped, she took them outside and stowed them in her saddlebags. She tied a sack of grain for Sundown to her bedroll behind the saddle. Feeling that she at least owed her five companions an *adios*, she went looking for them in the saloon behind the store. They did, after all, tell her that Snakehead Kalpana had been in south Texas, running horses across the border. If he had killed someone, especially a lawman, he might be long gone. She found all five of the men were gathered around a table, playing poker.

"I'm ridin' out," Danielle announced. "I just came to say *adios*."

"Watch your back, kid," said Cass Herring.

It was an underhanded compliment, for no man was likely to face her down when she drew with blinding speed. Potter, Brooking, and Slacker had words of farewell. Leroy Lomax glared at her murderously, for he was a big loser, having few chips before him.

"Don't expect nothin' from Leroy," Stubbs Potter said. "His ma weaned him on sour pickles, and he's went downhill from there."

There was laughter, some of it from strangers who had overheard the conversation. For a second, Danielle's eyes met Leroy's, and she knew if their trails again crossed on the frontier, one of them would die. Danielle rode out slightly to the southwest so that she might avoid Waco, which lay due south of Fort Worth. She had no doubt that eventually she would be riding back to Waco, for with the whole town, including the sheriff, looking out for Gaddis, Byler, and Burke, it was a safe enough haven for the outlaws. She took heart in the possibility that Kalpana might not have been working alone, that some of the other killers she sought might be riding with him. From what she had learned at Fort Worth, Laredo, Texas, was a border town over four hundred miles to the south. Since San Antonio was along the way, Danielle decided to stop and talk to the old ranger Sage Jennings.

SAN ANTONIO, TEXAS. DECEMBER 7, 1870.

Captain Jennings had heard of the killing of Alan Steele of the Kansas Pacific. Danielle filled in the details, and shaking his head, Jennings spoke.

"No damn wonder the frontier's neck-deep in outlaws. I reckon you've been to Waco?"

"I have, right after I left here before," Danielle said. She explained her run-ins with the sheriff and the Gaddis, Byler, and Burke families.

"I frankly don't know what we're going to do about that situation," said Jennings. "If we had some way of knowing when those three varmints slip back into Waco, I reckon we could take a posse and go after them. But it would be hell, trying to buffalo a whole town the size of Waco. Somebody would die and not necessarily the outlaws."

"I got word that Snakehead Kalpana, one of the men I'm hunting, has been rustling on the other side of the border and bringing the horses into Texas. Do you know anything about that?"

"I didn't know the last time you were here," said Jennings, "but I do now. Kalpana has three men riding with him. He killed two men. One of them a Mexican officer, and the other a Texas Ranger. We want him, and we want him bad. He's worth twenty-five hundred dollars, dead or alive."

"If I find him," Danielle said, "you won't be getting him alive. I'm bound for Laredo."

"He hasn't been heard from around there since the killings," Captain Jennings said.

"I'm not surprised," said Danielle, "but there's a lot of border from Laredo south to Brownsville. I aim to ride all of it if I have to."

"I could swear you in as a ranger," Jennings said, "but it might hurt you more than it would help. A varmint that's killed one ranger couldn't hang any higher for killing another one. Just be careful, and remember, it's against federal law for you to cross the border into Mexico."

"Wherever Kalpana is, that's where I'm going," said Danielle, "and that includes south of the border."

"I didn't hear you say that," Jennings said. "Do what you have to do, and good luck."

Weary from the long ride from Fort Worth, Danielle stabled Sundown and took a room for the night. She lay down and slept awhile after supper, then decided to visit the Alamo Saloon. She had heard it was a favorite watering hole for King Fisher, Ben Thompson, and other gamblers. The saloon was even more luxurious than she had imagined. Instead of sawdust floors, there were deep-pile carpet, drapes on the windows, a mahogany bar, and two dozen tables devoted to poker and faro. Danielle wondered if her lucky streak had played out, or if she could still win. Placing five double eagles on a faro table, she bought in.

"Ten dollars a bet," the house dealer said.

It was the highest stakes Danielle had ever played for. At ten dollars a throw, she could lose her hundred dollars in a matter of minutes. On the other hand, if she won, the higher stakes put more money in her pocket. She quickly lost fifty dollars before she began winning. She almost immediately recovered her fifty dollars, and for an hour she averaged winning two pots out of three. Her companions at the table took their losses in stride, for they seemed to be affluent men. When Danielle had won three hundred dollars, she withdrew from the game. It didn't pay to win too much, too soon. She couldn't help wondering what these men would have thought or said, had they known she wasn't a man. Thinking back, she was amazed at the changes in her. She had learned to control herself and her emotions so that nothing men said or did caused her to blush. It bothered her, for when she reached the end of her vengeance trail, suppose she had become a hard woman, comfortable in saloons among drunks and whores? She often thought of Tucker Carlyle, but she dared not ride back to the Carlyle ranch. Her goodbyes had been difficult enough, and she didn't want to go through them again. She returned to her hotel, and as usual, she slid the back of a chair under the doorknob.

Danielle arose early and had breakfast in a nearby café. She then took her saddlebags and headed for the stable where she had left the chestnut mare. During their months on the trail, she had become much closer to Sundown, and the mare nickered her pleasure when Danielle came near. She rode slightly to the southwest, toward Laredo. If there had been trouble on the border at Laredo, it wasn't likely the outlaws were still there, but she couldn't overlook the possibility that they had simply holed up somewhere in the wilds of old Mexico until the incident was forgotten. Rustling horses in Mexico and driving them into Texas had become relatively easy, for as Captain Jennings had pointed out, even the combined efforts of the United States and Mexico were not enough to patrol the hundreds of miles of border.

LAREDO, TEXAS. DECEMBER 10, 1870.

Compared to San Antonio, Laredo wasn't much more than a wide place in the trail. The hotel was a single-story affair, the rooms were cheap, and there were only two cafés. But as Danielle noted with amusement, there were six saloons. Darkness was falling when she reached town, and to her dismay, she found the livery closed. She pounded on the door with the butt of one of her Colts until the door creaked open. An old Mexican peered at Danielle in the fading light. Under his arm was a Winchester rifle.

"What you want, *señor?*"

"I want to stable my horse for the night," Danielle said. "What the hell's the idea of closing before dark?"

"*Mejicanos* come from across the river and take our horses," the old one replied.

"Tarnation," Danielle said, "don't you have a lawman or a sheriff?"

"*Sí*," said the Mexican, "but he is one *hombre*. The border, she be great, *señor*."

The old man had told her essentially what she had already heard from Captain Sage Jennings, but she had learned something more. Apparently in retaliation, Texas horses were being run across the border into Mexico, or so it seemed. But suppose it wasn't Mexicans stealing Texas horses? Who could say that, after several killings, American outlaws hadn't holed up south of the border and begun running Texas horses into Mexico? Danielle took a room at the hotel and went to the nearer café to eat. Tomorrow morning she would seek out the sheriff and question him.

Three men were in the café when Danielle entered, and they turned to stare at her. Each wore a high-crowned Mexican sombrero, and their faces were obscured by maybe a week's growth of beard. Their tight-fitting black trousers and their red embroidered vests showed much trail dust. Their ruffled, once white shirts were sweat stained, and tied low on his right hip, each had a revolver. Danielle paused in the doorway, her eyes on the three, and they hastily resumed eating. The cook looked fearfully from Danielle to the Mexicans, and relaxed. The three were eating, apparently oblivious to Danielle. She spoke.

"Bring me a double portion of whatever you have."

"Beef stew, potatoes, apple pie, and coffee," said the cook. "Tequila if you wish."

"No," Danielle said. "Coffee."

It was obvious the three men who had stared at Danielle were drinking tequila, for on their table sat a bottle a third full of the potent liquor. Danielle watched them out of the corner of her eye and, from their flushed faces, decided they were drunk or close to it. When the cook brought Danielle's meal, she ate slowly, allowing the trio to finish ahead of her. They did and left the café without looking at Danielle again. It was just her and the cook, so she spoke.

"I thought it was illegal for Mexicans to cross the border into Texas or for Texans to cross over into Mexico."

"That fool law was wrote in Washington," said the cook, "and that's a hell of a long ways from here. If the Mexes want to wade the branch and spend their pesos in Laredo, I ain't about to complain. I reckon you've noticed this ain't a very big town."

"I've noticed," Danielle said, "and I'm not concerned with Mexicans. I'm looking for Snakehead Kalpana, an American. I have business with him."

"Never heard of him," said the cook.

The furtive look in his eyes told Danielle he was lying. Drinking the last of her coffee, she paid for her meal and left the café. Returning to the hotel, she locked the door to her room and placed the back of a chair under the doorknob. Tomorrow she would seek out the sheriff, and for a long while, she lay awake, wondering if his attitude toward the border crossings would be the same as that of the man in the café. If Kalpana and some of the other men felt safe south of the border, finding them would be all the more difficult.

D anielle arose at dawn, had breakfast, and went looking for the sheriff. There were only two cells in the jail, both empty. The sheriff looked to be in his forties, and he got to his feet when Danielle entered the office.

"Sheriff, I'm Daniel Strange, from St. Joseph, Missouri."

"Pleased to meet you," said the lawman. "I'm Tom Carson. What can I do for you?"

"Tell me if you know anything about Snakehead Kalpana," Danielle said.

"I know he's an outlaw and a killer, and that the Texas Rangers would dearly love for him to be the guest of honor at a necktie party. What's your interest in him?"

Quickly, Danielle again told the story of her father's murder in Indian Territory.

"I can't say I blame you," said the sheriff, "but you're almighty young to be ridin' the vengeance trail."

"Maybe," Danielle said, "but there was nobody else. My two brothers are younger than I am."

"I'll help you in any way that I can," said the sheriff, "but I suspect Kalpana and the bunch he's ridin' with have moved on. It was Kalpana who shot two men. One of them was a Mexican officer, and the other was a Texas Ranger."

"Speaking of the bunch Kalpana's riding with," Danielle said, "do you know the names of any of them?"

"No," said Sheriff Carson. "I'm familiar with Kalpana only because he spent his time in the saloons, gambling. Of course, that was before we learned he was rustling Mex horses and selling them in Texas, and before he shot and killed the Mexican and a ranger. He's got a hair-trigger temper, and when he loses at the poker table, he has a bad habit of accusing somebody of cheating him. I threatened to arrest him several times, but he would always back down. I reckon it's lucky for me that he did, because he carries a couple of tied-down Colts. From what I've heard, he's faster than forked lightning."

Danielle sighed. "I'm obliged, Sheriff Carson. I didn't really expect Kalpana to still be here, but this trail's not quite as cold as that I've been following. How much border is there between here and Brownsville?"

"A good two hundred miles," said Carson, "and all manner of little villages where a man on the dodge can hole up. He could even be south of the border. Mexicans are poor, and if an *Americano* has money, they'll take him in, whatever he's done."

"The border situation being what it is," Danielle said, "can you suggest anything that might be helpful to me?"

"Maybe," the lawman said. "As you ride on to Brownsville, follow the river. There's Del Rio and Eagle Pass, about a day's ride between them. You probably won't learn much at Del Rio, but King Fisher has a ranch near Eagle Pass.* It's common knowledge

---

* King Fisher's ranch was the Pendencia. He was a cowboy, a rustler, and a killer—he was fifteen when he killed his first man.

that King rides across the border, rounds up wild horses, and drives them into Texas, but you would be wise not to mention that. He might be willing to identify some of the men you're looking for if he understands your reason. But he's almighty swift with a pistol, and he don't like company. Are you familiar with him?"

"Yes," said Danielle. "I ran into him and Ben Thompson once when I rode through San Antonio."

"Drunk, I reckon," Sheriff Carson said.

"Roostered to the eyeballs," said Danielle. "They looked just about drunk enough to want to fight, so I avoided them."

"Good thinking," Sheriff Carson said. "It's a damn shame King Fisher walks on both sides of the law. He could use his guns to help rid the border of thieves and killers."

DEL RIO, TEXAS. DECEMBER 12, 1870.

It seemed there was nothing more Danielle could learn in Laredo, so she rode along the Rio Grande toward Del Rio. It was, as Sheriff Carson said, a good day's ride, and the first stars were winking from the heavens when Danielle rode in. The town seemed smaller than Laredo, for Danielle counted only four saloons. For some reason, there were two liveries, and Danielle left Sundown at the one nearer the hotel. She then took a room for the night and went to a café for supper. Since it was already dark, she decided to wait until the following morning to seek out Sheriff Lon Guthrie. The café was nothing fancy, having a big hanging sign outside that said simply EATS. Besides the cook, there was only one man in the café, and he wore a lawman's star. Danielle ordered her meal, then took a chair across from the lawman. He looked questioningly at her.

"I reckon you're Sheriff Lon Guthrie," Danielle said. "Sheriff Carson, in Laredo, said I should talk to you."

"I'm Guthrie," said the lawman. "Who are you, and why do you want to talk to me?"

"I'm Daniel Strange, and I'm looking for a varmint that's been rustling horses south of the border and driving them to Texas. He's one of ten outlaws who robbed and murdered my pa in Indian Territory. His name, far as I know, is Snakehead Kalpana."

"I've heard the name," Sheriff Guthrie said, "but I don't think he's spent any time here in Del Rio. Seeing as how we're right on the border, I'm always watching for strangers in the saloons and cafés."

"I'm obliged for the information," said Danielle. "In Laredo, Sheriff Carson suggested that on my way to Brownsville, I talk to Sheriff Rim Klady in Eagle Pass. He told me that I should also talk to King Fisher, since he gathers wild horses in Mexico and drives them across the border into Texas."

"King Fisher's a hell-raising coyote that walks on his hind legs like a man," Sheriff Guthrie said. "I doubt he'd help you if he could, because some of those horses he rounds up in Mexico ain't wild. They're wearin' Mex brands. You'd best avoid him."

"If I don't learn anything in Eagle Pass," said Danielle, "I'll be riding on to Brownsville. With so much border, I can't believe these rustlers would give up easy pickings."

"Maybe you're right," Sheriff Guthrie said, "but Sam Duro's sheriff there, so don't be expecting too much."

"I'm obliged, Sheriff," said Danielle.

Sheriff Guthrie had finished his meal. He slid back his chair and stood up.

"Good luck, kid."

Danielle nodded, for the cook had just brought her supper. She ate, mulling over what Sheriff Guthrie had told her. While he hadn't really told her anything about the sheriff at Brownsville, he had implied much. Among the many good lawmen on the frontier, there was always an occasional one—if the price was right—who would turn his back on rustlers, outlaws, and killers. Danielle paid for her meal and returned to the hotel. Having already talked to Sheriff Guthrie, in the morning she could get an early start to Eagle Pass.

The border town of Eagle Pass wasn't that much different from Del Rio. There were the same weather-beaten saloons, but only four this time. Danielle arrived before dark and, finding a livery, stabled Sundown. She then set out to find the sheriff's office. The door was locked, and peering through a window, Danielle could see no sign of life inside. There was an hour of daylight remaining, so Danielle decided to make the rounds of the saloons. In the third one, called the Eagle's Claw, she found the sheriff involved in a poker game.

"Sheriff," Danielle said, "I have some business with you."

Sheriff Rim Klady turned and looked her over, his eyes pausing when they reached the two tied-down Colts on Danielle's hips. Finally, he spoke.

"Have you been robbed or shot somebody?"

"No," said Danielle. "I'm Daniel Strange, and it's about another matter."

"Then see me at the office in the morning," Sheriff Klady said.

The lawman had just won another pot. Dismissing Danielle, he raked in his winnings. Danielle left the saloon, furious. She took a room at the hotel. Tomorrow she might or might not be questioning the sheriff. It seemed that a talk with King Fisher might be far more beneficial if she could get to him.

The next morning, Danielle was sitting on the steps to the sheriff's office and the jail when the lawman arrived. She got up, allowing him to mount the steps and unlock the door. She followed him into the office.

"All right," said the sheriff, "I'm Rim Klady. Sit down and have your say."

Klady sat down in his chair behind his desk while Danielle took a ladder-back chair facing him. She quickly told her story, and by the time she was finished, the sheriff was shaking his head.

"The name Kalpana don't mean nothing to me," Sheriff Klady said. "There's hundreds of miles of border, and rustlers ain't likely to drive stock across the border where there's a town with a lawman."

"I understand King Fisher has a ranch near here," said Danielle, "and that he rounds up wild horses in Mexico, driving them back into Texas."

Sheriff Klady's manner changed abruptly, and there was something in his eyes akin to fear. Finally, he spoke.

"I don't bother King Fisher, and he don't bother me. I don't see nothin' wrong with him capturing wild horses in Mexico."

"Except that the United States government has a law against him going there," Danielle said. "That doesn't concern you?"

"Hell no," said the lawman. "The Federals passed that damn law. Let them enforce it. If Mexicans want to come into Texas or Texans want to go into Mexico, there ain't enough lawmen on both sides of the border to stop 'em."

"You haven't been much help, Sheriff," Danielle said, "and I'm going to ask just one more favor of you. How do I find King Fisher's place?"

"Just ride along the river toward Brownsville," Sheriff Klady said. "The Rio borders his place to the south, and you'll see a sign pointin' toward the ranch. Just don't complain to me if he greets you with a Winchester and orders you to get the hell off his property."

"I'd never think of bothering you over a small matter like that, Sheriff," said Danielle. "I'm armed, and I'm not afraid to shoot back. *Adios*."

The sheriff said nothing, and Danielle left, closing the door behind her. Mounting Sundown, she rode south, keeping the Rio in sight. As Sheriff Klady had said, there soon was a fork in the trail. A board with crude lettering had been nailed to a tree. It read: THIS IS KING FISHER'S ROAD. TAKE THE OTHER.

CHAPTER 16

Ignoring the warning, Danielle took King Fisher's road. Of her welcome, she was very uncertain, for the only times she had seen King Fisher had been in San Antonio when he and Ben Thompson had been very drunk. She finally rode out into a clearing and could see the ranch house in the distance. The place seemed deserted, but suddenly the stillness was shattered by a gunshot.

"Don't come any closer," a voice shouted. "You're not welcome here."

"I only want to talk to you," Danielle said. "I'm not the law."

"You're still not welcome here," said the distant voice.

Gritting her teeth, Danielle rode on. Would the man shoot her out of the saddle? She eventually reined up forty yards from the front porch. King Fisher stepped past the door, a Winchester under his arm. His dress could be described only as gaudy. His trousers were black with pinstripes, and over a white ruffled shirt, he wore a bright red tie. Around his middle was a red sash that matched the tie. His boots were fancy, and a white Stetson hat was tipped low over his eyes. On each hip in a tied-down holster was a revolver.

"I could have shot you dead and been within my rights," he snapped. "Haven't I seen you somewhere?"

"In San Antonio," said Danielle. "You and Ben Thompson were drunk."

"Since you're here," Fisher said, "who are you, and what the hell do you want of me?"

"I want some information," said Danielle, "and it in no way concerns you. I am Daniel Strange, and I'm hunting some men who robbed and hanged my pa in Indian Territory in the spring. One of those still alive—Snakehead Kalpana—has been rustling horses in old Mexico and driving them across the border into Texas. He killed a Mexican and a ranger near Laredo, but I doubt that he's given up rustling. I think he's just moved to another location along the border."

"Well, if you think he's here or that I'd have any dealings with the likes of him, then you're barking up the wrong damn tree," Fisher said.

"I've been told that you trap wild horses in Mexico and drive them into Texas," said Danielle. "I was hoping you might have seen or heard of Kalpana."

"I want nothing to do with the kind that rustles another man's stock," Fisher said. "I've shot some *hombres* that was needful of it, but I've never stole a horse or a cow."*

"If you know nothing about Kalpana," said Danielle, "maybe you'll recognize some of these other varmints I'm looking for."

Quickly, she told him the names of the other six men, and Fisher shook his head.

"I'm obliged anyway," Danielle said.

"You got sand in your craw, kid," said King Fisher. "How old are you?"

"Old enough," Danielle said.

Fisher laughed. "A regular two-gun man, huh? Can you use them irons, or do you just carry 'em to scare hell out of folks?"

In a lightning cross-hand draw, Danielle drew the butt-forward Colt from her left hip. She fired once, the slug kicking up splinters from the porch. Then she spoke.

---

* Despite his assurances to the contrary, King Fisher had been known to rustle. He was only fifteen when he stole his first horse.

"I could have shot your ears off, but you've been decent to me. *Adios.*"

Holstering the Colt, she wheeled the chestnut mare and rode away. King Fisher stood there watching her until she was out of sight. Then he laughed to himself.

"You'll do, kid. You'll do."

When Danielle reached the river, she rode southeast. She had no idea how far she was from Brownsville and decided not to attempt to reach it in what was left of the day. She was rapidly running out of trails and needed to think. There was always a chance, she concluded, that she had miscalculated. Suppose Kalpana *had* left Laredo, but instead of riding deeper into south Texas, he had ridden west toward El Paso? He might even have gone to southern Arizona, for there he would be just across the river from Mexico. There were so many possibilities, Danielle had to rest to put them all out of her mind.

BROWNSVILLE, TEXAS. DECEMBER 16, 1870.

C learly, nobody was enforcing federal law in Brownsville, for Mexicans were virtually everywhere. From the saloons there were drunken shouts in Spanish, and as Danielle rode along the main street, she saw many dark-eyed *señoritas* with their hair tied back, and some peons with colorful serapes about their shoulders. It appeared that most of the cafés and restaurants, if not Mexican owned, were at least Mexican operated. Before most of them, in colorful clothing and a high-crowned sombrero, a young boy praised his establishment's bill of fare in rapid Spanish. It looked like a wide-open town, Danielle thought, and might well be just the kind of place where Snakehead Kalpana would try to lose himself. Getting past the saloons, cafés, and street vendors, Danielle reached a quiet street down which she rode. She came upon a huge old house, and above the front door was a neatly painted sign that read **AMERICAN HOTEL**. Reining up, she dismounted and knocked on the door. When it was eventually opened, there stood a gray-haired old man.

"I just rode through town," Danielle said, "and I like the look of your sign. I'll need a room for maybe two or three days."

"Come in," said her host. "My name is Ephiram Delaney. My wife, Ethel, is upstairs. I'll get her. Make yourself at home."

He proceeded to summon Ethel by shouting for her at the top of his voice.

"Damn it," Ethel shouted back, "do you have to wake the dead? I'm coming."

She came down the stairs, taking her time, a wisp of a woman as gray as old Ephiram. She looked at Danielle, a question in her eyes. Danielle spoke.

"I'm Daniel Strange, and I'll need a room for maybe three nights."

"Two dollars a night for the room," said Ethel, "or three fifty if you want some grub twice a day."

"I'll take the room and the grub," Danielle said, handing her a gold eagle.

"Good choice," said Ephiram. "In these Mex cafés and cantinas, they load everything with chili peppers 'cept the coffee."

"Now," Danielle said, "is there a place close by where I can stable my horse?"

"Behind the house across the alley," Ephiram said, "but we can't afford no hostler."

"I won't need one," said Danielle.

"I'll get you a room ready while you're gone," Ethel said. "Just come on up. It'll be at the head of the stairs on the right."

Danielle led Sundown around the house and into the stable. It appeared to be empty, and Danielle chose a stall for the mare. She unsaddled the horse and, seeing hay in the loft above, climbed up and forked some down.

"Chew on that awhile, Sundown," said Danielle. "I'll be back before dark and bring you some grain."

Danielle found Ephiram seated on the front porch. Nodding to him, she again entered the house and mounted the stairs.

"In here," Ethel said.

The room could only be described as luxurious. There was a thick gray carpet on the floor, with rose-colored drapes at the window. The bed was brass with a multicolored coverlet. There were several extra chairs, upholstered in rose, and a wide dresser on which stood a porcelain water pitcher and a matching basin. On the back of the door was a mirror, full length and uncracked.

"The chamber pot's under the bed," said Ethel with a wink.

"I'm obliged," Danielle said. "You have a fine place. I've never had better."

"Thank you," said Ethel, pleased. "We cater to Americans. Ephiram says one day we'll wake up and there won't be anybody but *Mejicanos* as far as the eye can see."

"It already looks that way uptown," Danielle said.

"It just about is," said Ethel. "Don't let 'em sell you any of that Mex whiskey either. It's about a hundred and forty proof. Then when you're layin' there stiff as a post and can't get up, them human turkey buzzards—*Anglos* or *Mejicanos*—will pick your pockets clean."

"I'm obliged for the information," Danielle said, "but I don't drink or smoke."

"Praise be," said Ethel. "Last time we had a drinking man in here he passed out and his cigarette set the bed afire. Supper's at five, breakfast at seven."

As Danielle left the house, Ephiram sat nodding on the front porch. The Delaneys were in a residential section of quiet homes, and the area seemed a world apart from the center of town with its noisy *Mejicanos* and shifty-eyed *Anglos*. Danielle had already been warned not to expect too much of Brownsville sheriff Sam Duro, but she went looking for the lawman anyway. She found his office and he was there, his booted feet on the desk and his hat tipped over his eyes. From somewhere came the sound of three rapid gunshots and a cry of anguish, but the sheriff remained where he was.

"Draw, you lazy varmint," Danielle shouted, kicking the desk.

Duro's swivel chair went over backward, coming to rest on top of him. He cursed as he fought to draw his revolver, and Danielle laughed. Finally, he sat up, shoving the chair off him, and began beating his crushed Stetson back into shape. Danielle stood there chuckling, allowing the disgruntled lawman to get to his feet and right his swivel chair.

"Damn you," Duro shouted, "that's a good way to get yourself shot dead. Who the hell are you, and what business do you have here?"

"Killing business when I find the right man," said Danielle. "I'm after an outlaw and a killer. You being the law here, I reckoned I'd better talk to you first."

"The law hereabouts don't work with bounty hunters," Sheriff Duro said.

"I'm not a bounty hunter," said Danielle. "I'm after the yellow coyotes who robbed and murdered my pa in Indian Territory. One of them in particular is Snakehead Kalpana, and I have reason to believe he's here. Do you know him or know of him?"

"No," Sheriff Duro said, "and I won't tolerate vigilantes any more than I'll tolerate the bounty hunters. The first damn sign of trouble that involves you, I'll lock you in the jail till hell freezes. You got that?"

"If I find the *hombre* I'm looking for, I aim to do what I came here to do," Danielle said steadily, "and if you try to stop me, you'd better be pretty damn sudden with a pistol. *You got that?*"

Danielle turned and left the sheriff's office, not even bothering to ask Duro about the rest of the men on her death list. There were more gunshots from the area where most of the saloons were. She decided that Duro was even more useless than Sheriff Rucker in Waco. She had little choice except to make the rounds of the saloons, hoping to gather a bit of information that might suggest a new trail. The biggest and noisiest of the saloons seemed to be a place appropriately called the Border Saloon. There were poker and faro games in progress, but Danielle didn't like the looks of the men gathered around the tables. She watched a faro game for a while and learned her suspicions had been well-founded. A bearded man suddenly leaped to his feet, drew a Bowie knife, and lunged across the table. But the Mexican he had gone after was just as resourceful with his own blade, and under their weight, the table collapsed. They rolled around on the floor, each man seizing the wrist of the other's knife hand. Two bouncers arrived to break up the fight, and their method was simple. Each of them seized a chair, slamming it down on the head of one of the men on the floor. When the two knife wielders were beaten bloody and unconscious, the bouncers carried them outside, one at a time, and flung them into the street. By then, another table had been set up, and the interrupted faro game was again in progress. Danielle was about to leave, when a woman screamed. It was one of the saloon girls. She lay on her back on the floor while a man astraddle her was ripping her clothes off. Danielle looked for the bouncers, but they were nowhere in sight. Nobody tried to help the unfortunate girl, and some of the men had gathered around to watch, laughing. Danielle drew her Colt, crossed the room, and slammed the muzzle of the weapon against the back of the attacker's head. He tumbled over, allowing the terrified girl to get to her feet. Drawing the remnants of her torn dress together, she ran up the winding stairway that led to the second floor. The saloon had become deathly silent, and not a man among them could meet Danielle's eyes. She holstered her Colt, awaiting she knew not what. Slowly, the man she had buffaloed got to his hands and knees, shaking his head. He then got unsteadily to his feet.

"Which one of you sons of bitches hit me?" he snarled.

"I did," said Danielle, "and I'm only sorry I didn't do it sooner."

He went for his gun, only to find himself covered by Danielle's Colt. Baring his teeth like a wolf, he snarled at her.

"Do you know who I am?"

"No," Danielle said calmly, "but I know *what* you are. You're a woman-beating coward, a yellow-bellied coyote that walks on his hind legs like a man."

"I'll kill you for that!" he shouted. "Reece McCandless swears it."

"I'm obliged for the warning," said Danielle. "I'll watch my back. Now get out of here, and the next time you reach for a gun, I'll kill you."

McCandless was a big man, and given a choice, he would have preferred being gutshot to the humiliation he had endured. His face flaming red, he stumbled out of the saloon. As Danielle stepped out onto the boardwalk, she encountered Sheriff Sam Duro.

"Where the hell have *you* been?" Danielle asked. "The brute that just left here had a woman down on the floor, ripping her clothes off."

"I reckon you stepped in and saved her," said Sheriff Duro.

"I did," Danielle said, "and I only regret that I didn't shoot him."

"God help you if you had," Duro said. "That's Reece McCandless. Old Simon, his pa, owns half of Brownsville."

"Does he own you along with it?" Danielle asked.

"Kid," said Sheriff Duro, "I'm gonna pretend you didn't say that, because you're in enough trouble already. With any luck, you can mount your horse and be long gone from here before Simon McCandless learns what you've done."

"Sheriff," Danielle said, "I'll go when I'm ready, and I'm not ready. I called McCandless a woman-beating coward and a yellow-bellied coyote walking on his hind legs like a man, and I don't regret a word of it. I'm sticking to what I said, and I don't care a damn if old Simon McCandless is nine feet tall and feeds on raw meat."

Danielle left Sheriff Duro speechless. She went into one of the smaller cantinas, where a faro game was in progress, and decided to sit in.

"Five-dollar limit," said the dealer.

Danielle lost fifty dollars and was about to quit the game when one of the men across the table spoke to his companion.

"I'm tired of this damn town, neck-deep in *Mejicanos*. If Kalpana don't show up by tomorrow night, I'm ridin' on."

The other laughed. "After what he done in Laredo, he'll likely have to spend the rest of his life south of the river."

Danielle listened eagerly, hoping to hear more, but the conversation took a new turn and Kalpana's name wasn't mentioned again. The reference to what Kalpana had done in Laredo led Danielle to believe it might have been him who had killed the Texas Ranger. After losing most of her hundred-dollar stake, Danielle began to go over her options. She wanted to remain in the game so that when the two strangers left, she could follow them. Their reference to Kalpana was the only mention of the man's name she had heard after many months on the trail. It wasn't a common name, and she believed it was the outlaw she sought. The two strangers had a run of extremely bad luck, and to cut their losses, they withdrew from the game and started toward the bar. Danielle won another hand just as the pair finished their drinks and were about to leave the saloon. She waited until they were outside on the boardwalk before following them. Eventually, they reached a two-story building, the bottom floor of which was a saloon. A faded sign read **ROOMS FOR RENT UPSTAIRS**. Danielle watched the pair ascend the outside stairs, waiting for a lamp to be lighted in one of the rooms. Lamplight soon flooded one of the front rooms facing the street. Since the two had returned to their room instead of going on to other saloons, Danielle didn't expect them to leave again before the next morning. When they did, she would be waiting for them. She returned to the Delaney house, finding Ethel on the front porch.

"Come set with me awhile," Ethel Delaney invited.

"Maybe later," said Danielle. "I promised my horse some grain."

She walked on around the house to the stable, and the chestnut mare nickered as she drew near. She grained Sundown and then drew enough water from the well to half-fill the horse trough. She then returned to the front porch and sat down in a cane-bottom rocking chair.

"I thought I heard shooting a while ago," Ethel said.

"You likely did," said Danielle. "A couple of drunks. I reckon nobody got hurt."

"Wouldn't be nothin' done about it if somebody had been killed," Ethel said. "You met Sam Duro?"

"Yes," said Danielle cautiously.

"He's a disgrace to the star that he wears," Ethel said. "Outlaws get run out of other towns, and they come here."

"I heard that," Ephiram said, joining them.

"I don't care," said Ethel. "It's the truth. I think they pay Sam Duro to leave them be. I wish a company of rangers would come here and clean up this town."

"Would do no good," Ephiram said. "Damn outlaws would just ride into Mexico and hole up there until the rangers were gone. Who are you after, son? Maybe we've heard of him."

He had caught Danielle entirely by surprise, and she was forced to gather her thoughts before she replied.

"Who says I'm looking for anybody?"

Ephiram laughed. "I do. You don't pack them two guns for show. I figure you got to be a peace officer or a bounty hunter. In either case, this is your kind of town."

"Ephiram," said Ethel, "when are you goin' to learn to mind your own business?"

"No offense intended," Ephiram said sheepishly.

"None taken," said Danielle, "but you're wrong. I'm no lawman and no bounty hunter."

She had already told Sheriff Sam Duro her purpose for being in town, and could think of no reason why she shouldn't tell these friendly people the truth. Quickly, she did.

"I can't do nothin' about it," Ephiram said, "but I hear things. This Snakehead Kalpana was here, but he's spooked after shootin' that ranger in Laredo. He's somewhere on the other side of the border, and God only knows how many other outlaws are with him. You don't aim to ride into Mexico after him, do you?"

"Not unless there's no other way," said Danielle. "I overheard two men talking in one of the saloons a while ago, and Kalpana's name was mentioned. They're waiting for him, and startin' tomorrow, I aim to follow them."

"Watch your back, son," Ephiram said. "There's talk around town that the McCandless boy's gunning for you."

"Reece McCandless?" Ethel asked. "What on earth for?"

Ephiram laughed. "I forgot to tell you. Our young friend Daniel here was in one of the saloons where Reece McCandless was mistreating a saloon woman. Old Reece got himself buffaloed with the muzzle of a Colt, and he was laughed out of the saloon."

"I have no patience with women who work in saloons," said Ethel. "She was likely just getting what she deserved."

"Sorry," Danielle said, "but no woman deserves being mistreated by a bully."

"The McCandless family is a vicious flock of buzzards," said Ephiram. "Reese is the only son, and it's shameful what he gets by with in this town. Long as you're here, you'd better ride carefully."

"I aim to," Danielle said. "I may have a long day tomorrow, so I think I'll turn in."

BROWNSVILLE, TEXAS. DECEMBER 18, 1870.

Danielle was up and about well before breakfast time at the Delaneys', so she stopped to eat at one of the many cafés. While she was eating, she felt eyes upon her. Looking up quickly, she recognized the face at the window as that of the girl she had rescued from Reece McCandless. Just as quickly, the face was gone. Danielle paid for her breakfast and left the café, looking in both directions along the deserted street. She started along the main street's boardwalk to the old house to which she had followed the outlaws the night before.

"Look out, cowboy," a voice shouted.

Danielle went down on her left side, rolling off the boardwalk into the dusty street as shots rang out. She drew her right-hand Colt as she fell and, belly down, began returning fire. But her assailant was firing from cover, the slugs kicking up dust all around her. Lead splintered the hitch rail over her head while others slammed into the front wall of a store that had not yet opened for the day. It was a shoot-or-be-shot situation, and Danielle's only hope lay in rooting the bushwhacker out into the open. He had a Henry or a Winchester, for slugs kept coming, screaming closer with each volley. Danielle rolled to her knees and sprang to her feet. She ran, zigzagging her way toward the gunman's position. From the powder smoke, she found him firing from the window of a vacant building that faced the street. Danielle fired twice, and her lead came close enough to spook the bushwhacker. The firing from the window ceased. Danielle reloaded and holstered her Colt. The girl who had warned her stood fearfully in a doorway.

"I'm obliged to you," Danielle said. "I don't suppose you know who that was."

"Reece McCandless," said the girl. "He's been telling everybody who will listen that he intends to kill you."

"He won't if I kill him first," Danielle said. "What's your name?"

"Mary," said the girl. "If you kill him, old Simon McCandless will have every gunman in town after you. You'd better ride away while there's still time."

"When I'm ready, Danielle said, "and I'm not ready."

She continued along the boardwalk until she was across the street from the old house to which she had followed the two outlaws the night before. It would have been far simpler if Kalpana came to them, she thought. Otherwise, she might have to trail them across the border. Danielle took up a position behind a vacant building. From there she could observe the stairway to the second floor of the house across the street. When the duo finally left, Danielle followed them, only to find they had gone out for breakfast. Finished, they returned to their room and Danielle saw no more of them the rest of the day. Not being in a mood for further conversation with the Delaneys, she returned to the Border Saloon, where her trouble with McCandless had begun. It was barely dark outside, but the place seemed unusually crowded. Sheriff Sam Duro was there, and to her surprise, so was Reece McCandless. It was he who was shouting angrily.

"Damn you, I'll have your badge for this. I've been here all afternoon, and I got plenty of witnesses to prove it."

"Maybe," said Sheriff Duro, "but somebody slit that girl's throat, and I can't think of anybody with more reason than you."

"Whose throat's been slit?" Danielle asked.

"Mary," said a bystander. "You saved her from McCandless last night."

It was more than Danielle could stand. She approached Reece McCandless, and everybody backed away, including Sheriff Duro. When she spoke, her voice was like ice.

"You've been threatening to kill me, and you tried to back-shoot me this morning. All that saved me was Mary's shouted warning, and you got even with her for that, didn't you?"

"I don't have to answer your damn questions," McCandless said. "You ain't the law."

"No," said Danielle, "and for that reason, I only have to answer to my own conscience. I hear you've been threatening to kill me, and I'm going to offer you the chance. But this time you won't be under cover, trying to shoot me in the back. It's light enough outside. I'll meet you in the street."

"I won't do it," McCandless bawled. "I didn't shoot you this morning, and I ain't said nothin' about shootin' you."

"The hell you ain't," a salty-looking bystander said.

There were shouts of agreement from other men, and not liking the turn the situation was taking, Sheriff Duro yelled for quiet. Then he spoke to Danielle.

"You can't accuse a man of trying to bushwhack you without evidence, and you have only your suspicions. Get out of here and go about your business."

"I'm getting out," Danielle said, "but McCandless has threatened to kill me. Now I aim to offer him the satisfaction of doing just that if he's man enough to face me."

It became an intolerable situation for Reece McCandless as men shouted their approval. If a man was called out and refused to go, he was branded forevermore a coward. Those in the saloon began to bull-rag him while Sheriff Duro tried in vain to stop it. Danielle stepped out on the boardwalk, looking over the saloon's batwing doors. McCandless was literally shoved toward the door and out onto the boardwalk. Danielle waited on the other side of the street, then issued a challenge.

"When you're ready, McCandless, make your play."

"I'm no gunfighter," McCandless whined. "I won't do it."

"You cowardly, back-shootin' coyote," said Danielle, "the next time you come after me, you'd better make it good, or I'll kill you."

It was a calculated risk, and Danielle took it. For a split second, she turned her back on Reece McCandless, and then she did something none of the onlookers had ever witnessed before. She whirled, drawing her right-hand Colt as she did so, and dropped to one knee. Three times McCandless fired, the slugs zipping over Danielle's head. She fired once, and the force of it slammed McCandless back against a hitch rail. The rail broke, and McCandless fell to the boardwalk on his back.

"Damn you," Sheriff Duro shouted, "I ought to lock you up for forcing a gunfight."

"I don't think so, Sheriff," said Danielle. "Would you have jailed McCandless if I'd let him back-shoot me?"

It was a question Sheriff Sam Duro dared not answer. Red-faced, he started up the boardwalk toward his office. But as he rounded a corner and out of sight of those who had witnessed the gunfight, he headed straight for the town's bank and the office of old Simon McCandless. Somebody had to tell McCandless that his cowardly son had been gunned down while trying to shoot another man in the back. Sheriff Duro sighed. Hell was about to break loose, with the lid off and all the fires lit, and there was nothing he could do.

CHAPTER 17

Nobody spoke to Danielle after Reece McCandless had tried to shoot her in the back and had been gunned down. It was an undeniable case of self-defense, for McCandless had fired three times before Danielle had gotten off a shot. Nobody followed Danielle, and she had no idea what to expect. She stopped across the street, watching the house where she hoped there were two outlaws who might lead her to Snakehead Kalpana.

Sheriff Duro had no stomach for what lay ahead, but he had little choice. Somebody had to tell Simon McCandless that his gutless son had been gunned down after he'd tried to shoot another man in the back. Duro knocked on the door.

"Who is it?" McCandless asked.

"Sheriff Duro."

"Come on in," said McCandless gruffly as Duro closed the door behind him. "Now whatever you have to say, speak up. Don't waste my time with trivial things you could have taken care of yourself."

"Some things I don't do," Sheriff Duro said, "and standin' between two *hombres* with guns is one of 'em. That loudmouth boy of yours just got himself shot dead after he tried to shoot another man in the back."

Simon McCandless's expression didn't change. He was overweight, with gray eyebrows, gray hair, and a ruddy complexion. Kicking back his chair, he got up and walked to the window. For a long moment he looked out, seething, and when he again turned to Sheriff Duro, his face was white with rage.

"Just where the hell were *you* when this was taking place?" he thundered.

"Watching Reece go up against the fastest gun I've ever seen," said Sheriff Duro. "He started it, and besides being a damned fool, he was a coward, too."

"Nobody guns down my boy and lives to talk about it," McCandless shouted. "Nobody. Do you understand that?"

"I understand that it was a more than a fair fight," said Sheriff Duro. "Reece had a mad on because when he was stripping a girl in a saloon, this young gunfighter buffaloed him. It didn't do a hell of a lot for the McCandless image. Since then, the saloon girl has had her throat cut, and I think we have the brave Reece McCandless to thank for that."

"Are you done?" McCandless asked in a low, dangerous voice.

"For the time being," said Sheriff Duro. "I put up with a lot in this damn town, but I won't side with a yellow, back-shootin' coward, even if he is a McCandless."

"Then you just tell me who this young gun thrower is," McCandless said, "and I'll see that he pays."

"His name is Daniel Strange," said Sheriff Duro. "He's after the outlaws who murdered his pa in Indian Territory. Snakehead Kalpana's one of them."

"Kalpana's the gun-happy bastard who shot a ranger in Laredo," McCandless said, "and you let him hang around here?"

"Hell, I didn't know about the ranger in Laredo," said Sheriff Duro. "You ain't in the habit of checking references on none of these owlhoots. Why should Kalpana be that much different from the others?"

"He shot a ranger, and the rest of them will trail Kalpana all the way to hell and then go in after him," McCandless said. "Where is he now?"

"Across the river," said Sheriff Duro. "Dirk and Malo, a couple of his *amigos*, have a room here in town. I reckon they'll know where he is."

"Then get them," McCandless said, "and see that they take a message to Kalpana. Tell him there's a gunfighter in town looking for him, and unless he gets rid of this troublesome kid, he'll get no protection from me."

"Suppose the kid, Daniel Strange, guns down Kalpana?"

"Then you can report to the rangers that Snakehead Kalpana's dead," McCandless said, "and that ought to keep the law off our backs."

"And if Kalpana guns down this Daniel Strange?"

"He will have paid for murdering my son," said McCandless, "and I'll see that Snakehead Kalpana is put where his reputation won't harm us."

"So either Snakehead Kalpana or Daniel Strange is to die in a gunfight," Sheriff Duro said, "and you aim to take care of the survivor."

"In my own way," said McCandless. "If this Daniel Strange survives a shoot-out with Snakehead Kalpana, he *still* must pay for killing my son. As long as Kalpana's alive, we're up against the possibility the rangers will come looking for him. I'm sure they'll be asking some embarrassing questions. It'll be better for us if Daniel Strange guns Kalpana down. It'll take ranger eyes off us, and I can still see that Daniel Strange pays. Now get out of here and find those men who have been riding with Kalpana."

All Danielle's suspicions of Sheriff Duro were confirmed when she saw the lawman mount the outside stairs of the boardinghouse she was watching. Sheriff Duro knocked on the door, it opened, and he entered. Danielle would have given all her worth to hear what was being said. Sheriff Duro wasted no time.

"One or both of you have to ride across the river and find Snakehead Kalpana. You do know where he is, don't you?"

"Maybe," said Dirk cautiously.

"Damn it," Duro shouted, "you either know or you don't. Which is it?"

"All right," said Dirk, "we can find him, but he ain't the kind to spook easy. What do we tell him?"

"Tell him there's a young gunfighter in town gunning for him," Sheriff Duro said. "If Kalpana don't shut this kid up, we'll have the rangers after us. McCandless said if Kalpana don't ride over here and cut the kid's string, that he can stay in Mexico until he croaks because he won't get protection from us. You knew Kalpana killed a ranger in Laredo."

"Well . . . uh . . . yes," said Malo, "but that's a long ways from here."

"Not when it concerns the death of a ranger," Sheriff Duro said. "Now get going. We want Kalpana on this side of the river when he faces Daniel Strange."

"That ain't hard to figure out," said Dirk. "You figure this young gunslinger can take Kalpana. Then you'll turn his carcass over to the rangers so's they don't show up here."

"Don't do too much thinking," Sheriff Duro said. "You ain't equipped for it. Just tell Kalpana this kid's got vengeance on his mind and a draw as quick as a rattler. Kalpana's finished here unless he guns down this troublesome kid."

With that, Sheriff Duro stepped out the door, closing it behind him. He had no doubts that Dirk and Malo could find Kalpana, for they had ridden with him from Laredo after Kalpana had gunned down the ranger.

"What you reckon we ought to do?" Malo asked after Sheriff Duro had gone.

"We got to find Kalpana," said Dirk. "He's a marked man. If

he can gun down this Daniel Strange, we can hide out here a while longer."

Danielle watched Sheriff Duro descend the stairs, mount his horse, and ride away. Sundown was picketed nearby, and Danielle led the chestnut mare back to her vantage point, where she could see the outside stairs. Sheriff Duro had been gone only a few minutes when the two men she had been watching descended the stairs. Danielle watched them go to the nearest livery, which was two blocks away. When they rode out, she followed, keeping them in sight, but far enough behind that they wouldn't grow suspicious. The duo kept to side streets, and it soon became apparent they were headed for the river. Danielle followed them, convinced they were on their way to warn Snakehead Kalpana. Having the rangers after him, as well as a vindictive gunfighter, might convince him to remain in old Mexico, and Danielle couldn't abide that. She was breaking the law just crossing the border, and a gunfight with Kalpana could get her thrown into a Mexican prison. Still, she followed, not sure as to how she would get past the border sentries. But there were no sentries, and no evidence there ever had been. It seemed the border was open to Mexican and American outlaws, the alliance being sanctioned by corrupt officials on both sides of the border.

In less than an hour, the two men Danielle was trailing reined up before a crude cabin. A tendril of smoke trailed from the mud-and-stick chimney. A single horse stood outside on a picket rope. One of the two men pounded on the door.

"Who is there?" demanded a voice from inside.

"Dirk and Malo," said one of the men loud enough for Danielle to hear. "We got a message for you."

The door was opened, and Dirk and Malo entered. They wasted no time.

"There's a young gunfighter, Daniel Strange, looking for you," Dirk said. "Sheriff Duro brought the word from old man McCandless that if you don't silence this damn kid, you'll be stuck in Mexico for the rest of your life."

"Perhaps it is a trap to lure me into the hands of the rangers," Kalpana said. "Could this Daniel Strange be one of them?"

"No," said Dirk. "This kid ain't even old enough to shave. He told Sheriff Duro you're one of a bunch of outlaws that robbed and hanged his pa in Indian Territory."

Kalpana laughed. "And he seeks revenge. Well, my *amigos*, he will have his chance. Then you can bury him."

Dirk and Malo shuddered, for they had seen Snakehead Kalpana in action. He carried two thonged-down revolvers and could draw and shoot with either hand. He was as fast as the serpent whose name he had taken.

"Then saddle up and let's ride," said Dirk. "I always get the feeling these *Mejicanos* are watching us. It gives me the creeps."

Kalpana took his saddlebags, and the trio went out. Dirk and Malo waited until Kalpana had saddled his horse. Mounting, the three of them rode north. Following, Danielle sighed with relief. She had every reason to believe the third man was Snakehead Kalpana, and it appeared, for whatever reason, that he was riding back across the border into Texas. She would have gunned down Kalpana south of the border, had there been no other way, but the threat of Mexican prison was very real. Now Danielle concerned herself with where Kalpana would go once he reached Brownsville.

"What do you aim to do first?" Malo asked Kalpana.

"I aim to have me a talk with old man McCandless," said Kalpana. "I ain't takin' orders from that old buzzard."

"Then you ride on over to the bank and have it out with him," Dirk said. "We already locked horns with him once."

The three outlaws separated, Dirk and Malo riding back toward their rooming house. Virtually certain the third man was Kalpana, Danielle followed him. He reined up outside the bank, tied his horse to the hitch rail, and went inside. When he reached McCandless's office, he didn't bother knocking. Closing the door behind him, his cold, hard eyes met those of Simon McCandless.

"Don't you *ever* again walk into my office without knocking," McCandless hissed.

Kalpana laughed. "You scare the hell out of me, old man."

McCandless struggled to control himself. However arrogant and disagreeable Kalpana was, McCandless had need of him. He swallowed hard, managing to speak in a near normal tone of voice.

"There's a loudmouth kid gunning for you. Not only does he have a damn good reason, but he's seen fit to tell others why he's after you. Now you got two choices. You can gun down this Daniel Strange, or you can ride out of Brownsville and keep going."

"You wasn't so high and mighty when Malo, Dirk, and me rode in," said Kalpana. "You was only too glad to take a cut from the horses we sold after running 'em across the river from Mexico."

"That was before I learned you had killed a ranger in Laredo," McCandless said. "That put a considerable price on your head, and one way or another, this Daniel Strange knows you're here. If he keeps shootin' off his mouth about you and what you done in Indian Territory, we'll have the rangers in here. I don't aim for that to happen. Now you can silence this Daniel Strange, or you can get the hell out of here. What's it gonna be?"

"I got a feeling Dirk and Malo didn't tell me everything," Kalpana said. "Why don't you tell me the *real* reason you want me to cut this gun thrower's string?"

"Besides spreading the word that you—a ranger killer and first-class bastard—are in town, he shot and killed Reece, my only son."

Kalpana laughed. "Why? Was your kid playin' with his marbles, or did he stand up on his hind legs like the big boys do?"

Again McCandless struggled to control his temper. Lying would gain him nothing, for Kalpana would learn the truth. Finally, he spoke.

"Reece got into a quarrel with this Daniel Strange, and pulled a gun," McCandless said. "The kid carries two guns, and he's fast as greased lightning."

"There's a chance he might be faster than me, then," said Kalpana. "I don't aim to risk my neck just to avenge your idiot son, and I can't see it's to my advantage to silence this Daniel Strange. If the town ends up neck-deep in rangers, I can just ride on. It'll be you and your pet sheriff that get kicked off your thrones."

Things weren't going right at all. Snakehead Kalpana had stayed alive by always being a cut above the average outlaw. Mc-Candless sighed and spoke.

"All right, I'll admit my argument with Daniel Strange is two-fold. I want him silenced permanently before he endangers my position here, and I want him to pay for killing my son. I'll pay you five hundred dollars."

"Double that," Kalpana said, "and we'll talk."

"Half now, and half when the job's done," said McCandless.

"Deal," Kalpana said. "Show me your money."

From a desk drawer, McCandless took a small canvas sack and he counted out twenty-five gold double eagles. He shoved the money across the desk to Kalpana.

"Now," said McCandless, "when do you aim to take care of him?"

"Soon as I can find him and force him to pull iron," Kalpana said.

Kalpana then left the office, mounted his horse, and rode back to join his companions, Dirk and Malo. Danielle followed. Kalpana reached the boardinghouse, mounted the outside stairs, and knocked on the door. He was let in, and Danielle settled down to wait. Whatever the trio did, it seemed highly unlikely they would remain in their room very long.

"Well," said Dirk when Kalpana entered, "I see you met the old grizzly and come out with a whole hide."

"I done considerably better than that," Kalpana boasted. "Mc-Candless wants this Daniel Strange to pay for killing that fool kid, Reece. He wants it bad enough to pay me for the job. That's a thousand in gold."

"That's somethin' to your credit," said Dirk, "provided this kid don't kill *you*. He's as fast as anybody I've ever seen, and he leads a charmed life."

"Yeah," Malo agreed, "and I reckon McCandless didn't tell you that his fool kid tried to shoot Strange in the back. McCandless wouldn't draw, and when Strange turned his back on McCandless, the yellow coyote went for his gun. But Strange was expecting that. He hit the dirt, and all three shots McCandless fired missed. Then the kid shot him dead."

"He won't have to worry about turning his back on me," said Kalpana. "I'll face him in an even fight. Where do I find him?"

"Generally at the Border Saloon," Dirk said. "He's as lucky at the faro table as he is behind a gun."

"The saloon don't open for another two hours," said Malo. "You might as well take a rest until then."

D anielle waited impatiently, realizing the trio probably wouldn't venture out until the saloons opened. In Brownsville there was absolutely nothing to do except frequent the saloons to drink and gamble. It was a few minutes past noon when the trio left on foot. By the time they reached town, the saloons would be open. Reaching the Border, they went inside. Danielle waited a few minutes before following. She went in through the batwing doors, stepping aside until her eyes grew accustomed to the dim interior. Besides the trio of outlaws who had just entered, there were four other men bellied up to the bar.

"That's Daniel Strange that just come in," Dirk said quietly. "He must have followed Malo and me across the border and then followed the three of us back to Brownsville. He must want you almighty bad."

"I'm still not convinced he ain't a ranger," said Kalpana, "but they can't string me up any higher for killing a second one. You, there by the door. I'm Kalpana, and I hear you have been looking for me. Is it asking too much for you to tell me why, *señor*?"

When Danielle spoke, her voice was low and deadly, and even in the gloom of the saloon, her eyes were like green fire.

"You and your bunch of yellow coyotes hanged my pa in Indian

Territory last spring. I'm going to give you more of a chance than you gave him."

"No gunplay in here," the barkeep shouted, taking a sawed-off shotgun from beneath the bar. "I'll cut down the first one of you makin' a move. Take your fight outside."

None of the three outlaws moved. Quickly, Danielle stepped through the batwing doors to the boardwalk outside. Crossing to the other side of the dusty street, she leaned against a hitch rail, waiting. Snakehead Kalpana stepped out on the boardwalk, his two companions moving out of the line of fire. Something about an impending disaster drew men like flies to a honey jug, and observers were already everywhere, some of them looking out upstairs windows for a better view.

"When you're ready, Kalpana," said Danielle, still leaning against the hitch rail.

A chill crept up Kalpana's spine. The kid was just too confident. But Kalpana had taken money for the job, and he had placed himself in a position where he dared not back down.

"This will be a fair fight," Sheriff Duro shouted. "Any man pullin' a gun besides these two and I'll gun you down myself."

Most of the observers were aware that Kalpana was an undesirable who had killed a Texas Ranger, and they waited in anticipation. Eyes darted from Kalpana to Danielle and back again. Danielle made no move, for Kalpana had issued the challenge. It would be up to him when he chose to draw. Finally, just when it appeared he might not draw, he did. He was fast. Incredibly fast. But Danielle Strange was faster. Without seeming to move, the butt-forward Colt from her left hip was in her hand, spouting flame. Her first slug ripped into Kalpana's chest as he pulled the trigger, and his shot went wild. Stumbling backward, he leaned against the saloon's front wall, raising his Colt. Danielle fired again, and Kalpana collapsed on the boardwalk. Her eyes on the bystanders, Danielle punched out the empty shell casings and reloaded her Colt, returning the weapon to its holster on her left hip.

There was murmuring among the crowd who had observed the

fight, and Danielle chose to wait until it subsided before making a move. Sheriff Duro came to her aid.

"All of you break it up and get back to what you was doing," Duro shouted.

Dirk and Malo stared in disbelief at the body of Snakehead Kalpana.

"By God, I wouldn't have believed it if I hadn't seen it," Dirk said.

"Me neither," said Malo. "I've never seen a cross-hand draw as fast as that. I wouldn't go up against that little hellion with anything less than a Gatling gun."

Sheriff Duro had Kalpana's body taken to the carpenter shop, where a coffin would be built. He then returned to the bank building and knocked on the door to McCandless's office.

"Come in," McCandless said.

Sheriff Duro closed the door before he spoke.

"Kalpana's dead," said Sheriff Duro. "This Daniel Strange is the fastest gun I ever saw. He didn't get a scratch. What do we do now?"

"Kalpana had five hundred dollars of my money in gold," McCandless said. "I want it back."

"I took it off him," said Sheriff Duro, digging a handful of coins from his pocket.

The sheepish look on Duro's face told McCandless that the sheriff had intended to keep the money, but McCandless let it pass. Feeling the need to change the subject, it was the sheriff who spoke.

"Strange has done what he come here to do. He'll be leaving."

"He won't be goin' anywhere," McCandless said. "I want you to find me a dozen men, all good with guns. I'll pay fifty dollars a day and provide ammunition. The man who guns down Daniel Strange gets a thousand-dollar bonus."

"Kalpana was no slouch with a Colt," said Sheriff Duro, "and him layin' dead may make it hard as hell finding gunmen to go after the kid."

"I'm leaving that up to you, and I want it done today," Mc-Candless said. "We have to get the kid before he rides on."

"I'll do the best I can," said Sheriff Duro. "You want me to send these *hombres* to see you?"

"Hell no," McCandless growled. "The last thing I want is a bunch of killers coming to and from here." He handed Sheriff Duro a canvas sack. "There's six hundred and fifty dollars in here. That's enough for a first day's pay for a dozen men, and fifty dollars for you to buy the necessary ammunition."

It was clear enough, and Sheriff Duro had his hand on the doorknob when McCandless spoke again.

"One more thing. I want you to telegraph every Texas Ranger outpost. Tell them that Snakehead Kalpana, who killed the ranger in Laredo, is dead. That should keep them away from here."

"There's a price on his head," said Sheriff Duro. "Suppose they want proof?"

"Then they'll have to dig up his carcass and study it to their satisfaction," McCandless said. "If they got to know who killed him, all you know is that it was a gunslinger who was passing through and has since rode on."

"Yeah," said Sheriff Duro, "you're layin' it all on my back. The damn rangers are goin' to wonder how long Kalpana's been here, and why, when he got his, it was at the hand of another outlaw."

"Then damn it, tell the truth," McCandless snarled. "Tell 'em it was a revenge killing for Kalpana's part in a murder in Indian Territory. That won't reflect on us, and we'll see that they don't find Daniel Strange. Now get going."

Danielle returned to the Delaney house, let down and without any sense of triumph. It had been the anticipation of avenging her father's death that had led her on, but when a man, even the likes of Snakehead Kalpana, lay dead, she was strangely remorseful. To her mind came some Bible scripture she had learned

long ago: *Vengeance is mine, saith the Lord.* She found Ephiram and
Ethel Delaney on the front porch.

"We heard shootin'," Ephiram said. "We wondered if you was
involved."

"I was," said Danielle. "Snakehead Kalpana heard I was looking for him and came after me. I reckon I'll be ridin' on tomorrow."

"We'll miss you," Ethel said. "I hate to rent to this dirty, un-
washed bunch around here and from across the border. I'd swear
some of 'em ain't had a bath since the Flood."

"Wake me for supper," Danielle said. "I'm going upstairs to
rest."

"I didn't want to say anything," said Ephiram when Danielle
had gone, "but I simply can't believe old man McCandless won't
try something to avenge his no-account son. This young man,
Daniel Strange, ought to be riding out today, getting as far from
here as he can."

"It's curious you should speak of that," Ethel said. "I'm wondering if somebody didn't *pay* Kalpana to kill Daniel Strange. Someone with a reason for wanting Daniel dead."

"We know who that someone is," said Ephiram, "and it's best
we say no more about it. We got to live here."

Removing her boots, gun belts, and hat, Danielle stretched out
on the bed. Dead tired, she found herself unable to sleep, for a sense
of foreboding had her in its clutches and wouldn't let go. After
several hours she got up. Donning her hat, tugging on her boots,
and buckling on her gun belts, she went downstairs. There was no
sign of Ephiram, but Ethel was in the parlor.

"Do be careful," Ethel warned. "It may not be over."

"That's what I aim to find out," said Danielle. "I'll be back for
supper."

The town seemed strangely silent. Danielle visited some of the
saloons, receiving only curious looks. Meanwhile, Sheriff Duro
had a dozen hard-eyed men crammed into his small office. They
leaned against the walls, avoiding the windows. Every man packed
at least one revolver, while some had two.

"Fifty dollars a day, plus ammunition," Sheriff Duro said, "and I got your first day's pay. All you got to do is gun down this Daniel Strange. The *hombre* that cuts his string gets a thousand-dollar bonus."

"I reckon we know who's bankrollin' this," said one of the men. "I think the *hombre* we're bein' paid to kill done the town a favor. I ain't never liked McCandless's bigmouthed kid."

"Me neither," another man said.

"This is business," said Sheriff Duro. "Money business."

"Well, I ain't about to brace this Daniel Strange in no stand-up, face-to-face fight," one of the men said. "Kalpana was a fast gun, but he didn't have a prayer."

"Nobody said you got to face him," Sheriff Duro said. "Hell, there ain't nothin' honorable about bushwhacking a man. Shoot him in the back."

"I've seen some dirty, stinking, low-down coyotes in my day," said one of the men, "but this is the first time I've seen a lawman pay to have a man dry-gulched."

"This is a wide-open town," Sheriff Duro said, "and things are done different here. If it wasn't for me and certain others, the whole damn lot of you would be rotting behind bars somewhere. If this Daniel Strange is allowed to ride out of here, he's likely to go to the nearest ranger outpost and tell them he gunned down Kalpana. Rangers have a way of figurin' things out. They're likely to wonder how long Kalpana was here, without the law layin' a hand on him, and how many more there may be just like him."

"I reckon that makes sense," said one of the gunmen. "We got to stop the varmint."

There was mostly agreement among the rest of the outlaws, except for Malo and Dirk.

"Duro," said Dirk, "you'd better be right. If I end up with my neck in a noose, I aim to see that you're hanging beside me from the same damn limb."

"Damn right," Malo said. "You ain't pullin' the trigger, but you're as much a killer as any one of us."

Sheriff Duro swallowed hard. If the worst happened and Daniel Strange escaped, the town might be invaded by a company of Texas Rangers. Simon McCandless had wisely used Duro to arrange the killing of Daniel Strange, and would in no way be implicated, unless Sheriff Duro talked. He quickly reached the unhappy conclusion that even if he talked, he would still be neck-deep in trouble. There was no way he could accuse McCandless of anything without admitting that he, Duro, had arranged it.

CHAPTER 18

BROWNSVILLE, TEXAS. DECEMBER 21, 1870.

Danielle lay down across the bed to rest, and the longer she lay there, the more she was sure that Kalpana had been brought back across the border to kill her. His having failed in no way lessened her danger, and she sat up, then tugged on her boots. She would leave Brownsville tonight, taking word of the situation there to the Texas Rangers in San Antonio. But she had waited too long. There was a knock on her door, and answering it, she looked into the frightened face of Ethel Delaney.

"Daniel, there's a group of horsemen across the street watching the house. Ephiram believes they've come after you."

"I reckon he's right," said Danielle."I should already have ridden out. Now I'll have to face up to them."

"But they're here to kill you," Ethel protested. "You can't go out there."

"I can, and I will," said Danielle. "They haven't yet surrounded the house, but there may be men watching the back door. Is there a way out without going through the front or back doors?"

"Through the cellar," Ethel said. "Come on, I'll show you."

Carrying a lighted coal-oil lamp, Ethel Delaney led the way down the stairs from the kitchen to the cellar below. The door was barred from the inside, and Ethel lifted the bar.

"As soon as I'm out," said Danielle, "put that bar back in place."

"Go with God," Ethel said through her sobs.

Danielle stepped out into the night. There was no moon, and she could hear the mutter of voices across the street. Finally, there came a challenge.

"We want Daniel Strange," a voice shouted. "If we have to come in and get him, you Delaneys are gonna be sorry."

"He's been expecting you," Ephiram said, "and he ain't here."

"Duke," said the voice across the street, "look in the stable behind the house and see if his horse is gone."

Duke made his way around the house, his Colt drawn. Danielle stepped out of the darkness behind him, slamming the muzzle of her Colt against the back of his head. Without a sound, he collapsed. Taking his revolver, Danielle slipped it under her waistband, then waited. Her next move would depend on the men hunting her.

"Damn it, Duke," a voice shouted impatiently, "what's keepin' you?"

Only silence greeted him, and Danielle could hear angry voices. Obviously, the men were deciding what they should do next, and the gruff voice that had spoken before again threatened the Delaneys.

"You Delaneys, we're goin' to surround the house. You got ten minutes to get Daniel Strange out here. If you don't, we'll set the place afire and drive him out."

There was no reply from either of the Delaneys, and Danielle knew she couldn't allow them to suffer for her deeds. She moved away from the house into the shadow of a huge oak tree. Finding a stone the size of her fist, she waited until two of the men began to make their way along her side of the house. Once they were past her, she threw the stone against the side of the house. The two men whirled, firing at the sound. Danielle fired at their muzzle flashes, and they fell, groaning.

"The bastard ain't in the house!" a voice shouted. "He's shot Turk and Bender."

Danielle heard the sound of running feet and stepped back into the shadow of the oak. Her trick had worked once, but it would not a second time. There would be too many of them, and before she could cut them all down, some of them would be shooting at *her* muzzle flashes. Six men crept through the shadows alongside the house.

"Damn it," said one of them, "here's Duke, and he's out colder than a bullfrog."

One of the pair Danielle had shot groaned, drawing their attention.

"A couple of you help Turk and Bender back to the horses," a voice commanded.

"Bender's dead, and Turk's hard hit," said another voice.

"Then take their carcasses away, and then get the hell back over here."

Danielle waited until the two fallen men had been removed. She then stood behind the huge trunk of the oak and issued a challenge of her own.

"You're covered. Drop your guns."

The four drew and began firing. Lead slammed into the oak. Danielle, leaning to one side, fired around the trunk at the muzzle flashes. She then hit the ground, rolling into a new position, belly down.

"Oh, God," a voice moaned, "I'm gutshot!"

Two of the men were down, and the other two stood there, waiting. They well knew their muzzle flashes could be their undoing. Slowly, they began to back away toward the front of the house, and Danielle let them go. When they reached the far side of the street, an argument ensued, and Danielle was sure she recognized the gruff voice of Sheriff Sam Duro.

"Sheriff," Danielle taunted, "you're done. The rest of you men, if you come after me, be prepared to die."

"Come on, damn it," Duro bawled to the rest of the men, "we're goin' after him."

But only two of the men followed. Dirk and Malo mounted their horses. They left town, riding north. Two other men watched them uncertainly. Then, mounting their horses, they followed Dirk and Malo. As Sheriff Duro and his two companions crept alongside the house, there was a shadow directly ahead of them. The unconscious Duke had staggered to his feet, only to have Sheriff Sam Duro cut him down at close range. It was all Danielle needed. She fired at the muzzle flash, and the force of the slug slammed Duro against the side of the house. He slumped to the ground, and the two men who had accompanied him ran back the way they had come. Seconds later, there was the thud of hooves as the survivors of the ill-fated ambush galloped away. Danielle walked around the house, mounted the porch, and knocked on the door. Ethel Delaney opened it.

"Is it over?" Ethel asked fearfully.

"Not quite," said Danielle. "I want to get my saddlebags, and then I want to talk to Ephiram."

When Danielle came back down the stairs, the Delaneys were waiting in the parlor.

"There are at least six men wounded or dead," Danielle said. "Sheriff Sam Duro is one of the dead, but he's not the head of this damn snake. Ephiram, who is the man who runs this town?"

"Simon McCandless," said Ephiram.

"That explains a lot of things," Danielle said. "He brought Kalpana in to gun me down and, failing in that, sent Duro after me with a bunch of killers. Where am I likely to find McCandless?"

"He's got an office at the rear of the bank," said Ephiram, "but he lives at a hotel. It's the Rio, I think."

"He'll be at the office, then, waiting to hear that I'm dead," Danielle said. "I'll be back for my horse."

She stepped out the door, leaving the Delaneys speechless.

The bank building, having three floors, was the tallest building in Brownsville. There was a back door, and to one side of it a coal-oil bracket lamp burned. Danielle turned the knob, and the door opened on silent hinges. At the end of a short hall was yet another door with lamplight bleeding out beneath it. Danielle made no noise, for the hall was carpeted. Standing to one side of the door, she turned the knob. When the latch let go, she kicked the door open, slamming it against the wall. Simon McCandless sat behind the big desk, staring at her unbelievingly.

"Your pet sheriff's dead, McCandless," said Danielle, "along with some of the other owlhoots you sent after me. The rest of them ran like the yellow coyotes they are. Since you want me dead, do your worst. It's just you and me, McCandless."

"You've got sand, kid," McCandless said, "and I wouldn't kill you if there was another way. But you gunned down my boy, and as soon you could get to a ranger outpost, I think you'd tell the rangers all about me. What do you aim to do with me?"

"I'm going to put you on a horse and take you to the rangers," said Danielle. "I want them to see the daddy skunk in the flesh, and then I want to hear your excuses as you try to save your miserable hide. Get up. We're riding out tonight."

"You won't deny me a last cigar, will you?" McCandless asked.

"Go ahead," said Danielle. "Just be damn careful what you do with your hands."

McCandless opened a desk drawer and took out a cigar box. Danielle was barely in time, dropping to one knee as McClandless raised a Colt from the box and fired twice. The lead went over Danielle's head, splintering the door behind her. Danielle drew and fired twice, and McCandless was driven back into his swivel chair. He lay there, blood pumping out on his white ruffled shirt. He was trying to speak, and Danielle leaned across the desk.

"We'd have . . . made . . . an unbeatable team, kid. Too bad . . . you was on . . . the other side. . . ."

Those were his last words, and Danielle left him there. The town had some cleaning up to do before the rangers rode in.

The Delaneys were still in the parlor when Danielle got back to the house. They waited for her to speak.

"McCandless drew on me, and he's dead," said Danielle. "You decent folks in town had better get together and take control of things. I aim to report all this to the rangers just as soon as I reach San Antonio. There must be one honest man you can elect sheriff, and I hope your bank's got no more skunk-striped varmints like McCandless."

"McCandless has kept the town terrorized and under his thumb for years," Ephiram said. "Without him and his hired guns, we'll manage, I think. But tell the rangers we'll be welcoming them, just in case there are some undesirables who don't want to leave."

"I'll tell them," said Danielle. "I'm going to saddle my horse and be on my way."

"I hate to see you go, Daniel," Ethel said.

"In a way, I hate to go," said Danielle, "but I still have some manhunting to do."

Danielle saddled Sundown and, mounting, rode north toward San Antonio. It was more than two hundred miles, and she took her time, for it was a two-day ride.

SAN ANTONIO, TEXAS. DECEMBER 23, 1870.

Danielle rode in just before sundown on her second day out of Brownsville. She hoped to find Captain Jennings in his office, for it was important that the rangers reach Brownsville before the rustlers and killers had time to reorganize. Jennings was there and made no move to conceal his pleasure when Danielle entered the office.

"Captain," Danielle said, "we have to talk. There's been hell to pay in Brownsville, and the decent folks there are going to need some help."

"Then let's go eat," said Jennings. "Supper's on me."

They went to a small café where the ranger was known, and since it was early, there were few other patrons. While they waited for their food, sipping coffee, Danielle told her story.

"I thought there was something unusual about the telegram informing me that Kalpana had been gunned down," said Jennings. "It carefully avoided telling me who actually did the shooting, but I suspected it was you."

"I don't think I'd have had a chance at him," Danielle said, "if I hadn't been forced to shoot Reece McCandless. I think after Reece was shot, Simon McCandless hoped Kalpana could finish me. When he failed to, Sheriff Duro and maybe a dozen men came looking for me. In the dark, Duro shot one of his own men. I accounted for five others, including the sheriff himself."

"There's nothing worse than a lawman selling out," said Captain Jennings. "I'll need the names of some honest folks in Brownsville who will stand behind what you've told me. Not that I doubt you, but the rangers who'll be riding down there will find it helpful in getting at the truth of it."

"Ephiram and Ethel Delaney," said Danielle. "They stood by me through it all, even as Sheriff Duro threatened to burn their house to drive me out."

"We'll talk to them," Captain Jennings said. "I'll have two rangers on their way in the morning."

Their food was ready, and Danielle ate hungrily, for she had eaten little, the situation in Brownsville bearing on her mind. When they were down to final cups of coffee, Captain Jennings spoke.

"It's interesting, what you've told me about Simon McCandless. I've heard of him. He was one of the carpetbaggers who moved in after the war, and I suspect he may have been wanted by the law somewhere up north. I aim to find out. By the way, there's a three-thousand-dollar price on Kalpana's head, dead or alive. I aim to see that you get it."

"I don't really want it," Danielle said. "You know why I was after Kalpana. The reward had nothing to do with it."

"I know that," said Captain Jennings, "but I want you to have it. If you don't need it, send it to your ma and your brothers in Missouri. It's been hard times there, too."

"You're a thoughtful man, Captain," Danielle said. "That's exactly what I'll do."

"It'll take maybe a week to get the money," said Captain Jennings. "Why don't you just rest here for a few days until I make the arrangements?"

"I'm thinking of riding back to Waco," Danielle said.

"Rucker's still sheriff there," said Captain Jennings, "and it'll be the same old Mexican standoff all over again. There's still too many folks around who haven't gotten over the war, and they resist all authority, even to hiding their outlaw kin."

"I know," Danielle said, "but when I return, I won't be the same *hombre* who rode in there before."

"Disguise?"

"Yes," said Danielle, thinking of the female clothing in her saddlebag.

"Since you'll be in town for a few days," Captain Jennings said, "how do you aim to spend Christmas Day? It's the day after tomorrow."

"Christmas," said Danielle with a long, painful sigh. "It'll be the first time I've ever been away from my family at Christmas. I don't know what I'll do. I feel like I'm so old, Captain. A thousand years old, in just the few months since leaving Missouri. I've ridden so long on the dark side, there's no light to guide me."

"All the more reason why you need a few days' rest," Captain Jennings said. "I have two friends in Austin—Rangers Elmore and Williams—and like me, they have no family. They generally ride down here on Christmas Eve, and just for a day or two, we become as close to being a family as any of us will ever get. This Christmas, I'd like for you to join us."

"I . . . I don't know, Captain," said Danielle, touched.

"My last Christmas at home, I was seven years old," Captain Jennings said. "A week later, the Comanches struck and burned our house. Ma and Pa died in the attack, and a kindly old aunt took me in."

While his eyes were on Danielle, he wasn't seeing her. His mind was far away, at a different time and place.

Danielle spoke, breaking his reverie. "I'll spend Christmas with you and your *amigos*, Captain. I think I'd like that."

"Bueno," said Jennings. "Find yourself a hotel and get some rest. Elmore and Williams will be here sometime tomorrow, and we can meet for supper."

Danielle left Sundown at a nearby stable and chose one of the better hotels in which there was a dining room. There was a chill wind from the west, bringing with it a hint of snow that might blow in from the high plains. Removing her hat, gun belts, and boots, Danielle stretched out on the bed and slept. Far into the night, she awakened to the howling wind outside. Thankful that she and Sundown had a roof over their heads, she undressed and went back to sleep.

SAN ANTONIO, TEXAS. DECEMBER 24, 1870.

Danielle joined Captain Jennings for breakfast.
"Be here at the office at five o'clock tonight," said Captain Jennings. "Our ranger *amigos* will be here by then."

The threat of last night's storm had passed, and it being Christmas Eve, the streets were alive with people. Danielle had started across the street to her hotel when a shot rang out. Suddenly there was a blinding pain in her head, and she felt herself blacking out. At first there was only merciful darkness, and then through slitted eyes, she could see daylight. A man in town clothes was bending over her. Captain Jennings stood at the foot of the bed, watching with concern.

"You have a concussion," the doctor said. "For the next few days, don't do anything foolish that might jolt you around."

"No riding, then," said Danielle.

"Especially no riding," the doctor said. "Spend as much time in bed as you can. I'll be back to look in on you the day after tomorrow. Where are you staying?"

"Come by my office, Doc, and I'll take you there," Captain Jennings said. "Is he in a good enough condition to make it back to the hotel?"

"It all depends on him," said the doctor. "Young man, can you stand?"

"I don't know," Danielle said. "I'll try."

Holding on to the bed's iron footboard, she got to her feet, only to be engulfed by a wave of dizziness. But it soon passed, and she spoke to the doctor.

"I can make it, Doc."

"I'll go with him," said Captain Jennings.

"Take this bottle of laudanum with you," the doctor said. "There may be more pain, and this will help you sleep."

Captain Jennings said nothing until they reached Danielle's room on the first floor of the Cattleman's Hotel. Then Jennings had a question.

"Do you have any idea who might have fired that shot?"

"No," said Danielle. "It came from behind me. Some of those outlaws who rode out of Brownsville may be here."

The bushwhacker had been firing from cover, and when Danielle fell, he didn't fire again. Only when someone helped Danielle to her feet did Leroy Lomax curse. This damn little gunman had shamed him in Indian Territory, leading to a falling-out with the four men Lomax had been riding with. Now he intended to get his revenge. The kid seemed to have just been creased. When he was again up and about, Leroy would try again, and this time, he wouldn't miss.

Alone in her hotel room, Danielle removed her hat, gun belts, and boots. She stretched out on the bed and was soon asleep. She was awakened by knocking on the door.

"Who's there?" she asked.

"Captain Jennings. I stopped by to see how you're feeling."

Danielle got up and unlocked the door, and Jennings entered.

"There's no pain," said Danielle, "but the side of my head's sore."

"Elmore and Williams are in town," Captain Jennings said, "and they'd like to meet you. That invite to supper still stands if you feel up to it."

"I'm hungry," said Danielle, "and I feel steady enough. I'll try it."

"I thought you would," Jennings said, "so we're eating in the hotel dining room."

After meeting Jennings's friends Elmore and Williams, Danielle was glad she had been asked to join them. While they were a little younger than Jennings, they showed no less enthusiasm for their work.

"Captain Jennings told us about you," said Elmore while they waited for their food, "but he's gettin' old. I got a feeling he left some of it out."

"Yeah," Williams said, "what you've done is worthy of a company of rangers. Tell us all of it."

Danielle told them, stressing the loyalty of Ephiram and Ethel Delaney. They listened in silence, and when Danielle had finished, there seemed little to be said. Captain Jennings spoke.

"Daniel, take off your hat."

Danielle did so, revealing the bandage around her head.

"That happened on the street yesterday, right here in San Antonio," said Jennings. "A bushwhacker firing from cover."

"Then you have no idea who he is," Williams said.

"No," said Jennings. "It could easily be one of the outlaws from Brownsville. They had a death grip on the town until Daniel evened the odds."

"If he hated you enough to bushwhack you once, he'll try again," Elmore predicted. "I think we'll have Christmas dinner here at the hotel restaurant tomorrow to keep you off the street for a while."

"Good idea," said Williams.

After supper, the three rangers saw Danielle to her room before departing.

"We'll see you at eleven o'clock tomorrow morning," Captain Jennings promised.

Again Danielle stretched out on the bed, restless. She was starting to regret having promised Captain Jennings she would remain a few days in San Antonio. The hotel had gone to great lengths to decorate the lobby and the restaurant for the holiday, but it did not cheer Danielle. She thought only of her family in faraway Missouri, who had to spend this holiday not knowing if she was alive or dead. She drifted off into troubled sleep, only to be awakened by the distant clanging of a church bell. She sat up on the edge of the bed, listening. Finally, she pulled on her boots, buckled on her gun belts, and reached for her hat. When she reached the street, the sound of the bell was much closer. Following the sound, she came to a church just as the bell was silenced. From within the church came the glorious sound of several hundred voices singing the old hymns and Christmas carols. There was no music except in the melodious voices. Danielle stood there listening, and it was as though her feet had minds of their own. When she entered the church, she slipped into a back pew. Some of the congregation, seeing the pair of tied-down Colts, looked at her curiously, but kept singing.

For at least an hour, Danielle lifted her voice in singing the old songs she had learned as a child. Long-forgotten memories came alive, and she closed her eyes, relishing the images. The words of the old songs, like long-forgotten friends, came rushing back to her. After the last song had been sung, Danielle slipped out the door during the closing prayer. She considered visiting the Alamo Saloon, but suddenly it seemed like a tawdry place, filled with boastful, cursing men. She returned to her hotel room and, with the joyful chorus still ringing in her head, was soon asleep.

SAN ANTONIO, TEXAS. DECEMBER 25, 1870.

Many of the cafés were closed, so Danielle had breakfast in the hotel dining room. She wasn't surprised to find her three ranger friends already there. Danielle pulled out a chair and sat down.

"We forgot to mention breakfast this morning," said Captain Jennings, "and I thought you might want to sleep late."

"I can't hide out forever," Danielle said. "Sooner or later, the varmint that's out to get me will have to show himself. When he does, I'll be ready."

"If he doesn't shoot you from behind," said Williams. "That's one thing you can count on. A coward never changes."

After breakfast, lacking anything better to do, Danielle returned to her room, unaware that hostile eyes had been watching her. Leroy Lomax sat in the hotel lobby, an unfolded newspaper shielding his face. He watched to see how far down the hall Danielle was going, and then he went to the hotel desk.

"I want a room for the night," said Lomax. "Bottom floor."

Given a key, he was gratified to learn that his room was almost directly across the hall from that of the little gunman he hated. The kid had to eat, and Lomax would try again at dinner or supper. Lomax lay across the bed, waiting. The kid seemed to have a habit of eating with Texas Rangers, and Lomax didn't want to make his play as long as any of the famed lawmen were in the hotel. He would go after Daniel Strange after he had left the dining room and was on his way down the hall.

Danielle reached the dining room just a few minutes after eleven. Jennings, Elmore, and Williams were already there.

"Feeling better?" Jennings asked.

"Considerably," said Danielle. "I feel like I could eat a whole turkey, goose, or double portions of whatever's being served."

The meal was an occasion to remember. Prodded by Danielle, the three rangers spoke of trails they had ridden, outlaws they had captured, and violent brushes with death. Only then did Captain Jennings take from under his belt a Colt, laying it on the table before Danielle.

"It's a .31-caliber Colt pocket pistol, from the three of us to you," said Jennings. "It will fit neatly under your belt or under your coat. It's a short barrel, but no less a Colt. It'll stop a man dead in his tracks."

"I . . . I don't know what to say," Danielle said.

"There's nothing to say except Merry Christmas," said Jennings.

"But I have nothing for any of you," Danielle protested.

"You gave us our Christmas early," said Williams, "when you salted down that ranger killer Snakehead Kalpana."

"I'm obliged," Danielle said, slipping the short-barreled Colt beneath the waistband of her Levi's.

When dinner was over, Danielle left her friends and started down the hall to her room. Softly, a door opened behind her, and a cold voice spoke.

"Unbuckle them belts and let 'em fall."

Danielle paused and felt the muzzle of a gun poking her in the back. Slowly she loosed her gun belts, allowing her Colts to slide to the floor.

"Now go on to your room, where you was headed," said the voice.

Danielle had her key in her left hand, and while fumbling for the keyhole, she eased her right hand to the butt of the pocket pistol. Suddenly the door opened, and Danielle seemed to fall forward into the room. Rolling over on her side, she fired twice, slamming Lomax into a door on the other side of the hall. He fired twice, but his arm had begun to sag, and the lead plowed into the carpet at his feet. Men came running down the hall, three of them the rangers who had not yet left the building. Danielle's Colts lay on the floor in the hall, but in her hand she held the Colt pocket pistol.

"That's Leroy Lomax," Danielle said. "I had trouble with him in Indian Territory."

She stepped out in the hall, retrieved her gun belts, and buckled them on. She then slid the Colt pocket pistol under her waistband and, facing the three rangers, spoke.

"You gave me the best Christmas gift of all. My life."

"You still aim to stay a few days, don't you?" Captain Jennings asked.

"Yes," said Danielle, "but then I'll be riding on. There's six more killers I must find before my pa can rest easy. I want the varmints to know they're living under the shadow of a noose."

THE SHADOW
OF A NOOSE

PROLOGUE

ST. JOSEPH, MISSOURI. JUNE 15, 1871.

J ed," said Tim Strange to his twin brother, "now that Ma is in the ground, I don't rightly know what to do next. I wish there was some way to get in touch with Danielle and let her know what happened here. But I don't reckon anybody's heard a word from her since she took out after the bastards that killed our pa. That's been about a year ago."

For Jed, looking into his twin brother's face was like looking into a mirror. "It's going to plumb break her heart even hearing about Ma's death from *us*, let alone if she had to hear about it from a stranger," Jed replied miserably.

They both gazed across the barren, empty garden near their farmhouse. The house was in sore need of repair and had been long since before their sister, Danielle, had left.

"Look at this place." Tim sighed. "It's all worn down to dust and sorrow. We don't even have the price of seeds. You and I have been left in sorry straits, brother. If we're going to go hungry, we might just as well do it on the trail. We might even find work out there somewhere, if we kept our ages a secret. We won't find any around here, not with Reconstruction going on. If not for that old double-barreled rabbit gun in the house, I reckon we'd starve."

"I know what you mean," said Jed. "Everybody around here is having it as rough as we are. Never thought I'd say this, but I'm so sick of rabbit, I can't stand it."

"Well, even rabbit is starting to get scarce," Tim said.

Tim and Jed Strange were only fourteen when their sister had left them about a year ago on the hardscrabble farm to take care of their grieving, ailing mother, Margaret Strange. Try as they did, the two boys had not been able to make ends meet for themselves and their mother.

"Then we both know what we have to do, don't we?" said Tim. "We'll have to go find Danielle and make sure she hears the bad news from us."

Jed looked at his brother, knowing that while neither of them wanted to admit it, they had both been a little bit envious of the fact that it was their sister, Danielle, who had taken up the vengeance trail, hunting for the murderers of their father, Dan Strange. Both boys shared the thought that hunting for cold-blooded killers was man's work. They had been too young to go after the outlaws themselves at the time. While it was an indisputable fact that their sister Danielle was as good with a gun as any man, her going after the killers alone still didn't set right with them.

But Tim and Jed Strange were a whole year older now, and every spare minute they had was spent practicing their draw and their aim. The Colts they used had been custom fitted by their father, who had been known as the best gunsmith in Missouri. Before his demise he had seen to it that his children knew how to *use* as well as repair a gun, starting when they were hardly more than babies.

With their sweat-stained beat-up Stetsons in their hands, the twins looked down at their mother's grave and at the wildflowers they had placed on the fresh-turned mound of earth.

"Ma," Jed said, his head hung down low, "I wish we could've buried you in the cemetery proper-like the way you deserved. But this is the best we could do."

"Don't talk like that," Tim said. "You know as well as I do that Ma would as soon be here in the yard near this old house as she would in the finest cemetery in the world."

"You're right," Jed said to his brother, holding back the tears that were about to spill from his eyes. "I'll tell you one thing—the men who killed Pa just as well had killed Ma, too. She started dying the day Pa was put down. It just took her longer to do it. I want to find Danielle, and I want all three of us to find the bastards that caused all this."

They stood silently for a few minutes, each mulling over his own private thoughts. A small cool breeze cut through the hot air and made the petals of the wildflowers rustle over their mother's grave.

Finally, Tim said with a tightness in his chest, "We still have our Colts, and one tin of bullets between us."

Lifting his eyes from the grave, Jed said, "Yes, and we still have the two good bay horses, except that they're run-down in their flanks from want of grain."

"Then what are we waiting for?" said Tim. "Talking ain't going to get it done."

Tim stepped back from the grave with a last, sorrowful look. He took down one of the gun belts that they had hung on a stubbed branch of a cottonwood tree a few feet away, rather than wearing them to their mother's grave. Jed watched his twin brother for only a moment as Tim strapped the belt around his hips and began to tie the holster down to his thigh with a length of rawhide.

Jed realized that what they both had dreamed of for the past year was about to come true. He hurried over to the cottonwood tree, took down his gun belt, and strapped it on in the same manner as Tim had done.

"You're right. What *are* we waiting for?" Jed Strange said, echoing his twin brother's words.

As Jed and Tim Strange stood inside the barn, saddling the two bay geldings, preparing the gaunt horses for what both boys knew would be a long and treacherous journey, the sound of a buggy rolling into the yard caused them both to turn from their tasks and step back out into the sunlight. At first they thought it might have been one of the many families who had come by earlier to pay their last respects, perhaps someone who was arriving late. But when they saw it was Orville Myers, the new land speculator who'd been plying his profession in the St. Joseph area of late, they knew the purpose of his visit before he stepped down from his buggy and walked toward them.

"Damn," said Jed to Tim, "you'd think he could wait till after the funeral dust settled."

"Men like Orville Myers don't wait for nothing," Tim said. "But he could have saved himself a trip in this case."

Orville Myers seemed to have an idea that they were talking about him, for he kept his eyes lowered, unable to face them head-on, something their father had taught them always to be leery of. Dan Strange had always told his sons, "If a man can't face you directly, most likely he's hiding more than just his eyes."

Before Orville came to a complete stop, Tim Strange hooked his thumbs into his gun belt and said, "You weren't here when our friends and neighbors were, so you just as well might have not come at all."

"Boys, I know you don't like me. Nobody around here does. But I don't let them stop me from doing my job. I know the fix you're in, and I felt it only obligin' of me to ride out and make you an offer on this old place before it ends up on the auction block."

"What's he talking about, Tim?" Jed asked, keeping his eyes narrowed on Orville Myers's weasely face.

"I don't know, Jed. What *are* you talking about, Myers? The taxes are paid up on this place. Ma sent Danielle into town to pay them before Danielle left last summer."

"Indeed. But that was for last year's taxes." Orville Myers adjusted the wire-rimmed glasses on the bridge of his long thin nose, then took out a folded piece of paper from his black linen suit. "I reckon you boys are too young to realize that taxes ain't a onetime thing. You owe the same amount now as you did then, except this year the government is upping the total by twenty-six dollars to get back some money it spent fighting that blamed war. I guess that's the government's way to make a bunch of yellow rebels think twice before they decide to kick up their heels again."

"Mr. Myers, I don't mean no disrespect," said Tim, "but you'd best be careful calling these men around here *yellow*. The feelings over the war haven't cooled that much. There's some who'd leave you swinging from a tree over talk like that."

Orville Myers looked startled and quickly said, "Boys, don't get me wrong. I'm a businessman. I took no side in the war, and I take none now. I make my profit no matter who wins or loses. But back to the subject at hand. I'm making you an offer of two hundred dollars for this place just like she sits. It's a fair offer, and I advise you to take it. It'll put a little traveling money in your pockets."

"Why, you snake!" Tim Strange took an enraged step forward, but brother Jed grabbed his arm, stopping him. "We'd stand in one spot and starve to death before we'd sell you this place!"

"Take it easy, Tim," Jed said, holding his brother back. Jed shot Orville Myers a threatening look, saying, "And you'd best follow your heels back to that buggy and clear out of here!"

Myers backed away, talking as he went, pointing a finger at them. "Boys, you'd best see the wisdom in taking my offer. If you let me walk away from here today, I might change my mind before morning. If I haven't, you know where my office is. Don't let pride keep you from doing what's best for you."

The twins stood and watched the rise of dust drift away behind the buggy. Only when Orville Myers was out of sight did Tim Strange cool down a mite. Even so, his breath still rose and fell hard and hot. "It's a good thing you were here," he said to Jed, who stood beside him. "I saw red there for a minute. Funny, how the two of us are the same in every other way, yet when it comes to keeping a rein on our tempers, you're always the calmer one."

"Yes, but not by much in this case," Jed said. "It was awfully tempting to let you give that snake a sound thrashing. But let's always remember who we are and how we were raised, especially once we get out there on the road. Try to always ask yourself what

Ma and Pa would have us do before we go acting in haste. That's what I try to do, anyhow."

"That's good thinking, Jed," said Tim, "and I'll try remembering it. But there just might be things come up out there where we won't have time to stop and think what Ma and Pa would expect of us. I reckon wherever Danielle is, she's learned that by now. If she ain't, she might already be dead herself."

"Let's not think that way, brother," said Jed, patting Tim on his shoulder. "Come on, let's get the horses and get under way. We'll go to town and see where we stand on these taxes before we ride on."

Afternoon shadows had begun to stretch long across the land by the time Tim and Jed Strange rode into St. Joseph, hitching their gaunt horses to the iron rings in front of the town hall. Elvin Bray, the tax assessor, had already pulled down the hood on his oaken roll-topped desk and closed up the wooden file cabinets along the back wall behind the counter. He followed the same routine every day before he left his office. His next step would have been to lock the front door, pull down the shade, then count the cash he had collected before locking it away in the small Mosler safe beside his desk. But just as he reached out to lock the door, Tim and Jed walked through it. Elvin Bray jumped back a step and spoke in a startled voice.

"My goodness, young men, I wasn't expecting anybody this late in the afternoon!" Elvin touched his thin, nervous fingertips to his chin, trying not to look too shaken. "Is this something that can wait till tomorrow?"

"Pardon us, Mr. Bray," Tim said, taking off his battered Stetson and, out of force of habit, batting it against his right leg. "Now that Ma's dead, Jed and I are leaving the county for a while. We just wanted to see how much taxes is owed on our place before we head out."

"Head out?" Bray looked back and forth between them. "But your ma's funeral was just this morning. Sorry I couldn't make it out there. My wife, Cheryl Kay, and my boy, Thomas, was there, though, right?"

"Yes, sir, they was," Tim Strange said, "and we appreciated the turnout."

"I've been meaning to come out and talk to you boys anyway," said Bray. "Come on in here, and let's close this door a'fore somebody else shows up," said Bray, ushering them farther into the office. He closed the door and locked it. "I always get a might anxious this time of evening when there's money on hand."

"We understand," said Jed as he and Tim moved closer to the counter.

Elvin Bray stepped back behind the counter through a waist-high swinging door. He straightened the garters on his shirtsleeves, then spread his hands along the countertop.

"All right now, young men. What can I do for you?"

"Well, sir," Tim said, "as you know, our sister, Danielle, has been gone this past year. We haven't heard from her, nor she from us. We were fixin' to head out searching for her when Orville Myers come by the place. He's talking like we owe some taxes, and if we don't get them paid real quick, we could lose the farm. Can you give us an idea what we owe? We want to find a way to pay it."

Elvin Bray raised a thin hand, stopping Tim Strange from saying any more. He said, "Boys, let me ease your minds. As of right now, your taxes are paid in full for this year. They were paid by mail less than a month ago."

"Huh?" Tim and Jed looked at each other, puzzled.

"That's right," said Bray. "I can tell you without looking it up. Neither of you have been to town lately or I would have told you sooner. My Cheryl Kay would have told you today at your ma's funeral, but we didn't think it was the time and place to mention it."

As he spoke, Bray pulled up the hood of his roll-top desk, then picked up a ledger book and turned back to them with it. The twins noticed the metal cashbox sitting on the desk as Bray spread the ledger open and ran a thin finger down to the name "Strange."

"See here? You're paid in full for the year." He raised his eyes to them and smiled. "Maybe you haven't heard from Danielle, but we sure have. She mailed a bank draft in a letter to us. In fact, she overpaid by fourteen dollars."

"Well, thank God for that." Jed Strange sighed. "Not only for her paying the taxes, but also for letting somebody know she's still alive."

"Was there a return address on the letter?" Tim asked.

"Hold on. I'll find it for you," said Elvin Bray as he turned to his desk again and rummaged through a drawer full of opened envelopes.

Tim and Jed looked at each other, waiting on Elvin Bray. "Why do you suppose Orville Myers tried pulling a stunt like that on us, Tim?" Jed asked.

Before Tim could respond, Elvin Bray, hearing their conversation, said over his shoulder, "Because Orville Myers is a cuss. He most likely figured you boys being young, he'd get you scared of losing your home for taxes, then buy it on the spot before you even checked out his story."

"Being young don't mean we're stupid," Tim said defensively.

"I know that, boys." Elvin Bray found the letter and said, "Here it is," handing it over to them. "But somebody like Myers who ain't from here, and has no regard for anybody anyway, just figures you both for a couple of wet-nosed pups."

As Tim and Jed inspected the back of the bank draft envelope, Bray went on talking. "If you boys are headed out on your own for the first time, you're going to find a lot of Orville Myerses along your way or worse. It don't matter what you know or what fine upbringing you've had. Out there you'll meet some unsavory characters who'll be out to snare you, taking advantage of your inexperience."

"Thanks, Mr. Bray. We'll be careful," Tim assured him.

"This letter was mailed from Dallas, Texas," Jed noted, tapping a finger on the envelope, "but it gives no return address. I reckon Danielle must have known she wasn't going to be there long when she sent it." He shook his head. "I swear, it ain't like Danielle to not keep in touch."

"If she's moving around a lot on her own," Bray said, "you might be surprised how much she's changed in the past year. She might not want to say much, for fear it'll reveal things about herself she might not want known."

"What are you saying, Mr. Bray?" Tim asked, seeming to take offense.

"Now, don't get your dander up," Elvin Bray said. "I'm only saying people change once they get out there and get knocked around some. Be prepared, boys. That's all I meant by it."

"Not our sister!" Tim said, irritated. "She'll be the same as always once we find her."

Jed intervened. "Tim, all Mr. Bray is saying is that a year can make a difference in a person. He's not saying anything bad about Danielle. Are you, Mr. Bray?"

"No sirree. I've known you and your folks too long, and we've always been good neighbors to one another. I suppose what I'm trying to do is give you some parting advise. I apologize if it's been mistaken."

Tim cooled off and said, "No, I'm the one who needs to apologize. I'm sorry I took offense. I've got a lot on my mind today." He nodded at Jed. "We both do. Jed just don't show it as easily."

"Well," said Bray, smiling patiently, "I won't offer no more advice. The road is the best yet harshest teacher I know of." Bray sighed and shook his head slowly. "But as for your taxes, you can see you're in good shape till next year. Knowing that ought to make you feel some better."

"Thanks again, Mr. Bray," Jed said. "Suppose we can keep this envelope?"

"Sure." Elvin Bray shrugged. "In fact, if you're in need of some traveling money, I can let you have that extra fourteen dollars."

"Can you?" said Jed. "We'd sure be obliged!"

"Be glad to," Bray replied. "I'll just need one of you to sign a receipt for our records."

Jed and Tim nodded in unison. Elvin Bray went to the cashbox on his desk, counted out fourteen dollars, then picked up a receipt pamphlet and returned to the counter. Once the money changed hands and the receipt was signed, Bray smiled.

"There you are. When you find Danielle, you be sure and tell her she's missed by all of us here."

"We will, sir," Tim said, folding the money and shoving it down into his shirt pocket. "She'll be glad to hear you said that."

Elvin Bray stayed behind the counter and watched them leave. When the brothers were at the door, he called out to them, "Will you do me a favor? One of you pull that sash down on your way out?"

"I will," said Jed. But as he took a hold of the long sash cord and pulled down, it broke off in his hand. "Sorry, Mr. Bray," he said, turning to Bray with the cord dangling from his hand.

Elvin Bray raised a hand toward him. "It weren't your fault. That cord was getting old. Just pitch it away for me first chance you get."

He smiled, leaning on the counter, and watched them shuffle out through the door, Jed Strange winding the length of sash cord around his finger. When the door closed behind them, Elvin Bray shook his head, thinking of the long trail that lay before the two young men. Then he went back to his roll-top desk, picked up the metal cashbox, and pulled the hood down.

Across the street from the assessor's office, in the darkness of a narrow shadowed alley, two outlaws by the names of Duncan Grago and Sep Howard stood watching Tim and Jed Strange as the twins mounted their horses and rode out of sight along the quiet afternoon street. Sep Howard took note of Jed's short-barreled ten-gauge, the butt stock sticking out from beneath his blanket roll.

"What do you think, Dunc?" Sep asked. "We've been eye-balling this sucker for three days. This is the first time we haven't seen him lock the door this late in the evening."

"I believe we'd better make our run at him," said Dunc. "If we do this quiet-like, there's a good chance the last ones seen leaving the office will be those two." He nodded his ragged hat brim in the direction of Tim and Jed Strange. "One thing I learnt in prison—anytime you can shift the blame to somebody else, do it." He spread a thin, wicked grin.

"Sounds good to me," said Sep Howard. "But we'll have to kill that assessor to make it work that way."

"So?" Dunc Grago squinted at him. "You got any qualms against killing? If you do, I doubt if my brother, Newt, would have sent you to look for me. He knows that wherever I'm at, there's killing aplenty."

"I've got no qualms against puttin' anyone under snakes," said Sep. "Just tell me what you want done."

Dunc Grago reached down and drew a long Bowie knife from his boot well. He tucked the knife into his waistband, smoothing his vest down over it. "Move these horses closer and be ready in case anything goes wrong. I'll be coming out of there before you know it, so be ready."

Inside the assessor's office, Elvin Bray counted the dollar bills, stacked them neatly, and laid them down on his desk beside the cashbox. It was the first time in seven years that he'd failed to lock the door before making his daily tally and entering the figure into his accounting ledger, as the arrival of Jed and Tim Strange had broken his routine. Just as it dawned on him what he'd done, he heard the door ease open quietly, and he turned toward the stranger with his ledger book in his hand.

"I'm sorry, sir, but we're closed for the day. If you've come to town to pay your taxes, we'll be open again early in the morning."

"Taxes, huh?" said Dunc Grago. "Never paid any, never will." As Dunc spoke, his arm went behind his vest. He raised the Bowie knife by its handle and flipped it around in his hand to where he held it by the blade. "Catch this for me."

His arm shot forward as if he were cracking of a whip, sending the blade through the air in a shiny streak. The force of the blade striking Elvin Bray in his chest from fifteen feet away sent him staggering back against the oaken desk. Bray stood frozen for a second, staring down wide-eyed in disbelief at the knife handle pinned to his chest, the blade sunk deep in his heart. His face stiffened, then went slack as he sank to the floor.

"There now, all done," Duncan Grago said to himself, locking the door and pulling the shade down by its broken stub of a cord. He walked quietly over behind the counter, placed a boot on Elvin Bray's chest, and pulled the big knife free, wiping it back and forth on Bray's white shirt.

"If you could talk right now," he said to the wide, dead eyes staring blankly up at him, "you'd have to admit, that's the fastest thing you ever saw."

As Duncan Grago had predicted, nobody noticed him and Sep Howard leave town through the back alley, leading the horses slowly through the afternoon shadows until they were a good quarter of a mile from Elvin Bray's office. They had both kept quiet, looking back over their shoulders occasionally. Finally Sep Howard raised his lowered hat brim and spoke.

"I have to tell you," he said, the two of them finally stepping up onto the horses on the road out of town, "that was slicker than socks on a rooster. No wonder your brother, Newt, wants you back riding with him. I feared you might be a bit rusty, spending four years in stir."

The Colt in the tied-down holster on Duncan's hip streaked up toward Sep Howard, causing the older gunman's breath to catch in his throat. "Does that look rusty to you?" Duncan sneered.

"Lord, Dunc, give a feller a warning!" Sep Howard mopped his gloved hand across his brow, and settled as Duncan spun the Colt back down into his holster. "You know I wasn't making light of you."

"If I thought you was," said Duncan, "you wouldn't be sitting there right now." He offered a thin, tight grin. "Let's get on down to the Territory, see what Newt and his boys have got cooking for us."

"Sounds good to me," said Sep Howard.

He heeled his horse forward, yet he purposely kept a few feet back behind Duncan Grago. Sep Howard was getting on in age, and one reason he'd managed to stay alive as long as he had was because he'd learned not to show his back too long or too often to a man like Duncan Grago. When Newt Grago had asked him to ride all the way to Arizona to meet Duncan as he got out of prison, Sep Howard's first thought was, why didn't Newt go meet his brother himself? But ever since Newt Grago had more or less become the leader of a small gang of cutthroats and cattle rustlers down in Indian Territory, Sep saw Newt grow increasingly full of himself and staying wound pretty tight. Newt Grago had shot one of his own men for sassing him over a cup of coffee, and Sep and some of the others had watched him do it. So Sep hadn't backtalked him. He'd done as he was told, taking along a spare horse for the young convict.

He'd met Duncan Grago as soon as the young man stepped out through the iron gates of the prison with his belongings tied in a bandanna spindle. It took all of about five minutes for Sep Howard to decide that this young man was as wild as a buck and madder than a slapped hornet. Sep had already given some thought to saddling up and disappearing into the night. But now, seeing how cool and quiet this young man had just breezed in and out of the assessor's office, bringing back close to five hundred dollars, Sep decided to stick around a while longer and see how things went from here. As he was thinking about these things, Duncan Grago turned in his saddle, looking back at him as he spoke.

"Get on up here beside me, Sep," he said. "I've grown edgy about having an *hombre* shadowing me."

"I don't blame you. I'm the same way, Dunc," Sep Howard said, nudging his horse up a notch.

He took a guarded glance at the tight, grit-streaked face beneath Duncan Grago's hat brim, seeing the narrowed eyes, the crooked bridge of his nose, the shaved sideburns—prison style— and even the way Duncan sat loose and easy in his saddle. There was an ever-present tension about him like that of a coiled viper.

"I reckon my brother told you why I was in stir, didn't he?" Duncan Grago asked.

"Well, he mentioned a knife fight," said Sep, not wanting to appear too curious about it. "He didn't say what you was charged with, just that you was given five years."

"A knife fight, huh?" Duncan Grago laughed and slapped his thigh. "Yeah, you could call it a knife fight. But after it was over, you could've called it a quilting bee, it took so much thread to piece him back together. I cut him everywhere but the soles of his feet . . . and that's only cause he was wearing boots. Lucky for me he was part Mexican, or I'd be in that sweat hole the rest of my life."

"You mean, the man lived through all that cutting?" Sep Howard asked, feeling a little queasy the way Duncan Grago seemed to relish giving him the gory details.

"Yeah, he lived, if you call that living. Top of his head looks like an Arkansas road map." Duncan Grago spat, then kicked his horse up into a canter, liking the feel of the evening breeze on his face. Posting high in his saddle like a kid out on an evening lark, he shot a glance back at Sep Howard and called out, "Keep up with me, ole man, you might learn a thing or two!"

Under his breath, Sep Howard whispered, "Lord have mercy," and he spurred his horse forward.

Sep was getting tired of all the new faces showing up in Indian Territory of late. These younger outlaws seemed wilder than ever, he thought. Most of them were kill crazy, out looking to make themselves a reputation with a gun. Many of them were bent on revenge of some sort. Sep Howard had seen them come and go. They came from the prisons, the badlands, and from hell itself, it seemed—all of them hot for spilling blood.

He thought about the one he'd been hearing a lot about lately, the one who rode a chestnut mare and carried a crossed brace of Colts on his hips. Dan something-or-other was the kid's name. Sep Howard had never met the young gunman and couldn't say he had much of a hankering to do so. But he'd heard talk, the kind of talk that got a person's attention. Word of the young gunman had sure enough gotten Newt Grago's attention.

Apparently everywhere the young gunman showed up,

somebody turned up dead—usually somebody close to Newt Grago. In the past year four outlaws that Sep Howard knew of had met their match. Sep wondered if his going to fetch Duncan Grago had anything to do with the fact that Newt Grago was getting a little concerned, wondering why so many men he'd ridden with were dying in their boots.

Trying to keep up with Duncan Grago, Sep Howard ran names and faces through his mind. Bart Scovill, Snakehead Kalpana, Levi Jasper, Brice Levan. These were all bold, hardened killers. But now these men were dead. Sep thought this was a good time to watch his back real close and be ready to drop out of sight at a minute's notice. He didn't know if any of the others had made the connection between these men dying and the young gunman on the chestnut mare, but *he* sure had, and he was pretty sure Newt had, too.

Sep Howard heeled his horse harder, trying to stay by Duncan Grago's side. This was a good time to keep his mouth shut, Sep thought. He was getting older and slowing down, unable to handle himself with these young gun slicks like the one with the crossed Colts. He'd heard enough to know that he didn't want to find himself on some dusty street somewhere, all of a sudden having to look into those icy green eyes he'd heard so much about.

CHAPTER 1

Sheriff Matthew Connally had taken his supper at a small restaurant off the main street and a block from his office. Oil lamps had already begun to glow in windows as he strolled back along the boardwalk with his shotgun under his arm. While he still wore his Colt .45 making his evening rounds, the ten-gauge was his choice of weapons when it came to searching into darkened doorways and alleys. St. Joseph was not a wild, unruly town at present, but it had long been Sheriff Connally's experience that the only way to keep a town peaceful was with a tight hand and a ready load of buckshot.

In the darkness, Sheriff Connally saw the one-horse buggy pull up out front of the assessor's office, and as he walked closer, he saw Elvin Bray's wife, Cheryl Kay, hurry down from the buggy seat and to the door of the darkened office.

"Elvin, are you still in there?" Cheryl Kay said, knocking on the glass pane in the door. She tried peeping around the edge of the drawn window shade, but saw nothing in the silent blackened office. "Do you hear me, Elvin? Are you there?"

She reached down to shake the doorknob but, in doing so, felt the door give away and swing open a few inches. She gasped and stepped back.

"What's the problem here, Mrs. Bray?" Sheriff Connally asked, hastening up beside her.

"Oh, Sheriff," Cheryl Kay Bray said, looking at Connally with a hand to her cheek, "Elvin wasn't home for supper. I got worried. I came here and . . ." Her words trailed as she nodded at the partly opened door.

"I see," Sheriff Connally said, already on the alert, guiding her to one side of the doorway. "You wait out here, ma'am."

He slowly opened the door the rest of the way and stepped inside. Cheryl Kay Bray waited in breathless anticipation. In a moment, she leaned slightly around into the open doorway and spoke.

"Is everything all right, Sheriff?"

She started to step into the dark office, but when Sheriff Connally heard the floor creak beneath her shoes, he spoke to her from within the darkness.

"Don't come in here, ma'am. Something terrible has happened."

Within minutes, word had spread up and down the street. The assessor's office was soon brightly lit by lamps and lanterns, and a couple of young women from the nearest saloon stood comforting Cheryl Kay Bray out front on the boardwalk until the minister arrived. Bystanders milled in the street.

A town councilman by the name of Carl Hundley, who had been playing poker at the saloon, now stood in the center of the floor of Elvin Bray's office with his bowler hat in his hand. He rocked up onto his toes and craned a look over the counter to where Sheriff Connally and Doc Soble rolled Elvin Bray's cold body onto a gurney. Councilman Hundley winced at the sight, shook his head, and spoke to Connally.

"Sheriff, I hope you're prepared to act swiftly on this. Hattie McNear said she saw the Strange twins leaving here right about closing time. Said one of them was twirling a length of cord around his finger."

"Which one?" Sheriff Connally asked, riffling through the receipt pamphlet and seeing where Tim Strange had signed his name.

"Which one?" Councilman Hundley blustered. "How the hell could she tell which one? They're identical!"

"Oh," Sheriff Connally said, purposely busying himself with

the receipts. He'd asked the question only to slow Hundley down, not wanting to let the councilman step in and try to call the shots. "Do me a favor, Councilman," he said, without raising his eyes to Hundley. "Send one of those saloon girls for some coffee. I'd ask them myself but you seem to know them so much better."

"What?" Hundley fumed. "How dare you imply such a thing!"

But Sheriff Connally had already moved around the counter and past him to the door. He looked out into the gathering of people and called Hattie McNear into the office. As Hattie scurried forward, Sheriff Connally said under his breath to one of the saloon girls, "Will you fetch us a pot of coffee, Wanda Lee? We're going to be a while." He also pointed a finger at two men and motioned them inside to carry Elvin Bray's body to the mortician's.

Councilman Hundley still fumed silently as Sheriff Connally spoke to Hattie McNear.

"The councilman tells me you saw Tim and Jed Strange leaving here this evening, Hattie. Is that so?"

"Yes, Sheriff, I did see them whilst I was out searching for my cats," Hattie McNear said, her eyes large and watery behind a pair of wire-rimmed spectacles. "One of them was winding a string around his finger."

"I see," said Connally, cutting a glance to the broken stub of cord on the door shade. "Were they in any hurry, Hattie?" Sheriff Connally asked. "Which direction were they headed in?"

"No, they didn't seem to be in a hurry, Sheriff. They rode south. And I never said a word about thinking they might have done something like this." She cut a harsh glance at Councilman Hundley. "I've known those boys since they were babies. They wouldn't do such a thing."

"I know, Hattie," Sheriff Connally said. "But it's my job to ask questions."

Councilman Hundley interjected, saying, "It's your *job* to get on those boys' tail and bring 'em back here. This looks awfully suspicious on their part."

"Quit acting a fool, Councilman," said Sheriff Connally. "They didn't do this, and if they had done it, they'd be riding hell-bent right now. I'd never track them in the dark."

"Well," Hundley huffed, "just what *do* you intend to do, besides have coffee, that is?"

"I've sent somebody to find the telegraph clerk," said Connally. "The first thing we're going to do is send out a wire to the towns south of here. If Tim and Jed were riding south, they weren't headed home. I know those boys wouldn't do Elvin no harm, but I want to hear what they might know about who *did*. Come morning, I'll get on their trail by myself and see if I can't locate them in a way that won't scare the hair off their heads."

"I think you're making a terrible mistake, Sheriff," said Hundley. "How in the world do you know those two didn't do this!"

"I just know, that's all," Connally said in a firm tone. He turned to the faces pressing closer through the door of the office. "Let me ask you people," he said, raising his voice above their murmurs. "Do any of you believe Tim and Jed Strange killed Elvin or had something to do with this in any way?"

"No," the voices replied in unison.

"Hell no!" one voice trailed behind the rest.

Sheriff Connally turned to Councilman Hundley. "See? We all know these boys, and until something tells me otherwise, I'll not jump down their backs and accuse them of being murderers."

"We'll see about this," Hundley hissed, his face turning beet red.

He wheeled around and left, forcing his way through the throng of onlookers. He went straight to the telegraph office, a pencil stub in his hand, already writing down what he intended to say to the authorities in the surrounding communities.

THE SOUTH TRAIL. JUNE 15, 1871.

Tim and Jed Strange had made good time before dark. They'd stopped at a small mercantile outside St. Joseph where they knew the price of grain and supplies would be a little less expensive. They'd taken on some hardtack, coffee beans, three pounds of fresh pemmican, and dried red beans. After they'd left with their supplies tightly packed into their saddlebags, they made twelve more miles before darkness seeped in around them. They struck a camp not far from the banks of a river where they grained their gaunt horses and picketed the animals for the night. With a small fire glowing, the boys drank coffee and ate hardtack, being careful to ration themselves for the long unsure road ahead.

Jed lay the battered ten-gauge rabbit gun on the ground beside him. "Tim," he said, studying the fire and stirring a hickory stick into the small bed of embers, "do you suppose what Mr. Bray said is right about how the road has a way of changing everybody, teaching them some hard lessons?"

"I don't know," Tim said, attending to his Colt pistol, which he had disassembled on his spread bandanna close to the crackling flames. "All's I know is Pa taught us how to shoot, ride, and rope, and Ma taught us to respect others and read the Good Book. I reckon all a person can do is take these things and go forward with them. That's what Danielle done. We'll have to get her take on the rest of it. Whatever lessons are out there, hard or otherwise, we'll face them as we go. There's no turning back from life. We both know that already."

He held up the Colt's cylinder, having cleaned and oiled it, and rolled it back and forth between his palms, looking through it, inspecting each shiny part in the firelight.

Jed, his own Colt already cleaned, inspected, and reassembled, nodded in agreement and started to speak. But at the sound of one of the bays nickering low in the darkness, he fell silent and stopped stirring the hickory stick in the fire, looking furtively at his brother.

"I hear it," Tim whispered, his hands already working hastily, clicking parts back together on his Colt, then punching cartridges into it.

Jed rose into a crouch, picking up the short-barreled rabbit gun, and stepped back out of the firelight, his thumb over the shotgun's hammers, cocking them both at once. They heard the bays nicker softly again and now heard the sound of footsteps brushing through a stretch of broom sage. Tim shoved the sixth cartridge into his pistol and purposely spun the cylinder loud enough to be heard, then he, too, rose to his feet.

At the sound of Tim spinning the cylinder on his Colt, a voice called out from the darkness, "Hello, the camp!"

Tim Strange let his hand hang down his trouser leg, shielding the pistol from view. He cut a quick glance at Jed standing in the shadows with the shotgun poised, then spoke to the inky night.

"Hello as well," Tim said, taking a step farther to one side, putting distance between him and Jed. "Come forward," he added, his voice calm and friendly, yet his eyes searching the darkness with caution.

A silence passed. Then Sep Howard called out, "It don't sound too friendly in there. We just heard you spin one up."

"Yes, you did," said Tim Strange, "but not until we heard you slipping up unannounced."

"Sorry about that," Duncan Grago called out, putting a short, friendly laugh into his voice. "We're new around here and don't know the ways yet. Are we welcome?"

Tim looked at Jed, not certain what to do, for it was only good manners to invite a fellow traveler in. Jed nodded slowly. Then Tim called out, "Come on in. We're having some coffee and hardtack."

"Much obliged," Sep Howard said, stepping closer into the outer edge of firelight, Duncan Grago beside him.

Watching them, Tim and Jed both could have sworn the two men had slipped their pistols into their holsters just as the light fell upon them. Sep Howard and Duncan Grago could both see that the two young men had not moved back to the campfire.

Duncan Grago spoke. "Hell's bells, who wants to eat a handful of hardtack this close to town?" He paused and looked back and forth at the two shadowy figures of Tim and Jed Strange. "Are you boys scared or what? Come on into the light. We're pilgrims same as you."

"No, sir, we're not scared," Jed said. He started to step forward, but then the sound of Tim's voice stopped him.

"Stand fast, Jed," said Tim. He kept his attention on the two rough-looking gunmen as he spoke. Eyeing Sep Howard and Duncan Grago up and down, Tim could tell they were not new-comers to the ways of this country. "If hardtack don't suit you, then I reckon you've come to the wrong place."

"Yeah, I reckon," said Duncan Grago, rubbing his chin, lean-ing forward a bit, trying for a closer look at Tim and Jed. "Tell me, though, is that a new Colt you're holding down your leg?"

"This?" Tim moved the pistol just enough to make it clearly seen. "No, it's just well kept, in case a rattlesnake raises its head. My pa built this Colt for just such a purpose."

"Let's go, Dunc," Sep said under his breath.

But Duncan would have none of it, not yet. He laughed, speak-ing to Tim.

"Then I expect your pa must be Samuel Colt his-self," he said.

"You know what I mean, mister," said Tim. "Colt made it, but my pa turned it custom to fit my hand and work slick as silk."

"Oh! I'd truly like to see it," said Duncan Grago.

"You're fixin' to," Tim said, his tone of voice taking on a cold edge.

Jed joined in, saying, "Yep, and this double barrel as well."

"Let's go, Dunc," Sep Howard whispered again, his voice growing tight and shaky.

Duncan Grago hesitated for a second longer, then sneered, "Keep your sorry hardtack, then. We're leaving." He backed away a step and added sarcastically, "It's getting plumb dangerous out here, all these plow jockeys carry firearms." He chuckled and faded back into the darkness. "We'll be looking for yas, though."

Tim didn't answer, finding it more prudent to ignore the threat than to spark a shooting. He and Jed stood stone-still, listening to the sound of their footsteps move away through the broom sage. Jed faded backward into the darkness himself, circling to their right, where he put a hand on one of the bays' muzzles, settling it.

When he found the other bay, he unhobbled both of them and led them quietly the few yards to the dark edge of the camp. He stood with the horses beside him, the rabbit gun in his hands. After another moment of silence he spoke in a hushed voice.

"Newcomers, my foot. Did you get a look at them two? They've been on these trails longer than the dirt."

"Shhh," Tim said, silencing him. They stood stone quiet, the night around them still lying in deathlike silence. Then at length Tim spoke in a guarded whisper. "They're still out there. Back the horses into the dark. I'll kill this fire and bring our saddles and gear. This reminds me too much of what happened to our pa."

With Jed leading their horse, and Tim hurrying a few yards behind, wrestling with their saddles and loose sleeping rolls, they stopped at the river's edge long enough to right their gear and sling their saddles up onto the bays. Suddenly, in the darkness from the direction of their abandoned campsite, came the sound of heavy gunfire. They ducked in reflex, but then stood back up watching the muzzle flashes as the two gunmen fired on the campsite in vain. From fifty yards away, Jed and Tim heard one of the gunmen's voices call out to the other, "Stop shooting! They've slipped out on us!"

Tim drew the cinch beneath his bay's belly, speaking to Jed. "I reckon we just learned one of them hard lessons, didn't we?"

"Yeah," Jed replied, "never trust strangers out here. That's a shame, too, because people ought not have to live this way."

"Come on," Tim said, still keeping his voice low, "you can preach on the ills of the world once we're farther away from those varmints."

TRACY SIDINGS, MISSOURI. JUNE 17, 1871.

The town of Tracy Sidings had a temporary look to it and rightly so. The railroad company had erected the town primarily for their workers, and as a repair station and water stop along the route between St. Joseph and Kansas City. Not far behind the railroad workers came the drinking tents and gambling shacks. Not far behind the shacks came the whores, the traveling minstrels, and the peddlers. Soon, sparse houses sprang up for the wives and children of the railroaders, who demanded more respectable living quarters. Like in all such transient towns, the few residents of Tracy Sidings lived with the uncertainty of knowing that any day the railroad might change its operation and leave them all sitting stranded in its dust.

Standing outside a makeshift telegraph office, the town's acting sheriff, Martin Barr, stood watching the two young men ride in across the open plains from the north on gaunt-looking bays. In his left hand he held two telegraphs that arrived on the night of the fifteenth. Without taking his eyes off the approaching riders, he said to the telegraph clerk beside him, "Looks like this might be our killers coming here, Willard. The horses sure fit the description."

"Killers?" said Willard Chapin. "That depends on which telegram you want to believe. The one from Sheriff Connally said he only wants to talk to these boys."

"Yeah," said Martin Barr, "but the one from the councilman says they're looking pretty good for the crime. I'll just follow my hunch and take them into custody."

Martin Barr hadn't been wearing a badge very long and was doing so now only because the railroad had appointed him sheriff until the town could hold a proper election. Arresting a couple of killers was all Barr figured he needed to make a name for himself, dampening anybody's chances at running against him for the position.

"You might want to go along with Sheriff Connally on this thing," said Willard Chapin. "He knows the people around St. Joe better than some councilman. He's saying these are good boys and that you'd better not crowd them. They've had lots of grief lately."

"*Boys* is right," said Barr. "They're fifteen years old if the councilman is correct. I don't think they'll be giving me any trouble."

"Still," said Willard, "you'd be wise to take heed."

"Hush, Willard," Barr said over his shoulder, still watching Tim and Jed Strange riding closer. "Get around to Copley's Tavern and tell some of them night switchmen and hostlers they've just been deputized. Tell them to bring their guns if they're sober enough to hear you."

Willard Chapin whistled under his breath and shook his head, but did as Barr asked him. Within minutes there were seven men with liquor on their breath and weapons in their hands. As the whiskey-lit railroaders showed up, Martin Barr had them spread out and take cover along the rutted street, forming a large horseshoe-shaped trap into which Tim and Jed Strange would have to ride.

"If that's the sheriff up ahead," said Jed Strange, "first thing we'd better do is tell him about those gunmen night before last."

Both of them had seen the group of railroaders appear, then disappear, leaving the man with the large shiny badge on his chest facing them as they rode in closer.

"Hold it, Jed," said Tim. "Something ain't right here. Don't go no closer."

They slowed their horses down to hardly a walk. Something about the determined way the man stood in the street caused Tim to turn his bay sideways to a halt. His brother followed suit.

Jed sidled his horse a few feet away from Tim, letting his hand rest near his Colt. Tim called out loud enough to cover the distance between them and Martin Barr.

"Morning, Sheriff! We're just down from St. Joe."

Tim caught a glimpse of a railroader's cap appear above the edge of a rain barrel, and he suddenly grew wary. Across the street, Jed saw a glint of gun metal and felt his heart quicken a beat.

"Is there something wrong here?" Tim asked Barr.

"Come on in closer, boys. We'll talk about it," said Barr.

"Like hell," Jed whispered to his brother, seeing more signs of men in hiding along the boardwalk. "Tim, we're covered over here."

"I know. Over here, too," said Tim. "Sit tight." He turned his voice back up, calling out to Martin Barr, "Sheriff, we're not looking for any trouble. We're just passing through."

"Nope, not today you're not," said Barr, his right hand on his pistol butt. "We got a wire from Sheriff Connally in St. Joe night before last. He said to take you two into custody till he gets here. Now ride in here slow-like, raise those pistols with two fingers, and let them fall."

But the twins only cast each other a glance before Tim spoke again to Barr. "What for, Sheriff? We haven't broken any law that we know of."

"Then you'd better be advised that *murder* is breaking a law. Ride in closer and drop those pistols right now. I'm not asking again."

"Murder?" Tim gave Jed a bewildered glance. "What's he talking about?"

The lump in Jed's throat kept him from responding right away. When he did manage to speak, his voice wavered. "These men are fixin' to shoot us, Tim. What're we going to do?" As he spoke, the first of the railroaders rose up from behind a stack of nail kegs, the barrel of his rifle starting to swing toward them.

"We're going to shoot them back," Tim said, seeing no room for plea or reasoning.

He spun his big bay in a fast, full circle, the Colt in his hand out at arm's length, then fired, the sound exploding hard along the narrow street. The railroader's head snapped back as if it were on a spring hinge. Blood flew. Tim's horse reared as a rifle shot whistled past its ear. As it touched down, Tim's Colt exploded again. Another railroader fell screaming as Tim's bullet tore through the man's shoulder in an explosion of crimson and white cotton coat lining.

"Wait, damn it! Stop!" Martin Barr shouted amid the roar of gunfire, seeing too late that he'd stepped on the wrong cats' tails.

But the fight had commenced and there was no stopping now. Jed had sailed from his saddle into the street, a bullet striping up the length of his forearm. His horse bolted away as he rolled to his knee, firing shot after shot in rapid succession. Dust swirled high beneath Tim's bay as he swung it back and forth, taking his shot at one side of the wide street, then the other. But when a load of buckshot kicked dirt high near the bay's hooves, Tim, rather than risk harm to the animal, flung himself from his saddle and slapped the big bay's rump.

Tim's pistol never missed a beat until it clicked on an empty chamber. He worked quickly, reloading while Jed covered him. A bullet grazed Tim's thigh, spilling a streak of blood down his leg.

Two more railroaders had fallen, one as he ran from cover along the boardwalk and was hammered by a bullet in his ribs, another as he jumped out with a loud curse and raised a shotgun toward the twins in a drunken rage.

"Damn it to hell! Cease! Stop firing," Barr screamed. Then he made the mistake of running toward the twins with his pistol waving in the air. Tim, unable to hear through the gunfire, mistook Barr's action and stopped him short, putting a slug through his chest.

As suddenly as it had started, the fighting stopped. Tim and Jed were each propped up on one knee, back to back in the middle of the street beneath a lingering halo of burned powder and dust.

"My Gawd!" shouted one of the three remaining railroaders. "They've kilt Martin Barr!"

Tim punched out his spent cartridges and shoved new ones into their place, saying over his shoulder, "Jed, are you all right?"

"I'm shot, but not that bad," Jed replied, his voice straining against the pain along his bloody forearm. "What about you?"

"Same here," Tim said. "Let's back away to some cover while they figure out what went wrong."

CHAPTER 2

Tim and Jed Strange slowly moved away from the center of the street. Tim was limping from the bullet in his thigh. Jed helped him as much as possible, although the bullet that had torn up his own left forearm left him weak and nauseous. With the burned gunpowder smoke adrift around them, the twins retreated like wounded wolf pups, bloodied but still game. The two frightened bays had backed off twenty yards and milled about in the street. Onlookers had come forward cautiously, making the horses more nervous until Jed whistled to them. At the familiar sound, the bays ventured over to them at a trot, snorting and nickering under their breath.

"Easy, horse," Jed whispered, helping to support Tim and at the same keeping an eye on the stunned railroad workers, making sure they hadn't yet gotten over their shock and begun to retaliate.

On the boardwalk across the street, more men had come running to see the aftermath of the gunfight that the firing had stopped now. One of the three railroaders lifted his head up enough to look from the bodies on the ground over to Tim and Jed, huddled against their horses.

"There they are!" the stunned railroader shouted. "They're getting away!"

Jed struggled, trying to shove his wounded brother up into the saddle. "Help me, Tim. Pull up!" he pleaded. But Tim couldn't swing his bleeding leg over the saddle, and together, spent, they both crumbled to the ground. "If they come at us now, we're done for," Jed said in a trembling voice.

But as the railroaders drew together for courage and stalked forward, the sound of a fast-moving horse resounded from north of town. Two pistol shots suddenly sounded. Jed almost turned Tim loose to return fire. But then as the men came closer, Jed and Tim saw them stop abruptly and raise their hands up chest high. Sheriff Connally slid his big brown paint horse down onto its haunches and slipped from his saddle before the animal righted itself. His pistol covered the men in the street as he spoke.

"I'll shoot the next man that takes a step!" the sheriff bellowed. He gave a sidelong glance to the twins. "Tim? Jed? Are you boys all right?" Neither of them answered, but seeing them both still alive was enough for Connally. He shifted his gaze back to the men in front of him. "You drunken bunch of bastards," he raged, looking into the bloodshot eyes. "For two cents I'd haul back and let them kill the lot of yas!"

"We're deputies!" one railroader offered, pointing at Martin Barr's body in the street. "He deputized us! They kilt him! So don't jump on us! What about them? They're murderers, he said."

"He ain't saying nothing now, though, is he, you gandy-dancing, bo-shanked bunch of peckerwoods!"

The railroaders backed off, but not before Connally forced himself through the throng toward the one doing the talking, and swiped a hard blow across his forehead with his pistol barrel. The railroader went down, a thick hand clutched to his forehead.

"Get him up and out of my sight!" Sheriff Connally commanded.

The other men reached down, grabbed their dazed friend by his shoulders, and pulled him back. "What about them two, Sheriff?" one man ventured. "They *did* kill Martin Barr."

"As stupid as he was, somebody *had* to kill him," Connally shouted. "I just wish it was his mother on the day he was born! Now git, all of yas, before I cut loose."

The men moved farther away, one of them grumbling aloud, "You've got no jurisdiction here."

"What?" Connally shouted. "*Jurisdiction*, you say?"

A shot from his pistol kicked up dirt at their boots. They scurried back like frightened rats until the lot of them stood behind the protection of an abandoned buckboard wagon.

Sheriff Connally hurried over to the twins. "Take it easy, boys," he said, seeing the cocked Colt still in Tim's hand. "This is all a mistake." He moved in and looped Tim's arm over his shoulder, pistol and all. "Let's get him off the street. He's bleeding like a stuck hog."

Willard Chapin hurried in as Jed and Sheriff Connally helped Tim along the dirt street, the two bays following behind them. One of the horses raised its head toward Chapin's buckboard wagon and let out a threatening nicker.

"I'm not with them," Willard Chapin said, seeing the cold fury in Sheriff Connally's steel gray eyes. "How can I help?"

"Is there a doctor in this mud-sucking hole?" Connally hissed. "This boy don't know it but he's about to bleed out on us."

"Follow me," said Willard Chapin, ignoring Sheriff Connally's insult. "We'll take him to Doc Eisenhower's, if Doc ain't already headed out to help those wounded men back there."

"To hell with their wounds! Let 'em pour whiskey on them. These boys have been unjustly bushwhacked, far as I'm concerned."

Propped up between Sheriff Connally and Jed Strange, Tim's head started to droop from loss of blood. Yet he still tried to ask Connally, "What was . . . they talking about . . . murder?"

"Shut up, Tim," Sheriff Connally said, still coiled tight in his rage and unable to shed it. "I'm here to straighten things out."

In an upstairs office above a rickety saddle shop, the white-haired doctor stood up from dressing Tim's wound and sighed, shaking his head. Tim faded in and out of consciousness from loss of blood and the short dose of laudanum he'd taken. "You boys are down to feathers and bones, the both of you," the doctor said, turning his tired eyes to Jed Strange. "I'm afraid to give him any more for pain, lest it kill him."

"It . . . don't hurt none . . . Doctor," Tim managed to say in a weak voice.

"Hell, it never does," Doc Eisenhower said in a gruff, wizened tone. "That's why everybody enjoys getting shot, I reckon." He turned back to Jed Strange, asking, "What have you boys been eating lately? His blood's thinner than mountain air."

"We've been doing all right," Jed responded, his face flushing red with stung pride.

"Yes, I can see that." Doc Eisenhower looked at Willard Chapin and said in a blunt tone, "Willard, step yourself over to Gertie's, and tell her I said to cook up a mess of calf liver about half raw. This boy needs something pumping in his veins real quick." He jerked a nod at the bandage he'd placed on Jed's arm while waiting for Tim's wound to congeal, adding, "Tell her to fix double helpings. This one's wounded, too, and paler than Cull's mustache."

"I ain't hungry," Jed lied grudgingly as Willard Chapin headed for Gertie's boardinghouse.

"Of course you're not, but indulge me," the white-haired doctor said to Jed Strange. The room was hot, and thick with the metallic stench of drying blood. Doc Eisenhower wiped his hands on a blood-soaked towel, then pitched it on a pile in a corner. "Now, then, Sheriff, if you'll permit me, I'll go attend those railroaders, if they ain't gotten drunk and forgot all about it."

"Thanks, Doctor," Sheriff Connally said, rising from his spot against the wall.

"Don't thank me. Just pay me," Doc Eisenhower quipped with a faint grin. Rolling down his shirtsleeves and picking up his black bag from his desk, he left the office and walked down the squeaking stairs.

On the surgery table, Tim raised his head with much effort and looked down the length of his torn trousers and at the bandage wrapped around his thigh. "My only . . . pair of jeans gone," he offered.

"Don't worry. They still make trousers," Sheriff Connally said. "The main thing is you're both alive. I knew full well that you boys had nothing to do with Elvin Bray's murder."

While the doctor had attended the wounded twins, Sheriff Connally had filled them in on what had happened in St. Joseph. Tim shook his exhausted head and let himself slump back down on the table. "I swear . . . we must've been talking to Bray . . . shortly before he died. It don't seem right, a good man like him . . . stabbed to death."

"Don't talk right now, Tim," the sheriff said, resting a hand on Tim Strange's shoulder. "Let your brother tell me." He turned to Jed Strange. "Was there anybody else around when you left the office?"

"No, Sheriff, not that we noticed anyway." His mind went to the two men they'd encountered later that night. "We had some unwelcome company on the river trail. They might have been coming from the same direction. They were definitely the types who might do that sort of thing. They sure tried to kill us. I think they might have been following us."

Connally knew Jed was telling the truth, for he had seen the tracks of two other riders on his way to Tracy Sidings. "All right, tell me all about them," Sheriff Connally said. "But start back to where you two first rode into St. Joe. Tell me everything—where you were headed and why. Don't leave anything out. I know you're both innocent, but it's important that I hear everything, in case somebody else tries accusing you."

Sheriff Connally listened as Jed told him everything, from the time after their mother's funeral right up to when they'd ridden into Martin Barr's ill-fated trap. Connally looked at both of them as Jed spoke and couldn't help but feel sorrow for them. They were too young to have had so much go wrong for them, yet they carried it well, he thought. They were just two kids who should still be in school, but were instead sitting here hungry, whip handle thin, and nursing wounds that were cast upon them for no good reason.

Sheriff Connally sat silent for a long moment after Jed had finished talking. Finally when he spoke, he did so with a wince and a sigh, his eyes cast down at the wooden floor. "Boys," he said, unable to face either of them, "it seems like you two have been handed a raw deal ever since your pa's death."

"His murder, you mean," Jed cut in.

"Well, yes, his murder," said the sheriff. "I know it's been rough on both of you, what with your sister gone and your ma turning sick and dying. I know you've been living on a lick and a promise—"

"We . . . ain't complaining," Tim offered in a weak voice.

"I know you ain't," Connally said, "but I reckon I *am* on your behalf. Now, I know you ain't going to like hearing this, but I need for you to stay here for a day or two, just till I get this thing ironed out for you. Most likely a circuit judge will want to hear what you've got to say. After that I promise you'll be free to go."

"Free to go?" asked Jed. "You mean, you'll be holding us in custody? Why? You know we didn't kill Elvin Bray."

"Because that's just the way the law works, Jed," Connally said. "I don't like the thought of detaining you any more than you do, although to be honest, you'd be better off never stepping foot into the Territory. But the fact is, you can both use some food and rest, and so could your horses. I saw how poorly they look. Holding you here is the best thing that could happen to you, if you'll look at it in the right light."

"Sheriff Connally," Tim said, raising his head slightly, "you have always been . . . a man we trust. But . . . we've got to find our sister . . . and the men who killed Pa. You'd do the same . . . if it was you."

"I know, boys. You needn't convince me. If it weren't for my responsibilities in St. Joe, I'd be seriously considering riding with you. But back to right here and now. Look, boys, I'm trying to ask you as a favor . . . to stay here, help me get this thing settled. You want to help see Elvin's killers brought to justice, don't you?"

"You know we do," said Jed Strange.

"All right, then. Will you do this for me?" Sheriff Connally looked back and forth between them.

A silence passed as the twins looked at each other. Then Tim said from his surgery table, "All right, Sheriff Connally, we'll do what you say . . . but then we're headed to Indian Territory." Tim relaxed back down, then asked, "Sheriff . . . how did you feel the first time you . . . killed a man?"

"I felt terrible, Tim, the same as you're feeling right now. But like you, it was forced on me." Something passed over Connally's eyes for a second. "To tell the truth, if I could go back and change it, I'd as soon it be me that laid dead in the street that day." He took a long breath, then let it out with resolve. "But that's what was dealt me, and that's what I done with it. Try not to think about it. That's all I can tell you."

"I—I didn't kill anybody out there, did I?" Jed asked.

"No, but you shot the hell out of a couple, according to Willard. The only one dead is Martin Barr. That's no big loss. The stupid bastard would've walked off a cliff sooner or later, I reckon. Don't worry about the charges, though. Willard Chapin saw it all. Said Barr started the whole thing. The railroaders fired first. If they had a real sheriff here, he'd be charging *them* with assault. Don't worry about it. The ground is full of fools and want to be's. Martin Barr was just shining his play badge on the wrong corner."

"Did you know him well?" Jed asked.

"As well as I cared to," said Connally. "He spent the first half of life on the wrong side of the law. The second half I reckon he wanted to spend upholding it. They say he rode with Coleman Younger and his brothers for a while after the war."

"The Younger gang? The James boys?" Jed appeared stunned by the revelation.

"Yep, so rumor has it." He turned his gaze to Tim. "I reckon if there's any truth to it, you can rightly say you dusted down one of the original Boys."*

---

* "The Boys" was a name commonly given to the original members of the James-Younger gang.

"I don't want to . . . say nothing about it. Period," said Tim, his voice a bit stronger now. "To tell you the truth, I feel sick thinking about it."

"That's a good sign, young man," Connally said. "I'd be worried for your immortal soul if I thought you felt otherwise."

Willard Chapin returned with a large platterful of well-done steak and red, rare calf beef liver, covered by a grease-stained and bloodstained white cloth. "Gertie said she holds no responsibility for the rare liver. I told her it was Doc's orders to serve it that way."

"What's the word on the street?" Sheriff Connally asked, ignoring Willard's remarks.

"Just what you'd expect," said Willard. "The railroaders are gathering at Copley's Tavern, cussing, talking about hanging. Saying, how the hell do these boys get steak served to 'em right after shooting the blazes out of Martin Barr and the night crew?"

Connally nodded, thinking things over. "Have they built a jail here yet?"

"Yep. Halfway up the block, a brand-new three-cell beauty, as Barr called it. Why? You can't arrest those men. You've got no jurisdiction. . . ." His words trailed, remembering how Connally had reacted to that same statement earlier.

"I'm not planning on arresting anybody," replied Connally. "I need a safe place for these two to hole up and heal till they're well enough to ride."

"Well, it's probably the safest place in this town for them, and you, too," Willard said. "Barr had the key in his pocket. I'll go by the barbershop and get it for you—the barber here being our undertaker as well. The night workers will soon go off to their shacks. But it's the ones coming in tonight you'll need to worry about. There's a lot more of them."

"I figured as much," said Sheriff Connally. He looked at the faces of Jed and Tim Strange, and saw the concern in their eyes. "Don't worry, boys. We'll be all right here."

O rdinarily, Duncan Grago would have ridden wide of any nearby town after what he and Sep Howard had done in St. Joseph, but this was different. They'd come upon the hoofprints of Tim and Jed Strange's bay horses near the river where the twins had given them the slip, and had been trailing them ever since. When the two outlaws had heard shooting, they pulled off the trail and took cover in a dry creek bed. From there, they'd seen Sheriff Connally ride toward Tracy Sidings like a bat out of hell as the sound of gunfire continued unabated. After an hour of silence had passed and no more shots were heard, Duncan Grago spoke with a grin.

"I can't resist seeing what happened to those two pumpkin busters, can you?"

Sep Howard was hesitant. He said, "Dunc, your brother, Newt, is awfully anxious for us to get back down to the Territory. We're supposed to meet Julius Byler on the way. He's waiting on us outside of Fort Smith."

"We've got time," said Duncan.

With no more word on it, he jabbed his horse up from the creek bed and urged it on toward Tracy Sidings. Coming into town along an alley that passed by the town dump, the two outlaws rode toward the sound of angry cursing coming from a run-down tavern off the main street. Out front of Copley's Tavern, they reined their horses loosely for a quick getaway if needed, then slipped inside among the gathered railroad workers. As they ordered two beers and a bottle of rye whiskey, a railroader with a pistol-barrel welt on his forehead noticed them and fanned three of his fellow railroaders aside.

"What have we got here?" he asked, scowling at Duncan Grago and Sep Howard. "More strangers riding in on us?"

As the others turned to the two outlaws, Duncan Grago lowered his beer mug toward the drunken workers. "Whoa, boys. We heard the shooting from a mile off and just came to investigate." He jerked his thumb toward Sep Howard. "This here is Al Townsend. I'm Earl Jones. We've been tracking a bunch of cattle rustlers all the way from the other side of St. Joseph. Two of them split off from the others and headed this way over three weeks ago. The two we're after are look-alikes, riding a couple of underfed bays."

"Tarnation, that's them!" one of the railroaders exclaimed. The drunken men all looked at one another, then the one with the blue welt on his forehead stepped forward.

"What are you, stock detectives or bounty hunters?"

Duncan Grago shrugged and sipped his beer. "We're a little bit of both, you could say. But that's not important. What was all the shooting about here?"

"I'm Denton Perkins. A couple of wanted killers rode in here a while ago, shot our sheriff down like a dog, and wounded some of the men trying to help him uphold the law. Now the sheriff from St. Joe is protecting them—feeding them steak and biscuits if you can believe that!"

Duncan Grago shook his head in disgust and said, "I can believe just about anything when it comes to that sheriff in St. Joe. Most detectives like us don't even bother asking for his help anymore, for we know we won't get it. But he is a lawman, so what can you do about it?"

Denton Perkins gritted his teeth, running his fingertips across the bruise on his forehead. "You just watch, mister. You'll see what we can do about it!" he said to Duncan Grago. "When the law don't work for decent folks, it's time to get rid of the law! Am I right, men?"

"Damn right!" one of the railroaders shouted. Beer mugs tipped in agreement.

Denton Perkins swiped a hand across the bar, snatching up a half-full whiskey bottle. He threw back a long swig, and when he caught his breath, he banged a fist down on the wet bar top with a look of solemn finality. "Get a rope," he growled at the others.

In the wake of shuffling boot leather and drunken threats, the railroaders spilled from the dirty tavern, busting the plank door off its hinges on their way. At the bar, Duncan Grago turned to Sep Howard and laughed under his breath. "See? Wasn't this worth stopping for?" He raised his beer mug as if giving a toast and added, "I say anytime you can take a few minutes and get some poor bastard hung, it's always worth doing."

"Damn," Sep Howard whispered almost to himself, "and them boys are innocent."

Duncan Grago turned to him incredulously and said, "*Innocent?* Innocent of what?" He cut a sharp glance to Sep Howard. "The last innocent man on this earth was Jesus. You heard what he got for his effort. I ain't worried about innocent men getting hung. It's when they hang the guilty that troubles me."

CHAPTER 3

Sheriff Connally heard the large rock slam into the door of the doctor's office. He stood up and walked to the small window overlooking the narrow dirt street. "They're quicker than I thought they would be," he said over his shoulder to the twins, Willard Chapin, and Doc Eisenhower, who had returned from tending the wounded railroad workers in the lobby of a small hotel. "Willard, are you sure the horses are safely tucked away out of sight?"

"Yes, Sheriff," Willard replied, moving over to the window beside him to peer down at the angry mob. "I stabled them at the old express station. Nobody uses it anymore."

"How far it is from the jail?" Connally asked.

"Less than two blocks," Willard replied. "But don't worry—when you need them, I'll go fetch them for you and take them around back."

"Much obliged, Willard," said Connally, "but you've done plenty already. You have to live with these folks after it's over."

Another rock hit the door; then Denton Perkins's voice shouted in a drunken rage, "Come on out, Sheriff! Hand them killers over to us!"

Instead of opening the door, Sheriff Connally raised the window a little more and called down to them, "These boys are not charged with anything, and they won't be. You're making a big mistake here. The next rock that hits this door is going to cost somebody their fingers!"

On the street, one of the railroaders holding a rock at his side let it drop to the ground. Denton Perkins saw him and raged at him, "Pick that up, Wilson, you coward! We're not backing off till we've finished this!" He looked around at the other men behind him, and shook the rope on his shoulder. "That goes for *all* of yas! We'll burn them out if we have to!"

"This is insane," Doc Eisenhower said, hearing Denton Perkins shout at the others. "Let me see if I can talk sense to these men."

"Don't go out there, Doc," Connally cautioned him. But Doc Eisenhower wouldn't listen to him.

"I know all of these men, Sheriff, and I'm getting tired of dressing their bullet wounds." He moved quickly to the door and swung it open before Sheriff Connally could stop him. He looked down at the drunken, angry faces from the second-floor landing, then said to all of them, "You'd best watch your mouth, boys. Torch this building, and I'll leave here and never look back! Then who'll you go limping off to next time you crack your ankle with a bull hammer?"

"Stay out of this, Doc!" Denton Perkins warned him. "Those boys are outlaws! Two stock detectives just identified them over at the tavern. They been on their trail the past month ever since their gang split up! We're taking 'em to a pole and stringing 'em up!"

As Doc Eisenhower and the railroaders shouted back and forth, Sheriff Connally looked back over his shoulder at Willard Chapin and asked, "What's he talking about? These boys never left the farm except to hire out for a day's work when they were lucky."

Willard replied, "I have no idea, but there was two strangers headed into the tavern when I came by there."

"Well, hell." Connally sighed. "There's no telling who that is. Could be the bushwhackers these boys ran into coming here."

"It don't matter who it is," Jed Strange said, pushing himself up from his chair with his good hand, his bullet-creased arm in a sling. He walked over to Sheriff Connally and Willard Chapin by the window. "This is mine and Tim's fight, Sheriff. Just let us go down there."

"That's right," said Tim, trying to swing his wounded leg over the edge of the table. "You've done all you can for us."

"Both of yas, hush," said Sheriff Connally. "Stay back from the window, Jed. I didn't ride all this way just to see you both hang!"

On the landing, Doc Eisenhower had been arguing with the railroaders when his voice stopped short in a grunt as a rock skipped off his head and bounced through the open door. "Damn it all!" he shouted, staggering back inside with his hand raised to a bloody gash. "That's it! I'll shoot them myself, the drunken bunch of gandy dancers!"

"Hold on, Doc," Sheriff Connally said, seeing Doc Eisenhower reach for Jed and Tim's rabbit gun, which Willard Chapin had brought in from the express stables. "Take care of your head. I'll handle this bunch."

"Not by yourself you won't," said Jed, snatching the rabbit gun from the doctor with his good hand. "Not as long as I can swing a load of buckshot."

"No, Jed, trust me on this," Sheriff Connally said, reaching out for the shotgun. "Seeing you armed will only make them madder. This ain't the first time I've had to handle a bunch of drunks. They're whiskey brave right now, but it won't last."

Reluctantly, Jed turned the shotgun loose when Sheriff Connally closed his hand down over the front stock. "That's good, Jed," Connally offered in a quiet tone. "Now if you'll let me borrow this for about five minutes, we'll all feel a little better."

"Careful down there, Sheriff," Doc Eisenhower warned.

"Is there another way out of here?" Connally asked, checking the action of the short-barreled rifle as he spoke.

"Yep, there's a set of stairs leading down to Pelcher's saddle shop," said Doc Eisenhower. "The shop's closed till Pelcher gets back from Arkansas. There's also a back door out to the alley."

"Good deal," said Connally. "Suppose the two of you can get Tim over to the jail while I turkey these railroaders down?"

Doc Eisenhower looked Tim Strange up and down, and replied to Connally, "Well, moving him this soon is gonna start that leg bleeding again, but I reckon we're down to slim choices." He looked at Willard Chapin. "You up for it?"

"I'm game," said Chapin.

"All right, then," Connally said, swinging the rabbit gun under his arm, then lifting his Colt from his holster. "Count to fifty once I step out the door, then make your move."

"But, Sheriff," said Jed Strange, "I can't let you do this—"

"Jed," Connally said stiffly, cutting him off, "it's been years since anybody's *let* me do a damn thing. You can best help by doing like I say. Get ready now, all of yas."

When Sheriff Connally stepped out on the landing, the railroaders greeted him with loud jeers. A rock thumped against the side of the clapboard building, then fell at the sheriff's boots. Slowly, Connally looked down at the rock, the butt of the rabbit gun propped against his hip, the Colt in his right hand still hanging down his thigh. The crowd grew quiet for a second, seeing his slow, calm manner as he looked out at them and spoke.

"Count your fingers, boys. What I said about rock throwing still goes."

Connally stepped down, one slow step at a time, his calm aura seeming to give the men pause. But as he stepped off the bottom stair, the nine or ten railroaders drew closer together like cautious wolves. Denton Perkins crouched a bit and began slapping the coiled rope on the dusty ground, a noose now tied in the end of it.

"Come on, Sheriff, just try to stop us," he said, the slapping rope raising a low stir of dust. "There's only one of you. You've overplayed your hand."

"I'm sorry to hear you say that, mister," Connally said, raising the Colt, eyeing down the barrel at Denton Perkins's leg, "because I know you came all this way to work and make wages. I figure a busted kneecap's gonna lay you up at least six weeks, provided there's no infection. You can spend the rest of your life telling everybody why you limp."

"You won't do it," Denton Perkins sneered. "Those stock detectives told us the color of your stool."

He slapped the coiled rope harder and faster on the ground, the sound of it seeming to turn the rest of the men bolder. They all inched forward behind Perkins.

The sheriff's Colt cocked beneath his thumb. "Slap that rope one more time, and it's done, you ignorant peckerwood," Connally hissed through clenched teeth.

The conviction in his words caused Perkins's coiled rope to stop midswing, but Perkins hadn't backed down altogether yet.

"Sheriff, we all move at once, we'll plow right over you," Perkins said with a sneer.

"Some of you might," Connally said, pulling back both hammers on the rabbit gun, "but most of you won't feel nothing but a hot blast." He homed back into Perkins's eyes. "Then you won't have to explain the limp. I'll kill you graveyard dead. That's the sum of it."

As Sheriff Connally spoke, he made his advance, pressing closer, so close to Denton Perkins that the man had to inch back lest the barrel of the rabbit gun poke him beneath his chin. With Perkins backing up, the men behind him had no choice but to back up, too. Those who didn't had to spread to the side, Connally moving into their midst, his eyes and guns fanning back and forth slowly.

Connally saw that second when the whiskey alone wasn't enough to sustain them. The men wanted to turn and run now; he could sense it. Yet there was one more thing he needed to bring it about, and Denton Perkins opened his mouth and gave it to him.

"We ain't going to be—"

Before Perkins could get the words out, Connally dropped low almost to his knees, swinging the Colt a full fast circle and slamming the barrel upward into the big man's crotch. Perkins buckled forward, his arms wrapping around his lower belly. He hung there as if suspended, a long string of saliva swinging from his wide-open mouth. The onlookers groaned with him. A couple of them cried out as Connally's pistol whipped around in another hard fast circle and the butt of it crashed down hard on Perkins's thick neck. The force of the blow lifted Connally up onto this tiptoes.

"Lord—God!" a thin man in striped bib overalls yelled. "Don't kill him!"

"Do something, Roberts!" a voice from the crowd called out to the thin man.

Connally stalked toward him now, the rest of the men's spirits breaking fast as they hurried away quarter-wise, still staring back. Connally reached out with his boot and kicked the coiled rope forward. Roberts jumped from it as though it were a snake.

"Go on, *Roberts*!" Connally shouted. "Pick it up! This man's down. Now you take the lead!"

Roberts broke backward in a run, a startled look on his face. "Sheriff, you can't do this! We're just hardworking—"

His words were cut short as well, a blast from Connally's pistol throwing dirt up against his shins. "Who's gonna take the lead now?" Connally bellowed at the dispersed men. "Come on, somebody pick it up!" He stood for a moment in the echo of his words, his eyes moving from one man to the next as they cowered back at a safe distance. "All right, I'll take it myself!"

Connally jammed the pistol down into his holster, snatched up the coiled rope, and stepped back to where Denton Perkins lay heaving on his face, his buttocks still raised in the air, his arms still tight across his belly.

"You've . . . ruint me," Perkins groaned, strained and breathless.

"Not yet I ain't," said Connally. He dropped the noose over the big man's neck and jerked up, making Perkins rise stiffly to his knees. "Now we're gonna see who your friends really are." He jerked more, forcing Perkins to his feet. "He's going with me," Connally announced to the rest of the men. "You want to see a hanging? Just come give me some guff. I'll swing him off a chair from a jailhouse rafter."

The men only watched, their mouths agape, as Sheriff Connally shoved Perkins forward ahead of him. Perkins staggered in the dirt, his waist still badly bent, his boots dragging and having a hard time staying straight. Perkins heaved up a spray of sour whiskey as they moved in the direction of the new jail.

My goodness," Doc Eisenhower exclaimed, taking Denton Perkins by his bowed-over shoulder and helping him through the door, "you've nearly nutted this man."

"He's all right," said Sheriff Connally, shoving Perkins forward until the man slammed against a desk and fell into a ball on the plank floor. "He's lucky I didn't kill him." Connally bent slightly, placing a boot down on Perkins's shoulders and yanking the noose enough to make Perkins face him. "Anybody rushes this jail, and I'll take it out on your hide. Because *they* know, *you* know, and *I* know that I will hang you dead. Are we clear on that?"

"I—I didn't do . . . nothing but try to . . . see justice done."

"I'll see to it that they carve that on your marker," said Sheriff Connally. "Now tell me about these two so-called stock detectives. What did they look like? What are they riding?"

"I paid no attention to what they're riding," Denton Perkins said in a strained voice. "They said their names were Al Townsend and Earl Jones. Jones was the one doing the talking. He's young, with rusty yellow hair. Wears his hair and sideburns bristly short, almost shaved. He sports a leather Mexican vest and a beat-up brown Stetson." Perkins stopped and gulped a breath of air, then continued, his arms still clutched across his belly. "The other is older, heavyset, and unkempt. Wears a big drooping gray mustache and a black-and-white-checkered shirt. His hat's too far gone to describe."

Willard Chapin cut in, saying, "I looked over at the hitch rail outside of Copley's Tavern on our way over here, Sheriff. Those two horses are gone. One was a lineback dun. The other was a roan with three white stockings."

"Thanks, Willard," said Sheriff Connally. He turned his eyes to Jed Strange standing inside the open cell door, and asked, "Does that sound like the men you ran into?"

"Yep," said Jed, "that's them all right. We didn't see their horses."

Jed shot Denton Perkins a glare of contempt, saying, "You took their word that we're outlaws. Mister, my brother and me have gone hungry the past year when it would be easy to walk in somewhere with guns and take what we wanted. I hope you're *damn* proud of yourself."

"Easy, Jed," Sheriff Connally said, seeing the rage in the young man's eyes. "He's only one more fool in a world full of many." Connally straightened up and turned to Dr. Eisenhower, asking, "How's Tim's leg, Doc?"

"It's bleeding again, like I was afraid it would," Doc said, nodding toward the open door of the cell where Tim lay on a bunk. Jed and Willard Chapin stood beside him. "The bullet nicked an artery. I put a stitch down deep in it. I'm going to let it alone for a few more minutes. If it don't stop, I'll cauterize it." He sighed, then added, "My fear is that when the day workers come in off the road, they'll liquor up and start things all over again. If they do, it'll be hard to stop them." He nodded at Tim Strange. "And that boy has no business on a horse, making a run for it."

"Damn it," Connally said under his breath. He looked all around at the small office, the three cells, and the door on the back wall. "Get his leg fixed up the best you can for traveling, Doc. Having Perkins here will buy us some time. I'll hold up this bunch as long as I can, but this evening me and these boys are going to *have* to clear out of here. Once they're safe back in St. Joe, I want to catch up to Townsend and Jones real bad. I'm getting a hunch they're the ones who robbed and killed Elvin Bray."

As the sheriff spoke to Doc Eisenhower, Tim listened from the bunk in the cell. He looked down at his ripped trouser leg and at the blood-soaked bandage around his thigh. Then he looked up at Jed and caught his eyes for a second, just long enough for something to pass between them. Jed Strange got the message his twin was sending him. He eased closer to the rabbit gun, which sat leaning against the wall. Then he stopped and stood near it. Without bringing attention to himself, Jed picked the rabbit gun up and cradled it in the crook of his good arm.

In the midafternoon, Doc Eisenhower stood back from checking on Tim's leg wound and let a sigh of relief. "Well, the bleeding's stopped. I'm going to have to get over to the hotel lobby and
check on them wounded railroaders." He turned to Sheriff Connally and said, "The day crews will start straggling in anytime now.
Keep a close eye toward the tavern."

"I will, Doc," said Sheriff Connally, "and thanks for all your
help."

"Oh, I'll be back in a little while, Sheriff. I want one more look
at that leg before you put this boy on a saddle." Doc Eisenhower
rolled down his shirtsleeves, gathered up his black bag, and headed
for the front door.

"What about me, Doc?" Perkins, who was still lying with the
rope around his thick neck, pleaded from the floor. "I'm sicker than
a dog. My guts ache something awful, the back of my neck, too."

"Oh, really? I hate to hear that, Perkins," Doc Eisenhower said.
Then without another word to him, Doc turned and left.

Sheriff Connally chuckled under his breath.

"I'm afraid I must also leave for a while also, Sheriff," said Willard Chapin. "I need to check for any incoming messages. But I'll
be back, too."

"How about bringing us some more grub, Willard?" Sheriff
Connally asked. "You've been so obliging, I hate to ask."

"Not at all, Sheriff. I'll be happy to bring back some food from
Gertie's."

Willard put on his bowler hat and left. Watching first the doctor, then the telegraph clerk leaving, Jed Strange slipped another
guarded look at his twin brother, then moved closer to the desk
where Tim's gun belt lay in a coiled pile, the butt of his Colt standing against it in its holster.

When Sheriff Connally saw a road wagon full of sweaty workers roll past the window, he reached down, pulled Perkins to his
feet, and shoved him toward one of the empty cells. "In you go,"

he said to the groaning man. "Looks like some of the workers are headed for the tavern."

He locked the door to the cell, shoved the key down deep into his pocket, and took a rifle from the rack along the wall. As he loaded it, he said to Jed Strange, "Keep an eye on your brother for me. I'm going to sit on the porch with a rifle across my lap for a while, just to make a show of force for them."

Jed Strange only nodded without answering, but from his cell, Denton Perkins whined, "Sheriff, you're not leaving me alone with these two, are you?"

"Shut up, Perkins. I've heard enough of your mouth to last me a lifetime," Connally hissed, swinging his hat onto his head and a rifle under his arm.

As soon as Sheriff Connally was out on the porch and seated in a low wooden chair, Jed Strange stepped wordlessly into the open cell and handed Tim Strange the rabbit gun.

"Hey, what are you fixin' to do?" Perkins asked, his eyes going wide.

Jed stepped over to Perkins's cell. "Open your mouth again, and he'll empty both barrels into your maw."

Perkins cowered back from the bars and watched Jed Strange slip out through the rear door, silently closing it behind him. After a few tense moments had passed, Perkins watched Jed Strange slip back inside and walk hurriedly to the open cell where Tim Strange was already struggling to get up from the bunk. Jed looped his twin brother's arm across his shoulder and helped him toward the rear door, stopping at Perkins's cell long enough to prop Tim against the bars and say to Perkins, "Come here, you."

Perkins came to the bars, ready to plead for his life, but before he got a word out, Jed reached through the bars, grabbed him by his hair, and yanked his head forward. Perkins's forehead struck the iron bars with a dull thud, and as Jed turned him loose, the big railroader slumped to the floor, half conscious.

"Come on, Tim," Jed whispered, holding his brother's arm over his shoulder, "the bays are right out back."

CHAPTER 4

A few railroad workers had begun to gather out front of Copley's Tavern. They stood with beer mugs in their hands and looked over at Sheriff Connally on the porch of the new jail, a block away. Willard Chapin had to hurry past a barrage of taunts and threats as he carried the large wooden tray of food and coffee from Gertie's restaurant. He stepped up onto the porch of the jail and, looking a bit frightened, said to Sheriff Connally, "They're getting started early on their drinking. I'll get a shotgun and make a stand with you, Sheriff."

"No, but thanks anyway, Willard," said Sheriff Connally, standing up and opening the door for him. "If it gets too bad, I don't want your blood on my hands. This is the work I chose. If it ends here, then so be it."

"Oh, no!" Willard exclaimed once he was inside, looking around for the twins and seeing they were gone.

"Well, I'll be," Connally said in a hushed tone. "They've lit out on us." He saw Perkins pulling himself up, another large ugly welt on his forehead. "How long have they been gone?" Connally demanded.

Perkins shook his aching head. "I don't know, Sheriff. The one with the arm wound cracked my head against these bars. I've been out cold ever since."

"Damn it!" said Sheriff Connally, walking to the rear door and throwing it open. He looked back and forth along the alley, noting the fresh hoofprints in the dirt. As he gazed off in the direction the twins had taken, he said almost to himself, "Those poor, dumb kids. They've no idea what their heading into out there." He turned back to Willard Chapin, who'd set the tray down on the desk and slumped down beside it.

"Will you be going after them, Sheriff? They've proven they can take care of themselves with a gun, but I hate to think of them two wounded kids out there alone."

"I know," said Connally. "I feel the same. But I can't go no farther on this thing. My responsibility is to the folks in St. Joe. I had hoped to get the boys back there and get some sense talked into them before I try hunting down the men who killed Elvin Bray. Now there's no telling what'll happen to Jed and Tim Strange. Their pa sure taught them how to use a gun, but young boys being that quick with the trigger can be a dangerous thing."

"Where do you suppose they'll go?" Willard Chapin asked.

"Oh, there's not a doubt in my mind, they're headed down to Indian Territory," Sheriff Connally replied. "If they don't get themselves killed first."

WEST OF KANSAS CITY. JUNE 18, 1871.

Jed and Tim Strange swung wide of the Missouri farm country and took to the open wild grasslands west of Kansas City. Their first night found them camped at a thin stream beneath the cutbank of a low-rising knoll. Jed's wounded arm was stiff and sore, but there was little swelling. He shed the cloth sling from around his shoulder and, soaking it in the clear stream water, used it to attend to Tim's leg wound, which was healing over but still trickling blood.

"Careful you don't break it open," Tim said in the gray evening light.

"I wish Ma or Pa or somebody who knew what they were doing was here," Jed replied, sounding worried.

"Well, they're not," Tim said. "Give it here. I'll clean it myself."

He reached down and started to take the wet rag from Jed's hand, but Jed drew it back.

"I'm doing it, Tim," Jed declared. "All's I said was that I *wish* somebody knew more about what to do." He carefully began dabbing the wet rag at the edge of his brother's wound.

"Wishing and wanting is a thing of the past," Tim said in a milder tone. "We've both seen how easy it is to get into trouble out here. From now on we trust nobody, and we guard each other's backs the same way we did in that gunfight. That's the only thing that's going to keep us alive. I've never seen so many people anxious to hang somebody."

"I know," said Jed. "I hated cutting out on Sheriff Connally. But it might have been the only way to save all our lives."

"He understands, Jed," Tim said. "I'll always be beholden to him for what he was trying to do. But we're not letting anybody take us back to St. Joseph until we finish what we've started. Agreed?"

Jed nodded firmly. "Agreed." He finished cleaning Tim's wound and rewrapped it in the same gory bandage. "I just hope wherever Danielle's at, she's doing better than we are."

FORT SMITH, ARKANSAS. JUNE 20, 1871.

Danielle Strange walked from the U.S. federal marshal's office to the boardinghouse where she'd seen the vacancy sign on her way into town. In her run-down boots, she walked with the wide gait of a drover. She carried her dusty saddlebags, chaps, and range spurs draped over her shoulder, her rifle in her left hand, her right hand always close to the tied-down holster on her hip. The palm of her hand brushed past the butt on her Colt with each step. She had wintered in Mobeetie, Texas, where a family by the name of Elerby had taken her in, helping to nurse a knife wound in her side and a deep cut on her cheek. Then Danielle joined the Elerby boys, Luke and Clinton, who along with their father, Lattimer Elerby, and a small crew of drovers had brought one of the first spring herds up to Abilene.

"Damn the luck, Buck Jordan," she said to herself, swear words coming more freely to her now than they had before spending the last year of her life as a man in a man's world. "Why did you have to go get yourself killed?"

Only moments before she'd learned of Jordan's death, having heard about it from some of the deputies and jail guards gathered outside the Hanging Judge's court.* Buck Jordan, like many of the Hanging Judge's lawmen, had met his death out in the Indian Territory at the hand of killers whose whereabouts and identities were unknown.

Amid the squeaking of passing wagons and the clop of hooves on the hard rutted street, she added in a whisper to herself, "You were my only contact with the law in Indian Territory. Damn it!"

Along with the cussing, other things now came more easily to her, like the biting taste of whiskey, the clicking of a roulette wheel, and the ability to swing up her Colt with no hesitancy and watch a man fall to the dirt on an empty street in front of her. This was where the vengeance trail had led her, and this was where she lived.

In her pocket she carried a wrinkled paper that listed the names of the men who had killed her father, Daniel Strange. Of the ten names she'd written down a year ago, only six remained. The other four she had crossed off one at a time after seeing to it they'd paid the price for leaving Daniel Strange hanging dead from a tree. Her quest for the killers had started with meeting U.S. Marshal Buck Jordan here in Fort Smith. Jordan was the man who'd found her father's body, and he'd given her directions to her father's grave.

From the grave site, fate and circumstance had led her wandering from town to town on the killers' trails. The first killer on her list had been Bart Scovill, who'd been wearing her father's inlaid

---

* "Hanging Judge" was a name given to Judge Charles Isaac Parker.

silver custom Colt when she caught up with him at a town dance. Dressed as a woman that night, Danielle had lured Bart Scovill on; then with the fiddle ringing light and melodious in the background, she'd left him hanging dead from a barn rafter after retrieving her father's pistol.

From there, she'd traveled on and rooted out three more of the outlaws, killing them quick and without mercy. But now she'd been off their trail for a while and hoped that Buck Jordan might give her some sort of a lead. When Danielle had taken the knife in her side last fall, it had shown her it was time to drop out of sight for a while and let her new name cool off. She'd started to develop quite a reputation as Daniel Strange, the young gunslinger with the cold green eyes and an even colder heart.

When the Elerby boys had found Danielle wounded along the trail outside of Mobeetie, she'd told them her name was Danny Duggin, and they had never questioned it. She had a feeling they knew she was really the young gunslinger who'd gotten shot two days before in town and had since vanished. But they never let on. All the people of Mobeetie knew was that the emerald-eyed gunslinger named Daniel Strange had ridden away lying low in his saddle and hadn't been seen or heard from since, his bones lying bleached somewhere, no doubt.

Well, she thought to herself, *so much the better.*

If the killers thought that Daniel Strange was not looking for them, they would have let their guard down by now. She would get back on their trail with a new identity. Stepping up onto the porch of the boardinghouse, she paused for a moment, touching her fingertips first to the scar on her cheek, then to the thin false mustache she'd purchased from a traveling theatrical company and taken to wearing. Once assured that her true identity was well concealed, Danielle raised the brass door knocker and tapped it soundly.

When Danielle had paid the two dollars for a room to a jovial heavyset woman wearing a white full-length cooking apron, she'd introduced herself as Danny Duggin. She watched the woman pocket the money beneath her apron and run a hand across her moist brow as she spoke.

"It's a pleasure to meet you. I'm Norena Chapin, Mr. Duggin, but most of my regulars just call me Ma. Will you be staying with me for long? Because if you are, you can pay by the week or month and save yourself some money."

Danielle answered in the lowered, gruff voice she had become accustomed to using. "No, ma'am. I expect I'll be headed out sometime tomorrow. I saw your sign out front and knew I'd rather stay here than in a hotel. For my money, nothing beats a good home-cooked boardinghouse meal."

Norena Chapin blushed, obviously flattered, and raised a hand to smooth a strand of loose hair. "Why, thank you, Mr. Duggin. My son, Willard, always says the same thing. He used to be on the road a lot until he settled down with a job operating a telegraph office in Tracy Sidings. I expect from your clothes that you're a cattle drover?"

"Yes, ma'am, of late anyway," said Danielle. "Although, having heard about the death of a friend of mine, Marshal Buck Jordan, I suppose I might just go hunting for his killers."

Norena Chapin touched her work-worn fingers to her cheek, saying, "Oh, my, wasn't that a terrible thing? And you were a friend of Buck Jordan?"

"Yes, ma'am, so to speak," said Danielle.

"He used to live here, you know," Norena Chapin added.

"No, ma'am, I didn't know that," said Danielle.

"Oh, yes. His room was the first one at the top of the stairs, the room you'll be staying in. It used to be Willard's room, too, when he lived at home. I still miss them both something awful. I'm always fearful for Willard, although he lives in a railroad siding town, and I'm sure the railroad keeps law and order there."

"Yes, ma'am, I'm sure they do," Danielle said, already anticipating a bath and a soft bed before supper.

"But it's getting terrible everywhere," Norena Chapin offered, keeping Danielle waiting as she searched beneath her large apron for a room key. "Only day before yesterday, Willard wired me and told me there had been a shooting there." She spoke as she searched one dress pocket, then the other. "The sheriff from St. Joseph arrived in the nick of time to keep some of the townsmen from lynching a couple of young boys for a murder they didn't commit."

"Oh?" Hearing word of her hometown, St. Joseph, got Danielle's attention. "Was that sheriff's name Connally?"

"Willard didn't mention his name," Norena said, still searching her pocket, "but the two teenage boys were look-alikes. Willard said the boys were both wounded and managed to slip away that evening. Said the sheriff was upset because he wanted to take them back to St. Joe for safekeeping."

Danielle stood stunned for a second at the news, her hand at first unable to reach out for the key when Norena Chapin finally found it and offered it to her. Could the two boys be her brothers, Tim and Jed? Of course they were, she thought. What other twin boys were around St. Joseph? None that she could think of, at least not around the age Norena mentioned. Then, taking the key, she asked, "How badly were the boys wounded?"

"Well, they were able to get away, so I don't suppose it must've been too bad," Norena said. Then, seeing the look on Danielle's face, she asked, "Why? Do you know anyone from St. Joseph?"

"Uh, yes, ma'am. But it's been a while since I've seen them."

Suddenly the foyer of the boardinghouse felt small and tight to Danielle. She had to get upstairs to her room and do some thinking without Norena Chapin's eyes on her.

"Willard said two men killed the St. Joseph town tax assessor. That's what started this whole incident apparently. At first some of the people thought it was the young twins. That's why the sheriff was following them. It turns out, the boys were innocent, and the two murderers are still running loose. That's something you'd better be leery of if you're going to be traveling."

"I certainly will do that, ma'am," Danielle said, already heading for the stairs. "Now, if you'll excuse me, I'd better get myself a bath and some rest."

"Yes, Mr. Duggin, you do that," Norena said as Danielle stepped upward. "I'll come wake you for supper."

In the room, Danielle undressed, peeling off the fake mustache and taking off the binder she wore to flatten her breasts. She then threw a towel around herself and went to the bathroom for a soak in the tub. The water in the large iron tub was only tepid, but it had been changed that morning, and Danielle was thankful for that. Too often in the past year she'd had to bathe in water that had accommodated five or six other people before her. As she lathered and scrubbed, she thought about what Norena Chapin had told her, and came to the conclusion that it had to be her brothers, Tim and Jed, that Norena's son Willard was talking about.

"But why?" Danielle asked herself aloud, in the stillness of the bathroom.

She pictured her brothers' faces in her mind, wondering who was looking after her mother. She refused to consider that something might have happened to her mother that would have freed the twins up and allowed them to leave the farm. She finished her bath, trying to guess where the twins might be after striking out from Tracy Sidings, wounded and on their own.

"You're headed this way, aren't you?" she murmured.

In silence, she went back to her room and stretched out naked on the bed, letting the slight breeze through the window dry her, offering her some comfort from the scorching heat of the day.

That evening at supper, she took her seat at the boardinghouse table amid six male guests and partook of roast beef, gravy, potatoes, and corn bread. Because she was there for only one night, the other guests made only polite conversation with her in passing. But when one guest, a jail guard named Lee Tate, told the others about the telegram that had arrived from Arizona earlier in the week advising law officers of the release of felons who had served their time, Danielle took note. Danielle's interest began to fade until Tate mentioned the name Duncan Grago. She jerked her attention toward Tate in such a quick manner that all conversation stopped, and all eyes turned to her as she spoke.

"Grago, you said? What was his first name?" Her intense stare was unsettling. The name Grago was the name on the top of her list of her father's killers.

Lee Tate was taken aback by this young stranger with the thin wispy mustache, the scarred cheek, and the cold verdant eyes. "Why, his first name is Duncan, like I just said," Tate answered with a bemused expression. "Why? Do you know him?"

"No," Danielle said, easing back into her chair, "but I've heard of Newt Duncan and wondered if they might be kin."

As Lee Tate considered it, a whiskey drummer named Bob Dennard cut in, saying, "Humph, they're kin, all right, like two rattlesnakes from under the same rock." Eyes turned to him as he continued. "I came across those two years back in El Paso. They were both young then, Newton being the oldest. They killed an old Mexican couple near there that never harmed a soul in their life. The Gragos punched their ticket for a bag of coffee and an old silver brooch the woman wore." He sucked a tooth and set his coffee mug down beside his plate. "Texas has had a price of five hundred dollars on their heads for the longest time. I hope you've got no truck with the likes of them, Mr. Duggin. If I thought you did, I'd have to call you a rotten, killing animal, no different than they are."

A tense hush fell about the table. Danielle looked at Bob Dennard and realized in an instant that he was not the whiskey drummer he had introduced himself as. What was he, then? she asked herself, staring into his hard gray eyes. A bounty hunter? She thought about it as she spoke.

"No, I have no truck with them—none that's your concern anyway. But you might have asked in a less insulting manner." Danielle set her coffee mug down as well and kept both palms flat on the table edge.

"I might have . . . but I didn't," said Dennard, his face pinching red as he spoke. "I saw what you are the minute you came in, Mr. Duggin, if indeed that *is* your name."

The tension thickened around the table. Chairs scooted back, the other men ready to distance themselves from what looked like a coming storm between the two.

Dennard continued. "You come in here unarmed, but where you wear your holster is the only spot on your trousers that ain't bleached out from the sun. Drover, you say? Hell, I know better. That ain't no brush cut on your face, and you didn't get them backed-out eyes staring up cattle's rumps. Who are you, Duggin? Why all the questions about ex-convicts?"

As Dennard spoke, Norena Chapin had stepped into the room with a fresh bowl of potatoes. She saw the trouble brewing and stopped in her tracks. "Now, see here, both of you. I don't allow quarreling and such at my table—"

"Easy, Norena," said Dennard, who was well-known at the boardinghouse from years of frequent lodging there, "this young man is about to explain something to all of us. Let's hear what he has to say."

Danielle held Dennard's stare and thought about the derringer in her boot well. She could get to it if she needed it. That was not an issue. Her first concern was for the innocent people around the table. Her second concern was for Dennard himself. He was rude and short with her, but only because he'd mistaken her for the very kind of person she herself was hunting for. There was irony here, but she wasn't about to explain herself to this man. She did not want to blow her new name, uncovering once again her intent.

"You don't want to hear the only thing I've got to say to you, mister," she said in a calm, even tone. "I came to this table un-armed, in respect for this woman's home. Now, if you'll excuse me, ma'am," she added with a nod toward Norena Chapin, "I'll take my leave."

"Not without answering me first, you won't," Dennard said in-sistently.

Leaving half her plate of food uneaten, Danielle scooted her chair back, stood up, and turned from the table. The sound of a pistol cocking caused her to freeze in her tracks, her hand poised, ready to drop down to her boot. But before she made her move,

Dennard said in warning, "Hear that sound? The next time you hear it will be when your pistol is riding your hip. You'll answer me today civilly, or you'll answer me tomorrow on the outskirts of town."

Without turning, Danielle said over her shoulder, "Will that sound I hear tomorrow be coming at my back? Or will you have the guts to cock it head-on?" She walked out of the room without another word, and retired to her room for the night.

FORT SMITH, ARKANSAS. JUNE 21, 1871.

Norena Chapin was up before daylight and met Danielle as she came down the stairs with her gear over her shoulder. "Mr. Duggin," Norena said, "I just couldn't let you leave without first apologizing for Mr. Dennard's behavior last evening. You poor dear, you didn't even get to finish your supper."

Not expecting anyone to be up this early, Danielle had placed her Stetson atop her head before leaving her room. She removed it in deference to Norena's presence and said with a smile, "It was not your fault, ma'am, nor was it the fault of the cooking. The meal was excellent, and I'll be stopping here anytime I'm in Fort Smith."

"I certainly hope so," said Norena. She raised a bag from behind her back and held it out. "Here, I prepared something for you for the road. I couldn't bear to see you leave here shortchanged. I even thought about giving you back your money, but I knew you'd be too proud to take it."

"You're right, ma'am," said Danielle. "I can't hold you responsible for the rudeness of one of your guests." Danielle took the offered bag. "But I'll accept this and thank you for your kindness."

Norena Chapin smiled. "I don't know what got into Mr. Dennard. I've never seen him act that way."

"Well, let's hope that's the end of it," Danielle said. She left through the front door in the gray light of dawn and looked back to return Norena Chapin's wave on her way to the livery barn.

At the barn, Danielle found the stable boy already going about his chores, tending a pile of hay with a pitchfork. Once Danielle had prepared her chestnut mare for the road and led it out into the main bay of the barn, she flipped the boy a silver dollar and asked, "Tell me, young man, does a whiskey drummer by the name of Bob Dennard keep his horse here?"

"Yes, sir, he does," the boy said, pointing a dirty finger at an empty stall, "but it's not there now. He rode out of here over an hour ago. He woke me up to let him in."

"I see," said Danielle, "and what kind of horse does he ride?"

"A big dapple gray. Not what you'd expect a whiskey drummer to ride, is it?" the boy added. "Most drummers travel by coach or buggy. But not Dennard. He carries a lot of weaponry, too." The boy grinned. "My pa says maybe Dennard don't want to be sassed by some saloonkeeper."

"Your pa might be more right than he thinks," Danielle said, leading the chestnut mare out the front door.

Looking down at the set of fresh tracks, she stepped up into the saddle. Turning the mare and following the prints out to the main street, she headed north, but not before seeing the hoofprints lead off across the street to an alley. It was the perfect place for Dennard to sit and wait for her, she thought. She heeled the mare forward, knowing that before she rode out of sight, Dennard would be on her trail.

CHAPTER 5

THE OLD PIKE ROAD. JUNE 21, 1871.

Headed northwest, Danielle kept the chestnut mare at a steady clip on the hard dirt and stone as the first thin line of sunlight mantled the sky. Topping a low rise in the road, she reined the mare up sharply, then held the animal still and listened to the sound of a single horse's hooves closing behind her. Danielle batted her boots to the chestnut's sides and raced forward another two hundred yards until she topped another rise and started down the other side, out of sight where the road turned through a stretch of rock. Upon entering the waist-high rocks and brush, Danielle slowed the mare down, swung from the saddle, and stepped down into cover as the mare galloped on.

She waited in the brush and rock and, in less than five minutes, saw the big dapple gray come into sight, moving at a slow trot. Dennard was looking down in the pale morning light, keeping an eye on the hoofprints of Danielle's mare. So intent was he in his tracking, he didn't see Danielle jump in front of his horse, causing the big dapple to rear up beneath him

"Damn it!" Dennard cursed as his horse's hooves touched down.

His hand had gone instinctively to the pistol on his hip, but it froze there at the sight of Danielle covering him with both of her Colts drawn and cocked at him from less than six feet away.

"Raise your gun with two fingers and drop it, Dennard," Danielle demanded. Seeing the hesitancy in his eyes, Danielle added, "Try anything and I'll clip your thumb off."

Dennard replied in defiance, "I'm not going to die out here in the dirt, killed by some lousy outlaw."

His pistol streaked upward, but the shot from Danielle's Colt lifted it spinning from his hand. The dapple gray shied back a step, whinnying as Dennard clasped his left hand around his now bleeding right hand.

"I'm not an outlaw, Dennard, but you will die here in the dirt if you don't do like you're told." Danielle cocked the pistol again.

As Dennard stepped down grudgingly from his saddle, Danielle whistled up the chestnut mare, and by the time Dennard had turned to face her, still holding his bleeding hand, the mare came cantering up to Danielle's side. Danielle holstered her left Colt and raised a hand to the mare's muzzle, saying, "Good horse, Sundown." Then she said to Dennard, "I know you think you were tracking an outlaw. That's the only reason you're still alive. But you called this one wrong, Dennard. I'm not on the dodge. I'm on a manhunt myself."

"Yeah?" Dennard said skeptically. "I know a hard case when I see one. You look like one. You even smell like one. You got the jump on me. Now go ahead and shoot. Get it over with. I won't beg for my life."

"It's starting to sound tempting, Dennard," Danielle said. "Hold your coat open. Show me what else you're packing." As she spoke, Danielle circled around him to his horse and pulled his Henry rifle from the saddle boot.

"I'm clean," Dennard said, opening his lapels with his bloody hands. "I never need a hideout gun. I face a man straight up, or I don't face him at all."

"Is that the way you were planning to do with me?" Danielle asked, stepping back to pick Dennard's pistol up off the ground. "You were going to follow me, then ride in and invite me to a shoot-out?"

"No. I was going to get the jump on you, hog-tie you, and make you tell me everything you know about Newt and Duncan Grago or any other outlaws you ride with."

"Then you're sure in for a disappointing day, mister," Danielle said. "Now, get your boots off and pitch them to me." She reached down and took up the reins to the dapple gray.

"You can't leave me out here afoot," Dennard said, steadying himself on one foot as he yanked off a boot and pitched it over on the ground. "Horse theft is still a hanging offense, young man," he said, taking off his other boot.

"Not when somebody's on your trail about to dry-gulch you," Danielle said.

"I'm a bounty hunter," Dennard said with a scowl, getting bolder now that he saw his life was not in danger. "I've got a right to do my job."

"Not on me, you don't. There's no bounty on my head. I've got business to take care of. I'm not going to have you hounding me out here."

"Then you explain yourself, young man," said Dennard. "Why were you asking about the Grago brothers?"

"I'm not explaining a damn thing to you, Dennard," Danielle said, stepping toward her chestnut mare, leading the dapple gray. "But you're going to tell me what you know about the Gragos."

"Like hell I will," Dennard said defiantly.

"Oh, you will, Dennard." Danielle aimed the Colt at his left foot. "You can tell me now while you've got ten toes, or you can tell me five seconds from now when you've only got nine."

"All right, hold on!" Dennard placed one foot over the other, as if to protect them. "Newt Grago is holed up down in the Territory, gathering himself a gang. He's hard to get to. Some gunman killed off four of his buddies. I believe he thinks that gunman is looking for him, too."

"Name some men who ride with him," Danielle demanded, "and don't lie. I already know some of their names."

Dennard hesitated, then let out a breath and said, "There's Leo Knight, Morgan Goss, Sep Howard, Chancy Burke, Julius Byler,

Rufe Gaddis, Saul Delmano, Cincinnati Carver, and Blade Hogue. There's others, too. They come and go down in the Territory. But that's all I can think of with a gun pointed at my toes."

"Forget Goss, Knight, Howard, and Carver," said Danielle. "Where can I find the others when they're not with Grago?"

"If I knew the answer to that, they'd already be dead," said Dennard. He thought about it for a second. "But I heard tell that Rufe Gaddis and Saul Delmano were tossing Mexican horses down near Laredo, what time they're not robbing stagecoaches and raising hell."

"And the others?" Danielle probed.

"Well"—Dennard thought some more—"Chancy Burke is border trash, a killer and a drifter. What time he's not riding with Grago, you're apt to find him in any Mexican whorehouse that'll have him. As far as Blade Hogue and Julius Byler"—Dennard shrugged—"that's anybody's guess, I reckon." Dennard eyed Danielle closely. "I'll tell you one thing, young man. If you're really not an outlaw, you'd best not go horning into my business. I make a living killing these dogs. Nobody messes with my livelihood."

Danielle nodded, running the names through her mind and realizing most of these men were on her list. "I'm no bounty hunter, Dennard."

She'd never heard of Leo Knight, Morgan Goss, or Cincinnati Carver, but the others were the men who'd had a hand in killing her father. For a moment she was tempted to ask Dennard to join her, him taking the bounty on their heads and her taking her vengeance. Yet she had sworn at her father's grave that she would track down his killers one by one, and this was not the time to change her tactics.

"I'm taking your horse a mile up the road with me," Danielle said. "You'll find it tied beside the trail, along with your shooting gear. I'm throwing your boots away. I figure by the time you get there, then get back to town and get yourself some boots and a hat, I'll be cleared out of here. If you're smart, you'll stay off my back. Now give me your hat."

Dennard swore under his breath, yanked his bowler hat from his head, and sailed it to her. Danielle caught it and tucked it up under her arm, turning sideways to him just enough to step up into her saddle. "What if somebody passes by before I get there and steals my horse and guns?" Dennard said.

"Then you'd better walk quick, Dennard," Danielle said with a thin smile. She turned the chestnut mare and heeled it forward, leading the dapple gray. If her brothers, Jed and Tim, were headed this way, she would find them.

Danielle left the dapple gray where she'd said she would, and taking the trail through the rocky brush country, she rode on. At noon she stopped only long enough to rest the mare while she partook of the vittles Norena Chapin had given her. Then she pressed north for the rest of the day. Evening shadows were drawing long across the land when she stopped to water her mare and make camp at a run-out spring beneath a low rock ledge.

She saw the tracks of four horses as she stepped down to fill her canteen. Two sets of tracks were older than the others. These led off upward and off the trail. The other two sets of tracks circled away from the water and wound upward toward the ledge above her. She could feel eyes on her back as she capped the canteen, stood up, and looked around while the chestnut mare drew its fill.

"Easy, Sundown," she whispered, running a hand along the mare's dust-streaked side.

Danielle knew this was no time for any sudden moves. She draped the canteen strap over her saddle horn and walked slowly around the mare as if inspecting her saddle and tack. On the other side of the animal, Danielle stooped down pretending to inspect the mare's forelegs, and in doing so managed to scan the rocky slope above her. The slightest rustle of brush along the narrow ledge caught her attention. On her way back around the mare, she stopped short, yanked the rifle from her saddle boot with one hand, and as quick as a whip slapped her other hand on the mare's rump, sending the animal darting away along the stream bank as she flattened to the ground behind a low stand of rock.

Danielle aimed deliberately high, two shots from her rifle kicking up chips of rock from the terraced ledge, her third shot going low into a scrub cedar sapling.

"The next shot will take some bone with it!" she called out to rustling brush where she could tell someone had just hugged the dirt, taking cover.

"Whoa now! Take it easy, mister," a nervous voice called down to her. "We mean you no harm!"

It had been over a year since Danielle had heard the sound of her brother Jed's voice, yet she recognized it instantly, and her heart leaped for joy. But she stilled herself and called back to him, lowering her voice back into a husky tone, "Then why are you up there watching me like a bushwhacker?"

"I— That is, *we* are sorry, mister," Jed Strange replied, rising slowly from the mound of brush, his hands chest high in a show of peace. "We thought you were somebody else. There's two outlaws on this trail. That's their hoofprints leading up into the hills. We already had trouble with them once. We weren't taking any chances."

"Whose *we*?" Danielle demanded of him, already knowing, but playing her role as a wary traveler. She had to fight herself to keep from running upward along the ledge and throwing her arms around her brothers. "How many of you are up there?"

"There's two of us, mister," Jed answered. "Me and my brother. Can we come down there? We need to finish watering our horses."

"Both of you come down here real slow-like," Danielle said. "The light's failing, so don't make no sudden moves. I might get the wrong idea."

"Yes, sir," Jed called down to her. "We'll come down with our hands in sight."

Danielle smiled to herself. She knew how fast her brothers were with a gun. Even with their hands raised a bit from their holsters, they could pull iron quicker than most men. In the darkening dusk, she rose from behind her cover of rock and waited, hearing the horses' hooves clack along the ledge, then down onto the softer ground and toward her.

Once they were ten yards away, keeping her Stetson brim low across her brow, she said, "That's close enough," and looked Jed and Tim up and down, taking note of Tim's limp and the bandage around his thigh. "What happened to him, a snakebite?"

"No," Tim said, speaking for himself, reaching his free hand down and trying to close the gap in his ripped trousers. "I was shot in the leg. A railroad crew mistook me for a wanted outlaw. But they were wrong, mister, just so's you don't think we mean you any harm."

"If I thought you meant me harm, young man," said Danielle, "the conversation would never have made it this far." She jerked a thumb toward the run-out stream, saying, "Go on, finish watering your horses whilst I go get mine and picket it to graze. If you boys want to share a camp here, I have some coffee beans and jerked beef."

"Lord, mister," Tim said, "we'd love some hot coffee. We've been living hand to mouth on squirrel and possum since we left Tracy Sidings. I'm Tim Strange. This is my twin brother, Jed."

"Twins, eh?" Danielle pretended to eye them closer. "I suppose the light's too dim to tell it right now. I'm Danny Duggin, a drover up from Texas. Why don't one of you gather us some fire kindling? I'll be right back with that coffee. I'd like to hear about these outlaws you had problems with."

Tim and Jed Strange looked at each other as Danielle walked along the stream to where her mare stood drinking.

"He's sure a trusting sort, Jed," said Tim.

Jed let out a breath and relaxed. "Yeah. It's good to know that not everybody is out to rob or kill you."

Luckily Sundown was streaked with sweat and road dust, or else Tim and Jed might have recognized her right away, Danielle thought as she reached down and gathered the reins. She led the mare away from the stream a few feet and picketed her in a graze of sweet grass. When Danielle had taken down her saddle and saddlebags, she walked back to where Tim and Jed were already busy starting a small fire.

"I'll go picket our horses with yours, mister," said Jed Strange, taking up both sets of reins.

But before he could lead them away, Danielle spoke, stopping him.

"No. My horse is just up from Texas on a trail drive. He's ornery and cross," she lied. "Besides, you never know what illness he might be carrying. Do us all a favor and picket your horses closer in, away from him."

"Thanks for the warning, mister," Tim said. "Our horses ain't in the best of shape right now anyway."

"Oh?" said Danielle to Tim, watching Jed lead the two gaunt bays to a separate stretch of grass nearer by. "Have you young men been on hard times?"

"Not to complain, Mr. Duggin, but it's been rougher than a cob the past year," Tim said, breaking a match loose and bending down to strike it. "We lost our pa to some murderers over a year ago. Jed and I haven't been able to find work."

Before Tim could say more, Jed called over to them in the darkening evening light, saying to Danielle, "Then we ran into those two outlaws no sooner than we left St. Joe. They came near to pinning a murder on us and getting us hung. Lucky for us, the sheriff from St. Joe showed up to vouch for us and keep a lynch mob off our backs."

He walked back into the growing glow of the small campfire as it fed upward on a pile of cedar and pine twigs.

Not wanting to sound too prying, but still wanting to hear all the news they had from home, Danielle dropped her saddle and gear back out of the coming firelight, and asked, "What about the rest of your family back in St. Joe? Couldn't they have vouched for you as well?"

"We've only got one sister, Mr. Duggin," Tim said as Jed walked back with their saddles and dropped them to the ground, "and she left home after Pa's death. That's who we're looking for out here. We've got bad news for her, but there's no telling where she's at."

"I see," said Danielle quietly, cutting him off for the moment, for she already knew there was bad news coming about her mother. She prepared herself for it, wanting to postpone hearing it for as long as she could.

Her heart had leaped at the sight of her brothers, the two of them looking a little more like men since last she'd seen them. She had missed them terribly and it had taken much control to keep from revealing who she was and throwing her arms around them. Yet, for their sake, she thought, Danielle held her feelings in check and took the small bag of coffee beans and the battered pot from her saddlebags.

Pitching the bag to Jed, she said to him, "Bust us up some beans. I'll get us some water, and we'll brew up a pot."

It was a few minutes later when Danielle heard the news of her mother's death. As they sipped their hot coffee, Tim went on to say that he and Jed had buried their mother before leaving home. When Danielle heard it, she could not let on how terribly crushed she was. But as unbearable as the news was, all she could do was keep her hat brim tipped forward and down, hiding her eyes from them in the glow of the fire. Even more crushing was the fact that she could take no comfort from her brothers, nor could she offer them any in return. For all the twins knew, they were strangers here on a lone frontier trail. She dared not reveal herself to them, tempting though it was, for while she had long grown accustomed to this terrible vengeance trail, she did not wish it for her brothers. She managed to keep her tears hidden beneath her hat brim. When she could speak without her voice betraying her, she did so with a harder edge than she'd intended.

"Boys, I'm sorry to hear about your troubles. But has it occurred to you that maybe your sister wouldn't want you joining her? Has it occurred to you that maybe she isn't even in the country? If she left home hunting those kind of men, she could be halfway across Mexico by now."

"Then that's where we'll find her, Mr. Duggin," Tim said with determination. "We're not turning back if that's what you're getting at. There's nothing for us back there."

Danielle considered it, then said, "No, that's not what I'm getting at. It's none of my business what you do. But for all you know, maybe your sister already found the men who killed your pa. Maybe they're all dead by now." She hesitated for a second, then added, "Maybe she's even dead herself."

After a silence, Jed said, "Then we won't stop until we find where she's buried. We have to tell her about Ma even if we have to say it to a grave marker."

Danielle felt the tears well in her eyes again, and she fought them back. Nothing was going to stop these two and she knew it. The best she could hope for was to get some miles between them and continue her search. Hopefully she would rid the world of the remaining men on her list before her brothers ever had to face any of them. For her money, it was even odds that one of the outlaws the boys had encountered was Duncan Grago. She wasn't about to let an opportunity like this slip by. She was too close to be dissuaded now. Come morning, she would find the outlaws' trail and stick to it.

"Well, then, boys," she said in a softer tone of voice, "all I can tell you is, be careful in Indian Territory. If you think it's tough here, you ain't seen nothing yet. There's outlaws there who'll cut your throat just to see which way you'll fall. Don't trust anybody. Don't ever let your guards down."

"Thanks, mister," said Tim. "We don't intend to."

As Tim spoke, Jed eyed Danielle's half-hidden face in the licking flames. "Mr. Duggin, I can't help thinking that you look familiar. Have you ever been to St. Joseph?"

Danielle thought about it quickly. Deciding it would better to give him some reason for recognition than to deny it altogether, she said, "Yes, indeed I have, several times over the past few years. There's a gunsmith there who did some work for me on my pistols. Did some fine custom work. Can't remember his name, though."

"Well, I'll be danged!" exclaimed Tim. "That was our pa, for sure. Pa was known as the best gunsmith in Missouri. If he did some custom work on your Colts, you've got some good ones." He leaned slightly forward. "Can I take a look at them?"

With her riding dust still on, Danielle had made it a point to keep her father's Colt handles out of sight. Now she adjusted her duster across herself and said, "Out here, you never hand your gun to a stranger, young man, no matter how friendly the circumstance."

"Sorry," said Tim. "I should have learned better by now."

"No apology necessary, young man," said Danielle. "I only mentioned it for your own good." She finished her coffee, then slung the grounds from her cup. "I reckon we best all get some shut-eye. It's been a long day."

Jed and Tim looked at each other. "But, Mr. Duggin, we've been doing all the talking. What about you? What are you doing out here?"

"Just passing through, boys," Danielle said, reaching around and adjusting her blanket. "There's nothing much to tell you about myself. I'm a drover, working the spreads up from Texas. Of course if you're looking for work, I can give you some names of ranchers and trail bosses."

"Would you, please?" Tim asked, he and Jed both leaning forward eagerly. "We'll be needing work whether we find our sister or not."

This was a good way to get them off the trail for a while, Danielle thought. "Ever worked a herd?" she asked, already knowing the answer.

"No, but we handle a horse as well as the next, and we ain't afraid of a day's work, no matter how hard," said Jed.

"Then go down to Mobeetie, Texas, to the Riley spread," Danielle said. "Tell Jacob Riley you're new at droving but you need work. Better not waste any time getting there. He'll be pushing a big herd to Dodge before long. Jobs fill up quick."

"We'll head there tomorrow," Tim said, excited about the prospect of work. "Which way is it from here?"

"Swing west from here," Danielle said. "Pick up the Arkansas River the other side of Fort Smith toward the Canadian, then follow the Canadian past the grasslands into Texas. After about a day's ride into east Texas, head due south across the Washita. Follow the cow tracks from there. Ask anybody where the Jacob Riley spread is, if you have trouble finding it."

"But what about hunting for Danielle?" Jed asked his brother.

"We need to eat, don't we?" Tim replied. "Besides, Mobeetie might be as good a place as any to look for her. Right, Mr. Duggin?"

"I would think so," said Danielle. "One trail's as good as the next when you've no destination to begin with."

"But we were headed down to Fort Smith, to talk to a marshal by the name of Buck Jordan," Jed cut in. "He's the one who sent us Pa's belongings. We figured maybe he could tell us something about our sister."

"I'll save you both some time," Danielle said glumly. "Buck Jordan is dead. I heard about it coming through Fort Smith. The Hanging Judge loses about one marshal a month to badlands outlaws. Last month it was Buck Jordan." Danielle offered a thin, sad smile beneath the cover of her hat brim and her fake mustache. "That tells you something about Indian Territory, I reckon." She smoothed her blanket, lay back with her head on her saddle, and flipped half the blanket across herself. "Go on to Mobeetie, boys. Get yourself a stake of money. Then go hunt for your sister." She pulled her hat brim farther down over her face. "That's my advice. Good night, boys," she added with finality.

During the night, while the twins slept, Danielle raised her brim and looked from one to the other of them. The news of her mother's death still stung her down deep. For a long moment she watched her two brothers sleep, longing to gather them both into her arms. She thought of happier times on their Missouri farm and saw visions of the entire family gathered around the kitchen table. Her eyes watered again, but she caught herself and rubbed her eyes dry with her knuckles. She stood up silently, gathering her gear. From inside her saddlebags, she took out her only other pair of jeans and, slipping over closer to her sleeping brothers, laid them near Tim's head. Then she took out most of her jerked beef and the bag of coffee beans and laid the supplies atop the folded trousers.

"God be with you both," she whispered to herself, resisting the urge to place a hand on their cheeks. Then, like a passing breath of night wind, she was gone.

THE OLD PIKE ROAD. JUNE 22, 1871.

At dawn, Jed shook his brother's shoulder, saying, "Wake up, Tim. Duggin is gone."

"Gone?" Tim sat up and rubbed sleep from his face. "Where? Why?" He looked all around, acquainting himself with the campsite in the early light.

"I don't know," Jed replied, standing back a step. "But he left us food and coffee . . . and look." He held up the jeans and shook them out. "He's even left you a pair of blue jeans."

"Well, I'll be." Tim stood up stiffly on his wounded leg, then snatched the trousers from Jed's hand, looking at them in disbelief. "For all his tough tone of voice, I reckon Danny Duggin is surely—"

Tim's voice failed him for a moment, and he swallowed a tight knot in his throat.

"I know," said Jed, looking at the bag of coffee beans and jerked beef in his hand. "There's some decent folks out here. It just takes some sifting to find them, I reckon."

Tim collected himself, holding the trousers tight against his chest. "It's charity, no matter how you look at it. He must've known that if we'd been awake, I'd never accepted him giving me these trousers." He squeezed the jeans tighter. "But *damn*, I'm awfully glad he did it!"

Jed looked off toward where the chestnut mare had been picketed before Danny Duggin had slipped away in the night. "I swear, Tim," he said, "there was something I liked about that man. I know we never met him before, but he seemed almost like kin, didn't he?"

"Yep, I felt that way, too." Tim gazed off with his brother, the two of them feeling small against the magnitude of the land. "If we ever get back on our feet and run into him again, I want to repay Mr. Danny Duggin for these jeans, and thank him for his kindness."

CHAPTER 6

INDIAN TERRITORY. JUNE 24, 1871.

The hoofprints Danielle followed led her on a three-day meandering loop, southwest around Fort Smith and deeper toward the heart of Indian Territory. On the third evening, she'd heard distant gunfire and followed the sound of it. Then she spotted a black rise of smoke, which guided her to the burned hull of an abandoned wagon. The bodies of an old teamster and his four mules lay scattered among the ruins. Danielle took note of the jagged upthrust of rock standing above a sunken basin of brush and sage. The hoofprints she'd been tracking led in that direction. While there was no reason for the riders to have tarried here, she still played it safe, swinging fifty yards to the west so that she would ride in with the sinking sun to her back.

At the crackling embers that were once the wagon bed, Danielle kicked through the teamster's load of scattered bolts of cloth and hand tools. She shook her head at the pillaged remains. Whatever the old man had carried in his pockets was all the outlaws could have found any use for. What had this gotten them, she wondered, a twist of tobacco, a few dollars, maybe the old man's rifle or pistol? The senselessness of it angered her, and she kicked at the spoilage on the dusty trail.

Above the smoldering coals and the whir of the wind, Danielle hadn't heard the two horses slip in close at a silent walk until the sound of a rifle cocking behind her caught her attention. Before she could turn and draw, the voice of Duncan Grago said with the low hiss of a rattlesnake, "Go on and try it, peckerwood. We ain't above shooting you in the back."

Danielle froze for a second, then turning her head slightly, she said over her shoulder, "I'm surprised you haven't already. From the looks of that ole man, back shooting *is* your strongest suit."

"There's only one reason we haven't," Duncan Grago said. "I want to know who you are and why you've been breathing down our necks the past three days. I don't like people following me. It always spells law dog or bounty hunter to me."

"Following you?" Danielle chuckled, taking her chances on turning a bit farther around. As she faced them now, her hands were poised chest high, but still able to get a fast grab on her Colts. "I wasn't *following* you. I was leading you from behind." She leveled her gaze at them, inching her hands down as she spoke. "I figured if there was any bushwhackers or renegades running loose, I'd hear them killing you and get myself a head start out of here." She shrugged. "Better you than me, I always say."

Sep Howard only stared suspiciously, taking note of the cold green eyes and the big dust-streaked chestnut mare. But after the second it took for Danielle's words to sink in, Duncan Grago allowed a grin to form on his parched lips.

"Well, hell, I can't argue with that kind of thinking," he said. "There was a couple of plow jockeys back along the trail. Don't suppose you ran into them, did you?"

Danielle thought about it, then said, "Yeah, our paths crossed. They told me what you did to them back in St. Joe, then again in Tracy Sidings."

"No kidding?" Now Duncan Grago grinned openly. "What did you tell them?"

"I told them they'd better kill you the first chance they get, or else you'd be causing them trouble the rest of their lives," said Danielle.

Duncan Grago laughed aloud, but Sep Howard still sat staring, his hard, unyielding gaze leveled on Danielle. Finally he cut in, saying to Duncan Grago, "I never mentioned it to you, Dunc, but last year there was a young gunslinger kicking up dust across the Territory. He had green eyes, went by the name Daniel Strange, and he rode a big chestnut, just like that one right there." Sep Howard nodded at Sundown without taking his eyes off Danielle. "What's your name, mister?"

"My name's Danny Duggin, mister," said Danielle, her hand poised lower now, nearer to her pistol. "What's yours?"

"Never mind my name," said Sep Howard. His voice turned to Duncan Grago but his eyes stayed on Danielle. "That's pretty close, wouldn't you say, Dunc? His name's Danny. The gunman's name was Dan. They both have green eyes; both ride a big chestnut."

Duncan Grago's smile faded. "You're saying this is him?"

"I'm saying everything about him is awfully familiar," Sep Howard replied. "We all heard that young gunslinger got himself carved to death by Comanche Jack Pierce, but we could have heard wrong."

"You didn't hear wrong," Danielle said. "I heard all about that gunslinger myself. Comanche Jack Pierce cut him to pieces over a card game. He died outside Mobeetie." Danielle jerked her thumb toward Sundown. "For all I know, that might have been his chestnut. I bought her from a stable owner when her owner never came back for her. Now that's about all the explaining I plan on doing here. Besides, if I was a gunslinger wanting to hide my name, I could do a lot better than changing it from Dan to Danny, don't you think?"

"He got you there, Sep," said Duncan Grago with a short laugh. "I figure he just bumped the pot on you. Now are you going to call him or fold? To tell you the truth, I like the man's style. He ain't afraid, standing there, knowing any second we might pin a couple of slugs to his chest."

"Yeah?" said Sep Howard. "Well, I don't believe him, and I sure don't like him. For my money he's the same one who—"

His words were cut short by the blast of fire from Danielle's smoking Colt. She'd seen the faintest movement of his hand toward his pistol as he'd spoken. As Sep Howard's body flew backward from the saddle of his rearing horse, Danielle's Colt leveled and cocked on Duncan Grago before his hand could even close around his pistol butt.

"I wouldn't do it if I were you, *Dunc*," said Danielle, mimicking the name Sep Howard had called him.

Duncan Grago froze, then relaxed as Danielle's thumb let the Colt's hammer down to half cock. He shot a glance at Sep Howard lying dead in the dirt, then cut his eyes back to Danielle as she punched the spent cartridge from her Colt and replaced it with a new round.

"What the hell did you do that for?" Duncan rasped.

"I could tell he was getting ready to go for his gun," Danielle said. "Why beat around the bush about it?" She spun the cylinder on her Colt, flipped it around across her palm, and slid it back into her holster. "Anyway, I knew we weren't going to be friends, he and I," she added. "Now what about you?"

Duncan Grago had never seen a cross draw that quick in his life. He sucked a slice of air through his teeth, calmed himself, then said, "I'm Duncan Grago." He nodded at the body sprawled on the ground. "That *was* Sep Howard. I don't think he even saw what hit him, and he was more than a fair hand with a gun."

"Can't tell it by looking," Danielle said. She walked over to Sep Howard's body, stooped down, and rifled through his shirt pockets, taking out a twist of tobacco and a small fold of sweat-dampened dollar bills. She fanned the bills, then refolded them and stuck them down into her riding duster. "You want his pistol?" she asked.

"Naw, it didn't do much for him," Duncan Grago said. "What about that money, though?"

Danielle looked up at him and said, "If you wanted his money, you should have shot him yourself." She pitched Grago the twist of tobacco and watched him chuckle and bite off a plug, working it in his jaw as he spoke.

"No offense, Danny Duggin, but I believe you're as crazy and wild as I am." Grago spat a brown stream of juice for emphasis.

"Too bad this fool didn't see it," she replied. "It might have saved him a fast ride to hell."

Danielle had only gone through Sep Howard's pockets for show. She wanted Duncan Grago to see her as a hard case, and it had worked. She took her time dropping the saddle and bridle from Sep Howard's horse and slapping it on its rump. She wanted Duncan Grago to have the time he needed to work things out in his mind, for she knew that was exactly what he was thinking.

"What's your plans now?" Grago asked over his chaw.

Danielle turned from watching the horse run freely away in a drifting wake of dust and said, "Well, I thought I might go invest this money in a bottle of rye, maybe see if I can double it on a faro table. What about you? Where were you two headed before I stopped his clock?"

"I just pulled me a bunch of prison time in Arizona," replied Grago, "so naturally I've been wandering here and there, taking the long way around, raising myself a little hell." He nodded at the bodies of the old teamster and the mules. "But I've got a brother waiting on me down in the Territory. He has a good-sized gang riding with him off and on. If you really want to double that money, you might want to ride along with me. We'll be making some easy cash, quick enough. He's always looking for good gunmen."

Danielle felt her heart leap in her chest at the prospect of finding Newt Grago and perhaps all the other killers in one spot. But she hid her eagerness and said, "No, thanks. I work better alone." She looked up at him with a cool, level stare and decided to see just how far she could push him. "We might not get along, you and me. Then I'd have to be going through your pockets, too."

She offered a tight trace of a smile, watching his eyes for any sign of a comeback. If he was smart, she thought, he wouldn't stand still for this game of big dog, little dog she was playing on him. Danielle was going to ride with him; there was no doubt in her mind. But first she wanted to knuckle him under a little, just enough to let him know she was going to be in charge.

"Hell, I ain't hard to get along with," Duncan Grago said as if having not heard her veiled threat. "Ride on down with me. We've got a stop to make along the way. Sep and I was supposed to meet one of my brother's men, a fellow by the name of Julius Byler, outside of Fort Smith. After that we'll all three head down and join my brother. It'll be worth it to you. I can guarantee it."

That's the wrong way to respond, Dunc, Danielle thought to herself, staring up at him.

He should have come back with something tougher, letting her know he wasn't the least bit intimidated by this Danny Duggin with his fast draw and his sharp tongue. But it was too late now. Duncan Grago had just rolled over and shown his belly. She was the big dog now.

"Well . . ." Danielle paused as if considering it for a second. Then she turned and stepped up into her saddle and reined Sundown around beside him, letting him see her palm brush past the butt of her Colt. He almost flinched at the sight of it. "I hope you're right, Dunc," she said, watching him settle as her hands dropped harmlessly down onto her saddle horn. "I hate being disappointed."

"You won't be," he said, nudging his horse forward. "Once we hook up with Newt and his boys, there'll be action aplenty. You can count on it."

"I already am," Danielle said, nudging the big chestnut mare along beside him. "Just lead me to him."

THE ARKANSAS RIVER. JUNE 26, 1871.

Julius Byler had grown cross and restless waiting for Sep Howard and Newt's younger brother, Duncan Grago. He'd been holed up in a shack eighteen miles out of Fort Smith for most of the winter, and had run out of supplies over two weeks ago. His last trip into Fort Smith had ended in a shoot-out at a mercantile store when he'd stolen a new Winchester while the owner wasn't looking. He'd been afraid to show his face there ever since. With Judge Parker holding court there, the town swarmed with marshals

and deputies. If a man didn't want to end up on the end of Maledon's* rope, Byler thought, Fort Smith was a good place to avoid.

Julius Byler had been watching the river trail through the dirty
window, and at the sight of the two horsemen coming up into sight
through a sparse pine thicket, he snatched the stolen Winchester
from its spot inside the door and levered a round into the chamber.

Danielle was the first to see the movement through the dingy
window glass, and upon seeing the pane rise two inches, she stopped
Sundown and said to Duncan Grago, "If this is the place, you'd
best get ready to explain yourself, Dunc."

Duncan Grago caught sight of the rifle barrel slip across the
windowsill and level toward him. He called out from twenty feet
away, "Don't shoot! I'm Duncan Grago. If you're Julius Byler, my
brother, Newt, sent me and Sep Howard to meet you."

From inside the window, Julius Byler called out, "Then where's
Sep? I been expecting yas the past week."

"Sep's dead," said Duncan Grago, "but I'm here. If I wasn't who
I say I am, I'd never have found this place."

"How did you find it?" Byler asked, still aiming down the rifle
barrel.

"My brother, Newt, brought me here years ago. We spent a
month hiding out from a bunch of detectives out of Tennessee."

Byler hesitated, eyeing them through the dirty glass. Finally he
asked, "Who's that with you? What happened to Sep Howard?"

"It's a long story, what happened to Sep Howard," Duncan
Grago replied, "but this is Danny Duggin. He's a friend of mine."

Danielle smiled to herself and sat still, letting Duncan Grago
set things up for her. She was back on the killer's trail now, the
very air around her thick with their scent, she thought. She'd take
Julius Byler down and cross off his name from her list before they
ever left this place. She just had to figure a way to do it without
spooking Duncan Grago.

---

* George Maledon was the hangman for Judge Charles Isaac Parker.

The two of them watched the rifle barrel draw back inside the window; then they heard a bolt lift from the plank door. They stepped their horses closer as Julius Byler came out, hooking his galluses up over his shoulders, the rifle still in his hand and pointed loosely in their direction. "I don't like waiting. Never did." As he spoke to Duncan Grago, he eyed Danielle, taking close note of the dust-streaked chestnut mare. "And you," he said, turning his words to her, "I don't know you from Adam. Far as I'm concerned, you can turn tail and follow your tracks out of here."

"I don't turn tail real easy," Danielle said in a low tone. She stepped the mare closer. The rifle rose in Julius Byler's hands.

But Duncan Grago moved his horse sidelong in between them, speaking down to Byler in a harsh voice.

"Listen to me, Byler. Sep Howard said my brother wanted us to bring you along. Now I don't give a damn if you come or not. But you'd best think twice before you go shoving iron at Danny Duggin. He's with me. If he don't kill you, I will."

"You're vouching for this man?" Byler asked. "Because if you are, I'll take it your brother, Newt, is vouching for him, too."

"Damn right I vouch for him!" Grago snapped. "Think I'd ride with a man I wouldn't vouch for?"

"All right, then, take it easy," said Byler, backing off. "Once you get to know me, you'll realize I'm a cautious man."

"That's good to know, Byler," Danielle said. She swung down from her saddle, slow and easy. "Now you suppose we could get some hot grub and coffee before we head down to the Territory?"

"We could, except I don't have the makin's of a hot meal, and no coffee either. I been stored out over two weeks, living on hard-tack and water, unless I can shoot a muskrat on the riverbank."

"Damn," said Duncan Grago, swinging down from his saddle and stretching his legs. "You expect me and my partner to eat a stinking muskrat? We'll have to get some supplies before we head out of here."

We're partners now? Danielle smiled to herself, liking the way

Duncan Grago was implying that they were friends. She'd kept him good and buffaloed ever since she shot Sep Howard. The night before last, when Duncan had told her his grisly story of why he'd gone to prison, she hadn't shrunk from his knife-fight story the way Sep Howard had. Instead, when Duncan had finished telling her, she'd only told him in a calm voice that had she been that Mexican, she would have hunted him and killed him. His jaw had twitched, but he hadn't rebutted her threat in any way. His attitude would probably change once he was reunited with his brother and had more guns around to protect him. But for now Danielle had him where she wanted him. With someone who was his match, Duncan Grago was a coward, she thought. A coward who would take her where she wanted to go.

"Me and Danny will rest here a day while you go into Fort Smith and pull up some supplies, Byler," Duncan Grago said, taking charge now that everything seemed to be settled.

"I can't do it." Byler shook his shaggy head. "I stole a rifle and shot a store owner in the leg. They see my face in Fort Smith, they'll likely blow it off my shoulders."

"Well, hell's bells," said Duncan Grago, letting out an exasperated breath. "Is there anyplace else around here? Damned if I want to ride back that way."

Danielle cut in, saying, "I'll go, since you're both too afraid."

"I never said I'm afraid," Duncan Grago sneered, careful not to come back too strong at Danielle's cutting remark. "I just hate backtracking myself."

Looking at Danielle, Byler said, "I'd prefer keeping you in my sight for a while, Danny Duggin, till I know you better."

"You don't want to know me any better, Byler," Danielle said in warning.

"Cut it out, both of you," Duncan Grago demanded. "I'll go round up supplies. Think you two can get along till I get back?"

"We'll be fine," Danielle said, keeping a cold stare on Byler. "Ain't that right, *Julius*?"

It was later that evening when Danielle decided to make her move on Julius Byler. It would take Duncan Grago most of the night to ride back from Fort Smith, if he didn't decide to spend the night camped along the river and head back in the morning. After rubbing Sundown with a handful of straw and picketing her on a hilly rise behind the shack, Danielle had sat down on a cedar stump in the dusty front yard and taken her time cleaning and oiling her pistols one at a time, making sure to keep one ready and loaded across her lap.

The look she'd last seen on Julius Byler's face before he'd gone inside and bolted the door told Danielle he knew something was up between them. She kept an eye on the closed window for any sign of him or his rifle barrel. When she'd finished with her pistols, she stood up and swung her gun belt around her waist, buckled it, and adjusted it, taking her time, knowing full well that Byler was watching through a crack somewhere in the sun-bleached walls.

For a moment Danielle only stared at the shack, knowing the moment to wreak her vengeance was at hand. She let the long-controlled anger inside her come to the surface now, preparing for her task. Only yards away inside the shack stood another of the men who had killed her father, and like the other murderers she had found over the past year, she would see him dead. Danielle swallowed back the bitter taste in her throat, took a deep breath, and let it out slowly. She reached down at her feet and picked up a small rock.

"Julius Byler, it's time you pay up for murder," she called out, tossing the rock against the door of the shack.

"What the hell are you talking about?" Julius Byler called out. Inside the shack, his face was streaked with sweat. "I've never seen you before in my life!" He stood with his back pressed to the wall, his eyes fixed on the front door. "I never should have let you ride in with Grago! That's what I get for being hospitable!"

"You've never seen me before, but you know who I am," Danielle said. "You had me pegged as soon as you saw the chestnut mare. I'm that gunslinger who was killing you bastards last year. Come on out—it's time we reckoned up, just the two of us, the way it was with Bart Scovill, Snakehead Kalpana, Levi Jasper, and Brice Levan. They all died by my hand. Now you'll do the same."

"What's this about? Don't I have a right to know?" Julius Byler demanded.

"You don't have a right to nothing, far as I'm concerned." Danielle stepped sideways in the dusty yard, then took a fighting stance twelve feet from the plank door. "But I'll tell you anyway. Remember the man you and your outlaw friends robbed and hung in Indian Territory, back last year?" She paused, waiting for a response.

A silence passed. Then Byler called out, "Hell, I don't remember. That's a long time ago. He weren't the only man we killed, whoever he was."

Danielle felt her jaw tighten, her teeth clench. "That was my pa, you murdering son of a bitch. Now wipe the sweat off you palms, keep your hands from trembling near your guns, and get on out here!"

"Well, I'll be damned," Byler said, stalling as he stepped quietly over to the door, lifting the latch ever so slowly. "I remember you now. That's the reason all those boys died last year, huh?" He opened the door just a sliver of an inch, looking out at the figure of the gunfighter standing to the left in shadows.

"That's the reason, Byler. That front door is the only way out for you. Let's not put it off any longer."

"So you're his son, huh?"

"No . . ." Danielle let her words trail. Then she said with an air of finality, "I'm his daughter."

Her words stopped Byler short and left him stunned for a second. He shook his head in disbelief. "Well, I'll be. All this time, the green-eyed gunslinger everybody talked about was just a *girl*? Now that's one worth telling about." He felt bolder now, and he grinned to himself, peeping through the crack. "Bart Scovill and the others killed by a girl. They ought to have been ashamed of themselves." He took a deep breath, leaned the rifle against the wall inside the door, and loosened his pistol in his holster.

When Danielle made no response, Byler added, "Let me get this straight now. You really want a straight-up gunfight? No tricks or nothing?"

"That's right, Byler," Danielle said calmly. "You and me, no tricks." She braced her feet beneath her, knowing what was about to come.

Byler slipped the pistol from his holster, cocked it quietly, then said, "Well, then, why didn't you just say so in the first—"

He slung the door open and leaped out into the dirt, his pistol already out and up. Danielle's Colt streaked out in a cross-hand draw, her first shot hammering into his chest, slamming him back against the plank door frame. The second bullet hit his chest less than an inch below the first, just as his hand struggled to right his pistol toward her. Her next three shots jerked him along the front of the shack, his boots and body twisting in a crazy dance.

"There now, Pa," Danielle whispered, "I'm back in the hunt."

She reached down to the hot, smoking pistol, punching out the empty cartridges and replacing them. Then she walked back to the cedar stump, sat down with a long sigh, and stared at the bloodied body in the dirt until darkness fell around her.

CHAPTER 7

THE ARKANSAS RIVER. JUNE 27, 1871.

It was midmorning when Duncan Grago rode up from the river trail. Danielle had cleaned up around the door of the shack and dragged Julius Byler's body out of sight, a few yards up the rocky slope behind the shack. She had also taken Byler's horse from the open-front stall and sent it away with a slap on its rump. As soon as Duncan Grago rode into the yard, she started right in on him in a way to keep him off-balance.

"What the hell took you so long?" she demanded in a testy voice. "You should have been back last night."

Duncan was taken aback and offered a weak defense. "Damn, Danny, I got caught in a rain outside of Fort Smith. Nothing to get riled about! I figured you'd realized it might be morning before I got back."

"If all you boys do is sit around and wait for one another, I ain't sure I want to be a part of this bunch," Danielle hissed. She reached out with a boot toe and kicked a rock across the yard. "I'm like Byler when it comes to waiting. I can't stand it."

Duncan Grago stepped down from his mount and looked all around the yard and the front of the shack. "Where is Byler?" His eyes stopped for an instant at the sight of a fresh bullet hole in the front wall of the shack, where one of Danielle's shots had gone through Byler and lodged there.

"How the hell should I know?" Danielle snapped in reply. "We got into it last night after you left. He said this shack wasn't big enough for both of us. Wasn't going to let me inside. I had to straighten him out."

"You—you killed him?" Duncan Grago took on a curious look.

"No, I didn't kill him," Danielle lied, "but I should have. The son of a bitch threw down on me with his rifle. I creased his scalp and he ran off." She narrowed a cold stare at Duncan Grago. "If you've got a complaint about it, get it said." Her hand rested on the butt of one of her Colts.

"To hell with him." Grago shrugged. "I only came here because Newt asked me and Sep to bring Byler with us. If he don't like our company, he can do otherwise, I reckon." Duncan Grago looked relieved as Danielle dropped her hand from the pistol. "I'm glad you didn't kill him, though. Him and Newt's been friends for years."

Her voice still tight and cutting, Danielle said, "Look at me, Dunc. Do you think I'm a fool? I wouldn't kill one of your gang unless I had to."

"I understand, Danny," Duncan said, his right hand raised as if to hold her at bay. "I was just speculating, is all. There's no problem between us. We're *amigos*, far as I'm concerned."

"Good, then." Danielle pretended to cool down and spread a guarded smile to herself. "I like you, Duncan. I hope we can ride together without any misunderstandings. The last *amigo* I had went bad on me. I had to leave him lying in the dirt with his brains spilling out of his hat."

Duncan Grago wasn't used to somebody talking this way to him. This gunslinger had him rattled. He was used to being the one telling the tough stories, making everybody a little wary of him. Danny Duggin was a whole other thing. Duncan liked him, but he was scared to death of him, if the truth was known.

"We'll never have that kind of problem, Danny," he said. "You and me are cut from the same cloth. We're both mean as hell, and we'll die that way, eh? Ain't that right?" He offered a bold grin, putting a lot of chin into it.

"Yeah," Danielle said, "for me anyway. I'm still wondering about you." She said it half jokingly, leaving Duncan guessing where he really stood with her. "Now, are we ready to ride or not?" Danielle stepped over to where she'd reined Sundown to a weathered post in the ground.

"Sure thing," said Duncan Grago, stepping back up into his saddle. "But don't you want to eat something first?"

"We'll eat on the trail," Danielle said, making it sound like an order. "Unless you can't go a few hours on an empty belly."

"Me? Hell, I'm fine. Had some coffee and jerked beef at daybreak."

"That's good to hear, Dunc," Danielle said over her shoulder, nudging the mare forward and taking the lead. "Get up here beside me. I don't like nobody fanning my trail."

"Sure thing, Danny." Duncan Grago sidled his horse closer to Sundown. "I was thinking on the way back here. It's a long ride to where we're headed. Maybe we ought to swing in somewhere and rob us a bank or something. What do you think?"

Danielle only stared ahead. "We'll see, Dunc," she said. "We'll see."

MOBEETIE, TEXAS. JULY 10, 1871.

By the time Jed and Tim Strange rode into the small town of Mobeetie, Texas, they had been out of supplies for the past four days, living once more on jackrabbit and creek water, much to Jed's dismay. They found the Riley spread, but Jacob Riley and his regular drovers had ridden out a few days ago to deliver a small herd to an army encampment near the Mexican border. The old ranch blacksmith, Barney Pitts, had speculated to the boys that it would be another three or four days before Riley and his men would return. Pitts had offered Jed and Tim a spot in the bunkhouse and a place at the table, but until the two knew they would be working for Riley, their pride would not allow them to accept Pitt's hospitality.

"It would have been different if we were experienced cow-hands," Tim said as the two of them rode along the dusty street of Mobeetie, "but if we ended up not getting the job, staying there would be no more than a handout." He looked sidelong at Jed. "Pa always said if a man takes one handout, he'll soon take another."

"I know we did the right thing turning it down," Jed said with a grimace, "but it sure would be nice looking at some food that didn't smell like rabbit for a change."

As Jed spoke, Tim saw something ahead of them above a boardwalk that caused him to stop his bay in its tracks. "Well, get ready to eat, brother Jed," said Tim. He nodded at a hand-painted sign swaying on the hot breeze out front of a busy saloon. "Do you see what I see?"

The sign read: EAT YOUR FILL WITH THE PUR-CHASE OF A FIVE-CENT MUG OF BEER.

"I see it," Jed replied in a hushed tone, "but I don't believe it."

"I do," Tim said, batting his heels to his horse and pushing it forward. "Come on, Jed, let's get in there and eat before they change their mind."

At the crowded hitch rail out front of the saloon, they jumped down, spun their reins, and started up toward the batwing doors. But they had to jump to one side as the doors flew open and a burly bartender hurled a drunk through the air, then stood back dusting his hands as the man rolled in the dirt street and rose up onto his knees, cursing loudly.

"Don't mind him, boys," the bartender said to Jed and Tim. "Go on in and make yourselves to home."

On the street, the drunk raged, shaking a grimy fist in the air. "Yeah, that's it. Go on inside! See what you get for your nickel beer! These sonsabitches will rob yas blind! Look what they've done to me!" He jerked the inside lining up out of his empty pocket. "Don't think they won't do it to you, too! The rotten sonsabitches!"

"Well, you boys coming in or not?" the bartender asked, throwing open the batwing doors for them.

"Much obliged," Tim said, stepping inside with Jed right behind him.

Both of them stood in awe for a second at the sight and sound of a spinning betting wheel and the rattle of a snappy piano through a blue haze of cigar smoke.

"Find yourselves a spot and squeeze in, boys. Drink and eat your fill," the bartender said, stepping past them across the sawdust floor and disappearing around behind the crowded bar.

The twins looked at each other and seemed to snap out of a trance.

"He don't have to invite me twice," Jed Strange said, eagerly moving to the crowded bar, where men raised sandwiches thick with roast beef and fried chili peppers.

The two of them managed to secure enough elbow room to rake up slices of bread, and had begun piling on the beef when across the bar the same bartender looked them up and down as he spoke.

"You got to order a mug of beer, boys. That's the only rule to it. The rest is on the house."

Tim reached his hand down into his boot well as he chewed a mouthful of meat and bread. He pulled out the two folded dollar bills from inside his damp sock—all that was left of the fourteen dollars they'd drawn from Elvin Bray before leaving St. Joseph. He peeled the two damp dollars apart and handed one to the bartender. "Must we both buy a beer, or can we share one?" Jed asked.

The bartender snatched the dollar and smiled behind his thick dark mustache. "Both of you have to buy one if you both plan to stuff yourselves on my wife's roast beef."

"Give us each a mug, then!" Tim said, grinning and shoving the other dollar down into his shirt pocket.

Down the bar from them, a hefty man named Mose Epps, who had a reputation as the town bully, gigged his drinking buddy with his elbow and nodded at Jed and Tim Strange.

"Look at these two sodbusters, Randy," Mose Epps said, making no attempt at keeping his voice lowered. "They act like they ain't et in a month."

The other drinkers heard him above the din of the crowd and the rattle of the piano, and most ignored his rudeness. But his drinking buddy, Randy Farrel, laughed loud enough to get Jed and Tim Strange's attention. They looked up from counting their change in Tim's palm, and seeing Mose Epps's expression of disgust and the man beside him laughing, the twins gave them both a questioning look.

"That's right. You heard me," Epps said scornfully. "I said you two act like you ain't et nothing for a month. Now what about it?"

He stood with his hand on the pistol at his hip. Three drinkers at the bar between Epps and the twins picked up their beer mugs and slunk back out of the way.

Tim swallowed a mouthful of roast beef and bread, then washed it down with a gulp of beer. "Mister, you're mighty close to being right about that," Tim said, making light of the insult. "My brother here claims he's been seeing jackrabbit in his sleep for the past four nights."

A couple of the drinkers offered a nervous laugh, hoping Mose Epps would see the humor of it and let these haggard-looking boys alone. But Epps would have none of it. He stared coldly at the twins as he raised his beer mug, drained it, and set it down solidly on the wet bar top.

"Give me another, Frank," he said to the bartender. "I've got enough sense and manners to not take your generosity on the cuff."

"Leave it alone, Mose," Frank the bartender said in a lowered voice. He filled Epps's mug, slid it before him, and picked up the nickel from the bar. "Lunch is on the house for one and all. You know that."

"Yeah, I know it," Epps said, raising his voice for the twins' benefit. "But it's meant to draw business, not to draw a couple of look-alike saddle tramps in so's they can line their flues."

The saloon fell silent, save for the clicking of the spinning wheel. Even the piano player had to turn his attention to the bar.

Tim and Jed Strange stopped chewing their food. Jed reached out and set his beer mug on the bar.

"Tim, let's go," he whispered. "This is just a come-on to get folks to gamble."

"Now you've got it," Mose Epps sneered. "Nickel beer and free food is for the rollers, not for a couple of—"

"Hold on now," the bartender said, cutting Epps off. "Nickel beer and lunch is for anybody shows up. Boys, enjoy yourselves," he insisted to Tim and Jed Strange. "You don't *have* to gamble to eat and drink here. You're welcome all the same."

"Much obliged, sir," Tim Strange said to the bartender, keeping a cold stare fixed on Mose Epps. In a tight, calm voice, he said to Epps, "Let's get back to what you said about look-alike *saddle tramps*."

Mose Epps was used to bullying his way around in the streets and saloons of Mobeetie, Texas. Although the white-hot fire in Tim Strange's eyes told him he might have pushed the wrong man this time, Epps wasn't about to let himself get backed down in front of the drinking crowd.

"You heard me just fine the first time, sodbuster," Epps growled, his hand wrapping around the butt of the big two-handed horse pistol standing high on his stomach. "Now, if you don't want me to box your jaws, you both better crawfish out that door and—"

His words stopped at the sight of Tim's Colt, out of its holster now and cocked at his chest. The move was so sleek and fast, Mose Epps didn't even have time to grip his pistol, let alone try to draw it.

"But I want to hear you say it again, that part about look-alike saddle tramps lining their flues," Tim said. "I *dare* you to, you bag of hog guts."

"Easy, Tim," Jed whispered beside him. "He ain't worth killing."

Mose Epps stood stunned, helpless before the barrel of the cocked Colt. A few feet to his side, Randy Farrel started to inch his hand toward the pistol on his hip, but just as suddenly as Tim Strange had drawn and cocked his pistol, Jed Strange now did the same.

"Don't do it, mister, please," Jed said to Farrel, "or I will kill you."

Randy Farrel's hand crept back up chest high and stopped there in a show of submission.

"Now, you," Tim said to Epps. "I'm still waiting. Are you going to say it again or crawfish out that door the way you told *us* to?"

Epps's lips twitched as he tried to form a nervous smile. "Boys, I don't know how this got so out of hand. I was just making a little joke, you know? I didn't mean nothing by it."

"Yeah, you did," Tim said, not letting Epps off the spot. "I know your type. You like to belittle a man every chance you get. But when it comes down to guts and muscle, you've got neither one. That's when you decide to call it a joke."

"Please, buddy, I'm sorry," Mose Epps said in a low, shamed voice, not wanting the whole saloon to hear him beg.

"That's better," Tim said. He stalked forward, his eyes ablaze, and poked the tip of his barrel against Mose Epps's sweat-beaded forehead. "Now crawl out of here," Tim hissed, "before I blast the top of your head off!"

Mose Epps backstepped across the floor, his face flaming red in humiliation, all eyes watching him. Once he had stepped through the batwing doors, with Randy Farrel right behind him, Tim and Jed holstered their Colts and turned to the bartender. The saloon still stood in hushed silence.

"Sir," Tim said to the burly man behind the bar, "I apologize if we took advantage of you here. We've been on the road awhile, and the sight of that sign out front got the best of us, I reckon."

The bartender shook his head with a sigh of relief. "Boys, that sign means exactly what it says. Buy a nickel beer and eat your fill. To hell with Mose Epps. This is *my* place. I make the signs *and* the rules. Now drink up, and eat all you want." He looked around at the other patrons, who still stood back in stunned silence. "Well, what are you all waiting for?" the bartender said, waving them closer to the bar with both arms. "Next beer is on the house."

Jed reached out and stacked roast beef between two more pieces of bread, this time eating a little slower. Tim drained his beer mug and pushed it forward for a refill.

"That was some wicked gun handling, boys," said a voice beside them.

They both turned to see a smiling face and watched the man lower a black cigar from his lips and let out a long stream of smoke. "Permit me to introduce myself," the man said, his grin widening. "I'm Arno Dunne, and I couldn't help but notice how quick you boys grabbed up a handful of iron."

Tim and Jed had both settled down now, but they still had their bark on. More interested in eating than making conversation, Tim acknowledged Arno Dunne only with a nod, saying over a mouthful of food, "He was in the wrong, mister. That's the short of it."

"I agree," said Dunne, having to speak to their backs as both the twins had turned away from him. "It's a bad mistake, getting in a man's way when he's hungry. You had every right to drop him once his hand went to his pistol butt."

Tim and Jed turned back to Dunne as the piano struck up a fresh tune. "I knew it wasn't going to go that far," Tim said. "He was a windbag and a bully, and just needed to be took down a notch." This time as Tim ate and spoke, he noticed the brace of polished Colts on Arno Dunne's hips.

"He may be just a barroom bully," said Dunne, "but I wager you haven't seen the last of him. This is his perch. He'll have to make a move to save face here."

"Well, we hope you're wrong, Mr. Dunne," said Jed. "We came looking for food, not trouble."

"Call me Arno, boys," Dunne insisted. "I didn't catch your names."

"I'm Tim. This is my twin brother, Jed. We're just in town for a couple of days. We came to look for work at the Riley spread."

"The Riley spread, eh?" Arno Dunne seemed to think about something for a second, puffing his cigar. Then he said, "I hate to tell you, but Riley's not going to be hiring anybody for a while. If that's your only prospect for work, I'm afraid you've drawn a blank."

"How do you know?" Jed asked.

"Word has it him and his boys were hit by rustlers while they was taking a herd down to the army. If I know Jacob Riley, he'll be hunting down his cattle if it takes him a month. Meanwhile there'll be no work at his place."

Tim studied Arno Dunne's face, saying, "We just talked to his blacksmith earlier today. He never mentioned cattle rustlers."

"Barney Pitts is lucky he knows his own name." Arno Dunne shrugged, working his cigar between his lips. "I just got word myself, at a friend's house on my way here." He paused and blew out a breath of smoke. "I didn't catch your last names, boys."

Tim started to tell him, but before he could speak, the piano player stopped playing abruptly and dove from his bench onto the sawdust floor, shouting, "Shotguns! Look out!"

Jed, Tim, and Arno Dunne spun toward the slapping sound of the batwing doors just in time to see Mose Epps and Randy Farrel spread two feet apart, each of them raising a double-barreled shotgun.

"Nobody makes me a crawfish!" Epps raged.

But he'd have better spent his time shooting instead of talking, for Tim and Jed Strange both drew and fired in one blinding swift motion. Arno Dunne barely cleared leather before the sound of the twins' pistols roared in unison.

A blast of buckshot fired up into the ceiling, taking down a wagon-wheel lantern frame as Randy Farrel slammed backward through the batwing doors, his shotgun flinging from his hands. At the same time, two slugs from Tim's Colt drove Mose Epps back against the wall beside the doors, where he slid down to his knees and fell face forward, dead. His shotgun went off, sending a streak of fire and a spray of splinters across the floor. A deathlike silence hung in the air after the blasts. Smoke curled and drifted from the barrels of the twins' Colts.

"Lord, have mercy," the bartender whispered, breaking the silence. He looked at the body of Epps, then through the broken doors at Randy Farrel stretched out dead in the street.

"You all saw it!" Arno Dunne shouted, fanning his unfired pistol back and forth across the stunned onlookers. "Epps and Farrel started it, didn't they?"

"That's right," said the bartender. "When the sheriff gets here, that's what we'll say. Epps and Farrel caused the whole thing."

"Sheriff, hell," said Dunne. He shot Tim and Jed a warning glance. "If you boys are smart, you'll clear out of here. You want to take your chances with the sheriff? He's Mose Epps's cousin."

Tim and Jed looked at each other, their last encounter with angry townsfolk still fresh in their memory.

"We ain't staying," said Tim. He turned to the bartender. "Mister, you saw it. Will you tell the law we were only defending ourselves?"

"That's exactly what I'll tell him," said the bartender, "but you'd be wise to stay and tell him yourself."

"Yeah," Arno cut in sarcastically, "and take a chance on him jackpotting you for shooting a couple of snakes. Come on, boys, I'm getting you out of here for your own good." He turned back and forth with his pistol covering the drinking crowd. "Any objections?"

The crowd cowered back.

Jed said to his bother, "Tim, maybe we ought to stay and explain."

"No, come on. Dunne's right." He backed toward the door, limping slightly as he punched out the two spent cartridges from his Colt. "Why do we need to explain anything? Everybody here knows the truth."

Jed backed away with him as Arno Dunne ushered them both out the doors to the hitch rail. Jed stood frozen for a second when he looked down at the body of Randy Farrel lying dead in the dirt.

"Come on, Jed, damn it!" Tim shouted, untying both of their reins and pitching Jed's over to him. "Let's ride!"

"Listen to your brother, boy," Arno Dunne demanded. He'd

already stepped atop a buckskin Spanish barb and spun it around in the street. "The sheriff'll be here any minute!"

They rode hard and fast out of Mobeetie, Arno Dunne at the lead on a well-beaten road headed south. At a fork two miles out of town, Arno slid his barb horse to a halt and jerked it around, facing the twins as they followed suit. He laughed and slapped his thigh.

"Boys, you sure know how to stir up a slow day in Mobeetie," he said.

But Tim and Jed Strange saw no humor in his remark, and their expressions told him so.

"Aw, come on, now," Arno said, "those two got what was coming to them. We all know it. Be thankful I was able to warn you before they shot you both in the back. Ease up on yourselves a little. Life goes on."

"As I recall, it was the piano player who warned us," Tim said, still looking solemn.

"Well, however it went, just be thankful we're all alive and kicking." Arno chuckled, taking out a fresh cigar from inside his coat and biting the tip off it. "That's what it's all about, ain't it? Staying alive?" He struck a match, lit it, and flipped the match away. He propped a boot across his saddle fork and relaxed, eyeing the twins and blowing a long stream of smoke.

Jed spoke, pushing up his sweaty hat brim. "Now we have no way of seeing Jacob Riley about work, for sure."

"I already told you, there's no work there for yas," Arno Dunne said, sounding a bit put out. "Besides, if work's what you're after, I know a better bunch to work for than Jacob Riley any day." He wagged his cigar at the Colts on their hips. "The way you boys swing iron, you'd be foolish eating dust and staring up a longhorn's rear end from sun to sun. Believe me, there's better ways to make a living."

"You mean gun work, don't you, Dunne?" Tim said, starting to distrust this smiling stranger and his slick style. "My brother and I ain't hired guns, and we don't intend to be. We might be young, but we ain't stupid."

"Of course you're not," Arno Dunne said without conviction. "But you're new out here and just got a taste of how fast things can happen. There's two kinds of people in this world—the givers and the takers. This is hard country, boys. If you want to give, it'll take everything you've got, down to the hide on the soles of you feet. When it's through with you, it'll spit you in the dirt and let the wind cover you over." He grinned. "But it don't have to go that way. Look at me."

He spread his arms, showing his new but dusty clothes, his fine hand-tooled holster, his well-blocked Stetson, and his shiny leather riding gloves. "I drive cattle myself when I can't keep from it, only I don't do it for a dollar a day and found. No sirree. If I mess with longhorns, I make as much as Riley and don't have to stand near the expense he does."

Jed spat, crossing his wrists on his saddle horn and looking away. Tim stiffened a bit and said to Arno Dunne, "What you're telling us is that you're a cattle rustler, no different than the ones who stole from Jacob Riley."

"Cattle rustler? A thief? Naw, not me." Arno Dunne laughed under his breath. "But let's put this way: It ain't stealing if they're just running around loose. Same way with Mexican horses. If the *patrónes* can't keep their horses on their side of the border, they shouldn't complain about losing them."

"We see what you're getting at, Dunne," Tim answered, barely hiding his disgust. "I reckon we'll just say *adios* here and go our way."

"Boys, you oughta think about it first," Arno Dunne cautioned them before they had time to turn their horses. "Where you going to go right now? You're broke and hungry—you said so yourselves." He reached a gloved hand back and patted his bulging saddlebags. "I've got supplies for over a week and money to buy more once these run out."

"We don't take handouts, Dunne," Jed Strange said, now turning his bay. "Let's go, Tim."

"Not so fast," Tim said, reaching a hand out and taking Jed's bay by its bridle, stopping it. "Dunne, you said you and your bunch handle cattle when you can't keep from it. What do you do the rest of the time?"

"Tim, you don't mean it," Jed said, stunned by his brother's interest.

Dunne spread another slick grin. "Attaboy. Now you're starting to use your head." He tapped his cigar to his temple. "We do whatever comes up the trail to us. Most make enough money that most times we don't have to do anything at all. Think you could handle that? Learn to take life easy, enjoy the spoils of the land?"

Tim stared at him for a second, then asked, "And where are your friends? Where are you headed?"

Arno Dunne pointed southeast with his cigar. "They're waiting for me right now, boys. Right down there, smack in the heart of Indian Territory."

"That's it for me. I'm leaving, Tim," Jed murmured, "and you're leaving with me."

Again Jed tried to turn his bay, but Tim held it firm by its bridle as he spoke to Dunne.

"Will you excuse me and my brother for a minute, Dunne?" Tim asked.

Arno Dunne said with a sweeping gesture of his cigar, "Take your time, boys. Talk it over real good. We're in no hurry here."

CHAPTER 8

Arno Dunne looked on from twenty feet away as Jed and Tim Strange talked between themselves. At first Jed was strongly opposed to riding any farther with a rustler like Arno Dunne. While Dunne watched, he smiled to himself and blew long streams of cigar smoke into the hot passing breeze. He couldn't make out Jed Strange's words, but he could tell by the way the boy shook his head that he wasn't at all interested in Dunne's proposition.

"How can you even consider taking up with this man, Tim?" Jed whispered to his twin brother. "If we get tangled up with a bunch like he's talking about, we'll never find Danielle. We'll be lucky if we don't hang."

As Jed spoke, he took from his pocket the window-shade cord that he'd been carrying ever since St. Joseph. Out of habit now, he anxiously coiled it back and forth around his finger.

"Listen to me, Jed." Tim spoke in a firm tone, reaching out and clasping his hand down on Jed's, stopping him from toying with the window-shade cord. "I've been thinking about it ever since this man opened his mouth about Indian Territory. If Danielle's down there hunting down killers, this is the kind of men she'll be after. She could be on their trail right now. For all we know, Dunne could *be* one of Pa's killers, or know of them anyway. I can see what he is, but he might have come along at just the right time to be some help to us. He knows the Territory, and we don't."

"Yeah," Jed interjected, "but remember what Danny Duggin said? There's men in the Territory who'll cut your throat just to see how you fall. That's Dunne, if you want my opinion."

Jed reached into his pocket and took out his small whittling knife. He cut the length of window sash cord in half as he spoke.

"I know it is, Jed. That's why I figure nobody will bother us so long as we're with him. All we got to do is keep an eye on him. We'll stick with him and his friends until we know our way around. When it comes to taking care of ourselves with a gun, we've got no problem. We just have to watch our step. What do you say?"

"I say, we ain't going to get started breaking the law, Tim. It's easy enough to get in Dutch out here without going looking for it."

"I know," Tim said, "but we've got to make a move of some kind or we'll never do what we set out to. The job didn't pan out. Now I say we get to looking for Danielle before that plan goes wrong on us as well. If we ain't got enough sense to keep from becoming outlaws, we ought not to be out here in the first place. Now, are you with me on this?"

"Are you going on with him even if I'm not?" Jed asked, his eyes searching Tim's.

Tim let out a breath, then replied, "No, brother, you know better than that. I'm just saying we'd better get to doing something or else go on back home and forget it."

Jed looked away for a moment, considering it. He took one of the lengths of window-shade cord and deftly fashioned a miniature thirteen-knot noose into it. He laid it on his knee, then picked up the other length and formed another small noose.

Finally he looked back at Tim and handed him one of the nooses and said, "All right, let's do it. Just make sure we watch each other's backs."

"That goes without saying," Tim whispered. "But what's this for?"

"Just to remind us we're riding in the shadow of a noose," said Jed.

He spun his own miniature noose around on his finger and slipped it down around his saddle horn.

"Good idea," Tim said, slipping his miniature noose down on his saddle horn the same way. "We'll always remember that it's just you and me against the rest of the outlaw world, brother."

When they both turned their bays back around and heeled them toward Arno Dunne, the man smiled even wider than he had before, seeing the looks on their faces.

"All right, then," Arno Dunne said jovially, jerking his horse around to the thin trail leading off to the southeast toward a stretch of low badlands hills. "Let's press some saddle leather, boys. We've wasted too much time as it is."

THE WASHITA RIVER, INDIAN TERRITORY. JULY 20, 1871.

Fortunately for Danielle Strange, Duncan Grago had made no more mention of swinging out of their way to rob a bank on their way deeper into Indian Territory. Danielle would not have gone along with it even if he had. She remained ever mindful that her task was to hunt down a band of outlaws, not become one herself. Yet the farther they traveled without any incident, the more restless and angry Duncan Grago became. He directed none of his anger toward her, for he knew better. But toward everything else, including the land itself, Duncan Grago became seething mad and hardhanded. Even his horse became a victim of his rage and would have suffered much abuse, had it not been for Danielle stopping him. When the poor animal had stumbled coming down a slope of loose rock, Duncan Grago had jumped down from his saddle, picked up a hand-sized stone, and screamed at the helpless animal.

"You worthless buzzard-bait son of a bitch!" he raged, drawing his arm high and wide, ready to smash the horse between the eyes.

But Danielle had already seen the attack coming and was down from her saddle in a flash. She caught Duncan's arm with her left hand and, with her right hand, swung her pistol full circle, cracking Grago across the top of his head with the barrel. It was nearly a half hour before Duncan Grago became conscious. During that time, Danielle dragged him into the shade beneath a high, wide pine tree, propping him up against it.

She stood back with her hand near her pistol butt, just in case he awoke and made a move on her. But as he raised his bleary eyes to her, he only asked in dull confusion, "What—what happened?"

Danielle took a hard tone with him, saying, "I busted your head with a gun barrel. That's what happened."

Duncan Grago's eyes flashed white-hot for a second, but noting her hand near her Colt, and having already seen what that Colt could do, he checked himself, raising a hand to his throbbing head and asking with a groan, "What the hell for? Last I remember, I was going to knock that cayuse's head off."

"That's right. You were, you damn fool," Danielle spat, leaning down and lifting him by his shoulder. "Then you'd be afoot the rest of the way, or else I'd be stuck with you against my back."

Duncan Grago looked bewildered for a moment, considering it. "I reckon I just saw red when the horse faltered under me."

"Well, you'd best start seeing some other color," Danielle said, helping him steady himself on his wobbly feet. "This ain't the kind of country to be in without a horse. Do something that stupid, and I'll leave you to the coyotes." She shoved him slightly, guiding his horse.

"I—I didn't mean to," Grago said. "I don't know what came over me."

Danielle only watched and shook her head as Duncan struggled up into his saddle and gathered his reins. Then she stepped atop Sundown and heeled the big chestnut forward, keeping Duncan beside her and in her sight. Duncan Grago was like a storm in a clay jar, she thought, aching to bust loose and destroy something at every turn in the trail. Little did she know that his opportunity would come that very evening when they met a small crew of drovers leading a herd from the Texas panhandle toward Fort Smith.

Had Danielle seen the rising dust of the herd sooner, she would have diverted around them. But by the time she and Duncan rode up a wide, rocky basin, the lead rider was already in sight, moving toward them slowly with some forty head of cattle trudging a few yards behind him.

"Well," Duncan said with a grin, "looks like we don't have to cook tonight."

"Yeah," Danielle replied, already getting a bad feeling. "Let's mind our manners. We don't need to draw attention to ourselves."

But she could tell by the look on Duncan's face that he had no idea what she meant. She nudged Sundown forward grudgingly, seeing the lead drover raise a gloved hand toward them from a hundred yards away.

"Hello, the herd!" Danielle called out as she and Duncan Grago drew nearer and pulled their horses to one side, waiting for an invitation to approach.

"Hello, yourselves," called out the lead man, waving them toward him. "Come on over. These cattle have no spook in 'em."

Danielle and Duncan moved in, sidling up to the young man who had looked more and more familiar as Danielle drew closer. "Dan?" said the young drover, peering at Danielle. "Is that you?"

Danielle recognized him now through the caked dust on his cheeks and a week's worth of beard stubble. It was Tuck Carlyle, a young man her age with whom she'd worked the past summer running a herd of cattle. Seeing Tuck made Danielle's heart soar for a second. But then she reminded herself of Duncan Grago being with her, and realized she had to find a way to let Tuck know what she was up to. Luckily for her, Tuck had only called her Dan, and not Daniel Strange as he might have done. Tuck had no idea that the person he knew as Daniel Strange was really a woman. He did know that Daniel Strange had been on the vengeance trail the last time they'd seen each other.

"Yep, it's me, Danny Duggin," Danielle said, staring intensely at Tuck, hoping he'd get the message.

He did, and right away.

"I knew that was you riding in, Danny," Tuck said without a hitch. "But you do look different, having grown yourself a lip duster. And ya got yourself a scar, I see."

"Yep," Danielle replied, touching her finger to her cheek. "I had a little disagreement over a card game. How've you been, Tuck?"

"Fine as can be," Tuck said, letting his gaze drift from Danielle to Duncan Grago.

"This is Dunc," Danielle said. "We're riding together these days." The way she said it gave Tuck Carlyle an idea that the two were not close friends. "Dunc, this is Tuck Carlyle, a trail buddy of mine."

Duncan Grago only lifted his chin in a short nod and said nothing, even as Tuck acknowledged him with a howdy and a friendly smile.

Tuck turned back to Danielle, saying, "What about you? Are you still—?" Tuck caught himself and reshuffled his words. He was about to ask whether she was still hunting the outlaws who had killed her father, but he changed the question quickly and asked, "Are you still doing what you were doing the last time I saw you?" The way he said it worked out perfect for Danielle, for it sounded as if Danielle might have been up to something on the sly.

"Yeah, I'm still dodging the law," Danielle said. "It's all right to say it in front of Dunc. He's had some run-ins with the law himself. Right, Dunc?"

"Yeah." Duncan Grago sneered, looking away as he spoke. "And I plan on having some more before I get too old to enjoy it."

Tuck Carlyle gave Danielle a guarded nod, letting her know he understood. "Hope you'll be staying for supper, Danny," Tuck said. "Long as it's been, I reckon we ought to get caught up."

"Thanks for the invite," Danielle said, "but we'd best be moving along."

"What's our hurry?" Grago asked, taking on a bolder tone now that someone was around to see and hear him.

Before Danielle could come up with a reply, Tuck Carlyle cut in, saying, "Sure, Danny, what's your hurry?" He jerked his head back toward the rest of the drovers strung out along the herd. "Nobody back there knows you." This was Tuck's way of letting Danielle know that nobody would slip up and say the wrong thing. "Have supper with us. We're just a greasy-sack outfit,* but we eat as good as anybody."

Danielle relented. "Well, why not, then? Whose small herd is this anyway?"

"These hide racks belong to the old Scotsman Connery. He lost them in a poker game to Dubb Macklin in Fort Smith. He's paying me and the others to deliver them for him. I reckon delivery was part of the bet." Tuck grinned. "Evidently the age or condition of the animals wasn't, though. There's a couple in there you'd swear came over with Noah on his ark. I'll be glad to get shed of them. Keep hoping rustlers will take 'em off our hands, but so far we've had no takers."

Danielle laughed with him, then asked, "How's your sister, Carrie, and your ma?"

"Ma's fine. Carrie, too." Tuck lifted a gaze to Danielle, adding about his sister, "She still talks about you all the time. I tried telling her there's more than one moony-eyed cowhand prowling the range. She won't hear of it, though."

"I wish she would," Danielle said. "There's no place for her with me."

Danielle let herself reflect back on the summer past, when there had been a peculiar situation between herself, Tuck Carlyle, and his sister, Carrie. Danielle had never let the Carlyles know

---

* "Greasy-sack outfit" was a term for an outfit with no chuck wagon. Such outfits carried their provisions in flour sacks and canvas bags.

that she was really a woman disguising herself as a man. Because of it, Carrie Carlyle had become deeply infatuated with the person she knew as Daniel Strange. To make matters worse, Danielle had herself fallen head over heels for Tuck Carlyle for a time. Thinking about it reminded her of how much she'd learned over the past year on the trail. Becoming attracted to a man was the one thing she must avoid at all cost. There would come a day when Danielle would shed her disguise and take up the normal life of a woman. But until that day came, she would be careful not to let her feelings as a woman come between her and what she must do.

"Well, so much for wishful thinking," Tuck Carlyle said as if in answer to Danielle's thoughts.

Danielle gave him a questioning look, and seeing it, Tuck went on to explain, "I mean, about Carrie still wanting you to come back and sweep her off her feet."

"Yeah," Danielle said, looking Tuck up and down longingly, then turning her face forward to the open land, "so much for wishful thinking."

"So what time will this bunch be stopping to pull down some grub?" Duncan Grago asked, his tone rude and impatient.

Tuck Carlyle passed a glance at Danielle, then replied, "This is no sun-to-sun drive. I reckon we can gather down as soon as we get to the basin up ahead. Can you wait that long?"

"I reckon I can if I have to," Duncan Grago grumbled under his breath.

There were only four other cowhands working the small drive, Tuck Carlyle taking up the roles of trail boss, line rider, and point man. At suppertime, a young man named Curtis Lotts, who doubled as cook, prepared a pot of beans with pork seasoning and a platter of what he called fried chicken, which was really nothing more than a wishful term for thick bacon rolled in flour and fried to a crisp turn.

Around the campfire sat Tuck Carlyle, Curtis Lotts, and an old drover from Abilene known only as Stick. The other two men were a couple of brothers named Clarence and Tolliver Martin, who worked full-time for the old Scotsman's spread. These two sat watch on the small herd, waiting to be relieved for supper by Stick and Curtis Lotts.

As soon as Danielle found a moment alone with Tuck Carlyle, she quickly explained to him about the knife fight she'd had and how she was going by the name Danny Duggin, hoping the reputation she'd built as Daniel Strange would die down. Inspecting Sundown's hooves while the two of them stood a few yards away from Duncan Grago and the others, she told Tuck who Duncan was and why she was traveling with him. Tuck Carlyle only shook his head.

"I swear, Dan, the farther you ride this vengeance trail, the less I recognize you, and I'm not talking about just the mustache and the scar on your cheek."

"I know, Tuck," Danielle responded, straightening up from Sundown's hooves and dusting her hands together. "Sometimes I don't rightly recognize myself. But I'm praying it'll all be over soon. When it is, I hope to run into you again. There's things I'd tell you that I can't tell you now."

She longed for the day when she could reveal her true identity to him and settle down to a normal life.

"We're *amigos*, Dan," Tuck said, "so anything you've got to tell me, I'll be ready to listen. Meanwhile, I've sure got some news for you. Remember the Flagg family, the ones who threw some of their cattle in on the drive we made last year?"

"Yep, I remember them," said Danielle. "Good folks as I recall."

"That's right they are. Well, ole man Flagg's sister in St. Louis passed away and her widower husband sent their daughter, Ilene, to live with the Flaggs whilst he works the steamers." His eyes got excited as he continued. "The thing is, Dan, she and I have struck up quite a romance. The next time you see me, there's a good chance she'll be my wife, that is, if she'll have me."

They had turned and started back toward the campfire as Tuck spoke. Now his words stopped Danielle in her tracks. She stood speechless, trying hard to hide the disappointment in her eyes.

After a moment of seeing how his words had affected his friend, Tuck Carlyle laughed and said, "Damn, Dan, don't look so troubled by it! I just told you I might be getting married, not that I was about to get myself snakebit."

Danielle shook the weight of sadness from her shoulders and forced herself to laugh along with him. "I know, Tuck. It just took me by surprise for a second there. I'm happy for you, real happy. If I'm around, I'd better get an invitation to the wedding."

Tuck slapped her on the back. "Hell, that goes without saying. What about you, Dan? Have you met yourself a good woman yet?"

"Naw," Danielle said, "you know me. I've got no time for anything but the hunt for my pa's killers."

"Maybe once that's over, you'll run into the right person," Tuck said encouragingly.

"Yes, maybe so," Danielle said, looking away from him as they stepped in closer to the campfire so that he couldn't see the hurt in her eyes.

All went well throughout the evening meal. Duncan Grago was sullen, and while not the friendliest man the drovers had ever met, he at least managed to keep quiet and eat his meal. But about the time Danielle thought the evening might pass without incident, Duncan's mood took a sharp turn for the worse. Once Stick and Curtis Lotts had left to relieve the Martin brothers, Clarence Martin tried to show an extra stretch of hospitality by pulling out a bottle of rye he'd been saving in his saddlebags.

"Whoa, boys, no drinking on the trail," said Tuck Carlyle, seeing Clarence hold the bottle up in his hand.

Clarence's intention had been to ask Tuck's permission before passing the bottle around the campfire. Yet the bottle of rye seemed to strike a chord in Duncan Grago's brain. He snatched the bottle as he butted in, cutting Tuck Carlyle off.

"Don't mind if I do, buddy," Grago said, already pulling the cork from the bottle with his teeth.

Tuck Carlyle saw it was too late to stop him, so he tried instead to alter the course. "Well, one drink each, boys," he said, "but only because we have a couple of supper guests."

Saying that was also a mistake, Danielle thought, watching the words sink into Duncan Grago's mind. Knowing it was going to be his only drink for the night, Duncan took a long, deep pull that drew everybody's rapt attention until he lowered the bottle and blew out a tight breath.

"Lord, that's good!" he exclaimed, his face glowing red in an instant from the rush of alcohol.

Danielle had no desire for a drink. Her only purpose in reaching for the bottle was to get it out of Duncan's hand before he threw back another long guzzle.

"Then let us in on it," she said, snatching the bottle from him.

"Dang it," Clarence Martin said in a half-joking tone, "I didn't mean for yas to drink it all."

"Then you shouldn't have brought it out," Duncan Grago shot back at him. There was no mistaking the lack of humor in Duncan's voice.

Danielle saw the long drink of whiskey wrap its tentacles around Duncan Grago's mood, and she almost held her breath at what she knew could turn ugly as quick as a streak of heat lightning.

"I was only joshing," said Clarence Martin, taking the bottle back and rubbing his hand across the top of it. "Whiskey's meant to be drunk, is what I always say."

But Duncan Grago took Clarence's words as a sign of weakness and gave him a look of contempt. "Is that so, huh? Then give me that bottle and watch me drink it."

"I said one drink each," Tuck Carlyle cut in. Being the trail boss, Tuck knew it was up to him to clamp down before things got out of hand. "I never allow my drovers to drink on the trail. It's a bad practice." He held his hand out for the bottle, but Duncan only looked at it with a dark chuckle as he spoke.

"I ain't one of your drovers, and I don't need no *practice*. I been drinking right handily for years."

He raised the bottle to his lips and threw back a shot, but Danielle's hand shot out and once again snatched it from his lips. Whiskey spilled. Clarence Martin muttered under his breath in disapproval.

"Here you go, Tuck," Danielle said in a low tone, keeping her eyes on Duncan Grago as she picked the cork up from the ground, wiping it on her thigh and shoving it down into the bottle. She pitched the bottle up to Tuck, who stood above the rest of them seated around the fire.

"It's time we shove off, Dunc," she added to Duncan Grago, seeing his eyes fixed coldly on Tuck Carlyle.

"Why?" Duncan asked, the heat of the whiskey boiling inside his head and chest. "No need in us going somewhere and making a camp when there's one right here."

His eyes were still locked on Tuck Carlyle, and Tuck hadn't backed down an inch. Danielle knew Tuck wouldn't, not for Duncan Grago or anybody else. She acted quick, reaching out with her boot and nudging Duncan.

"I said, it's time we go. Now come on, or I'll leave you where you're sitting." As she spoke, her hand rested poised near her pistol butt.

Duncan Grago hesitated a second longer; then he let out a breath and said grudgingly, "Hell, all right, then." Rising up and dusting off the seat of his trousers, he gave a smug parting glance to Tuck Carlyle, then turned it to Clarence Martin. "You ever need me to show you how to drink whiskey, just come looking."

The words stung Clarence Martin's pride, and as Duncan and Danielle turned to walk to their horses, Clarence rose from the ground, muttering under his breath, "By Gawd if he didn't spill as much as he drunk."

Duncan Grago let out a sarcastic laugh over his shoulder, saying in a belittling voice, "If you're going to weep over it like a woman, send me a bill for it, you steer-licking peckerwood."

That did it. Clarence Martin threw his hand to his pistol, shouting as he raised it, "You belligerent bastard!"

Three shots resounded as Duncan Grago ducked to one side, turning, drawing, and firing back at the flashes of muzzle fire in the graying evening light. All Danielle could do at that split second was move aside, crouching as the bullets flew. Tuck Carlyle and Tolliver Martin did the same, for no matter what kind of man Duncan Grago was, and no matter how he'd provoked the fight, at that moment he was within his rights to defend himself.

A total of eight shots were fired between them. Clarence Martin's shots went wild as he sank backward to the ground, one of Duncan Grago's first bullets nailing his chest. Tolliver Martin had recovered from his shock and went for his pistol, but one of Duncan's shots sliced deep into his shoulder. He flew backward across the campfire with flames licking at his wool shirt.

"You all saw it!" Duncan Grago screamed, backing toward his horse, his pistol fanning back and forth between Tuck and Danielle. "He tried back-shooting me! I had to kill him!"

Danielle and Tuck Carlyle gritted their teeth and fought the urge to go for their Colts. But they knew they couldn't dispute Duncan Grago. Clarence Martin had done the unthinkable, and it had left him dead on the ground. His brother, Tolliver, rolled back and forth on the ground, smothering the fire from his wool shirt, his pistol lying a foot from his hand. He tried lifting himself to his feet, his left hand clenched tight to his wounded shoulder.

"Nobody move!" Duncan Grago shouted, backing farther away to his horse. "Don't nobody try to follow me!"

"Wait, Dunc," Danielle called out to him, stepping forward.

But Duncan Grago was wild and scared, not even hearing her. He swung up into his saddle with his pistol still pointed at them and batted his horse away from the campsite at a fast clip.

"Help me find my pistol," Tolliver Martin cried out, his voice strained against the pain in his bleeding shoulder.

He staggered in place. Tuck Carlyle caught him as he fell, and helped sit him on the ground as blood poured freely.

"I'm going after him! I'll kill him. Look what he done to my brother!"

"Easy now, Toll," said Tuck, trying to console him as he tore open his shirtsleeve to inspect the wound. "I hate saying it, but that man was in his rights. I don't know what got into Clarence, doing a thing like that. But you getting yourself killed ain't going to change a thing."

Hearing the gunfire from camp, the small herd of cattle milled in a spreading circle, spooked. Stick and Lotts pressed their horses dangerously close to the frightened beasts, keeping a firm hold on them, folding the circle back upon itself.

"Thank the Lord these old dowds ain't breech loaded!"* Stick called across the restless tangle of horns. "They're too old to run or they'd be gone by now!"

"Reckon you've got them?" Lotts called back to him. "I'll go see what's the matter!"

"Go on! These hides have no run in 'em! I'll join you once they 'plete down!"

Lotts turned, booting his horse toward camp. As he slid his horse to a halt, dropping from its back before it had settled, he saw Clarence Martin's body and saw Tuck and Danielle leaning down over Tolliver.

"What's happened?" Lotts shouted.

"Just what it looks like," Danielle said stiffly. "Clarence and Dunc went at it. Dunc killed him and wounded his brother."

Even as Danielle spoke, she took a step back and gazed off at the lingering dust left by Duncan Grago's horse. "Damn, I'm awful sorry, Tuck," she said. "It was a mistake thinking that lunatic could go a meal without causing trouble."

"It wasn't your fault," Tuck said, looking up from tending to

_____
* "Dowds" was a term for bulls past their prime; "breech loaded," a term for uncut bulls.

Tolliver's wound. "Things got said that couldn't be made right. You're wanting to get right after him, ain't ya?"

"I won't leave you shorthanded, Tuck," she replied. "It ain't my style."

"I know it ain't, Dan," Tuck said with a grimace, "but go on. If there's anything good to come of this, it'll be you taking care of that bastard once and for all."

Tuck looked around at Curtis Lotts and asked, "How's the herd?"

"Stick's got 'em steadied. He's coming directly."

"No, he ain't," said Tuck. "Get out there and tell him to hold tight. You, too. Nothing you can do here. This is done."

When he looked back toward Danielle, she had taken another step back toward her chestnut mare, a questioning look in her eyes, until Tuck nodded hard, saying, "Yes, go on. This ain't changed nothing between us. We're still *amigos*."

"Thanks, Tuck," Danielle said in a quiet voice, taking another slow step before breaking into a run toward Sundown. In a second she was mounted and gone, Sundown's hooves pounding the hard earth beneath them.

CHAPTER 9

INDIAN TERRITORY. JULY 21, 1871.

Duncan Grago had gotten a good head start, and with no regard whatsoever for his horse's safety, he'd kept a good distance between himself and Danielle throughout most of the night. Danielle, keeping Sundown at a steady but safe pace in the rugged rock and brushland, kept on Duncan's trail by following the looming dust in the night air. From time to time, she dropped down from her saddle and found his horse's hoofprints in the pale moonlight.

Around an hour before dawn, Danielle heard the distant sound of a horse nickering long and loud in pain. Knowing it had to be Duncan's horse, she pushed her chestnut mare a little harder toward the sound until at last she found the horse limping in a slow circle beside the narrow trail.

Swinging down from her saddle, Danielle called out to the black shadows on a hillside to her right, "Dunc, it's me, Danny. I'm by myself. Don't do nothing stupid."

Footprints on the ground wandered in a short circle, then led up into the brush on a steep slope.

Danielle gathered the reins of the limping horse, straightened the saddle hanging down on its side, and called out again, "I know you hear me, Dunc. Come on down. Nobody's going to bother you."

After a moment of silence, Duncan Grago's voice came out of

the purple darkness, saying, "Nobody is with you, Danny? Are you sure?"

"Damn it, Dunc, I told you I'm alone, didn't I? Get down here right now, or I'm going to leave you behind. Why'd you keep me tracking you all night anyway?"

"I'm coming, Danny, all right?" Duncan Grago scurried down through sand and brush. "I was just afraid you'd taken their side against me."

"You were in the right back there, Dunc, even Tuck Carlyle said so," Danielle said to Duncan's dark figure as he stepped out of the inky night. She didn't mention the fact that he had provoked the fight, for it would do no good now. What she needed now was to get the two of them back on the trail, headed for the men who'd killed her father.

"I knew it was self-defense," Duncan Grago said, stepping closer in the moonlight, his pistol hanging loose in his hand, "but I wasn't sure that it would make any difference to your friends."

Danielle shook her head, saying, "Holster your pistol, Dunc. Tuck saw how it happened. He didn't like it, but he had to abide by it. He's the trail boss. What he says goes with his cowhands."

"It's because you were with me, wasn't it?" Duncan asked, slipping his pistol inside his holster. "If it hadn't been for you, they'd have been right on my tail."

"Maybe," Danielle said. She leaned down beside Duncan's horse as she spoke, and gently ran a hand along the swollen tendon in its right leg, then upward along the lumpiness in its knee. The horse whinnied low in pain. Letting out a tired breath, Danielle said as she straightened and dusted off her hands, "This poor animal's done for out here. You should have known better than to push it so hard in the dark on this kind of ground."

"I—I wasn't thinking as clear as I should have been," Duncan said, his voice sounding ashamed. "That whiskey had me a little *loco* for a while. I drank it too fast, I reckon."

"Yeah, I reckon," Danielle said with a snap of sarcasm. "Now I have to decide whether or not I want you breathing on my back until we can find you a horse somewhere."

"I don't know what comes over me sometimes," Duncan Grago said.

Danielle took note of how much he sounded like a schoolboy caught in some kind of mischief. She almost felt sorry for him, were it not for the body of Clarence Martin lying dead in the distant darkness and the countless others who'd suffered at Duncan Grago's hand.

Duncan continued. "It seems like something's inside me that just busts out all of a sudden. I can't help it."

Danielle didn't answer as she reached down, loosened the cinch from beneath his horse's belly, and dropped the saddle to the ground. She dropped the bridle from around the horse's muzzle and watched it wander for a moment on its shattered leg, nickering pitifully.

"Finish it," she said to Duncan in a low, solemn tone. Then she stepped away and turned to Sundown, holding on to the reins until the sound and flash of Duncan Grago's pistol filled the night, and the pain-filled nickering of his horse was cut short into silence.

When they'd both stepped atop Sundown, Duncan Grago adjusted himself against Danielle's back, his saddle and bridle resting down along his leg. "I've never liked thanking a person," Duncan said, "and the fact is I've never had much reason to." His voice softened. "But I'm obliged to you, Danny Duggin. Nobody has ever befriended me this way. I kind of wished they had over the years. You've been straight with me."

Danielle felt the slightest twinge of guilt for a second and had to remind herself of what a low piece of work Duncan Grago really was. "Well, like I said, Dunc, you were in the right back there. Once I side with a person, I try to stick with them." She gave the chestnut mare a slight nudge, letting the mare make her own pace at a walk. "From now on, though, you're going to have to act like you've got some sense," she added.

"I will, Danny. . . . I'll try," Duncan said.

In the clammy coolness before dawn, Danielle became more and more aware of the heat of Duncan Grago against her back. The feel of him evoked an uncomfortable urge inside her that she didn't want to admit to. She had no passion for the likes of Duncan Grago, yet the closeness of a man stirred something inside her that she could not deny. As the first thin reef of sunlight spread across the horizon, she felt Duncan Grago slumber against her, his head lying over her shoulder and his warm breath caressing the side of her throat. She shifted uneasily in her saddle.

Unable to escape the closeness of him, she finally gigged him gently with her elbow and said, "Wake up, Dunc. You hear me? Wake up. It's daylight."

"Huh?"

As he stirred from his sleep, he became unsteady and threw his arm around her chest to keep from slipping off the mare's rump. Duncan noticed nothing out of the ordinary when his hand clutched the binder she used to flatten her breasts, but she did, and her natural impulse was to shove his hand away.

Her reaction stunned him from his drowsiness for a second, and he said, "Oh sorry, Danny," before he even realized why he'd said it.

"It's time we got down and rested the mare," Danielle said, her cheeks feeling flushed. Yet Duncan had slumped forward against her again and seemed to have relaxed back to sleep.

"Just a few more minutes," he whispered dreamily, too drowsy to notice the warm comfortable feeling that sleeping against Danny Duggin induced in him.

Danielle prodded him again, harder this time, saying, "Hey, what the hell is wrong with you? Wake up. I'm not your pillow!"

The shock of the situation struck a sharp note in Duncan Grago's mind, and he flung himself off the mare, looking confused and embarrassed as he staggered in place. "Oh, Danny! Damn it! I— I'm sorry! I must have been dreaming."

"Forget it," Danielle snapped. Unable to face him directly for a moment, she looked back along the trail, then at Duncan's empty hands. "Where's your saddle and tack?"

Duncan shook sleep from his eyes and lowered his head. "Damn it, I must've dropped them both somewhere."

Danielle slumped a bit in disgust, saying, "Well, hell. You've just about lost everything but your boots." Then she swung down from her saddle and stretched her legs. "We're going to have to take turns on this mare, to not wear her out. We'll also have to rest her in the hottest part of the day.

"I'll ride the first hour," Danielle continued. "Then you take the next hour. How much farther is it to your brother and his men?"

"Not far," Duncan Grago said. "We should be there tomorrow sometime. There's an old relay station thirty miles ahead. If I'm lucky, I can pick up a horse there."

SALT FORK OF THE RED RIVER, INDIAN TERRITORY. JULY 22, 1871.

Traveling with Arno Dunne, Jed and Tim Strange had kept ever mindful of what they told him about themselves. Dunne had a way of trying to pry information out of them in what appeared to be normal conversation. But the twins had revealed little to him. When Dunne had asked them what their last name was, Tim told him it was Faulkner, their mother's maiden name being the first name that had popped into his mind. They had been riding their horses at a walk along a winding ridgeline when Dunne asked, and looking back and forth at their faces as he stopped his horse and let the twins drift past him, he couldn't judge whether or not they were telling him the truth.

"Faulkner, huh? Well, that's good enough for now," Dunne whispered to himself, watching the twins turn their bays on the thin trail and sit looking back at him.

"What's the holdup?" Tim asked, his hand relaxed and comfortable on his lap near the butt of his Colt.

Jed Strange let his bay take a sidelong step, putting a couple of feet between him and his brother.

"Nothing," said Arno Dunne with a shrug. "Just got tired of riding lead. Thought I'd drop back for a while." He caught the look of distrust in their eyes and shook his head. "Boys, I've never saw two young men so full of suspicion in my life."

Tim offered a faint smile and spoke in a polite manner. "It's not that we don't trust you, Dunne. It's just that you're the only one who knows the way we're going."

"Oh, I see." Arno Dunne chuckled, nudging his horse forward. "I'm glad you cleared that up for me. I was about to think you didn't trust me behind your backs." He passed between them, tipping his fingers to his hat brim, once more taking the lead.

As Dunne rode a few yards ahead of the twins, Tim looked at Jed, saying, "See how easily he does things? We let down for a second and he puts us right at his advantage."

"I know," Jed replied, watching Arno Dunne's back. "But it won't happen again." As he spoke, he toyed with the miniature noose hanging from his saddle horn. "How's your leg feeling?"

Tim patted his healing wound gently. "It's mending right along," he said. "How about your arm?"

"It's almost good as new," Jed said, stretching his arm, working his fingers open and shut. "I'm ready for whatever's ahead."

"Good." Tim nodded, the two of them heeling their bays closer behind Arno Dunne.

Dunne looked back over his shoulder at them, saying, "Did you ever stop to think what a big chance *I'm* taking? Why should I be so sure I can trust you two behind me?"

"You invited us, Dunne," Tim said. "If it's not to your liking, just let us know."

Dunne let out a short laugh. "Naw, I'm only joshing with you. If I had any doubts, we wouldn't have come this far. The truth is,

I can see you two haven't had as much experience as you let on. But that's okay by me," he added quickly. "I saw how handy you are with those Colts." He paused as if thinking something over, then said without turning to them, "Tell me something, though. How would you feel about an ole-fashioned duel?"

"What do you mean?" Jed asked, the two of them moving their bays up closer as the trail broadened.

"You know," said Dunne, "stepping off ten paces, looking a man in the eyes until somebody gives a signal, then trying your best to blow the hell out of him before he does the same thing to you? Think either one of you can handle that?"

"You sound like you're talking about a sporting event," Jed responded.

"Yeah," Tim interjected, "and gunfighting is not a sport, Dunne. Why would any man consider doing something like that?"

"Why, for money, of course." Dunne chuckled. "I mean, *serious* money, the kind you can unroll onto your palm and feel the weight of it. The kind of money that makes women swoon and makes men green with envy." He tossed them a glance over his shoulder, smiling slyly. "Think about it, boys. I'm talking about the kind of money that instead of pinching a nickel for a beer and a free lunch, you'd be setting up the house and leaning with your thumbs hooked under your arms."

"You're talking to the wrong men, Dunne," Jed replied. "That kind of money has blood all over it."

"Just making conversation, is all," Dunne said, stepping his horse off the trail toward a ridge overlooking a wide stretch of flatland. "But in case you don't know it, blood washes right off of money. The bigger the money, the less of a stain blood leaves on it."

"But still," Jed said, "we were taught that the only time to use our Colts is in self-defense. It ain't right, what you're talking about—"

"Exactly how much money are you talking about, Dunne?" Tim Strange asked, cutting his twin brother off.

Arno Dunne had stopped his horse close to the edge of the ridge. He rose up in his stirrups, gazed out across the flatland, then backed his horse so it faced the twins. He smiled, tapping a finger to his forehead. "Now there's the proper question—*how much money?*" He winked and looked back and forth between them. "For twins, you two sure have some different ways of looking at things, don't you?" He gestured his hand toward Jed, saying, "Jed's only concern is whether something is right or wrong. But you"—he pointed his finger at Tim—"you go right to the business end of it. You want to know what it's worth to you in dollars and cents. I like that." Arno Dunne's smile broadened as he stared at Tim Strange.

Tim shrugged. "What's the harm in asking? You said you were only making conversation. That's true, ain't it?"

"What's the difference whether or not I was just making conversation?" Arno Dunne asked. "The question is still on the table—would you fight a duel like that or not?"

"It depends on the kind of man I was up against," Tim replied, his gaze fixed right on Arno Dunne.

"Hell, boy, we already know what kind of man he is. He's the kind of man who would kill you for money, or else he wouldn't be standing there. Now that we've settled that, would you do it or not?"

Tim looked away from Dunne, saying, "You're talking crazy. I don't want to hear any more about it."

Dunne laughed and shook his head. "Then let me ask you both this: Are you tired of riding those lank-sided bays? Because if you are, we've got a fresh change of horse coming." He jerked his head toward that flatland below the ridgeline. "They should be getting here most anytime."

"What are you talking about?" Jed stepped his bay forward and peered out ahead. At a distance of less than three hundred yards, he noticed seven men moving toward them across the flatlands, leading a ten-horse string stretched out between them.

"He's right," Jed said to Tim, stepping his bay back from the ridgeline. "It looks like a group of seven cowhands coming up from the Red."

"You counted seven," said Dunne, "but unless I've missed my guess, there's two more you didn't see."

"Seven or nine, what's the difference?" Tim said to Dunne. "We're not trading these bays. They're good horses. They're just a little bit off their weight right now. But they'll fill out once we get them on some steady grain."

"Trade?" Dunne chuckled. "Who the hell is talking about a trade? I swear, boys, do I have to spell everything out for yas? You don't trade for nothing out here, not if you've got any guts at all."

"Hold it, Dunne," Jed cut in. "We're not horse thieves and bushwhackers. Those are just some hardworking drovers down there."

"Oh, you think so? Well, you're wrong." Arno Dunne's face turned solemn, and he added, "Maybe it's time both of you decide exactly *what* you are. So far all I've heard is what the two of you *won't* do." Dunne stepped down, pulling his rifle from his saddle boot. "You can either side with me or stay out of my way. There's a fight coming up out of that draw."

"Not for me and Tim, there ain't," Jed said.

Arno Dunne turned to Tim, wiped a hand along his rifle barrel, and checked it. "What about it, Tim? You with me on this or not?"

"What are you saying, Dunne?" Tim asked. "That those men aren't drovers at all?"

"That's exactly what I'm saying." Arno Dunne levered a round into his rifle chamber. "They're headed this way because their two scouts spotted us and gave them a signal from somewhere, probably from behind us. Now you'd both best get to deciding where you stand on this."

"Like hell!" Jed swung his horse to the edge of the ridge, his pistol streaking up from his holster.

Seeing what his twin bother was about to do, Tim shouted, "Wait, Jed!"

But it was too late. Jed fired three warning shots into the air, the sound of them echoing out across the basin below as he yelled down, "Hello, the basin!"

"You damned fool!" Arno Dunne hissed. "Now you've done it! Get back from that edge. You've got yourself skylighted!"

But Jed didn't rein his bay horse back. Instead he turned the bay toward Dunne, his pistol covering him.

Two hundred yards below on the flatland, the riders heard the shots and scattered into brush, fanning out into a broad circle surrounding the ridgeline.

"I'm not moving until they're safely around us, Dunne," Jed replied.

"Then like as not, you've gotten us all killed," Dunne said. Paying no attention to Jed's pistol pointing at him, Dunne stepped away, taking a position behind a small cluster of rock and gazing down onto the flatland.

At the edge of the ridge, dirt and chips of rock suddenly sprang up at the hooves of Jed's bay beneath the sound of the rifle fire from below them. The horse shied back.

"Get down, Jed!" Tim shouted.

He didn't have to shout twice. A bullet whistled past Jed's head as he ducked, jerking his horse back from the edge.

From his position behind the rocks, Arno Dunne returned fire into the basin, already seeing the men moving into a widening circle around them. He tossed a quick glance at Jed and Tim Strange, watching them jerking their horses farther back out of the rifle fire.

"You boys have a lot to learn," he shouted to them. "Too bad you ain't going to live long enough to learn it."

"Never mind about us, Dunne," Tim called out to him as Dunne raised his rifle and continued firing. "We'll live through this. How'd you know they weren't drovers?"

Arno Dunne shook his head in disgust. "There's some things you just know, boys, if you want to see the next sunrise."

CHAPTER 10

From their position in the rocks along the ridgeline, Tim turned to Dunne as the rifle fire drew closer around them. "Maybe there's still enough time for us to make a run back along the trail we came up on."

Arno Dunne let out a dark chuckle under his breath, scanning the puffs of rifle shots below them. "I've got a feeling that's what they would like for us to do." He jerked his head back toward the winding, narrow trail. "Those two scouts I was talking about will be waiting back there for us, up in the rocks. They'll pick us off like ducks in a shooting galley."

"How do you know that, Dunne?" Jed asked in a critical tone.

"Because that's what I would do if I was them," Arno Dunne snapped. As a shot clipped a rock near his head, Dunne flinched back and cursed under his breath.

"Then what are we supposed to do," Jed asked angrily, "just sit here while they get a tighter grip on us, kill our horses, then take what they want?"

"Nope," said Dunne, eyeing the two of them, "but horses *are* what they want. So they'll try their best not to kill them." He ducked slightly as another shot sliced through the air close to them. "Since you boys don't have rifles, what you're going to do is leave me here close to the horses while the two of you belly-crawl out through the firing and get behind them." He spread a thin smile.

"It'll give you both a chance to use those big Colts you're so proud of."

Tim and Jed looked at each other for a second, then realized that what Dunne said made sense.

"All right, then," Tim responded, nodding toward the ten-gauge rabbit gun beside Jed, "we'll leave this with you in case they get in close enough for you to need it."

"Okay, leave it," said Dunne with a shrug, "but if they get that close, I'll be dead anyway."

"What if I pull the horses in closer to you?" Jed asked. "Won't that make them quit firing?"

"Naw, that'll just make 'em mad," said Dunne. "They'll know why you did it. Then they'll say to hell with it and make a rush, killing everything. We got to keep the horses safe for bait. As long as they know they've got a chance at gaining some live horses out of this deal, they'll move a little easier."

Two shots whistled past, forcing Tim to duck his head down as he asked Dunne, "Do you know these men?"

"Probably some of them, by name anyway. But I wouldn't exactly say any of us were ever saddle mates. It wouldn't matter now if we were. They're making their play. They don't care who it is up here."

A shot whined in and blasted up bits of rock at Dunne's shoulder. He ventured a return shot over his cover of rock, then dropped back down and looked at the twins, saying, "They're moving closer. Are you going or not?"

Jed swallowed against the tight knot in his throat and looked at Tim.

"Yeah, we're going," said Tim.

"All right, then," Dunne said. "Get behind them, but don't cut them off. Leave them room to fall back if they feel the urge. Keep them flanked, but be careful. You'll be firing toward each other."

"Let's go," Tim said to his brother.

Jed nodded, checked his pistol, then dropped down flat onto his belly beside Tim.

They crawled away in opposite directions beneath the rifle fire, which was now growing heavier and closer. Yet, Tim noted to himself as he put the distance of a few yards between himself and Arno Dunne's position, the rifle fire had not followed him. They hadn't caught a glimpse of him crawling away. He hoped the same was true for his brother. He glanced back over his shoulder in the dirt, but saw no sign of Jed.

"Watch yourself, Jed," he whispered to himself. Then he turned forward and continued crawling, gradually circling to his left.

Thirty yards on the other side of Arno Dunne, Jed Strange hugged the ground. Also noting that the rifle shots had not followed him, he breathed a short sigh of relief, then inched forward, circling to his right until he knew from the sound of the rifle fire that he'd gotten past the men's positions. He lay flat for a second, getting a feel for his next move. The sound of two rifles firing in unison lay less then twenty yards away.

He crawled closer toward the sound, then stopped cold as he heard one man say to the other, "I'm reloading. Keep them pinned."

"Take your time, Kelsy. I've got all day," the other voice replied.

Jed Strange held his breath for a moment, lest the sound of it be heard as he inched closer toward the backs of two men who lay beneath the cover of a short stretch of rock and pale broom sage. Busy with their rifle fire, the two men never looked around, for if they had, they would have seen Jed clear as day. He crept to within twenty feet of them, his pistol cocked in their direction. The wise thing to do would have been to shoot them both in the back with no warning. Yet as he raised his pistol and aimed it dead center on a sweat-streaked leather vest, he hesitated. He could not abide shooting a man in the back.

As the two men fired repeatedly toward Arno Dunne's position, Jed stood slowly to his feet, took a deep breath, and said, "Both of you, drop your guns! Raise your hands!"

"What the—?" The two men turned quickly to face him, neither of them making an attempt to lower their rifles.

"You heard me. Drop them!" Jed demanded.

The riflemen would have none of it. "You bet," said one, a killing grin on his whiskered face. Their hands tightened on their rifles, and when he saw the looks on their faces, Jed's Colt exploded twice, bucking in his hand.

Both men went down, one pitching backward across the low stand of rock. The other man spun in place as he fell. His rifle went off, the shot going wild as his rifle jumped out of his hand and fell to the ground.

Jed threw himself to the ground as a voice called out from twenty feet away, "Hey, Kelsy, Dermot? What are you two doing over there? I heard pistol shots."

Jed hurried forward on his belly, snatched up the fallen rifle, checked it, and levered a round into the chamber. The voice called out again, "Somebody get over there, see what's going on with Dermot and Kelsy."

As the voice spoke, the firing lulled for a second. Jed hurried to the covered low rock and turned himself toward the voice. Just as he did, he heard the sound of Tim's Colt bark out from across the wide circle of riflemen.

"What the hell is going on out here?" the voice cried out.

"I don't know, but I'll damn sure find out," another voice responded.

Jed waited for a second, aiming the rifle but holding his fire as the sound of footsteps rustled through the broom sage. When the man stepped into view, crouched and moving forward, he lifted his eyes to Jed Strange and started to swing his rifle to his shoulder when Jed's shot nailed into his chest.

"They've gotten around us!" a voice shouted, seeing the man Jed had shot fly backward in a spray of crimson.

Tim Strange had heard the shots from his brother's Colt at the same time he'd begun making his move on one of the riflemen at the other side of the firing circle. Now he rose to his knee with his own newly acquired rifle in his hand, wiped the smear of blood from the stock, and fired toward the sound of the voices. Arno Dunne, taking advantage of the commotion, acted quickly, firing straight ahead into the center of his attackers.

With the tables clearly turned on them, the three remaining outlaws drew close together, forced to do so by the deadly accurate rifle fire from Tim and Jed on either side. Huddled in the dust and looking back longingly toward the spot where they had left their horses, the leader, a man named Brenton Belcher, spoke to the two men beside him.

"How the hell did you boys let this happen? We're cut off here!" Shots spat overhead, pinning them down as Belcher raged. "Where's our scouts, Paco and Logan? I know damn well they hear all the shooting!"

Beside Belcher, a thin outlaw named Cody Renfrow raised his cheek from the dust just enough to answer. "I reckon they cut out on us, Belcher. But to hell with them. What are *we* going to do?" His words were partly drowned out beneath the rifle fire.

Belcher looked past Cody to the other man, a young Texan named Arliss Sidlo. "Arliss, crawl back to the horses and get them in here as close as you can. We'll keep you covered."

"Keep me covered?" said Sidlo. "Hellfire! You can't even get a shot off without them clipping your ears."

"Go on, damn it!" Belcher demanded. "Either get moving or I'll shoot you myself!"

Arliss Sidlo turned on his belly and crawled away, rifle fire nipping at the ground around him.

When he'd gotten out of sight, Cody said to Belcher as the two of them managed to throw a couple of slugs toward the sound of Jed and Tim's rifles, "Arliss ain't coming back, Belcher, in case you're wondering."

"He'd better," said Belcher. "I meant what I said about shooting him."

"He knows that," said Cody. "That's *why* he ain't coming back."

Belcher thought about it for a second, then said in bitter disappointment, "Damn it all. We're really in a fix here." He took advantage of a lull in the rifle fire and called out toward Arno Dunne, "Hey, out there, any chance of us surrendering?"

From Tim's position behind a low rock, he heard Arno Dunne call back to Belcher, saying, "Not a chance in hell, mister. You bit this off. Now chew on it." Two shots from Arno Dunne's rifle resounded, making sure the outlaw understood.

Belcher plastered his face to the dirt as the two shots struck the ground near his shoulder. Then he rose up an inch, spat grit from his lips, and said, "I recognize your voice. Is that you, Dunne?"

"You bet is it," Dunne replied. "Is that you, Belcher?"

"Yes, it is," Belcher called back to him. As soon as he spoke, he rolled away a few inches, for he knew Dunne was taking aim at the sound of his voice in the brush. "It don't seem right, ole boys like us killing each other, does it?"

"A while ago I might have agreed with you, Belcher," Dunne called back with a humorous chuckle. "But I see nothing wrong with it now." He levered a round and fired, the bullet thumping into the ground, causing Belcher to roll farther away.

"Hold your fire!" Jed Strange called out to Arno Dunne. "If they've had enough, let them go."

"You're out of your mind!" Arno Dunne yelled at him. "If they had kept the upper hand, there's no amount of begging and pleading that would have kept them from killing us."

"But we're not them," Jed shouted, moving closer toward the two pinned-down outlaws as he spoke to Dunne. "We'll let you go, if you promise to ride on," he added to Belcher and Cody.

"Yes, sir!" Belcher called out. "We promise. Let us clear out to our horses and you'll see no more of us."

"Your horses are gone, Belcher," Arno Dunne said. "Your buddy is beating a path out of here right now, taking everything with him."

"Well, damn him!" swore Belcher.

From his position on the other side of the two outlaws, Tim saw his brother, Jed, move closer to them and called over to him, "Stay back, Jed! You can't trust these vermin."

"We're letting them go, Tim," Jed replied. "They're done for. They don't want to fight."

"He's right!" Belcher called out. "All we want is to get out of here."

Tim, seeing that Jed wouldn't be dissuaded, moved in a little closer and called out to his brother, "All right, Jed, they can leave. But stay back from them."

Arno Dunne shook his head and said to himself, "You damned idiots have no idea what you're fooling with." Then he levered his rifle and moved forward, the three of them forming a circle around the two outlaws in the brush. "Go on, then, Belcher," Arno Dunne called out, "both of yas get the hell out of here."

The two scouts—a Mexican named Paco and his partner, a Kansan named Turly Logan—had not run out on Belcher and the others. They had stayed back along the trail until they caught sight of Arliss Sidlo riding off with the string of horses. Now they were riding in hard and fast along the trail. When Belcher heard their hoofbeats, his courage returned. He stood up slowly with his rifle cocked and aimed at Arno Dunne as he spoke.

"One thing I forgot to mention, Dunne," said Belcher. "We're going to be needing a couple of your horses. Just call it a loan among ole buddies."

But Tim, having caught sight of the two riders charging toward them, dropped Belcher with a quick shot, then turned to face the two returning scouts. He dropped his rifle to the ground and his Colt came streaking up from his holster. Twenty yards away, Jed Strange also saw the two riders charging and drew his pistol as well. Arno Dunne spun with them, just in time for a bullet to graze his shoulder. Tim, Jed, and Arno Dunne fired as one, their volley lifting both riders from their saddles and hurling them backward to the rocky ground.

"Look out, Dunne!" Tim shouted, spinning back toward Belcher and Cody.

Belcher had managed to stand up, blood running freely from

his chest. With Cody beside him, both men started to fire on Dunne from behind.

Jed and Tim responded ahead of Dunne, their shots dropping both men into the brush. Dunne stared, realizing how close he'd just came to dying. "Hell's bells, boys, I believe you saved my life."

"You're welcome, Dunne," Tim said in a clipped tone as the brothers stepped forward to the bodies in the brush. Arno Dunne stood silent for a moment with his hand pressed to his grazed shoulder.

Lying on the ground with one hand to his gaping chest wound and his other hand raised in surrender, Brenton Belcher gasped and said to Jed and Tim as they encircled him, "Don't . . . shoot no more. I . . . really am through now."

"Good of you to let us know," Tim said wryly. He reached out with his pistol pointed at Belcher's face and started to squeeze the trigger.

"Wait, Tim! Don't do it," said Jed. "He's done for. It ain't self-defense now."

"I don't give a damn," Tim hissed through clenched teeth. "Dunne was right. Show them no mercy."

But still he hesitated, knowing that what Jed had just told him was true. No matter the circumstance, this man was no longer a threat.

"Shoot that lousy bastard, Tim!" Arno Dunne ranted, moving up beside Tim. He pushed his rifle barrel forward toward Belcher, seeing Cody lying dead in the dirt. "He's the last of the bunch. This way nobody comes back later on, carrying a grudge!"

"No," said Tim, shoving Arno Dunne's rifle barrel away from Belcher. "Jed's right. This ain't self-defense any longer. He'll be dead soon enough."

"Not soon enough to suit me." Dunne sneered. But under Tim's frigid gaze, he made no attempt to repoint his rifle at the dying outlaw.

"We never did . . . like each other, Dunne," Belcher said, his voice thick with blood. "Seeing these . . . boys shoot. I reckon . . . you're headed to . . . the big contest with them, eh?"

"Shut up and die, Belcher," Arno Dunne snapped. "We don't have all day to waste on you."

"Yep, that's it," Brenton Belcher said in a low rasping laugh. "These boys . . . are your entries. You always was one . . . to play the angles."

As his words ended, his eyes glazed over and grew more distant until a long, low breath rattled from his chest. He slumped back onto the ground and lay limp.

"Son of a bitch," Dunne cursed, leaning forward and spitting in the dead man's face. "He was right about one thing—we never did get along."

"What contest was he talking about?" Tim asked, taking a step back and holstering his Colt.

"Nothing," said Dunne. "You never could pay attention to anything this horse-thieving fool had to say."

Dunne avoided any further explanation. Instead, he directed his attention to Jed, who stepped forward now and slipped his pistol into his holster.

"There, Jed, you see what your little ounce of mercy almost cost us?"

"I saw it, Dunne," Jed replied, "but we still tried to do the right thing. That's all we have to answer to the Lord for."

"Ha!" Dunne said. "You keep that attitude, you'll be going to heaven all right, but it might be too damn soon to suit you."

"Back to what he said about a contest," Tim interrupted, nodding at Belcher's body on the ground as he spoke to Dunne. "He seemed to know what he was talking about."

"You just ain't going to turn it loose, are you?" Dunne asked, trying to fake an innocent smile.

"That's right. I ain't," Tim said firmly, his hand resting on the butt of his Colt, "so spit it out."

Arno Dunne took a patient breath and shook his head, saying,

"All right, I'll level with you—not that it makes any difference. Newt Grago is cooking up a shooting contest, just something to see who's the fastest gun. I have to admit, seeing the way you two boys handle them Colts, it entered my mind that you might stand a chance to win yourselves some big money. To be honest, I hoped I might make a few dollars myself, betting on yas."

"That's what you were getting at earlier, ain't it?" Jed asked. "When you started all that talk about facing a man off in an old-time duel?"

"Yep, it was. But it was only speculation, boys, so don't get on no high horse over it." Dunne raised his hat brim, wiped sweat from his forehead, then lowered it and tucked his rifle up under his arm. "The more I see of you Faulkner twins, the more I realize you're not about to do anything you don't want to do. So let's forget the whole matter. I owe you both for saving my life. Far as I'm concerned, the best way I can repay you is to get on my horse and ride away from yas. You're both good boys. You've got no business out here. If you ever change your minds and decide to throw into this kind of life, look me up." He half turned and started toward his horse when Tim's voice stopped him.

"How much money?" Tim asked.

"What?" Arno Dunne looked taken aback. So did Jed Strange.

"You said maybe Jed and I could make some good money in this shooting contest. How much?" Tim's face was a mask of re-solve.

"Well, now." Arno Dunne scratched his jaw thinking it over. "It's what you call a matched shoot-out. Every time you beat a man, the stakes on your next fight gets higher. Take it all the way to the top, we're talking about as much as ten thousand dollars."

"That's ten thousand after you take your cut?" Tim asked.

Arno Dunne looked embarrassed, but only for a moment. "Yes, that's after I take my cut. Let's face it. You boys would never known about this if it weren't for me."

"And how much is your cut, Dunne?" Tim asked.

Before Arno Dunne could answer, Jed cut in, saying to his brother, "Tim, you don't mean it. We're not going to do something like this. This is deliberate murder."

"No, it's not, Jed," said Tim, staring at Dunne as he spoke. "It's like Dunne said earlier—these men are there for the same reason we'll be. Everybody knows the risk going in. Ain't that right, Dunne?"

Dunne chuckled. "You've been paying more attention than I thought, Tim Faulkner. Now see if you can talk some sense to your brother, the *deacon* here"—he thumbed toward Jed—"and we've got ourselves a business arrangement."

"You still never said how much your cut is, Dunne," Tim persisted without taking his eyes from Arno Dunne's.

Dunne stalled for a second, then let out a resigned breath, saying, "Hell, you're going to find out anyway. The pot gets cut straight down the middle every time you win, fifty to you two, fifty to me."

"Huh-uh," said Tim. "We'd be better off leaving you to lay here in the dirt, find this Newt Grago, and take our chances with him."

"Easy now," said Dunne, his smile back at work. "You're catching on to how things work, but don't get ahead of yourself. Grago's men would kill you both, seeing you ride in without me or somebody to vouch for yas."

"You get ten percent, Dunne, not a dollar more," Tim said as Jed stood listening in disbelief.

"Huh-uh." Arno shook his head. "Thirty or else I ride."

"Fifteen, or you can go *ahead* and ride, Dunne," said Tim.

Dunne considered it, once more scratching his jaw. "You're getting hard to deal with, Tim Faulkner. But let's make it twenty percent and get out of this heat."

Tim offered a faint smile in return. "Okay, twenty percent every time we win."

"What about if we lose?" Jed asked, looking back and forth between the two of them.

When neither Tim nor Arno Dunne answered him, he asked again. But Tim and Arno Dunne just walked off toward the horses and Jed trotted to catch up to his brother, asking him in a lower tone as they stepped farther away from Dunne to their bays, "Do you know what you're agreeing to, Tim? This is no different than being a paid assassin."

Tim replied, nearly whispering, "Damn it, Jed, you saw he was about to leave. Where would that put us as far as finding these men and possibly Danielle? Agreeing to do it don't mean we're going to. Just stick with me on this. Once we're inside this bunch of outlaws, we can deal with what to do next."

Jed let out a tight breath of relief. "Tim, you had me worried there for a second, but now that you've explained your reasons, I see what you mean. I'm sorry I doubted you. I should have known better than to think you'd go along with something like this."

"Just keep that in mind, Jed," Tim said. "No matter what I go along with, always realize that I've got our best interest at heart."

"I know that, Tim. You was just so convincing, it fooled me for a minute. I'm back on track now."

"Good," Tim said. "Now play along with things and keep quiet. Don't be asking questions like what happens if we lose. You know as well as I do—if we lose, we're dead."

CHAPTER 11

INDIAN TERRITORY. JULY 23, 1871.

At a remote spot along a nameless creek, Danielle Strange and Duncan Grago had spent a day in the shade of a tarpaulin lean-to, where an old horse thief named Uhl Hobbs kept a fresh string of stolen horses. Hobbs had welcomed them into his camp only after recognizing Duncan Grago. While Danielle rested and grained Sundown, Duncan Grago picked out a copper-colored Spanish barb that had gone a long time without a rider on its back. Danielle and Hobbs stood at the rail of a makeshift corral and watched Duncan get the barb used to a saddle. After a moment of studying Danielle with a guarded gaze, Hobbs asked, "Don't suppose you caught sight of any lawmen along the Red, did you?"

"Nope," Danielle answered, keeping her attention on Duncan as he wrestled with the headstrong copper barb.

Hobbs looked her up and down again, and asked, "That's a powerfully good-looking Colt you're carrying, Danny Duggin. Don't expect you'd be willing to trade it out for some riding stock?"

"Not at all interested," Danielle replied, her hand resting instinctively on the butt of her Colt. She knew Hobbs was more interested in finding out everything he could about this newcomer, Danny Duggin, than he was in trading for a gun or a horse.

"Being a trader, I always like to ask," Hobbs said. Then after a moment of silence, he asked in a bolder tone, "How come I've never seen you before, Danny Duggin? Dunc says you've been around Fort Smith and down in Texas for a while. I go to both places quite often."

Danielle dealt him a level stare, saying, "I guess you just weren't looking where I was standing, Hobbs. Now if you've got any more questions to ask about me, get it done. You're starting to rub against my grain."

Hobbs jerked back a step and kept his grimy hands chest high in a show of peace. "No offense, Mr. Duggin. You can't blame me for being a little cautious. Hell, it ain't even legal for me being here, let alone holding a string of horses with no paperwork on them."

Danielle allowed a faint smile. "No offense taken, Hobbs. Dunc and I will be moving on once he gets the air out from under that saddle. Until then, you might just as well settle down and stop wondering who I am or where I've been. You ought to know I'm not going to tell you anything I don't want you to know."

Hobbs cackled across broken yellowed teeth and shook his head. "Reckon I'm just curious by nature." He raised a crooked finger for emphasis. "But I want to tell you this for your own good. I heard there's a whole posse of deputies from Parker's court getting ready to make a sweep through here. So the two of you'd best keep an eye turned back to your trail. Be sure and mention it to Dunc first chance you get."

"I will. Much obliged for the information," Danielle said, seeing Duncan Grago wrestle the barb over closer to them. "We always keep an eye on our trail."

When Duncan had paid Hobbs for the copper barb and a Mexican saddle, he and Danielle rode on. They spent the rest of the day and part of the following morning pushing forward through tangles of brush across jagged terrain more fitting for mountain goats than horses.

ROBBER'S ROCK, INDIAN TERRITORY. JULY 24, 1871.

Two shots from the smoking pistols echoed in the ledges and canyons surrounding Robber's Rock. Newt Grago tossed aside a handful of beef rib bones he'd been eating and wiped his hands on a soiled bandanna. He stepped off the porch of the newly built plank shack and looked across the wide encampment of men and horses. There had to be as many as sixty or seventy men there, he estimated to himself, the thought of it making him smile. When the men had drifted in, two and three at a time over the past couple of weeks, they'd brought with them stolen cattle and Mexican horses. Two large tents had arrived a week earlier with a grifting gambler named Merlin Haas, who had come at Newt Grago's request. Along with the tents, Haas had also brought along some gaming tables, as well as six painted ladies all the way from Austin, Texas. The atmosphere at Robber's Rock was like that of a carnival, and that was just what Newt Grago wanted.

"Damn fine shooting," Newt Grago said to Chancy Burke.

Burke punched out the spent cartridge shell from his pistol and replaced it with a new round. He only nodded at Newt Grago and watched him walk toward the body of Curly Lyndell lying flat in the dirt.

Newt Grago finished wiping his hands, wadded up the greasy bandanna, and shoved it down into his hip pocket. Looking down at the body closely, Grago sucked at a tooth and loosened a fleck of beef from it with his fingernail. Then he spat the fleck away and turned, facing the gathering of onlookers, saying loud enough for all to hear, "Boys, Curly Lyndell is deader than hell."

Among the gathered spectators came sighs of disappointment as well as whoops and cheers for Chancy Burke. Newt Grago gave the crowd a second to spend itself down; then he raised a stack of dollars from his lapel pocket and fanned it in the air above his head as he stepped back over to Chancy Burke.

"That means ole Chancy here has just made himself the easiest two hundred and fifty dollars he ever made in his life." Newt

Grago handed Chancy Burke the money, then turned back to the crowd, saying, "I know damn well some of you might have made just as much, or lost just as much, depending upon how you bet. But the fact is, the only way to *win* big here is to *play* big here!"

The crowd stirred, and Newt Grago raised his hands toward them. "Boys, I ain't going to try to talk you into anything. But the man who challenges Chancy Burke and beats him gets his two hundred and fifty, plus another two hundred fifty for being the winner. I'm talking about *five hundred dollars*! Do I have any takers?"

While Newt Grago looked the crowd over for a show of hands and saw none, one of the women from Austin freed herself from an outlaw's arm around her waist and slinked forward a step. She threw her hand on her hip, striking a pose as she turned and said to the crowd, "Boys, I'd shoot any one of you here for five hundred dollars. Can I get in on this?" she asked Grago.

"Haw!" Newt laughed, throwing his head back. "You get over there where you belong, Lulu. This is man's sport."

"Man's sport, my aunt Fannie's drawers," Lulu said sarcastically, cutting her gaze to the gathering of outlaws. "There must not be a man in the bunch. What's the matter with you bunch of gutless coyotes?"

"Shut up, Lulu," said a drunken voice, "or I'll put a bullet in you for free, just to see what color your blood is. If you've got any, that is."

The crowd roared its approval. Newt Grago silenced them down with his raised hands. "Like I said, nobody's going to talk you into anything, but go have a few drinks and think it over. Chancy Burke is now the man to beat. He'll be ready when any one of you are. Right, Chancy?"

"That's right," said Burke, fanning his winnings with one hand while spinning his Colt down into his low-slung holster. "The sooner the better far as I'm concerned. I came here to win. I plan on leaving with both boots full of money."

The same drunken voice called out again to Burke from amid the crowd. "If that kid shows up who killed Scovill, Levan, and the others, you might fill your boots with something entirely different."

The crowd roared with laughter.

Chancy Burke's face flared crimson red. "Who said that?" he shouted, stepping forward with his hand near his tied-down Colt. "I want the bigmouthed son of a bitch who said that to come forward and say it again!" His eyes scanned the crowd as the laughter settled into cold silence. "Who was it? Was that you, Blanford? You're always shooting off your soup hole. Come on out here and say it again!"

The crowd parted and Ollie Blanford, a tall Arkansan with a drooping red mustache, stepped forward. "It weren't me said it, Burke. If it was, I wouldn't be at all hesitant to saying it to your face. Now what about me always shooting off my soup hole? I don't recall ever speaking more than a word or two to you in my whole life. We never rode together. Why'd you single me out?" His long arm hung loose but poised, his fingertips turned slightly in toward his pistol butt.

"Because it sounded like your voice, Blanford," said Burke.

As the two outlaws spoke, Merlin Haas had moved in beside Newt Grago. Now, seeing trouble brewing quickly between Burke and Blanford, Haas took his cigar from his mouth and said to Grago, "I'd best stop this before it gets too far out of hand."

But Grago took Haas by the arm, stopping him, saying, "Naw, what's your hurry? Let it go a minute. This might be just the thing to get this ball rolling." He chuckled and pulled Haas back beside him.

"Hell, maybe you're right," Haas whispered.

Ollie Blanford responded to Chancy Burke, "It might have sounded like me, but it weren't. As far as my bad-mouthing, I never say a damn thing I ain't prepared to back up with knuckle or lead either one."

"Then let's do her up," Chancy Burke hissed, scraping a boot sidelong in the dirt, taking a fighting stance.

"That suits the hell out of me, boy," Ollie Blanford replied.

The crowd moved aside as Blanford's hand slipped down slowly, removing the strip of rawhide from across his pistol hammer.

"Whoa, now, boys," said Newt Grago, seeing his opportunity to reap some benefit for himself, "let's take a second to get the pot right. This is exactly what I was talking about. You're going to shoot each other anyway, one of you might as well make something from it—the rest of us, too."

He glanced around at the crowd for support. "If any of you want in on this, you'd better get over to Haas right away before these two commence skinning leather." He took a step back, turned to Blanford and Burke, and said to them both, "You boys can give us just a minute here, can't you?"

"I'm ready anytime he is," Burke said, keeping his gaze fixed on Blanford.

"Same here," Blanford said. "I can wait a minute or two before killing him if it's worth five hundred dollars to me."

"Don't start spending that money yet, Blanford," Burke threatened. "All you're buying is a ticket to hell."

"That's the spirit, boys," Grago said, stepping back and hurrying over to Merlin Haas. "This is all working out just fine, Haas," he said, leaning close to Merlin Haas's ear while the grifter counted the money being shoved at him by the excited crowd.

"It's the craziest, wildest thing you've ever come up with, Grago," Haas replied, scratching down numbers and names with a pencil stub as the wad of cash in his hand grew ever larger, "but I ain't complaining . . . no, sir!" He shook his fistful of money.

Lulu waded in among the bettors, waving a ten-dollar bill out before her. "Ten dollars on Burke? Anybody? What do you say?"

Newt Grago grabbed her by her arm and pulled her away from the crowd. "That's enough, Lulu. You've done your part. Now put your money away, settle back, and watch the show."

Lulu lowered her voice, speaking to him. "You said to get them stirred up and keep them that way, Grago. That's exactly what I'm trying to do."

"I know, Lulu, and you've done a good job. Between you and

that loudmouthed drunk a while ago, they'll be at one another's throats the rest of the day. We'll all make a bundle on it." While he spoke, Newt Grago took out a big double eagle coin and shoved it down the front of her tight-fitting bodice. "Relax now."

Lulu giggled and patted the coin inside her dress. "Whatever you say, Grago, but I still don't see what you're going to gain, getting a bunch of your own gang killed off this way."

"It makes good sense, Lulu," said Grago. "Even the best of herds needs some careful culling now and then. I want only the fastest and the best riding with me. This is one way of making sure I get them. At the end of this, I'll have a gang of men so tough, they'll make the James-Younger gang look like a bunch of pickpockets."

"Meanwhile, you and Merlin Haas make a tidy bankroll, covering the bets and cutting a percentage of the pot, right?" she asked.

"Of course, Lulu." Grago smiled. "Only a damn fool works for free. Me and Haas will make our money, but don't worry—you and your girls will be well taken care of in the process."

"That's all that matters to me." Lulu giggled. She shoved two fingers down into her bodice, fished out the double eagle, and flipped it, catching it sideways out of the air on its way down.

While the sun boiled white-hot in the afternoon sky, Danielle and Duncan Grago crossed a stretch of land that had appeared flat from a distance. Yet, angling now toward a pair of slim, rising buttes, Danielle saw that they would be moving through nothing more than a rocky maze of gulches, cutbanks, and dropoffs for the next ten miles.

Once across the rugged furnace, the land leveled in between the buttes, and it was at that point that they heard the two quick pistol shots resound in the distance. Duncan only grinned, looking up among the high ledges into the shadows the buttes, saying, "Yep, that'll be Newt and the boys. We'll be running into some lookouts here any minute. So let's not make any sudden moves until they see who I am." He squinted in the sun's glare, his eyes scanning back and forth above them.

Danielle searched also, reminding herself of how dangerous and difficult this would have been on her own, without an insider like Duncan leading the way. The ledges along the slope of the buttes were perfect for an ambush, the land beneath them offering little protection.

"Let's hope they recognize you," she said. "After all, you've been gone for a while."

"Don't worry. Brother Newt has them watching for me. They won't do nothing that'll get him down their collar."

He gigged the copper barb forward, the horse still resisting slightly but getting used to a rider on its back. Before they had traveled another mile, two more pistol shots echoed in the distance. Duncan only smiled and nodded them forward.

As they drew deeper between the two buttes, a flash of evening sunlight glinted off a rifle barrel fifty yards above them. Instinctively, Danielle's hand went to her Colt, but a voice from behind a large rock alongside the trail called out, "Keep your hands in sight, mister," and Danielle froze.

"It's me, Grago," said Duncan, turning his horse in the direction of the voice, keeping his hands in view. "Don't shoot. This is my friend Danny Duggin."

"Dunc?" the voice said. "I thought that was you when we saw you crossing the scrubs. It's me, Chester."

Danielle watched as the man stepped in view from behind the rock, a cocked rifle in his hands.

"Newt's been wondering what took you so long getting here."

"Chester Gibb," Duncan said, relaxing now and letting his hands down, "it's been a long time since I laid eyes on you. Who's up in the rocks?"

"That's Clet Eldridge," said Gibb. "Me and him's been waiting for somebody to relieve us so's we can get a couple drinks of whiskey. Your brother's got quite a gathering in there. They've been whooping it up, sure enough." He raised an arm to the man in the rock shadows above them and waved back and forth slowly, letting him know everything was all right.

"Yeah, we heard some shooting earlier," Duncan said. "What's going on in there?"

"It's the wildest thing you ever saw, Dunc," said Gibb. "Newt's got a contest going to see who's the fastest gun. So far, nobody has beat Chancy Burke. He killed ole Marvin Parrish this morning. Shot him right through the heart."

At the sound of the name Chancy Burke, Danielle perked up, remembering the name from her list of killers.

Duncan looked astonished and asked Gibb, "You mean, it's a contest where they're really shooting each other?"

"Yep." Gibb chuckled. "I told you, it's the wildest thing ever. A man can either make himself some money or end up dead in the dirt." His eyes went to Danielle Strange. "What about you, mister? Are you any good with that tied-down Colt, or do you wear it to keep your shirt tucked in?"

Danielle said from beneath her lowered hat brim, "Don't concern yourself about my Colt or my shirttail."

Duncan Grago cut in, saying, "Chester, I might as well tell you right now: Danny Duggin don't tolerate much guff off of nobody. As far as his Colt goes, you can take it from me—it does whatever he wants it to. He's a friend of mine, and I vouch for him." Duncan's hand rested on his pistol butt. "Is there any more that needs to be said on the matter?"

"Hell no, Dunc," Chester Gibb said quickly. "You know how I am. Sometimes I like to aggravate." His eyes went to Danielle. "No harm intended, Danny Duggin. Any friend of Dunc's is a friend of mine. Right, Dunc?"

Duncan Grago stared at him with a tight, fixed grin. Danielle saw the wild look that had been missing for a while come back into his eyes. "Let's hope so, Chester," he said. "Otherwise I'd put a bullet right where your—"

Danielle cut him off, saying to Chester Gibb, "How fast is this Chancy Burke?"

Chester Gibb swallowed a dry knot in his throat, glad to change the subject. "He's damn fast. Right now he's the cock of the walk. But there's others on their way here that are just as fast, if not faster."

"Oh? Who's coming?" Danielle asked, knowing she was on the verge of standing face-to-face with her father's murderers and barely able to keep from riding in with her Colts blazing. Still, she kept calm, wanting to find out everything she could about these men.

"Well, let's see," said Chester Gibb, scratching his beard-stubbled jaw, thinking about it. "There's what's left of the regulars— Rufe Gaddis, Saul Delmano, and Julius Byler—not to mention some others Newt sent for. Arno Dunne's supposed to be on his way. If I know Arno, he's gone and got himself a gunslinger he figures is fast enough to make him some money here."

"Yeah, that's Arno Dunne, all right," said Duncan, "always playing an angle." He tilted his head slightly and asked, "You mentioned Julius Byler? Hell, I figured Julius would have already arrived by now. We met up with him, but then him and Danny here had a falling-out. When Danny ran him off, I thought he probably came on out here."

"Nope, he ain't here." Chester Gibb looked from Duncan to Danielle, and asked, "You ran Julius Byler off? I don't know how you did that unless you shot him."

Feeling both Duncan's and Gibb's eyes on her, Danielle shrugged, saying calmly, "That's what I did. I shot him, six times in the chest, then sent him packing. Told him if he came back, I'd shoot him some more." She stared blankly from beneath her lowered hat brim and waited.

For a second Chester Gibb only stood with a puzzled look on his face. Then he chuckled and said to Duncan Grago, "Well, I see your friend Danny Duggin here has a sense of humor. For a minute there, he had me believing it." He waved them past him on up the narrow trail toward Robber's Rock. "You two go on, Dunc. Tell somebody to come out and relieve us. Me and Eldridge has been out here long enough. Besides, there ain't no lawmen foolish enough to ride into Robber's Rock nohow."

"I'll tell Newt to send somebody," said Duncan, straightening the copper barb onto the trail.

Danielle followed Duncan Grago closely. Hearing Chester Gibb's words caused a guarded smile to alight on her lips. *Just keep believing that, Gibb,* she thought to herself as her eyes searched upward around them. In the shadows of rock fifty feet above them, a rifleman stepped forward and waved them along the narrowing pass.

Danielle hadn't said a word to Duncan Grago about the posse out of Fort Smith that the old horse thief Hobbs had told her about. She hoped Hobbs was right, but she wasn't about to mention it to Duncan Grago. As far as she was concerned, the law could have whatever was left of this band of outlaws. She wanted only the ones whose names were on her list. If the law was coming, she needed to get her killing done and clear out of here, for once the posse hit, they wouldn't know Danny Duggin from the rest of this bunch. Danielle nudged her chestnut mare forward, anxious to bring her vengeance to a head.

"Once we get to the camp, you stick close to me for a while, Danny," Duncan Grago said over his shoulder. "Just till everybody sees you're all right."

"Sure, Dunc, no problem," Danielle said, staring straight ahead, preparing her mind for the killing task that lay ahead.

CHAPTER 12

S tanding on the porch above the crowd, Newt Grago and Merlin Haas were the first to see the two horses come into view
from the trail leading down to the encampment.

"Think it's your brother, Duncan?" Haas asked, still holding a
thick stack of dollars in his sweaty hand.

"I'd bet on it," Newt Grago replied. He stepped down and el-
bowed his way through the gathered outlaws who were still milling around the corpse of Ollie Blanford. "Get him away from here
before he starts drawing flies," Newt demanded of the crowd.

"You heard him, boys," said Haas, stepping along behind Newt
Grago toward the two riders in the distance. "Get Ollie out of
here—Curly Lyndell, too." He gestured toward the body of Curly
Lyndell lying a few yards away. "We can't have another round
until somebody does some cleaning up here."

"What are we supposed to do with them?" a voice called out
from amid the crowd.

"Hell, I don't know," Haas said in passing. "Tie a rope around
their ankles and drag them to a gully somewhere, I reckon. Just get
them out of here before they turn ripe on us. I'll tell Lulu to give
a free bottle of rye to the man who gets rid of them."

"What the hell are we waiting for, boys?" the same voice called
out. "Somebody get a rope!"

A few yards past the gathered crowd, Newt Grago and Merlin Haas stopped and stood at the edge of the dusty clearing, looking out at the two approaching riders.

"Yep, that's Dunc on the left," Newt Grago said, a smile spreading on his sweat-streaked face. "We'll see some action now. He was meaner than a sack full of rattlesnakes when he went to prison. He'll be even meaner now, I expect. You never met Dunc, did you, Haas?"

"Nope, can't say I ever had the pleasure," Merlin Haas replied, squinting in the mellow evening sunlight. He saw Duncan Grago lift his hat and run a hand back across his short-cropped hair. "Looks like they sheared him to the bone before they turned him loose. Who's that with him?"

"I don't know who it is," said Newt, himself squinting in the sunlight. "But it ain't Julius Byler or Sep Howard either one. That's for sure. Damn it! I told Sep to make sure he and Dunc stopped by Byler's hideout and brought him along with them." He lifted his hat from his head and swung it back and forth, waving at his brother and the rider beside him. "Well, whoever it is, if he's riding with Dunc, he's got to be all right."

"Yeah," said Haas, grinning. "If he gets himself killed here, I've got first claim on that big chestnut he's riding."

Newt Grago had been so excited to see Dunc riding in that he'd paid no attention to the horse the other man was riding. But now he stiffened a bit at Haas's words as a thought dawned on him. "We'll see," he said, his tone of voice changing, growing cautious now as he tried peering closer at the face of the other rider. After a moment, he called out over his shoulder to the men a few yards behind him, "Boys, get on over here. My brother, Dunc, is riding in. Let's make him feel welcome!"

The outlaws moved in closer behind Newt Grago and Merlin Haas, two of them dropping the rope they'd looped around the ankle of Ollie Blanford's body and leaving him lying in the dirt.

"What's up, boss?" Chancy Burke said, stepping in beside Newt Grago. "You sound worried."

"Worried? Naw, not me," said Newt. "Just keep your eyes skinned on this man riding with Dunc."

"I've got him covered," Chancy Burke said, lowering his voice as the two horses cantered in the last few yards and came to a halt. Burke's right hand rested on the butt of his Colt, jiggling it in his holster.

"Hot damn, brother Newt!" Duncan Grago cried out joyously, jumping down from the copper barb's back and running forward, his hat flying back off of his head.

Danielle instinctively touched her fingers to her fake mustache, checking it. Then she adjusted her hat brim low and level, crossed her wrists on her saddle horn, and watched the Grago brothers throw their arms around each other as they laughed and cursed between themselves. She swallowed back the bitter taste of anger and fought the urge to swing her Colt from her holster and drop Newt Grago on the spot.

"Dunc, you don't look a damn bit different than when I last saw you!" Newt Grago said, shoving his brother back at arm's length and looking him up and down. "I take it you've been properly rehabilitated, though? I'd hate to think that in all this time, they failed to teach you the error of your ways."

Duncan Grago stepped back, laughing, and looked all around at the gathered outlaws as he spoke to Newt. "You bet they showed me the errors of my ways. They taught me the most important lesson a man ought to know." He hesitated for a second, making sure all eyes and ears were upon him. Then he said, laughing even louder, "They taught me to never be taken *alive!*"

The outlaws whooped and roared with laughter. Danielle smiled only enough to go along with Duncan Grago's show. Even as she did so, she noticed Newt Grago and the man on his left cutting their eyes at her, then looking away. She knew they were checking out this stranger on the chestnut mare sitting before them, and she knew why. The man who'd killed some of their friends had been riding a big chestnut mare. But she stayed calm, already knowing the questions would come, already preparing herself for them.

In a moment, when the laughter and greetings had died down, Newt Grago turned toward her with his left arm looped up around Duncan's shoulder. His right hand hung loose and natural near the pistol on his hip. "So, Dunc," Newt Grago asked, his eyes hooded and his thin smile fixing on Danielle, "who is your friend here? Somebody from prison, I reckon?"

"Naw, this is my pal, Danny Duggin," Duncan Grago said. "We met on the trail coming here from Fort Smith. Danny saved my bacon. Hadn't been for him, I'd be dead."

"Is that a fact?" Newt Grago asked, eyeing Danielle. "In that case, I'm mighty obliged to you, Danny Duggin." He jerked a thumb toward Haas on his right, then Burke on his left, saying, "Meet Merlin Haas and Chancy Burke, a couple of the boys. You can meet the rest, providing you'll be sticking around for a while."

Danielle nodded at the two men in turn, careful not to let the white-hot vengeance show in her eyes as she looked upon the face of Chancy Burke. "I plan on staying awhile," she replied, "if it's all right by you. Dunc said it would be."

"Well, hell yes, it's all right with him," Duncan cut in, speaking for his brother. "Right, Newt?"

Newt Grago gave only a grudging nod, stepping forward, looking closely at the chestnut mare as Duncan Grago continued. "I had the awfulest time getting Danny here to come along with me. He mostly keeps to himself. A real loner, you might say."

"A real loner, huh?" Newt said almost to himself, running a hand down Sundown's muzzle. Sundown shied and pulled her head to one side. "A fine mare you've got here, Danny Duggin," Newt said, inspecting Sundown closely as he spoke. "Had her long?"

Here goes, Danielle thought to herself, knowing she had to play this just right. "A few months," she replied in an offhand manner. "I've got no paper on her, but she ain't stolen, if that's what you're wondering." Danielle pulled the reins, moving Sundown away from Newt's hand.

"It wouldn't matter to me if she was stolen or not," Newt chuckled. "Hell, most of the horses here are stolen. But I am curious as to where you got her."

Danielle took on a testy tone. "You can stay curious, then. I came here with Dunc because he said there was money to be made. He forgot to mention that a man had to explain where he gets his riding stock."

"Easy, Danny," Duncan Grago said, trying to keep the air friendly. "Newt's only making conversation. Ain't you, Newt?"

"Maybe . . . maybe not," said Newt, keeping a suspicious gaze on Danielle. "The fact is, there was a young man about your age who rode a big chestnut mare last year. He killed some pals of mine. Rumor has it he's riding a vengeance trail—"

"Save your breath, Grago," Danielle said, cutting him off with a sigh of exasperation. "I've already heard this story." She allowed herself a slight laugh. "Hell's fire, you're the third person that's brought it up in the past few weeks. If you thought I was that man, why didn't you just come out and say so in the first place?"

Newt Grago slid a glance around to Chancy Burke, then looked back at Danielle.

Danielle noted how Chancy Burke and the others were ready to make a move at Newt Grago's slightest signal. She stayed calm, not even lifting her wrists from her saddle horn.

"If it makes you feel any better," she said, "the gunslinger you're talking about is dead. I know because I found his body. He was cut all to hell. This *was* his mare." She reached out a hand and patted Sundown's neck, then let her hand lie back on her thigh, not near her pistol just yet but close by, should the need suddenly arise. "I found this big chestnut wandering around and took her. That's as much as I can tell you about it."

Newt Grago seemed to be weighing her story. Danielle was unsure if he believed it or not. Finally he said, "You're sure that gunslinger is dead, huh?"

Danielle made a relaxed shrug in reply. "He was dead when I found him. He was dead when I left. It ain't likely his condition has changed since then."

Faint laughter rippled across the outlaws. Newt Grago even grinned a little. For a second he seemed satisfied, but then his grin faded somewhat and he said, "Yeah, that's funny. There's only one thing that puzzles me." He raised a finger and feigned a curious expression. "See, this gunslinger's name was *Dan* Strange. Your name's *Danny* Duggin. You can see the similarity, I'm sure?"

Danielle let out another breath, this time shaking her head slowly. "Yep, and I've been asked that question before by Sep Howard. I'll tell you the same thing I told him. I'd have to be a damned fool to change my name from Dan to Danny, now, wouldn't I?"

Another wave of laughter stirred among the outlaws until Newt Grago silenced it with a harsh glance backward. Then he said to Danielle, "You mean, Sep Howard already asked you about it?"

"Yep," Danielle said.

"By the way, where is Sep?" Newt asked, turning to Duncan Grago.

But before Duncan could answer, Danielle said in a flat tone, "I shot him dead."

The crowd tensed as Newt Grago jerked back toward her with murder in his eyes. "You what? You shot Sep Howard?"

"That's right."

"But it was a fair fight, Newt," Duncan cut in. "Danny only did what he had to do. I vouch for him. Sep Howard tried gunning him, and bang! Danny put him down."

"Sep Howard was no small piece of work," Newt said, looking back at Danielle.

"He is now," Danielle replied quietly.

"He was a pal of mine, too," Newt said.

"Well, maybe you ought to pick pals who can keep themselves from getting killed," Danielle offered, knowing it to be the best answer she could possibly give to a man looking for fast and hard gunmen. She spread a flat, mirthless smile. "We both know this is a tough world we live in."

"I sure can't argue that with you." Newt Grago chuckled, seeming to loosen up. The others followed suit, one passing a bottle of rye to another as the tension seemed to lift. "Where's Julius Byler?" he asked Duncan Grago. "You were supposed to swing by his place and bring him along."

"He bad-mouthed Danny and Danny ran him off," Duncan Grago said proudly.

Again, Newt looked surprised and swung his attention back to Danielle. "The hell you say!"

Danielle shrugged one shoulder, tossing the matter aside. "Like I said about picking pals."

Chancy Burke saw that this Danny Duggin was stealing some of the thunder he'd built up among the men, and he didn't like it. He took a step forward, saying, "Sounds like you're pretty cocksure of yourself, Duggin. Maybe you need a good lesson in manners."

"I'm always willing to learn," Danielle said, answering him in a way that left no margin for doubt. "How good are you at teaching?"

"Hold on, boys," said Merlin Haas, stepping in before Newt Grago got the chance to himself. "This ain't the place for it. Anybody wants to show their fangs, let's do it by the rules, like we've been doing it."

"The rules?" Danielle asked, having used the exchange with Burke as a good reason to drop her hand back to her Colt. "What are you talking about, rules?"

Newt Grago saw the opportunity to further his shooting contest, and he took it. "Danny Duggin, if you're a man who likes action, my brother, Dunc, has brought you to the right place." He poked a thumb over his shoulder, pointing back toward the shack. "Come on, all of yas. Let's get Dunc and Danny some rye whiskey, make them both feel at home here."

"Sounds good to me," Duncan Grago said, stepping back and swinging up onto his copper barb. "What do you say, Danny?"

"I'm right beside you," Danielle responded, nudging Sundown forward, giving Chancy Burke a cold, lingering stare as she stepped the mare past him.

As the whole motley collection of gunmen moved back toward the shack, Newt Grago said to Chancy Burke, "Kill that son of a bitch so quick, he won't know what hits him. You hear me?"

"I hear you," said Burke. "But what about Dunc? He seems real taken by this Danny Duggin. I don't want Dunc coming down on me over it."

Newt grinned. "That's why we want it to be just one more part of the shooting contest. That way Dunc can't blame nobody."

"Good thinking," said Chancy Burke. "You figure this is that gunslinger from last year, don't you?"

"I don't know. He fits the description. But whether he's that gunslinger or not, there's no mistaking that mare. Remember the man we left hanging from the tree last year? The big chestnut I wanted before it managed to get away?" He nodded toward the chestnut mare as Danielle slow-stepped it toward the shack. "If that's not the same animal, I'll eat my shirt."

Chancy Burke nodded slowly. "If that's him and the rumors we heard are true, he's after me the same as he is you and the rest of us."

"That's right," Newt Grago said in a grim tone. "So that's something you'd better keep in mind when you face him tomorrow."

"Tomorrow, hell. What's wrong with tonight?" Chancy Burke asked.

"Because if he really is that gunslinger, you'll need the rest of the evening to go somewhere and practice your draw. I don't want no slipups here. I want him dead the first time he toes the mark."

"He's dead right now, Newt." Burke chuckled confidently, watching the chestnut mare move away in a low stir of dust. "He just don't realize it yet."

On their way to the shack, Danielle cast a sidelong glance at the body of Ollie Blanford lying in the dirt, a rope looped around one ankle leading to a saddle horn on a dusty paint horse standing obediently, waiting. Danielle looked farther across the flat clearing out front of the shack, at the other body in the dirt. "Your brother likes some pretty tough games," she said to Duncan Grago, who was riding beside her. "Is he as keen on participating as he is on promoting?"

"Ha!" Duncan laughed. "Newt is the best gunman I ever saw, and I've seen plenty. The thing is, he don't have to do his own gun-handling anymore unless he wants to. Newt's the man on top now. He can get somebody else to do his shooting for him. But that don't make him soft." Duncan grinned. "That just makes him smart. I already see what he's doing here. He's getting rid of the deadwood. I figure he's making something on it at the same time. By the time this is over, he'll have the damnedest bunch of killers you ever saw working for him. Then the world had better step aside. Won't you be proud, pulling iron with a gang like this?"

"Yeah," said Danielle. "I can hardly wait."

At dark, Danielle slipped away from Duncan Grago long enough to go to the crowded rope corral, where she had left Sundown after watering, graining, and rubbing her down with a handful of dried wild grass. To remove the temptation of anybody stealing the big chestnut, Danielle led her nearly fifty yards away from the encampment and left her at the mouth of a dry wash where long strands of clumped grass leaned in the night breeze. She didn't hobble the mare, but left her free to roam and graze, knowing Sundown would stay close by unless someone or something came upon her. In such an event, it would be better to leave the mare free of any restraints.

Returning to the camp, Danielle walked to the glow of lanterns spilling out through open tent flies. The tent on her right appeared less crowded than the one on her left, so she veered over to it and stepped inside to the sound of both profane curses and drunken laughter as the outlaws stood lined along the banks of a row of battered faro tables. Past the tables, Danielle saw Duncan and two other outlaws drinking at a bar that was merely a long pine plank lying across two wooden whiskey casts. Seeing Danielle, Duncan motioned her forward with his whiskey bottle in his hand.

"Where've you been?" Duncan asked in a friendly tone. "You're way behind on your drinking! Newt will be here any minute. We'll go to his shack, drink some more rye, and talk about old times." He pushed the half-full bottle of rye into her hand, then gestured with a nod toward the two men beside him. "This here is Morgan Goss and Cincinnati Carver. Boys, this is Danny Duggin, my best pal."

"Yeah, so we heard," said Cincinnati Carver, a ratty-looking outlaw with a sawed-off shotgun slung over his left shoulder and a small hatchet riding in his belt. "We was there when you rode in, remember?"

Both outlaws gave Danielle a cautious but respectful nod, then attended to the dirty shot glasses of rye in their hands. Danielle knew nothing about the two men, yet she recalled Bob Dennard mentioning them the day she got the drop on him on the trail out of Fort Smith.

Morgan Goss stood well over six feet tall and was slim as a rake handle. He wore a tall black Mexican sombrero that had a bullet hole in its crown, an aged bloodstain surrounding it. His wrists were girded with tall silver-studded leather gauntlets. Bandoleers of pistol ammunition crisscrossed his chest. He leaned forward along the plank bar and spoke to Danielle in a guarded voice. "Don't want to say this too loud, but I hope to hell you shoot Chancy Burke's head off in the morning. Me and Cincinnati is putting our whole bankroll on you."

Danielle gave Duncan a surprised look, and he raised a hand in defense. "Don't ask me, Danny," he said. "I had nothing to do with it. The way you and Burke nearly locked horns earlier has got everybody speculating, I reckon. Everybody figures you two will be going at it."

Nothing would please me more, Danielle thought. But she didn't want to seem too eager about it at first. "I didn't come here for this kind of business," she said. "In fact, if I knew what was going on, I might not have come at all." She raised the bottle of rye, appearing to take a long drink, but actually only taking a short sip. "If this is what you had in mind, Dunc, I might just take my leave come morning and clear out of here."

"I didn't know nothing about this, Danny, I swear," said Duncan Grago. "But you have to admit, if there's some money to be made drawing and shooting that big Colt, why not make it?"

"He's telling you right, Danny Duggin," said Cincinnati Carver. "If a man can spin a bullet out faster than the next, he'll fare well here."

"What about you?" Danielle asked him. "Are you going to be facing anybody?"

"Me? Hell no!" Cincinnati Carver patted the side of his trousers, showing he had no sidearm. "I don't even trust myself to *carry* a pistol, I'm so bad with one." His hand went to the stock of the sawed-off shotgun slung over his shoulder. He stroked it lovingly. "Now, if they'd let me use Little Milly here, I'd be game as a wild mustang."

Beside Cincinnati Carver, Morgan Goss laughed and said, "The trouble is, one blast from Little Milly would not only kill his opponent. It'd also wipe out half the spectators."

"What about you?" Danielle asked Morgan Goss. "Are you going to face anybody out there?"

"I ain't a fancy gunslinger," Goss responded. "I don't kid myself about it. I can shoot as straight as the next man, but I'm not fast on the draw." He tossed back a shot of rye and wiped the back of a leather wrist gauntlet across his mouth. "Besides, I've been outlawing too long to have to prove myself, and I'm slick enough at stealing horses that I'm never scarce of cash."

"You figure that's what this is all about, money or fame?" asked Danielle. She offered a trace of a smile, looking into Morgan Goss's large watery eyes.

Morgan Goss shrugged, saying, "That's all most things are about, ain't it? A man steps up to kill another man in a shooting contest, it's because he either needs to line his pockets or wants to broaden his name."

"Or both," Cincinnati Carver added, raising his glass of rye.

"What the hell do you two old horse thieves know about any damn thing?" Duncan Grago snapped at them, somehow finding a way to take offense at what the men said. "My brother organized this whole thing. I won't have you bad-mouthing it."

As he spoke, Danielle noticed the wild gleam that was back in his eyes, brought on no doubt by the whiskey and the excitement of being back among his own kind.

Morgan Goss and Cincinnati Carver both shied back a step, seeing Duncan Grago's hand drop to the butt of his pistol.

"Hold on, Dunc," Goss said. "We weren't speaking ill of Newt. Hell, we're just speculating on why a man—"

"Don't tell me to *hold on*," Duncan seethed, cutting Goss off. Eyes turned from the faro tables toward the sound of Duncan Grago's raised voice. "So what if a man wants to gain himself a reputation shooting some sonsabitches? So what if he wants to make himself money for doing it? This is a free country!"

The longer Duncan raged, the more Danielle could see that he was spinning out of control. His hand had gripped the butt of his Colt, his fingers tightened around it. She saw him start to jerk the gun from his holster, and as quick as the snap of a whip, she drew her own Colt and swung the barrel sidelong against his forehead.

Duncan Grago crumbled, but Danielle swooped down, looping him across her back as he fell, then raised him up on her shoulders. She turned with her pistol still out, letting the crowd see it, saying, "Everybody, stay calm. No harm done. My buddy Dunc just got a little too much rye in him."

The weight of Duncan Grago on her shoulders was staggering, yet she managed to stand straight and turn toward the fly of the tent. The faro players chuckled, dismissing it, and turned back to the tables.

"Damn, Danny Duggin," said Morgan Goss, "we both owe you our thanks. Dunc always was crazy as a June bug once he got to drinking."

"I know," said Danielle. "I've seen it before." She didn't know how long she could stand the weight on her back, and she wasn't about to let anybody see her have to drop him. "Tell his brother he's all right. He just needs to sleep it off a couple of hours."

"We'll tell him," said Cincinnati Carver.

Danielle forced herself to walk steadily and upright beneath the crushing load until she'd left the tent and gotten out of the glow of lantern light. She staggered a few yards farther to the spot where the two of them had pitched their saddles and gear on a clear spot of ground. Dropping Duncan to the ground, her breath heaving in her chest, she dragged him by his ankles the few remaining feet to his rolled-up blanket.

"I don't know . . . why I'm wasting my . . . time on you," she whispered, out of breath.

When she'd finished spreading Duncan's blanket and rolling him over onto it, Danielle wet her bandanna with tepid water from her canteen and pressed it to the welt on Duncan's forehead. He groaned, and she sat down and adjusted his head over into her lap.

"What—? What hit me?" he asked in a dazed voice.

"Damn it, Dunc, I hit you, you fool," she said.

"But . . . why?" he asked, closing his eyes and relaxing in her lap.

"Because you were about to kill a couple of your brother's men, Carver and Goss." She pressed the wet rag gently with one hand while she held her other hand beneath his chin.

"Oh, I see," Duncan said, his mind drifting.

In his addled state, he nuzzled his cheek against her stomach. Danielle smiled to herself, knowing that once he came to enough to realize what he was doing, this would jolt him the rest of the way to his senses. Not wanting to confuse his already unstable mental condition, she started to shift herself out from underneath him. But he managed to stop her by raising a limber arm and holding her in place.

"Don't go," he said in a dreamy half-conscious voice. "I—I could lay here . . . all night. Couldn't you?"

Danielle smiled again to herself without answering. She sat still for a few minutes longer, touching the wet rag to his swollen forehead. When Duncan Grago finally opened his eyes and looked up at her face with some clarity, he gasped at the realization of where he was lying and how comfortable he'd been there.

"Oh, my God," he rasped. Yet Danielle noted that he still made no attempt to raise up.

"It's all right, Dunc," Danielle said, shifting her weight once more in order to move from beneath him. But before she could free herself and stand up, Newt Grago's voice called out in the moonlight.

"What the hell is going on here?" Newt bellowed.

He stomped closer as Duncan flung himself upward to his unsteady feet and hurriedly dusted the seat of his trousers. Danielle stood up as well, the wet bandanna hanging from her hand. She quickly raised her fingers to her mustache, making sure it was in place.

"Nothing, Newt," Duncan said, his words sounding shaky. "Danny here was just tending this bump on my head."

"Yeah, I heard about that bump and how it got there." Newt's eyes narrowed on Danielle. "I don't know what kind of man you are, Danny Duggin. But by God, my brother's coming with me to the shack right now!" He reached out, grabbed Duncan's wrist, and yanked him away from beside her. Behind Newt Grago, Danielle caught sight of Chancy Burke standing with his hand on his pistol, a wizened grin on his face.

"Jesus, Newt!" Duncan Grago cut in, taking a wide, staggering step away from his brother. "What the hell are you thinking? Danny and me are pals! My God! You don't think we—?"

"Shut up, Dunc!" Newt spat at him. "Get to the shack, damn it to hell, before somebody else comes along here."

Before Duncan could offer anything more in his and Danielle's defense, Newt moved in and shoved him away toward the path. As Duncan staggered out of sight, Newt spun back to Danielle. But he reined himself down at the sight of her drawn Colt cocked toward him and Chancy Burke.

"Settle down, Newt Grago," she said, knowing how easy it

would be right then to kill him and Chancy Burke on the spot. Yet in doing so she also knew she would be throwing away her chance at getting the rest of her father's killers once they'd all arrived. "Whatever you're thinking, put it out of your mind. I cracked Dunc's head because I figured you wouldn't want him killing a couple of good horse thieves. I was soaking his head and nothing more when you came in here."

Newt Grago only stood broiling in his rage and shock. Finally he said in a voice barely under control, "Come morning, you're going to face Chancy Burke. We'll see what you are once and for all."

"What if I say no?" Danielle asked, not wanting to appear too anxious. "What if I just ride out of here tonight?"

"I hope you try riding out of here," Newt Grago warned. "I've got guards at every trail in and out. You're here, and you'll die here come morning. Don't let me see your face near my brother again." He wheeled around and left, calling over his shoulder to Chancy Burke, "Come on, Burke, leave this sorry coyote to think about it all night."

"Right, Newt," Chancy Burke said. Before turning away from Danielle, Burke said to her in a lowered tone, "See you in the morning, Danny boy."

"My pleasure, Burke," Danielle whispered to herself as they stepped out of sight. Before the sound of their boots faded, Danielle gathered her blanket and saddle and moved away in the moonlight, not about to sleep here where they would expect her to be. At any time these men could change their minds and slip up on her in the night.

Newt Grago stomped back to his shack, Duncan staggering forward a few feet in front of him and Chancy Burke moving up beside him. "Don't you ever breathe a word of this to a soul," Newt said without facing Burke, "or I'll rip your tongue out. Do you hear me?"

"I hear you, Newt," said Burke. "But I've got to ask, just between you and me, is poor Dunc gone crazy on us? Maybe from being in prison too long?"

"There ain't a damn thing wrong with Dunc!" Newt stopped in midstride and grabbed Chancy Burke by his shirt, raging close to his face. "It's that bastard Danny Duggin or whoever the hell that pansy really is! He's got Dunc's mind all twisted out of shape. Can't you see that?"

"Sure, Newt, I see it. Take it easy," Chancy Burke replied quickly, although deep down he had some doubts about Duncan Grago after seeing the way he'd acted back there.

"I want that man dead in the dirt, Burke. And I don't want to hear another word about something being wrong with my brother!" He turned Burke's shirt loose and huffed away.

Burke stood for a second grinning to himself, casting a glance back toward the spot where they had left Danielle. "Hell," Burke said aloud to himself in the darkness, "you ain't fooling me, Danny Duggin. You might be quick. You might even shoot straight. But I've got you pegged now, Danny boy. This is going to be too damn easy."

CHAPTER 13

Before daylight, Danielle got up from her blanket, having slept on and off throughout the night without a campfire, and carried her saddle and gear to the place where she'd left Sundown. She saddled the mare, walking her closer to the encampment but not bringing her all the way in. Instead, she left the mare hitched to a white oak tree several yards away from the rope corral, where all the other horses were kept. There were more horses there now. All through the night, Danielle had heard the sound of drunken laughter emanating from the big gambling tents. More than once she'd heard the sound of pistol fire. She hoped the men on her list were among the outlaws that had arrived in the night.

The clearing in front of the plank shack was almost empty now in the early-dawn light. Across from the shack, three men sat on the ground out front of one of the big tents with a bottle of rye, passing it back and forth between them. Danielle recognized Morgan Goss as one of the men, his tall sombrero now slumped forward. One of Lulu's girls sat on his lap with her arms around his neck. As Danielle came closer, one of the other men gigged Goss in his ribs. Morgan Goss looked up at Danielle and blinked his large bloodshot eyes.

"Danny Duggin, you'd best clear out of here for your own good," he said in a whiskey-slurred voice.

"I've been told I can't," Danielle said, trying to sound regretful. "Looks like I'm in this contest whether I want to be or not."

"Yeah, that's what I heard," said Goss. "Damn, I feel like it's mine and Cincinnati's fault, causing trouble with Dunc, and you cracking his head for him. I never figured he'd take it so hard."

Danielle cocked her head, curious. "I meant, having to face off with Chancy Burke today. What are you talking about, Goss?"

Morgan Goss blinked his big watery eyes again, saying, "Hell, you don't know? Dunc is all stoked up over you busting his head. Came back in the tent late last night, wild-eyed crazy, swearing he was going to shoot you dead."

"Damn it," Danielle whispered under her breath.

She got the picture now. Duncan was so ashamed of what his brother, Newt, and Chancy Burke had seen that now he had to prove something to them. He had to turn against his friend Danny Duggin just to save face. *The poor stupid fool,* Danielle thought. Duncan Grago thought there was something wrong with himself because he felt an attraction for her. It was an attraction he could think of only as unnatural, having no idea Danny Duggin was really a woman.

"Where is Dunc?" she asked Goss.

"He passed out a couple of hours ago," Goss said. "They carried him inside the shack."

"Who else is in there?"

"Nobody." Goss shrugged. "Newt, Haas, and Chancy Burke all three rode out an hour ago to check on the guards. Three more men showed up during the night. There's supposed to be more coming still."

"Who are they?" Danielle asked, hoping it was the men on her list.

"One of them is Mysterious Dave Mather.* The other two are

---

* Mysterious Dave Mather was a young gunman known to work both sides of the law and a friend of Doc Holliday, Wyatt Earp, and other notables.

Bill Longley* and Briley Whitfield. Briley ain't nothing. He just rode here with them. But Longley's a straight-up killer. Said he heard about this shooting contest all the way over in Evergreen, Texas, when Rufe Gaddis rode through and told him about it."

"Is Rufe Gaddis here yet?" Danielle asked, recognizing his name from her list.

"Naw, but he will be before long," said Goss, "along with Saul Delmano and the rest of them. Bill Longley says he plans to make himself a thousand-dollar grubstake here, then quit. Mather said a man had to be crazy to take part in something like this, but he'll be betting on Bill Longley. If I was you, I'd be careful. This thing is drawing gunmen like honey draws flies."

"Thanks, Goss. I will be."

Danielle let out a breath, then turned and walked to the door of the plank shack. She knocked low and quietly. Then seeing the door open a few inches from the touch of her knuckles, she eased inside and closed the door behind her.

"Dunc?" she inquired, taking a step forward toward the snoring figure stretched out on a bunk beneath a wad of blanket.

When Duncan Grago didn't stir, she stepped closer and said his name again. This time, Duncan Grago heard her and sprang up onto the side of the bunk, gathering his open shirt across his chest. His gun belt hung from a ladder-back chair beside the bunk.

"It's me, Danny Duggin," Danielle said, taking a step between Duncan and his pistol belt.

"I know it's you, Danny," Duncan said in bitter voice, "and you've got no business here. If Newt sees you here, he'll kill you. What do you want?"

"I heard you were making threats against me, Dunc," Danielle said. "Don't do something stupid and make me have to kill you."

---

* Bill Longley was a young Texan who killed a black lawman at the age of fifteen, and spent the rest of his life as a gunman and outlaw.

His red-streaked eyes lifted to her, full of anger. "What makes you so damn sure you'll be the one doing the killing?"

"I'm not here to argue, Dunc. I just came to let you know. I don't want us to face off out there. If it happens, it'll be your call, not mine."

Duncan looked down and rubbed his face with both hands. "I was drunk when I said it, Danny." He hesitated for a second, then added, "But I told my brother I was going to do it . . . so I reckon I will. He thinks there's something—" Duncan cut himself off, then shook his head and held his face in his hands. "Hell, I don't know *what* he thinks. I don't even know what *I* think. There's something about you, Danny. You make me have crazy thoughts. I feel like I'm losing my mind when I'm around you."

Danielle felt sorry for him, seeing how confused he was over his feelings. But there was no way she could explain it to him. In all her time posing as a man, this was the first time something like this had happened. Somehow her womanhood had reached through her rough disguise, and although neither she nor Duncan Grago had meant for it to happen, he seemed to have fallen for her. He didn't realize that what he felt was only the natural draw of a man to a woman. All he knew was there were feelings inside him that he could not fathom.

"Dunc, listen to me," she said, almost having to bite her tongue to keep from telling him the truth. "There's nothing wrong with you. You're not losing your mind. But you need to get away from here, clear your head somewhere, get yourself a woman. You've been away all these years. Everything is crowding you. Don't let yourself get tricked into thinking that you have to prove yourself to your brother or anybody else."

"Prove *what* to my brother?" He stood up from the bunk, his fists clenched at his sides. "What the hell are you trying to say is wrong with me?"

Danielle didn't back down an inch. She could tell he wanted to step forward in his rage and his shame, but she also knew he wasn't about to have her pistol come up from her holster and crack his head again.

"Stand down, Dunc," she warned in a low tone. "I'm not saying anything is wrong with you. It's you who's thinking it."

"Damn it to hell! Get out of here!" Duncan shouted hoarsely at her. "This is a shooting contest! I'll choose who I want to face on the street! If you don't want a shoot-out with me, crawfish out of this camp and don't come back! Or I'll kill you, Danny Duggin. I swear to God I will!"

Danielle took a slow step back, her hand on her Colt, mindful of Duncan's pistol in the holster hanging on the chair back. She raised a finger, pointing at him as she spoke. "All right, Dunc, I've asked you not to do it. I'll face Chancy Burke in the street. I'll kill him. There's not a doubt in my mind. Whether or not I face you next is up to you. Think it over. That's all I ask."

Danielle backed to the door, opening it behind her. Before she stepped back from the shack, she saw the disturbed, hurt look in Duncan's eyes.

"Danny," he said, shaking his head slowly, "I'm sorry. I've got to do it, don't you see? I hate to . . . but I've just got to."

"Yeah," she said, almost in a whisper. "So do I, Dunc. So do I."

Danielle walked back to the front of the large gambling tent where Morgan Goss stood talking to the three men who had arrived during the night. Other men had stirred from their blankets and they came drifting in out of the morning haze. Lulu came walking up to Morgan Goss and the others at the same time as Danielle.

"What was all the shouting about?" she asked, barely stopping long enough for an answer as she headed inside the large tent with a metal cashbox under her arm.

"Ask Danny Duggin," Goss said, pointing in Danielle's direction.

But Lulu only tossed Danielle a glance in passing and let the tent fly fall behind her.

"Danny Duggin?" one of the newcomers inquired as Danielle stepped in among them. He was a thin young man with small pinched eyes and a drooping dark mustache. A bottle of rye hung from his right hand. Next to him stood a taller young man, equally thin, wearing a long goatee. "I knew some Duggins back in Pennsylvania. Any kin there?"

"No kin that I know of," Danielle replied.

"Say, you're the one Burke and some of the others were talking about last night," said the one with the goatee.

"Oh?" Danielle just looked at him.

"Yep, he's the one, all right," said Morgan Goss. "He's a good *hombre*, in my opinion, and I don't say that often about anybody."

"Hell, Goss, you don't even say that about your own pa." The man with the goatee chuckled.

"Danny," said Goss, "this here is Billy Longley and Dave Mather."

Danielle gave the two men a respectful nod.

"Good to make your acquaintance, Danny Duggin," said Longley, the one with the long goatee. "I'm glad to get the chance to size up the competition." He spread a tight level grin. "Looks like one of us will soon be laying dead while the other strikes a match on his belt buckle."

"I won't be shooting with you, Bill Longley," Danielle said firmly, "so you might just as well forget it. Go check out some other competition."

"Bet you a dollar I can goad you into it." Longley grinned.

"No bet, Longley," said Danielle. "This contest ain't my style. I'm only shooting against Chancy Burke because there's no way out of it," she lied. "Newt Grago is forcing me into it."

"Aw, come on now, Danny Duggin," said Bill Longley. "You don't look like a man easily forced into anything he don't want to do in the first place."

Danielle just stared at him.

"Don't let Bill get under your skin, Danny Duggin," said Dave Mather. "He's come here with the notion of making a thousand dollars. It's got him a little edgy, just thinking about it."

"Ain't a damn thing edgy about me," Longley said to Mather, keeping a fixed stare on Danielle. "I'll make my thousand any way they want to do this thing. I'll kill one son of a bitch for a thousand, two sonsabitches for five hundred a piece, or a *thousand* sonsabitches for a dollar a head. Makes me no difference."

"Good luck, then," said Danielle. "I won't be one of them."

"Are you sure, Danny Duggin?" Longley asked, leaning a bit toward her.

"Cut it out, Bill," Mather said laughingly, pulling Longley back and sticking the bottle of rye in his hand. "Here, have some breakfast." Mather turned to Danielle. "What's the story on you and Dunc Grago? Goss said he's talking about killing you."

"Talk won't get it done," Danielle said. "He was drunk. I cracked his head. I'm hoping he'll get over it before the shooting starts."

"Some men get over a head cracking sooner than others," said Mather with a wince. "Some don't get over them at all. If I was you, I'd shoot Duncan Grago as soon as his face hits daylight coming out of the shack." He grinned. "It might save you a lot of trouble down the road."

"I'll take my chances," Danielle said. "Now, if you'll all excuse me, I'm going to see what this place feeds for breakfast before the morning drinkers show up."

"Better hurry, then." Mather grinned. "They're dragging in already."

No sooner had Danielle stepped out of sight inside the large tent than Bill Longley leaned closer to Dave Mather and asked, "What do you say, Dave? He doesn't look like much to me. After I trim a couple other of these gunslingers down, talk Danny Duggin into trying me, then put a couple of hundred on me with Merlin Haas. We'll make a bundle."

"He doesn't strike me as the kind of man you can talk into anything," Mather replied. "Besides, I ain't sure I'd put a hundred on you against this Danny Duggin, if that's his real name. He impresses me as a man on a mission. Get between him and whatever that mission is, I could see him killing you without batting an eye."

"Thanks for your support, partner," Longley hissed, giving Mather a rough shove.

Mather rocked back on his feet, then came forward and snatched the bottle of rye from Bill Longley's hand, grinning. "Don't mention it, partner," he replied, raising the bottle to his lips.

By the time Danielle had washed down a bowl of loose hash with a mug of warm beer, the tent was alive and kicking with outlaws still drunk or hungover from the night before. Halfway through her meal, Danielle caught sight of Duncan Grago coming into the tent. Duncan had Lulu set him up a bottle of rye and a glass. But upon seeing Danielle down the bar from him, Duncan sneered, backhanded the glass from the bar, jerked up the bottle, and left with it. Danielle stood still for a moment, just staring at the open tent fly.

"What's the matter, Danny Duggin?" said Lulu's voice behind the bar. "You and your buddy not waking up eye to eye this morning?"

Danielle turned to face her across the plank bar. "Do we know each other, ma'am?"

Lulu saw the flare of fire in her eyes before Danielle managed to conceal it. "Honey, you don't know me, but I sure know you." Lulu tossed a hand. "Leastwise, I know of you. You're the one giving Newt Grago his worst night's sleep in years."

"If that's true, then I'm glad of it," said Danielle, laying down a coin for her breakfast and beer.

"Ready for another?" Lulu asked.

"No, thanks. I wasn't even ready for that one until you said you're out of coffee." Danielle offered an amiable smile to make up for the look in her eyes when Lulu had first approached her.

"I'm Lulu Dorsey. Glad to meet you, Danny Duggin," Lulu said, returning the smile. She cocked her head to one side. "Tell me something—what is it about you that's got the Grago brothers and Chancy Burke so stirred up?"

"Beats me, Lulu," said Danielle. "I reckon they were just looking for something to get stirred up over, and I happened along. That's just my opinion." Now Danielle cocked her head in return, asking, "Why do *you* think it is?"

"I think it's because you remind them of things they'd sooner forget. Newt thinks you recognize him from somewhere, like maybe you've got a grudge to settle or something."

"If that's so, why hasn't he made a move to try to settle up with me?" Danielle asked. "Or better yet, why haven't *I* made a move to settle that grudge if there is one?"

"Oh, I don't know. . . ." Lulu fluffed her curly hair with her fingertips, flirting with what she thought was the handsome young Danny Duggin standing before her. "But if you're not busy tonight, we could go over all the reasons—" Her words were cut short at the sight of Duncan Grago stepping back inside the tent with his pistol out at arm's length, aimed and cocked at Danielle.

"Damn you to hell, Danny Duggin!" Duncan Grago screamed, his face contorted, tears running freely down his cheeks.

Lulu jumped to the side and down to the dirt floor. Men dove away from the bar and the faro tables, taking cover. But Danielle stood firm, her eyes riveted on Duncan Grago, both her hands coming up slowly and spreading along the edge of the bar behind her.

"You'd better grab for your Colt, Danny! I'm going to kill you!"

Danielle saw the anger and the madness in his eyes. Yet she saw something else there that told her if she didn't make a move, she wouldn't have to kill him. She held firm, resisting the urge to go for her pistol, praying she wasn't calling this thing wrong—if she was, she'd surely die.

"I mean it, Danny! Damn you!" Duncan bellowed. "Go for your Colt, or I'll cut you in half! I swear it!"

Danielle never wavered an inch. The first shot from Duncan's pistol exploded, the bullet whistling past her shoulder two feet away. Behind the bar a stack of beer mugs shattered in a spray of glass. Danielle only stared. Her hunch was confirmed. If Duncan meant to shoot her, he wouldn't have missed, not by that wide of the mark. The next shot went past her other shoulder, this one farther away than the first. She allowed herself a tight breath, still holding ground.

"I mean it!" Duncan raged.

Two more shots exploded, one on either side of her, wood splinters showering down from where one bullet nipped the tent pole behind the bar.

"What do you want from me, huh? Want me to holster up? Give you a chance to draw? All right, there!" Duncan uncocked his pistol and shoved it into his holster. His trembling hand was poised close to the butt of the weapon. "Now draw, damn you! Draw, or I'll kill you in cold blood, so help me God!"

Danielle still only stared, making no effort to prepare herself for a gunfight.

"All right, then! You're dead!" Duncan screamed. He streaked the pistol up from his holster, cocked and pointed.

In that second Danielle saw clearly what Duncan Grago was asking of his friend Danny Duggin. In his confused and tortured state of mind, Duncan was asking to be killed. Like with some injured, hopeless animal, his every move begged for him to be put out of his misery.

"I won't fight you, Dunc, not like this," Danielle said in a level, unyielding voice.

Duncan Grago's hand shook even worse, then slumped toward the dirt floor. He let out a tormented scream, firing the two remaining shots into the ground. "Damn it to everlasting hell! What's happening to me?" he sobbed, crumpling to his knees in full view of the other outlaws.

"Nothing you don't have coming, you son of a bitch!" said Bill Longley, stepping in behind him and planting a hard boot on his slumped shoulder. Duncan Grago flew forward on his face. Bill

Longley jumped forward, yanking a pair of brass knuckles from his hip pocket. "What kind of low poltroon makes a play like that and then don't follow through? I'll work your head over like it's a hickory stump."

He reached down, grabbed Duncan Grago by the back of his shirt, and lifted him up halfway, drawing back the brass knuckles for a good solid punch to Duncan's face.

"Turn him loose, Longley," Danielle said, stepping forward.

"Like hell," said Longley, drawing his arm farther back, widening the arc of his swing. But his arm stopped suddenly as the tip of Danielle's pistol barrel jammed against his ear and cocked.

"I said, turn him loose. Nobody takes up my fight unless I ask them to." Danielle leaned some pressure into the Colt, causing Longley's head to tilt beneath the weight of it.

"For God sakes, don't beg for my life, Danny!" Duncan Grago sobbed into the dirt.

"Shut up, Dunc," Danielle snapped.

"You're making a bad mistake, Duggin," Bill Longley snarled, trying to look sideways as he spoke. "Let me lay into this piece of punkwood. I want to beat him real bad."

"You'll die, Longley. That's a promise," Danielle warned.

"Aw, come on. I saw how you just stood there, wouldn't do nothing. You won't shoot me, not really."

"Ten dollars says he will," Mysterious Dave Mather said, stepping inside the tent, his short-barreled Hood .38 caliber out of his shoulder harness and pointed at Danielle. "Of course I'll kill ole Danny Duggin here as soon as he pulls that trigger on you, if that's any consolation."

Longley stared sideways at Dave Mather, thinking about it. Seeing the small Hood pistol, he let out a sigh, saying, "Damn it, Dave, why'd you draw that little cork popper when you see he's got a big Colt pinned to the side of my head?"

Dave Mather chuckled, dark and low. "Call it poor judgment, Bill. I dressed in a hurry this morning. What're you going to do? I'm ready to back your play."

"Well, hell," Bill Longley said, relenting, lowering his arm slowly and letting the brass knuckles drop from his fingers. "I hate somebody poking a pistol in my ear, Duggin. It's cause to kill a man, I always say."

"You just can't turn nothing loose easy, can you, Bill?" Dave Mather said, stepping forward, his pistol still trained on Danielle. He bent down and picked up the brass knuckles. "Now let him up, Danny. Let's all move slow and easy, keep from splattering brains all over the day drinkers. What do you say?"

"Sounds good to me if you really mean it," said Danielle. "If this is a setup, we're all going to die here."

"It's no setup, Danny Duggin," said Dave Mather. "If I was going to shoot you, it wouldn't matter whether or not you held a gun to Bill's head. Show a little trust here." He grinned.

When Danielle stepped back and relaxed her grip on her Colt, Bill Longley raised Duncan Grago to his feet and shoved him through the fly of the tent. "Here, don't forget this." He snatched Duncan's pistol from the ground and pitched it out behind him. "You might need it to go somewhere and blow your brains out."

He turned back to Danielle, dusting his hands together. "No hard feelings, Danny Duggin, but the next time you point a pistol at me, you'd better make sure it comes out smoking." He smiled flatly and without expression. "Come on, Dave, before I change my mind and wipe this whole place out."

"In a minute, Bill," said Mather. He stood beside Danielle and watched until Bill Longley left the tent. Then Mather turned to Danielle, holstering his Hood pistol up under his arm. "Tell me, Danny Duggin, does this sort of thing happen everyplace you go?"

"Lately it seems like it," said Danielle. She stepped back to the bar and slumped back against it. "Am I going to have to watch my back with Bill Longley around?"

"I doubt it. In his own way, he thought he was doing you a favor. He might challenge you in this shooting contest. Otherwise, like he said, no hard feelings."

"That's good to know," Danielle said. "I've got enough trouble here as it is. I don't need any more."

No sooner than she'd spoken, Morgan Goss stuck his head inside the tent, announcing to the drinkers who were now getting back to the bar and the faro tables, "New riders coming in, boys. Looks like Arno Dunne brought a couple of shooters with him. Reckon we'll be starting the contest again most anytime."

"Is there anybody else you recognize?" Danielle asked, hoping to hear some of the names on her list.

"Nope, just these three, Arno Dunne and couple of look-alikes on a pair of bay horses."

Danielle stood stunned for a second, knowing it must be her brothers, Jed and Tim.

"What's wrong, Danny?" Dave Mather chuckled. "You look like you just fell down a long, dark hole."

"It feels like it, Mather," Danielle responded, and leveling her hat low on her forehead, she walked toward the tent fly.

CHAPTER 14

"Stick close to me, boys," Arno Dunne told Jed and Tim Strange as they rode into the encampment, "and say no more than you have to." The twins only nodded, looking all around at the grizzled faces, the tents, and the lay of the rugged land, in case they had to make a quick getaway. "None of these men know you or how good you are with those Colts." Arno laughed under his breath. "We want to keep it that way as long as we can. By the time they find out, we'll have most of their money in our pockets."

"We understand," said Tim.

He recalled the events of the morning as they rode along. They had met up with Newt Grago, Merlin Haas, and Chancy Burke along the trail. When Arno Dunne explained how he'd brought these two along to join the contest, Chancy Burke looked them up and down with a sneer, sizing them up as a couple of greenhorns fresh off of the farm.

"What's the story on those little dead man's knots hanging from your saddle horns?" he'd asked, pointing at the two miniature nooses made from the window-blind cord.

Before either Jed or Tim could respond, Arno Dunne cut in. "That's a secret, Burke," Dunne said. Then he looked away from Chancy Burke and at Merlin Haas and Newt Grago. "In fact, everything about these boys is a secret, except their names." He nodded toward Jed and Tim. "This here's the Faulkner twins, Tim and Jed. Anybody wants to know more about them will have to step up face-to-face and find out for themselves."

"Are they any good with them Colts?" Burke asked. "You must think so or you wouldn't have brought them here."

Arno Dunne gave a playful wink to Newt Grago as he answered Chancy Burke. "Of course I think they're good. The question is, *how* good? And that's the part that'll cost you to find out."

Newt Grago had caught the glint in Arno Dunne's eyes, and knew he was up to something. That was fine with Newt, so long as there was a way for him and Haas to make their money as well. Arno Dunne had some crack shooters here, and Newt Grago knew it. He'd smiled and swept a hand back toward the encampment.

"Any friends of Arno Dunne's are friends of mine. Head on in, Arno. We'll be back as soon as we check on the last guard position."

That had been over an hour ago, and now, drawing closer to the encampment, the twins had prepared themselves for anything. "I hope we ain't made a bad mistake here," Jed Strange whispered to Tim, the two of them dropping their bays back a few feet behind Arno Dunne.

Less than fifty yards ahead, men began to gather along the edge of the camp clearing. These were tough-looking men, Jed thought, men who stared at them with eyes like vultures. Thumbs hooked into gun belts as Dunne led them forward.

"Get on up here with me, boys," Dunne said to Tim and Jed over his shoulder. "Don't get bashful on me now. We've got some work cut out for us."

Jed and Tim gigged their bays forward. "Notice how he keeps saying 'we' or 'us'?" Jed asked under his breath. "He makes it sound like he's the one going to be doing the shooting."

"Yeah," Tim replied. "If this thing goes wrong or he doublecrosses us, he'd *better* be ready to do some shooting. I'll kill him if it's the last thing I do."

At the line of gathered men, Arno Dunne sidled his horse the last few steps and said down to Cincinnati Carver, "Heard some shooting a while back. Have you started the contest before Newt and Haas get back?"

"Naw," said Carver, "Newt would have a fit if we did something like that. All you heard was Dunc going crazy, shooting at an ole boy named Danny Duggin. They got into it last night, and Duggin cracked his head. Dunc's acting like the world came to an end because of it. Hell, you know how Dunc is." Cincinnati Carver looked the twins over, noting right away how young and inexperienced they looked. "Who's your friends, Arno?"

Dunne spread a crafty smile, looking from Carver to the rest of the faces. Bloodshot eyes looked back at him. "Boys, this is the Faulkner twins, Tim and Jed. Newt met us along the trail and welcomed them in. I told him these two were about half good with a pistol. He said, bring them in and we'll see what they can do."

Carver said, "Dunne, this thing has gotten big. Bill Longley has shown up, claiming he's going to make himself a thousand dollars here."

"Bill Longley, huh?" Arno Dunne reined his horse back a step, looking over the heads of the men and toward the two big gambling tents.

A voice laughed amid the gathered men, calling out, "Does that change any plans you might have had, Dunne?"

Arno Dunne collected himself, took a cigar from his coat pocket, and stuck it into his mouth. "Hell no," he said after a short pause, "the more the merrier. Come on, boys," he said to Tim and Jed, jerking a nod toward the big tents. "Let's go cut some dust from our throats."

The crowd of men parted and Arno Dunne and the twins stepped their horses through them. As the men dispersed behind them, Tim said to Jed, "Did you hear them mention Danny Duggin? I wonder if Danny is in on this shooting contest."

Hearing Tim, Arno Dunne cut in, asking, "Who's this Danny Duggin? Does he know how fast you boys are?"

"We met Danny along the trail, back before we rode to Mobeetie. He's the one who gave us a tip on where to find work."

"Okay, okay," Dunne said impatiently, "but does he know how good you are with a gun? That's what I need to know."

"Not really," Tim replied. "We only met him, shared a camp and coffee with him. He seemed like a good enough *hombre*. Never thought he'd be a part of something like this. He didn't strike us as being an outlaw."

"You'd be surprised who's an outlaw and who ain't. People can fool you," Dunne replied.

"I don't want to face Danny Duggin if he's a part of this," said Jed.

Dunne sighed in exasperation. "Boys, if he's in the contest and wants to face you, doesn't that tell you something? If he's willing to kill you, shouldn't you be just as willing to kill him?"

Jed started to speak in protest, but Tim saw it was pointless and cut him off, saying, "Damn right, Dunne. Whoever's facing me has just as much to think about as I do. So to hell with them. I'm out to win." As he spoke, he cut Jed a guarded glance, letting him know he was just going along with Dunne.

"Tim," Dunne said over his shoulder, drawing his horse to a halt outside the first large tent, "you are a joy to behold. I believe in time, you'll have your mind straight and be as good an outlaw as ever outran a rope." He reached a hand out and jiggled the miniature noose on Tim's saddle horn as the twins stopped their horses beside him. "But you, *deacon*," he added, looking at Jed, "I don't know what we'll ever make of you."

"Never you mind about me, Dunne," Jed said as the three of them swung down from their saddles. "I'll handle whatever flies at me."

Watching from beside the large tent, Danielle listened to the sound of her brothers' voices. Hearing and seeing them gave her mixed feelings. She wanted to run out and fling her arms around them both. At the same time she felt like running out and cursing them and sending them packing. But no matter what she felt, this was no time for her to divert from her course. She would have to deal with her brothers being here, keeping out of their sight as much as possible and going on with her plans once the rest of her father's killers arrived.

"Damn it, Jed and Tim," she whispered to herself, seeing them spin their reins around a makeshift rail and step inside the tent, "why couldn't you just be content to stay in St. Joe?"

In saying it, she felt a little guilty, for they could have very well asked her the same question last year when she began her journey. Reminding herself of this fact caused her to take a deep breath and not judge her brothers too harshly.

When she'd first heard Morgan Goss mention Arno Dunne and a couple of look-alikes riding a pair of bays, she'd gone straightaway to where she'd hitched Sundown and moved the mare back to where she'd left her last night. She couldn't risk Jed and Tim seeing Sundown. That would destroy everything.

Now with the mare safely out of sight, all Danielle could do was wait. She moved quietly back alongside the tent, then cut away toward the shade of a white oak, where she planned to watch the camp for any sign of Newt Grago and Chancy Burke. As soon as the contest started, she wanted to get her shot at Burke and take him down. That would mark one more name off her list. Then she would find a way to stay off to herself and keep an eye on the trail leading in. She repeated the other three names on her list to herself, knowing them by heart now: Rufe Gaddis, Saul Delmano, Blade Hogue. Once these other killers rode in, she would no longer care about Jed and Tim recognizing her. Nothing else would matter then, as she'd gun them down, every one of them, and Newt Grago, too. Or else she'd die trying.

It was high noon when Newt Grago, Merlin Haas, and Chancy Burke rode back into camp. By that time the outlaws had grown restless and eager for the shooting to begin. Several of the lesser gunmen had taken to drawing names among themselves, fearful of facing the likes of Chancy Burke or Bill Longley. A couple of fistfights and a knifing had broken out in the clearing of Lulu's gambling tent, and shots had erupted over one of Lulu's girls, leaving a Montana outlaw by the name of Herk Evans with a bullet in his thigh. Bill Longley had gotten a little drunker than he'd intended to, and he'd starting shooting beer mugs from atop one of the girls' heads until Dave Mather came along and stopped him.

Now Mather and Longley stood at the center of the clearing, drinking strong coffee, the rest of the outlaws giving them wide berth as they watched Grago, Haas, and Burke ride into camp.

"I don't know about you," Longley said, "but the more sober I get, the worse this pigsty starts looking to me."

"You want to head out?" Mather asked, sounding astonished. "What about the thousand dollars you promised yourself?"

"Oh, I'll stand a couple of rounds if they got anybody who'll try me," Longley said, stroking his goatee. "But I've been thinking. The only man here who's game for all takers is Chancy Burke. If he kills this Danny Duggin, nobody else will be bold enough to face up to him, except me." Longley shrugged. "Then, once I kill Burke, there won't be a soul here who'll face me. That means, I can only make five hundred or seven hundred at the most."

"That's not bad money," said Mather, "and who knows? When some of these others show up from Newt Grago's old bunch, you might even get some other challengers." A guarded smile came to Mather's face. "Do me a favor. Lay off of Danny Duggin if you can. There's something I like about him."

"Yeah? What's that?" Longley asked.

"I can't say," Mather replied, looking away from Longley's questioning gaze. Then as if dismissing the subject, he pointed at the group of outlaws who had drawn names among themselves and were getting itchy to start the contest. "You've also got to figure, some of them will get more bark on once they commence facing one another and winning. That's just human nature."

Bill Longley nodded, thinking about it. "Yeah, I reckon you're right. We'll just have to play this thing by ear for a while. Think you'd better get over to Merlin Haas right away, get us a few dollars bet on Danny Duggin?"

"Sure thing," said Mather. He reached inside his coat, took out a stack of bills, and headed over to the shack, where Newt Grago, Haas, and Burke had just stepped down from their horses.

At the shack, eight or ten outlaws had crowded around Newt Grago, each of them waving dollars in his face.

"Hold it, boys!" Newt shouted, shoving them back from him. "One at a time."

Beside him, Chancy Burke butted a man back with his chest, keeping a hand on his pistol butt.

"You heard him, damn it!" Burke shouted. "Newt ain't the one taking the bets. You need to get with Haas." He nodded at Merlin Haas, who stood clasping his coat lapels, a black cigar standing straight out from his teeth.

"But he won't take our bets unless Newt here okays it," a man named Quince Matine said. "This ain't about the regular pot. This is some matching a few of the boys have done on their own."

"The hell are you talking about, Matine?" Newt Grago asked, looking around at the gathered men.

"Edwards here has challenged his cousin Bennie to a shoot-out." He pointed around at the others. "Cotton Pate has challenged Anderson. Hell. We've got enough matches here to last into the night, if you'll just give us the go-ahead."

"No kidding?" Newt Grago chuckled. "So, some of you have gotten together and done a little figuring on your own, eh?" He looked at Merlin Haas and laughed. "What do you say, Haas? Want to cover some extra bets? Looks like we're going to have a whole other level of shooters here. Everybody's wanting to get into the action."

"Bring 'em on," Haas said, reaching into his coat and pulling out a pencil and paper. "We ain't turning nothing away. Step over here and give me the information. Who's fighting who?"

The men hurried over and surrounded Merlin Haas. Chancy Burke saw Dave Mather coming toward them, and he leaned close to Grago, saying, "What about these two, Newt? What are we going to do about Longley wanting in on this shooting contest?"

"I told you last night not to worry about it when him and Mather rode in, didn't I?" Newt Grago whispered, seeing Mather draw closer. "You're starting to sound like you're afraid of Longley."

"Hell, Newt, I ain't no damn fool," Chancy Burke whispered in reply. "There ain't a man here can beat Bill Longley."

"Maybe not one man," Newt said, "but I bet a few men can handle the job."

He winked at Burke, then stepped forward as Dave Mather arrived with the stack of dollar bills in his hand. Chancy Burke smiled and let out a breath of relief.

"Howdy, Mather, what can I do for you?" Newt Grago asked.

"I got five hundred dollars says the kid Danny Duggin is going to put your boy Burke here in the ground. No offense, Burke," Mather added, casting Burke a glance.

Chancy Burke's face reddened, and he looked away without reply.

"You need to see Haas, Mather. He's the one what handles the betting," said Grago.

"Huh-uh." Mather shook his head. "Merlin Haas has been known to disappear come pay-up time. I'd rather you hold the bet. It might keep me from chasing Haas down and putting a bullet in his eye."

Newt Grago laughed thinly as he took the money.

"Hell. Okay, then. Even money on Burke and Danny Duggin. We'll be starting as soon as Duggin shows up. Meanwhile, have you seen Dunc?"

"Nope," Mather said. "He hasn't shown his face after what happened over at Lulu's earlier."

"What happened at Lulu's?" Grago asked in stunned surprise.

Before Mather could answer, they recognized the voice of Danny Duggin calling out from forty yards away. "Chancy Burke! Let's get to it!"

The men gathered in the clearing stepped away at the sound of the voice. They formed a wide path for Danielle to walk through. She came forward slowly but steadily, her right hand passing close to the big Colt on her hip with each step. Among the crowd, she caught a glimpse of Tim and Jed standing beside Arno Dunne.

Jed stepped forward, saying, "Danny? Danny Duggin? Remember us?"

"Not now," Danielle said, staring straight ahead. "There's killing to be done."

Tim reached out and pulled Jed back while Arno Dunne shook his head in disgust at Jed's action.

"You've been wanting it, Burke. Now come and get it!" Danielle said with finality, stopping at ten yards and planting her feet a shoulder width apart.

A few feet to one side of the crowd, Bill Longley sipped back the last of his coffee and moved forward, watching with keen interest.

Beside Newt and Chancy Burke, Dave Mather chuckled, saying to Burke, "Well, Chancy, here's where the bullet meets the bone. Don't let the fact that you're about to die throw you off your game none."

"Go to hell, Mather," Chancy Burke hissed, stepping past him and starting a wide, slow half circle to his left, wanting to get to where he could put the sun in this young gunman's eyes.

"Take your time, Burke. Get it where you want it," Danielle called out to him. "It's a high-noon sun, so it won't help you much. Get your hand steady and your mind clear. I'm ready when you are."

"That's real obliging of you," Burke replied, moving sidelong, one slow step at a time, putting wide clearance between himself and Newt Grago and the others. Then he stopped, seeing the noon sun was indeed no help to him at all. "This will do just fine for me, Duggin." But Burke raised a hand toward Danielle, putting the fight off for a moment as he half turned to Newt Grago, calling out to him, "Are all the bets in place, Newt?"

Newt Grago nodded.

"That's all I wanted to know," Burke said, keeping his left hand raised toward Danielle. Without lowering his left hand, Chancy

Burke spun suddenly, his hand coming up with his pistol, cocking it on the upswing. The crowd gasped, unprepared for his surprise move. But Danielle was ready. She'd known his play when he'd raised his hand and turned toward Grago. Her Colt exploded before Burke even got his pistol all the way up.

One loud burst of fire filled the clearing, followed by a grunt from Chancy Burke as he staggered backward, turned a full circle, then sank to his wobbling knees. Danielle could tell his world was spinning around him as she stepped forward with her Colt hanging in her hand.

"That's what it feels like, Burke," Danielle said, bending down with him as he rocked back flat on the ground. His pistol spilled from his hand, and his fingers tried clawing at it. "Go ahead, pick it up. Die with it in your hand." She bent down face-to-face, and whispered in his ear, "That was my pa you and your rats killed last year. You left him hanging from a tree. I just wanted you to die knowing that there's one killing you didn't get away with."

"You . . . you son of a bitch," Chancy Burke gasped. His fingertips managed to wrap around the butt of the pistol, struggling to raise it.

"Wrong again," Danielle said. "I'm no *son* at all. I was his *daughter*." She paused for a second, letting it sink into his fading eyes. Then she said, "Be sure and tell the devil it was a *woman* who sent you to hell."

Straightening and taking a short step back, she waited until the pistol in his hand moved forward, shaky, trying to level up on her. She fired a round down into his forehead, then opened the cylinder on her Colt, punching out to the two spent cartridges and replacing them. As she closed the cylinder and spun it down her forearm, Newt Grago, Dave Mather, and Merlin Haas stepped in beside her.

"You didn't have to do that!" Newt Grago said angrily. "You could see he was dying!"

"It's your contest, not mine, Grago," Danielle said. "One man dies. One man wins. What's next on today's events?"

She turned, facing him up close, resisting the urge to unload her Colt into his belly. Grago held her stare. She could see he was on the verge of going for his pistol, and she almost hoped he would.

"Well, now," Dave Mather said, seeing trouble about to erupt between them and moving forward to stop it, "I believe you owe me a thousand dollars, Newt." He snapped his fingers, grinning at Newt Grago. "I'll have it now, if you please."

Newt Grago pulled back a step and forced his eyes away from Danielle to Mather. He took out a huge roll of bills and counted them off into Mather's palm. The crowd sifted forward toward Chancy Burke's body. Tim and Jed looked up from the bullet hole in Burke's head, and stared at Danielle.

"Lord, Danny Duggin," Jed whispered, shaking his head slowly.

Danielle could not face him, so she turned and walked away toward Lulu's tent.

"So I guess that's that," said Bill Longley, giving Newt Grago a sarcastic smile. "We all see who's the man to beat now, don't we?"

"You're up with Danny Duggin anytime you want it, Longley," Newt Grago growled. "Just say the word. I want that man dead, for reasons I ain't even going to explain."

But Longley only laughed, taking half of the thousand dollars Dave Mather handed to him.

"What for, Newt? I just made half of the amount I came here for without having to fire a shot. I might double it up at Lulu's tonight and head out come morning. Never let it be said that I ain't a man of peace."

Bill Longley turned to walk away with Dave Mather, but Grago stopped him, calling out, "Don't rush off, Bill. I might have a proposition for you."

"Oh?" Longley turned back, smiling toward him. "Why, Newt, I'm always pleased to listen to anything you've got to say. Go on to Lulu's, Mysterious Dave. . . . I'll be along directly."

CHAPTER 15

Danielle had Lulu's tent to herself for a few moments while all the outlaws and gunmen milled around the body of Chancy Burke. The first person to arrive a few minutes behind her was Dave Mather, and he did so with a look of respect in his dark eyes as he sidled up to the bar and tipped his hat back.

"You're not drinking, I see," Mather said to Danielle, flagging down Lulu to order himself a whiskey with a beer chaser.

"No," Danielle said in a flat tone, standing with her back against the bar and a boot propped up behind her. "You might not want to stand too close to me, Mysterious Dave. I've got a feeling Newt Grago ain't real happy with the outcome of the first match of the day. There could be a hail of gunfire come through this tent any minute."

"I'll take my chances," Mather said, raising the whiskey and sipping it. "But you're right. Newt ain't at all pleased." He savored the taste of the whiskey for a second, then took a drink of beer and wiped his hand across his mustache. "I have no doubt he's out there right now, trying to get Bill Longley to challenge you into a match."

"Bill Longley can challenge all he wants to. I'm not fighting him," Danielle said.

"They'll goad you down, Danny Duggin, and you know how that goes." Mather smiled. "They'll call you a coward, try to get under your skin."

"Yep, they can do that." Danielle cocked her head toward Dave

Mather. "But I don't fall for kid games. Newt Grago made threats on Chancy Burke's behalf, and Burke made some on his own. I didn't do it for the money or the name of doing it. I did it because I was told by both of them that I would have to if I ever wanted to leave here alive. Now Burke's dead and I'm still standing. That's as simple as I can call it. To hell with Newt Grago and what he wants."

She wasn't about to tell Mather the truth—that she had come here for the sole purpose of killing not only Burke, but Grago and the others as well.

"I'll say something to Bill Longley if he goes for Grago's deal, whatever it is," Mather said. "If I can, I'll keep him from raining down your back."

"I appreciate your offer, Dave, but don't worry about my back. It's rainproof. I know Bill Longley's reputation. If he makes a move on me, I'll burn him down—same as I did Chancy Burke, same as I would anybody else."

"By God, you sure ain't short on confidence, are you, Danny Duggin?" Mather chuckled.

"Nope. If I was, I'd have been dead a long time ago." Danielle turned her head and spoke down the bar to Lulu. "Maybe I'll take a beer, after all. Bring Dave another one, too."

Lulu quickly filled two mugs and slid them down the plank bar. Danielle hooked one and raised it to her lips. When she lowered it, she looked at Mather curiously, asking, "Why would you do that for me, Dave?"

"What? Speak to Bill Longley on your behalf?" Dave Mather shrugged, raising his fresh beer. "Hell, I don't know. If I needed a reason, I reckon I'd say it's because you strike me as a man on a mission. I don't believe you belong here in this bunch, and I don't believe you're here by choice. Something brought you here, Danny Duggin, some task you can't let go of till it's finished." He sipped his beer and sat it down. "Am I right?"

Danielle didn't answer right away. Instead she looked off for a moment. "If I was here on some sort of mission like you say, do you think I'd admit it?"

"Of course not," Mather said, getting the message. He raised his beer in salute. "But all the same, here's to missions and those of us who carry them out."

They drank their beer as others began arriving at the tent in twos and threes, talking about the shooting and speculating on the matches coming up. Lulu got busy behind the bar, setting up bottles of whiskey and sliding frothing beer mugs into eager hands.

When Bill Longley came in, he walked straight to Danielle and Dave Mather. A few drinkers scooted away, giving him plenty of elbow room, something Longley had grown accustomed to, owing to his deadly reputation. "I don't know what the trouble is between you and Newt Grago," Longley said to Danielle, "but he's sure bent on seeing you dead."

Danielle stared at him for second, then said, "I notice he's not bent enough to come do it himself."

Bill Longley laughed under his breath. "I noticed that myself. Still, the fact remains, you are the man to beat now. If I'm the only one here who has the grit to challenge you, I reckon that means it's you and me, first thing in the morning. That'll give these boys the rest of today to kill one another off." He nodded toward the other drinkers, who were hurrying with the beer, some of them headed back out into the clearing with a mug in one hand and a bottle of whiskey under their arm.

"What if I say no?" Danielle asked.

Bill raised a finger as if trying to work something out in his mind. "See, that's the same thing I just asked Newt Grago. He said if you refused to face me, he'd go ahead and pay me to shoot you down where you stand."

"Whoa now, Bill," Dave Mather said, seeing that Danielle wasn't backing down an inch. In fact, she straightened from against the bar with her hand poised near her Colt. "Danny and I were just talking about that. Danny Duggin here won't admit it, but there's something between him and Grago that we don't know about. I told him if he wanted to drop out of the contest, that was his business. Don't you agree?"

Longley looked as if he couldn't understand why on earth a gunman with the skill he'd just witnessed would turn down a chance to
better himself. He glanced at Mysterious Dave Mather, then looked
back at Danielle. "Didn't you come here for the contest?"

"I came here with Duncan Grago because he said his brother
was looking for new men to ride with him. I had no idea about this
contest." Danielle looked hard at Mather, adding, "And I never
admitted there was anything between me and Newt Grago."

"Well, it's easy enough to see," said Bill Longley. "Speaking of
Dunc Grago, that's one more thing that's got Newt Grago all worked
up in a lather. He ain't been able to find his brother since he came
back. Seems to think you might have dealt ole Dunc some dirt."

Danielle shook her head. "Then he should be standing here
asking me about it, instead of you. Fact is, I haven't seen Dunc
myself, not since you tossed him out of here earlier. The shape he's
in, he might have rode out, not wanting anybody to see him. But
that's no concern of mine. What about this offer Newt made you,
Longley? Did you take him up on it?" She stood firm, knowing she
was looking into the eyes of one the fastest, most cold-blooded
gunmen in the West.

Longley rubbed his neck with his left hand, apparently having
a hard time deciding. "Damn," he said finally, "I knew if I turned
it down, Newt'll have no trouble at all getting a few of his regulars
to gang up on you. I hated turning down hard cash." He looked at
Dave Mather. "Do you see my point, Mysterious Dave?"

"Yep"—Dave Mather nodded—"but you're the one who always
says you have no respect for a man who hires somebody to do his
fighting for him. Danny Duggin here says he don't want to fight
you, and we both saw it ain't because he don't know how. Turn it
loose, Bill. We made some money. It's not as much as you wanted,
but once some of the other gunmen show up, you might still get
your chance at your thousand-dollar mark." He smiled, polishing
off the last drink from his mug, and added, "Meanwhile, if you
want to do something that makes good sense, buy us all a beer."

Bill Longley looked Danielle up and down again, then spread

a thin, crafty smile. "I turned Newt's offer down. I just wanted to see how you reacted. I came here for the match, not to get into Newt Grago's favor. Let him do his own shooting. I never liked the coyote that much to begin with." He looked past Danielle, to Lulu behind the bar, waving her over to them to order a round.

At the tent fly, Cincinnati Carver stuck his head in and said to the remaining outlaws still waiting to be served, "Better get a move on, boys. Cotton Pate and Little Joe Anderson are getting ready to face off!" As the men hurried out through the fly, Cincinnati Carver stuck his head back in and said to Mather, Longley, and Danielle, "What about y'all? Ain't you gonna watch it?"

"Naw, get on out of here, Cincinnati," Longley said in a bored tone. "Once you've seen one hog killing, you've seen them all."

The sound of distant pistol fire caused the horses to twitch their ears, but the six riders only passed knowing glances back and forth at one another as they rode on slowly between the two slim buttes and turned off the main trail toward the encampment. Once off the narrow trail they rode abreast, Rufe Gaddis in the center. On his right rode Blade Hogue; on his left, Saul Delmano. The other three men were Jack Pitch, Max Dupre, and Billy Joe Earls, hardcase gunmen who'd been riding with them in south Texas the past few weeks and welcomed the chance to throw in with Newt Grago's gang.

When word of a shooting contest had reached them, Jack Pitch had bought himself a new customized-model Remington and had been practicing with it at every opportunity. Seeing they were turning off the main trail and eager to get to the encampment, Jack Pitch asked the others, "What the hell are we being so cautious for? There's nobody there but ole boys like ourselves. Nobody could have snuck past the guards."

Rufe Gaddis barely turned a glance at him, saying, "I'm always cautious. I'd rather swing wide by a mile than ride with the sun to my face. Have you got a problem with that?"

"Just asking," Jack Pitch said, spurring his horse forward.

They rode on, circling wide of the encampment and turning back toward it from the west once the afternoon sun was at their backs. They rode in silence until they entered a stretch of scrub oak surrounding a small basin. The riders fell back into a line as they rounded the edge of a tall stand of rock. Then, where the stand of rock ended and the trail began to widen again, Rufe Gaddis stopped his horse short with a jerk on its reins and said in a stunned voice, "Good God almighty!"

Staring at the body hanging from the rope tied to an overhead branch of a white oak tree, the men pressed their horses close together. "That poor *hombre* ain't been hanging there long," Blade Hogue said under his breath, scanning the area. "Reckon them lawmen we heard about managed to slip in here?"

Rufe Gaddis stepped his horse to one side, looked around at the other riders, and said gruffly, "Damned if I know. But the way we're squeezed up here, one shot would just about hit every one of us."

Billy Joe Earls and Blade Hogue traded confused looks with each other for a second.

Rufe Gaddis swung an arm through the air impatiently. "I mean, spread out some, damn it! Take some cover somewhere."

The men yanked their horses apart as Rufe Gaddis stepped down from his saddle. Drawing his rifle from its boot, he said over his shoulder to Saul Delmano and Jack Pitch, "You two, come with me. Watch my back."

The three men walked the twenty-yard distance slowly, casting glances all around the small clearing surrounding the white oak. When they stopped ten feet back and looked up once more at the body swaying in the air, its blue hands hanging limp at its sides, Rufe Gaddis reached down and drew a knife from his boot well and pitched it over to Saul Delmano, saying in a low guarded tone, "Get over there, Saul, and cut him down." He nodded to where the rope led down from the limb and was drawn tight, tied off around the bottom of the trunk.

Gaddis and Pitch took a step backward, watching as Saul

Delmano sliced through the rope. When the body thudded on the ground at their feet, Rufe Gaddis leaned down close and looked at the swollen purple face, its black tongue bulging.

"Who is it, Rufe? You recognize him?" Jack Pitch asked, seeing the look on Rufe Gaddis's face as he pushed up his hat brim and shook his head.

"Yeah, I recognize this poor bastard," Rufe Gaddis replied without turning to face Jack Pitch or Saul Delmano. Instead, he spoke down to the blank dead face in the dirt, saying, "Dunc, you crazy son of a bitch. You look even worse than the last time I saw you."

"Whooee," Jack Pitch said in a hushed whisper, staring at Duncan Grago's dead hollow eyes. "There's something about a man stretching hemp that always runs a chill right through me. How's Newt Grago going to take somebody hanging his brother?"

"I don't think anybody hung ole Dunc," Rufe Gaddis said, looking around in the dirt. "There's only one set of hoofprints. His hands aren't tied. I got a feeling Dunc hung himself. He always was on the verge of blowing his stack. Looks to me like he finally did it."

"You might want to tell Newt that," Saul Delmano said, reaching a hand up to the others, who watched from the cover of rocks and scrub oaks. He waved them in, then looked back down at Rufe Gaddis. "Newt thought a lot of Dunc, crazy bastard that he was. He's going to go blind, staggering wild over this. I damn near rather leave ole Dunc laying here and not mention it at all."

"No, we've got to take Dunc in and let Newt know about it," Rufe Gaddis said with a wince. "Let the chips fall where they will, I reckon. Let's scout around for his horse, and get him up on it. We ain't taking him in to Newt until after dark. If this was my brother done something like this, I wouldn't want everybody in camp knowing about it."

"Damn," said Saul Delmano, "this is turning into a rough day."

I n the tent, Arno Dunne had directed the twins away from Bill Longley and Mysterious Dave Mather and to the far end of the

bar. Like most people, Dunne walked a little lightly around Longley. Evening had started to darken, and with the shooting matches
over for the day, the outlaws had converged on the tent to talk
about the four gunfights they'd seen and the money they had either won or lost on them. In spite of Arno Dunne cautioning them
against it, as soon as Jed and Tim got themselves a mug of beer,
they moved down to where Bill Longley stood slightly back from
the bar with a thumb hooked in his gun belt, speaking to Duggin
and Dave Mather.

They stood back politely until Bill Longley finished what he
was saying. Then stepping closer, Tim said, "Pardon me for interrupting, but we saw Danny Duggin and wanted to—"

Bill Longley stopped him short, blocking him from joining
their private circle with a raised forearm. "Hey, boy, can't you see
we're talking here?"

Tim Strange's eyes flared. Seeing it, Danielle cut in, saying to
Bill Longley, "It's all right, Longley. I know these two."

"But I don't," said Longley, "and I can't stand a person waltzing
right in and including themselves." He looked Tim up and down,
then turned his eyes to Jed, giving him the same cold look. "Who
are you look-alikes anyway? If it weren't for those big Colts on your
hips, I'd swear you just fell out from behind a plow somewhere."

"That's right," Danielle said quickly, knowing by the look on
Tim's face that the next words out of Longley's mouth would be
all it took to spark a fight between them. "These boys are straight
off of a farm over near St. Joe. Let me handle this, Longley," she
said, stepping in between Bill Longley and her brother Tim.
"Look, you two farmhands. I met you along the trail, and we had
some coffee together. Don't go thinking that makes us friends. I'm
here on business, *my* business." Her eyes cut from Tim to Jed.
"When you called my name out in the clearing a while ago, you
could have diverted my attention for just a split second and gotten
me killed. Didn't you know that?"

Both twins looked stunned at Danielle's words, and she hated
talking to them that way. But the shock of her gruff demeanor

toward them diverted Tim from saying anything to Longley, which was all she wanted.

"Danny," said Jed, "I wouldn't have done it if I thought it might cause you trouble. You was decent to us back on the trail. I was pleased to see you and just spoke before I thought."

"Yeah," said Danielle, reining in her anger somewhat, "that's the trouble. You didn't *think* first. Out here, if you don't think the first time, it's usually the last chance you get. Now go on back down there with your friend. And stay the hell away from me."

Arno Dunne had been watching from his spot down the bar, and seeing Danielle nod toward him, he picked up his mug and moved down among them. "Excuse me, gents," he said. "I'm Arno Dunne. I couldn't help but notice that my two men here seemed to have rubbed you the wrong way."

"Now we've got another one crowding in," Longley said. "I bet I have to start clearing us a place here any minute."

Drinkers scooted farther away along the bar as Longley's right hand dropped from its perch on his gun belt and rested near his tied-down holster.

Dave Mather allowed himself a muffled laugh, and said to Arno, "We know who you are, Dunne. You're the flushingest saddle sore Texas ever scraped off its backside. What brings you to our end of the bar?"

Arno Dunne jerked a thumb toward Tim and Jed. "I've got a couple of shooters here that I believe stand a chance in the contest. I saw that you seem to be having some cross words with them, and just wanted to remind you that if any iron gets drawn, let's make sure it happens tomorrow out in the clearing, where we all stand to make some money on it. Once these boys prove themselves, they might be the ones you have to face off with."

"I draw iron when and where it suits me, Dunne," said Bill Longley. "You don't tell me a damn thing."

"Easy, Bill," Dunne responded. "I'm just their promoter, you might say. Have you got anybody lined up to shoot against? If not, let's talk business, and think of the possibilities."

Danielle seethed, hearing Dunne talk about her brothers this way, knowing he couldn't care less if they lived or died, and knowing that right here and now there wasn't a thing she could say about it, except, "Mr. Dunne, if you're so interested in this contest, why don't you stick your own name up for tomorrow's matches? I wasn't going to enter against anybody, but in your case, I'll gladly make an exception."

Still stinging from Danielle's words a moment earlier, Tim said firmly, "Danny Duggin, you've made your opinion of me and my brother clear. We don't need you speaking on our behalf." He looked at Bill Longley, then Dave Mather. "If anybody wants to call on me or my brother in the morning, we'll oblige them. You might all be surprised at what a couple of farm boys can do."

"Twenty dollars on Bill Longley," a voice called out, the drinkers obviously listening to what was being said and wanting in on the action.

"You're covered," another drinker replied.

"Wait just a damn minute," Arno Dunne called out above the din of the excited crowd. He stilled the drinkers, then turned back to Bill Longley. "I didn't mean one of them might face you first thing tomorrow. They still have to prove themselves. I meant if all goes well, maybe you and one of them—"

Longley cut him off boldly, saying, "To hell with *one* of them, and to hell with later on. If these sodbusters are as game as they talk, I'll face them both at once, come morning, when the sun peeps over the rooster's ass."

Arno Dunne felt pressed now, knowing if somebody like Longley killed the twins first thing, he'd have no chance to make any money putting them up against some of these lesser gunmen. "No way," Arno Dunne said, "not tomorrow leastwise. They're not ready yet."

Tim had been listening, barely in control after Longley's insults and Danny Duggin's rejection. "I'm ready," Tim said. "But not two on one. First thing in the morning, I'll sign up to fight you. I'm not afraid."

Danielle winced, saying to herself, *No, Tim! Think about what you're getting into!* But she was helpless to make her thoughts known. She had to keep silent and wait. Hopefully, she prayed, she would find a way to stop it before the match tomorrow, even it meant facing Bill Longley herself.

W here'd you say you found him?" Merlin Haas asked Rufe Gaddis.

Both of them looked at the body of Duncan Grago, which Newt Grago had placed on a blanket in the corner of the shack. Newt Grago stood directly over his brother's corpse, staring down at it, shaking his head slowly in the glow of the lantern clenched tight in his fist.

Rufe Gaddis answered Merlin Haas in a near whisper. "We found him about two miles west of here when we swung wide out of the sun. Looked liked he'd been hanging there most of the day."

"Who would have done this?" Haas asked. When neither Gaddis nor Grago answered, Haas asked again, thinking they hadn't heard him.

This time when he asked, Newt Grago turned toward him, the lantern's light causing Newt's face to look even grimmer.

"Go get yourself a drink, Merlin," Grago said in a low, controlled voice.

"No, thanks. I'm fine," Haas replied, not getting the message that Grago just wanted him to leave.

"I *said*, go have a drink, *damn it*!" Newt repeated, this time his voice rasping like a file on hard metal.

"Oh! Why, yes, I believe I will." Haas backed to the door, took his bowler hat from a peg, and leveled it down onto his forehead with nervous fingers.

"And keep your mouth shut about this," Newt Grago added. "I mean, don't breathe a word to a soul about it, or I'll rip your tongue out of your head."

"No, sir, Newt! Not a word," Haas stammered. "I swear it!" His hand trembled as he opened the door just enough to slip through and disappear into the night.

As soon as Merlin Haas was gone, Rufe Gaddis gave Newt Grago a knowing look, saying quietly, "You see how it happened, don't you? Dunc did this to himself."

"Yeah, I see," Newt murmured in a low, tortured voice.

"I knew you wouldn't want the word out," said Gaddis. "That's why I waited till dark and slipped in by myself. Delmano and the rest are camped a mile out, waiting for me."

"You did right, bringing him in to me this way, Rufe," said Newt Grago. "He ain't acted like his old self since he rode in. I reckon prison made a mess out of him."

"Prison's rough," said Gaddis, "but damn." He shook his head, looking over at the body on the floor. "I can't imagine ole Dunc doing something like this. He must have really lost his mind."

Newt stood in silence for a second, then said, "Yes, he did, but he had some help. That snake Danny Duggin he's been riding with caused this. He's what pushed Dunc over the edge."

"Who's Danny Duggin?" Gaddis asked.

"Some two-bit gunslinger Dunc brought here with him," Newt hissed. "I've got some sneaking suspicions about that bastard."

Gaddis looked confused. "I don't get it. How'd this Duggin cause Dunc to do this?"

Newt Grago snapped his eyes onto Gaddis in the flicker of lantern light, saying in a sharp tone, "Never mind how he caused it. But he did, sure as hell. Dunc got his head screwed on wrong some way, and this Danny Duggin took advantage of it."

"Damn, Newt," said Gaddis, "I reckon some crazy things have been going on. Why's this man Duggin still alive if you saw he was causing Dunc trouble?"

"It's a long story, Rufe. But I'll tell you something else about Duggin. The first time I laid eyes on him, I suspected him to be the young gunslinger that was shooting everybody up last year."

"My God, Newt," Gaddis said, stunned at the fact that Newt hadn't killed this Danny Duggin outright.

"I know, Rufe." Newt rubbed his lowered forehead. "I shoulda killed him right off, but he was a friend of Dunc's. I didn't want to make a move till I was dead sure of it. Now my waiting has cost Dunc his life."

"Where is this Duggin?" Gaddis asked. "I'll just go put a bullet into his brain."

"No, it's not that easy tonight," Newt Grago said. "He's over at Lulu's with Dave Mather and Bill Longley. You never know who those two will side with."

"Longley and Mather are here?" Gaddis looked worried all of a sudden and stepped away from the door.

"Yes, both of them are here. Longley heard about the contest and came here, saying he was drawing himself a thousand dollars' worth of blood, then moving on." Newt rubbed his forehead again. "Things ain't gone quite the way I planned them to. But don't worry about Longley. He wouldn't go along with what I had planned for Duggin. So I've got four men all set to cut his boots out from under him, soon as he leaves Lulu's tonight and heads to his bedroll."

"What do want me and the boys to do? Just tell me, Newt. We're ready for anything," Gaddis said.

"Ride in come sunup," said Newt Grago. "Longley will be dead. Mather, too, if he gets in the way. You and the boys will have Danny Duggin all to yourselves. We'll tell everybody he ambushed Dunc. Then we'll take our time and kill him good and slow."

"Sounds good to me, Newt." Rufe Gaddis backed to the door and opened it a crack, looking out into the darkness, then turned to Grago. "See you first thing in the morning. Me and the boys will all have our mean on."

CHAPTER 16

ROBBER'S ROCK, INDIAN TERRITORY. JULY 26, 1871.

It was in the dark hours of morning when Bill Longley and one of Lulu's girls left Danielle and Dave Mather in the gambling tent and headed to where Mather and Longley had set up a campsite for themselves. No sooner had Longley and the woman left than Danielle looked around the tent at the few remaining bleary-eyed drinkers. Arno Dunne and the twins had left over two hours ago. Only three old hard cases stood at the faro table, arguing in a drunken stupor, one of them with an arm looped around one of Lulu's girls. Lulu herself had retired to a cot in the back corner of the tent, leaving another one of her girls tending bar. Danielle looked at the girl tending bar, seeing she was half asleep as she poured Mather a shot of rye.

"Something's not right, Dave," Danielle said suddenly.

Mather gave a drowsy smile, saying, "There's a lot of things not right, Danny. But who are we to question the workings of the universe?"

"No, Dave, damn it! Listen to me," Danielle demanded. "That woman who left with Bill Longley. Did you notice how wide-awake and sober she was?"

Mather perked up a little, his shot of rye in his hand. "Yes, come to think of it." He set his glass down, a look of consternation washing over his face.

Danielle continued. "And how she just seemed to pop up out of nowhere all of a sudden? It was like she'd been biding her time, waiting just for Longley."

"You're right, Danny," Mather said, pushing his glass back with his fingers. He turned quickly to Danielle, but Danielle was already headed out of the tent. Mather hurried, his hand coming up with his pistol. "Longley's being set up!" he said aloud to himself, swinging the tent fly back with his forearm.

Mather caught up with Danielle a few yards from the tent as rifle fire streaked out of the darkness toward the path Longley and the woman had taken. From the center of fire, Longley's pistol exploded repeatedly, fighting back. The woman screamed in pain as Mather and Danielle hurried forward, firing at the muzzle flashes, trying to give Longley some cover fire. Two of the rifles streaked lead toward them, Danielle diving in one direction and Mather in the other. But they stayed down for only a second; then both of them came up in a crouch, firing and moving forward.

"Bill!" Dave Mather called out to Longley through the roaring gunfire. "Are you all right in there?"

Longley's only reply was three shots from his Colt, one of them causing a loud whimper followed by the sound of breaking brush as one of the riflemen toppled down from his perch a few feet above the clearing.

"Good, he's holding his own," Mather said to Danielle while rifle fire flashed like heat lightning. "I'm going around to the right. You circle left. Don't fire on me if you can help it."

Danielle and Mather moved quickly, their pistols blazing their way in the darkness. Of the three remaining riflemen, only two were firing, their shots centered on Bill Longley. Danielle held her fire for a second, hearing the sound of running boots breaking through the brush toward her. Seeing the outline of a man in the pale moonlight, she stood straight up in his path and fired one well-placed round into his chest. He grunted, rolling and sliding to a halt almost at her feet. She fired another shot into him for safety's sake, then crouched back down and hurried forward.

Dave Mather, seeing the two rifles firing at Bill Longley, stood up and stalked forward, two pistols now in his hands, both of them pounding like drums. Joining Longley's fire, Mather saw one rifle cease to fire in the darkness. To his left he heard Danielle's Colt and saw the flashes of flame as Danielle moved forward, the three of them forcing the last rifleman to make a run for it.

"Bill," Mather called out to Longley, "it's me and Danny Duggin! Hold your fire. We're coming in."

"Then come in slow," Bill Longley replied in the darkness. "Let me get a good look at both of you."

Danielle moved in with caution, letting Mather arrive a moment ahead of her as she scouted the darkness for any more ambushers. She heard Mather and Longley talking as she finally stepped in closer and saw the two of them bent down over the woman.

"You're hit pretty bad," Longley said down to the gasping figure on the ground. "Newt Grago put you up to this, didn't he?"

"Yes," she said, struggling for breath. "Them . . . cowardly bastards. They was . . . supposed to wait till you were lying down on your blanket."

"They should have warned you first, honey," said Longley, brushing a strand of hair from her fading eyes. "I'm one hard ole dog to kill."

"Well," she rasped, "it looks like I'm not. . . ."

Her words trailed and ended in a spent breath. Longley let her head down from his forearm and folded her arms across her stomach wound.

"That does it," Bill Longley said with venom. "I'm going over to the shack and shoot Newt Grago's eyes out." He grunted, trying to rise to his feet and not making it. "Damn it, give me a hand here, Dave. Get me on my feet."

"Bill, you're hit?" Mather asked, taking him by a shoulder and lifting him up.

Bill Longley came to his feet, staggering to one side, and went back down.

"Yes, damn it all! I caught a bullet in my hip. But I'm still game. I'll get him. I hate an ambusher worse than anything."

"Hell's fire, Bill," Dave Mather said, he and Danielle both moving in to take a closer look at the flow of blood from Bill Longley's hip wound. "You're not going anywhere if we don't get this bleeding stopped."

"It's clean through, ain't it?" Longley asked, his fingers searching the wound in the darkness.

"Yeah, but it's bleeding bad," Mather replied.

"Bleeding never hurt nothing. Get me to my feet, damn it!" Longley demanded. "I've got time to kill that skunk yet."

In the darkness behind them, voices called back and forth asking one another about the gunfire. Boots thrashed through the brush toward them.

"Listen back there, Bill," Mather said. "Every one of them is Newt Grago's man in some way or another. We don't stand a chance against all of them, especially with you shot up."

"Mather's right, Longley," Danielle joined in as she punched out her spent cartridges. "Let's get you away from here. We'll get your blankets and gear and get off a ways. It'll be daylight in another hour. You can come back for Newt Grago once we get you taken care of. I'll even help you kill him."

"I don't need no help killing him," said Longley, again struggling to stand up. On his feet with an arm looped across Mather's shoulder, he asked, "What tipped you off that it was a setup, Dave?"

"You can thank Danny Duggin here for that, Bill," Mather replied, adjusting Longley's weight against his side. "He caught on to it no sooner than the two of you left the tent."

"Much obliged, then, Danny," Longley grunted. "I reckon you're right. Let me get patched up. Then we'll go kill us a whole slew of rats."

"What about this poor woman?" Danielle asked as Mather and Longley lumbered away toward their dark campsite.

"What about her?" Longley said over his shoulder. "She played the hand Grago dealt her. She lost. Burying her ain't my responsibility."

Danielle sighed under her breath, looking down at the dead

woman on the ground. But then she shook her head and caught up
to Mather and Longley for a moment.

"I've got something to take care of. You two, go on. There's a
little creek down over the rise. You'll see my mare along there. I'll
meet you there."

"Where are you going, Danny?" Mather asked. "This place is
going to blow wide open once Newt sees his boys didn't get the job
done. He'll try to kill you the second he lays eyes on you."

"I know," Danielle said, "but I've got to take care of something.
It's important."

"Part of your *mission*, I take it?" Mather asked.

"Yeah," Danielle said, backing away, "you could call it that."

Inside the shack, Newt Grago seethed at the wounded rifleman who had fled there to escape the hail of gunfire once
his companions had fallen. "Tanner, you cowardly cur!" Grago
shouted in his face, grabbing him by his shirt and yanking him in
close. "You mean to tell me that *four* riflemen couldn't handle Bill
Longley?"

"It weren't just Longley, Newt, I swear!" the frightened Lloyd
Tanner insisted. "There was that gunman Duggin and Mysterious
Dave Mather! I heard them call out to one another!"

"Damn it to hell!" Grago raged, shoving Tanner away from him
and pacing back and forth, needing to think.

"They'll be coming, Newt," said Tanner. "What are we going
to do?"

"Shut up, Tanner!" Newt Grago barked at him. He paced some
more, rubbing his temples. Then he abruptly stopped. "All right,
here's the plan. You ride out a mile along the west trail. You'll find
Rufe Gaddis and some others camped there. Bring them back here
as fast as you can. Get back before sunup. I'll round up the whole
camp and tell them what that bastard Duggin did to my bother,
Dunc. We'll get this straightened out. You can count on it."

"What did he do to your brother, Dunc?" Tanner asked, holding his left hand tight against the bullet graze on his right shoulder.

"I'll show you what he did!" Grago screamed, dragging Tanner to the body of Duncan Grago lying in the corner. "There, take a look at him! That's what he did! Duggin killed him! Left poor Dunc hanging from an oak limb. Now get out there and get Rufe and the boys and get back here pronto!"

"But, Newt, what about my shoulder? I'm bleeding like a stuck hog," Tanner pleaded.

"You haven't seen bleeding yet if you don't get moving," Grago said through clenched teeth.

He stomped across the shack, picked up his gun belt from a chair back, and slung it around his waist. Before he got it buckled, Tanner was out the door and running toward the corral, snatching a saddle and bridle up from the ground out front of the shack on his way. The gunfire had awakened the encampment, and as Tanner fumbled with the rope, loosening the corral gate, Arno rushed up beside him.

"Tanner, what the hell's going on?" Dunne asked, seeing the blood on Tanner's shoulder.

"Get away from me, Arno! I've no time for you. All hell has busted loose here!" He hurried into the milling horses, grabbed one by its mane, and pitched the bridle around its head, tossing his saddle up across the horse's back. "Duggin kilt Dunc Grago and left him hanging in a tree! Newt's coming now to get everybody after Duggin, Mather, and Longley!"

"Mather and Longley?" Dunne asked. "Did they have something to do with it?"

"I don't know!" Tanner yanked the saddle cinch tight. "But I'm gone to bring in Rufe Gaddis and the boys. Now get out'n my way!" He shoved Dunne back, then hurled himself up onto the saddle and kicked the horse forward.

Dunne watched him ride away, then closing the rope gate, he cursed to himself, "Damn it. Today was my day for making a killing here."

Danielle stood back out of the chaos in the encampment clearing, searching among the torchlit faces for her brothers, Tim and Jed. Around the corner from Lulu's gambling tent, she saw men strap on their pistols and check their rifles while others came running forward, hitching up their galluses, rubbing sleep from their eyes. Danielle finally spotted Tim and Jed as Arno Dunne came hurrying up to them, standing too close for her to say anything. She hunkered down against the side of the tent and waited, feeling precious seconds tick by. In another few minutes, the first rays of sun would begin peeping up over the horizon, shedding her cover of darkness.

She listened to Dunne, only making out part of what he was telling the twins. But she did manage to hear him tell Tim and Jed that Tanner had gone to get Rufe Gaddis and the boys, and that they would be here in just a few minutes. Hearing it caused her blood to race. In the glow of lantern and torchlight, she saw Arno Dunne step back from the twins.

"Stay here," Danielle heard Arno Dunne instruct her brothers. "I'll get my rifle and be right back."

As soon as Dunne moved away, Danielle called out in a hushed voice, "Tim, Jed, over here, by the tent."

They looked around at the sound of her voice. "Danny Duggin?" Jed asked, barely lowering his voice.

Tim caught the secretive manner in which Danny Duggin was addressing them and poked Jed in the ribs, whispering, "Keep it down, Jed."

Looking all around first to make sure no one had heard them, Tim nudged Jed toward the side of the tent, where he saw Danielle's green eyes flashing at them from beneath her lowered hat brim.

"Hurry up!" Danielle hissed at them.

"Danny!" Tim said as he and Jed hunkered down out of sight. "Arno Dunne said you killed Newt's brother Dunc. Is it true?"

"No," Danielle whispered, "but it might as well be. Now listen to me. We don't have much time. Duncan Grago is one of the two outlaws who killed Elvin Bray back in St. Joe and tried to ambush you on the trail."

"What the—?" Tim and Jed looked at each other, stunned.

"Don't talk—listen!" Danielle said, cutting them both off. "The men who killed your pa are on their way here. I heard Arno Dunne just tell you they would be here anytime now."

"Hey!" Tim said, interrupting her. "What do you know about our pa? Or about Elvin Bray?" His hand went to the butt of his pistol.

Danielle lowered her head, seeing she wasn't going to get by with the explanation she had planned to tell them. "All right, Tim," she said, "just pay attention. We're in a bad spot here." She peeled the fake mustache back from her lip and looked up, pushing her hat brim up for a better view. "It's me, your sister . . . Danielle." Then she stared in silence for a second, letting it sink in.

"Oh, Lord God," Tim finally whispered in astonishment.

"My goodness gracious, it *is* you," Jed murmured, his voice beginning to tremble. "Danielle . . . we came looking for you! We were going to snoop around, see what we could find out, try to find you—"

Jed's voice stuck in his throat, and they both leaned forward. Tim joined him, and all three of them, kneeling in hiding, threw their arms around one another.

"I know. . . . I know," Danielle whispered, holding back her sobs, taking up extra precious seconds to hold her brothers to her bosom. "It's been hard on you . . . on all of us. I wanted to tell you sooner, but I couldn't risk it."

Tears streamed down her cheeks. She smelled the road dust and dried sweat on her brothers and found comfort in it, knowing that they smelled the same scent on her, and that it was the scent of their long journey bringing the three of them together.

"My brothers," she whispered, "at last I can say those words . . . *my brothers*."

Even in their stunned surprise, Jed and Tim Strange looked at each other, each knowing that their venture had just taken a change for the better. Their family was reunited now, their destinies the same.

At the sound of boots running past them, close to their position, Danielle held them back at arm's length. She ran a sleeve across her eyes, then said, "Listen to me. We'll talk later. Right now Bill Longley and Dave Mather are hiding out down by where I hid Sundown. You two can walk right into the corral while everybody's busy wondering what's going on. Get your horses, and get back here with them. We've got lots to do this morning."

"Danielle," Jed asked, "you mentioned the men who killed Pa are coming? Shouldn't we wait here for them?"

"Come on, Jed," Tim said before Danielle could answer. "Danielle knows what she's doing. Let's get our horses and get them back over here. It's turning daylight on us."

Danielle hunkered down and watched them hurry to the corral. On their way back with their horses, Arno Dunne ran up beside them, trying to grab Tim's reins, but Tim shook him loose. Dunne ran behind them on foot, cursing and waving his rifle in the air.

As Tim and Jed turned their horses in alongside the big tent, Arno Dunne followed right behind them, ranting, "You lousy plowboys! You're not going to run out on me! I came to see you make me some money or else watch you die trying! You think you're gonna run out on me?" He levered a round up into the rifle chamber and raised it. "You low-down—"

At the sound of the rifle lever, Tim and Jed had both swung around in their saddles, their pistols out and aimed. But they froze, seeing the knife handle sticking out of Dunne's chest, Danielle's hand wrapped around it as she stood behind him with her left arm wrapped around his throat.

"I'm sorry I don't have time to kill you proper-like, Arno Dunne, you rotten snake," she rasped in his ear, "for using my brothers, turning them into the likes of you and your kind."

Across the clearing behind them, Newt Grago had stepped out onto the porch and called out to the gathering outlaws, waving them in closer to him. Danielle looked around over her shoulder at the sound of Grago's voice but knew that killing him would have to wait until she returned.

"I haven't forgotten you, Grago," she whispered to herself, tightening her grip on the knife handle in Dunne's chest.

Tim and Jed both winced, seeing Danielle twist the knife blade deeper into Arno Dunne's heart. Dunne's mouth opened in a silent scream.

"Lord, Danielle," Tim whispered, watching Arno Dunne's gloved hands jerk and quiver, then fall limp at his sides.

Danielle let Dunne drop to the ground, leaving the knife still sunk in his chest.

"Let's go," she said, wiping blood from her hand as her brothers stared at her as if in disbelief.

Danielle stepped forward, tossed herself up onto the rump of Tim's horse, and threw her arm around Tim's waist. Before Tim or Jed could respond, she batted her heels to the horse's sides and sent it lunging into a full gallop.

Jed Strange looked back at the body of Arno Dunne lying on the ground in a dark circle of blood. "I'm glad you got the killing you've been looking for, Arno Dunne. I just wish it had of come from me." He jerked the horse away and kicked it out behind his brother and sister.

CHAPTER 17

The last few yards, riding double to where Dave Mather and Bill Longley stood waiting for them, Danielle looked over Tim's shoulder and saw the bodies of two outlaws lying on the ground. Mysterious Dave Mather stood back in the silver gray light of dawn, waving her and her brothers in. He smiled, a rifle hanging from one hand and a pistol from the other, as they rode in closer and sidled their horses up to him.

Longley sat on a mound of earth with his right leg stretched out before him, a blood-soaked bandanna pressed against his hip. Sundown's reins were in Longley's other hand, along with his pistol.

"Well," Dave Mather said, grinning up at Danielle, noting that her mustache was gone, "I see you took the time to shave before returning."

"It's a long story, Mather," Danielle said, dropping down from behind Tim. "These two are my brothers. I didn't tell you before, but I'm telling you now so you'll know they're both on our side."

Mather's grin widened. "Nothing like a little surprise on the verge of a gun battle, I always say." He nodded at the two bodies on the ground. "Now here's a surprise for you. We caught three of them coming in from the buttes, riding like hell. Said there's a forty-man posse coming down on this place." He nodded at one of the bodies, saying, "This one told us before he died. They were hightailing it back to Newt Grago. The one who got away should be getting to Grago about now. I felt bad having to shoot these two"—Mather shrugged—"but we needed their horses worse than they did."

"A forty-man posse?" Danielle glanced back in the direction of the tall, slim buttes. "Damn it, why now? I've got things to take care of!"

"Oh, the mission?" Mather asked.

Behind him, Bill Longley struggled to his feet, dusted his seat, and walked forward, leading the chestnut mare, not looking at all happy about it.

"Yeah, the mission," Danielle said. She let out a breath. "Well, I've sided with you, Mather. Tell me how you two want to handle this thing. I won't back out on it."

"Far as we're concerned, there's nothing to back out on," Bill Longley said in a gruff tone. "Do we look like fools to you? Dave and I ain't facing no forty-man posse, not with all the charges I've got hanging over my head. They'd have to hang me eight or nine times just to get caught up."

"Then what are you going to do?" Danielle asked, looking back and forth between the two. "A posse that size will leave some guards at the passes. How do you plan on slipping past them, especially when Longley's wounded?"

Mather looked off in the direction of the buttes, then looked back at Danielle. "Oh, I'll think of something. They don't call me Mysterious Dave for nothing."

Bill Longley cut in, saying, "Hope you've got no objections, but I'll be taking this chestnut mare with me. You can ride one of those dead mongrels' horses." He nodded at the two horses they'd taken and hitched to a stand of scrub cedar.

Danielle's first impulse was to throw her hand to her Colt and tell him he'd have to kill her before he'd ride away on Sundown. But she held herself in check, seeing something in Bill Longley's eyes that said he was just testing her. "Be my guest, Longley," she said. "There's nothing I'd like better than to send you off on that mare."

But Longley hesitated, looked at Mather, and said, "This peckerwood thinks he's tricking me into something, don't he?"

"It appears that way to me, Bill," Mather said. "If I was to guess, I'd say Danny Duggin here knows that somebody in that posse is going to recognize that mare. Am I right, Danny Duggin?"

"Yep, you guessed it," Danielle said. "Hell, I can't do you this way, Longley, not even as a joke. If anybody in the posse spots that mare, you'll never shake them off your tail."

"A joke, huh?" Bill Longley flung Sundown's reins over to Danielle. "I don't see a damn thing funny about it." He turned to Mather, adding, "Let's get out of here before I take a notion to start shooting everybody around me. I hate killing a man after he helped me out of a tight spot." He eyed Danielle closely for a moment, then grumbled, "Watch your backside, Danny Duggin. I'm beholden to you." He turned and limped over to the other two horses.

Mather spread a playful smile at Danielle. "I think Longley has taken a liking to you. You're the first person I've ever seen that he's let talk to him this way." Mather took a step closer, looking into Danielle's eyes. "It's too bad about this mission of yours, Danny Duggin," he said, close to her face.

"Why's that, Dave?" Danielle asked, not backing up an inch, but getting an uncomfortable feeling from him standing so close. Mather's eyes searched hers in a way she hadn't felt for a long time.

Mather leaned nearer to her and whispered close to her ear, "Because without that mustache and low-slung Stetson, you are one fine-looking young woman . . . whoever you are."

Danielle felt her cheeks flush. She stepped back, ready to issue her denial and make some tough-sounding statement. But before she could say a word, Dave Mather's lips found hers and pressed a deep kiss on her, muffling her protest. Then before she could do anything else, he had moved back away from her. She stood enraged, yet powerless and somewhat pleased that he had seen through her disguise. He was the first one who had done so in all her time on the outlaw trail.

"You bastard," Danielle cursed him in a whisper, trying to sound like she meant it.

But Mather winked, seeing that her heart wasn't in it. "If I'm wrong, may lightning strike me dead on the spot. But there's some things a beautiful woman just can't hide. And even if you could, there's some men you just can't hide it from." He then added in an even lower tone, "Don't worry. Mysterious Dave knows how to keep a secret like nobody's business. I won't tell if you won't."

On the bays behind her, Tim and Jed Strange lowered their hat brims and chuckled to themselves. Bill Longley stood to the side with the two horses' reins hanging from his hand, his mouth agape at what he'd just witnessed. He stared at Dave Mather as Mather walked over nonchalantly and took a set of reins from his hands.

"Come on, Bill, thought you was in a hurry to leave," Mather said as he swung up into the saddle.

"God Almighty, Dave!" Longley said, still staring in disbelief as he struggled into the saddle, taking care not to further aggravate his wound. "What the hell is the matter with you?"

"Let's just say I got caught up in the moment." Dave Mather chuckled, tasting his lips.

"Caught up in the moment?" Longley said, having to shake his head in order to clear it. "I'll be dipped and dragged! That's the damnedest thing I ever saw you do! Am I going to be all right riding with you?"

Mather looked back at Danielle, who still stood in silence, watching him tap his horse forward. He tipped his dusty hat brim to her, then turned to Bill Longley, saying, "Yeah, Bill, you mudugly yard goat . . . you don't have a *thing* to worry about."

Rufe Gaddis, Saul Delmano, Jack Pitch, Max Dupre, Billy Joe Earls, and Blade Hogue followed Tanner around the last turn along the trail into the encampment. Coming in from the west, where they'd spent the night, they now spread out single file, riding the last quarter of a mile through a narrow rocky pass that opened into a stretch of rolling flatlands. On the other end of the flatland, the top of Lulu's tent stood visible above a rise of clump grass and scrub cedar. In the distance beyond the encampment, a rise of dust stood high, drifting sidelong in the air. It was the plumes of dust that prompted Rufe Gaddis to pull back on his reins and cause his horse to rear slightly as it came to a halt.

"What is it, Rufe?" Jack Pitch asked, his own horse spinning in place as Pitch reined it down harshly. The other men bunched up behind them.

"I don't know," said Gaddis, "but I sure don't like the looks of it. The last time I saw that much dust that high in the air, it turned out to be a whole company of Yankee cavalry come to clean up our gun smuggling down along the border." He backed his horse up a step.

"Think the law got word of Newt's contest?" asked Blade Hogue, moving in between Gaddis and Pitch. "Figured this was a good place to round up a bunch of us at once?"

"It wouldn't surprise me," said Gaddis. "Newt didn't mind letting the word out."

"What do you think, Rufe?" asked Pitch. "Want to ride on in, take our chances?"

Gaddis gave him a sarcastic look. "You really are itching to use that new Remington, ain't you, Jack?"

"Tanner said Newt Grago needs our help," Pitch responded, red-faced. "That's all I was getting at. I don't want to be looked at as ducking out on trouble."

"Just shut up, Jack, before I wear that shiny new Remington out over your head," Rufe Gaddis snapped at him.

"Rufe," said Blade Hogue, hoping to divert Gaddis and Pitch from locking horns, "maybe a couple of us oughta swing around and—"

"Quiet, Hogue!" Rufe Gaddis said, listening closely with his head cocked toward the flats. "Did you hear that?"

"Yeah," said Saul Delmano, stepping his horse forward through the others, "that was rifle fire."

As they all sat focused toward the distance, the sound of gunfire resounded in a long, hard volley. The men looked at one another with wary eyes.

"It damn sure is rifle fire," Rufe Gaddis said. Then he turned to Tanner and asked, "How many men was Newt talking about killing?"

Tanner stared wide-eyed at the distant explosions, saying, "Just three that he told me about. There's that gunslinger Danny Duggin. Then there's Bill Longley and Dave Mather, if'n he got in the way, is what Newt said."

"Well, that's not the sound of three rifles," Saul Delmano said, moving his horse in beside Jack Pitch.

"Damn right it's not," said Gaddis. He jerked his horse around and forced it into the other riders, making them part for him. "Come on, boys, we're going to sit this one out for a while, see what that's all about." He gigged his horse forward into the narrow rock pass.

Jack Pitch called out to Gaddis, "Maybe that's all of Newt's boys firing at those three men. Did you stop to think of that?"

"No, I didn't, Jack," Rufe Gaddis called back over his shoulder to Jack Pitch as the others turned their horses and fell in behind him, "but why don't you go check it all out for us? You seem to be the one so interested in finding out." He spurred his horse into a trot before Jack Pitch could answer. Beside Jack Pitch, Saul Delmano stepped down from his horse and lifted its right front hoof, inspecting it closely.

"Ain't you coming?" Jack Pitch asked Delmano.

"I'll be right along," Delmano replied, "soon as I see why this horse is favoring its hoof."

He watched as Jack Pitch shook his head and kicked his horse forward. As soon as Pitch caught up to the others, Delmano dropped the horse's hoof, swung up into his saddle, and rode off in the opposite direction. With a posse coming, he wasn't about to get caught riding with Rufe Gaddis, Blade Hogue, and the rest of them. Delmano had had a bad feeling all night about riding in and killing this Danny Duggin, especially after Gaddis said Duggin was riding with Bill Longley and Dave Mather. Delmano decided he'd rather take his chances slipping around the posse on his own.

A hundred yards back into the narrow rock pass, Rufe Gaddis stopped his horse again, this time at the sight of the single rider atop the chestnut mare sitting sideways across his path. "Now what do we have here?" Gaddis said to Tanner, who reined down beside him.

Tanner's hand went to the butt of the rifle in his saddle boot as the other riders stopped behind him.

"Something we can do for you, mister?" Rufe Gaddis called out to Danielle from thirty feet away, already having a pretty good idea what was about to happen.

Gaddis was talking only to give the men behind him a chance to spread out as much as possible in the tight space of the pass. He knew it was no coincidence that this rider had met them at this spot. Above them on either side, rock walls rose up fifty feet, providing for a perfect ambush.

Danielle raised her hand, and in it was the worn list of names she'd been carrying so long. Not having to look at the list, she recited the names from memory. In a flat tone, she said, "Blade Hogue, Rufe Gaddis, Saul Delmano."

"Yep," said Rufe Gaddis, "that's us, all right." He could tell where this was going. His hand drifted to his pistol butt.

"You know why I'm here," Danielle called out. "If the rest of you want to live, back your horses and get out of here."

A couple of the men stifled a short laugh at the thought of one rider sounding so sure of himself in the face of these odds. But Rufe Gaddis didn't laugh. Neither did Blade Hogue. As Gaddis replied, Hogue ventured a glance along the rising rock to their left and right.

"You're that gunslinger from last year, ain't ya?" said Gaddis.

"Yep," Danielle replied. And that was all she said.

"You're name's not Danny Duggin, though, is it?" Gaddis asked, hoping the men behind him were ready for what was coming.

"Nope," Danielle said. Then she fell silent again.

"I heard somewhere that this is all about somebody killing your pa and leaving him hanging from a tree," Gaddis said.

As Gaddis spoke, Danielle stepped down slowly from her saddle and pushed Sundown on the rump, sending the mare out of harm's way. "You heard, right," Danielle said, stepping forward slowly, fanning her riding duster back behind her holsters.

"What if I told you me and these boys had nothing to do with it?" Rufe Gaddis asked, his right hand poised near his pistol butt.

Danielle ignored his question. "Let's get to it," she said, coming closer yet.

Rufe Gaddis offered a tight, edgy smile, not sure if he should step down from his saddle or not. Uncertain how many men were atop the rock with rifles pointed down at him, he said, "I'm no fool. You think I don't know an ambush when I see one? Who's up there? Longley? Mather?" He allowed himself to turn his eyes from Danielle just enough to call up along the rock ledges, "Is this your style? Come on down and face us like men!" His words echoed along the narrow pass.

"We already have," said the voice behind them.

Gaddis and the others jerked around in their saddles and saw the two figures standing afoot in the trail behind them. Tim and Jed Strange stood five feet apart, their gun hands poised, their eyes level and determined.

Jack Pitch grinned. "Ragged-assed farm boys wearing guns too big for them," Pitch murmured. But nobody seemed to hear him as he sized the brothers up. *These two are mine,* he thought to himself. All that practice with his new Remington wasn't going to waste, after all. He sat staring at Tim and Jed as Rufe Gaddis turned his attention back to Danielle.

Now that Gaddis had some idea of what he was facing, he swung down slowly from his saddle. Had there been men covering them from above, he would have been better off staying mounted, maybe being able to make a run for it once the rifle fire got too hot and heavy. But this was no ambush. These three wanted it face-to-face. *So be it*, he thought, getting some solid earth beneath his boots. This was going to work out fine. Didn't these fools realize they would be shooting into one another in a cross fire like this? He smiled again and spread his feet a shoulder width apart, facing Danielle, knowing Hogue and the others would take care of the two men behind them.

"All right, boys," Gaddis said over his shoulder without taking his eyes off Danielle, "let's hurry up and get this over with. We ain't got all—"

Danielle's first shot tore Rufe Gaddis's words from his chest and sent him reeling backward. Her next shot slammed into Tanner, who had drawn his rifle from its boot but seemed confused as to which way to point it. Behind him, Tim's and Jed's pistols exploded, taking Blade Hogue from his saddle as his horse reared high with him. Tanner's horse reared as well. Danielle's shot flung him from his saddle into Max Dupre. A loud curse came from Dupre as Tanner's blood splashed on his face. Before he could raise a hand and wipe his eyes, two shots hit him front and rear. He spun from his saddle into a tangle of frightened hooves and falling bodies.

Jack Pitch had gotten off three shots from his new Remington before a bullet from Jed's big Colt went through Billy Joe Earls's neck and sliced through Pitch's shoulder. Jack Pitch dove from his horse and rolled away from the heart of the melee to where he could find room to rise up onto his knees and use his new pistol to its best advantage. He raised the Remington, taking his time even as the battle raged. Getting a perfect aim on Tim Strange's chest, Pitch said to himself, "Got ya!" and pulled the trigger. But the hammer didn't fall. Wild-eyed, Pitch shook the gun, then slapped it against his palm, desperately trying to dislodge the dirt inside the open hammer that had been scraped up as he'd rolled across the ground.

"Damn it! Wait!" Jack Pitch screamed at Tim and Jed, seeing both of their pistols swing around toward him, trailing smoke. He shook the Remington again as if to show them that his pistol wasn't working. But neither of them seemed to care, he thought, feeling the hard blasts of .45 slugs pound into his chest.

In seconds it was over. Silence moved in beneath the drifting echoes and settled onto the narrow trail. With the smell of burned gunpowder heavy around her, Danielle poked out the spent cartridges from her smoking Colt and replaced them. Doing so, she kept an eye on Rufe Gaddis, who lay writhing back and forth on the ground, his hands clasped to his bleeding chest. His right hand still held his pistol.

"Tim, Jed!" she called out across the fleeing horses through a swirl of dust. "Are you okay?"

"We're all right," Tim answered, sidestepping the frightened animals as they pounded away along the trail. "Jed got a bullet through his shirt, but he's fine. What about you?"

"I'll do," Danielle said, feeling the warm blood seep down her side. She looked back at Rufe Gaddis, who had managed to squirm upward onto one knee, his blood-slick hand grasping his pistol tighter, trying to raise it.

"I'll . . . kill you," Gaddis rasped, "you lousy . . . good-for-nothing . . . gunslinger."

"Come on," Danielle said, stepping toward him, "you can do it. Raise that pistol. Come on! Raise it!" she bellowed.

Gaddis struggled, using all his waning strength. "Damn you . . . to hell!"

Danielle's Colt hung in her hand at her side. She raised the barrel just enough to send a fatal slug between Rufe Gaddis'd eyes. His pistol flew from his hand and he pitched backward in the dirt.

Tim and Jed had stepped forward through the swirl of hoof dust and looked down at Gaddis, then over at Danielle.

"You're hit," Tim said to her.

Both of them rushed forward, but Danielle stayed them back with a raised hand.

"I'm all right." She nodded toward the distant sound of rifle fire, noting that it had moved closer across the flatlands. "We need to make tracks. That posse is heading this way."

"But we ain't outlaws," Jed offered. "We've got nothing to worry about."

"They don't know what we are," Danielle said. "Anyway, we've got no time for their questions. If Newt Grago's still alive, I want him. He's the last of Pa's killers." She pressed her hand to her wounded side and limped toward Sundown, who stood off to one side of the narrow trail. "Get your horses. Let's go."

Tim and Jed looked at each other; then Jed called out to Danielle, "At least let us take a look at your side first, Danielle. You can't go around bleeding like that."

"It'll dry," she said, picking up Sundown's reins. "Grago's not getting away from us."

"Danielle, for God sakes," Jed started to plead.

But Danielle cut him short, saying, "Listen, there's horses coming! Now get ready!"

As soon as she said it, two horses rounded the pass into sight.

"Whoa!" Morgan Goss shouted to his horse, which slid almost down onto its haunches in stopping. He looked around at the bodies on the ground, then at Tim and Jed, who stood on either side of the trail. His hands went up in surrender.

Behind him came Cincinnati Carver lying low in his saddle and staring back at the trail behind him. When Carver turned forward and saw Goss's hands in the air, he reined his horse down and flung his shotgun away.

"Don't shoot! You've got us!" Cincinnati Carver shouted, still not recognizing them from the encampment.

"Settle down, Cincinnati," Danielle said, stepping into better view, flipping her Colt back into its holster, which caused Carver and Goss to breathe a little easier. "It's me, Danny Duggin."

"Duggin?" Cincinnati Carver looked surprised. He looked at the bodies on the ground, then back to Danielle. "What's going on here? Who shot Gaddis and these boys?"

"I did, Cincinnati," Danielle replied.

"Damn it, you're the law," said Morgan Goss, "and to think I trusted you, even drank with you . . . bet my money on you!"

"I'm not the law, Goss. I just had something to settle with Newt Grago and this bunch."

Goss lowered his hands as Danielle stepped forward and picked up his shotgun from the dirt, dusting it off against her leg. "Danny Duggin, you're shot there," Goss said, nodding at the blood on Danielle's side.

"I'm all right," she said. "How far back is that posse?"

"Not far enough," said Cincinnati Carver. "They're sweeping through here like a hay sickle any minute. Me and Goss decided we best get down to *Mejico*, where folks have better manners. You're welcome to come, all three of yas."

"Naw, we're not wanted by the law," Danielle said, handing Carver's shotgun up to him. "Is Newt Grago dead?"

"Humph," said Cincinnati Carver, "not unless he fell off his running horse and broke his neck. The snake cleared out of there first thing. Left all of us to face that posse alone." He looked back along the trail as he spoke. "Don't mean to appear rude, Danny, but we'd best get our shanks in the wind. They're awfully close."

"Which way did Newt Grago head?" Danielle asked.

"Hell, the same way he always heads when things get too hot for him. He's got a woman named Bertha Stillwell he always runs to. She's opened a saloon in that whistle-stop town they just named Newton. She's got lots of connections there with men from the Atchison, Topeka and Sante Fe Railroad. Newt says they just named the town after him. Says it'll bring him luck. The damned fool— the town's really named after a place in Massachusetts! Are you going to kill Newt, too, when you find him? Because if you are, tell him I said good riddance before he dies, the no-good yellow bastard."

Danielle didn't answer. Hearing the rifle fire moving closer, she stepped back and said, "Good luck down in Mexico, boys," then slapped Morgan Goss's horse on its rump. The two outlaws wasted no more time. They bolted off along the trail, leaving a wake of dust behind them.

When they were out of sight, Tim asked, "Do you think they're telling the truth about Grago?"

"Yep, I think so. If not, we'll find out in Newton." She stepped toward Sundown without another word, swinging up into her saddle and heeling the mare forward.

"I've heard of that place, Newton, Kansas. It's already supposed to be the toughest place in the West," Jed said to Tim as they walked to where they'd hitched their horses. "If Newt Grago has a lot of friends there, we'll be in for a rough time."

"Then we'd both best be ready for it," said Tim, staring straight ahead, "because it looks like that's where we're headed, come hell or high water."

CHAPTER 18

Leaving the narrow trail and riding wide of the encampment to the northwest, Danielle, Tim, and Jed Strange avoided the posse, keeping close to a stretch of low rock cliffs along a dry creek bed. For the first half hour, they pushed the horses hard until they were sure the sound of rifle fire had turned away from them, following a more southerly direction. Most of the outlaws who had managed to get away from the encampment had fled southwest toward Texas. From there they would head for the Rio Grande, crossing into Mexico the way Cincinnati Carver and Morgan Goss planned to do.

When Danielle and her brothers stopped to rest their mounts, they did so atop a rock ledge that faced the encampment from less than half a mile away. From there, the site of the encampment looked like a place struck by a cyclone. Danielle, Tim, and Jed gazed out across the wavering heat toward the flattened tent. Gambling tables lay broken and scattered. Bodies of outlaws lay strewn within the wide clearing across a fifty-yard stretch of surrounding land. Lulu and her girls were handcuffed and sitting on the ground, along with four wounded outlaws who sat with their heads bowed. Two Cherokee trackers stood guarding the prisoners with their rifles propped on their hips.

Danielle stood up, dusting her trousers, and backed away from the rock ledge. "Well, that does it for Newt Grago's shooting contest," she said. "All he managed to do was get a bunch of men killed."

Jed and Tim both stood up and backed away from the ledge beside her.

"One good thing came out of it, though," Jed said. "If Arno Dunne hadn't been so eager to bring us here, we might not have found you."

"That's right," Tim joined in. "Plus, we got to meet up with some of Pa's killers face-to-face." He looked at Danielle. "Of course, Jed and I didn't know which one was which, but I reckon you did, didn't you?"

Danielle shook her head, saying, "No, I never laid eyes on those men back there. But don't worry. They're Pa's killers all right. One of them gave me all their names last year before he died. Newt Grago is the only one left."

Just saying Grago's name caused her to grow anxious, wanting to get back in the saddle. She walked to Sundown and took up the reins. "Come on," she said to Tim and Jed, "time's a-wasting."

The three mounted up and rode away. In a thicket of scrub cedar not twenty feet from where they had stood, Saul Delmano lowered his rifle and watched their backs until they disappeared around a turn in the trail. Delmano had heard every word they'd said. It would have been easy to take aim and ambush them, but a shot from his rifle would have alerted the Cherokee guards and any other deputy who might have been in the encampment.

"I'll get my chance," Delmano said to himself.

He waited a few minutes longer, then led his horse from the thicket and followed their tracks wide of the slim buttes toward the northern boundary of Indian Territory. For the next three days, he managed to stay within a mile of them, keeping to the brush and dry washes, cautiously keeping an eye on the rise of dust Danielle and her brothers left in their wake.

THE CANADIAN RIVER. JULY 29, 1871.

Newt Grago had not traveled alone these past three days. At the first sign of the posse converging on the encampment, he'd collected Merlin Haas and three other hard cases to ride with him. He'd taken Merlin Haas along because Haas still held most of their winnings. Once Newt Grago took the large roll of money from Merlin Haas, it became apparent to Haas that Grago had no more use for him. Merlin Haas kept as quiet as possible, hoping to get away from the outlaw leader as soon as they crossed into Kansas. The three other men with Grago were the two Stanley brothers, Hop and Renfrow—both former guerrilla riders from the old Quantrill's Raiders days—and a Missouri stagecoach robber named Willis McNutt, who had ridden off and on with Newt Grago over the past few years. Grago had left the Stanley brothers along the Washita River the day before to ambush anyone who might be following their tracks. He'd promised the Stanleys two hundred dollars apiece once they met up with him later in Newton, Kansas.

"The Stanley brothers won't have a chance in hell if they get into a shoot-out with a posse that large," McNutt said in a guarded tone to Merlin Haas as the two of them huddled near a low fire. Newt Grago stood a few yards away at the river's edge, checking his horse's hooves.

Merlin Haas whispered to McNutt in reply, "I'm thinking it ain't so much the posse he's concerned about now as it is that gunslinger Danny Duggin. Grago wants Duggin dead awfully bad. Says he's the one what left Dunc hanging from a rope. Besides, the posse most likely has their hands full with everybody headed across Texas for the border."

McNutt looked Merlin Haas up and down, a trace of a cruel grin showing through his red beard. "You think you know so much, Haas? Then think of this. Newt's going to close his trail behind him once he gets on over to Kansas. He don't like leaving witnesses behind him. When he leaves here in the morning, only one of us will be going with him. The other is going to be sitting here with a rifle, waiting for whoever comes along."

"You're wrong, McNutt," Haas said, but his voice lacked conviction.

McNutt stifled a laugh, saying, "Yeah, you hope I'm wrong, Haas, but you know better. When Grago gets to Newton, he won't need neither one of us. He's got protection there. He'll be walking the streets in a suit and tie, smoking a big cigar."

Merlin Haas swallowed back the dryness in his throat and said, "Well, he knows I can make him money. He'd be foolish to let something happen to me."

"Yeah?" McNutt patted the pistol standing in a holster across his stomach. "Maybe you can grift and gamble, but I can help him stay alive. Which one would you pick if you was him?"

Merlin Haas started to respond, but then stopped himself and sat silent as Newt Grago walked back to the small fire and crouched down on his haunches, saying, "Boys, the horses are in bad shape, us pushing them so hard." He picked up a short stick of kindling and stirred it around in the bed of glowing embers. "Resting tonight will help them some, but we'll be lucky if they make it all the way into Kansas."

"Then what do you suppose we do?" McNutt asked Grago, giving Merlin Haas a knowing glance as he did so.

"I don't know," said Grago, shaking his head slowly. "I've got to think about it and figure something out." He stood back up and stepped over to unroll a blanket on the ground. "Meanwhile, let's get some rest ourselves. Tomorrow's going to be a long day."

But Merlin Haas got very little rest that night. In spite of his long day in the saddle, he rolled back and forth from one side to the next in his blanket. More than once he thought about easing over to the horses, cutting one out, and slipping away into the darkness. His hand went now and then to his share of the winnings in his coat pocket, reassuring himself that it was still there. At one point he came close to rising up and making his move to the horses, yet before he got to his feet, McNutt's voice spoke to him from across the campfire.

"What's the matter, Haas, can't sleep?" McNutt murmured, a dark, playful tone to his voice.

"I—I thought I heard something out there," Haas replied.

"You didn't hear nothing, Haas," McNutt said. "If you did, don't worry about it. That's why I'm sitting guard."

"Oh, all right, then," Haas said, feeling his heart pound in his chest. He lay back down and turned away from McNutt, his hand resting inside his coat on the small Uhlinger pistol he kept there.

THE CANADIAN RIVER. JULY 30, 1871.

I n the gray hour before dawn, Merlin Haas had finally dozed off when he felt Newt Grago's boot nudge him roughly in his side. "Wake up, Haas," Grago said, standing above him. "I've made us a plan that'll work out best for all of us."

Merlin Haas rolled onto his back, his hand still beneath the blanket, on the pistol inside his coat. "What's the plan?" Haas asked, suddenly aware of the tip of Grago's rifle barrel hovering near him. The rifle was not pointed at Haas, but it was close enough that he got the message.

Behind Grago, McNutt sat stooped over the low-glowing embers, his face shadowed by the low brim of his hat.

"Like I told you last night," said Grago, "these horses are blowing out on us. I figure it's best you stay behind here on the Canadian and keep an eye on the trail. Me and McNutt will take your horse as a spare. If we find fresh horses up ahead, we'll come back for you. If not, you take up with the Stanleys when they come through here."

"But—but what if they don't come?" Haas asked, getting a sick feeling low in his stomach.

"Then somebody has killed them," Grago said, leaving no room for questioning in his voice. "You'll take a horse from whoever comes along next." His rifle barrel tipped slightly closer to Merlin Haas's face. "Do you see any problem with that?" he asked.

Merlin Haas knew better than to push it, so he said, "Well, no, anything you say, Newt. Leave me a rifle though, won't you?"

Grago seemed to think about it, then said, "No, that's probably not a good idea. You've got that little Uhlinger. It'll do the job for you." He paused, then added, "It'd be best if you gave me your share of the winnings, just for safekeeping till we meet up again, don't you think?"

Merlin Haas reached his free hand inside his coat pocket, feeling his legs tremble, knowing better than to resist. "Yes, that's a good idea, Newt." He handed the thick roll of money up to him. "Here, take it all. I want you to have it. . . . I mean, to keep for me, that is."

He knew his voice sounded shaky. Behind Grago, Haas heard McNutt chuckle under his breath.

"What's so funny?" Grago asked McNutt, turning a wary eye toward him as he shoved the money down into his pocket.

"Nothing," said McNutt. "Just recalling something that happened to me once a long time ago."

"Well, keep it to yourself." Grago sneered. "Go get the horses. We've got a long ride ahead."

As McNutt stood and moved away to where the horses stood saddled and ready, Newt Grago turned back to Merlin Haas. "We made some money together, Haas. If you make it to Newton, just look me up." He smiled in the darkness. "I won't be hard to find. Hell, the town's named after me."

Merlin Haas tried to calm himself, unable to speak without his voice betraying him. He only nodded, trying to return the smile, but finding his lips stiff, he was unable to do so.

When McNutt walked the three horses over to the low circle of firelight, he looked down at Haas and winked, saying in a hushed voice, "I told you, didn't I?" Then he turned to Grago, handed him the reins to one of the horses, and in a moment all that remained of the two was the low drumming of hooves moving along the bank of the river.

It took Merlin Haas a few minutes to collect himself and stand up without his knees feeling too weak to support him. Once he was sure the two men were gone, he staggered in place and rubbed his face in his hands. Then he took a deep breath, pulled the Uhlinger pistol from inside his coat, and turned it over and over in his hand. What were the odds of his staying here and picking up a horse? Even as he asked himself, he already the answer.

"Slim to none," he said aloud, his voice sounding hollow to him in the still dawn air. He sighed and sat back down in the low glow of the firelight and looked around bleakly at the deserted camp.

THE WASHITA RIVER. JULY 30, 1871.

I t was not anything that Danielle heard or saw riding closer to the rise of ground near the banks of the Washita. It was something she felt, something she'd learned to pay attention to this past year on countless trails through the lawless frontier. The tracks they'd been following swung to the left, toward a low spot where the river crossing would be shallow. Yet something told her there was trouble waiting behind the low rise forty yards to the right. From the low rise, the crossing lay bare and unprotected. It was the kind of spot that was perfect for an ambush. Once at the crossing, she and her brothers would be in the open, helpless in the sights of a good rifleman.

"Hold up," she said suddenly to Tim and Jed riding beside her. She reined Sundown to a halt and scanned the low rise and the river crossing a hundred and fifty yards ahead of them.

"What is it?" Tim asked, the three of them squinting in the midmorning sun's glare.

"We're not going in there just yet," Danielle said, stepping Sundown back and forth. "Don't let your bays stand still. Keep them moving. I've got a hunch there's rifles looking at us from that rise."

"So do I," said Tim as he and Jed kept their bays moving back and forth now, "but I've been feeling like there's somebody behind us, too. Maybe it's just nerves."

"Nope," Danielle said, "there is somebody behind us, probably has been ever since we left the buttes. I caught a glimpse of dust a while ago. But this is different. Keep moving. Let's cut west, see if we can tip their hand. If they see us leaving, they'll take a long shot instead of letting us get past them."

"Good thinking," Jed replied, gigging his bay quarter-wise, not letting it stand still beneath him.

When Danielle cut west on Sundown and heeled forward, Tim did the same, Jed dropping in behind him. Before they had gone ten yards, two rifle shots thumped into the ground at the hooves of Tim's and Jed's bays, causing the horses to rear sideways as the sound of the shots echoed around them.

"Hurry up!" Danielle called out behind her, giving Sundown more heel. "They're still too close for comfort!"

Sundown bolted west, and Jed's and Tim's bays followed, all three of them staying back from the riverbank until Danielle had put another hundred or more yards between them and the crossing. When she cut back toward the river, she slowed enough to let Tim bring his bay in beside her as he spoke.

"What now?" Tim called out above the sound of hooves beneath them.

"They've got to come out of their cover if they want us," Danielle said, drawing her Colt as she shouted to him. "Let's see if they will!"

Behind the low rise, Hop Stanley stood up, dusting his knees, cursing aloud to his brother, Renfrow. "Damn it to hell! Look what we've brought on. Can't you hit anything with that Winchester?"

"Me? What about you?" Renfrow shouted, jerking his horse's reins up from the ground and swinging up into the saddle. "I didn't see you doing so hot yourself! You was afraid they'd get out of range, and now by God they have!"

"Come on," said Hop Stanley, also snatching up his horse's reins and levering another round into his rifle chamber. "If we don't get them now, they'll be all over us. Keep them on the run!"

Bringing up the rear behind Tim and Danielle, Jed Strange looked back over his shoulder as they headed into a wide, sloping turn toward the riverbank. He saw the two riders pounding hard on their trail and shouted forward to Tim and Danielle, "Here they come—looks like there's only two of them!"

"Good!" Danielle shouted without looking back. "Make this turn out of sight, then stop!"

Hop and Renfrow Stanley pressed their horses flat out along the trail, the dust of the other three horses still looming in the air, stinging their eyes and faces. Hop Stanley had his rifle cocked and ready to raise as soon as they made the wide turn toward the river. But straightening out around the bend, both Hop and Renfrow sat back hard on their reins, trying to slide their horses to a halt. They failed to do so before the blasts of pistol fire lifted them from their saddles. Danielle, Tim, and Jed stood in the center of the trail, their pistols smoking as the Stanley brothers rolled dead to the ground, a red mist of blood seeming to hang in the air for a second, then settling with the dust.

The twins stared, their pistols still trained on the two lifeless bodies. Danielle stepped forward, watching one of the Stanley brothers' horses stand up from where it had faltered and tumbled in the dirt. The horse nickered and shook itself off, then trotted to one side, its saddle loose and drooping beneath its belly.

"Get those horses," Danielle said over her shoulder. "We might need them for spares."

"Are they Newt Grago's men?" Tim asked, stepping forward beside her and nodding at the two bodies.

"You can bet on it," Danielle replied. She cut her gaze off along the rise and fall of the land behind them. "That takes care of them. But we've still got somebody trailing us."

Two hundred yards away, lying on his belly in tall grass, Saul Delmano cursed to himself, seeing the two bodies lying on the trail. He wasn't sure from this distance, but it looked like it had been the Stanley brothers riding in, making a stupid fatal mistake. *Well, so much for that,* he thought, sliding backward to where the land sloped down behind him. Once behind the cover of the rise, he walked over to his horse and shoved his rifle back into its boot. He wasn't about to get those three on his tail. He would stay back and play it safe. They still had a long way to go.

CHAPTER 19

NEWTON, KANSAS. AUGUST 7, 1871.

The town of Newton sat on the Chisholm Trail, where only a year before there had been nothing but a few dust-blown shacks, stacks of cross ties and steel rails, and a crew of determined gandy dancers.* Judge R. P. Muse, an agent for the Atchison, Topeka and Santa Fe Railroad, had chosen the spot as a likely site for a rail terminal, owing to the big herds of cattle coming up the trail from Texas and the settlers and businessmen coming in from the East. The stockyards and loading chutes seemed to swell with longhorns from daylight to dark. With the longhorns came the men who drove them: good, hardworking men for the most part. Yet among them came the lawless element: the grifters, the thieves and killers, whose only interest in cattle lay in the large amounts of cash that the industry generated. Newton, although still in its infancy as a rail town, had already been labeled the wickedest city in the West.

Newt Grago stood on the boardwalk out front of Bertha Stillwell's saloon and looked at the stir of passerbys in the morning heat, chewing a cigar. With his thumbs hooked to the lapel of his new swallow-tailed dress coat, he smiled.

"Damn, Berth," he said to the big woman standing beside him, "I do believe you've hit the jackpot here."

---

* "Gandy dancers" was a term for men who worked in a rail-laying crew.

A shot rang out from the direction of another saloon at the far end of the street. A woman screamed. The crowd outside Bertha's only looked back over their shoulders and hurried on about their business.

Bertha and Newt Grago glanced across the top of the moving traffic toward the sound of the shot, then looked away.

"I knew you'd like it here once you arrived," Bertha replied. She was a hefty woman who carried herself well and dressed in the latest fashions. She fanned looming dust with a delicate flowered kerchief and smiled at Newt Grago. "As far as anybody bothering you here, leave that to me and the boys. I sent Jake Reed up to Cottonwood Station last night. He'll be back this evening with Spurlock, Quince, and some of the others by this evening. There should be as many as seven or eight guns in all. Think that's enough to keep you out of trouble? If not, we'll hire more. I aim to please," she added in a coy tone.

Newt Grago blushed a bit, then said, "I just hope Spurlock and his boys ain't forgot who's always in charge when I'm around. I'm the one who'll be calling the shots."

"I told Jake to be sure and make that clear to Spurlock," Bertha interjected.

"If I ain't mistaken," Grago went on, "there's a gunslinger on my trail that's going to require my strictest attention as soon as he gets here."

"Whatever you need, Newt," Bertha replied, reaching over and squeezing his hand. "I already put the word out—anything you want, you get, including the use of my two bodyguards, George Pipp and Star-eye Waller."

"You are a jewel, Berth."

Newt Grago smiled. He ran a clean hand down the front of his white boiled shirt, and looked himself up and down, realizing that he hardly resembled the man who'd ridden in here two days ago, dust-streaked, leading a gaunt, spare horse behind him. When he and McNutt had arrived at the outskirts of Newton, Grago instructed McNutt to hang back awhile and then come into town alone. No one had any idea they were together, except for Bertha Stillwell. McNutt had kept close to Grago and watched his back. There was no sheriff in Newton at present, but lawmen came and went on an almost daily basis, hunting wanted fugitives who'd broken the law inside their towns and jurisdictions across Kansas. Newt Grago always liked to play it safe when he could. Willis McNutt was his ace in the hole.

But neither Newt Grago's watchful eyes from the boardwalk, nor Willis McNutt standing across the street leaning on a hitch rail, caught sight of the four riders who had slid around the perimeter of Newton and slipped in from the other end of town. Danielle led the way, followed by Merlin Haas, then her brothers, Tim and Jed, who had kept a close eye on Haas since they'd found him along the banks of the Canadian River. Amid the busy cattle chutes at the far end of town, Danielle reined Sundown to a halt and pressed a hand to the tender, swollen wound throbbing painfully in her side.

Tim and Jed both knew what was bothering her as soon as they stopped beside her, and Tim said, "We've got to get that looked at before we do anything else, Danielle."

"I'm all right." She looked at each of them in turn, then looked at Merlin Haas and asked, "Are you good for your word, Haas? You said you'd do some scouting around for us. Can we trust you?"

"Damn right you can," Haas replied without hesitation. "After what that bastard did to me, left me afoot, took all my money, I've got no qualms whatsoever about handing him over to you. Let me get going and see what I can find out."

"Go on, then," Danielle said. "Check things out. We'll meet you here this afternoon." She nodded toward a drover's shack where saddles hung along a rail fence, and blankets and gear lay piled on a plank porch. In a circle of stones, fire licked beneath a tin coffeepot sitting atop a greasy blackened roasting rack. "We'll stay here. It looks like there's room for a few more blankets on the ground."

"I'll be back," Merlin Haas said. "You can count on it."

Tim and Jed both turned to her as soon as Merlin Haas drifted away from the chutes and onto the crowded street. "Think we can trust that cur?" Tim asked.

"Nope, not much," Danielle replied. "That's why I want you two to keep an eye on him from a distance. I'm going to take your advice and get this wound looked at. It's paining me something awful. I just didn't want to say anything in front of Haas." She stepped Sundown back from between her brothers, then said as she turned the mare away, "Both of you, be careful. I'll find a doctor and meet you back here."

Tim and Jed nodded and watched her ride off toward the busy street.

Danielle made her way along the rutted dirt street, keeping the mare near the boardwalk, where she hoped to be less noticeable, should the eyes of Newt Grago or any of his outlaw friends be searching the crowd for her. Because she was without the fake mustache and kept her hat brim low on her forehead, the only thing recognizable about her was Sundown, and even the mare would be hard to spot, all covered with road dust and streaked with sweat. At a hitch rail she pulled the mare in beneath a freshly painted sign that read: DOCTOR LANNAHAN. Casting a glance back and forth along the street, she stepped down from her saddle, hitched Sundown, and walked up the boardwalk and in through the single wooden door.

Inside the empty office, a thin young doctor looked up from his desk in a corner and put on his wire-rimmed spectacles as he stood to face her.

"I'm Dr. Philip Lannahan," he said, adjusting his vest. "May I help you?" No sooner had he asked than he saw the dark circle of dried blood on her side and moved forward as Danielle swayed a step before catching herself.

Danielle moved her hand from her side, saying, "I took a bullet a couple of days back, Doctor. It's still inside me. Got me feeling weak and fevered all over."

"Oh, my goodness!" Dr. Lannahan said, moving with her, ushering her past the front office into the next room, where a gurney stood covered with a clean white sheet. "You can't let something like that go unattended, young man. What on earth were you thinking?"

Before Danielle answered, the doctor pressed her back onto the gurney and began unbuttoning the bib of her shirt. Danielle raised a hand and stopped him. "I'll tell you why I had to let it go for a while, Doctor," she said. "I'm in the midst of a manhunt and the men I'm hunting were too close for me to take the time to stop."

"I see," the doctor said. "That's foolish of you, but I suppose I understand." His finger went back to the buttons, but again she stopped him.

"There's something you're about to find out that you must promise never to mention to anyone," she said.

The doctor looked deep into the serious eyes demanding secrecy of him. "I treat wounds, young man. I don't harbor fugitives if that's what you're about to tell me."

"No, Doctor, that's not it at all." She sighed and let him open her shirt, knowing that as soon as he saw the binder around her chest, he would begin to understand.

As he pulled the open shirt back across her shoulders, he caught sight of the binder and hesitated for a second. Then he continued undressing her, saying, "I see what you're asking me now. Don't worry. Your secret is safe with me, Miss . . . ?"

"I'm Danielle Strange," she said, letting out a breath and trying to relax. "I go by the name Danny Duggin." She pointed to the binder around her breasts. "This is also why I couldn't stop and get the bullet taken out. By the time my brothers and I had a chance to stop and attend to my wound, we ran into another man who traveled on with us. I couldn't risk him knowing I'm a woman."

"Well," said the doctor, stepping over to a metal tray where shiny instruments gleamed in the sunlight that streamed through a window, "I hope you haven't waited too long. You're burning up with fever."

As he spoke, he reached out and gently pressed her back flat against the gurney and touched a finger to the swollen flesh surrounding the bullet hole. "This is infected," he said almost to himself, studying the condition of the wound. "It's not the worst I've ever seen, but it's certainly not the best either. I hope you have nothing planned for the next few days, Miss Strange. It looks like you're going to be boarding right here."

"Don't get into the habit of calling me Miss Strange," Danielle said in a firm tone. "Call me Danny Duggin. And yes, I'm afraid I do have something planned for the day. Something most urgent."

"But, Miss— I mean, Danny Duggin," the doctor said, quickly correcting himself, "you won't be able to be up and around for a while once I remove this bullet! To attempt it would be insane."

"Then what can you give me for the fever and the pain until I finish my business and get back here?"

"No, that's out of the question," the doctor said, shaking his head. "I must insist you stay here right now, get the bullet removed, and then rest and recuperate. Whatever you have to do in Newton will simply have to wait."

"It can't wait, Doctor," Danielle said, rising slightly onto one elbow, the pain of her wound throbbing deep inside the inflamed flesh. "Give me something to take and send me on my way."

"Anything I give you for the pain is only to put you to sleep. Anything I give you for the fever and infection isn't going to have a great deal of effect until we get that bullet out of you. I can clean it, soak it in alcohol for now, and dress it in a bandage. But the alcohol is going to burn like the dickens."

"Let's get to it, Doctor," she said with resolve. "It'll have to do for now."

"Are you certain about this?" Dr. Lannahan asked. "I assure you this will burn like nothing you've ever felt."

"Stop talking about it and get it done," she demanded. "I can stand the pain."

"As you wish," said the doctor.

He stepped back over to the tray and returned in a moment with a fresh dressing and a bottle of alcohol. Danielle lay clutching the sides of the gurney with both hands as the white-hot liquid seemed to sear the flesh from her bones. She kept herself from screaming aloud until finally through the pain came a queasy numbness. As the doctor finished soaking the wound and wrapping it in clean gauze, she lay shivering beneath a clammy patina of sweat.

"There, now," the doctor said at length, stepping back from her. "If you think that was bad, wait until that infection gets worse. I've seen men beg someone to shoot them."

"I'll keep that in mind, Doctor," Danielle said, forcing herself to sit up on the gurney and swinging her legs down over the edge. Stiffly she pulled on her shirt, closed the bib shut across her chest, and began buttoning it up. "How long before this fever starts knocking me off my feet, Doctor?" she asked.

The doctor shook his head in exasperation. "Oh, a couple of hours, a day. Who knows? I'm surprised you're on your feet right now."

Danielle gave him a stern gaze. He relented, saying, "Oh, all right. I'd say by this afternoon you should expect it to get to its worst stage. But mind you, once you get to that point, I can't promise you're going to pull through. Blood poisoning is not a pleasant death."

Danielle finished buttoning up her shirt, thinking of her father's death and saying, "Neither is hanging from a tree in the middle of nowhere, Doctor." She stood up and took a second to clear her head before taking a step. Then she said, "I'll be back tonight, I promise," and walked back across the front office and out the door.

I t was already afternoon when the twins came back to the shack beside the rail chutes. Danielle sat near the rail fence, her face looking ashen and drawn. Tim noticed that she shivered a little as they stepped down from the bays and walked over to her.

"What did you find?" Danielle asked them right away.

Before answering, Tim asked a question of his own. "What'd the doctor say? Are you doing all right?"

"He said I'm fine," Danielle replied. "What did you find out? Did you see Newt Grago?"

"Yep, we saw him from a distance," said Jed. "Merlin Haas went right up to him. You couldn't tell anything had ever happened between them. They even shook hands. We saw Grago give him some money. Then they went inside a saloon, and that's the last we saw of them."

"How many men are hanging around Grago?" Danielle asked.

"None that we saw," Jed answered.

"Good," Danielle said in an expelled breath. "This time it's just me and him. Then it's over," she added, looking up at her brothers. "We can go back home."

"Are you sure you're feeling all right?" Tim persisted. "You don't look so good."

"Yes, I feel fine," Danielle said, a bit testy. "It's just a graze like I told you before," she lied. "The doctor cleaned it and bandaged it. Told me to come back tonight, and he'd take a closer look at it."

"What for?" asked Tim. "If it's only a graze, what else is he going to do?" He looked suspicious.

"How do I know?" Danielle snapped at him. "I told him I had business to take care of. He said I'd be fine so long as I came back tonight and had him look at it again."

"All right," Tim said, backing off, "take it easy. I'm just worried about you, is all."

Danielle took a deep breath, calming herself, then said, "I know, but we don't have time for your worrying. As soon as Haas gets back, if his story sounds real enough, you two are going to watch my back. I'm going to call Newt Grago out in the street and settle all accounts."

Tim and Jed both nodded, but Tim saw the glazed, hollow look in Danielle's eyes. He knew better than to say anything right then, yet he couldn't help but wonder if she was really up to doing what she'd come so far to do.

At the bar inside Bertha Stillwell's saloon, Merlin Haas wiped foam from his upper lip and set his mug of beer back down on the bar. He looked at Newt Grago standing beside him and resisted the urge to pull the Uhlinger pistol from inside his coat and put a bullet between Grago's eyes. But killing Newt Grago was not why he had come here, he reminded himself, managing a smile. That was something Danny Duggin would do, once Haas got back and told him that Newt Grago was here alone, with nobody around but a couple of Bertha's bodyguards. From what Haas had seen of Danny Duggin's gun handling, the two bodyguards wouldn't bother him a bit, especially since he had a couple of helpers of his own.

"I have to admit, Newt," Merlin Haas said, still managing a tight smile, "I was pretty damn sore at you, leaving me that way. To tell the truth, I never believed you'd give me my money back even if I made it here."

"Well," Grago responded, "to be honest myself, I never thought you'd make it. I figured there was no sense in that money laying out there in the dirt somewhere while the buzzards picked your bones. But since you did make it, here's to you." He raised a shot of rye in salute to Merlin Haas. After he threw it back, smacking his lips with a hiss, he asked, "Now, tell me again, how was it you got ahold of one of the Stanley brothers' horses?"

Haas shrugged. "Just like I said. I was hiking back along the trail toward the Washita, and first thing you know, there it came trotting up to me. All's I did was raise my hands, stop it, and step into the saddle." He raised his beer again, and this time when he set it down, he added, "Of course, I figure it must mean that either Hop or Renfrow or maybe even *both* of them are dead."

"But you saw no sign of either the posse or that young gunslinger Duggin?"

"Not a trace," said Haas. "I figure he must've got in the wind with everybody else and headed for Texas. That's the last you'll see of him, I reckon."

"Yeah, I think you're right," Newt Grago said, eyeing Haas closely. "So where are you headed now, Haas?" Grago asked, refilling his shot glass from the bottle on the bar.

"Wherever the action takes me." Merlin Haas shrugged. "I hate losing all the gambling equipment. Sure hate seeing Lulu carted off in handcuffs that way. But she'll show in Texas before long. They've got nothing worth holding her on. I figure me and her'll be back in business before you know it." He finished his beer in one last long swallow, then slid the empty glass across the bar top. "Well, it's been a hell of a spree, Newt. I 'spect I'll push on now."

"Glad you made it, Merlin," Grago said, slapping Haas on the back with a laugh. "You watch your backside out there."

"I'll do it, Newt Grago," said Haas, "and you do the same. Thanks for taking care of my money for me." He patted his coat pocket.

"My pleasure, *amigo*," said Newt Grago. Now that he had heard what Haas had to say, Grago's hand swept upward with his pistol cocked. "Come to think of it, I might just hang on to it a while longer." He spread a nasty grin. "Give it back, Haas, all of it."

Haas knew that to resist would bring himself sudden death. "I should've known better," he murmured, lifting the money and handing it back to Grago.

"Yep, you should have," Grago agreed, stuffing the inside of his coat. "Now clear out before I shoot you for the hell of it."

As Haas slunk out the door, Bertha Stillwell came up beside Newt Grago as he watched Merlin Haas disappear through the swinging doors. "Is everything all right, Newt?" Bertha asked, slipping a fleshy arm around his waist.

"Naw, everything is not all right at all," Grago said, rolling the cigar in his lips, considering things as he stared at the swinging doors. "I don't believe a word that grifter said. He didn't get this far on his own, and he didn't just walk up and find one of the Stanleys' horses trotting along the trail."

"Then how did he get here?" Bertha Stillwell asked.

"I don't know, but I'd sure like to," Grago said, still staring at the doors. "What time did you say those boys will be here from Cottonwood Station?"

"This evening sometime," Bertha said. "Why? Are you expecting trouble before then? Did you tell Haas that Spurlock and his boys are coming in from Cottonwood Station?"

"Hell no, I didn't tell him about Spurlock and his boys. But as far as *trouble* goes, I've been expecting it since the day I was born," said Newt Grago, tossing back a shot of rye and banging the empty glass down on the bar. "Why would today be any different?"

CHAPTER 20

Saul Delmano slipped into town, using the same trail Danielle, her brothers, and Merlin Haas had ridden in on earlier. When he saw the familiar horses hitched along the rail fence, he quickly ducked his own horse away and stepped it in between two holding pens full of steers. From there he sat watching for a moment until Merlin Haas came riding in from the main street and stepped down from his saddle. Delmano realized that Merlin Haas was the only one of the four who could recognize him. After seeing the way these three young gunmen fought, Delmano debated whether or not to stick here and side with Newt Grago, or to get out, hoping that these three thought him dead along with Blade Hogue and Rufe Gaddis. He weighed his decision as he sat watching them talk among themselves.

"What did you find out?" Danielle asked Haas, listening closely for any waver in his voice or any sign of him lying. "Did you see Newt Grago?"

"Yep, I saw him all right. Even drank a beer with him," said Merlin Haas.

The twins stood watching his face, listening along with Danielle. "How'd you tell him you got here?" Tim asked.

"I told him one of the Stanley brothers' horses came along while I was hiking back toward the Washita. Since I am riding one of their horses, I figured if he saw me on it, the story would match up." Haas grinned. "I know how to stretch the truth some when I need to. I ought to know how—it's been my occupation my whole life."

"I know," Danielle said. "Did he mention having any men here? Was there anybody around him? Don't forget, we followed two sets of hoofprints here. What about this McNutt you told us about?"

"Didn't see hide nor hair of McNutt. Maybe he lit out. As far as any others, there's only a couple of Bertha Stillwell's bodyguards hanging around. But they'd be around anyway if Bertha's nearby." He paused for a moment, then looked at Danielle and the twins with sincerity, saying, "Listen, I know you've got some doubts about me, but I'm talking straight to you. What Newt Grago did to me, leaving me stranded that way, there's no patching that up as far as I'm concerned. I don't care what you do to him. You can believe that or not."

Danielle considered what he'd told them. It went along with what the twins had seen, Haas and Grago going into the saloon. "If you are lying, Haas, there's not enough land out here to keep us from finding you."

"You think I don't realize that?" Haas said. "I gave it all some good thinking before I ever went looking for Newt for you. That's the God-honest truth."

Danielle looked at the twins, then back to Merlin Haas. "All right, Haas. You're free to take off. Keep the horse. But once you leave, don't come back sticking your nose into things."

Stepping back to the horse and collecting the reins from the ground, Merlin Haas said, "Don't worry. I'm already gone. If you shoot that bastard more than once, tell him the second one is from me."

They watched Merlin Haas step into his saddle and turn the horse away toward the trail they had had come in on. Danielle stood up and brushed the dust from her trousers. A feverish shiver racked her body, but she held firm until it passed. Then she took her Colt from her hip, checked it, and spun it back into her holster.

From between the rail chutes, Saul Delmano couldn't hear

what Merlin Haas and the others had been saying, but seeing Haas leave on such friendly terms was all Delmano needed to see. Knowing that went a long way in helping Delmano make up his mind. He leveled his hat brim low on his forehead, then turned his horse and slipped along between the rail chutes until he found a place where he could get past any watching eyes and get onto Merlin Haas's trail.

From the northwest, on the trail from Cottonwood Station, Bertha Stillwell's bartender, Jake Reed, and a group of eight riders moved along at a steady trot. At the head of the riders beside Reed, Mace Spurlock rode with a rifle across his lap. Behind Spurlock rode Quince Evans and six gunmen who'd thrown in with them four months ago, robbing banks and stagecoaches. They were thieves and killers to the man. In riding order behind Quince Evans, they were: Earl Peach, Richard and Embrey Davenport, Duke Sollister, Joe Stokes, and Slim Early. There was no talk among them. They knew why they were headed to Newton when they left Cottonwood Station. They were going there at Bertha Stillwell's request to protect Newt Grago. That was good enough for them.

Coming onto the dirt street as the afternoon traffic had just begun to settle, the riders spread wide and rode abreast slowly, forcing people aside and out of their way. A young boy whose mother pulled him out of the horse's path picked up a lump of dried horse droppings and hurled it at the riders. Duke Sollister turned in his saddle, his hand on the butt of his pistol, and almost drew and fired before realizing it was only a child.

"Teach that kid some manners, woman," he hissed. "Nobody's too young to die."

The woman gasped, jerked the child away, and ducked inside a mercantile with her kid under her arm. At the far end of the street, Danielle, Tim, and Jed had stopped for only a moment, long enough for Danielle to look around and form a quick plan for them to cover her back in case of a surprise. She nodded at an alley on one side of the street, and Tim veered off toward it without a word. She looked at the rabbit gun in Jed's hand, then jerked her head toward a stack of nail kegs standing on the boardwalk across the street from Bertha Stillwell's saloon.

"You be careful, sister," Jed whispered before moving away and leaving her in the middle of the dirt street. Danielle only nodded, knowing the raging fever inside her would not let her speak plainly without her voice wavering in her chest.

With the twins in position, she stepped to the middle of the street out front of the saloon and planted her feet squarely in the dirt beneath her, a shoulder width apart. She did not see the riders pushing their way slowly through the traffic along the rutted street, fifty yards away from the other end of town. She saw only in her mind the vision of her pa swaying in the breeze at the end of a hangman's rope.

"Newt Grago!" her voice boomed through the waning afternoon pedestrians toward the swinging doors. "Come out, you murdering son of a bitch! It's time I put you facedown in the dirt!"

At the sound of her words, boots shuffled out of the way on the boardwalk and a lady's parasol fell to the ground. Buggy and freight wagons squeaked to a halt, both teamsters and businessmen alike abandoning their seats and running for cover. Even at forty yards away, over the street traffic, Mace Spurlock heard the voice and saw the commotion of people getting out of the way. He raised a hand and brought the others to a halt.

"Give it a minute," he said over his shoulder.

The horsemen milled in place, pistols coming out of holsters and eyes riveting on the lone figure in the middle of the street.

From his spot in the alley, Tim Strange saw the riders more clearly as the street emptied. He could tell Danielle hadn't seen them, her eyes pinned as they were on the saloon doors. He drew in a tense breath, stepped up onto the boardwalk, and moved unseen along the front of the buildings, hoping for a better position before the nine riders made their move.

Behind the stack of nail kegs, Jed Strange had seen the riders as well, and knew instantly why they were here. He flashed a glance across the street toward Tim's alley position, but saw Tim moving forward along the boardwalk. Then his eyes caught sight of McNutt's red-bearded face venturing a peep from around a tall striped pole in front of a barbershop.

"Oh, Lord, Tim, look out," Jed whispered to himself.

For a split second McNutt's eyes locked on Jed's from across the street. Then McNutt drew back out of sight behind the barber pole.

"I'm coming, Danny Duggin!" Newt Grago's voice shouted out above the saloon doors.

But watching the saloon, Danielle didn't see him. Instead, in the open windows above the saloon, she saw the glint of evening sun flash off of a rifle barrel, and she dove sidelong, whisking out both her Colts, one firing on the window to her left, the other to the right. White lace curtains streamed forward and down as one of Bertha Stillwell's bodyguards tumbled to the overhang above the boardwalk and fell to the street. At the same time, from the other window, a body slumped forward, a rifle falling from its hand and sliding down the overhang.

Danielle spun back toward the saloon doors in time to hear the pistol fire from inside. Her fever was playing tricks on her eyes, causing the front of the saloon to sway like reeds in a breeze. As Newt Grago burst through the doors, her shot only clipped his shoulder and sent him spinning along the front of the building. He dove down behind a wooden cigar Indian and fired back at her.

Jed Strange saw that McNutt had spotted Tim moving along the boardwalk. "Look out, Tim!" Jed shouted, coming up from his cover.

The blast of the short-barreled rabbit gun rattled the store windows along the street, the impact of the heavily loaded buckshot slamming McNutt full in his chest and leaving little of him in its wake.

At the saloon, Grago fought hard from behind the wooden Indian, chunks of the thick statue flying in all directions as Danielle's Colts riddled it with holes.

"Come on, boys, enough sightseeing," Spurlock called out, waving the men forward, batting his heels to his horse's sides.

The riders charged forward with a loud yell, their pistols gunning for Danielle in the middle of the dirt street. But coming into the play now were Tim and Jed Strange. Each of them stepped into the fray from their side of the street, centering themselves toward the oncoming riders like statues of iron, their big customized Colts bucking in their hands. As each shot rang out, another rider flew from his saddle. Catching the brunt of their fire, the riders broke rank and dove for cover, leaving their confused, terrified horses to fend for themselves.

As the riders collected themselves and returned fire from safer positions, Jed and Tim could not withstand that many guns.

"Come on, Danielle, run for it!" Tim shouted, stepping forward, one gun empty in his left hand, his right hand pounding out shots as bullets whistled past him. "For God sakes, Danielle!" he screamed. The searing pain of a bullet through his shoulder caused him only to flinch as he continued to cover his sister in the street.

But Danielle fought on as if in a trance, unhearing, unresponsive to anything, save for the sight of Newt Grago lying dead at her feet. And Newt Grago was proving himself to be no easy kill. He'd rolled from behind the wooden Indian and scurried along the boardwalk, blood spewing from his shoulder, his ribs, and his forehead. Still he fought on, pitching down from the boardwalk as Danielle's bullets kicked up splinters behind him. He hugged the side of a water trough for cover while he hurriedly reloaded his pistol. In the street, a shot had caught Danielle high in the back and spun her to the ground.

"You dirty bastards!" Jed Strange screamed in rage, seeing his sister down and his brother, Tim, propped up on one knee, still firing, blood matting his chest, arm, and one side of his face.

The blast from Jed's shotgun didn't hit any of the men, but it blew away the side of the abandoned freight wagon in which three of them had taken cover. They fled like roaches, Jed's Colt coming into play, taking two of them down just as a bullet sliced through his side. He fell to the ground, a hand pressed to the wound for a second as his Colt continued firing. He saw one of the men rise up and aim at him, taking his time, getting it right. But just before the man fired, a bullet sailed in above Jed and punched out the man's right eye, letting Jed know that Tim was still back there, still fighting, helping his brother all he could.

Jed reached a bloody hand inside his coat pocket and took out two fresh loads and poked them into his rabbit gun. Then he fired both barrels, lifting a cloud of splinters and glass from the front of a store. He heard Tim's Colts bark behind him in the street, taking two men down in a spray of blood.

"Pull back, boys!" Mace Spurlock shouted to his men, hurrying backward in a crouch toward where his frightened horse stood in an alley, away from the gunfire.

Taking a quick look around, he saw none of the men standing except for Earl Peach, who wandered aimlessly with an empty gun clicking over and over on empty chambers in his right hand. Peach's left hand clasped tight against his stomach, keeping his innards from spilling out.

"To hell with this! I'm quits here!" Mace Spurlock shouted, flinging his pistol aside as a bullet whistled past his ear. He ducked his head to one side, his hands held high in the air. "Damn it! I give it up! Don't shot!" Blood spread down his raised arms and ran in a thin stream from his elbow. "Lord God Almighty!" he shouted, looking around at the carnage in the street. "What's got into you people?"

Using all her strength, Danielle managed to roll up onto her knees, keeping the Colt in her left hand aimed toward Newt Grago's position behind the water trough, her right Colt cocking toward Mace Spurlock as he stepped closer. Ten feet behind her, Tim rose up and staggered forward, only to collapse back down onto his knees.

"Watch him, Tim," Danielle warned in a shaky voice, the fever taking its toll on her, getting worse by the minute now, it seemed.

"I—I can't," Tim rasped, trying to raise his pistol, but failing to do so.

Jed Strange limped forward, using the empty rabbit gun now as a crutch, his right hand raising his pistol toward Spurlock. He, too, was having a hard time keeping it steady in his blood-slickened hand.

Around the edge of the water trough, Newt Grago ventured a look at Danielle, seeing the big Colts weave back and forth in her unsteady hands. He cut a glance to Mace Spurlock. Their eyes met for only an instant, yet at that moment each of them understood the other. They made their move in unison. Spurlock jumped to one side out of Danielle's aim. His hand went to the hideout pistol behind his back as Newt Grago flung himself up from behind the water trough and fired at Danielle. Grago's bullet ripped the Colt from her left hand, spinning it high in the air.

"Get him, Spurlock! Kill that bastard!" Newt Grago screamed.

But Danielle's right Colt exploded just as Spurlock swung his pistol from behind his back. The bullet ripped through his heart and dropped him backward, dead before he hit the ground. Grago fired again, his shot grazing Danielle under her arm, slicing through the binding that held her breasts flattened to her chest. She fell backward to the dirt with the impact, but fired up at Newt Grago as he tried pulling off another round. He let out a loud grunt as the bullet lifted him from behind the water trough and up onto the boardwalk.

Danielle collapsed for a moment, then shook her head to make the street stop spinning. Through sheer will alone, she struggled up to her feet and stalked forward toward Newt Grago, one halting step at a time. Tears streamed down her drawn, fevered cheeks.

"Tim?" she asked over her shoulder. "Jed . . . ?" Her words trailed.

"Yeah," Tim said, gasping, "I'm alive . . . so's Jed. Ain't you, Jed?"

"So far," Jed replied, his words squeezed out through the pain.

Danielle made it to the water trough, catching a hand to it for support, her other hand raising the Colt toward Newt Grago, who lay trying to catch his failing breath. Along the street, townsfolk began venturing forward from hiding, a hushed murmur of voices rising up as if from the dirt.

"At last," Danielle sobbed, "I've killed you . . . you and every one of your murdering sonsabitches who killed my pa."

"Yeah, so what?" Newt Grago rasped, the hole in his chest stifling his breath, the flowing blood sapping his last moments of life. "You've . . . got yourselves . . . killed, too. You . . . ain't going to make it, none of you are."

"You're wrong, Grago. I'll live. So will my brothers," Danielle said, the Colt wobbly in her hand.

"Your brothers?"

Grago tried to focus on Tim and Jed as they managed to move forward, holding each other up. But by now all Newt Grago could make out were dark images. He heard the gunslinger Danny Duggin go on to say something close to his face, something that didn't make any sense to him. Danny Duggin was a woman? That couldn't be right, Grago thought, trying to sort it all out as the darkness circled in closer around him.

Grago heard Danny Duggin's voice again, this time faintly above the cocking of the big Colt close to his face. Grago tried to speak, but couldn't as he caught the smell of burned powder still curling from the pistol so close to his face.

"Dunc," he finally managed to whisper. "You was . . . all right, after all."

Newt Grago's world stopped as a silver flash rose up and exploded in front of his closed eyelids, then all turned black, black and silent, as Danielle Strange stepped back, faltering, poking out the spent rounds from her Colt and trying with all her strength to replace them.

NEWTON, KANSAS. AUGUST 14, 1871.

A full week had passed before Danielle fully opened her eyes and looked up into the faces of her brothers, Dr. Lannahan, and of all people, Tuck Carlyle. She was still drowsy and weak. The bullet from her side had been removed, and the fever that had nearly killed her had broken only the night before. There were parts of the aftermath of the gun battle that she remembered, but most of what had happened was still a blur. She remembered dropping down on the boardwalk with one Colt still in her right hand, her reloads spilling from her left hand and rolling around on the planks beside her. After that, she recalled the doctor appearing through a gray fog and carefully scooping her up. Then she heard some mention of a bed in a separate room off the doctor's office. Her last thought had been of how good a soft bed would feel beneath her. She offered a tired smile now as she spoke.

"Tuck, is that really you?"

Tim and Jed gave each other a knowing glance, feeling not the least neglected that her first attentions went to the handsome young drover.

"Yes, it's really me, Danny," Tuck said. "I was just pushing a short herd to the holding pens when I heard what had happened. I'm sorry I wasn't here in time to lend a hand, especially once I heard that Gragos was part of it. Damn, you gave us all a scare."

"Dunc's dead, Tuck. This was his brother and some other outlaws."

"They told me about Dunc," said Tuck, nodding toward Tim and Jed.

She looked over at Tim and Jed, who stood bandaged and bruised two feet back from the bed. "I expect you know by now that these two scarecrows are my brothers, Tim and Jed." She offered the twins a smile as Dr. Lannahan looked her over, carefully making sure the blanket covering her stayed up close to her chin, hiding her breasts.

"Yep," said Tuck. "They told me everything."

"Everything?" Danielle gave Tim and Jed a look, asking them in a guarded manner.

Tim cut in, saying, "Yep, we told him you're our older brother. Told him how we've all been searching for our pa's killers."

"Good." Danielle sighed. Then she turned to Tuck. "You told me on the trail that you're interested in a young woman named Ilene."

"Yep, that's right," Tuck said. "Why do you ask?"

"Because as soon as I get out of this bed, we need to go someplace and talk. Now that I'm coming off this vengeance trail, I've got something I need to tell you."

"Really?" Tuck asked, looking curious at the serious manner she'd used. "Is it something important? Because if it is—"

Tim cut him off, saying, "It'll have to wait. Not to be rude, but Jed and I really need to talk to our brother alone for a few minutes, if you don't mind."

Tuck Carlyle looked back and forth between them, then said, "Sure. Family business. I understand." He looked back down at Danielle. "We'll talk later, then, Danny. I'll be in town a couple of days till the train arrives and loads these steers for St. Louis. Meanwhile, you take it easy." He raised his hat in his hands, nodded to Tim and Jed, and stepped back to the door. "Glad you're doing well, *amigo*."

Danielle smiled, lifting a hand toward him as he turned and stepped out the door. She knew something was up from the way Tim had acted. She waited until she heard the outer door close behind Tuck Carlyle; then she turned her face back to her brothers, asking Tim, "What was that all about? What's going on?"

Tim and Jed hesitated, looking down at the floor for a second before Tim finally said, "I was afraid you were about to tell him you're really a woman, Danielle. We couldn't let you do that without first making sure you really wanted him to know."

"Why not?" she asked. "This whole mess is over now. I'm free to get back to living my own life." She looked at their grim expressions, then added, "Ain't I?"

Jed spoke now in a quiet voice, saying, "Some drovers found Merlin Haas lying alongside the trail three days ago. They brought him here and he asked for you before he died. We told him the shape you were in, so he told us instead." Jed paused, then went on. "He said the man who shot and robbed him was Saul Delmano."

Danielle looked away. A silence passed as she let the news sink in, feeling the familiar tightness once again growing inside her. When she looked back at her brothers, she asked, "How's Sundown and the bays doing?"

Jed and Tim looked at each other. "They're all three fine. The bays are filling out in the flanks now that they've been on steady grain for the past few days. What are you thinking, Danielle?"

She felt her eyes grow moist, but she struggled against her emotions and swallowed a knot in her throat. "You already know what I'm thinking." She looked at each of them in turn, adding, "I'm thinking you'd best keep calling me Danny Duggin."

"You don't have to go, Danielle— I mean, Danny," said Jed, correcting himself. "Me and Tim can finish up from here. You've more than done your part."

"I made a vow standing beside Pa's grave," she said. "It's not even a choice I can make. I'll be there when Saul Delmano dies, or else I'll die in the trying."

"I told you so," Tim said to Jed in a lowered voice. He looked back at Danielle, asking, "What about this Tuck Carlyle? We saw how you looked at him. It ain't right, you having to deny yourself this way."

Danielle didn't answer. Instead, she turned to Dr. Lannahan, asking, "How soon can I ride, Doctor?"

"It all depends," he said, cutting a glance to Tim and Jed, trying to get a feel for what they wanted him to say. "A week maybe? Two weeks if you don't get your strength back the way you should."

Danielle gave him a solemn stare, saying, "My strength is coming back right now. Don't stall me, Doc. Tell me the truth—when can I ride?"

He shrugged and offered a slight smile. "In that case, as soon as you pay your bill."

Danielle returned his smile and struggled up onto the side of the bed. "Tim, go get the horses. Jed, go into my saddlebags, get some money, and pay the doctor. Are you both able to ride?" she asked in afterthought.

"Yep," Tim said, taking a step back. "But there's something else we need to tell you. There's a bounty hunter named Bob Dennard. He was also there when they brought Haas in. He says he knows you. Said you and him had some trouble back near Fort Smith."

"That's right. We did. What about him?" asked Danielle, taking the freshly washed but bullet-riddled shirt Dr. Lannahan handed her and stiffly putting an arm into it.

"He says he wants to forget the trouble between you. Said if we go after this Saul Delmano, he wants to go with us. He knows a lot about Saul Delmano, says Delmano will duck into Mexico, where he has lots of friends and connections. Dennard says we'll be outgunned if we face Delmano down there."

"Dennard's not riding with us," Danielle said with finality.

She slipped the shirt the rest of the way on and stood up on weak legs, reaching for her clean trousers as the doctor draped them across the foot of the bed.

"He's only in it for the blood money." She paused, considering it, then said, "There's a big difference between him and us."

She pulled on her trousers, stepped into her boots, and reached for the gun belt and the pair of matched Colts hanging on a ladder-back chair beside the bed. Strapping on the gun belt, she looked from Tim to Jed, saying, "The three of us are riders of judgment."

Ralph Compton stood six foot eight without his boots. He worked as a musician, a radio announcer, a songwriter, and a newspaper columnist. His first novel, *The Goodnight Trail*, was a finalist for the Western Writers of America Medicine Pipe Bearer Award for best debut novel. He was the *USA Today* bestselling author of the Trail of the Gunfighter series, the Border Empire series, the Sundown Riders series, and the Trail Drive series, among others.

Ready to find
your next great read?

Let us help.

Visit prh.com/nextread

Penguin
Random
House